select
editions

THE READER'S DIGEST ASSOCIATION LIMITED, LONDON

contents

even money
dick francis and felix francis
9

A new, vintage-calibre English mystery from the Francis duo, their third collaboration as a father-and-son writing team. This time, the competitive world of the bookmaker is their focus and it's odds on that you'll want to devour the story in a single sitting.

the sign
raymond khoury
181

This thriller has an opening scene as dramatic as any you're likely to come across. A massive, blazing sphere of light appears in the skies over Antarctica. What does it portend? Is it man-made? Or is it something of greater significance? Read on to find out . . .

endal
allen and sandra parton
361

He was irresistible, loyal and brave, and he was named 'Dog of the Millennium' as well as winning numerous awards and medals. To find out how Endal became a hero in ex-Royal Navy officer Allen Parton's life, dip into this heart-warming true story.

hell bent
william g. tapply
441

Brady Coyne is a good lawyer to know—likable, humble and moral. Which is why his ex-girlfriend, Alex Shaw, seeks his advice on her brother Gus's divorce. Before Brady can help his new client, though, Gus is found dead. Who drove him to suicide—and why?

**select
editions**

Reader's
Digest

Reader's Digest

The condensations in this volume
are published with the consent of the authors
and the publishers © 2009 Reader's Digest.

www.readersdigest.co.uk

The Reader's Digest Association Limited
11 Westferry Circus Canary Wharf London E14 4HE

For information as to ownership of
copyright in the material of this book,
and acknowledgments, see last page.

Printed in Germany
ISBN 978 0 276 44437 1

authors in focus

Allen and Sandra Parton have written an honest
and moving account of the uphill struggle they
faced after Allen suffered a serious head injury
while serving in the Gulf War. Not only had he lost
the use of both his legs, he also had no memories
of his wife and children, and could not talk or write.
Then, after five years of anger and misery, a chance
encounter with a Labrador puppy—Endal—raised
him from despair. The remarkably perceptive Endal
became Allen's aide with everyday tasks and gave
him the strength to live again. This is an uplifting
story of devotion, companionship and healing love.

in the spotlight

Many of the challenges facing our planet at the start
of the twenty-first century are apocalyptic in scale and
global in scope. So Raymond Khoury's bold and dramatic
new international thriller about powerful men with ambitious plans to control the political agenda and bring about
radical change to protect the environment, touches on the
zeitgeist. How would *you* react if you saw a shimmering
ball of light in the sky? Would you assume it be of divine
origin, something from outer space, or perhaps a piece of
technological trickery? In 2009, anything is possible and
politicians are prone, more than ever before, perhaps, to
adopt extreme measures to get things done.

DICK FRANCIS
AND FELIX FRANCIS

EVEN MONEY

As a bookmaker, Ned Talbot has seen it all,
from the euphoria of big race-day profits to glum
disappointment when not many punters turn
out at the track.

But Ned's never had a shock like the one he
gets when a stranger comes up to him at Ascot,
claiming to be his long-lost father.

And it's a dead cert that there's trouble ahead
when the stranger is then stabbed to death
just a few hours later . . .

CHAPTER 1

I sank deeper into depression as the Royal Ascot crowd enthusiastically cheered home another short-priced winning favourite. To be fair, it wasn't clinical depression—I knew all about that—but it was pretty demoralising just the same.

I asked myself yet again what I was doing here. I had never really enjoyed coming to Ascot, especially for these five days in June. It was usually much too hot to be wearing morning dress, or else it rained, and I would get soaked. I preferred the informality of my usual haunts, the smaller steeplechase tracks of the Midlands. But my grandfather, who had started the family business, claimed that the Royal meeting gave us some form of respectability, something he had always craved.

We were bookmakers. Pariahs of the racing world. Disliked by all, and positively hated by many. I had discovered over the years that my clients were never my friends. Whereas city investors might develop a close relationship with their stockbrokers, punters never wanted to be seen socialising with their bookies. Most of my regulars didn't even know my name. I suppose that was fair: I didn't know most of their names, either. We were simply participants in transactions where each of us was trying to bankrupt the other—not a situation likely to engender mutual respect.

'Score on seven,' said a top-hatted young man, thrusting a banknote at me.

I glanced up at our board to check the odds we were offering on horse number seven. 'Twenty pounds on number seven at eleven-to-two,' I said, taking his note and adding it to the wad of others in my left hand.

A small printer in front of me whirred and disgorged a ticket, which I handed to the man. He snatched it from me and moved quickly away into the throng. His place was taken by a short, portly gentleman whose multi-coloured waistcoat was fighting a losing battle against his expansive stomach. He was one of my regular Royal Ascot customers. I knew him only as AJ.

'Hundred on Silverstone to win,' he wheezed at me.

'Hundred on two at even money,' I said, taking his cash and checking the amount. Another betting slip appeared out of the small printer and I passed it over. 'Good luck, AJ,' I said, not really meaning it.

He looked surprised. 'Thanks,' he said, and departed.

In the good old days, when bookmaking was an art rather than a science, every transaction was written down in 'the book' by an assistant. Nowadays, everything was recorded on a computer. It kept a running tally of all the bets that we had taken, and also constantly updated our profit or liability for every possible outcome of the race. It used to be down to the gut reaction of the bookmaker to decide when and by how much to change the prices we displayed. Now the computer decided.

When I started working for my grandfather, I had been his 'runner'. It had been my job to take cash from his hand and use it to back a horse with other bookmakers—a horse on which he had taken some large bets—in order to spread his risk. If the horse was beaten, he didn't make so much, but conversely, if it won, he didn't lose so much, either. Nowadays even that was done by computer, betting and laying horses on the Internet exchanges. Somehow, the romance and the fun had disappeared.

Another man was taking the plunge. 'Twenty pounds, horse two,' he said.

'Twenty on two at evens,' I repeated, so that Luca Mandini, my assistant, could enter the bet on his computer.

Luca was my magician, my Internet whiz kid with a razor-sharp mathe-matical brain who stood right behind me, tapping on his keyboard until the betting slip duly appeared from the printer.

Without Luca I was sure I would have given up by now, forced out by the relentless bully-boy tactics of the big bookmaking firms, who did all they could to squeeze the profit out of the small independents. I was the sole shareholder in my bookmaking business, and I felt the pain.

I handed the betting slip to the man standing patiently in front of me.

'Are you Teddy Talbot?' he asked.

'Who wants to know?' I asked him back.

'I know your grandfather,' said the man, ignoring my question.

My grandfather's name had indeed been Teddy Talbot, and it was his name that was still prominently displayed on our prices board. The slogan actually read TRUST TEDDY TALBOT, as though the extra word might somehow encourage punters to bet with us, rather than the next man.

'My grandfather's dead,' I said, looking beyond him for my next customer and hoping he would move away. He was disrupting my business.

'Oh,' he said. 'I'm sorry. When did he die?'

I stared down at him from my lofty position on a foot-high metal platform. He was grey-haired, in his late fifties or early sixties, and wearing a cream linen suit over an open-necked shirt.

'Look,' I said, 'I'm busy now. If you want to talk, come back later. Now please move aside.'

'Oh,' he said again. 'Sorry.'

He moved, but only to a short distance away, from where he stood and watched me. I found it quite disconcerting.

'Weighed in,' announced someone over the public address system.

A lady in a straw hat came up and handed me a betting slip with TRUST TEDDY TALBOT printed on it. It was a winning ticket from the previous race, the first of rather too many. Nowadays, the potential win amount had to be printed on the slip, so I scanned the details and paid her out for her win. The transaction was wordless—no communication was necessary.

A line of winning-ticket holders was forming in front of me.

Betsy, Luca's girlfriend, came and stood on my left. She paid out the winners while I took new bets on the next race. Luca scanned his screen and adjusted the prices on our board according to the bets I took and the bets and lays he made on the Internet gambling exchanges. It was a balancing act, comparing potential gains against potential losses, always trying to keep both within acceptable ranges. A predicted return greater than 100 per cent was called the overround and represented profit; anything less indicated loss. We tried to keep the overround at about 9 per cent by continuously adjusting our prices. The punters didn't always cooperate, however, so Luca tried to compensate by betting and laying on the Internet.

We liked to think that the computer was our slave, doing the jobs we gave it more efficiently than we could have done them. But in reality the computer was the master and we were its slaves. Technology had replaced instinct.

And so our day progressed. I became hotter and hotter, both over and under the collar, as the sun broke through the veil of cloud and heavily backed short-priced winners continued to push our return into the red.

I didn't, in fact, need to wear my stifling morning suit as I wasn't actually in the Royal Enclosure. There were no bookmaker pitches that side of the fence. But my grandfather had always worn formal dress at this meeting and, since my eighteenth birthday, he had insisted that I did so, too.

Another favourite won the fifth race to huge cheers. I sighed audibly.

'It's not so bad,' said Luca in my ear. 'I had most of that covered.'

'Good,' I said over my shoulder.

The string of short-priced winners had forced us to try to limit our losses by adjusting down the offered prices on our board, which meant that we didn't do as much business. Even our regular clients tended to go elsewhere, chasing the fractionally better odds offered by other bookies.

The man in the linen suit still stood about five yards away and watched.

'Hold the fort,' I said to Betsy. 'I need a pee.'

'Will do,' she said.

I walked across to the man. 'What exactly do you want?' I demanded.

'Nothing,' he said defensively. 'I was just watching.'

'Why?'

'No reason,' he said.

'Then why don't you go and watch someone else?' I said forcefully.

'I'm not doing any harm,' he almost wailed.

'Maybe not, but I don't like it,' I said. 'So go away. Now.'

I walked past him and into the grandstand in search of the Gents.

When I returned, he'd gone.

The last race of the day was won by a twenty-to-one rank outsider, the favourite having been boxed in against the rails until it was too late.

'That saved our bacon,' said Luca with a broad grin.

'Saved your job, you mean,' I said, smiling back at him.

'In your dreams,' he replied.

In my nightmares, more like. I lived in fear that Luca would be enticed away from me by some other outfit.

'So what's the total?' I asked him.

He consulted his machine. 'Down fifteen hundred and sixty-two.'

'Could be worse,' I said, but I couldn't actually remember a previous first-day Tuesday at Royal Ascot when we had lost money.

'Sure could,' he said. 'If the favourite had won the last, we would have been off another grand more, at least.'

I raised my eyebrows at him and he grinned.

'I didn't manage to take as much of the favourite as I wanted on the exchanges,' he explained. 'Damn Internet link went down.'

'Just us or everyone?' I asked seriously.

'Dunno,' he said. He seemed intrigued. 'I'll find out.'

Luca and I started to pack up our equipment as Betsy paid out the occasional winning ticket. Most of the racegoers were streaming for the exits to try to beat the traffic jams. By the time the crowd had dispersed to the car parks, we had loaded most of our gear onto the little trolley that doubled up as a base for our computer during the racing. The betting ring was deserted save for a few other bookmakers who, like us, were still packing up.

'Do you fancy a beer?' Luca asked as I fastened an elastic strap.

'I'd love one,' I said, looking up. 'But I can't. I have to go and see Sophie.'

He nodded knowingly. 'Some other time, then. Betsy and I are going to have one. We're taking the train into town later to go to the party in the park.'

'Right,' I said. 'You go on. I'll pack up the rest of the stuff. I'll see you both in the morning. Usual time.'

'OK,' said Luca. 'Thanks.'

He and Betsy went off, leaving me standing alone next to the tarpaulin-covered trolley. I watched them go, hand in hand. At one point they stopped and embraced before disappearing out of my sight into the grandstand. Just another happy couple on their way to the bandstand bar for a drink.

I sighed. I supposed I must have been that happy once, a long time ago. What had happened to all the happy times? Had they deserted me for ever?

I wiped my brow on the sleeve of my jacket and thought about how I would adore a nice cooling beer. I wanted to change my mind and go to find the other two, but I knew it would be more trouble than it was worth.

I sighed again and stacked the last of our equipment boxes onto the trolley, then fixed the rest of the elastic cords across the green tarpaulin. I took hold of the handle, released the brakes from the wheels and tugged hard.

'Do you want a hand with that?' a voice shouted from behind me.

I stopped pulling and turned round. It was the man in the cream linen suit. He was about fifteen yards away, leaning up against the metal fence between the betting ring and the Royal Enclosure. I hadn't noticed him as we'd packed up and I wondered how long he'd been there watching me.

'Who's offering?' I called back to him.

'I knew your grandfather,' he said again while walking over to me.

'You said,' I replied.

Lots of people knew my grandfather, but few had liked him. He had been a typically belligerent bookie, who had treated both customers and fellow bookmakers with the same degree of contempt they clearly held for him.

'When did he die?' asked the man, taking hold of one side of the handle.

We pulled the trolley together in silence up the slope to the grandstand and stopped on the flat of the concourse. I turned and looked at my helper. His grey hair was accentuated by the deeply tanned skin of his face.

'Five years ago,' I said.

'What did he die from?' he asked. I could detect a slight accent in his voice but I couldn't quite place it.

'Nothing, really,' I said. 'Just old age.' And bloody-mindedness, I thought.

'But surely he wasn't that old,' said the man.

'Seventy-five,' I said. 'And two days.'

'That's not old,' said the man, 'not these days.'

'It was old enough for him,' I said.

The man looked at me quizzically.

'My grandfather decided that his time was up so he laid down and died.'

'Silly old bugger,' he said, almost under his breath.

'Exactly how well did you know my grandfather?' I asked him.

'I'm his son,' he said.

I stared at him with an open mouth. 'So you must be my uncle,' I said.

'No,' he said, staring back. 'I'm your father.'

CHAPTER 2

'But you can't be my father,' I said, nonplussed.

'I can,' he said with certainty, 'and I am.'

'My father's dead,' I said.

'Is that what your grandfather told you?'

My legs felt detached from my body. I was thirty-seven years old and I had believed for as long as I could remember that I was fatherless. And motherless, too. An orphan. I had been raised by my grandparents, who had both told me that my parents had died in a car crash when I was a baby.

'But I've seen a photo,' I said.

'Of what?' he asked.

'Of my parents,' I said.

'So you recognise me, then?'

'No,' I said. But the photo was very small and at least thirty-seven years old, so would I actually recognise him now?

'Look,' he said, 'is there anywhere we could go and sit down?'

IN THE END I did have that beer.

We sat at a table near the bar overlooking the pre-parade ring, while the man in the cream linen suit told me who I was.

'Your mother and I were in a road accident,' he told me. He looked down. 'And then she died.' He paused, as if wondering whether to carry on.

I sat there looking at him in confusion. I couldn't understand why my grandparents would have lied to me, but, equally, why would this stranger suddenly appear and lie to me now? It made no sense.

'Why have you come here today to tell me this?' I said. I began to feel angry that he had disrupted my life in this way. 'Why didn't you stay away?' I raised my voice. 'As you have done for the past thirty-seven years?'

'Because I wanted to see you,' he said. 'You are my son.'

'No, I'm not,' I shouted at him.

There were a few others enjoying a quick drink before making their way home, and they were looking in our direction.

'You are, Edward,' he said quietly, 'whether you like it or not.'

It was the first time he had used my name and it sounded odd. I had been christened Edward, but I'd been known as Ned all my life.

'What's your name?' I asked him.

'Peter,' he said. 'Peter James Talbot.'

My father's name was indeed Peter James Talbot. It said so on both my birth certificate and his. I knew by heart every element of those documents, which had been the only tangible link to my parents, apart from the small, creased photograph that I still carried with me everywhere.

I removed my wallet from my pocket and passed the photo over to him.

'Blackpool,' he said with confidence, studying the image. 'This was taken in Blackpool. We were there for the illuminations in November. Tricia, your mother, was about three months pregnant. With you.'

I took the photo back and looked closely at the young man standing next to a dark green Ford Cortina, as I had hundreds of times before. I glanced up at the man in front of me, then back at the picture. I couldn't say for sure that they were the same person, but, equally, I couldn't say they weren't.

'It is me, I assure you,' he said. 'I was nineteen and that was my first car.'

'How old was my mother?' I asked.

'Seventeen, I think,' he said. 'Yes, she must have been just seventeen.'

'You started young.'

'Yes . . . well.' He seemed embarrassed. 'You weren't actually planned.'

'Oh, thanks,' I replied somewhat sarcastically. 'Were you married?'

'Not when that picture was taken, no.'

'How about when I was born?' I wasn't sure that I wanted to know.

'Oh, yes,' he said with certainty. 'We were by then.'

Strangely, I was relieved that I was legitimate. It meant that there had been some commitment between my parents, maybe even love.

'Why did you leave?' I asked him. It was the big question.

He didn't answer immediately but sat quite still, looking at me.

'Shame, I suppose,' he said eventually. 'After your mother died, I couldn't cope with having a baby and no wife. So I ran away.'

'Where to?' I asked.

'Australia,' he said. 'Eventually. First I signed on to a Liberian-registered cargo ship in Liverpool docks. I went all over the world for a while. I got off one day in Melbourne and just stayed there.'

'So why come back now?'

'It seemed like a good idea,' he said.

It wasn't.

'What did you expect?' I asked. 'Did you think I would just welcome you with open arms after all this time? I thought you were dead.' I looked at him. 'I think it might be better for me if you were.'

He looked back at me with doleful eyes. Perhaps I had been a bit hard.

'Well,' I said, 'it would definitely have been better if you hadn't come back.'

'But I wanted to see you,' he said.

'Why?' I demanded. 'You haven't wanted to for the last thirty-seven years.'

'Thirty-six,' he said.

I threw my hands up in frustration. 'That's even worse,' I said. 'It means you deserted me when I was a year old. How could a father do that?' I was getting angry again. So far my own life had not been blessed with children, but it was not from a lack of longing.

'I'm sorry,' he said.

I wasn't sure it was enough.

'You can't just have decided suddenly you wanted to see me after all this time,' I said. 'You didn't even know that your own father was dead. And what about your mother? You haven't asked me about her.'

'It was only you I wanted to see,' he said.

'But why now? Don't try to tell me you had a fit of conscience after all these years.' I gave an ironic laugh.

'Edward,' he said somewhat sternly, 'it doesn't befit you to be so caustic.'

The laughter died in my throat. 'You've no right to tell me how to behave,' I said with equal sternness. 'You forfeited that when you walked away.'

He looked down like a scolded dog.

'So what do you want?' I asked him. 'I've got no money.'

His head came up again quickly. 'I don't want your money,' he said.

'What, then?' I asked. 'Don't expect me to give you any love.'

'Are you happy?' he asked suddenly.

'Deliriously,' I lied. 'I leap out of bed each morning with joy in my heart, delighting at the miracle of a new day.'

'Are you married?' he asked.

'Yes,' I said, giving no more details. 'Are you?'

'No,' he replied. 'Not any more. But I have been. Widowed twice and divorced once,' he said with a wry smile. 'In that order.'

'Children?' I asked. 'Other than me.'

'Two,' he said. 'Both girls.'

I had sisters. Half-sisters, anyway.

'How old are they?'

'In their late twenties, I suppose. I haven't seen them for, oh, fifteen years.'

'You seem to have made a habit of deserting your children.'

'Yes,' he said wistfully. 'It appears I have.'

'Why didn't you leave me alone and go and find *them*?'

'But I know where they are,' he said. 'They won't see me, not the other way round. They blame me for their mother's death.'

'Did she die in a car crash, too?' I said, a touch of cruelty in my voice.

'No,' he said slowly. 'Maureen killed herself.' He paused and I sat still, watching him. 'I was made bankrupt and she swallowed enough tablets to kill a horse. I came home from the court hearing to find bailiffs sitting in the driveway and my wife lying dead in the house.'

His life was like a soap opera, I thought.

'Why were you made bankrupt?' I asked.

'Gambling debts,' he said.

'I thought gambling debts couldn't be enforced in a court.'

'Maybe not technically, but I had borrowed against everything and I couldn't afford the repayments. Lost the lot. The girls went off to live with their aunt. I never saw them again.'

'Are you still bankrupt?' I asked.

'Oh, no,' he said. 'That was years ago. I've been doing fine recently.'

'As what?' I said.

'Business,' he said unhelpfully. 'My business.'

One of the bar staff came over to us. 'Sorry, we're closing,' he said. 'Can you drink up, please?'

I looked at my watch. It was past six o'clock. I finished my beer.

'Can we go somewhere to continue talking?' my father asked.

I thought about Sophie. I had promised I would go and see her straight after the races. 'I have to go to my wife,' I said.

'Can't she wait?' he implored. 'Call her and say you've been held up.'

I thought again about Sophie, my wife. She wasn't at home. She would be sitting in front of the television in her room watching the six o'clock news. I knew she would be there because she wasn't allowed not to be.

Sophie Talbot had been sectioned under the Mental Health Act 1983 and detained for the past five months in secure accommodation. It wasn't actually a prison, it was a hospital, a low-risk mental hospital, but it was a prison to her. And this wasn't the first time. In all, my wife had spent more than half the previous ten years in one mental institution or another.

'How about a pub somewhere?' my father said, interrupting my thoughts.

I needed to be at the hospital by nine at the latest. I looked at my watch.

'I have about an hour, maximum,' I said. 'Then I'll have to go.'

'Fine,' he said.

'Do you have a car?' I asked him.

'No,' he said. 'Came on the train from Waterloo.'

'Where are you staying?' I asked.

'Some seedy little hotel in Sussex Gardens,' he said. 'Guesthouse really. Near Paddington Station.'

'Right,' I said, deciding. 'We'll go somewhere for a drink; then I'll drop you at Maidenhead and you can get the train back to London.'

'Great,' he said, smiling.

'Come on, then.'

We pulled the trolley out through the main gate and across the road.

'What sort of business are you in now?' I asked him as we hauled our load through the deep gravel at the entrance to the car park.

'This and that,' he said evasively.

'Is it legal?' I asked.

'Sometimes.' He smiled at me and pulled harder on the trolley.

'Are you going to go back to Australia?' I asked, changing the subject.

'Expect so,' he said. 'But I'm just lying low for a while.'

'Why?' I asked.

He just smiled again. Perhaps it's better, I thought, if I don't know why.

I had parked my car, my trusty twelve-year-old Volvo estate, in car park number two, behind the owners' and trainers' area. As always, I'd had to pay for my parking. The racecourses gave bookmakers nothing.

Bookmakers' pitches had once been held on the basis of inherited seniority, as they still were in Ireland. From 1998, however, pitch positions in Britain had been offered for sale at auction and, once bought, remained the property of the bookie, to sell on if he wished. Whoever owned number one had the first choice of where to stand in the betting ring, number two had second choice and so on. My pitch number, bought by my grandfather for a king's ransom, was eight.

My bookmaker's badge fee, which allowed me to stand on any day at the races, was set at five times the public-entry cost. So if a racegoer paid forty pounds each day to get into the betting ring, as they did at Royal Ascot, then the badge fee was set at £200. Plus, of course, the regular entrance cost for Betsy and Luca to get in. On any day at this meeting, I was many hundreds out of pocket before I even took my first bet.

'How long are you staying?' I asked my father.

'A while,' he replied unhelpfully.

'Look,' I said, 'perhaps it's better if you go straight back to London now. There's little point in going for a drink if you ignore all my questions.'

'I want to talk about the past, not the future,' he said.

'Well, I don't.'

We were still pulling the trolley towards my car, passing through a gap in the hedge to the back of car park two, when I heard running footsteps behind us. I turned my head and caught a glimpse of someone coming straight at me. He ran up onto the tarpaulin-covered trolley and kicked me in the face.

Shit, I thought as I fell to the ground, I'm being robbed. Didn't this idiot know what a dreadful day it had been for the bookies?

I was down on all fours with my head hanging between my shoulders. I could feel on my face the warmth of fresh blood and I could see it running in a bright red rivulet from my chin onto the grass beneath me.

I half expected another blow to my head, or even a boot in my guts. I managed to manoeuvre my right hand into my deep trouser pocket and pull out the envelope containing a small wad of banknotes, all that remained of the few grand of readies I'd bought with me that morning.

I threw it on the grass. 'Here,' I shouted. 'Take it and leave us be.'

I rolled over onto my side. I didn't really want to see my attacker's face, but I needn't have worried. The young man—and I was sure from his strength and agility that he was young—was wearing a scarf round his face and the hood of his dark grey sweatshirt was pulled up over his head.

He turned to face my father. 'Where's the money?' he hissed.

'There,' I said, pointing at the white envelope. 'That's all I have.'

The man ignored me.

'Go to hell,' my father said to him, lashing out with his foot.

The foot caught the man in the groin. 'You bastard,' he hissed with anger.

The man appeared to punch my father twice rapidly in the stomach. He sat down heavily on the ground with his back up against the hedge.

'Where's the bloody money?' hissed our attacker once again.

This time my father said nothing.

'Leave him be,' I shouted at the hooded figure. 'It's there,' I said, once again pointing at the envelope on the grass. The man continued to ignore me and turned back to my father, so I screamed, 'Help! Help! Help!'

The car park was mostly deserted, but there were still some after-racing parties taking place in the owners' and trainers' area. Heads turned our way and three or four brave souls took a few steps in our direction.

The man took one look over his shoulder at the approaching group and ran off, disappearing over the wooden fence on the far side of the car park. I sat on the grass and watched him go. He never once looked back.

The envelope of money still lay on the grass next to me. I picked it up and thrust it back into my pocket, then struggled to my feet.

Three of the waistcoated revellers had arrived, still clutching their champagne glasses.

'Are you all right?' asked one. 'That's quite a cut on your face.'

I could still feel the blood, now running down my neck.

'I think I'll be fine,' I said. 'Thanks to you. He didn't get away with any-thing.' I took a couple of steps over to my father. 'Are you OK . . . Dad?' I asked him. The word 'dad' sounded strange to my ears.

He looked up at me with frightened eyes.

'What is it?' I asked urgently, taking another step towards him.

He was clutching his abdomen and now he moved his hand away. The cream linen jacket was rapidly turning bright red. My father hadn't been punched in the stomach by the young man; he'd been stabbed.

THE AMBULANCE took an age to arrive. One of the champagne revellers had made the 999 call while I knelt down on the grass next to my father. The blood had spread across his abdomen and his face had turned ashen grey.

'Lie him down,' someone said. 'Put his head lower than his heart.'

Quite a crowd had drifted over from the various car-park parties. It seemed absurd for people to be standing around sipping champagne while my father was fighting for breath at their feet.

'It's OK,' I told my father. 'Help is on the way.'

He nodded very slightly and then tried to say something.

'Save your energy,' I instructed, but he continued to try to speak.

'Be very careful.' He said it softly but quite distinctly.

'Of what?' I replied.

'Of everyone,' he whispered. He coughed and blood appeared on his lips.

'Where is that damn ambulance?' I shouted at no one in particular.

But it was the police who arrived first. Two officers appeared on foot, and one of them was immediately on his radio calling for reinforcements. The other one knelt down next to me and tended to my father by putting pres-sure on the wound with his hand. My father groaned.

Eventually the ambulance arrived, with the driver apologising for the time taken. 'Going against the race traffic,' he explained. 'Jams everywhere and half the roads made one way—the wrong way.'

My father was rapidly assessed and given oxygen through a face mask, and intravenous fluids via a needle in his arm. He was lifted carefully onto a stretcher and loaded into the vehicle. I tried to climb in with him, but was stopped by one of the policemen.

'You wait here with us, sir,' he said.

'But that's my father,' I said.

'We will get you to the hospital shortly,' he said. 'It looks like you need a stitch or two in that head anyway.'

The paramedics closed the ambulance doors and bore my father away just as the police back-up arrived in two blue-flashing cars.

I SPENT MUCH of the evening in a hospital, but not the one where I'd planned to be. According to one of the nurses, my father had still been alive when he arrived at Wexham Park Hospital. But the combination of massive shock and drowning in his own blood killed him before he could make it into the operating theatre. So sorry, they said; there was nothing they could have done.

I sat on a chair in a curtained-off cubicle in accident and emergency, next to the body of my dead parent, a parent I hadn't known existed three hours previously, and wondered how the world could be so cruel.

I was numb. I had grieved for my father when I was about eight, when I was just old enough to begin to realise what I was missing. I could still remember it clearly. I had seen my school friends with their young mums and dads, and realised for the first time that my aged grandparents were different. I remembered the tears I had shed, longing for my parents to be alive and with me. I had wanted so much for my father to be there and to be like the other dads, shouting encouragement from the touchline during my school football games, carrying me high on his shoulders when we won, consoling and wiping away the tears when we lost.

I looked at the figure lying silently on his back beside me, covered by a crisp white sheet. I folded the sheet down to his chest so I could see his face. He looked as if he was just asleep, peaceful, with his eyes closed, as if he could be wakened by my touch. I stroked his suntanned forehead for the first and last time in my life and considered what might have been.

I should be angry with him, I thought. Angry for leaving me all those years ago. Angry that he'd taken so long to come back. Angry that I'd had sisters for nearly thirty years whom I'd never met. And angry that he had come back and added complications to my already complex existence.

But it seemed pointless and wasteful of my energy to direct anger towards my father's corpse. I would save my anger, I decided, for the young man who had so abruptly taken away any chance I might have had to make up for time lost in the past. I grieved not so much for the death of my father but for the loss of the opportunity that had come so close.

A man in a light brown suit came into the cubicle. 'Mr Talbot?' he asked.

'Yes,' I said, turning towards him.

'I'm Detective Sergeant Murray,' he said, showing me his warrant card. 'Thames Valley Police.' He looked down at the inert form beneath the sheet. 'I'm very sorry about your father, but we need to ask you some questions.'

'Yes, of course,' I said.

One of the nurses showed the two of us into a small room provided for families, and a second plain-clothes policeman came in to join us.

'This is DC Walton,' said Sergeant Murray, introducing his colleague. 'Now, what can you tell us about the incident in the car park at Ascot?'

'I'd call it more than just an incident,' I said. 'I was attacked and my father was fatally stabbed.'

'We will have to wait for the post-mortem to determine the actual cause of death, sir,' said the sergeant rather formally.

'But I saw my father being stabbed,' I said.

'So you did see your attacker?' he asked.

'Yes,' I said. 'But I don't know that I'd recognise him again. His face was covered. All I could see were his eyes, and that was only for a split second.'

'But you are sure it was a man?' he asked.

'Oh, yes,' I said. 'He had a man's shape. He ran at me and came straight up onto my equipment trolley and kicked me in the face.' I instinctively put my hand up to the now-stitched cut in my left eyebrow.

'Was he white or black?' he asked.

'White, I think,' I said slowly, going over again in my mind the whole episode. 'Yes, he was white,' I said with certainty. 'His eyes were those of a white man.' I remembered that I'd thought at the time that they were shifty-looking eyes, rather too close together for the shape of his face.

'Can you describe what he was wearing?' the sergeant asked.

'Blue jeans, charcoal-grey hoodie, black scarf over the lower part of his face,' I said. 'And black boots, like army boots with deep-cut soles. I saw one of those close up.' The constable wrote it all down in his notebook.

'Tall or short?' the sergeant asked.

'Neither, really,' I said. 'About the same as my father.'

'Tell us about your father,' he said, changing direction. 'Can you think why anyone would want him dead?'

'Want my father dead?' I repeated. 'But surely this was just a robbery that went wrong?'

'Why do you think that?' he asked.

'I just assumed it was,' I said. 'It wouldn't be the first time a bookmaker was robbed in a racecourse car park. Not even the first time for me. Some people will try anything to get their money back.'

'But you say you weren't robbed on this occasion,' said the sergeant.

'No,' I admitted, feeling for the envelope of cash in my trouser pocket. 'I simply imagined the thief took off when he found he had an audience.'

'Now, about your father,' he said. 'What was his full name?'

'Peter James Talbot,' I said. The constable wrote it down.

'And his address?' the detective sergeant asked.

'I don't know his address, but I believe he lived in Melbourne, Australia.'

'Then can you tell us, Mr Talbot, why the man you claim was your father had a credit card and a driving licence in his jacket both in the name of Alan Charles Grady?'

'ARE YOU TELLING US that you didn't know your father existed?' the chief inspector asked.

'Well . . .' I said slowly. 'Yes and no.'

'Which?' he demanded.

'Yes, obviously I knew that he existed thirty-seven years ago, but no, I didn't know until today that he *still* existed.'

I was again with Detective Sergeant Murray and DC Walton but we had transferred as a group from the hospital to a stark interview room at Windsor Police Station. We had been joined by Detective Chief Inspector Llewellyn, who did not extend the nicety of expressing sympathy for my dead father. I decided I didn't like him very much, and he clearly didn't like me.

'Are you absolutely certain that this man was your father?' He stabbed his finger at the driving licence that sat on the table in front of me, its photograph clearly being that of the man lying dead at the hospital.

'No,' I said, looking up at him, 'I can't say I am absolutely certain. But I still think he was. It was not so much what he looked like or what he said but his demeanour that convinced me. He picked at his fingers in the same way I watched my grandfather do a million times, and there was something about his lolloping walk that is somehow reminiscent of my own.'

'Then why is this licence in the name of Alan Grady?' he asked.

'I have no idea,' I said. 'Is it genuine?'

'We're checking,' he said.

'Well, I still believe the man in that photograph is my father.'

The chief inspector clearly didn't share my confidence. 'The DNA will tell us for sure one way or another,' he said. I had been asked for, and had given, a sample of my DNA at the hospital. 'And you say he's lived in Australia for the past thirty years or so?'

'That's what he told me, yes,' I replied.

'And you believed him?'

'Yes. Why would he lie to me?'

'Mr Talbot,' he said, 'in my experience, people lie all the time.' He leaned forward and looked at me closely. 'You might be lying to me right now.'

'Well, I'm not.'

'We'll see,' said the chief inspector, standing up abruptly and walking out of the room.

'Chief Inspector Llewellyn has left the room,' said the sergeant, for the benefit of the audio recording machine that sat on the table to my left.

'Can I go now?' I asked.

'You can leave any time,' said the sergeant. 'You are not under arrest.'

Maybe not, I thought, but I had been questioned under caution.

'Then I would like to go home,' I said. 'I have to be back at Ascot Racecourse at ten thirty in the morning.'

'Interview terminated,' said the sergeant, glancing up at the clock, 'at twenty-two forty-five.' He pushed the STOP button on the recorder.

'Please can I have a photocopy of that driving licence?' I asked him.

'What for?'

'The photograph. The only one I have of my father was taken before I was born. I would like to have another.'

'Er,' said the sergeant, looking at Constable Walton. 'I'm not sure I can.'

'Please,' I said in my most charming manner.

Constable Walton shrugged his shoulders.

'OK,' said the sergeant. 'But don't tell the chief inspector.'

I wouldn't, I assured him. I wouldn't have told the chief inspector if his flies had been undone.

Sergeant Murray disappeared for a moment and returned with a blown-up copy of the licence, which I folded and placed in my trouser pocket, alongside the envelope of cash.

'Thank you,' I said.

'Yeah,' he said wistfully. 'Lost my dad too, about three months ago.'

'Sorry,' I said.

'Thanks,' he replied. 'Cancer.'

He walked me to the door of the police station, where we shook hands warmly, the comradeship of those with recently deceased fathers.

'Now, how do I get home?' I said, turning my morning-coat collar up against the chill of an English June night.

'Where's your car?' he asked.

'In the car park at Ascot, I expect. That's where I left it.' With, I hoped, all our equipment still safely in the boot. The uniformed boys had helped me load everything in there before insisting they drove me to the hospital. 'The car park will be locked, and there's no chance of getting a hotel room now.'

'Where's home?' asked the sergeant.

'Kenilworth,' I said, 'in Warwickshire.'

'Er . . .' He seemed to be undecided. 'I suppose you'll have to get a taxi.'

'Do you have any idea how much a taxi to Kenilworth would cost?' I asked in exasperation. 'Especially at this time of night.'

'Sorry, sir,' he said rather formally. 'Nothing else I can do.'

'Don't you have a spare cell I could use?' I asked.

'We can't go offering cells as hotel rooms, can we?' he said sarcastically.

'If I was drunk and disorderly you'd put me in a cell to sleep it off.'

'But you're not,' he said.

'I could be,' I said, grinning. 'It'd be cheaper than a taxi to Kenilworth.'

'I'll see,' he said. 'Wait here.'

He disappeared into the police station for a few minutes.

'OK,' he said. 'On compassionate grounds only. I've had to say that you are distraught over the death of your father and in no state to be allowed to go home. And for God's sake don't tell Chief Inspector Llewellyn.'

I DIDN'T SLEEP very well but, in fairness, it was mostly due to having a thumping headache rather than the starkness of my surroundings. My night's accommodation hadn't been designed with comfort in mind, but the kindly night-custody sergeant had provided me with a second plastic-covered mattress, which made the concrete sleeping platform almost bearable.

'We're not very busy tonight,' he'd explained. 'Just a couple of drunk drivers from the races. Bit too much of the champers, silly buggers.'

I was luckier than the two other residents as I slept with the light off and the door ajar. Even though my cell had its own basic en-suite facilities in the corner, I was invited in the morning to make use of the more salubrious staff washroom, where I found a shower, shampoo and a disposable razor. My hosts also provided me with breakfast.

'We are required to feed the drunks before their court appearances, so I ordered you a breakfast too,' said the custody sergeant.

'Thanks,' I said, taking the offered tray of cornflakes and toast with a mug of sweet white tea. 'Don't have a copy of the *Racing Post* as well, do you?'

'Don't push your luck, Mr Talbot,' he said with a grin.

My opinion of the police had risen a few rungs—except, that was, for Chief Inspector Llewellyn. But fortunately there was no sign of him as I took my leave and rode in a taxi back to the racecourse.

I walked into the still-closed car park two at 7.50 to find my old Volvo exactly where I had left it the previous evening. It stood all alone on the grass, not far from the gap in the hedge where there was now a white tent surrounded by blue-and-white POLICE DO NOT CROSS tape. A bored-looking constable stood guard on one side of the tent.

I went over to my car, started the engine for warmth and called Luca on my mobile phone. 'Sorry,' I said to him. 'I can't pick you and Betsy up today. Can you make it here by train?'

'No problem,' he said sleepily. 'See you later.' He hung up.

I sat in the driver's seat of my car and took stock of the situation.

The previous afternoon I had discovered that I hadn't been an orphan all those years, only to be violently orphaned for real less than an hour later. Or had I? Had the man in the linen suit really been my father? Did I really have two Australian sisters? If so, shouldn't someone tell them their father had been murdered? Were their names Talbot or Grady? Or something else?

I pulled the copy of the driving licence from my pocket and looked at the black-and-white photograph of my father. His eyes gazed straight into the camera. Alan Charles Grady, the licence read, of 312 Macpherson Street, Carlton North, Victoria 3054. I wondered, as I had done for much of my sleepless night, if the sergeant had been right and the purpose of the attack had been specifically to do my father harm, if he *was* my father, rather than to rob me. But why would anyone want to harm him?

'Where is the money?' the murderer had hissed at him. The police had shown me the contents of my father's pockets. Other than the driving licence and the credit cards with the name Grady on them, there had been a return ticket from Waterloo to Ascot, a packet of boiled sweets, the TRUST

TEDDY TALBOT betting slip I had given him myself and about thirty pounds in cash. Was there some other money that he had had? Or owed?

'Be very careful,' my father had said to me as he lay dying on the grass where the white tent now stood. 'Be very careful of everyone.'

I glanced around as if somebody might have been creeping up on me. But I was still alone in the car park, save for the police guard at the tent.

I tried to call Sophie, but she wouldn't answer her phone. She had been cross with me when I telephoned her from Wexham Park Hospital to say I wasn't coming to see her. I had decided not to mention the sudden appearance of a living father in my life, followed by his equally sudden permanent removal. Stress caused by unexpected situations could bring on a severe bout of depression. Currently she was improving and I was hopeful that she would soon be coming to live at home—until the next attack.

Sophie rode a rollercoaster life, with great peaks of mania followed by deep troughs of despair. Between the extremes there were periods of calm, rational behaviour. These were the good times when we were able to lead a fairly normal married life. Sadly they were becoming rarer, and shorter.

'Have you been drinking again?' she had asked accusingly.

Sophie, in her irrational mind, believed that I lived for alcohol. I wasn't an alcoholic, never drank to excess. In fact, I now rarely touched the stuff. It made for a quieter life. I'd had a single beer four hours previously but I had still promised her that I hadn't touched a drop.

She hadn't been convinced. 'You're always drinking,' she'd shouted down the line. 'You won't come and see me because you're drunk. Admit it.'

I had come close to telling her why I couldn't come to see her, but I held my tongue. 'I'm sorry,' I'd said, admitting nothing. 'I'll see you tomorrow.'

THE SECOND DAY of Royal Ascot didn't quite have the excitement of the first. But murder in the car park was the talk of the racecourse.

'Did you hear that the victim was someone involved in doping,' I heard one man confidently telling another.

'Really?' replied the second. 'Well, you never know what's going on right under your nose, do you?'

For all I knew they might have been right. There was scant factual information being given out by the police. Probably, I thought, because they couldn't be sure of the true identity of the victim, let alone the perpetrator.

Luca and Betsy were, surprisingly, not at all inquisitive about my rapidly darkening eye, but they were suitably sympathetic, which was more than could be said for my fellow bookmakers, or even my clients.

''Morning, Ned,' said Larry Porter, the bookie on the neighbouring pitch. 'Did yer missus do that?' He was obviously enjoying my discomfort.

'Good morning to you, too,' I replied. 'And no. I walked into a door.'

'Oh, yeah,' he said. 'Pull the other one.'

I felt sorry for people who really had walked into a door. No one must ever believe them. 'Actually, I was mugged,' I said.

'We were all mugged yesterday,' he said, laughing expansively at his little joke, 'by the bloody punters.'

I just smiled at him and let it go. Thankfully, no one else seemed to connect the murder in the car park with my black eye, and the novelty of it slowly wore off as the afternoon's sport progressed.

'Was it just us or was the Internet down for everyone yesterday?' I asked Luca during a lull after the third race.

'It seems the whole system was down for nearly five minutes,' he said. 'And you know what else was funny? The mobile phones were off, too. All of them. Every network. Nothing.'

'But that's impossible,' I said.

'I know,' he said. 'But it happened. No signal anywhere for about five minutes. The boys from the big outfits were going nuts.'

By 'the big outfits', Luca meant the five large companies that ran strings of betting shops across the country. Each had a man or two at the races who would bet for them with the on-course bookmakers to affect starting prices. The odds offered by on-course bookmakers often change before the race starts. If a horse is heavily backed, they will shorten its odds and offer better prices on the other horses to compensate. The official starting price is an approximate average of the prices offered on the bookmakers' boards on the racecourse just as the race starts.

Big winning bets in high-street betting shops are nearly always paid on the official starting price. So if someone loads money on a horse in their local betting shop, the company arranges for their man to bet on that horse with the racecourse bookmakers so that the odds on their boards drop and consequently the starting price will be shorter. But if both the Internet and the telephones are not working for the five minutes before the race, then the companies have no way of instructing their staff to make the bets.

'Any word on anyone being caught out?' I asked Luca.

'No, nothing,' he said. 'Quiet as a whisper.'

Word usually went round pretty quickly if a big company believed they had been 'done'. The big boys believed that it was their God-given right to control the starting prices, and if someone managed to get one over on them, it was unfair and they moaned about it ad nauseam. Most others believed that what was really unfair was how the major bookmaking chains could change the on-course prices so easily.

I shrugged my shoulders and took a bet from another customer. Luca pushed the keys on his computer and out popped the ticket from the printer.

'At least our computer and printer didn't go off as well,' I said to him over my shoulder.

'Well, they wouldn't,' he said confidently. 'Unless the battery went flat.'

Our system, like every other bookmaker's, was powered by a twelve-volt car battery hidden under the platforms we stood on. The batteries were provided freshly charged each day by the racecourse technology company, which also provided the Internet access. The same battery powered the lights that showed the horses' names and prices on our board. If the battery went flat, we would soon know about it.

The lights stayed on and we recouped most of our losses from the previous day as favourites were beaten in each of the first five races. I was just beginning to enjoy the day when Chief Inspector Llewellyn pitched up in front of me with DC Walton in tow.

'Making a bet, Chief Inspector?' I asked with a smile.

He didn't appear amused. 'We need to talk,' he said. 'Now.'

'Can't it wait?' I said. 'I'm busy.'

'No,' he said crossly. 'I need to ask you some more questions, now.' He emphasised the final word so sharply that Betsy looked up questioningly.

I smiled at her. 'Can you hold the fort for five minutes?'

'Sure, no problem,' she said.

I moved away with the policemen to a quieter spot on the grass.

'Now, what's so bloody urgent?' I said. 'I've got a business to manage.'

'And I've got a murder investigation to run,' he replied. 'But if you prefer you can accompany us to the police station for a formal interview there.'

'Here is fine,' I said.

'I thought so,' he said almost smugly. 'Now, Mr Talbot, have you anything to add to your account of the incident in the car park last evening that resulted in the death of a man?'

'No,' I said. 'I don't.'

'And you still believe that the man killed was your father?' he asked.

'Yes,' I said. 'I do.'

'It seems you may be right,' he said slowly. 'The DNA analysis suggests that you and the deceased were closely related. It's by no means a hundred per cent certain, but it would be enough to settle a paternity case.'

So at least my father had been truthful about that.

'However,' he said, 'the DNA results have thrown up something else.' He paused for effect. 'Your father was wanted for murder.'

'What?' I said, unable to properly take it in. 'Are you sure?'

'Completely sure,' he said. 'The DNA match is a hundred per cent.'

'But who did he murder?' I asked, almost as if in a trance.

'Patricia Jane Talbot. His wife.'

My mother.

CHAPTER 3

It was after eight by the time I made it to the hospital near Hemel Hempstead. Sophie was still cross, but at least she was speaking to me.

'I thought you weren't coming again,' she said accusingly.

'I said I would come,' I replied, smiling at her and trying to lighten the atmosphere. 'And here I am, my darling.'

'What have you done to your eye?' she demanded.

'Silly, really,' I said. 'I caught it on the corner of the kitchen cupboard, you know, the one by the fridge.' We had both done it before, often.

'Were you drunk?' she asked.

'No,' I said. 'I was not. I was getting the milk out of the fridge.'

I leaned down to give her a kiss and she made a point of smelling my breath. Finding no trace of the demon drink, she relaxed somewhat.

'Have you had a good day?' she asked, smiling at me.

'Yes,' I said. 'Particularly good. All six favourites lost and we recouped the entire amount of yesterday's losses, and then some.' I decided against mentioning anything about my visit from DCI Llewellyn.

'Good,' she said, sounding genuinely pleased.

We sat together in armchairs in front of the television in what might have been a normal domestic situation if not for the multi-adjustable hospital bed in the corner of the room and the uniformed male nurse who brought us in a tray of coffee, together with Sophie's medication.

'Good evening, Mr Talbot,' the nurse said to me. 'Glad you could make it tonight.' He smiled. 'Your wife was so disappointed yesterday.'

He gave the impression that I was being officially told off, which I probably was. Sophie's treatment relied heavily on having a steady routine.

'Good evening, Jason,' I said to the nurse, smiling back and resisting the temptation to make excuses. Now was neither the time nor the place.

Sophie and I watched the television news together before I departed into the night and onto the road to Kenilworth, heading home.

Our house was a 1950s three-bedroom semi-detached in what was still called Station Road, although the railway station to which it referred had closed in the 1960s. At 11.50 p.m. I gratefully pulled my Volvo into the parking space that used to be the front garden.

Sophie and I had moved here from a rented one-bedroom over-shop flat soon after our wedding. Her parents hadn't approved of the union. They were god-fearing Methodists who believed that bookmakers were agents of the Devil. So it was as if we were both orphans, but we didn't care. We were in love and we needed only each other.

The house in Station Road was the first home we had owned, and to begin with it was a struggle to meet the mortgage repayments. Sophie had worked in the evenings behind the bar at the local pub, and I had toiled six days a week on the Midland racecourses. Quite quickly, though, we paid down the mortgage to a level that allowed us to spend more time together at home.

I had always wanted children and I soon made mental plans to turn the smallest bedroom into a nursery. Perhaps it was the pain of having endured an unhappy childhood that had made me so keen to nurture the next generation. Not that my grandparents hadn't been loving and caring. They had. But they had also been somewhat distant and secretive. Now I knew why.

'How could God have taken Mummy and Daddy to Heaven?' I had constantly asked my grandmother. She'd had no answer to give me. Now I discovered that my father, not God, had been responsible for my mother's death, and he himself, far from going to Heaven, had gone to Australia.

In spite of her longing for a child, Sophie's illness had soon put our family plans on hold. And now, after ten years of witnessing the destruction of a bubbly, lively and fun-loving young woman from within, I knew that those plans were well and truly switched off. It was not just that Sophie was too often ill to look after a child; it was also the risk that a pregnancy would cause an upset to her hormones that could tip her over into a state from which she would never recover. Postnatal depression can debilitate even the sanest of mothers, so what might it do to Sophie?

I supposed I still loved my wife, although after five months of medically enforced separation I was sometimes unsure. It was true that, during those months, there had occasionally been some good moments, but they had been rare, and mostly we existed in limbo, our lives on pause, waiting for someone to push the PLAY button if things improved.

We had definitely been dealt a bum hand in life. Sophie's parents blamed me for their daughter's illness, while I silently blamed them back for rejecting her over her choice of husband. The doctors wouldn't say for sure if that had been a factor in her illness, but it certainly hadn't helped.

Alice, Sophie's younger sister, said I was a saint to stick by her. But what sort of husband would desert his wife because she was ill? 'In sickness and in health,' we had vowed, 'until death us do part.' Perhaps, I thought, death would indeed be the only way out of this nightmare.

I shook myself out of these morbid thoughts, let myself into the house, and went straight to bed.

THURSDAY AT ROYAL ASCOT is Gold Cup Day. It is also known as Ladies Day, when the female of the species preens herself in her best couture under an extravagant hat she wouldn't be seen dead in at any other time or place.

This particular Thursday, the sun had decided to play the game and was shining brightly out of a clear blue sky. The champagne flowed and seafood lunches were being consumed by the trawler-load. All was set for a spectacular day of racing. Even I, a cynical bookie, was looking forward to it all with hope and expectation for another bunch of long-priced winners.

'Didn't walk into another door, then?' asked Larry Porter as he set up his pitch next to ours.

'No,' I replied. 'No doors in the car park last night.'

He grinned at me. 'And all that cash yesterday.' He rubbed his hands. 'Fancy trying to rob you on Tuesday when you're broke, then let you off yesterday with bulging pockets. Bloody mad.'

'Yes,' I said, wondering again if it really had been an attempted robbery.

'Let's hope we have bulging pockets again today,' he said, still smiling.

Larry Porter and I could not be properly described as friends. In truth, I didn't have any friends among my fellow bookmakers. We were competitors. We fight for the custom of the general public, and we fought hardest and dirtiest among ourselves, doing our utmost to get one over on our neighbours.

Many in the racing industry, both privately and publicly, called all bookmakers 'the enemy'. They accused us of taking money out of racing. But we were only making a living, just like them. The big firms, though no friends of mine, spent millions on race sponsorship, and we all paid extra tax on gambling profits on top of the 'levy', a sum taken from bookmakers' profits and put back into racing via the Horserace Betting Levy Board.

The betting levy provided more than half the country's total race prize money. Plenty of the trainers hated all bookmakers with a passion, but they still bet with them, and they couldn't seem to see that the future of racing relied totally on the public continuing to gamble on the horses.

'Larry, did your Internet go down just before the last race on Tuesday?' I asked him.

'I believe it did,' he said. 'But it happens all the time. You know that.'

'Yes. But did you know that all the mobile phones went off, too?'

'Did they indeed? Anyone hit?'

'Not that I know of,' I replied.

'I'll bet there was quite a queue at the phone box on the High Street,' he said with a laugh. There was a public telephone just outside the racecourse, one of the few remaining, now that everyone seemed to have a mobile.

'Yeah,' I said, joining in with his amusement. 'I bet you're right.'

Business was brisk in the run-up to the first race. As always when there was a really big crowd, many punters liked to place all their bets for the whole day before the first so that they didn't have to relinquish their viewing spots between races. Acquiring seats in the Royal Enclosure viewing area on the fourth floor of the grandstand was as difficult as getting a straight answer from a politician.

'What did that copper want yesterday afternoon?' Betsy asked me.

'Just a few more questions about getting mugged on Tuesday,' I replied matter-of-factly. Even though I had initially asked Betsy to take over for just a few minutes, I had actually left her and Luca for the whole of the last race. They had also had to pack up all our equipment on their own while I spoke with Chief Inspector Llewellyn.

I thought back to what the chief inspector had told me.

'Your mother was strangled,' he'd said. It had turned me icy cold on one of the hottest days of the year.

'But how do you know that my father was responsible?' I'd asked him.

'Well,' he'd said, 'it seems it was suspected as much when he suddenly disappeared at the same time. But the DNA match has proved it.'

'How?' I asked, although I was dreading the answer.

'Your mother apparently scratched her attacker and his skin was found under her fingernails. At the time of the murder, DNA testing wasn't available, but samples were kept. During a cold-case review about five years ago, a DNA profile of the killer was produced and added to the national DNA database. As we have now discovered, it matches your father exactly.'

In less than a single twenty-four-hour period I had first met my father and realised that I was not the orphan I had thought I was, watched helplessly while my new-found parent was fatally stabbed, then discovered that he had been nothing more than a callous murderer, the killer of my mother. It wasn't my father's life that was the soap opera, it was mine.

THE AFTERNOON seemed to slip by without me really noticing. Luca had to keep reminding me to pay attention to our customers.

'For God's sake, Ned,' he shouted in my ear. 'Get the bloody things right.' He exchanged yet another inaccurate ticket. 'What's wrong with you today? You never usually make mistakes.'

I did. I was just usually more expert at covering them up. But today I felt lousy and my mind was elsewhere.

'Sophie's not good,' I said. It was the easy excuse.

Luca knew all about Sophie's condition. It had been impossible to keep it a secret over the years. Too often I had been forced to take days off work in order to be with her. Luca Mandini was a licensed bookmaker in his own right and he'd often covered for me.

'Sorry,' Luca said. He never asked for details. He seemed almost embarrassed. 'Bloody hell,' he suddenly shouted.

'What is it?' I asked, alarmed.

'Internet's gone down again,' he said, stabbing his keyboard with a finger.

I looked at my watch. A little less than five minutes to go before the Gold Cup was due to start.

'How about the phones?' I asked him, turning round.

He was already pushing the buttons on his mobile. 'Nothing,' he said, looking up at me. 'No signal. Same as before.'

I looked round the betting ring at the other bookmakers, especially those to my right along the Royal Enclosure rail. I could see a few of the boys from the big outfits pushing buttons on their phones with no success. One or two of them dashed away to seek other forms of communication.

'Two monkeys, horse six,' said a punter in front of me.

A 'monkey' was betting slang for £500. Two monkeys—£1,000—was a fair-sized bet, our biggest of the day. Was it a coincidence, I wondered, that it was laid just seconds after the Internet and the phones went off? I took a careful look at my customer. There was nothing about him that made me think he was up to no good. He was a regular racegoer with a white open-neck shirt and fawn chinos. I didn't recognise him, but I'd know him again.

I glanced up at our board as I relieved him of the bundle of notes he held out to me. Horse number six, Lifejacket, was quoted at four-to-one.

'Four thousand-to-one thousand on horse six,' I said over my shoulder. 'OK with you, Luca?'

Luca consulted his digital mate. 'We'll take it at seven-to-two,' he said.

'Seven-to-two,' I said to the man in the white shirt and chinos.

'OK,' he said. He didn't seem to mind the change in odds.

'A grand at seven-to-two, horse number six,' I said.

Luca pushed the computer keys and a ticket popped out of the printer. I gave it to the man, who moved on to put another bet on with Larry Porter.

'A grand on six at fours,' shouted Luca. He was laying the bet with Norman Joyner, a bookmaker whose pitch was in the line behind us, and he was trying to do so at a better price than we'd just given to the man in the chinos.

Norman was wise to his attempt. 'Hundred-to-thirty,' he called back. The price offered on horse number six was rapidly on its way down.

'OK,' said Luca. 'I'll take it.'

There was no money passed, no ticket issued. While none of us may have actually been friends, one bookmaker's word to another was still his bond.

'Internet still down?' I asked over my shoulder.

'Yup,' said Luca.

There was beginning to be a touch of panic in the ring. The men from the betting-shops chains wore frowns of concern, and technicians from the company that provided the Internet links seemed to be running round in circles.

'Fifty pounds on Brent Crude,' said a voice in front of me.

I looked down. 'Hi, AJ,' I said, noticing the fancy blue-and-yellow-striped waistcoat he was wearing. 'Sorry, what did you say?'

'Fifty on Brent Crude,' AJ repeated.

'Fifty pounds to win number one,' I said over my shoulder, glancing at our prices board, 'at fifteen-to-eight.'

The ticket appeared and I passed it over.

'They're off,' said the race commentator over the public-address system, announcing the start of the race.

'The Internet's back,' said Luca. 'Now is that a coincidence or what?'

'Phones too?' I asked.

'Yup.' He repeatedly pushed the buttons.

No coincidence, surely.

LIFEJACKET, HORSE NUMBER SIX, finished third in a close race with the second horse, both of them ten lengths behind the winner, number one, Brent Crude, the favourite, who was returned at the surprisingly long odds of fifteen-to-eight. Brent Crude had been the real class horse in the race, and he had been expected to start at evens at best, and quite likely at odds-on.

'I reckon there's been a bit of manipulating of the starting price going on here,' said Luca with a huge grin. 'Serves them right.'

'Who?' said Betsy.

'The big-chain bastards,' I said to her.

Luca nodded, laughing. 'I think someone's been playing them at their own game. Stopped them contacting their racecourse staff to make bets with us.'

'What do you mean?' asked Betsy.

'Someone's been placing largish bets on several less-fancied horses,' I explained, 'to shorten their odds, and so lengthen the price on the favourite.'

'I still don't get it,' said Betsy.

'Suppose,' I said, 'that really large bets were being placed in the betting shops on Brent Crude, all of them at the official starting price, then the shops wouldn't have been able to contact their staff here at the course to get them to bet on him with the course bookmaker and shorten his price.'

'It must have driven them bonkers in the shops to see the starting price lengthen,' said Luca, 'just when they wanted it to shorten.'

'Isn't that illegal?' asked Betsy.

'Probably,' I said. 'But the big companies are forever controlling the starting prices. I think they just got a taste of their own medicine.'

'It's almost certainly illegal to interrupt communications,' said Luca. 'But I think it's brilliant.'

'But how can they do that?' asked Betsy.

'They use an electronic jammer. I saw it on a television programme. The police can do it, too. When there was a bomb scare at Aintree one year, they shut down all the phone systems. Perhaps this was the same thing, but I doubt it. We'd be evacuating the racecourse by now.'

'How did the prices change in the minutes before the off?' I asked him.

He consulted his micro-processing friend. 'Lifejacket came right in from four-to-one to two-to-one,' he said. 'Five other horses tightened as the race approached but Brent Crude drifted all the way from even money to fifteen-to-eight. He was very nearly not even the favourite.'

'That's a lot,' I said.

'Yeah,' said Luca, 'but there was a whisper in the ring that he was sweating badly in the paddock. Colic was even mentioned.'

I knew; I'd heard the talk. 'Was it true?' I said.

'Dunno,' he said, grinning again. 'I doubt it.'

THERE WAS AN UNUSUAL feeling of bonhomie among the bookies in the ring as we waited to see who had been taken to the cleaners. Except, that was, for the on-course teams from the big outfits, who had been as much in the dark as the rest of us and who would, no doubt, carry the blame for something over which they had had no control.

Rumours abounded, most of which were false, but by the end of the day there was strong evidence that all the big boys had been hit to some extent.

From our own point of view, it hadn't made a whole lot of difference. I had taken two large bets of £1,000 each, with quite a few smaller ones following as punters chased the big money. Three-quarters of that had been laid by Luca with other bookies as their prices had tumbled, and he had laid a little more on the Internet during the race. Both the horses that had been heavily backed with us had lost, of course, while we had taken only a very few last-minute wagers on the favourite, including that fifty pounds to win from AJ. Most of the bets with us on Brent Crude had been taken earlier in the day, when his price had been even money, not fifteen-to-eight. Unlike the betting shops, we always paid out at the price offered at the time of the bet and not on the starting price. A satisfactory result all round, I thought. And a bloody nose to the bullies, to boot. Now, that was a real bonus.

LUCA, BETSY AND I remained in good spirits as we packed up for the day after the last. There had been no repeat of the earlier excitement but the betting ring was still buzzing.

'A great day for the little man,' said Larry Porter.

'They'll cry foul, you know,' said Norman Joyner from behind me.

'Probably,' Larry agreed. 'But it'll make them uncomfortable, and it's fun while it lasts.'

Luca and I hauled the trolley up the slope to the grandstand while Betsy carried our master, the computer, in its black bag.

'No drinks at the bandstand bar tonight?' I said to them.

'No,' said Luca. 'We're going straight from here to a birthday party.'

'Millie, my kid sister, she's twenty-one today,' said Betsy. 'Big family party tonight at my aunt's house.'

'I hope you have fun,' I said. 'Wish Millie a happy twenty-first from me.'

'Thanks,' she said warmly. 'I will.'

I thought about my own kid sisters in Australia and wondered if anyone had told them yet that their father was dead.

Luca, Betsy and I made it to the car park, on this occasion unmolested, and we loaded our gear into my capacious Volvo estate.

'Do you need a lift?' I asked.

'No, thanks,' said Luca. 'Not tonight. We'll take the train from here to Richmond. That's where the party is.'

'Look,' I said to him. 'I fancy giving it a miss tomorrow. Having a day off. What do you think? You're welcome to work with Betsy if you want.'

Even though I paid Luca and Betsy a salary as my assistants, they made easily as much again from sharing the profits. Over the last couple of days we had far more than recouped our losses from Tuesday, and the days at Royal Ascot were some of our busiest of the year.

'What about the stuff?' he said, nodding towards my car. 'We planned to stay at Millie's place tonight. In Wimbledon.'

Luca and Betsy lived somewhere between High Wycombe and Beaconsfield in Buckinghamshire. I had collected them that morning, as I had often done, from a lay-by just off junction 3 on the M40.

'Isn't your car in the lay-by?' I asked. I had sometimes transferred the gear into his car there.

'No,' said Luca. 'Betsy's mum dropped us off this morning.'

Bugger, I thought. I would have to come to Ascot again tomorrow.

'OK,' I said with resignation in my voice. 'I'll be here. But I'm fed up with dressing like this. I'll be more casual tomorrow.'

Luca grinned. He loved the exhilaration of the big race days. 'Great,' he said. 'And you'd hate to miss another day like today, now wouldn't you?'

'I can't believe there will be another day like today. Not ever,' I said. 'But, no, I wouldn't want to miss it if there were.'

'We must dash,' said Luca. 'See you here tomorrow, then. Usual time?'

'Yes, all right,' I replied. 'Have fun tonight.'

JASON, THE NURSE, hadn't been very happy when I called to say that I'd be late at the hospital. I had a job to do. I'd hoped to do it the following day, but now I couldn't. I'd promised Jason I'd be there in time to watch the ten o'clock news with Sophie. I looked again at my watch. It was half past eight. I still might make it, but things were not going quite as planned.

Having left my morning coat, waistcoat and tie in my parked car, I was on foot in Sussex Gardens, in London, looking for a certain seedy hotel or guesthouse. But everywhere I looked there were seedy little hotels and guesthouses. After an hour and a half, I had drawn a complete blank.

'Do you, or did you, have a guest this week called Talbot?' I asked without much hope in yet another of the little places I had been in. 'Or one called Grady?' I pulled out the now rather creased copy of the driving licence that Sergeant Murray had made for me.

A young woman behind the reception counter looked down at the picture, then up at me. 'Are you police?' she asked in an Eastern European accent.

'No,' I assured her. 'Not police.'

'Who you say you want?'

'Mr Talbot or Mr Grady,' I repeated patiently.

'You need ask Freddie,' she said.

'Where is Freddie?' I asked, looking round at the empty hallway.

'In pub,' she said.

'Which pub?'

'I not know,' she said crossly. 'This pub, that pub. Always pub.'

This was going nowhere. 'Thank you anyway,' I said politely, and left.

This had been a stupid idea, I realised. I thought that if I found out where my father had been staying, and recovered his luggage, I might learn why he had really come back to England. There had to have been more of a reason than simply to see me after a thirty-six-year absence. After all, he had risked getting arrested for murder. But it was clearly a hopeless task. Over half the hotels and guesthouses I'd been into either had no proper record of their guests or they wouldn't tell me even if they had.

Just another couple of hotels, I decided, and then I must leave for Hemel Hempstead.

Many of the properties in Sussex Gardens had been constructed at a time when households regularly had servants. The grand pillared entrances had been for the family's use only, while the servants had access to the house via a steep stairway to a lower-ground floor behind iron railings.

The Royal Sovereign Hotel was one such property, though nowadays its name was grander than its appearance. The iron railings were rusty and paint was flaking from the stucco pillars on either side of the dimly lit entrance.

'Do you, or did you, have a guest this week called Mr Talbot or Mr Grady?' I asked again, placing the driving-licence photocopy on the reception desk and pushing it towards the plump middle-aged woman behind it.

She looked down at the photo. ''Ave you come for 'is stuff?' she asked.

'Yes, I have,' I said excitedly, hardly believing my good luck.

'Good,' she said, looking up. 'It's cluttering up my office. 'E only paid for two nights so I've 'ad to move it this morning. I needed 'is room, you see.'

'Yes, I do see,' I said, nodding at her. 'That's fine. Thank you.'

'But 'is name wasn't Talbot or Grady. It was Van something or other. South African 'e said 'e was. But it was definitely 'im.'

'Oh, yes,' I said. 'He sometimes uses different names. One's his real name, and the others are professional names.'

She didn't look any the wiser. ''Ad an accident, did 'e?' she asked.

'Yes, sort of,' I said.

'Looks like you did, too,' she said, putting her hand up to her own eye.

My left eyebrow remained swollen and my whole eye was turning a nasty shade of purple with orange streaks.

'Same accident,' I said, putting my hand up to my face. 'I'm his son.'

'Oh,' she said. 'Right. Back 'ere, then.' She disappeared through a curtain hanging behind her, and I followed her into a windowless alcove about eight foot square, with a narrow table on one side piled high with papers.

'There,' the woman said, pointing. 'That's 'is stuff. I 'ad to pack up some of 'is things. Wash kit and so on, 'cause, as I said, 'e only paid for two nights.'

There were two bags. One was a black-and-red rucksack, the other a small black roll-along suitcase with an extendable handle.

'Thank you,' I said to the woman with a smile. 'I'll let you have your floor back.' I picked up the rucksack and slung it over my shoulder.

''Ang on.' She dug around on the desk. 'Could you just put your name and signature?' She held out a pen and the back of a used envelope. 'You know. Just so I'm covered. And a phone number as well.'

'Sure,' I said. I took her pen and the envelope. *Van something*, she had said my father was called. I printed my name as Dick Van Dyke and signed the same with a flourish. The number I wrote down I just made up.

'Thanks,' she said, tucking the envelope back under a pile of stuff on her desk. ''E only paid for two nights,' she repeated yet again.

At last I worked out her meaning.

'Here,' I said, holding out a twenty-pound note. 'This is for your trouble.'

'Thanks,' she said, taking the money and thrusting it into a pocket. 'I 'ope 'e gets better soon,' she said. 'Give 'im my best.'

I promised her I would, then rapidly took my leave. I turned out of the hotel and walked quickly down Sussex Gardens towards my car. I looked down at my watch. It was five past nine. I would have to get a move on.

I was still looking down at my watch when a man came out of the building to my right and bumped into the roll-along suitcase I was pulling.

'Sorry,' I said, almost automatically.

The man hurried on, paying me no attention. I'd glanced up at his eyes and I suddenly felt an icy chill down my spine. I had seen those eyes before. They were the shifty, close-set eyes of the man who had twice punched a knife through my father's abdomen in an Ascot car park on Tuesday.

I didn't stop walking. In fact, I speeded up and forced myself not to look back. I prayed he hadn't recognised me with my swollen and blackened eye.

Only after a further twenty or so rapid strides did I step into another of the pillared entrances and chance a glance back. There was no sign of him. I must have stopped breathing when I first saw him, and I now gasped for air, my heart pounding in my chest like a jackhammer.

I peeped round the pillar again. I saw him come out of one of the hotels, then disappear into the one next to the Royal Sovereign. It looked as if he might be on the same errand as I had been. I could imagine the plump, middle-aged woman behind the reception desk. *Oh, yes*, she'd tell the man, *'is son's just been 'ere. 'E took the bags. I'm sure you'll catch 'im if you 'urry.*

Not if I could 'elp it, 'e wouldn't.

Surprisingly, I made it back to my Volvo without actually walking into any lampposts, so preoccupied had I been with looking behind me. I flung my father's bags onto the back seat and quickly climbed into the front. My hands were shaking so much that I couldn't get the key into the ignition. I took several deep breaths and told myself to calm down. This plan seemed to be working well until I saw the man again. He was jogging down the road, straight towards me. My heart rate shot up off the scale.

Still the damn key wouldn't go in, so I leaned to my right to see better and was still looking down, trying to match the key to the lock, when I heard the man walk past me and climb into the car parked right behind mine.

I slid down further so he wouldn't see me. It seemed like an age before he finally started his engine and drove away. I began to breathe again.

I should be grateful to Luca, I thought, that I hadn't waited until the following day to do my private-detective act. My father's bags would, by then, have been long gone. But it would have been much less stressful.

I sat in my car for a good ten minutes wondering if I should go and report the encounter to Chief Inspector Llewellyn. I had slipped down so low that I hadn't even seen the type or colour of the car the man drove, let alone the number plate. I wasn't much of a private detective after all. And I didn't relish having to explain to the chief inspector why I had said nothing earlier about the hotel in Sussex Gardens. In the end, I decided to have a look at the luggage first. I could call the police then if I wanted to.

My breathing and pulse had at last returned to their normal rates, so I started the Volvo and made tracks to Hemel Hempstead and the hospital.

AT MIDNIGHT, I sat in the sitting room of my house in Kenilworth, surrounded by the contents of my father's bags, wondering what it was among this lot that his murderer would bother spending an evening looking for.

I had made it to the hospital to watch the end of the news with Sophie. Jason had given me a stern look and tapped his watch as I arrived. What could I tell him? *Sorry I'm late; I've been dodging a murderer on the streets of west London.* Fortunately, Sophie didn't seem perturbed. She gave me a warm kiss on the cheek without even appearing to check if I'd been drinking. She hadn't even objected when I'd made my excuses and left.

So here I was, surrounded by piles of my father's clothes. There was little else in the bags. His washing kit was minimal, he didn't have any medications, and he'd obviously had a penchant for blue shirts, of which there were six. He had preferred an electric razor to a wet shave, and boxer shorts to briefs. But there was nothing remarkable, certainly nothing worth killing for.

'Where is the money?' the man had said to my father in the car park.

What money? I wondered. Had I missed something? I went through every-thing again, even taking the top off his electric razor in case a safe-deposit box key was hidden in the minute space beneath. Of course, it wasn't.

The only things that sparked my interest were his passport, a mobile tele-phone and some keys, which I found in one of the rucksack's side pockets.

Nothing happened when I pushed the buttons of the telephone. Either it was broken or the battery was flat. I put the phone to one side and picked up the keys. There were three of them on a small split-ring. House keys, I thought, and not very exciting without the house.

The passport was more informative. It was an Australian passport in the name of Alan Charles Grady. Tucked inside it was a print-out of a British Airways e-ticket receipt and a boarding card, also in the name of Grady. He had arrived at Heathrow ten days previously, I noted. So where had he stayed for the first week of his visit? Or had he flown elsewhere in the interim?

Again I pulled the driving-licence copy from my pocket and looked at the address: 312 Macpherson Street, Carlton North, in the Australian state of Victoria. Where exactly was Carlton North? I wondered.

I went upstairs to my office and logged on to the Internet. Google Earth provided a fine close-up view of Carlton North, a mostly residential suburb of Melbourne just two or three miles north of the city centre. Macpherson Street, appropriately for the address of a dead man, ran along the northern edge of an enormous cemetery.

As far as I was aware, both my parents had been only children and I had consequently grown up with no aunts, uncles or cousins. My mother's parents had died before I was born—at least that is what my paternal grandmother had told me, but I now wondered if I could take her word for it. Teddy Talbot, my father's father, was dead, but my paternal grandmother was still alive. She lived in a residential care home in Warwick. I visited her occasionally, but age and Alzheimer's had taken their toll and she was no longer the woman who had raised me. Thankfully, she wasn't unhappy with her lot; she was just mostly lost in a different existence from the rest of us.

In spite of all her troubles, I had always envied Sophie for having had several siblings and many cousins. Despite the rift with her parents, she had remained as close to the rest of her large family as her illness had allowed. I, meanwhile, had no one other than my demented old grandmother.

Except that I now knew I did have family after all. I had two half-sisters in Australia. The only problem was that I didn't know their names or where they lived, and they, in turn, would have no idea that I existed. I couldn't imagine my father had told them that he already had a son in England, the offspring of a wife whom he had strangled before fleeing to the Antipodes.

I went downstairs again and back into the sitting room.

Once more I sifted through the sad piles of shirts and underwear as if I would find something I had previously missed. But there was nothing.

I stared into the red-and-black canvas rucksack. As before, it appeared to be empty, but I tipped the whole thing upside-down and gave it a good shake, more out of frustration than in expectation of finding anything.

As I turned it over, back and forth, I could feel something move.

I peered inside once more. The rucksack had a waterproof liner sewn into the canvas with a drawstring at the top. There was a gap at the back and I slid my hand down between the liner and the canvas. A space about two inches deep across the bottom of the rucksack existed between the liner and the base, and here I found the treasure that the man had sought.

I pulled out three blue-plastic-covered packages and carefully used a pair of kitchen scissors to open them at one end. Each contained sizable wads of banknotes, two in British pounds and the other in Australian dollars. I counted each pack in turn and did some rough mental arithmetic.

My father had taken lodgings in a seedy one-star hotel in Sussex Gardens with about £30,000 in cash inside his luggage.

And he had died for it.

CHAPTER 4

There were five other items hidden in the space, in addition to the money. One was a South African passport in the name of Willem Van Buren. Another was a small polythene bag containing what appeared to be ten grains of rice but were, as closer examination revealed, frosted glass. Two others were photocopied booklets about six by eight inches with DOCUMENT OF DESCRIPTION printed on the front cover.

The fifth item was a flat black object about six inches long and two wide with some buttons on it. At first I thought it was a television remote control but it didn't appear to have volume and channel buttons, just 0 to 9 plus an ENTER button. I pushed one of the buttons and a small red light appeared in the top right-hand corner for a moment, then went out. Nothing else happened. I pointed the thing at the television and pushed again. Unsurprisingly, nothing happened other than the flash of the little red light.

I would show the thing to Luca, I thought. He was not only my whiz kid at using the computer, he also understood what went on under its cover. My own technical ability ran simply to giving something a sharp clout if it failed to perform as expected.

I looked up at the kitchen clock. It was 12.40. Suddenly I felt hungry. I hadn't eaten anything since breakfast sixteen hours ago. I looked in the fridge. There wasn't much there. I usually went to the supermarket on a Sunday but this last weekend I had somehow forgotten to go. I found a tin of baked beans in a cupboard and made myself beans on toast, carefully removing a few mouldy bits from the bread before placing it in the toaster.

I spread the bounty from the rucksack's secret compartment out on the kitchen table in front of me and looked at it as I ate.

I picked up the two booklets headed DOCUMENT OF DESCRIPTION. I hadn't seen one close up before but I knew what they were. Horse passports, they were called, and every racehorse had to have one. They were a detailed record of a horse's marking and hair whorls. A horse presented at a racecourse for a race had to match the one described in its passport. In the old days, unscrupulous trainers might have presented a 'ringer' that would run in another horse's place. The ringer was usually much better than the horse that should have been running, so it would start at much more favourable odds than if its true identity had been known. Many such a deception had raked in the cash before the introduction of horse passports put a stop to it.

But the two in front of me were photocopies, not the originals. I scanned through them but could see nothing out of the ordinary.

Next I picked up the human passport, that of Willem Van Buren from South Africa, and looked at the photograph. The face that looked out at me was that of my father. Van Buren must have been the name he had used to check into the Royal Sovereign Hotel.

Did I have yet more sisters, or perhaps some brothers, in Cape Town or Johannesburg?

I was also intrigued by the bag of rice-like grains. I took one of them out of the bag and rolled it between my thumb and index finger. It was, in fact, slightly larger than a grain of rice, about a centimetre long and about a third of that in diameter. I held it up to the light but I couldn't see through it. Why, I wondered, would anyone bother to hide a few chips of frosted glass?

I took my tomato-sauce-covered knife and recklessly crushed the grain against the table. It broke surprisingly easily. I could now see that the grain was not made of solid glass but was a hollow cylinder with what appeared to be a minute electronic circuit housed inside.

I scooped the broken bits back into the bag with the other nine. Again, I would ask Luca. If anyone knew what they were, he would.

And then, of course, there was the money. What should I do with it all?

Well, I told myself, I *should* go and give it to Chief Inspector Llewellyn. But how could I? He certainly wouldn't take it very kindly that I hadn't told him about my father's luggage earlier. He might even accuse me again of being somehow involved in his murder.

I decided to sleep on it, and went to bed.

FRIDAY AT ASCOT was wet, with an Atlantic weather front sweeping in from the west and bringing a ten-degree drop in temperature. Trust me, I thought, to choose this day to switch from my warm morning coat to a lightweight blazer. I took shelter under our large yellow TRUST TEDDY TALBOT emblazoned umbrella and shivered in the strengthening breeze.

'Good party?' I asked Luca and Betsy.

They had been uncharacteristically quiet as we had set up our pitch.

'Great,' said Betsy without much conviction.

'Late night?' I asked, enjoying myself.

'Very,' she said. 'But we could have done without the police.'

'The police?'

'My aunt called the police,' she said, clearly not pleased. 'About a hundred uninvited guests turned up at her house.'

'Yobs, you mean,' said Luca with a degree of bitterness I hadn't witnessed in him before. 'Your stupid sister. Ruined her own party.'

'She didn't ruin it,' Betsy retorted in a pained tone.

'What do you call inviting people on Facebook to a party?' he said. 'Not bloody surprising so many weirdoes turned up and trashed the place.'

'Look,' I said, interrupting them. 'I'm sorry now I asked. Calm down, both of you. We have work to do.'

They both fell silent, but their body language was far removed from the loving episode I had witnessed on Tuesday as they had walked, hand in hand, on their way to a drink at the bandstand bar.

Oh dear, I thought. It wasn't just the weather that had turned cool.

The afternoon progressed without any of the excitement of the previous day. The incessant rain understandably kept many punters away from the betting ring. They preferred the dry, warm surroundings of the grandstand bars and restaurants, where they could place bets with the Tote.

There were no outages of the Internet service, no disruptions of the mobile phones, no last-minute wild swings in the prices. Favourites won three of the six races, while a couple of rank outsiders gave us bookies some respite in the others. All in all, it was a remarkably unremarkable day, apart from the ongoing frosty relations between my staff.

'Do you two combatants need a lift home?' I asked as we packed up. Neither of them said a word. 'For God's sake,' I went on, 'do either of you want on go on living or what?'

It raised a slight, brief smile on Luca's face.

'The Teddy Talbot bus leaves for High Wycombe in five minutes whether you're on it or not,' I said with a degree of exasperation in my tone.

Still nothing.

'Do I assume, then, that we won't be back here tomorrow?' I asked as we made it to the car park unrobbed. Even muggers don't like the rain.

Royal Ascot Saturday had become one of our busiest days of the year.

'I'm game,' said Luca.

I looked expectantly at Betsy.

'OK,' she said grudgingly. 'I'll be here.'

'Good,' I said. 'And can I expect a thawing of the cold war?'

There was no answer from either of them.

I was getting bored with this game. 'OK,' I said. 'No talking—no lift.'

'I'm sorry,' Luca said.

'No problem,' I said.

'Not you, Ned,' he said irritably. 'I'm sorry to Betsy.' He turned to her.

'Oh . . .' Betsy burst into tears, gasping great gulps of air.

She and Luca dissolved into each other's arms and just stood there hugging each other, getting wet, like a scene from a romantic film.

'Oh, for goodness' sake,' I said. 'You lovebirds had better get in the back seat while I drive.'

I WAS QUITE thankful that Luca didn't, in fact, sit in the back with Betsy but sat up front next to me. I don't think I could have taken that lovey-dovey stuff all the way to High Wycombe.

'What do you think that is?' I said to him. I handed over the black plastic object that resembled a television remote, which I had put in the door pocket of the Volvo that morning.

He turned the device over and over in his hands, then started pushing buttons. He was rewarded by the brief flash of red whenever he pushed one.

'The light stays on a few moments longer if you press the "enter" button,' I said. He pressed it, and it did. 'Do you think it's a remote for something?'

'Dunno,' he said. 'It's obviously not for a television or a radio. There's no volume control. How about a garage-door opener or something?'

'But why the numbers?' I said. 'Surely garage-door openers just have one button?'

'Maybe you need to push a number code and then "enter".'

'Yeah, maybe,' I said. 'How about these?' I passed him the small plastic bag containing the unbroken grains, along with the one I had crushed.

He poured the tiny items out of the bag onto his hand; then he held the broken one up in between his thumb and forefinger. 'I assume this one was like the others before you stamped on it?'

'I used a knife actually,' I said. 'And yes, it was.'

'They're definitely electronic,' he said.

'Even I can see that,' I replied sarcastically. 'But what are they for? They don't seem to have any connections, so how do they work?'

He continued to study the tiny circuit. 'Passive electronics,' he said quietly.

'And what are they when they're at home?' I asked.

'Devices with no gain,' he said. 'They're called passive electronic components or passive devices.'

'So?' I said, none the wiser.

'Transistors provide gain,' he said. 'They can be used as amplifiers to give a signal gain, to drive a speaker in a radio, for example. The signal received by the aerial is very small, so it has to be amplified by a series of transistors.'

'The higher the volume, the greater the gain?' I said.

'Just so,' he said. 'But transistors need a power supply—either a battery or a mains connection—so this little sucker can't have transistors.'

'What are you two on about?' asked Betsy suddenly from the back seat.

'This,' said Luca, carefully handing her one of the unbroken grains.

'Oh, I know what that is,' she said, rather condescendingly.

'What?' Luca and I asked together.

'It's a chip for dogs,' she said. 'They're injected under the skin using a syringe. We had one put in our Irish setter so Mum and Dad could take her to France. When she came back, she simply got scanned by customs to check she was the right dog with the right vaccinations.'

'Like horses,' I said.

'Eh?' said Luca.

'Horses have them, too,' I said. 'To check they are indeed who their owner says they are. I read about it in the *Racing Post*, ages ago. I just didn't know what the chips looked like.'

Luca looked again at the tiny electrical circuit. 'It must be a passive arfid circuit,' he said. 'This little coil must be the antenna.'

'I'll take your word for it,' I said. 'What's an arfid when it's at home?'

'Radio-frequency identification, R-F-ID, pronounced arfid,' he explained. 'You put a scanner close to the circuit that emits a radio wave. The wave is picked up by the little antenna and that provides just enough power for the RFID circuit to transmit back an identification number.'

'Sounds complicated,' I said.

'Not really,' Luca replied. 'They exist all over the place. Those alarm things in shops that go off if you try to take things out without paying, they use RFID chips. The tube and buses in London use them in the Oyster cards. You put the card on the scanner and it reads the information to make sure you have enough credit to travel. Some people call them Spychips because they allow a person to be tracked without their knowledge,' he went on. 'But I think they'll soon be on everything. They already use RFID in cars to pay road and bridge tolls in lots of places. It's not much more of a step for them to calculate your average speed between two points and issue a ticket if you break the speed limit.'

'How do you know so much about these RFID things?' I asked.

'Read about them in electronics magazines,' he said. 'But I've never seen one this small before.' He held up one of the glass grains.

So why, I thought, had my father hidden ten of them in his luggage? Perhaps they were something to do with the photocopied horse passports.

'Is the black remote thing a scanner?' I asked.

'It doesn't have any sort of read-out, so I doubt it,' said Luca. 'I'll ask at my electronics club, if you like.'

'Electronics club?' I said.

'Yeah. Mostly teenagers,' he said. 'Making robots or radio-controlled cars and such. I help out Friday nights in the local youth centre.'

I thought about whether I should give the device to him, or to the police.

'OK,' I said. 'Ask at your club if anyone knows what it's for.'

'Right,' he said. 'I'll take it with me tonight. I'll let you know in the morning if we get anywhere.'

I DROPPED LUCA and Betsy in High Wycombe; then I went to see my grandmother, at the nursing home in Warwick where she had lived for the last two and a half years. Her room was a microcosm of my childhood memories. Every knick-knack, every photograph was so familiar to me. It was only my grandmother herself who was unfamiliar. As I sometimes was to her.

'Hello, Nanna,' I said, leaning down and kissing her on the forehead.

She briefly looked up at me with confused recognition, and said nothing. The nurses told me that she could still chat away quite well on some days, but I personally hadn't heard her speak now for quite a few weeks.

'How are you feeling?' I asked her. 'Have you been watching the racing?'

There was no reply, not a flicker of apparent understanding. Today was clearly not one of her good days.

I sat down on a chair facing her and took her hand in mine. She looked at my face with hollow, staring eyes. I stroked her hand and smiled at her.

'Nanna,' I said to her slowly, 'I've come to ask you about Peter. Do you remember your son, Peter?'

She went on looking at me without giving any sign that she had heard.

'Your son, Peter,' I repeated. 'He married a girl called Tricia. They had a little boy called Ned. Do you remember Ned? You looked after him.'

I thought she hadn't registered anything, but then she smiled and spoke, softly but clearly. 'Ned,' she said. 'My little Ned.'

I felt myself welling up with emotion. 'Yes,' I said. 'Your little Ned. Nanna, I'm right here.'

Her eyes focused on my face. 'Ned,' she repeated. I wasn't sure if she was remembering the past or whether she was able to recognise me.

'Nanna,' I said, 'do you remember Peter? Your son, Peter?'

'Dead,' she said.

'Do you remember his wife, Tricia?' I asked her gently.

'Dead,' she repeated.

'Yes,' I said. 'But do you know how she died?'

My grandmother looked at me with a quizzical expression. Finally she said, 'Secret,' and put one of her long, thin fingers to her lips.

'And Peter,' I said. 'Where did Peter go?'

'Dead,' she repeated.

'No,' I said. 'Peter wasn't dead. Tricia was dead. Where is Peter?'

She didn't say anything and her eyes had returned to their distant stare. *Secret*, she had said. So she must have known.

I pulled the photocopy of my father's driving licence from my pocket and put it on her lap. She looked down at its photograph. I placed the tiny photo of my mother and father at Blackpool there too.

She looked down for some time and I thought at one point that she had drifted off to sleep, so I took the pictures and put them back in my pocket.

I stood up to leave but, as I leaned forward to kiss her, she sat up straight.

'Murderer,' she said, quietly but quite distinctly.

I knelt down so that my face was close to hers. 'Who was a murderer?'

'Murderer,' she repeated.

'Who was murdered?' I asked, changing tack. I already knew the answer.

'He murdered Tricia,' she said. She began to cry, and I gave her a tissue from the box beside her bed. She wiped her nose and then she turned and looked at me, her eyes momentarily full of recognition and understanding.

'And he murdered her baby.'

CHAPTER 5

'It emits a radio signal,' said Luca in the car on the way to Ascot on Saturday morning. He was holding the black remote-type thing. 'You were bloody lucky this wasn't nicked,' he added with a chuckle.

'Why would it be nicked?' I asked him.

'Because most of the teenagers at the electronics club are hooligans,' he said. 'They're only there because the courts make them go. Supposed to be part of their rehabilitation. One of the little horrors had your scanner in his bag. God knows what he thought he would do with it.'

'What sort of radio signal does it emit?' I asked.

'Fairly low frequency. But quite powerful.'

'So what's the thing for?'

'I think it might be for writing information onto the RFID chips,' he said. 'The end slides off and you can fit one of the little glass grains into this hollow.' He pointed at it as I drove. 'When you push the "enter" button, it sends out a signal. I think that must program the RFID chip with the numbers you punch into it before pushing the "enter" button.'

'Is that really possible?' I said. 'There aren't any connectors.'

'It's easy,' he said. 'Writing to RFID chips occurs all the time. When someone puts their Oyster card near one of those round yellow pads on the tube gates, the system automatically deducts the fare from the available credit, then rewrites the card with a new balance. It's all done by radio waves.'

I was slightly disappointed. I had somehow hoped that the device was going to be more exciting than that.

Betsy had gone to sleep in the back. I yawned. Sleep had not come easily after my visit to my grandmother. I had lain awake for hours thinking about what she had said to me. What did you do when you found out that your son was a murderer? More to the point for me, what did you do when you found out that your father was one? Somehow, in spite of what I had learned, I still felt some form of affinity with the man who now lay silently in some mortuary cold storage. I still mourned for what might have been.

'It's the Wokingham today,' said Luca, rubbing his hands and bringing me back from my daydreaming.

'Sure is,' I said.

The Wokingham Stakes was the fourth race of the day on Royal Ascot Saturday. It was one of the most lucrative races of the meeting for us bookmakers, and fun as well. While most bets tended to be smaller than for some of the group races, there were plenty of them. It seemed like a happy race, with no one placing white-knuckle wagers that they couldn't afford to lose.

Luca looked through the *Racing Post* as I drove. 'They reckon here that Burton Bank will start favourite at about six- or seven-to-one.'

'Who trains him?' I asked.

'George Wiley.'

'Wiley trains in Cumbria, doesn't he?' I said. 'That's quite a way to come. He must think he's a good prospect. How about the others?'

Luca studied the paper. 'About ten with a realistic chance, I'd say, but the Wokingham is always a bit of a lottery.'

We discussed the afternoon's racing for a while longer. I thought we would need the unpredictability of the Wokingham after the first two races of the day. The Chesham Stakes and the Hardwicke Stakes were both renowned for producing short-priced winners, favouring the punter.

The previous day's rain had swept away eastwards into the North Sea and the sun had returned, bringing out the Saturday crowd that was streaming into the racecourse by the time we had negotiated the traffic jams and parked the car. It looked like being another busy day at the office.

CHIEF INSPECTOR LLEWELLYN and Sergeant Murray were waiting for me in the betting ring.

'We need to ask you some more questions,' the chief inspector said.

'What about?' I said, hoping it wasn't about finding bundles of cash in a missing rucksack. 'Can't it wait until after I've finished work?'

'No,' he said with no apology.

'Sorry, Luca,' I said. 'Can you and Betsy set things up?'

'No problem,' Luca said.

The policemen and I wandered away to a quieter area.

'Now, Chief Inspector,' I said, 'how can I help you today?'

'Did your father tell you which hotel he was staying at in London?'

'No,' I replied truthfully, 'he did not.'

'We have been unable to find any hotel where someone called Grady or Talbot checked in,' he said.

'He told me that he'd only recently arrived from Australia but not exactly when. Perhaps he arrived that morning and came straight to Ascot Races.'

'No, sir,' said the chief inspector. 'British Airways confirmed that he arrived from Australia on one of their flights the previous week.'

'I'm sorry. The first time he contacted me was on the day he died.'

'According to the airline, when he arrived at Heathrow he had a piece of hold luggage with him,' he said. 'We have been unable to trace it. Did he give you anything? A left-luggage receipt, for example?'

'No,' I said. 'I'm afraid not. He gave me nothing.'

Why, I wondered, didn't I just tell them I had the luggage? And the money, and the other things. Maybe it was a hope that my father was not a murderer, as everyone seemed to think, and a feeling that the only chance I had of finding out was somehow connected with the dubious contents of that rucksack. Or perhaps it was just down to my aversion to Chief Inspector Llewellyn.

'Do you have any further recollection of your attacker?' he asked.

'Not really,' I said. 'But I am sure he was a white man aged somewhere in his mid- to late thirties, wearing jeans and a charcoal-grey hoodie and a dark scarf. And army boots.'

'Any distinguishing marks, scars or so forth?'

'None that I could see,' I said, again truthfully. 'I think he had short, fairish hair that seemed to stand upright on his head.'

'How could you tell if his hood was up?' asked the chief inspector.

'Thinking back, I believe I could see it under the hood.'

'Mmm,' he said. 'You didn't say that on Tuesday night.'

'I hadn't remembered on Tuesday night,' I said. Or seen it, I thought.

'Could you do an e-fit for us?' he asked.

'An e-fit?'

'A computer-made image of the killer,' he explained.

'So he did actually kill my father?' I said, somewhat sarcastically. 'The post-mortem results are in, are they?'

'Yes,' he said. 'According to the pathologist, your father died from two stab wounds to his abdomen, one on each side of his navel. They were angled upwards and punctured both his lungs. It was a very professional job.' There was no sorrow in his voice. To him, I suppose, a murderous villain had got his just desserts after thirty-six years on the run.

'So what happens now?' I asked. 'Can there be a funeral? And how about any family my father may have in Australia? Have they been informed?'

'I understand the Melbourne police have been to his home address,' he said. 'They found no one there. It seems your father lived alone.'

'But he told me he had two daughters from a previous marriage,' I said. 'Has anyone told them?'

'Not that I'm aware of,' he said. His tone indicated that he didn't consider it in the least important. And he might have been right. According to my father, even he hadn't seen my sisters for fifteen years.

'How about the funeral?' I asked.

'That will be up to the coroner,' he said. 'The inquest will be opened on Monday. You should have received a summons to attend by now.'

I thought about the pile of unopened letters on my hall table. The opening of my mail, or rather the lack of it, was another of my failings.

'Why do they need to summons me?' I asked.

'For identification purposes,' he said. 'You're the deceased's next of kin.

Once the deceased has been formally identified, the inquest will be adjourned. The coroner may issue a certificate for burial. That will be up to him.'

Identification could be interesting, I thought. Talbot, Grady or Van Buren?

'Right,' I said, looking at my watch. 'Is there anything else?'

'Not for now, Mr Talbot,' said Llewellyn. 'But don't go anywhere.'

'Is that an official request?' I asked.

'You know, there's something about you I don't like,' he said.

'Perhaps you just don't like bookmakers,' I said back.

'You are so right,' he said. 'But there's something else about you.' He jabbed his finger onto my chest.

I thought he was trying to intimidate me, or provoke me into saying something I would regret. So I simply smiled at him.

'I can't say I'm very fond of you either,' I said. 'But I don't suppose it will cloud the professional dealings between us, now will it?'

It certainly would, I thought. At least, it would on my side.

'Don't pick a fight with me, Mr Talbot,' he said, his face now about six inches from mine. 'Because you'll lose.'

I decided that silence here was the best policy.

Eventually he turned on his heel and walked off.

'Be careful, Mr Talbot,' the sergeant said to me in a friendlier tone. 'He doesn't like to be crossed.'

'He started it,' I said lamely in my defence.

'Just take the warning,' he said. 'And I'd watch my back if I were you.'

'Surely Chief Inspector Llewellyn is not that malicious?' I said jokingly.

He smiled. 'No, not quite. I was thinking about the man who killed your father. You were a witness to that, don't forget. Witnesses to murders are an endangered species.' The smile had left his face.

'Thank you, Sergeant,' I said. 'I'll take that warning, too.'

He nodded, and set off to follow the chief inspector.

'Just a minute,' I called after him. 'Do you happen to know where my mother was murdered? And when?'

He stopped and came back. 'Thirty-six years ago,' he said.

'Yes, but when exactly? What date? And where was she found?'

'I'll have a look,' he said. 'Can't promise anything, but I'll read the file.'

'Thanks,' I said.

He went off, hurrying to catch up with his boss, leaving me to wonder if my father's killer knew who I was, and how to find me.

'WHAT WAS ALL that about?' asked Luca when I went back to our pitch. 'Those two coppers have been here to see you twice now. Don't tell me it was just because someone mugged a bookie.'

'Well,' I said, 'you know about the murder in the car park?'

'Yeah,' he replied. 'Of course.' Everyone was still talking about it.

'It seems the man who mugged me might have been the killer.'

'Oh,' he said. 'That's all right, then.' He seemed relieved.

'What do you mean?' I cried, exasperated. 'He could have killed me too.'

'Yeah,' he said. 'But he didn't.' He smiled. 'Betsy and I reckoned you must be in some sort of trouble with the law.'

'Oh, thanks,' I said sardonically. 'Such confidence you have in me.'

AS PREDICTED, the first two races, the Chesham and the Hardwicke Stakes, were each won by the favourite.

'That was fine by us,' said Luca into my ear after the second. 'We had that laid at better odds so, for a change, the favourite's done us a favour.'

'Well done,' I said back to him. 'Now for the fun and games.'

Betting on the third race, the Golden Jubilee Stakes, was brisk, with queues of eager punters forming in front of me. The favourite, Pulpit Reader, opened at four-to-one, but the race was wide open and the market reflected it.

'Fifty on Pulpit,' said the man in front of me.

'Fifty on number five at fours,' I said to Luca, who pushed his keypad. I took the ticket from the printer and handed it to the man.

'What price number sixteen?' asked AJ, the next man in the queue, who was sporting a rather traditional grey waistcoat today.

'Horse sixteen?' I asked Luca. Our electronic board was not big enough to have all the runners displayed at once.

'Thirty-threes,' he said.

'Tenner each way,' AJ said, pushing a twenty-pound note towards me.

The ticket duly appeared from the printer.

So it went on. Mostly smallish bets of ten or twenty pounds. A wager on the Golden Jubilee was more for entertainment than for making serious money.

We were still taking bets as the race started. A young woman in a black-and-white dress with a matching large-brimmed hat was my last customer, thrusting a ten-pound note my way even as the horses were passing the five-furlong pole. 'Ten pounds to win on horse number five, please,' she implored breathlessly. I took her money and issued the ticket.

'No more,' I said, but there were no more. Everyone was watching the race, most of them on one of the big-screen TVs opposite the grandstand.

The Golden Jubilee Stakes is the British leg of the Global Sprint Challenge and consequently it attracts horses from overseas. On this occasion it was an American horse that broke away from the pack in the final furlong to win by more than a length. Pulpit Reader, number five, could only finish fourth. The young woman in black and white had enjoyed less than a minute's run for her money, which would now remain firmly in my pocket.

Next up was the thirty-runner Wokingham Stakes, and that was even more of a lottery than the Golden Jubilee.

The race was always like a cavalry charge, flat out for three-quarters of a mile from the starting stalls along the straight to the winning post. It is also a handicap, which means that the better-rated horses have to carry the most weight as determined by the handicapper, whose aim it was that all the runners would finish in one huge dead heat. Wins by favourites are rare.

Again betting was brisk, with money spread fairly evenly on shorter-priced favourites and outsiders alike. There were few pointers to help the discerning punter in this race. Often, in sprints, one side of the track seems to produce more winners than the other, and the number of the starting stall a horse is drawn in could be a good indicator of its chances. At Ascot, however, the draw hadn't proved to be much of a factor.

Nearly every punter has a system, even if it's closing their eyes and sticking a pin into the list of runners in the racecard. In general, the punters who do best are the ones who are disciplined and who study the form. Disciplined in so far as they record everything, don't go mad on hunches, and don't panic when they have a losing streak.

The most successful are those who know about almost every horse in training. They learn, over time, which horses run consistently to form and which do not. They discover which horses prefer right-handed tracks and which do better left-handed, which jumpers like long run-ins and which short, whether they are more likely to win with uphill finishes or flat ones, and whether they run above or below par on firm or soft ground. They know where each horse is trained, if it runs badly after long journeys in a horse-box, and even if a horse tends to do better than its rivals in sunshine or rain. Horse racing is not a science and there will always be surprises, but over time, just like human athletes, good horses run well and bad horses don't.

Making a profit from gambling on horses involves identifying those occasions when the offered odds for a horse to win are better than the true probability of that outcome. So if the knowledgeable punter calculates that the chances of a horse winning a particular race are, say, one in two, and the odds offered by a bookmaker are better than evens, that is the time to bet.

'Ten each way Burton Bank,' said a man in front of me.

'Ten pounds each way number two at seven-to-one,' I called to Luca over my shoulder.

I took the man's twenty-pound note and gave him his ticket. Ten pounds 'each way' meant ten pounds on the horse to win, and ten to place, which in a handicap of over sixteen runners meant to finish in the first four.

The next person in the queue was the young woman in the black-and-white dress and matching wide-brimmed hat.

'Ten pounds each way on number eleven,' she said, tilting her head up so she could see me, and I could see her. She was gorgeous.

'Ten each way number eleven at sixteens,' I called to Luca.

The ticket appeared and I handed it over. 'Better luck this time,' I said.

She looked slightly taken aback that I had spoken to her, and she blushed a little. 'Thank you,' she said, taking the ticket. I watched her hurry away.

Betting became fast and furious as the race time approached. A probable long-odds winner was encouraging everyone to have a punt. Burton Bank was just about holding his favouritism at seven-to-one, although two other horses' prices had shortened to fifteen-to-two.

'Twenty pounds to win on Burton Bank,' said my next customer, a young man in morning dress.

'Twenty to win number two at sevens,' I said over my shoulder to Luca.

'Bloody hell,' he replied. 'The Internet's gone down again.'

'PHONES AS WELL?' I asked, watching Luca pushing buttons on his mobile.

He nodded. 'Same as before.'

The effect was startling. Suddenly there were men running everywhere with walkie-talkies in their hands and curly wires visible over their collars, leading, I presumed, to inserts in their ears. They scanned the bookmakers' boards, on the lookout for sudden changes to the odds.

'Twenty pounds to win on Burton Bank,' repeated the young man in front of me, slightly irritated at the delay.

'Sorry,' I said to him. 'Twenty to win number two at sevens,' I repeated, turning to Luca. He looked at me and shrugged his shoulders, then pressed the keys and out popped the ticket. The young man snatched it away.

'A tenner each way number four,' said the next punter, a large man in a blue-striped shirt and red tie.

'Ten pounds each way number four at fifteen-to-one,' I said, and the ticket duly appeared.

Ten pounds each way wasn't enough to significantly change the odds, not even on a relative outsider, and no one else tried to make any odds-changing bets with me before the race. But the chaps with the earpieces were still running up and down the lines of bookies, making bets and shouting at each other, both directly and through their walkie-talkies.

'What do you mean, it's busy?' one of them shouted into his two-way radio. 'Well, get her out.' He turned to one of the others. 'There's a damn woman in the phone box making a call.'

It was almost funny. Larry Porter clearly thought it was, and he stood full-square, laughing loudly.

'It's back,' said Luca just as the starting stalls opened and the cavalry charge began.

'What a surprise,' I said.

I watched the race unfold on one of the big-screen TVs. The handicapper didn't quite get his dream of a multiple dead heat but still there was a pretty close blanket finish.

'First number four,' announced the public address system. 'Second number eleven. Third number twenty-six. Fourth number two.'

So Burton Bank, horse number two, had finished fourth. He had been clear favourite with a starting price of five-to-one, so some of those bets made by the earpieces must have been to try to shorten his price. On Thursday, in the Gold Cup, Brent Crude, the favourite, had drifted badly when the Internet went down, so I thought the big boys' first instinct today must have been to back the favourite and drive down its price. It hadn't done them much good.

The winner had been returned at a starting price of fifteen-to-one. But there was nothing suspicious about that. The starting price of the winner of the Wokingham Stakes had regularly been at twenty-to-one or higher.

'What was all that about?' I asked Luca.

'Dunno,' he said. 'Where did all those blokes come from? They must have been hiding in the stands somewhere.'

'It was a bit of overkill, if you ask me,' I said.

'They must have lost a packet last time.'

'I'll bet they didn't do so well this time either,' I said, and laughed.

'Serves them bloody right,' Luca said, laughing too.

It really did serve them right, I thought. The big boys had no sympathy for independent bookies as they tried to squeeze the lifeblood out of us, so they couldn't expect any compassion when they got rolled over. The truth was, we absolutely loved it.

'Weighed in,' announced the public address.

The first in line to be paid out was the gorgeous young woman in black and white. 'Well done,' I said cheerfully, giving her fifty pounds for her ten-pound place bet on number eleven.

'Thank you,' she replied, blushing again. 'My first win of the day.'

'Would you like to use it to make another bet?' I asked, pointing at the cash in her hand.

'Oh, no,' she said in mock shock. 'My boyfriend says I should always keep my winnings.'

'Very wise,' I said through gritted teeth.

Betting was light on the last two races as punters drifted away, either to beat the race traffic, to have some tea and scones, or to sup a last glass of champagne in the bars. The men with the earpieces were still wandering around aimlessly, waiting for something untoward to happen.

It didn't.

The day fizzled out. The Queen went home to Windsor Castle, and Royal Ascot was over for another year.

I SPENT MOST of the next day with Sophie.

It was a lovely summer's day and we went for a walk in the hospital grounds. She had improved so much over the past five or six weeks and I was really hopeful that she would be able to come home very soon.

We walked round a small pond set beneath the overhanging branches of a great oak tree. The mental hospital had been created by transforming a minor stately home that had been bequeathed to the nation by someone in lieu of inheritance tax. The building had been greatly changed from its former glory but the grounds somehow remained rather grand, even though the formal flowerbeds had long ago been converted into simple lawn.

'Did you have a good week at Ascot?' Sophie asked as we sat on a bench by the pond.

'Yes,' I said. 'A very good week.' I still hadn't said anything to her about the events of the previous Tuesday. 'There was all sorts of excitement yesterday,' I went on. 'Someone managed to turn both the Internet and the mobile phones off. The big companies were having a fit.'

'I'm not surprised,' she said, smiling warmly at the thought. Sophie knew all about bookmaking. She had stood next to my grandfather and me as our assistant throughout our courtship and well into our marriage.

When Sophie smiled, the sun still came out in my heart.

I took her hand in mine.

'Oh, Ned,' she sighed. 'I hate this existence. I hate being here. The other residents are all bonkers and I feel I don't fit in.' Tears welled up in her eyes. 'When can I come home?'

'Soon, my love, I promise. The doctors say just another couple of weeks.'

'They always say that,' she said with resignation. She was right. It was as if they were afraid to make the decision to send her home just in case she had a relapse and then they would be blamed for discharging her too soon.

'You don't want to go home too soon and then have to come back, now do you?' I said, squeezing her hand in mine.

'I never want to come back here,' she said bluntly. 'I'm absolutely determined, this time, not to become ill again.'

If being well were simply a matter of want and will-power, Sophie would be fine for ever, but free choice had about as much chance of curing manic depression as a sheet of rice paper had at stopping a runaway train.

'I know,' I said. 'I don't want you to have to come back here either.'

It was a major step forward in her recovery that she even recognised that she had been ill in the first place. For me, one of the most distressing things about her condition was that, when manically high or depressively deep, she couldn't appreciate that her bizarre behaviour was unusual.

'Come on,' I said, 'let's go and have some lunch.'

We walked hand in hand back up the expansive lawn towards the house.

'I love you,' Sophie said.

'Good,' I said, slightly embarrassed.

'No, I mean it,' she said. 'Most husbands would have run away by now.'

Wow, I thought, she really is nearly better. For the time being, anyway.

'I haven't been much of a wife, have I?' she said.

'Nonsense,' I said. 'You've been the best wife I've ever had.'

She laughed. We laughed together.

'I will really try this time,' she said.

I knew she would. She really tried every time. But manic depression, or bipolar disorder as it was now called, couldn't be cured by trying alone.

'They have some new drugs now,' I said. 'We'll have to see how they do.'

We walked in silence up across the terrace, and made our way back into the building through the French doors of the patients' day room. What must have once been a spectacular salon with crystal chandeliers and great works of art was now a rather dull, blue-vinyl-floored, utilitarian space lit by fluorescent tubes hanging on dusty chains from a superb ornamental plastered ceiling. Such sacrilege.

Sophie and I sat down at one of the small square tables, on chairs that were so uncomfortable they must have been designed by a retired torturer.

Overall, the staff were very good with the patients' families, encouraging us to spend as much time as possible at the hospital, and we were not the only family group sitting down to a Sunday lunch of roast beef and Yorkshire pudding. More comfortable chairs, I thought, would have helped.

'Please can I come home for next weekend?' she asked me.

'Darling, you know it's up to the doctors,' I said. 'I'll ask them later.'

We ate our meal mostly in silence.

The only topic Sophie wanted to talk about was going home, and I had just put the stoppers on that. But it was up to the doctors and not up to me. Patients in secure mental-health accommodation could only be released back into the community on the say-so of a consultant psychiatrist and by agreement of a relevant Care Programme Approach Review.

It was the drugs that were the problem.

Over the years, the doctors had tried electric-shock therapy but, if any thing, that had made things worse, so Sophie's only option was to take a daily cocktail of brightly coloured pills. Some were antipsychotic and others antidepressant. Together they could usually prevent and treat Sophie's symptoms, but they all had side effects. Not only did they make her feel nauseous, they also tended to reduce the activity of her thyroid gland while increasing her craving for carbohydrates. Hence Sophie put on weight, and that in turn was bad for her state of mind, especially for her depression.

But the most problematic thing about her condition was that, when the drugs made her feel free of psychosis, she started to believe, wrongly, that she didn't need them any more. The pills, and their side effects, were then thought of as the problem rather than the solution and so she stopped taking them, and the whole wretched cycle started once more.

'Would you like some fruit salad and ice cream?' asked one of the staff, taking our main-course plates.

'Yes, please,' I said. 'How about you, my love?'

'Yes,' she replied rather quietly. 'Lovely.'

'Are you all right?' I asked.

'Fine,' she said, but her eyes were distant.

The doctors were right, I thought. She might need another couple of weeks in hospital to get the drug doses sorted out properly after all.

We finished our lunch and went up to her room. She regularly took a nap in the afternoons and I was hopeful that it had just been tiredness that had caused her to be somewhat vacant downstairs, and not the start of another inward-looking depressive episode.

The two of us sat down in armchairs in front of an old black-and-white war film on the television. Sophie drifted off to sleep while I read her news-paper, mostly the racing pages. Regular domesticity.

THE INQUEST into the death of my father was opened and then adjourned on Monday morning at the coroner's court in Maidenhead. The proceedings took precisely fourteen minutes.

Chief Inspector Llewellyn was called first and he informed the coroner that a violent assault had occurred in the car park at Ascot Racecourse on June 16, at approximately 18.20 hours, which had resulted in the death of a man at Wexham Park Hospital, Slough, at 19.30 the same day.

A written report from the post-mortem pathologist was read out, stating that the primary cause of death was hypoxemic hypoxia, a lack of adequate oxygen supply to the organs of the body. The hypoxia had been brought on as a result of punctures to each side of the deceased's abdomen, caused by a sharp-pointed bladed instrument approximately twelve centimetres long and two centimetres wide. The blade had been angled upwards during each strike and had, on both occasions, penetrated the diaphragm and ruptured a lung, causing both lungs to fill with blood. The resulting hypoxia had led to cardiac arrest, cerebral ischaemia and, ultimately, death.

I was then called to give evidence of identification. The letter of sum-mons had indeed been in the pile of unopened mail.

I was asked by the court usher to state my full name and address, and then to hold a Bible in my right hand and swear that my evidence would be the truth and nothing but the truth.

'You are the deceased's son?' asked the coroner, a small balding man, looking expectantly at me over a pair of half-moon glasses.

'Yes,' I said. I was standing in the witness box of the court.

'What was your father's full name?' he asked.

'Peter James Talbot,' I said.

'And his date of birth?'

I gave it. I knew every detail of my father's birth certificate as well as I knew my own. The coroner wrote it down in his notebook.

'And his last permanent address?' he asked, not looking up.

I pulled the photocopy of the driving licence from my pocket and consulted it. 'He lived at 312 Macpherson Street, Carlton North, a suburb of Melbourne, Australia,' I said.

'And when did you last see your father alive?' he asked.

'As he was loaded into the ambulance at Ascot Racecourse,' I said.

'So you were present at the time of the assault?' he asked.

'Yes,' I said.

The coroner glanced over at Chief Inspector Llewellyn. 'Are the police aware of your presence at the time of the assault?' he asked me.

'Yes,' I said again.

He wrote something down in his notebook, then asked, 'Did you observe the body of the deceased after death at Wexham Park Hospital?'

'Yes,' I said once more.

'Can you swear to the court—and I remind you, Mr Talbot, that you are under oath—that the body you observed was that of your father?'

'I believe it was my father, yes,' I said.

The coroner stopped writing his notes and looked up at me. 'That doesn't sound very convincing, Mr Talbot,' he said.

'Until the day of his death,' I said, 'I hadn't seen my father, or even known of his existence, for the past thirty-six years.'

The coroner put down his pen. 'And how old are you, Mr Talbot?'

'Thirty-seven,' I said.

'Then how can you believe that the deceased was your father if you haven't seen him since you were a year old?'

'He told me so,' I said.

The coroner appeared amazed. 'And you took his word for it?' he asked.

'Yes, I did,' I replied. 'We'd been speaking about family matters for some time before the attack on us in the Ascot car park, and I became convinced that he was, indeed, my father as he had claimed. In addition, I was informed by the police that DNA analysis had confirmed the fact.'

'Ah,' he said, turning towards Llewellyn. 'Is this so, Chief Inspector?'

'Yes, sir,' he said, standing up. 'The DNA indicated that Mr Talbot and the deceased were very closely related. Almost certainly father and son.'

The coroner wrote furiously for about a minute in his notebook before looking up at me. 'Thank you, Mr Talbot, that will be all.'

Nothing about Alan Charles Grady or Willem Van Buren. Identification of the deceased had been formally established as Peter James Talbot.

'May I arrange a funeral?' I asked the coroner.

He again turned towards the chief inspector. 'Do the police have any objection to an order being issued?'

Chief Inspector Llewellyn stood up. 'We would prefer it if the body were to remain available for further post-mortem inspection, sir. We have reason to believe that the deceased may have been connected with past crimes and we may wish to perform further DNA testing.'

'Do the necessary samples not already exist?' the coroner asked him.

'We may have the need to gather more,' said the chief inspector.

'Very well,' said the coroner. He turned back to me. 'Sorry, Mr Talbot, I will not issue a burial order at this time. You may reapply to my office in one week's time.'

'Thank you, sir,' I said.

I looked at the chief inspector with renewed loathing. I was sure he had only objected to me organising a funeral in order to irritate me.

'This inquest is adjourned,' said the coroner. 'Next case, please.'

Those of us concerned only with the death of Peter James Talbot stood up and filed out of the court. Ahead of Chief Inspector Llewellyn, Sergeant Murray and me were three other men and a young woman.

By the time I reached the lobby, one of the men and the woman were standing with Chief Inspector Llewellyn and asking him questions, one with a notebook, the other with a handheld recorder. Reporters, I thought. One of the other two men was chatting with Sergeant Murray, but I couldn't see the fourth stranger. I rushed out of the building, but he had disappeared.

I went back up the steps and into the building. Both the reporters saw me at the same instant and hurried across.

'Do you know why your father was killed?' asked the young woman.

'No,' I said. 'Do you?'

She ignored my question. 'Did you see the person who was responsible for his death?' she asked, thrusting her recording device into my face.

'No,' I said.

'Would you recognise the killer again?' asked the man, forcing his way in front of me and elbowing the woman to the side.

'No,' I said, hoping he would print the answer for the killer to read.

'Did he do that to your eye?' asked the woman, trying to push back.

'Yes,' I said. 'He kicked me. That's why I was unable to see the person responsible, or indeed anything else that happened.'

'But why was he killed?' implored the man.

'I have no idea,' I said. 'I hadn't seen my father for thirty-six years until the day he died.'

'Why not?' the young woman asked almost accusingly.

'He emigrated to Australia when I was one,' I said, 'and my mother and I didn't go with him.'

They suddenly seemed to lose interest in me. Maybe they could tell that I wasn't going to be much help to them.

What they really should have asked me was why my mother hadn't emigrated to Australia with my father. The answer was because she'd been murdered by him. Not that I'd have told them.

CHAPTER 6

Early on Tuesday morning I drove to south Devon and parked near a long line of painted beach huts behind Preston Sands, in Paignton. I had driven right past Newton Abbot Racecourse, where they were racing later that day. But I wasn't here for my work. Luca and Betsy had taken the equipment and would be standing at Newbury for the evening meeting. I hoped to be able to join them later.

I locked my old Volvo and went for a walk along the seafront.

It was still relatively early and Paignton was just coming to life, with the deck-chair rental man putting out his blue-and-white-striped stockpile in rows for the holidaymakers to sit on. There were a few morning joggers and dog-walkers about, and a man with a metal detector digging on the sand.

It was a beautiful June day and the sun was already quite high in the sky, its rays reflecting off the sea as millions of dancing sparkles.

I thought back to the inquest the day before.

'South Devon,' Sergeant Murray had said to me quietly as we stood in the lobby of the courthouse.

'What?' I'd said.

'South Devon,' he'd repeated. 'That's where your mother was murdered. In Paignton. On August the 4th, 1973. Her body was found on the beach under Paignton pier.'

'Oh,' I'd said inadequately. 'Right, thank you.'

'And don't tell the chief inspector I told you,' he'd said, keeping an eye on the door to the Gents through which his boss had disappeared.

'No,' I'd said. 'Of course I won't.'

He'd turned to move away from me.

'Did she have a baby with her that was murdered as well?' I'd asked him.

'Not according to the file I read,' he'd replied, then hurried away.

My grandmother had probably been confused, I thought.

I took off my shoes and socks, rolled up the legs of my trousers and walked along Paignton beach.

I wasn't really sure why I had come here. What did I think I would find? The previous evening I had used my computer to Google 'Paignton Murder', but I could find nothing about the murder of a Patricia Jane Talbot in August 1973. The Internet simply did not stretch back far enough.

So here I was, walking along the beach as if simply being here would give me some insight into what had gone on in this place all that time ago.

The tide was out, revealing a wide expanse of red sand, crisscrossed with patterns of ridges and grooves produced by the outgoing water. I strode purposefully southward towards the pier, past the imposing grey sea wall of the Redcliffe Hotel, carrying my shoes and digging my bare toes into the sand.

I stood on the beach in the shadow of the Victorian pier and wondered again what had happened right here to my mother. Where had I been at the time? Had I been with my parents here in Paignton on that fateful day? Was I here on this very spot when she'd died?

There was nothing much to see. I hadn't expected there to be. But something in me had needed to visit this place.

I pulled my wallet out of my trouser pocket and extracted the creased picture of my parents taken at Blackpool. All my life I had looked at that picture and longed to be able to be with my father. The grandparents who had raised me had been my father's family, not my mother's, and somehow my paternal loss had always been the greater for me.

Now I studied her image as if I hadn't really looked at it closely before. I stood there and cried for her loss and for the violent fate that had befallen my teenage mother in this place.

'You all right, boy?' said a voice behind me.

I turned round. A man with white hair and tanned skin, wearing a faded blue sweatshirt and baggy shorts, was leaning on one of the pier supports.

'Fine,' I croaked, wiping tears from my eyes with the sleeve of my shirt.

'We could see you from my place,' said the man, pointing at a cream-painted refreshment hut close to the pier. 'Do you fancy a cuppa?'

'Yes, please,' I said. 'Thank you.'

'Come on, then,' he said. 'On the house.'

'Thank you,' I said again, and we walked together over to his hut.

'He's all right, love,' the man shouted as we approached. He turned to me. 'My missus thought you looked like you were going to do yourself in. You know, wade out to sea and never come back.'

'Nothing like that,' I said, giving him a smile. 'I assure you.'

He handed me a large white cup of milky tea and took another for himself from the cheerful-looking lady behind the counter. 'Sugar?' he asked.

'No, thanks,' I said, taking a welcome sip of the steaming brown liquid. 'It's a beautiful day.'

'We need it to last, though,' he said. 'July and August are our busy times, when the families come. Mostly just a bunch of OAPs in June. We need the sun to shine all summer if we're to survive. At least most folk won't be going abroad for their holiday this year, with the pound so low. Too expensive.'

We stood together for a moment, silently drinking our tea.

'I must get on,' said the man. 'Can't stand here all day. I also run the pedalos, and they won't get themselves out, now will they?'

'Can I give you a hand?' I asked.

He looked at my dark trousers and my white shirt.

'They'll clean,' I said to him.

He looked up at my face and smiled. 'Let's get on, then.'

'Ned Talbot,' I said, holding out my hand.

'Hugh Hanson,' he said, shaking it.

'Right then, Hugh,' I said. 'Where are these pedalos?'

I SPENT MOST of the next hour helping to pull pedal boats out of two great big steel ship's containers, and lining them up on the beach. Then we went back to the hut for another cup of tea.

'Proper job,' said Hugh, grinning broadly. 'Thank you.'

'Thank *you*.' I grinned back. 'Best bereavement therapy I've ever known.'

'Bereavement?' he asked, suddenly serious.

'Yes,' I said. 'My mother.'

'I'm sorry,' he said. 'When did she die?'

'Thirty-six years ago,' I said.

He was slightly taken aback. 'Long time to grieve.'

'Yes,' I agreed. 'But I only found out where she died yesterday. It was just over there.' I pointed. 'Where I was standing on the beach.'

He looked over to where I had been, under the pier; then he turned back to me. 'Wasn't murdered, was she?' he asked me.

I stood there looking at him in stunned silence.

'Oh, I'm so sorry,' he said. 'I didn't think she'd been old enough to be anyone's mother.'

'She was eighteen,' I said.

'I'm sorry,' he said again.

'How did you know?' I asked him.

'I didn't,' he said. 'But the murder of that girl was big news around these parts. My father owned the business then, of course, but I was working for him. We were bigger then, with masses of boats for hire. That murder shut us down for a week, and the summer seasons took years to recover.'

I looked again at the space beneath the pier.

'They never caught the man who done it, did they?' he said. 'That's what really did for us all. No one felt safe with a killer on the loose. People stopped coming to Paignton for years. Stupid. The killer was probably from up the line, anyway. After all, your mum wasn't local, was she?'

I shook my head. 'Were you here the day they found her?' I asked him.

'Certainly was,' he said. 'It was Father who saw her lying under the pier and went over to wake her up. Hopping mad, he was. Sleeping on the beach isn't allowed. We're always having things damaged by people at night. Anyway, he couldn't wake her up because she was dead. White, he went. I thought he was going to be sick. It was me as called the police.'

'Did she really look like she was asleep?' I asked.

'I presume so,' he said. 'I didn't see her close to. By the time I'd made the call some security man had set up a load of rope to keep people away.'

'Is your dad still alive?' I asked.

'No,' he said. 'The old boy died about ten years ago.'

Pity, I thought. I must have looked disappointed.

'There was masses about it in the local paper for days and days,' Hugh said. 'They'll surely have copies of them in the local library.'

'Where is the library?' I asked.

'In Courtland Road,' he said. 'Not far. That direction.' He pointed.

'I might just go there later,' I said.

'Do you fancy a bacon and egg sandwich?' Hugh asked, changing the subject. 'I'm having one.'

'I'd love one,' I said.

We sat on chairs put out for the customers of the refreshment hut, and his wife brought each of us a fresh mug of tea and a huge sandwich with so much bacon and egg filling that it was falling out of the sides. I ate mine with eager relish. I hadn't realised I was so hungry.

'How much do I owe you for that?' I asked, downing the last of my tea.

'Don't be silly,' he said. 'You earned it.'

'Thanks, Hugh,' I said, and we both stood up and shook hands. 'I hope the sun shines for you and your customers all summer.'

'Thanks,' he said. Then he asked, 'Are you sure you want to find out more about your mother's death? You might find out something you don't like.'

How could anything be worse than finding out your own mother was murdered by your father? I thought.

'Thanks for the concern,' I said, 'but I have a need in me to find out more. My mother made me who I am and I desperately want to learn more about her. At present, I know almost nothing. This is the only place to start.'

He nodded. 'You know where to find me if you need any help.'

'Thanks,' I said, really meaning it.

I waved at his wife, who was busily making crab sandwiches behind the counter, and walked away in the direction he had pointed.

Paignton Library did indeed have a newspaper section but it only kept copies for the previous six weeks.

'You'll have to go to Torquay,' said a kindly lady behind the counter. 'They keep back issues of the local papers on microfiche. They'll have back copies of the *Herald Express* and the *Western Morning News* as well.'

'Thank you,' I said, and departed back to my car.

I SAT IN A DARKENED ROOM at Torquay Library at one of the microfiche machines and read all there was in the *Herald Express* newspapers of August 1973 concerning the eighteen-year-old Patricia Talbot, found murdered under Paignton pier.

Just as Hugh Hanson had said, there had been masses about it for days and days. But in spite of all the column inches, there was very little actual detail, and no reports of progress with the investigation.

I did discover that she had been found clothed, and there appeared to have been no evidence of any sexual assault. The local police were quoted as confirming that she had been strangled and that she had been dead for several hours before she was discovered on the beach at 7.20 in the morning by a Mr Vincent Hanson. Hugh's father, I presumed.

Most of the reports centred around the fear that an unsolved murder on the beach would have a detrimental effect on the local tourist industry. There was surprisingly little information about Patricia Talbot herself. No mention of whether she was on holiday in Paignton or had been working there. No report of any hotel where she had been staying, or even if she had been alone in the town or with her husband. Not a word about any fifteen-month-old son left motherless. Only once was my father even mentioned, and only then to report that he had nothing to say. 'I have no comment to make at the moment,' he was quoted as saying three days after the discovery of the body.

I had exhausted all the coverage in the *Herald Express*, so I went back to the reference-library desk. 'Do you have the *Western Morning News* for August 1973?' I asked a young member of the library staff.

'Sorry, we only have the *Morning News* back to '74,' he said. 'You'd have to go to Exeter for any earlier than that.'

'Ah, well,' I said. 'Thanks anyway.' I began to turn away.

'But we have the *Paignton News* for '73, if that's any good.'

The *Paignton News* had been a weekly publication, and the week of the murder it had reported nothing more than I had already read in the *Herald Express*. I almost left it at that, but something made me scan the following week's edition. There I found out what my grandmother had meant.

On the third page there was a brief account of an inquest at South Devon Coroner's Court that had been opened into the sudden and violent death of one Patricia Jane Talbot, aged eighteen, of New Malden in Surrey.

According to the paper, the post-mortem report stated that the main cause of death had been asphyxiation due to constriction of the neck consistent with manual strangulation. The piece concluded by stating that the deceased had been found to be pregnant at the time of her death, with a female foetus estimated at between eighteen and twenty weeks gestation.

Indeed, he had murdered her baby. He had murdered my sister.

I DIDN'T GET to Newbury for the evening racing. Instead I went straight home to Kenilworth.

I was angry. In fact, I was absolutely livid. How could my father have come to Ascot, just one week previously, and been so normal and so natural, even so agreeable, when he held the knowledge that he had murdered my mother, together with her unborn child?

It was despicable, and I hated him for it.

Why had he come back and turned my life upside-down? Had he come because of the glass RFID chips and the money? Surely it hadn't been just to see me? I lay awake for ages, tossing and turning, trying to sort it out, but all I came up with was more and more questions, and no answers.

Whose money was it in his rucksack? Was the money connected to the RFID chips and the black-box programmer? Was he killed because he hadn't handed over the money, or was it the black box and the glass grains that were so important? And what exactly were they for?

Every punter has a story of how they think a crooked trainer or owner has run the wrong horse in a race. How a 'ringer' has been brought in to win when the expected horse would have had no chance. But running a ringer has always been more difficult than most people believed, especially from a large, well-established training stable, and not only because horse identification has become more sophisticated with the introduction of RFID tags and horse passports. The real reason is that too many people would have to be 'in the know'. The horse's groom, the horsebox driver, the travelling head lad and the jockey, just for a start, in addition to the trainer and the owner.

It would be impossible to keep it a secret from any of them, because they would simply recognise that the horse was not the right one. People who work every day with horses see them as individuals with different features and characteristics, and would spot a ringer immediately. And it was too much to expect that a secret conspiracy of even a handful of people would hold for very long.

So what real good were the rewritable RFID chips?

I finally went to sleep, still trying to work out the conundrum.

I WAS NOT SURE what woke me, but one moment I'd been fast asleep, the next I was fully conscious, knowing that something wasn't quite right.

I listened intently, lying perfectly still on my back in the dark and keeping my breathing very quiet and shallow.

As usual in the summer, I had left open one of my bedroom windows for ventilation. But I could hear nothing out of the ordinary. Nothing except for the breeze, which rustled the leaves of the beech tree by the road.

I had begun to think I must have been wrong when I heard a sound that I recognised. Someone was downstairs, and was opening the kitchen cabinets. The cabinet doors were held shut by little magnetic catches. The sound I had heard was the noise made when one of the catches was opened.

I lay there wondering what I should do. I didn't really imagine my intruder was searching through my kitchen cabinets for tea bags.

Sergeant Murray had warned me that witnesses to murder were an endangered species, and now I wished I had taken his warning seriously.

I thought about making lots of noise, stamping down the stairs, demanding to know who was in my house in the hope that he'd be frightened away. Then I remembered the two stab wounds that had killed my father. Was my visitor the shifty-eyed man from the Ascot car park, and did he have his twelve-centimetre-long blade with him ready to turn my guts into mincemeat?

I stretched out my hand towards the telephone that sat on my bedside table, intending to call the police. I decided it was better to be still alive, even if it did mean I would have the difficult task of explaining why there was £30,000 of someone else's cash in my wardrobe. Much better, I thought, than drowning in my own blood.

But there was no dialling tone when I lifted the receiver. My guest downstairs must have seen to that. And, as always, I'd left my mobile in the car.

What, I wondered, was plan C?

There was nothing to be gained from simply lying there in bed waiting for him to come up and plunge his knife into my body. Clearly, he would rather have found what he had come for and departed silently, or else he would have come up and dealt with me first. But I was under no illusion that he would give up before he had searched everywhere, whether or not I was wide awake or fast asleep, or very dead.

I looked around in the dim luminosity that filtered through the curtains from the streetlight glow outside. Sadly, my bedroom wasn't equipped with any form of handy weapon.

Perhaps I should just throw the money and the other things from the rucksack down the stairs and let my visitor take them away. Anything to stop him coming up to get them himself, with murder in mind.

I gently levered myself out of bed and crossed the room to the wardrobe, but before I had a chance to open it I heard the third tread of the staircase creak. I had been meaning to fix that step for years but I couldn't be bothered to lift all the carpet. I had become so obsessed with the creak that I missed it out, always taking two steps together at that point.

My visitor hadn't known about the creak. Nor would he have known that the step always creaked a second time as the weight was removed.

I stood stock-still beside my wardrobe, listening. I was holding my breath and I could hear the blood rushing in my ears. There had definitely been only one creak. The intruder had stopped on the stairs in mid-climb and was, no doubt, listening for any movement from me as hard as I was from him.

I had to breathe.

I decided to snort through my nose like a pig. I snored loudly and then exhaled in a long rasping wheeze. Then, quite clearly, I heard the third step creak again as my visitor removed his weight from it. I assumed he was still on the way up, so I snored again, then grunted as if turning over in bed.

The wardrobe was behind my bedroom door. I flattened myself against the wall and stared at the brass door handle, my heart thumping hard.

The handle began to depress and my heart almost went into palpitations. Slowly the door opened towards me.

Attack had to be the best form of defence.

When the door was about halfway open I threw myself against it with all the force I could muster, attempting to slam it shut again. But the door didn't fully close because my visitor's right arm was preventing it. I could clearly see his gloved hand and his wrist protruding into my bedroom. There was a gratifying groan from its owner each time I pushed against the door, repeatedly throwing my weight against the wood.

'You've broken my bloody arm!' he shouted.

Good, I thought. Pity I hadn't torn it off completely.

'What do you want?' I shouted back through the door, still refusing to ease up the pressure to release his arm.

'I'm going to kill you, you bastard,' he shouted back.

I put my right foot down on the floor to stop the door from opening, leaned back and then threw my whole weight against it once more.

This time he didn't just groan, he screamed.

'What do you want?' I shouted again.

'I want to break your fucking neck,' he said, sounding very close indeed. I pressed again, the door squeezing against his damaged arm.

'And what exactly are you looking for?' I asked.

'The microcoder,' he said.

'What's that?'

'The flat black box with buttons on it,' he said. 'Give me the microcoder and I'll go away.'

'I don't think you're in a position to make demands,' I said, while still pushing hard on the door. 'What does this microcoder do?'

Instead of answering, he threw his weight against his side of the door to try and open it, but my foot was still preventing that. However, the wood bent sufficiently for him to extract his arm. The door slammed shut.

My advantage was over, but I couldn't hear him going down the stairs.

'What does the microcoder do?' I repeated, shouting through the door.

'Never you mind,' he said, still sounding very close. 'Just give it back.'

'I haven't got it,' I said.

'I think you have. Your father stole it and I want it back.'

'Was that why you murdered him?' I asked.

'I didn't murder anyone,' he said. 'But I could murder you, you bastard. I'm in agony, here.'

'Serves you right,' I said. 'You shouldn't come snooping around other people's houses uninvited.'

'It doesn't give you the right to break my arm,' he whined.

'I think you'll find it does. Now get out of my house and stay out.'

'Not without the microcoder,' he said.

'I told you, I haven't got it,' I said.

'Yes, you bloody have,' he insisted. 'You must do. Where else would it be?'

We didn't seem to be making any progress.

I hooked my left foot round Sophie's dressing-table chair and pulled it towards me. I then placed the back of the chair tight under the door handle. I should have done that in the first place, I thought.

Stalemate ensued for the next fifteen minutes or so. I was wondering what he was up to when he suddenly banged on the door, making me jump.

'I'll be off now, then,' he said quite casually. It was as if he'd just been round for a drink and it was time to go home.

'Who are you?' I said.

'Never you mind,' he said again. 'But I didn't kill your father.'

I heard him go down the stairs and the third step creaked twice as he descended. I heard the front door being opened. Then it was slammed shut.

I went across to my bedroom window and looked down. The man was walking across the car-parking area and onto the road. He appeared to be cradling his right arm and, at one point, he turned briefly to look up at me, as if intentionally showing me his face. I recognised him immediately. It wasn't the man with the close-set eyes who had stabbed my father in the Ascot car park; it was the elusive fourth stranger from his inquest.

WARILY I REMOVED the chair from under the door handle and peeped out onto the landing. I crept silently down the stairs, avoiding step three, listening carefully and ready to run back up at the slightest noise. There was no one there. He had gone, and he'd not come back again. I turned on all the lights and went round closing the stable door now that the horse had bolted.

In truth, I'd made it far too easy for him. Like the fanlight in my bedroom, the one in the living room had been open, and he had simply put his arm through it, opened the big window beneath and climbed in. He'd left some muddy footprints on the fawn carpet under the window. No doubt I should now call the police and they could take photos of the prints.

Instead, I used my handheld vacuum cleaner to clear up the mess.

The phone handset in the kitchen was off the hook. I picked it up and listened. Nothing. I replaced it on the cradle, then lifted it again and pressed REDIAL. The LED read-out just showed 0. A female computer-generated voice stated, 'The number you have dialled has not been recognised. Please check and try again,' and that phrase was repeated about six times before it shut off completely, leaving the line dead.

Apart from the mud on the living-room floor, my nocturnal visitor had been tidy in his search. The kitchen cabinets were open but hardly disturbed, as were the sideboard cupboards in the dining room.

However, far from answering any of the questions surrounding my father, my intruder had simply created new ones; in particular, was he working with Shifty Eyes or did they represent different interests?

After all, he had asked only for the microcoder. There had been no mention of the considerable cache of money that had been hidden with it.

But if the fourth stranger knew where I lived, then so could anyone else. I had, perhaps carelessly, freely given out my home address at the inquest, where he would have heard it. It would now be in the official record and could be obtained by any member of the public who really wanted it. Perhaps I should be on the lookout for another unwelcome guest, one with shifty eyes, in search of bundles of blue-plastic-wrapped cash.

ON WEDNESDAY I went to Stratford Races.

Whoever thought that jump racing in June was a good idea hadn't envisaged racing at Stratford after a prolonged drought, when the ground was as hard as concrete. Very few trainers were willing to run their steeplechasers and the overnight declared runners for Stratford had been so few that it was hardly worth the journey. Add the fact that Mother Nature had decided that this was the day the six-week drought would break, with numerous thunderstorms moving north from France, and one could understand why the midweek race-day 'crowd' was not really worthy of the name.

Only four bookmakers had bothered to turn up to try to wring a few pounds out of the miserable, rain-soaked gathering, and we huddled under our large umbrellas watching the raindrops bouncing back off the tarmac.

The first race was a two-mile novice hurdle. We watched as the four runners appeared on the course and went down to the two-mile start. A few hardy punters made a dash across the ring towards us to place a bet before hurrying back to the shelter of the grandstand.

'It's not much fun today,' said Luca in my ear.

'It was your idea,' I said, turning to him. 'I'd have been happy staying in bed on a day like this.'

After my disturbed night, staying in bed had seemed like an excellent plan, but Luca had called me twice during the morning to see if I was coming to Stratford that afternoon.

'You don't have to come,' he'd said in the second call. 'Betsy and I can cope on our own. We had a good night at Newbury without you.'

I had begun to feel that I was being eased out of my own business and that made me even more determined to be here. But now, as another rivulet of rainwater cascaded off the umbrella and down my neck, I wasn't so sure.

'We must be mad,' shouted Larry Porter, again our neighbouring bookie.

'Bonkers,' I agreed.

Business was so slow that Betsy had complained about the rain and taken herself off to the bar, and I was beginning to wish I could join her.

'Whose stupid idea was it to come to Stratford?' I said to Luca.

'You've got a waterproof skin, so what are you worrying about?' said Luca with a grin. 'As least it's not cold.'

'It's hardly hot,' I replied.

'No pleasing some people,' he said to the world in general. 'Why don't you just go home and leave Betsy and me to make you a living?'

He said it with a smile, but he meant it nevertheless. It seemed I really was being eased out of my own business.

'You mean it, don't you?' I said seriously.

'Absolutely,' he replied. 'We need to be more ambitious, more proactive, more ruthless.'

I wasn't sure whether the 'we' included me or not.

'In what way do you want to be more ruthless?' I asked him.

'All that stuff at Ascot last week has shown me that the big boys are not invincible,' he said. 'Someone gave them a bloody nose and good luck to them. Bookmaking should be all about what happens here.' He spread his arms wide. 'Well, not exactly here today, but you know what I mean: standing at a pitch on the course, not watching some computer screen.'

I was amazed. I thought it was the computer gambling that made Luca tick. 'But you love the Internet,' I said.

'Yes, I do,' he said. 'But only as a tool for what happens here. The on-course bookies need to set the prices and they should not be driven by the exchanges. By rights, it should be the other way round. We should be prepared to alter our prices for our advantage, not for those of anyone else.'

'You sound like you're at war,' I said with a laugh.

'We are,' he said seriously. 'And if we don't fight, we'll go under.'

I remembered back to the time when I had been assisting my grandfather. I'd had the same sort of discussion with him then. Bookmaking was an evolving science and new blood, like Luca, needed to be ever pushing the boundaries. Without it, as he'd said, we would go under.

As is so often the case with small fields, the four horses in the race finished in extended line astern, the favourite winning it at a canter by at least ten lengths. There was hardly a cheer from the measly crowd.

As Luca had said, it wasn't much fun.

A man in a suit came striding across from beneath the grandstand just as the rain began to fall in a torrent. He was holding an umbrella but it didn't appear to be keeping him very dry. Too much water was bouncing back from the ground. His feet must have been well and truly soaked.

He stopped in front of me. 'What the hell's going on?' he demanded.

'What do you mean?' I asked him in all innocence.

'With the bloody prices?' he said loudly. 'How come that winner was returned at two-to-one when everyone knows it should have been odds-on?'

'Nothing to do with me,' I said, spreading my hands out wide.

'Don't get bloody clever with us,' the man said, pointing his finger at me.

'And who is us, exactly?' I demanded, disregarding the implied threat.

He ignored me and went over to remonstrate with Larry Porter, who told him to go away and procreate, or words to that effect.

The man was far from pleased. 'I'm warning you two,' he said, pointing at both Larry and me. 'We won't stand for that.'

Larry shouted at him again, using language that made even me wince.

'What was all that about?' I asked Luca.

He grinned. 'I thought we might tempt a few more punters over here if we offered a better price on the favourite. That's all.'

I stood there looking at him. So that was why he had been so keen for me to stay at home and leave things to him and Betsy.

'You silly bugger. We don't play games with these guys,' I said seriously.

'Don't be so boring,' he said.

'I mean it. They are powerful people and they stamp on irritations.'

Was this what he meant by being at war?

The starting price was not set by a single bookmaker's prices. It was a sort of average, but was actually the mode of the offered prices rather than a true average. A mode is the value that occurs most frequently in a sample.

At Ascot last week the number of bookmakers was high, so a representative sample of, say, twelve bookmakers' prices was used. If, in the sample of twelve, five of the bookmakers had the price of a certain horse as the race started at three-to-one, say, then its starting price would be three-to-one, even if four of them had the price at seven-to-two, and the other three at four-to-one. Three-to-one was the mode: the price that occurred most frequently.

If there were two modes, because five of those bookies had the price at three-to-one, and five of them had it at seven-to-two, then the starting price was always taken as the higher of the two odds—i.e. seven-to-two.

At Stratford on this particular wet Wednesday in June, there were only four ring bookmakers and the sample included all four. Only two of them needed to offer higher prices than was 'true' for the starting price to be recorded as 'too high'. So Luca could not have affected the price on his own.

'Was it Larry's idea or yours?' I asked him.

'What do you mean?' he said, all innocently.

'It needed two of you,' I said.

'You were there, too,' he said, with a degree of accusation in his voice.

It was true. I was there, and it was my name on the board. So I would carry the can, if a can indeed had to be carried. But I now realised how much I had subconsciously delegated to Luca and his computer.

I knew full well that it was bound to have been Luca's idea. And how could I keep him on if I didn't trust him not to bring my business down, either in standing or in monetary terms? If my grandfather had taught me one thing, it was that reputation was important.

I could almost hear the cogs whirring in Luca's brain. He knew that if I let him go and he had to set up in business on his own he would have to purchase a number at a future pitch auction, which would require considerable outlay to obtain a decent spot in the ring.

From my own point of view, I had come to rely heavily on Luca. His expertise with our computer and the Internet gambling had been instrumental in keeping the name of Teddy Talbot in the higher echelons of bookmaking circles. We had been remarkably profitable over the last few years, and I was not naive enough to think that it was solely down to me.

The trouble was, Luca knew it.

'How about offering me a proper partnership?' he said with a smile.

I took that as a positive sign. 'I'll think about it,' I said.

'Don't take too long,' he said seriously, the smile having vanished.

Was he threatening me, I wondered, or warning me that he'd had offers from elsewhere? Luca was my full-time employee, but he could do equally well, maybe better, offering his expert services freelance on a daily basis to the highest bidder. There were half a dozen or so professional bookmaker's assistants who were all highly capable and in regular demand in the ring.

Maybe Luca was considering joining their ranks, or perhaps he'd had an offer from another bookmaker to become a partner.

I looked over at Larry Porter.

Surely not him, I thought. I had always considered that I was a better businessman than Larry, but maybe he thought the same about me.

'Hi, Larry,' I called over across the rain-swept deserted six feet between us. 'What price will you give me on the favourite in the next?'

'Piss off,' he shouted back. 'You self-righteous git.'

Charming. He might have been funny if it wasn't for the fact that he and Luca had put us all in jeopardy by so blatantly changing the prices.

The day progressed with, if anything, a deterioration in the weather. No doubt the gardeners of Middle England were delighted by the downpour, but the punters at Stratford plainly were not. We took just two bets on the big race of the day, if that was an appropriate way of describing it. The three-mile steeplechase on rock-hard going had attracted a paltry field of three.

In the betting ring, there was noticeably more activity than for the first couple of races, though that was due not to an increase in the number of punters braving the conditions but to the fact that several 'suits' from the big outfits had turned up. They stood around scrutinising our prices more closely than a stamp collector studying a Penny Black.

Nothing untoward occurred, of course, but I caught a glimpse of Luca and Larry Porter having a secret smile at one another. Just how long, I thought, would it be before they couldn't resist trying it again?

The race itself could hardly be described as exciting. The short-priced favourite, the only decent horse of the three, jumped off in front at the start and led the other two round and round the course by an ever-increasing margin, winning by a distance, almost at the trot. One of the remaining two slipped over at the last fence to leave the other to finish second, but so far behind the winner that the stands had long before emptied.

After weigh-in, the stewards decided to abandon the rest of the day's racing. It seemed that the heavy rain, coming down as it had on the rock-hard ground, was causing the top surface of the grass to skid off the under-lying dry compacted soil, making the going treacherous.

Personally, I thought the stewards had done everyone a favour and we gratefully packed up our stuff and made our way to the car parks.

'Are you still OK for Leicester tomorrow, without me?' I asked Luca.

'Yeah, sure,' he said. 'Looking forward to it.' He smiled at me. I stopped pulling the trolley. 'OK, OK,' he said. 'No funny business. I promise.'

'Let's talk at the weekend,' I said.

'Fine,' he replied. 'I want to talk things through with Betsy anyway.'

Betsy had appeared from the bar and had helped us to pack away the last few things. I was never quite sure what was going on in her head, and that day she had hardly said a word to me.

We loaded the equipment into the boot of his car while Betsy simply sat inside it in the passenger seat. She didn't say goodbye to me.

'Have a good day tomorrow,' said Luca. 'Good luck.'

'Thanks,' I said. 'I hope it all goes well.'

Sophie was due to have an assessment with a consultant psychiatrist from a different hospital. It was the final hurdle for her pass in order to be able to come home. Just as there needed to be agreement between two psychiatrists for her to be sectioned, there was also a need for such agreement for her to be, as they put it, released back into the community.

I wasn't at all sure whether it was a good idea to leave Luca and Betsy to go to Leicester together without me.

'Betsy and I will be fine,' Luca said, clearly reading the dilemma in my face. 'I promised, didn't I?'

I must have still looked doubtful.

'Look,' he said, 'we'll be doing the best for the business in every respect. No point in fouling it all up if you're thinking of offering me a partnership, is there?' He smiled at me.

'OK,' I said. 'But—'

'Like you said, we'll talk at the weekend,' he said, interrupting me.

He climbed into the car, next to Betsy, and drove away, as I stood there watching, wondering if life could ever be the same again.

THE RAIN HAD EASED a little as we had packed up the stuff, but now it began again in earnest, drumming noisily on the roofs of the cars around me.

I threw my umbrella in the back of my car, jumped in the front and started the engine. I was about to drive away when the passenger door suddenly opened and a man in a blue mackintosh climbed in beside me.

'Can you give me a lift?' he asked.

I looked at him in amazement, but he just stared forward through the windscreen, ignoring me.

'Where to?' I said finally. 'The local police station?'

'I'd really rather not,' said the man. 'Couldn't you just drive for a bit?'

'And what makes you think I'd want to do that?' I asked him icily.

He turned towards me. 'I thought you might want to talk.'

My audacious hitchhiker was the fourth stranger from the inquest, my unwanted nocturnal visitor of the previous night, complete with fresh plaster cast on his right arm.

I put the car into gear. 'OK,' I said. 'You talk and I'll listen.'

CHAPTER 7

'Well?' I said. 'Talk to me.' I took the Stratford to Warwick road.

'Why didn't you call the police?' he asked.

'How do you know I didn't?' I glanced across at him.

'I stayed to watch,' he said. 'You vacuumed up the mess I left and no one does that if they've called the police.'

I felt uneasy at the thought of him being outside my home, watching me. 'How long did you wait?' I asked him.

'Not long,' he said. 'My arm hurt too much.'

'Serves you right.'

'You broke my wrist.'

'Good.'

We sat in silence for a while.

'Who the hell are you, anyway?' I asked him.

'Just call me John,' he said.

'John who?'

'John Smith.'

Oh, yeah, I thought. Pull the other one. 'And what do you want?'

'The microcoder,' he said. 'Like I told you last night.'

'Even if I did have it, and I don't, what right do you think you have breaking into my house to look for it?'

'It seemed like a good idea at the time,' he said. 'And I didn't break in. You left a window open. You were just asking to be burgled.'

'So that's what you are, is it?' I said. 'A burglar.'

'Don't be stupid,' he said.

I looked across at him. 'I'm not the one with a broken wrist.'

'OK,' he said. 'I agree. That wasn't so clever.'

Again I drove in silence.

'Where to, then?' I asked.

'To wherever the microcoder is.'

'I told you, I don't have it.'

'I don't believe you.' He turned in his seat and looked at me. 'For a start, if you didn't know what I was talking about, you would have telephoned the police last night. And secondly, we know you retrieved your father's ruck-sack from the hotel in Paddington.'

'What rucksack?' I said, trying to keep my voice level and wondering again if this John Smith and Shifty Eyes were working together. He'd said 'we'. Was I on my way to meet the man with the twelve-centimetre knife?

'Oh, come on,' he said. 'We'd been looking for his luggage, too. And I'd been looking for your father ever since he stole the microcoder.'

'Who are *we*?' I asked.

He didn't answer. He just turned back and looked out at the road.

'Why did you murder my father?' I said slowly.

He kept looking ahead. 'I didn't,' he said.

'But you had it done,' I said.

'No.' He turned again to face me. 'I don't know who killed him.'

'And you expect me to believe you?' I said. 'Perhaps we should go to the police station and you can then explain to them exactly who you are and why you were in my house last night.'

'I'll deny it,' he said. 'You vacuumed up the evidence, remember.'

I pulled the Volvo into a lay-by and stopped the engine. I turned to him.

'And what is it you really want?' I asked.

'The microcoder,' he said flatly. 'That's all.'

'And what exactly is this microcoder, anyway?' I said. 'What does it do?'

He sat silently for a moment or two, clearly debating with himself as to how much he should tell me.

'It writes coded information onto animal identification tags,' he said.

'RFIDs,' I said absent-mindedly.

'So you *do* know what it is!' he said. 'Now, where the hell is it?'

Now it was my turn to sit silently debating with myself how much to tell.

'Who do you work for?' I asked. 'Are you some sort of secret agent?'

He laughed. 'What makes you think that?'

'You seem pretty secretive,' I said. 'And you talk about "we" and "us" as if you were part of an organisation.'

He again stared for a moment through the windscreen.

'Indirectly,' he said, 'I work for the Australian Racing Board.'

'Do they know you break into people's houses?'

'They would deny any knowledge of my existence.'

'You don't sound Australian.'

'I'm not,' he said.

'So this so-called microcoder is to do with Australian racing?'

'It's to do with all racing, everywhere. Now, where's my microcoder?'

'So it's yours, is it?' I asked.

'Yes,' he said. 'And I know you have it.'

'How?'

'I had a description of the man who collected your father's luggage from the Royal Sovereign Hotel, though I didn't know it was you until I saw you at the inquest. The lady described you perfectly, including the black eye, though how she didn't question the name Dick Van Dyke, I'll never know.'

I couldn't help smiling, and he noticed.

'What on earth made you come up with that?' he said.

Perhaps he was unaware that my father had checked in under the name Willem Van Buren. The hotel lady had said he was called Van something, and Dick Van Dyke had been all I could come up with at the time.

'If you know so much, how come you took so long to find him—so long, in fact, that I found his luggage before you did?' I asked.

'Because he wasn't using his real name,' he said.

'And what is his real name?' I asked.

'You tell me,' he said. 'You formally identified him at the inquest. So it's now officially recorded by the coroner as Peter James Talbot. But is that right? Who, then, is Alan Charles Grady?'

And who, I also thought, was Willem Van Buren, of South Africa?

'Tell me what you know about my father,' I said to John.

'Well, for a start, I knew him only as Alan Grady. I had been keeping a tight eye on him for some time. He was followed from Melbourne, but I lost him at Heathrow. I now think that he never came through immigration but took another international flight straight out. But I don't know where to.'

I thought about the e-ticket receipt I had found tucked into the Alan Grady passport in my father's rucksack. There had been no other flights listed there, other than his return to Australia.

'Was he using the name Grady?' I asked.

'I don't know that either,' he said.

'How long exactly have you been keeping an eye on my father?' I asked.

'For years,' he said. 'He used to run an illegal backstreet bookmaking business in Melbourne.'

'I thought bookmaking was legal in Australia.'

'Only on-course bookmakers are legal,' he said. 'Needless to say, Mr Grady was not one of those. But he was mostly very good at keeping one step ahead of the security service, just doing enough to keep himself out of court.'

I was pleased he was good at something. 'Only mostly?' I asked.

'He got convicted a couple of times,' he said. 'Small stuff, really. Did a short stretch inside for obtaining money with menaces. Unpaid gambling debts. Then he got turned over by another illegal outfit, ended up bankrupt.'

At least that bit of my father's story had been true, I thought.

'How come a man can go to prison and also be bankrupted and still no one realises that he's not using his real name?'

'But Alan Grady *was* his real name,' he said. 'Passport, driving licence, bank accounts, even a genuine birth certificate all in the name of Grady. I didn't hear the name Talbot until Wednesday, when someone I had lunch with at Ascot told me about the murder in the car park the day before.'

'But how did he get a genuine birth certificate in a false name?' I asked.

'There must once have been a real Alan Grady,' he said. 'Perhaps your father stole his identity. Perhaps the real Alan Grady died.'

Or he was murdered, I thought. 'So tell me about this microcoder,' I said.

'Seems you know already.'

'I know it can be used to write numbers onto RFID chips,' I said. 'But why was it worth chasing my father halfway round the world to get it back?'

'Fraud,' he said. 'Making one horse appear to be another.'

'But everyone knows that running a ringer in a race needs a conspiracy. Someone will always spill the beans.'

'Ah, yes,' he said. 'But you could easily sell a foal or a yearling as another, with no risk then of anyone recognising it as the wrong horse. Especially if you sell it to England from Australia, or vice versa.'

'But surely horses are DNA-tested for their parentage,' I said.

'Yes, but they're only retested if they eventually go to stud. And the DNA testing takes a long time. Not like scanning the ID chip, which is instant.'

'But if you switch a bad horse for a good one, then sell it,' I said, 'what would you do with the good one? You can't sell the same horse twice.'

'No, but if you put it into training under its new identity, it could make you a packet on the track. If it's so much better than people think it should be, it would win at long odds, to start with. Just don't breed from it.'

'And the bad one you sold would just be seen as another expensive failure?' I said. 'And there are lots of those about.'

'Exactly,' he said. 'You wouldn't do it with a mega-valuable yearling, obviously, as there'd be masses of checks made, but loads of horses go to the sales each year. Even the horses-in-training sales now attract huge prices.'

'But I thought those RFID chips were secure and unchangeable,' I said.

'So did we,' he replied. 'But it seems we were wrong. Someone has discovered that an intense, localised magnetic field can wipe the horse's unique number from the chip, just the same way those security tags stuck on merchandise in shops are wiped over a magnetic pad to clear them.'

'And, don't tell me,' I said, 'the microcoder can write a new number in?'

'Well, not quite,' he said. 'The magnetic field has to be so strong that the chip's electronics are completely destroyed. But the microcoder can write a different number into a new chip, which is then inserted in the horse's neck and, hey presto, you instantly have a different horse.'

'But how about the horse's passport, with all its whorls and such?' I said.

'That would be OK if people bothered,' he said. 'But too many people believe the technology without question. Like in tennis. If the Hawk-Eye computer system says a ball is out, then the players believe it's out. Same with this. If the RFID tag says that the animal is Horse A, then it's Horse A, even if it's got all the whorls for Horse B. The authorities try to get people to check both, but they still tend to believe the RFID tags. After all, it's the same authorities that insist on them being inserted in the first place.'

'Does everywhere use the same ones?' I said.

'Pretty much,' he said. 'Except the United States. They don't use chips at all; they tattoo the inside of the horse's lip. But if a horse comes from the States to race in Australia or Europe, it has to be chipped first.'

'Seems to me that the system needs changing,' I said.

'We need that microcoder back,' he said in reply.

'What's to stop someone making another one?' I said.

'Nothing, I suppose,' he said. 'But our boffins say it's not that easy.'

'How about the man who made the first one? Couldn't he make another?'

'Ah,' he said. 'Therein lies a tale. A trigger-happy Victoria State policeman shot him as he was trying to resist arrest.'

'Dead?' I asked.

'As good as,' he said. 'Got a bullet in his brain. Totally gaga.'

'Someone else will work it out,' I said.

'He'd have to have both the knowledge and the intent,' he said.

'If there are any with the knowledge, then there will be some with the intent. Trust me, I'm a bookmaker.'

He laughed. 'You're probably right.'

We'd been sitting in the lay-by for quite a while, and as we talked I'd been trying to think what to do. Why had he said nothing about the money? Did he not know it had been in the rucksack? And if he had a direct line to the Victoria State Police, then maybe he did to Chief Inspector Llewellyn, too. But why then had he entered my house uninvited in the middle of the night?

'Never mind the horses,' I said. 'How do I know you are who you say you are? Do you have any personal ID?'

'I told you,' he replied slightly uncomfortably. 'The Australian Racing Board would deny all knowledge of my existence.'

'And why is that, exactly?' I said.

'The nature of my job means I have to work undercover. If I was a normal employee, my cover would be blown. There are bound to be people in the organisation who'd pass on the information to the very people I am trying to investigate.' He turned to me again. 'So where exactly is my microcoder?'

'I gave it to a friend.'

'You did what?' he exclaimed. 'Who?'

'A friend who's an electronic specialist. To try to see what it does.'

He went pale. 'Well, get it back, now,' he almost shouted.

'I can't,' I said. 'My friend has gone on holiday to Greece. Won't be back until Sunday.'

I didn't really trust this John Smith. Not enough to hand over my trump card to him—not just yet, anyway.

'Where does this friend live?' John asked. 'And what's his name?'

'Her, actually,' I said. 'And what makes you think I'd tell you her name or address? You must be joking. You'd go and break into her house.'

'Mr Talbot,' he said seriously, 'I don't think you understand the trouble you might be in. I'm not the only person looking for that microcoder. And some of the others might not be so patient. There are some nasty people out there.'

Be very careful of everyone, my father had said. I certainly intended being very careful of Shifty Eyes and his twelve-centimetre knife. And I planned to be very careful of Mr John Smith here, as well.

'You call breaking into people's houses being patient?' I said.

He sat there in silence for a second or two, staring ahead.

'Where can I drop you?' I said. 'I have things to do.'

'Here will do fine. A colleague of mine has been following us since we left the racecourse.' He twisted round in the seat.

I looked in the rearview mirror. There was a dark blue Ford in the lay-by behind us, but it was some way off and I couldn't see the driver's face.

'Give me a call when your friend comes back from holiday,' he said, turning back and handing me a business card with just a mobile-telephone number printed on one side. 'Call me,' he said. 'For your own good.'

He opened the passenger door and eased himself out of my car.

'Go now,' he ordered, closing the door.

I watched him get into the dark blue Ford, feeling decidedly annoyed that someone had been following me. In fact, I was downright angry.

I started the engine but, instead of engaging forward gear, I reversed back down the lay-by towards the Ford. I would have rammed him, too, if he hadn't suddenly pulled out into the road and shot away, narrowly avoiding a collision with both a truck and a car towing a caravan. I snatched the Volvo into forward gear and pulled out to give chase, but I had no chance. Both the truck and the caravan were between me and the Ford.

Damn it, I thought, as the Ford sped away into the distance. That wasn't very clever. My first ever undercover, James-Bond-style car chase and I'd got stuck behind a bloody caravan. 'M' would not have been amused.

Sophie's assessment took all morning and went on into the afternoon. It mostly consisted of a case conference between the medical staff, discussing whether they considered that Sophie was well enough to go home. There was also an informal presentation by Sophie, explaining why she thought she was ready to leave their care. Then they, in turn, were free to ask her questions in order to try and determine her state of mind.

This was not the first time Sophie had been forced to go through this type of assessment. Six times before, she had endured sitting quietly while others discussed her mental health and then passed judgment on her fitness or otherwise to be released from hospital. Only on four of those six occasions had she been successful, and it was far from guaranteed this time.

'What about you, Mr Talbot?' asked the visiting psychiatrist in the session after lunch. 'Can you be at home to support your wife for the first few days?'

'Of course,' I said.

'Do you work from home?' he asked, looking up at me from his notes.

'No,' I said. 'But I intend being there when Sophie comes home.'

'And what line of business are you in?' he asked.

'I'm a bookmaker,' I said.

'In a shop?' he said, without a pause.

'No,' I said. 'I'm an on-course bookie, mostly at the Midlands meetings. But I will be at home whenever Sophie needs me.' I decided not to mention unwelcome night-time visitors, or men with twelve-centimetre knives.

'Thank you, Mr Talbot. I'm sure you will.' The psychiatrist's tone implied that he didn't really believe it. He looked down and wrote more notes.

'Excuse me,' I said. He looked up. 'I assure you that Sophie's well-being is far more important to me than my work. I want her home. And I will do everything within my power to ensure she remains safe. I love my wife.'

I had sat all day holding Sophie's hand, listening to these emotionally distant professionals discussing her most personal secrets in matter-of-fact detail, and I surprised myself now with the passion of my plea. But I did want Sophie home. I realised that I wanted it very much indeed.

'Yes, Mr Talbot,' said the psychiatrist, 'I believe you do.' He smiled at Sophie, who went on holding my hand very tightly.

He went back to writing a few more notes before looking up.

'Mrs Talbot, Mr Talbot, thank you both for your time. As you know, we shall require further discussion between us before we make our decision. Today is Thursday. We should have an answer for you by Saturday.' He looked around at the other medical staff as if enquiring whether any of them had anything more to say. They didn't. 'Thank you, then,' he said, rising to his feet.

'Thank you,' said Sophie.

We stood up in turn and made our way out of the conference room.

'I thought that went quite well,' I said to her quietly.

'Did you?' she said.

'Yes,' I said, being upbeat. 'I'm sure it's going to be all right.'

We walked together side by side along the corridor towards her room.

'Do you really love me?' she said.

'Yes,' I said. 'Very much.'

She didn't stop walking. But she did start smiling.

I SPENT THE EVENING at the hospital with Sophie, watching television. Neither of us spoke about the assessment or what conclusion the medics might come to; neither of us wanted to tempt fate by discussing the matter. But was I, in fact, being sensible in wanting Sophie to come home with so many unresolved issues surrounding my father?

John Smith, or whoever he was, had gone on and on about his blessed microcoder but he hadn't once mentioned any money. He would certainly know about the cash if he was working with Shifty Eyes. But had it been Shifty Eyes in the dark blue Ford, o-r was there someone else?

'Shall we have some coffee?' Sophie asked, interrupting my thoughts.

'Yes,' I said. 'That would be lovely. Shall I call the nurse?'

'No,' she replied. 'Since last week they've let me go down the corridor to the little kitchen. I'll get it.'

'Do you need any help?' I asked her.

'Ned,' she replied, looking at me sideways, 'I can make coffee on my own.' She smiled at me. My heart now did the same flip-flop that it had, all those years ago, when we had first met and she had smiled at me.

'Are you sure?' I said.

'Positive,' she said. 'I am trying very hard, you know. I haven't missed a single dose of these new drugs and I do honestly believe that they are helping. I feel really quite well now, and ready again for the world.'

I stood up and hugged her. There were tears in my eyes. She had come a long way even in the last week and truly did seem better than ever this time.

'Go and get the coffee,' I said.

She left the room and I wiped my eyes on my sleeve. Tears of happiness and hope, at last, after so many of despair and hopelessness.

I PULLED MY VOLVO warily into the parking area in front of the dark house and sat in the car for a few moments, looking around for anything out of the ordinary. Everything seemed fine.

I quickly locked the car and made it safely to my front door. Inside, there were a few letters and bills on the mat but no threatening notes.

Calm down, I told myself.

I tried to, but it didn't stop me going round the house, checking that the windows were closed and drawing the curtains in every room. After making sure that not the slightest chink of light escaped through the blinds in the kitchen, I laid the booty from my father's rucksack out on the kitchen table.

I sat there looking at it. Why didn't I deliver the whole lot to Chief Inspector Llewellyn and let him sort it out? Wash my hands of the affair and get on with my life, which was complex enough without microcoders, forged RFID tags and shifty-eyed men with long, sharp knives?

A good part of me thought that was a great idea.

But it had disadvantages. For a start, there would be the difficult task of explaining to the chief inspector why I hadn't given him the stuff as soon as I'd found it. He might charge me with obstructing the police, and then what protection would they afford me against a knifeman? None whatsoever.

Second, keeping hold of the microcoder and the money might give me some leverage, provided I kept alive long enough to use it.

I picked up my father's mobile telephone and tried again to turn it on, but without success. It was a Nokia, and my own was a Samsung, so my charger would not work. I took the SIM card out of my father's phone and put it in mine, but I couldn't get any details of his numbers. If there was anything there, he had stored it in the phone's memory, not on the SIM.

I picked up the Alan Charles Grady passport and examined it. It had been issued nine months previously and appeared genuine. I turned the pages and saw that he'd entered the United Kingdom the day before he came to see me at Ascot. It was the only UK stamp in his passport, but there was also one for Dublin dated the previous week. So he *had* flown straight out again from Heathrow after his arrival from Australia, as John Smith had thought.

I wondered what he had been up to in Ireland.

THE FOLLOWING MORNING, Friday, I was waiting outside the local mobile-telephone shop for it to open at nine o'clock sharp.

At 9.10 the door was unlocked by a female shop assistant who looked about twelve. 'Yes, sir,' she said in a bored tone. 'Can I help you?'

'I need a charger for this phone,' I said, holding out my father's Nokia.

'No problem,' she said. She went over to a display and took one of the chargers. 'This should be the one. Anything else?'

'Could you just check that it's the right one?' I said.

She obviously thought I was mad, but she took a large pair of scissors from a drawer beneath the desk and cut through the plastic wrap around the charger. She plugged it in to a socket and took the phone from me.

'There,' she said. 'It's charging. You can see from the little moving lines.'

'Thank you,' I said. 'Can you turn it on?'

She pushed a button on the top. The screen lit up and the phone played a five-note tune. She handed it back to me with it still connected to the charger. The message *Please enter your security code* was displayed on the screen.

'It's a long time since I used this phone,' I said to her, 'and I can't remember the security code. Can you bypass it for me?'

'No chance,' she said, sounding horrified at the suggestion. 'I'm not allowed to do that. How do I know it's your phone, anyway?'

'So theoretically you could bypass the security code?' I said.

'I doubt it,' she said. 'But I expect Carl could.'

'Who's Carl?'

'He works out the back,' she said. 'He mends mobiles. He's very clever.'

She disappeared and returned with a young man who didn't strike me as the very-clever type. He was wearing faded, torn and frayed blue jeans, a plain off-white T-shirt and a knitted brown hat that reminded me of a tea cosy. Tufts of fair hair stuck out from under the hat in all directions.

'Can you unlock this phone?' I asked him.

He didn't say anything but took the phone from my hand and looked at it.

'What's the phone's IMEI number?' he said.

'IMEI?'

'International Mobile Equipment Identity,' he said slowly.

'I have no idea,' I said.

'It's normally written inside the phone,' he said, taking off the back and removing the battery. 'Hello. This one's been removed. That's what people do with stolen phones,' he said, looking warily at me.

'How else can I get this IMEI?' I asked, ignoring his suspicions.

'You could input star hash zero six hash once it's unlocked,' he said unhelpfully. 'Or it would have been printed on a sticker on the box when you bought it.' He put the battery back into the phone and turned it on. *Please enter your security code* appeared again on the display.

'Can't you do it without the IMEI number?' I asked.

'No, mate,' he said, handing back the phone. 'Can't help you without the IMEI or the security code. Not without wiping clean the whole phone memory. Do you want me to do that?'

'No,' I said quickly. It was the phone's memory I wanted most.

I paid the girl for the charger and took it and the phone back home. I sat again at my kitchen table, and wondered what the security code might be.

I punched in 3105. My father's real birthday had been May 31.

The display momentarily read *Incorrect security code* before returning to *Please enter your security code.*

I inserted the year of his birth. *Incorrect security code.*

Next I tried 1234. *Incorrect security code.*

I looked at the copy of his driving licence. I typed in 0312, his house number. *Incorrect security code.*

The licence showed Alan Grady's birthday as March 15, 1948. I tried 1503. *Incorrect security code*. I typed in 1948. *Incorrect security code*.

It could be anything. I wondered how many wrong chances I'd have before the whole phone locked up for ever.

Just for a laugh, I entered *my* birthday, 2504, and suddenly there it was— *Correct security code*. I couldn't quite believe it. It was unlocked.

So he hadn't forgotten. My birthday.

The phone rang in my hand, making me jump.

I answered it.

'This is voicemail,' a disembodied female voice said. 'Please enter your security code.'

Not again, I thought. I tried 2504.

'You have three new messages,' said the voice. 'Message one received at ten thirteen a.m. on June the 18th.'

Two days after he died.

'Alan, this is Paddy, Paddy Murphy,' said a male voice with a strong Irish accent. 'Where are you? You were meant to call me yesterday.'

Messages two and three were also from Paddy Murphy, each with an increasing degree of urgency, pleading for Alan to call him back.

The caller's number came up as +353 42 3842. I grabbed a notepad and wrote it down. Plus 353 meant it was a Republic of Ireland number. Perhaps Paddy Murphy was the man my father had flown to Dublin to visit.

The rest of the telephone was less useful than I had hoped.

Unlike most people, my father had not used his mobile as his phone book. There were no entries on either the phone memory or on the SIM card. No convenient names for my sisters with their telephone numbers.

The only useful thing was a list in the calls register of the last ten numbers he had called and five that he had received. One of them in each of the lists was the +353 number of Paddy Murphy. I made a written note of them all, then used my father's phone to call Paddy Murphy.

'Hello,' said an Irish-sounding voice, the emphasis on the long final 'o'.

'Is that Paddy Murphy?' I asked.

'Who wants to know?' said the voice rather cautiously.

'This is Alan Grady's son,' I said.

There was a long pause. 'And who might Alan Grady be?'

'Don't play games with me, Mr Murphy. Call me back on this number if you want to talk.' I hung up.

He called back immediately.

'Yes?' I said.

'And what line of business might you be in?' he asked.

'Selling,' I said.

'Selling what, exactly?' he replied.

'Depends on what you want to buy,' I said.

'Are you the police?' he asked suddenly.

'Why do you ask?' I said. 'Have you been up to no good?' But the line was dead. Paddy Murphy had hung up.

Damn, I thought. That hadn't gone at all well. And he was possibly my only real lead. Perhaps he believed I'd been trying to trace the call. I wish I had. My father had flown into Dublin, but Paddy Murphy, if that was his real name, could be anywhere in the Republic of Ireland.

I sat for ten minutes waiting and hoping for him to call. He didn't.

So I tried him again, but he didn't answer. How, I wondered, did one find out where a certain telephone number was situated? I decided to ask Luca. If anyone knew, he would.

IN THE AFTERNOON I drove to Kempton Park for the evening racing. Luca was meeting me at the course as he and Betsy were spending the day somewhere in Surrey, visiting friends or something.

I'd asked him how things had gone at Leicester on the Wednesday.

'Fine,' he'd said. 'Good crowd. Plenty of business.'

'Profitable?' I asked.

'Very,' he'd replied without explaining further.

Why did I worry so much? Would it be better or worse if Luca was my official business partner? Indeed, should I sell him the whole enterprise and be done with it? But what else could I do? I had to earn a living somehow.

I turned off the congested Friday-evening M25 and fought my way against the commuter traffic to Sunbury and Kempton Park Racecourse. Race traffic was also starting to build up and I crawled the last two miles nose to tail with other cars before turning into the racecourse car park behind the stands.

I pulled into a spot as indicated by one of the parking marshals. Another car drew in beside me. I watched as a train pulled into the racecourse station and disgorged a mass of humanity that swarmed towards the racecourse. It was a beautiful evening and the good weather had brought out the crowds. A good night for business, I concluded, and stepped out of the car.

'Are you Talbot?' said someone behind me. 'Teddy Talbot?'

I turned round. There were two men standing between the cars, both wearing short-sleeved white shirts, open at the neck, with black trousers: uniform of the heavy mob. The shirts did little to hide the substantial size of their biceps, or the tattoos clearly visible on their forearms.

'Yes,' I said cautiously. 'Can I help you?'

Instead of replying, the nearer man stepped forward quickly and punched me hard in the stomach.

The blow drove the air from my lungs and I dropped to the ground.

'Oh, I say,' said the man from the neighbouring car. He had just removed a jacket and some binoculars from his boot, and he was looking horrified.

'Shut up,' said the puncher, pointing at him, 'or you'll get the same.'

The horrified man shut up immediately and moved rapidly away. I didn't blame him. I would have moved rapidly away too, if only I could have drawn some air into my lungs. I rather hoped he'd gone for reinforcements in the shape of a policeman or two, but I wouldn't have bet on it.

'I have a message from my boss,' the puncher said, returning his attention to me. 'Don't mess again with the starting prices.' He kicked me in the midriff. 'Get it?' he said. 'No more Stratford.' He kicked again. 'Get it?'

He kicked me once again for good measure; then the two of them turned and calmly walked away, leaving me lying curled up on the tarmac.

Once my diaphragm had recovered from its spasm, my breathing resumed with a rush. Using the door handle of my Volvo, I pulled myself semi-upright, relieved that the punch had been just that. There'd been no knife.

'Are you OK?' asked the horrified man, appearing tentatively round the back of his car.

'I'm fine,' I said, not feeling it.

'What was all that about?' he asked.

'Nothing,' I said, leaning wearily against the car and feeling sick.

'It didn't look like nothing,' he said accusingly.

'Could you identify those men to the police?' I asked him.

'Er,' he hesitated. 'Not really.'

'No?' I said. 'Then nothing happened. OK?'

'I'm only trying to help,' he said, somewhat pained.

'Sorry,' I said. 'And thank you for your concern.' If I'd been seriously hurt, he might just have saved my skin by coming back. 'I promise you I am very grateful. My name's Ned Talbot.' I held out my hand to him.

He hesitated again, not taking it. 'I don't want to get involved,' he said. 'I didn't like the look of those men.'

'It's OK,' I said. 'I understand completely. I won't be describing them to the police either.' One kicking was more than enough, I thought.

'Right,' he said, and he turned on his heel and walked briskly away.

He may not have wanted to get involved, but I still noted down the registration of his car on my notepad. Just in case.

LUCA AND BETSY were both waiting for me at our pitch in the betting ring. They had set up everything and were sitting on our metal platform in the shade of our large yellow TRUST TEDDY TALBOT umbrella.

'Hello,' I said. 'Have any trouble? Any problems in the car park?'

'No,' Luca said. 'But I forgot how bloody hard it is to get that trolley across from the centre of the course.'

'I've just been given a message,' I said. 'In the car park behind the stands.'

'Who by?' he asked.

'I don't know. Someone who's not very happy about what happened at Stratford on Wednesday.'

'What sort of message?' asked Luca with concern.

'Fists and steel toecaps.'

'What!' He seemed genuinely distressed. 'Here? In the car park?'

I nodded. 'And I could show you my bruised solar plexus to prove it.'

'God,' he said, clearly upset. 'I'm so sorry.'

'Why are you sorry?' said Betsy. 'You didn't do it.'

'Shut up, Betsy,' said Luca sharply.

'Don't talk to me like that,' she whined.

'Then don't say such stupid things,' he said to her. He turned back to me. 'Ned, I'm really sorry. Are you OK?'

'I'll live,' I said, without much warmth. It would do no harm, I thought, for Luca to realise that his little games had consequences, some of which were decidedly unpleasant, and not just for him.

Betsy went off towards the grandstand in a huff, and both Luca and I watched her go. 'Go after her, if you like,' I said to him.

He shrugged his shoulders and stayed where he was. It would appear, I reflected, that we might soon need another junior assistant. And I wouldn't be sorry. I decided I didn't really like Betsy much.

'How about Larry?' I said. 'Is he here this evening?'

'He should be,' said Luca.

'Really?' I said, wondering how Luca knew.

He looked at me sideways. 'Yeah, well. He told me last night. At Leicester, all right?' Luca was visibly flustered, and that was a rarity.

'Do you have his phone number?' I asked.

'Sure,' he said.

'Then call him,' I said. 'Warn him to watch his back. And his stomach.'

Luca pulled his mobile from his pocket and pushed the buttons.

'Larry,' he said. 'It's Luca.' He listened for a moment. 'So where are you now?' he said. He listened again for a moment. 'Right,' he said. 'I'll call you later.' He hung up and looked at me. 'Too late. He's in Ascot Hospital having X-rays for suspected broken ribs.'

'So who were they?' I said.

'How the hell would I know?' he said. 'I didn't see them.'

'Who did we upset so much?'

'All of them,' he said. 'The talk was of nothing else at Leicester. Some of the other bookies even congratulated us.' He was smiling.

What bloody fools, I thought. And it was me who got the 'message', not Luca, because it's my name on the board.

'I told you not to mess with the big outfits,' I said. 'At least, not so openly. We need to be more subtle, more devious.' I smiled back at him.

He was confused. 'What do you mean?'

'I don't know yet,' I said. 'But if they think they can get away with beating me up in racecourse car parks, they've got another think coming.'

Luca smiled broadly. 'Right,' he said. 'Great.'

THE REST OF THE EVENING was quiet in comparison, with not a single bully-boy to be seen. Business was brisk, with a string of tight finishes and a largely young crowd eager to be tempted into the evils of gambling. Many of them were actually there for the pop concert that was taking place after the racing. I was almost able to ignore the dull ache in my guts, which refused to go away, in spite of me swallowing a couple of painkillers.

A young woman stood in front of me, wearing tight jeans and a skimpy top that displayed a pleasing amount of sun-bronzed midriff.

'Remember me?' she said.

I looked up from her midriff to her face. 'At Ascot last week,' I said. 'Black-and-white hat. I didn't recognise you without your finery on.'

She laughed, and I laughed back. Then she blushed. I remembered that, too.

'Come on, Anna,' said a young man who was pulling at her arm.

I watched them go. She turned and waved at me before disappearing into the throng. At least someone thought of their bookie as a human being.

'I don't think Betsy will be coming back,' said Luca over my shoulder.

'Go and find her,' I said. 'I'll manage on my own for a while.'

'In your dreams,' he said, slapping me on the shoulder.

That was a good sign, I thought.

'She'll come back if she wants to,' he went on. 'I'm not going to go running after her. To tell you the truth, I don't really care if she comes back or not.'

I cared. Luca was much more fun without her.

The last race of the evening was a five-furlong sprint for two-year-old maidens. Many had never even been on a racecourse before, let alone won a race. Only one, East Imperial, had good previous form, finishing second twice. Naturally it was a short-priced favourite when the betting opened.

'Don't even think of disrupting the Internet tonight,' I told Luca.

He didn't deny it, but his jaw dropped open. 'How did you know?' he said.

'It didn't take rocket science,' I said. But in truth I hadn't known for sure. It had been a guess. 'You are a wizard at electronics,' I said. 'And you and Larry have been up to all sorts of stuff. It seemed an obvious connection. Who else was in on it?'

'Norman Joyner was. He was the only other bookie. It's just a bit of fun.'

My stomach didn't think it was funny, and I bet Larry's ribs didn't either.

'So were you going to do it again here, tonight?' I asked.

'That was the plan. But Larry had the kit with him and he didn't make it.'

We both knew why he hadn't.

'Was it this race?' I asked.

'Yeah, of course,' he said. 'Red-hot favourite and all that.'

'But why? Where's the gain? Are you betting on it elsewhere?'

'No,' he replied. 'That's the beauty of it. There's no trail for them to chase. No one who has anything to do with us does well out of it. It just produces a windfall for everyone who backs the favourite in a betting shop at the starting price. And there'll be masses of those. It makes the big outfits lose a bit and gives them a fit that someone else is playing them at their own game.'

'But it cost you money to change the odds for the bets in the ring at Ascot,' I said, remembering the man in the white shirt and fawn chinos who had bet £1,000, two monkeys, on a loser.

'Not really,' he said. 'A friend of Larry's started the betting with a grand of readies. Then the same money went round and round, with Larry and me backing with Norman, and him doing the same with us. The odds changed all over the ring but not much cash changed hands with anyone else, and what did was covered by a little wager on the favourite at home by Larry's wife.'

Very organised, I thought.

'Was that also what you were up to at Stratford?' I asked.

'Yeah, sort of,' he said. 'But, I grant you, that was a bit too obvious. We hadn't planned to do anything there, so we didn't have the kit with us, but there were so few bookies, and the weather was so awful, we decided to have some fun just by changing the odds on the boards.'

'Well, don't ever do it again,' I said. 'If you are seriously interested in a partnership in the business, there's no place for messing about with the prices. You could put our livelihoods in jeopardy. Do you understand?'

He looked like a scolded schoolboy. The truth was that he had thought of it as just a game. But I had the bruises to prove it wasn't.

'I mean it,' I said. 'Never again.'

'Oh, all right,' he said, clearly fed up, but accepting the inevitable.

East Imperial, the favourite, won the race easily and was returned at a starting price of eleven-to-ten on, which was about right.

Overall, Betsy apart, it had been a good night for us, and Luca and I packed up our stuff in good spirits.

'Tell me about the equipment you use,' I said to Luca as we pulled the trolley round the grandstand and out to the car park behind.

'What equipment?' he said, all innocently.

'You know. The kit you use to take down the Internet and the telephones.'

'The Internet's easy,' he bragged. 'It's the phones that are more testing.'

'Tell me,' I said.

'You don't actually make the Internet go down,' he said; 'you just make the access to it very slow.' He smiled. 'I use our computer Wi-Fi connection to give the racecourse server a virus that causes it to chase round and round making useless calculations of prime numbers. That uses up all its RAM, its random-access memory, so leaves it no space to do what it should be doing. Then, when I want, I turn the virus program off and, hey presto, the calculations stop and the Internet access is back to its rightful speed.'

It sounded all too easy. 'And the phones?' I said.

'Simple in principal,' he said. 'Emit a mass of white noise, that's a random radio signal, at the right frequency. It simply overwhelms the weaker signals from the telephone transmitters. Smothers them completely. Not very subtle, but effective over a smallish area like the betting ring.'

'How big is the device?' I asked him.

'Small enough to fit in Larry's boxes,' he said. 'And it's powered by a car battery, same as the odds boards.'

'How often have you used it?'

'Only the three times at Ascot,' he said. 'It was only finished last week. The first time, on Tuesday, was just a test to see if it worked. Thursday was the target, as you've worked out. Saturday was just for fun.'

'But on the Tuesday, surely we nearly came unstuck,' I said. 'You told me that we would have been off another grand if the favourite had won the last, because you couldn't use the Internet to lay it.'

'Yeah, well, we took a lot of late bets, and Larry had the switch.'

'Luca, retire the kit now, before it gets you into real trouble, and before it costs us in profits.'

'Yes, boss,' he said mockingly.

'I mean it.'

'I know,' he said more seriously.

'But keep it safe,' I said. 'Just in case.'

He looked at me questioningly, but I didn't answer. Instead, I started to lift the equipment into the back of my car. Suddenly, I doubled over in pain.

'Are you all right?' asked Luca, alarmed.

'I will be,' I croaked. My stomach muscles had cramped up.

'Do you need a doctor?' he said, genuinely concerned.

'No,' I said, straightening up and stretching. 'I'll be fine in a minute.'

'Oh God, Ned,' Luca said. 'I didn't plan for this to happen.'

'Of course you didn't,' I said. 'But I told you, I'll be fine.'

The cramp finally eased and I smiled at him. His worried expression improved slightly, and he lifted the rest of our stuff into the car.

'Now, tell me,' I said. 'What do you know about Irish telephones?'

'Not much,' he said. 'Why?'

'I wondered if you knew if they have area codes so you could tell where a number was in the country.'

'All I know is that Irish mobiles start with 85, 86, 87 or 88 after the 353.'

So Paddy Murphy's number hadn't been a mobile.

'How about 42?' I asked him.

'I don't know. Google it. If it's an area code, it'll be on the Internet.'

'Thanks,' I said. 'I will.' Now why hadn't I thought of that?

'When are we going to have our little chat?' he asked.

'About what?' I said, wanting him to be the one to raise the subject again.

'A partnership,' he said.

'We'll talk in the car tomorrow on the way to Uttoxeter,' I said. 'Be at my place by eleven.'

'Are you sure you're OK?' he said.

'Positive,' I replied. 'Now get on home before you miss the train.'

CHAPTER 8

I made it to the hospital in time for the last fifteen minutes of the news. Sophie jumped up and threw her arms round my neck when I arrived. 'I'm so glad,' she cooed. 'I thought you weren't coming as it's so late.'

'There was a pop concert after the racing,' I said. 'Masses of people, so it took a long while to pack up and get out.'

I sat down next to her and she held my hand as we watched the last few items and then the weather. Neither of us wanted to say anything about the outcome of the assessment. But perhaps it was time to discuss it. I had called the hospital twice that day, but there had been no news.

'Still no decision from the psychiatrists, then?' I said.

'No,' she replied. 'It's very frustrating. All the staff here think it's a fore-gone conclusion that I should go home.'

'So do I,' I said. 'Darling, you seem so much better now.'

She smiled at me with genuine happiness, and my heart went flip-flop once more.

'I know,' she said. 'I feel wonderful and these new drugs are great. Far fewer side effects than before. And I don't feel so bloated by them.'

Could I really hope that life's bumpy rollercoaster was now going to run smooth? It was far too soon to believe that, but the starting signs were good.

'Have a nice day at Uttoxeter tomorrow,' she said as I stood up to leave.

'I will,' I replied, giving her a kiss.

I debated in my mind whether to worry her about Luca. I really wanted her opinion, and I suppose she had a right to know if I was about to become a 50 per cent partner rather than a sole proprietor of the business.

'Luca Mandini wants a full partnership,' I said.

'Does he indeed?' she said. 'He's still very young.'

'He's twenty-seven,' I said. 'That's not so young. And he's very good.'

'Do you think you'll lose him if he doesn't get it?' she asked.

'Probably. He'll either start up on his own or go to someone who'll give him what he wants.'

'But can you afford it?' she asked.

'Yes, I think so,' I said. 'I'd save on his salary and it wouldn't be a lot different, money-wise. I already give him a sizable share of the profits. If he left, I could always employ another assistant to run the computer, but . . .'

'But they wouldn't be as good?' she said.

'Probably not,' I said.

'Seems a no-brainer to me, then. Give Luca what he wants.'

'You really think so?'

'Sure,' she said. 'Can you afford not to? But make sure you tie him down with a contract so it costs him to leave.'

Tie him down with a contract so he can neither leave the business nor destroy it with dodgy dealings, I thought. I had decided against telling Sophie about Internet outages, mobile phones that wouldn't work and fixing the starting prices. There were still limits to what was prudent.

But I was glad I'd asked her about Luca. Crystal-clear business thinking had always been her forte, when she was well, that is, and her current advice seemed as sound as her present mental state.

'Thank you,' I said to her. 'I'll do just that.'

We kissed good night, a joyous, loving kiss.

On this occasion, she was not even fed up at me for leaving her behind. I think we both knew she would be coming home with me on Monday, and a couple more days or so wouldn't matter.

DUNDALK, THE INTERNET told me. Paddy Murphy's telephone was in Dundalk, a large town on the northeast coast of the Irish Republic, some fifty miles north of Dublin, not far from the border with Northern Ireland.

I was sitting in my office after another undisturbed night in Station Road.

Under no illusions that Shifty Eyes would have given up in his search for the money, I had once again slept with the chair from Sophie's dressing table wedged under the bedroom door handle. I had also left the cash in the cupboard beneath the stairs. Perhaps he would then be cajoled into taking the money without also using my body for target practice.

I looked again at my father's telephone. I had tried Paddy Murphy's number a few more times after I returned from the hospital. I pushed the button once more and heard the familiar ringing tone.

'If you were the Gardaí you'd be here by now,' Paddy said, answering. 'So I'll assume you're not.'

'No,' I said. 'I'm not.'

'So who are you?' His Irish accent was stronger than ever.

'I told you,' I said. 'I'm Alan Grady's son.'

'He doesn't have a son,' he replied.

'Oh, yes, he does,' I said. 'I was born before he went to Australia.'

There was a pause. 'What do you want with me?' he asked.

'How well did you know my father?'

'What do you mean, did?'

'My father was murdered at Ascot Races. He was stabbed.'

There was a long silence. 'Have they caught who did it?' he finally asked.

'Not yet,' I said.

'Any suspects?'

'I don't know,' I said. 'I don't think so.'

'Don't they have any leads at all?' he persisted. Was he scared?

'The murderer was a man in his mid- to late thirties. Medium build with shifty-looking eyes,' I said.

'How do you mean, shifty?' he said slowly.

'Slightly too close together for his face,' I said.

He hesitated too long. 'Could be anyone,' he said.

'But you know who,' I said. It was a statement, not a question.

'No,' he said. But I didn't believe him.

'Denying it won't stop him coming after you. Who is it?'

'Do you think I'm bloody mad or something?' he said, a nervous rattle to his voice. 'Even if I knew, I wouldn't be telling you, now, would I?'

'Why not?' I asked him.

'Do you think I'm bloody mad?' he said once again. 'He'd kill me, too.'

'He might do that anyway,' I said.

It added to his discomfort. 'Blessed Mary, mother of Christ,' he said.

'Praying won't help you,' I said. 'But telling me or the police might.'

He didn't reply.

'Why would this man want you dead anyway?' I asked. 'Have you stolen money from him? Or is it something to do with the microcoder?'

'The what?' he said.

'The microcoder,' I repeated. 'A black box with buttons on it.'

'Oh, you mean the chipwriter,' he said.

'Yes,' I said. 'Who does it belong to?'

'I thought it was Alan's,' he said. 'But now I think he may have stolen it.'

'From the man with the shifty eyes?' I asked.

'No,' he said with certainty. 'Not from him.'

'I thought you didn't know who he was?' I said.

'I don't,' he said, but without conviction. 'But the chipwriter definitely came from Australia. I know that.'

'Why did my father come to see you two weeks ago?' I asked him.

'Who says that he did?' he said.

'I do,' I replied. 'But why? And what's your real name?'

'Inquisitive, aren't you?' he said.

'Yes,' I replied. 'And if I don't get some answers from you pretty soon, I might just go and give your phone number to the policeman investigating my father's murder. Then the Gardaí *will* be on your doorstep.'

Another pause. 'What do you need to know?' he asked.

'What my father was doing in Ireland, for a start,' I said.

A longer pause. 'He was delivering something to me,' he said at last.

'What?' I demanded.

'Just something I'd bought from him,' he said.

'What was it?' I asked him again. 'An electronic identification tag?'

'Yes,' he said slowly, without elaborating.

'And a horse passport?'

'Yes,' he said slowly again.

'A forged horse passport and ID tag?' I asked.

Another pause.

'Come on,' I said loudly with frustration. 'Tell me.'

'But why should I?' he said.

'Because with Shifty Eyes on the lookout, I may be the only friend you have, Mr Paddy Murphy, or whatever your real name is. And if he kills you, too, you'd want to know that he was then caught, wouldn't you?'

'But I don't know his real name,' he wailed.

It was like getting blood from a stone. 'Well, what *do* you know?' I asked.

'I know he kills horses,' he said.

'What!' I exclaimed. 'How?'

'In all sorts of ways. But he always kills them in a way that looks like it was an accident. For the insurance money.'

I did some quick thinking. 'So, you switch a bad horse for a good one,' I said, 'kill the bad one and claim the insurance money on the good one?'

'Exactly,' he said.

'What happens to the good horse?' I asked.

Now that he had started to tell me it came easier. 'It goes into training under the name of the nag, the bad one,' he said. 'If we're lucky, we make a killing backing it when it first runs in poor company, and wins at long odds.'

Clever, I thought, but risky. Making a horse's death appear accidental wouldn't be easy.

'How about the insurers?' I said. 'Don't they check?'

'To be sure, they do,' he said. 'They even have a special investigator who researches all claims relating to horse deaths.'

'So how come you can get away with it?' I asked.

'The insurer's investigator has his eyes set rather too close together.'

MUCH TO MY SURPRISE, and his, Betsy was with Luca when they arrived at my house at 10.50.

'She just turned up at my place this morning as if nothing had happened,' Luca said to me while she was in the bathroom. 'I can't believe it.' He seemed quietly laid-back about it, pleased even.

We set off for Uttoxeter just after eleven in my old Volvo, with Luca sitting up front, as usual, and Betsy in the back, listening to her iPod and dozing.

'I've thought about what you asked,' I said to Luca.

'And?' he said, unable to disguise his eagerness.

'I'm prepared to offer you a full partnership in the business, under certain conditions.'

'What conditions?' he said warily.

'Nothing too onerous,' I said. 'But if I'm to give up half my business, and half the profit, I need assurances on a number of things. You need to show your commitment to the business in the long term, for a start. That means we need a contract that would tie both of us to the business for at least five years, with penalties on either side for early departure. After five years, you would have fully earned your partnership with no financial input needed from you. Within that five-year period, however, I will have a casting vote when there is no agreement between us.'

'Agreement about what?' he asked.

'The way in which the business develops,' I said. 'I can see that you are eager to push the boundaries.' And go beyond them, I thought.

'Yes,' he said.

'Well, that has to be done by agreement. Now don't get me wrong. I'm not totally against change, and I will look at any suggestion you make, but for the next five years I will have the final say about what we do.'

'How about after that?' he said.

'After five years, as full partners, we'd have an equal say in how the business was run. If we couldn't agree, we'd both have to give and take a little.'

'But for the next five years I'd be doing the giving and you the taking?'

'Well, if you put it like that, then, yes, I suppose so.'

'So not much different from now,' he said, with resignation in his voice.

I was losing him.

'Yes, it is,' I said. 'You are asking for quite a lot here, Luca, and I'm prepared to hand over half of a highly profitable business to you, at no direct cost to yourself. I could be asking you to buy a 50 per cent share in the business from me, but I'm not. I'm giving it to you for free, but over five years.'

He sat in silence, thinking.

'I honestly think it's a great deal,' I said. 'And you don't have to make a decision right now. Think about it. We can go on just as we are for as long as you want. For ever, if that's what suits you.'

He remained sitting silently beside me for quite a long time.

'Can we call it Talbot and Mandini?' he said finally.

I wasn't sure that I would go that far.

LARRY PORTER was at Uttoxeter, feeling sorry for himself and spitting venom.

'Bloody bastards,' he said to me, and anyone else who would listen. 'Who do they think they are, beating up innocent people?'

I was the innocent one, I thought, not him.

'Calm down, Larry,' I said. 'You'll give yourself a stroke.'

'But aren't you angry as well?' he said.

'Of course. But I'm not going to just get mad—I'm going to get even.'

'Now you're talking,' he said.

'Who were they, anyway?'

'I don't know,' he said. 'Some bully-boys or other.'

Not too easy to get even, I thought, if we didn't actually know who had been responsible. But it was a fair bet that they had come from one of the big bookmaking firms. They were the only ones who would have suffered from Luca and Larry's little game at Stratford Races. But which big firm?

'So what are you going to do about it?' Larry demanded.

'I'm not sure yet. But first, I'm going to find out whose orders those thugs were working to. And, Larry,' I said, looking him straight in the eye, 'no more little games. Understand?'

'Why are you being so bloody self-righteous all of a sudden?' he said.

'Because I recognise when not to poke a hornets' nest with a stick. Let us wait and bide our time, and let's not get stung again in the meantime.'

'OK,' he said with resignation. 'I suppose so.'

Larry wasn't happy. He wanted to lash out at those who had hurt both his body and his pride. But lashing out at a great big grizzly bear would simply result in another claw-swipe to the head.

Getting even required far more cunning than that.

MR JOHN SMITH, or whoever, was waiting for me next to my car in the Uttoxeter Racecourse car park at the end of the day.

'Don't you have anything better to do than hang around in racecourse car parks?' I asked him sarcastically.

'Tomorrow's Sunday,' he said, ignoring me.

'How very observant of you,' I replied.

'Don't you be funny with me,' he said. 'Your friend is back from holiday tomorrow and I want the microcoder.'

'I don't know what time she lands. I'll call you when I've heard from her.'

'Make sure you do,' he said threateningly.

'I must warn you, I don't respond well to threats,' I said.

'Take my advice, Mr Talbot,' he said. 'Respond to this one.'

Gone was the patient good humour of last Wednesday afternoon. Mr John Smith, I imagined, was under pressure to get results.

He turned suddenly and walked away across the car park. I tried to see where he went but I lost sight of him among the departing crowd.

'What was all that about?' I turned at the sound of Luca's voice. He had just arrived at the car and had clearly witnessed the exchange.

I looked him in the eye, then shot a glance at Betsy, who was a few steps behind him. He quickly got the message that I didn't want to discuss it within her hearing, and started to help me load the equipment into the car.

After a few minutes we all climbed in and set off home. Soon Betsy was dozing in the back seat with her iPod on and her head against the window.

Luca turned to me. 'So, what was it all about?' he said quietly.

'The man wanted the black remote thing I showed you,' I said. 'He calls himself John Smith, but I very much doubt that's his real name. He also says he's working for the Australian Racing Board.'

'Why don't you just give it to him, then?' Luca said.

'I don't altogether trust him,' I replied, 'so I made up a story about giving it to a friend who had gone on holiday and would be back tomorrow.'

'Nice one,' said Luca sarcastically. 'So where did the RFID writer come from in the first place?'

'I was given it,' I said.

'Who by?' he asked.

'A man from Australia.'

'Not John Smith?' he said.

'No. Another man from Australia.'

'So a mystery man from Australia just gave you a device for writing RFID tags and now the Australian Racing Board wants it back?'

It sounded implausible even to me.

'Yes,' I said.

'But is it theirs?' he asked.

'I don't know.'

'Why don't you ask the mystery man who gave it to you?'

'I can't,' I said. 'He's gone away.'

'Back to Australia?'

'Not exactly,' I replied. Further than that, I thought.

'So are you going to give it to the man in the car park, this John Smith?'

'I might,' I said. 'What do you think I should do?'

'Well, it's not yours, is it? So why not give it to him? If you don't, you might get another dose of fists and steel toecaps. He looked quite determined.'

'Yes, you're probably right,' I said. 'But I feel that giving up the microcoder is like giving up my trump card.'

'Microcoder?' Luca said.

'That's what the man calls it. But I know my father called it a chipwriter.'

'Your father?' Luca said, surprised. 'I thought your father was dead.'

'He is,' I said, without further elaboration. I'd forgotten that I hadn't told Luca that the man murdered at Ascot had been my father.

'So how come your father knew about this microcoder thing?' he asked.

'It's a long story,' I said. I tried to move the conversation on. 'How difficult would it be to make another one exactly the same?'

'I don't know,' he said. 'As far as I remember, it's just a radio transmitter that concentrates the radio signal at a point where you would put the RFID chip. It didn't appear that sophisticated.'

'Could you make another one?' I asked.

'Well, I don't know about that,' he said slowly.

'I don't want you to,' I added quickly. 'I just wondered if you could.'

'Yeah, I reckon I might,' he said. 'Or if I couldn't, one of the little hooligans from the electronics club would probably be able to do it in no time. So do you want a copy of this microcoder?'

'No, not really,' I said. 'I just wondered why, if it's so easy to make a copy, it's so important to get this particular one back.'

'But they'd have to have something to copy,' he said. 'And they'd have to know the right frequency to set it at.'

'Is that difficult?' I asked.

'Not if you have the original,' he said. 'But much more difficult, maybe impossible, without it.'

'Still, you'd have thought that the Australian Racing Board would have access to whatever resources they needed to make a copy,' I said. 'I think that's why I don't trust him. He doesn't ring quite true.'

'So does that mean you won't give it to him?' Luca asked.

'No. But I might just ensure it doesn't work properly before I hand it over.'

'That might be dangerous,' said Luca, grinning.

'You think so?' I asked.

'Yeah, but why not? Live dangerously.'

Or not at all, I thought.

SOPHIE CAME HOME on Sunday, and her younger sister, Alice, came to stay at our house in Station Road to help out.

'I don't need any help,' Sophie said.

But we both knew she did. The change from institutional life to being at home was a huge step. There would be no one there to call on for help, for a chat or a word of encouragement, especially when I was away at the races.

Alice was just the person we needed. She was busy, efficient, loving and free. And I was very fond of her, but in small doses. One week of busy domestic efficiency was enough for any man.

On Sunday morning Alice arrived, very early, from her home in Surrey, and tut-tutted about the state of the house, especially the unmentionable leftovers in the deeper recesses of the refrigerator. In no time she had donned a pair of rubber gloves and was transforming the place.

By the time we left together in my Volvo for the hospital, the house was sparkling and fresh, and I was grateful. It wasn't just that Alice wanted everything to be clean and neat for her sister's homecoming, it was that we both knew that Sophie would otherwise feel pressured into doing the house-work, and her mania had always begun with obsessive cleaning. Still, at least I was confident that this time the drugs were doing their thing.

Sophie was packed and ready when we arrived. Her room was now bare and back to its 'hospital ward' status. Jason, her favourite nurse, was there to wish her goodbye and to help take her bags down to my car.

'Thank you,' she said to him, putting her arms round his neck and kissing him on the cheek. 'Thank you to all the staff.'

Jason looked embarrassed, but took this show of affection in good grace. 'I won't say it's been a pleasure,' he said to me. 'But Mrs Talbot has been a model patient.'

He stood by the door and waved as we drove down the driveway, through the high gates and out into the real world.

MR JOHN SMITH was waiting outside our house when we arrived home. As I parked the Volvo he climbed out of the dark blue Ford that I had last seen disappearing ahead of me from the lay-by near Stratford. I couldn't see who was in the driver's seat, because of the reflection from the windscreen.

Damn, I thought. I really didn't want to have to start explaining to Sophie about microcoders, bundles of banknotes and murders in Ascot car parks.

The last thing we needed was for him to force his way through my front door and disrupt Sophie's longed-for return home, so I marched straight across the road to talk to him. He came forward to meet me.

'Is that your friend?' he asked, nodding towards the house.

I turned and saw Alice lifting Sophie's suitcase from the car. It must have appeared to Mr Smith that someone was arriving back from holiday.

'Yes,' I said, turning back to him.

'Where's the microcoder?' he demanded.

'In her baggage, I expect,' I said. 'Wait here and I'll get it for you.'

'I'll come with you.'

'No,' I said quickly. 'If you want it, you'll have to wait here.'

'OK,' he said. 'But you have just two minutes. Understand?'

'Five,' I said. 'I'll bring it out in five.'

It wasn't just threats I didn't like. I didn't respond well to orders, either.

I didn't wait for him to reply but strode straight back across the road to follow Sophie and Alice through the front door.

'Who's that man?' asked Sophie, turning and looking back.

'Just a bookmaking friend. He's come to collect something.'

'Aren't you going to ask him in?' she said.

'I did,' I replied, 'but he's in a hurry to get home.'

'What is it?' she said.

'Just a TV remote that Luca has been fixing.' I went to the cupboard under the stairs and took out the microcoder. 'This,' I said, holding it up.

She lost interest. 'Fancy some tea?' she asked.

'Love some,' I said. 'I'll be back in a few minutes.'

Sophie went into the kitchen with Alice to put the kettle on, and I took the microcoder out to Mr Smith.

'Thank you, Mr Talbot,' he said, taking the device. 'And the chips?'

'You didn't ask for the chips,' I said.

'Well, I'm asking now.'

'Wait here.' I went back across the road, collected the little bag of glass grains from the cupboard and went out to hand them to him.

He studied the bag. 'There are eight of them,' he said. 'Where are the rest? There should be twelve.'

'That's all I have,' I said innocently. 'That's all there ever were.'

He didn't seem very happy. 'Are you sure?' he demanded.

'Certain,' I said. 'If I had any more I'd give them to you. They're no good to me, are they?' That might have been true, but it hadn't stopped me keeping a couple of them back, one complete chip and the one I'd broken, just in case.

Still, there had definitely been only ten chips in my father's rucksack. So, if there had been twelve originally, two were indeed unaccounted for. Perhaps Paddy Murphy could enlighten me as to their whereabouts.

'It will have to do,' he said, as if to himself. Then he looked up at me. 'Mr

Talbot, I won't say I've enjoyed our little business together'—he held up his plastered wrist—'but thanks nevertheless for returning the microcoder.'

He turned, walked over to the dark blue Ford, climbed in and was driven swiftly away by his unidentified chauffeur.

He might not still be thanking me, I thought, when he found out that his precious microcoder now wouldn't work.

I hadn't been lying when I told Sophie that Luca had fixed it. He'd fixed it good and proper, by scratching right through the minute connectors on the printed circuit boards using a Stanley knife.

SOPHIE'S FIRST NIGHT home was not quite an unbridled success, but nor was it a disaster. There was just the expected little spat between the sisters when Alice refused point-blank to allow Sophie to help prepare our supper.

'It's my house,' Sophie complained to me. 'And she won't let me do anything in my own damn kitchen.'

'Let her do it,' I replied soothingly. 'You know she means well.' I stroked Sophie's hand and she slowly relaxed. 'Come and sit down.'

We cuddled together on the sofa and watched experts on antiques trying to appear interested in dusty old junk salvaged from people's attics.

'It's ready,' said Alice, putting her head round the living-room door.

The three of us sat at the kitchen table eating grilled salmon fillets, with penne pasta and peas.

'That was lovely,' I said, laying down my knife and fork.

'Mmm,' said Sophie, agreeing. 'Much better than hospital food. Thank you, darling Alice.' Sophie smiled at her sister, then winked at me.

I beamed back at her. My Sophie of old was back. But for how long?

Coming home had tired her and we all turned in early, me taking Sophie up to our bed almost as I had done on our wedding night, and to do again the same things that all newlywed couples do.

For the first time in almost a week, my mind being on other matters, I went to sleep without wedging Sophie's dressing-table chair under the bedroom door handle.

THE CREAK OF SOMEONE walking over the third step brought me instantly from deep sleep to sharp awareness. It was already light. I lay there in bed holding my breath and trying hard to listen for any movement on the stairs. I looked at the door. Sophie still slept soundly beside me.

How could I have put her in such danger? I thought. What a fool I was.

The door handle slowly depressed and the door began to open. I could feel my heart pounding in my chest. What was I to do?

'I made you some tea,' said Alice, coming into the room carrying a tray.

'Oh, Alice,' I said with such relief that I almost cried. 'Thank you.'

'It's a beautiful morning,' she said in a whisper, looking at Sophie.

'Yes,' I replied in the same manner. 'I'll leave her to sleep.'

Alice put the tray down on my bedside table and, with a wave, she departed. I heard the step three creak twice, as usual, as she went down.

What was I doing? I thought as I picked up a mug of steaming tea. Was it time to go to the police and ask for their help and protection?

It was all well and good for me to perform a James Bond act when it was only my life and my future on the line, but what would Sophie do without me?

Shifty Eyes was still out there somewhere, and he would surely still be searching for his money. I was surprised he hadn't already found me.

SOPHIE SLEPT IN until nine thirty, while the mug of tea cooled on the bedside table. I took her up a fresh one and sat on the bed with her as she drank it.

'What a wonderful night,' she said, stretching her arms high above her head. 'This bed is just so comfortable.'

'It's been a very lonely bed without you in it,' I said.

'Oh, Ned,' she said, stroking my leg. 'Let's really try to make it work this time. I'm so tired of all this.'

If only, I thought. We had said this before. Hope had burned in our breasts so often, only to be dashed each time by seemingly unstoppable events.

'Yup,' I agreed, ruffling her hair. 'Let's really make it work this time.'

But first I had some unfinished business to deal with.

I left her to dress while I went downstairs to call the coroner's office to ask if an order had been signed to allow my father's funeral to take place.

'The Thames Valley Police are still apparently objecting to a burial order,' I was informed by one of the officials. 'You could try calling them and asking. It may be an oversight on their part.'

'Thank you,' I said. For nothing.

I called Thames Valley Police Headquarters and asked to be put through to Chief Inspector Llewellyn.

'Ah, Mr Talbot,' he said, coming on the line. 'The bookmaker.'

'Yes, Chief Inspector,' I replied. 'Just why don't you like bookmakers?'

'My father was addicted to gambling,' he replied with surprising anger. 'That, and the demon drink, stole my childhood.'

I was astonished that he'd told me. But it explained a lot.

'I'm sorry,' I said.

'If you were really sorry, you'd give it up,' he said.

'But that wouldn't make much difference now, would it?' I said, somewhat sarcastically. 'There are lots of other bookmakers.'

'One at a time,' he said. 'One at a time. All you bookmakers are scum.'

Realising that nothing I might say would make any difference to his firmly entrenched opinion, I changed the subject. 'Can I go ahead and bury my father?' I asked. 'The coroner's court says that the police still have an objection to the issuing of a burial order. What is the objection?'

'Er,' he said. 'I'll have to get back to you.'

I reckoned that he only needed more time to think up a new excuse.

'Good,' I said, and gave him my home telephone number. 'I will be in all day today and I want to get on and make the arrangements.'

'Right,' he said, sounding distracted. 'And, Mr Talbot, you still haven't provided us with an e-fit of the killer.'

'I'd love to come in and do an e-fit,' I said, feeling slightly surprised. At least he was no longer convinced I was the killer, I thought. 'I'd have expected you to have chased me before this. It must surely be a bit late? Any potential witnesses who saw the killer will have forgotten him by now.'

'We already have some e-fits from the other witnesses in the Ascot car park, but they're not very consistent. Anything you can add may be helpful.'

'Right,' I said eagerly. 'When and where?'

'Any Thames Valley police station will do, provided it has an e-fit computer. Banbury is probably closest to you. I'll find out and call you back.'

He did so about five minutes later.

'It's fixed for two this afternoon, at Banbury,' he said.

'Fine,' I said. 'I'll be there. And is there any news about the burial order?'

'I will inform the coroner that we have no further objection to the issue of the order,' he said formally. Was it my imagination or was the chief inspector warming slightly? 'But I still don't trust you, Mr Talbot.'

Yes, it must have been my imagination.

'I'm sorry about that, Chief Inspector,' I replied. But I suppose, if I were honest, I would have to admit that he had good reason not to fully trust me.

Next, I again used my father's mobile to call Paddy Murphy.

'Well, hello,' he said cheerfully, again with the emphasis on the final 'o'. 'I didn't think I'd heard the last of you.'

'What's the name of the man with his eyes too close together?' I asked, getting straight to the point.

'I don't have his real name,' said Paddy.

'What name do you have?'

'Just Kipper,' he said. 'It's a nickname.'

'Have you ever met him?' I asked.

'I haven't rightly met him, but I believe I saw him once.'

'In Ireland?' I asked.

'Hell, no,' he said. 'In England. Your dad was that frightened of him. Said he was a strange fellow, bit of a loner.'

If my father was as frightened of this Kipper as Paddy made out, why had he kicked out at him and told him to go to hell in the Ascot car park?

'Which insurance company does this Kipper work for?' I asked.

'Well, to be sure, I don't rightly know,' he said.

'Is the company Irish?' I asked. 'Or English?'

'I don't know that, either,' he said. 'All your father told me was that Kipper's job was as an investigator looking into horse deaths. Maybe I just assumed he was with an insurance company.'

Paddy Murphy wasn't being very helpful.

However, he went on to tell me a few interesting things about the two missing counterfeit RFID chips. A horse that had supposedly recently died from colic had in fact been switched, using the fake RFID chips, with a much less valuable animal, which had then been killed for a large insurance payout. And the horse had been a winner at the Cheltenham Steeplechase Festival the previous March. I remembered reading something only the other week in the *Racing Post* about a horse dying from colic.

'What was the horse's name?' I asked him.

'No, no,' he said. 'I've told you too much already.'

Indeed he had, but he had been boasting about his cleverness.

'Well, let me know if this Kipper fellow turns up,' I said.

'To be sure, I will,' said Paddy, sounding apprehensive.

'And let me know when you're next in England. Perhaps we can meet.'

'Well,' he said a little uncertainly, 'I'm not sure about that.'

'Who are you, anyway?' I asked. 'What is your real name?'

'Now, that would be telling,' he said with a laugh, and hung up.

CHIEF INSPECTOR LLEWELLYN himself was at Banbury Police Station to meet me. He was accompanied by Sergeant Murray.

'Hello, Chief Inspector,' I said cheerfully as he appeared in the entrance lobby. 'For what do I deserve this honour?'

'For telling me lies, Mr Talbot,' he said. 'I don't like people telling me lies.'

Oh dear, I thought, he must know about my father's luggage. 'What lies?' I said, trying to keep my voice even. 'I told you everything I know.'

'You told me that your father had given you nothing at Ascot,' he said.

'That's right, he didn't,' I protested.

'But I have reason to believe that he gave you a black box, like a television remote control.' He paused, and I said nothing. 'We understand from Australia that your father is thought to have stolen such a box. Now, quite by chance, one of my officers on the case helps with a club for young offenders in High Wycombe and he tells me he saw a similar black box there last week. This morning my officer called the person who brought the black box to the club and, surprise, surprise, that person says that you gave it to him.'

Thanks, Luca, I thought. But he could probably have said nothing else.

'Oh, that thing,' I said.

'So you *were* lying,' he said almost triumphantly.

In fact, I hadn't been. My father had not given me the box at Ascot.

'I'd forgotten about it, that's all,' I said. 'I was carrying it for him with our equipment. I found it the following day when I was setting up.'

Now I *was* telling lies.

'You should have given the box to me immediately you found it,' he said.

'Sorry,' I replied. 'Is it important?'

He didn't answer my question. 'Where is it now?' he asked.

'I don't know,' I said. 'It didn't seem to do anything. I thought it must have been a garage-door opener or something, so I just dumped it in the bin.'

'Which bin?' He was beginning to lose what little patience he had.

'The house wheelie bin, last weekend. But it's been emptied since then.'

'Didn't you think it was odd that he would carry his garage-door opener halfway round the world?' the chief inspector asked.

'Not really,' I replied. 'He'd just told me that he was my father, who I believed had died thirty-seven years ago. Now, I thought *that* was odd.'

'Are you now telling me more lies?' he said.

'No, of course I'm not,' I said crossly. 'I've come here to help you with an e-fit. Don't you think I want you to catch my father's killer?'

'I'm not so sure that you do,' he said slowly. 'And, Mr Talbot, don't go away anywhere without telling us first.'

'Why not?' I asked him sharply. 'Am I under arrest or something?'

'Not yet, no,' he said. 'Not yet.'

PRODUCING THE E-FIT was easy. I had dreamed so much about Shifty Eyes that I had little trouble transferring the image in my head onto a computer. The young e-fit technician, as he was called, was an expert.

'A little bit wider,' I said.

The technician turned the wheel on his computer mouse with his right forefinger and the face in front of me stretched out until it was just right. His eyes were added, rather too close together for the width of the face, and then a nose, mouth and ears, each in turn adjusted in height, width and thickness by the rotation of the mouse wheel. Finally, short straight fair hair was grown instantly and made to stand upright on the top of the head.

Now Shifty Eyes, or Kipper, as Paddy had called him, looked out at me from the screen and it sent a shiver down my back.

'That's it,' I said.

'Great,' the technician replied, punching the SAVE button on his keyboard. 'The chief inspector will be delighted.'

I doubted that. But I did wonder if my image was anything like any of those produced by the other witnesses. I had an advantage over them, of course: I'd seen the man again in Sussex Gardens, and without his hoodie.

By the time I arrived back at Station Road, peace had broken out between the sisters. Alice had conceded that Sophie would be allowed to enter her own kitchen to help with the dinner preparations, and Sophie, in her turn, had agreed to allow Alice to do all the cleaning up after her. It seemed like an excellent deal to me, especially as all I had to do was eat the meal.

'We're having Thai green chicken curry and sticky rice,' Sophie declared. 'They never served spicy food in the hospital and I'm desperate for some.'

'Great,' I said, meaning it.

'Where did you go?' she asked.

'Banbury.'

'What for?'

I thought quickly. 'I went to see someone who has a new device which he wants us to buy to put on our computer, at the races.'

'Oh,' she said, uninterested. 'And did you buy it?'

'No,' I said. 'It wasn't much good and it was too expensive.'

What was I doing? Lying to the police was one thing, but lying to Sophie was quite another. I didn't like it. And it would have to stop. Just as soon as Shifty Eyes was arrested for my father's murder.

I SPENT MUCH of Tuesday morning sitting in my office doing some research, using the Internet and the two printed volumes most familiar to anyone in racing: the *Directory of the Turf* and *Horses in Training*.

First I searched back through the online editions of the *Racing Post* until I found the piece I had read about a horse dying. The horse had been called Oriental Suite and, according to the newspaper, it had died of complications arising from a bout of severe colic. Oriental Suite had won the Triumph Hurdle, a high-class hurdle race for four-year-old novices, at Cheltenham last March. He had been tipped to be a future Champion Hurdler. The horse's owner was quoted as being distraught over the untimely death. Racing, he declared, had been robbed of a future megastar.

If Paddy Murphy was right, and the horse had been switched and wasn't actually dead, the truth was not that racing had been robbed of a future star, but that an insurance company had been robbed of a fair-sized fortune.

From a desk drawer I took the horse-passport photocopies I'd found in my father's rucksack. One of them was for a bay horse named Oriental Suite. According to the *Racing Post* website, in his short life, Oriental Suite had won nearly £200,000 in prize money. No wonder he'd been well insured.

But why would anyone want to effectively kill off his potential champion steeplechaser? Perhaps it was all down to cash flow, or maybe the owner believed he could have his cake and eat it too—collect both a big insurance payout *and* still have a champion horse under a different name.

I turned back to the Internet and started looking up the declared runners for the coming week. Bookmakers needed to keep abreast of all the winners and losers if they were to make a living from other people's folly. I also looked up anything about valuable horses that had recently died in unusual circumstances. But there was precious little information to be found. In spite of being strong and physically fit, thoroughbred racehorses were actually quite delicate creatures and, sadly, many of them died unexpectedly from injury or disease. Such events were unlikely to be newsworthy unless it was the death of a potential champion, such as Oriental Suite.

The aroma of coffee was drifting up from the kitchen, so I went down the stairs. As always, I carefully avoided treading on step three.

Alice and Sophie were both in tears, sitting at one end of the kitchen table, hugging each other. I said nothing, but walked over to the coffee maker, poured some of the hot brown liquid into a mug and drank.

'Sorry,' said Sophie, dabbing her eyes with a tissue. She was more laughing than crying. 'I meant to bring you up a cup. Alice and I have been talking.'

'So I see,' I said, smiling at them both.

'We've been talking about Mum and Dad,' said Sophie. 'They want to come over and see us.'

I stopped smiling. I hadn't spoken to Sophie's parents in nearly ten years, and I had no wish to start doing so again now. They had been so hurtful towards me when Sophie had first fallen sick, accusing me of bringing on the mania by acts of cruelty towards the wife I adored. Her father even said her illness was God's punishment for me being a bookmaker.

I had walked out of their house on that day and had never been back.

'You can go and see them if you want,' I said. 'But count me out.'

Sophie gave me a pained look.

I knew that Sophie had seen her parents at various times throughout the previous ten years but we never spoke about it. I knew only because she was always agitated after the visits, and I didn't like it. Once or twice those agitations had led on to full-blown mania, and the subsequent depression. And on at least one occasion, an argument between Sophie and her stubborn, self righteous father had resulted in her early return to hospital.

'You know it's not a good idea,' I said to her gently. 'It always ends in a row of one sort or another, and rows are not good for you.'

'It's different this time,' she said.

That was what she always said. I lived in the hope that it would be different this time, but I had to assume it wouldn't be. Still, I could hardly tell her not to see her own parents, and I didn't want her going secretly behind my back. And, most of all, I didn't want to argue with her.

'What do you think Sophie should do, Alice?' I said, sidestepping the problem and placing it on another's shoulders.

'I know Mum is very keen to see her,' she said.

'Then why didn't she visit her in hospital?' I asked. But I knew the answer.

'The hospital is so upsetting for them both,' said Alice.

It hadn't been a barrel of laughs for the rest of us, but Alice and I had visited almost every day. Even her two brothers had visited Sophie at least twice during her recent five-month stay. But of her parents there had been not a sign. The truth was, I thought, that neither of them could bear to admit that their daughter was mentally ill and, provided they didn't actually see her in an institution, they could go on fooling themselves that she was fine and well.

'You must do what you think is best,' I said to Sophie. 'But I would prefer it if they didn't come here. Go and see them at their place, if you like. And if you do go, I think you should go with Alice.'

'Fine by me,' said Alice. 'If Dad starts being a pain, I'll kick him.'

She and Sophie laughed, their heads close together in sisterly conspiracy.

She'd better take steel-toecapped boots, I thought.

CHAPTER 9

The first race at Towcester's late-June evening meeting started at 6 p.m. I always liked to be set up at least an hour before the first, to capture the early punters and to allow time to sort out any equipment problems we might have. Consequently, I drove into the main car park a little before five o'clock and parked in the shade of a large oak tree.

As the racecourse was roughly midway between our homes in Kenilworth and High Wycombe, Luca and I had agreed to travel there in separate cars, so I unloaded everything myself and pulled it on our trolley into the enclosure.

The betting ring at Towcester was in the space between the grandstands. Luca was already waiting for me there as I pulled the trolley to our pitch.

'Where's Betsy?' I asked.

'She's not coming,' he said. 'In fact, I don't think she'll be coming again, ever. She packed up yesterday and moved out of my flat.'

'I'm sorry,' I said, not really meaning it.

'I'm not,' he replied. 'Not really.'

We set up the stuff in silence for a while.

'I suppose we'll need a new junior assistant now,' Luca said.

'Yes,' I said. 'Any ideas?'

'There's a lad at the electronics club who might be good.'

'I don't want any juvenile delinquents.'

'He's a good lad at heart. He just fell in with the wrong crowd.'

'Talking about the electronics club,' I said, 'did you tell the police about that microcoder thing?'

'Oh, yeah,' he said. 'Sorry about that.'

'I should think so, too. I was nearly arrested yesterday.'

'God! I'm sorry. I didn't even know Jim was a copper until after he'd asked me about it. He helps out at the club, too. He called me up yesterday morning and asked about that black-box-device thing, which he'd helped me investigate. So he casually asks me where I got it from, and I told him that you gave it to me. I didn't think I was doing anything wrong to say so, but Jim then says his boss, some chief inspector, will be most interested.'

'You could have bloody warned me.'

'Sorry,' he said. 'Jim called right in the middle of my own domestic crisis. Betsy had just accused me of sleeping with her sister, Millie.'

I looked at him in surprise. 'And have you?' I asked, intrigued.

'That's none of your business,' he said, laughing. 'But no, not exactly.'

'And what the hell does that mean?' I said.

'I kissed her. Once. At her birthday party. But Betsy caught us.'

'Oh, come on. Everyone kisses the birthday girl at her own party.'

'Not with tongues,' he said. 'And not out in the garden, behind a bush.'

'Ah,' I replied. That explained a lot. 'So what are you going to do?'

'Nothing,' he said. 'Leave things to cool off. Then see how the land lies.'

'She may not have you back,' I said.

'Back? Are you crazy? I just thought I'd better let things settle for a while before I asked Millie out.' He grinned.

I wasn't sure whether he meant it or if he was just trying to shock his new business partner. Knowing Luca, it was probably both.

IT WAS A LOVELY summer's evening at the races, with a large crowd, many of them eager to have a flutter on the horses, and most of them dressed in shorts and T-shirts. It was a far cry from the formality of Royal Ascot, and much more fun. The bars were soon doing brisk business, helped by the unusually warm weather, and before long there was a party atmosphere all around the betting ring. Luca and I worked without a break, but it was still one of those times when being a bookmaker was a real joy.

No one becomes a bookie unless they have a bit of the showman in them. I just loved shouting the odds on my platform and bantering with the crowd.

'Come on, mate,' one heavyweight punter shouted. 'Call it fair to have

Ellie's Mobile at only three-to-one?' He looked up at the name at the top of our board. 'How can we "Trust Teddy Talbot" when you offer it at that price?'

'If you'll ride it, you can have it at tens,' I shouted back at him.

All his mates roared with laughter.

'He couldn't ride a bike,' one of them shouted.

'Not without bending it,' shouted another.

'Give me twenty on the nose,' said the heavyweight, thrusting a note at me.

'Twenty pounds to win, number two, and make it at four-to-one,' I said to Luca over my shoulder. 'Special favour.'

'Cheers,' said the man, surprised. 'You're a real gent.'

I didn't know about that but, if I couldn't repay a bit of initiative and colour, then I was in the wrong business.

Ellie's Mobile, the favourite, romped home to win by four lengths at a starting price of three-to-one, cheered with great gusto by the ten-strong band of well-oiled mates, who had stayed near our pitch to watch the race.

'Well done,' I said to the big chap, who was beaming from ear to ear.

'My God!' he said loudly. 'I've actually got one over on a bookie.'

'That makes a change,' chipped in one of the others.

They all guffawed, then ordered more beer. After weigh-in, I paid the big man his eighty pounds in winnings plus his twenty-pound stake.

'Cheers,' he said again, stuffing the cash into a pocket. 'I'll trust Teddy Talbot any day of the week.'

Giving him a better price had cost me twenty pounds. But the man and his nine friends more than repaid that amount in losing stakes in the remaining races. And they did so with smiles on their faces.

In fact, the whole evening was fun, and our overround, the measure of overall profit, hovered around 9 per cent throughout. Luca and I were tired but happy as we packed the equipment onto our little trolley after the last.

'Where are we the rest of the week?' I asked.

'Worcester tomorrow afternoon, Thursday evening and Friday afternoon at Warwick, then Leicester on Saturday,' Luca said.

'Better put everything in my car, then,' I said.

'Yeah,' he replied. 'I'll give you a hand.'

We dragged the trolley up the hill to the main car park where I had left my car. All around us were happy racegoers also returning to their vehicles.

'How about your young delinquent friend?' I asked. 'Can he come with you sometime this week so I can meet him?'

'I'll find out,' Luca said. 'And he's not a delinquent. He's a nice lad.'

'OK, OK,' I said, smiling. 'Ask him if he'd like to come and watch us one day this week. What's his name?'

'Douglas Masters,' he said. 'Can I tell him there's a job?'

'Sure,' I said. 'But tell him it's like an interview. No promises.'

Two large men were leaning on the oak tree waiting for us beside my car. I knew them from a previous encounter. As before, they were dressed in short-sleeved white shirts, black trousers and steel-toecapped work boots.

I stopped the trolley. 'What the hell do you want?' I shouted across.

Luca looked at me in stunned amazement. 'Eh?' he said.

'Luca,' I said, 'these are the two gentlemen who delivered a message to me in the Kempton car park.'

'Oh,' he said. Oh, indeed.

'We have another message,' one of the men said. He was the taller of the two, the one who had spoken to me at Kempton. The other one, still well over six foot, stood silently to one side, bunching his fists.

'What message?' I said. There was about ten yards between us, and I reckoned that if they made a move towards me there was enough of a start for me to reach the safety of a busy after-racing bar in the grandstand.

'Luca,' I said quietly to him, 'if they move, run for it. Run like the wind.'

The look on his face was priceless. I'm not sure that he'd realised until that point that he was in any danger.

'My boss says he wants to talk to you,' the man said.

'You can tell your boss to bugger off,' I said.

'He wants to buy you out,' he said, ignoring me.

I stood there looking at the man in complete surprise.

'What?' I said, not quite believing what I'd heard.

'He wants to buy your business,' the man said.

'He couldn't afford it,' I said.

'I don't think you understand,' said the man. 'My boss wants your business and he's prepared to pay for it.'

'No,' I almost shouted. 'I don't think *you* understand. My business is not for sale and, even if it was, I wouldn't sell it to your boss, whoever he might be, for all the tea in China. So go and tell your boss to get stuffed.'

The man flexed his muscles and began to get red in the face. 'My boss says you can either sell it to him the easy way or lose it to him the hard way.'

'And who exactly is your boss?' I shouted at him.

He didn't reply but advanced a stride towards me. My head start had just been reduced to nine yards.

'Stay there,' I shouted at him. He stopped. 'Who exactly is your boss?' I asked again. He ignored me. And he advanced another stride. Eight yards.

I was on the point of running when another voice came from behind me. 'Hello, Teddy Talbot. You all right?'

I turned, and breathed a huge sigh of relief. The big man from the betting ring was staggering up the car park towards me, with his band of brothers.

'You in need of some help?' he asked.

'That would be great,' I said. 'I think these two men are just leaving.'

I stared at the two bully-boys, and they finally decided to give up and go. Luca and I stood surrounded by the cavalry and we watched as the two men walked across to a black BMW 4x4 and drove away through the archway and out onto the London Road. I made a mental note of the number plate.

'Were those boys troubling you?' asked my mate, the large guy.

'Some people will do anything to get their losses back from a bookie,' I said flippantly. 'But, thanks to you, they didn't manage it today.'

'You mean those two were trying to rob you,' said another of the group.

'They certainly were,' I told him.

'You should have said so. I'm a policeman.'

He produced his warrant card from his pocket and I read it: PC Nicholas Boucher, Northamptonshire Constabulary. Off duty, I presumed, in multi-coloured tropical shirt, baggy shorts and flip-flops.

'I got their car registration,' I said.

'Good,' said PC Boucher. 'Now, were they threatening you?'

'Well, no,' I said. 'They hadn't quite, and you guys turning up must have frightened them away before they had a chance to.'

'Oh,' he said, rather disappointed. 'Not much I can do, then. We can't exactly arrest people for just looking threatening, now can we?'

'No,' I said. 'I suppose not. But I'd love to know who they were so I can watch out and avoid them in the future.'

'What was their vehicle registration?' he asked.

I gave it to him.

'No promises,' he said. 'It's against the rules really.'

He took his mobile phone from his pocket and called a number.

'Jack,' he said into the phone. 'Nick Boucher here. Can you do a vehicle check?' He gave the vehicle registration then waited for a while. 'Yes,' he said. Then he listened again. 'Thanks,' he said finally, and hung up. 'Sorry. That vehicle is registered to a company, so it won't help you.'

'Which company?' I asked him.

'HRF Holdings Limited,' he said. 'Ever heard of them?'

'No.' I looked at Luca, who shrugged his shoulders. 'Thanks, anyway.'

'Are you guys going to be all right from now on?' said PC Boucher. 'I've got to get this bunch of drunks home. I'm the designated driver.'

'Yes,' I said. 'Thanks.'

I watched the group lurch over to a white minibus and fall into it. The passengers all waved enthusiastically at me through the windows as poor, sober PC Boucher drove them away. I waved back at them, laughing.

'HRF Holdings,' said Luca. 'Do we know them?'

'Not by that name,' I said. 'HRF Holdings Limited is a parent company. And I think I know one of its children.'

IT TOOK ME less than an hour to get home, including a few extra trips round the roundabouts to ensure that I wasn't being followed by a black BMW 4x4.

I parked the car in the space in front of the house and made it safely, unchallenged, to my front door.

'Hello,' said Sophie, coming to meet me. 'Had a good time?'

'Very,' I said. 'I always like Towcester, especially the evening meetings.'

'Hiya,' said Alice, coming out of the kitchen with a glass of white wine in each hand. She gave one of them to Sophie with a smile. I wasn't sure that drinking alcohol was a good idea on top of her medication, but I wasn't going to say so for the moment.

'Have you had a good day?' I asked them. Sophie had told me they were going to Leamington Spa for the shopping.

'Lovely,' Sophie said, without elaborating.

'Have you eaten?' I looked at my watch; it was now past ten.

'We have,' said Sophie. 'But I've kept some for you. I know you're always hungry when you get home after an evening meeting.'

I suppose it was true, but it didn't mean I always had something to eat. During the past five months, I had more often than not had a stiff shot of Scotch and gone straight to bed.

'Do you know anything about a rucksack?' Sophie asked casually as she stood at the cooker reheating my supper.

'What?' I said sharply.

'A rucksack,' she said again. 'A man came here. Said he wanted to collect a rucksack. He said you knew about it.'

'What sort of rucksack?' I said, rather flustered.

'A black-and-red rucksack,' she said. 'The man told us you were looking after it for him. He was quite persistent, I can tell you.'

Oh God, I thought.

'So you didn't give it to him?' I asked her.

'No, I didn't even know we had a black-and-red rucksack. Where is it?'

'In the cupboard under the stairs,' I said. 'Did he try and get in?'

'No,' she said, slightly perturbed by the question. 'Why would he?'

'I just wondered, that's all,' I said. 'So tell me what happened.'

'I told him to go away and come back when you were at home.'

'We then locked the house up tight, opened a bottle, and waited for you to get back,' said Alice with a smile.

'Can you describe the man?' I asked both of them.

'He was rather creepy,' said Alice.

'In what way was he creepy?'

'I don't know. He just was. And he was wearing his hood up, and a scarf. You've got to be up to no good to be doing that on a night as hot as this.'

'Could you see his eyes?' I asked. 'Were they set rather close together?'

'Yes,' said Alice, throwing a hand up in the air almost excitedly. 'That's it. That's exactly why I thought he was creepy.'

So it had definitely been Shifty Eyes, the man Paddy Murphy had called Kipper. He had found me at last.

'What are we going to do?' Sophie asked loudly, suddenly becoming scared. 'I don't want him coming back here.'

'It's all right, my love,' I said, putting a reassuring arm round her shoulders. 'I'm sure he won't come back tonight.'

The doorbell rang and we all jumped.

'How sure?' Sophie said, looking worried.

'Ignore it,' said Alice. 'Then he'll have to go away.'

We stood silently in the kitchen, listening. The doorbell rang again.

'I know you're in there,' shouted a voice from outside. 'Open up.'

I went out of the kitchen into the hallway. 'Who is it?' I shouted.

'Mr Talbot,' said the voice, 'you've got something of mine. I want it back.'

'What?' I asked.

'A rucksack,' he said. 'A black-and-red rucksack.'

'But the rucksack belonged to Alan Grady, not you,' I said, without stopping to think. Damn, I should have denied all knowledge of it, I thought.

'I'm calling the police,' said Sophie, coming into the hallway. 'Do you hear me?' she shouted. There was a tremor in her voice.

'There'll be no need for the police,' said the man calmly through the door. 'Just give me the rucksack and I'll go away.'

'Give him the rucksack,' Sophie implored me, her eyes big with panic. 'Please, Ned, just give him the damn rucksack.'

'OK, OK,' I said. I went to the cupboard under the stairs and fetched it.

'Give it to him,' Sophie urged me again, her voice quivering with fear.

I lifted the rucksack and turned to go upstairs with it.

'Where the hell are you going?' Sophie almost screamed at me.

'If you think I'm opening the front door with him there, you must be . . .' I didn't finish the sentence. 'I'm going to throw it to him out of the window.'

I went up to our bedroom and opened the window. I couldn't see the man as he was standing under the overhanging porch.

'Here,' I shouted.

He moved back into my sight. He appeared just as I had seen him the first time in the car park at Ascot Racecourse: blue jeans, charcoal hoodie, with a black scarf over the lower part of his face. As before, all I could see were his eyes, which were set rather too close together for the width of his face.

I held the rucksack out through the open window at arm's length.

'What's your name?' I asked him.

'Drop the rucksack,' he said, ignoring my question. He didn't have a strong regional accent, at least not one I could notice.

'How did you find my house?' I asked him.

'Never you mind,' he said. 'Just drop the rucksack.'

'It's only full of Mr Grady's clothes,' I said. 'I've searched it. There's nothing else there.'

'Give it to me anyway,' he said, holding his arms ready to catch it.

'Who's John Smith?' I asked.

In spite of only being able to see his eyes, I could still tell that there was no recognition of the name. But then that wasn't his real name, was it?

'Give me the bag now,' he hissed, 'or I'll break your bloody door down.'

I dropped the rucksack. He failed to catch it before it hit the concrete path, but he snatched it up and was off, jogging down Station Road.

I wondered how he had found out where I lived. If he had obtained the information I had given the coroner at the inquest, why had it taken him so long to arrive at my door? Perhaps he'd been tipped off by someone at Banbury Police Station, or someone else in the Thames Valley Police who had seen the e-fit and recognised his face. I would probably never know.

He would certainly find that the microcoder and the glass-grain RFID chips were missing from the rucksack, as Mr John Smith now had them. I had also kept back the three house keys, and the passports, both the two photocopied equine ones and the two with my father's picture in them.

However, if Paddy Murphy was to be believed, it would be the stash of money that the man would be more concerned about. If he knew where to look, Kipper would find the three blue-plastic-wrapped packages of banknotes that I'd put back under the rucksack lining. But, if he counted the cash, he might also discover that he was £2,000 short from each package.

It had seemed a good idea at the time. But now I wasn't so sure.

'WHAT THE HELL was all that about?' Sophie demanded when I went down the stairs. Alice stood beside her, looking concerned.

'Just an impatient man who wanted something I had,' I said, trying to make light of the encounter.

'He was horrible,' said Sophie. 'Why did you give it to him?'

'But it was you who told me to,' I said slightly exasperated.

'Whose rucksack was it, anyway?' she asked.

'A man called Alan Grady,' I said. 'He gave it to me to keep safe.'

'Then he's not going to be very pleased with you for giving it away.'

She seemed to have forgotten the fear and panic that had gripped her when the man had been standing outside our front door.

'I don't think he'll mind too much,' I said, without elaborating further. I smiled at the two of them. 'Now, what's for supper?'

'He won't come back, will he?' Alice asked nervously as I ate my macaroni cheese, the three of us sitting round the kitchen table.

'I don't think so,' I said. 'He has what he came for.'

At least, he had most of it. But would he come back for the rest?

After my supper I went up into my little office to log on to the Internet while the girls took themselves off to bed.

HRF Holdings Ltd was indeed a parent company, and one of the businesses it owned I knew very well. Tony Bateman (Turf Accountants) Ltd, to give its full title, was one of the big five high-street betting-shop chains.

I made a search of the Companies House WebCHeck service, and down-loaded the most recent annual report for Tony Bateman (Turf Accountants) Ltd and HRF Holdings Ltd. They were both private limited companies and the report recorded the names of the directors and the company secretaries, as well as a list of the current shareholders of each entity.

There was no mention in the report of anyone actually called Tony Bateman. It must have been a name from the past, I thought, possibly the company founder. I did, however, recognise one name. Henry Richard Feldman was well known on British racecourses. Now in his late sixties, he had made his money in property development, and for the past twenty years or so he had been a prolific and successful racehorse owner. He was also the sole shareholder of HRF Holdings Ltd.

But why did he, or more precisely why did Tony Bateman (Turf Accountants) Ltd, want to buy my business?

Ever since betting shops were made legal in Britain in 1961, the big firms had been expanding their domains by buying out the small independent bookies. Mostly it had been the individual town-centre betting shops they had been after. But more recently they had also been turning up in the betting rings on the tracks, using their influence to further control the on-course prices. Now, it would seem Tony Bateman Ltd was after my business and my lucrative pitch positions at the racecourses. And it appeared that they were prepared to resort to threats and intimidation to get them.

Sophie was fast asleep when, well after midnight, I finally went along the landing to bed. I crept quietly into our bedroom, and once again I put Sophie's dressing-table chair under the door handle.

Just to be on the safe side.

ON WEDNESDAY MORNING I made the arrangements for my father's funeral.

I'd never realised how expensive dying could be. A basic, no-frills funeral would cost about £1,000, and that didn't include the substantial price of a grave plot or the charge for the use of the crematorium. Add to that the cost of the necessary certificates, as well as a fee for someone to conduct the service, and it soon became a hefty sum indeed.

Somehow it didn't seem quite fair that my father had turned up out of the blue when I had thought he'd been dead for thirty-seven years, only for me to be saddled with his funeral expenses. Still, I was his known next of kin, so I knew I would just have to shut up and pay up.

I called the first undertaker on the Internet list.

'We could fit you in this coming Friday,' the man said. 'We've had a cancellation at Slough Crem. It's a bit short notice, though.'

'What time on Friday?' I asked.

'Three o'clock,' he said.

Friday was just two days away, but I didn't think that really mattered. It wasn't as if there would be anyone else coming.

'Three on Friday will be fine,' I said.

'Right,' he said. 'Where is your father's body?'

'I presume he's still at Wexham Park Hospital,' I said. 'But I'm not sure. The coroner's office will know.' I started to give him their number.

'Don't worry, we've got it,' he said. 'We'll fix everything.'

For a fee, no doubt, I thought rather ungraciously.

'Do I need to book someone to take the service?' I asked.

'We can also fix that, if you like. But anyone can take the service. You can officiate yourself if you want to.'

'No,' I said. 'I think he would have wanted a vicar or something.' I wasn't a religious person myself, but I thought it would be better to have an expert.

'Any special request for music or hymns?' he said.

'No,' I said. 'Whatever the vicar thinks is fitting will be fine by me.'

'As it's such short notice,' the man said, 'could we have full payment up-front by credit card?'

'Is that usual?' I asked.

'Quite usual,' he assured me. 'Especially as the deceased was not resident in this country, with no estate to be probated by the courts.'

I could see that it would be rather difficult for the undertaker to take back the coffin due to lack of payment once the cremation had occurred.

I gave him my credit-card number and my address.

'Thank you, Mr Talbot,' he said. 'Of course, we will send you an itemised account after the day.'

'Thank you,' I said. 'Is there anything else I need to do?' I asked.

'Once the inquest is over, the death will need to be registered with the registrar,' he said. 'In the meantime, the coroner will issue a temporary death certificate. Everything else we need we'll get from the coroner.'

'Right,' I said. 'I'll see you on Friday afternoon.'

I sat in my office for a while, wondering who I should tell. I thought the police would want to know, but was I required to inform them? And should

I tell my grandmother that her son's funeral was on Friday? Perhaps not, I thought. It would be far less distressing for her if I didn't.

And how about Sophie?

She still thought my parents had both died in a car accident when I was a baby. Should I now explain to her that Alan Charles Grady, the man who had owned the black-and-red rucksack, the man who had been murdered in Ascot Racecourse car park, had actually been Peter James Talbot, my father? And did I tell her that my mother had also not died in a car crash, but had been strangled by my father on the beach under the pier at Paignton?

I decided that I would, in time, tell Sophie all about the events of the past two weeks, but not just yet. She had enough to deal with at the moment.

I would go to my father's funeral alone.

LUCA ARRIVED at Station Road at noon and he had a spiky-haired boy with him. Douglas Masters, I presumed. He looked about sixteen. He was wearing a red checked shirt, fawn denim trousers that looked like they were about to fall down off his hips, and dirty white trainers.

'Hello,' I said cheerfully, holding out my hand.

'Hi,' he replied. He shook my hand warily, leaning forward to grasp it.

'Is he old enough?' I asked Luca. Eighteen was the minimum age for working as a bookmaker, or as a bookmaker's assistant.

'I'm eighteen,' the boy assured me. He pulled out a driving licence from his pocket, which he held out to me. According to the licence, he was indeed eighteen, and two months.

'OK, Douglas, thank you,' I said. 'And welcome.'

'Duggie,' he said. 'Or Doug. Not Douglas.'

'OK,' I repeated. 'Duggie it is.'

He nodded. 'How about you?' he asked.

'Call me Mr Talbot for now,' I said.

'And him?' he said, nodding at Luca.

'Luca will be fine,' Luca said.

He nodded once more. 'Just so I know,' he said.

I think it was fair to say that young Mr Masters was economical with his words, and his expressions. I raised my eyebrows at Luca in silent question.

'Duggie will be fine,' said Luca, sticking up for him. 'He's just shy.'

'No, I'm not,' said Duggie with assurance, but no grace. 'I'm just careful. I don't know you.'

'Good,' I said exuberantly. 'That's what's needed in bookmaking. You can't be too careful, because you never know what your customers might be up to.'

He cocked his head to one side. 'Are you taking the mick?' he said slowly.

'Something like that,' I replied.

He smiled. It was a brief smile but a vast improvement while it lasted.

'That's all right, then,' he said.

'Come on, let's go,' I said with a smile, 'or we'll be late.'

We piled into my Volvo, with Luca sitting up front next to me and Duggie in the back. Sophie waved to us as we set off.

'How's she doing?' Luca asked me, waving back at her.

'Fine,' I said, not wanting to discuss things in front of Douglas, but the young man was quick on the uptake.

'Is she ill?' he asked from behind me.

'She's fine at the moment, thanks,' I said, hoping to end the conversation.

'Cancer, is it?' he said.

'No,' I said.

'My mum had cancer,' he said. 'It killed her in the end.'

'I'm sorry,' I said.

'Yeah,' he said wistfully. 'Everyone's sorry. Doesn't bring her back, though, does it?'

We sat in silence for a while and I warmed to the boy.

'Duggie,' I said, 'how well do you know the others in the electronics club? Would you trust them?'

'Maybe I'd trust them not to grass to the cops,' he said. 'That's about all.'

'How many of them are there?'

'Dunno,' he said. 'Quite a lot.'

'There must be sixty of them, at least,' said Luca. 'But they're not all there on any one night.'

'So how many of those sixty would you actually trust, Duggie?' I asked.

'With what?' he replied.

'With some money,' I said. 'Say to go and buy something, or place a bet.'

'Maybe half. The rest would spend it on themselves. On drugs, mostly.'

Half of them would be enough, I thought.

'Would you know which are the ones to trust?' I asked him.

'Sure,' he said with confidence. 'The ones who are my mates.'

I changed the subject. 'What did you do, Duggie? To be sent to the club?'

There was a long pause. 'Nicked cars,' he said finally.

'Do you still nick cars?' I asked.

'No,' he said.

'Do you have any recorded convictions?' I asked.

There was another long silence from the back of the car.

'Duggie,' I said, 'I'm not asking so that I can judge you myself, but I need to know under the conditions of my bookmaking licence.'

Under the terms for the issuing of licences in the Gambling Act 2005, prior convictions did not, in themselves, mean an individual was not a fit and proper person to hold a bookmaker's licence, or to work as a bookmaker's assistant, but convictions for fraud or violence would be a no-no.

'Yes,' Duggie said.

'Just for nicking cars?' I asked.

'Yes,' he said reluctantly. 'But I never done it. I was told to plead guilty.'

'Who by?' I asked.

'Our poncey lawyer,' he said. 'There was a group of us. We all got done for it. The lawyer said we'd get a lesser sentence if we pleaded guilty. So I did.'

'But why, if you didn't do it?' I asked.

'I was in the car, wasn't I?' he said. 'But I didn't know it was nicked. The poncey lawyer said I would get done anyway, so I should plead guilty.'

I wasn't sure whether to believe him.

'Is that all?' I said. 'Only the once?'

'Yeah,' he said.

'OK,' I said, and we drove on in silence for a while.

'I won't nick your money, if that's what you're wondering,' Duggie said eventually.

I wasn't, but I might keep a close eye on him anyway.

THE RACING at Worcester was quiet compared with the previous evening at Towcester. Not many punters had turned up, and those who had seemed to have little cash with them to gamble. It was not a very profitable afternoon.

One of the plus points, however, was Duggie. He gradually opened up as the day progressed and he clearly enjoyed himself. The more responsibility I gave him, the more confident I became in his ability.

'Where are we on Monday?' I asked Luca as we packed up after the last.

'Nowhere,' he said. 'It's a day off.'

'Not any more,' I said. 'We're going to Bangor-on-Dee. Tell Larry Porter he's going, too. And tell him to bring the box of tricks.'

Luca stopped loading the trolley. 'Right,' he said, smiling at me. 'I will.'

'And, Luca,' I said, 'I need you to do something for me on Friday.'

'We're at Warwick on Friday,' he said.

'Not any more we're not,' I said. 'Friday is now a day off from racing. I want you to go and see some of your electronic-club delinquents, the ones Duggie thinks are trustworthy. I need their help.'

I explained what I wanted him to do and his enthusiasm went off the scale. I didn't mention that I'd be spending Friday afternoon at my father's funeral.

'Duggie here will help you,' I said as we loaded the gear into the Volvo.

Duggie smiled. 'Does that mean I've got the job?' he asked.

'You're on probation,' I said. 'Until Monday.'

He looked at me uncertainly.

'Not that sort of probation,' I said with a laugh.

We discussed our plans as I drove back round the M42 in the rush-hour traffic, and then on to my house in Kenilworth.

'Warwick tomorrow evening, then?' said Luca.

'Definitely,' I said. 'Do you want to meet here first?'

'Yes,' Luca replied. 'First race is at six thirty. Here at five?'

'Five will be fine,' I said.

'I hope your wife will be all right, Mr Talbot,' Duggie said as he climbed into Luca's car.

'Thank you, Duggie,' I said.

He would do well, I thought.

CHAPTER 10

At three o'clock on Friday afternoon I sat alone in the chapel of Slough Crematorium as my father's coffin was carried past me and placed on the curtain-skirted catafalque at the front.

A clergyman in a white surplice over a black cassock came in and stood behind the lectern. 'Are you the son?' he asked.

'Yes,' I replied.

'Are we waiting for anyone else?'

'No,' I said.

'Right, then. We'll get started.'

The door at the back of the chapel opened with a squeak. I turned round. Sergeant Murray came in and sat down two pews behind me. I nodded to him and he responded in the same manner. I turned back to the minister.

The clergyman began: 'I am the resurrection and the life, saith the Lord; he that believeth in me, though he were dead, yet shall he live . . .'

He droned on, rushing through the funeral rite as laid down in the Book of Common Prayer, but I didn't really listen to the words.

Instead, I sat and stared at the coffin and tried hard to remember what the man inside it looked like. I had seen him alive only briefly, for hardly more than an hour, yet his reappearance had dominated my life since then in a way it hadn't done for the previous thirty-seven years.

It was difficult to describe my feelings, but anger was uppermost among them. Anger that he gone for ever, anger that he'd been here at all.

Undeniably, he was my father. The DNA had proved that. But it didn't feel like he had anything to do with me. I wished I'd had longer to talk with him on the day he'd died, and the opportunity to talk to him again, even if it was to rant and rave at his conduct, or to gather answers to so many unanswered questions: Why did he kill my mother? Why did he run away? Why didn't he take me with him? And, in particular, why did he come back?

I thought about his daughters, my sisters, in Australia, who probably didn't even know he was dead. Should I say a prayer on their behalf?

The minister was nearing the end.

'In sure and certain hope of the resurrection to eternal life through our Lord Jesus Christ, we commend to Almighty God our brother Peter, and we commit his body to the elements, earth to earth, ashes to ashes, dust to dust. The Lord bless him, and keep him, and give him eternal peace. Amen.'

As the minister was saying the last few words, my father's coffin slowly disappeared behind long red curtains, which closed silently around it.

My father's funeral had taken precisely nine minutes.

If only his influence could be so easily and quickly eliminated.

'Lovely service,' I said to the minister on my way out. 'Thank you.'

'My pleasure,' he said, shaking my hand.

Everyone always says it's been a lovely service at a funeral, I thought, even if it hadn't. In this case, it had been functional. And that was enough.

'Thank you for coming,' I said to Sergeant Murray as we stood together outside afterwards.

'Chief Inspector Llewellyn apologises for not being here himself,' he said.

'I hadn't expected him to come,' I said. I hadn't, in fact, expected anyone to be here, not least because I hadn't told a soul about the arrangements.

'The coroner's office let us know,' he said. I nodded. 'The police always try to go to murder victims' funerals if we can.'

'Just in case the killer turns up?' I asked.

'It has been known,' he said, smiling.

'No chance today,' I said. 'Not without being noticed, anyway.'

'No,' he said with a nervous laugh. 'Not much of a crowd to hide in.'

'Has my e-fit been of any use?' I asked.

'Yes, as a matter of fact, it has,' he said. 'It's been shown to some of the other witnesses and they now generally tend to agree with you. So yours has now taken on the mantle as being the most accurate.'

'I haven't seen it in any of the newspapers. Or on the television.'

'It's been in the *Bracknell and Ascot Times* and the *Windsor and Eton Express*,' he said. 'But no one's come forward yet to say they recognise him.'

'Perhaps it would have been better to have put it in the Melbourne papers,' I said. 'Or at least in the *Racing Post*.'

'Now that's a thought,' he said. 'Maybe I'll recommend it to the chief inspector.' And, with that, the sergeant made his excuses and departed.

That just left me and the undertaker, who had been hovering to one side.

'Was everything in order, Mr Talbot?' he asked.

'Yes, thank you,' I said. 'It was fine.'

'Good,' he said. 'And what would you like done with the ashes?'

'What are the choices?' I asked.

'We can put them in a container for you, if you want,' he said. 'They will be ready for collection tomorrow. Or they can be scattered here, in the garden of remembrance, if you would prefer,' he said.

'Oh,' I said. 'Just have them scattered here, please. I don't want them.'

'Right,' he said. 'That will be all, then. I'll send you an itemised receipt in due course.'

'Thank you,' I said. 'That will be fine.'

He nodded to me—it was almost a bow—and then he walked quickly across to his car and drove away.

I was left standing alone in the crematorium car park with that strange feeling of having mislaid something but I wasn't quite sure what.

Perhaps it was a childhood that I'd mislaid, with loving parents, family holidays and happy Christmases. But was it *my* childhood that I'd lost, or those of my non-existent children. I stood next to my car and wept.

A few early arrivals for the next funeral spilled out of their cars and made their sombre way to the chapel. None of them bothered me. Weeping in a crematorium car park was not only acceptable, it was expected.

EARLY ON SATURDAY MORNING I went to see my grandmother. I told myself it had nothing to do with having been to my father's funeral the day before, but of course it did. I desperately wanted to ask her some more questions.

Sophie had come to the front door to see me off, still in her dressing gown and slippers. As far as she was concerned I'd spent the previous afternoon at Warwick Races. I would tell her the truth, I thought, eventually.

'Give her my love,' she had said as I left.

'I will,' I had replied, but both of us doubted that my grandmother would remember who Sophie was. She might not even remember who I was.

She was sitting in her armchair looking out of the window when I arrived. I went over and gave her a kiss on the cheek.

'Hello, Ned,' she said. 'How lovely.'

Today was clearly one of her better days. She looked very smart in a dark skirt, a white blouse with yellow embroidered flowers and a lavender cardigan, open at the front. And she'd had her hair done since my last visit.

'You look beautiful,' I said, meaning it.

She smiled at me, full of understanding.

I sat on the end of her bed next to her chair. 'How have you been?' I asked.

'I'm fine,' she said. 'Julie will be here soon.'

'Who is Julie?' I asked.

'Julie,' she repeated. 'She'll be here soon.'

I decided not to ask again. 'Sophie sends her love,' I said. A small quizzical expression came into her eyes. 'You remember Sophie. She's my wife.'

'Oh, yes,' she said, but I wasn't sure that she really knew.

There was a knock on the door and one of the nursing- home staff put her head into the room. 'Everything OK?' she asked.

'Fine,' I said.

'Would you like some tea or coffee?'

'Coffee would be lovely,' I said. 'Milk and one sugar.' I turned to my grandmother. 'Nanna, would you like some coffee, or tea?'

'I don't drink tea,' she said.

'I'll bring her some anyway,' said the staff member with a smile. 'She always says she doesn't drink tea but she must have at least six or seven cups a day.' The head withdrew and the door closed.

'I like Julie,' my grandmother said again.

'Was that Julie?' I asked, but Nanna didn't answer. She was looking out of the window again. I took her hand in mine and stroked it.

We sat silently until the woman came back in with a tray and two cups.

'Are you Julie?' I asked her.

'No,' she said. 'I'm Laura. But we do have a Julie and your grandmother calls all of us Julie. We don't mind. I'll answer to anything.' She laughed. 'Here you are, Mrs Talbot.' She put the tray down on the bedside table.

'Thank you,' I said.

'Just pull the alarm if you need anything,' Laura said, pointing at a red cord that hung down the wall alongside my grandmother's bed.

'Thank you,' I said again. 'I will.'

I sat patiently drinking my coffee as my grandmother's tea slowly cooled.

'Here, Nanna,' I said, giving her the cup. 'Don't forget your tea.'

'I don't drink tea,' she said, but she still took the china cup in her thin, bony hands and drank from it. The tea was soon all gone, so I took the empty cup from her and put it back on the tray.

'Nanna,' I said. She went on looking out of the window. 'Nanna,' I repeated more loudly, and pulled gently on her arm. She slowly turned to face me.

'Nanna, can you tell me about my parents? About Peter and Tricia?'

She looked up at my face, but the sharpness of a few minutes previously had begun to fade. I feared I had missed my chance.

'Nanna,' I said again with some urgency, 'tell me about Peter and Tricia. Peter, your son, and Tricia, his wife.'

'Such a dreadful thing,' she said, turning away from me again.

'What was a dreadful thing?'

'What he did to her,' she said.

'What did he do to her?' I pulled gently on her hand to keep her attention. She turned back slightly towards me.

'He killed her,' she said slowly. 'He murdered her.'

'Tricia?' I asked.

'Yes,' she said. She looked back up at my face. 'He murdered Tricia.'

'But why?' I asked. 'Why did he murder Tricia?'

'Because of the baby,' she said, looking back at me.

'What about the baby?' I pressed her. 'Why did he murder her because of the baby?' I wondered if he had killed her because the baby wasn't his.

My grandmother stared into my eyes. 'He killed the baby, too,' she said.

'Yes,' I said. 'Whose baby was it?'

'Tricia's baby,' she said.

'But was Peter the father?'

'Peter ran away,' she said.

'Yes, I know,' I said. 'Peter ran away because he killed Tricia. But was Peter the father of her baby?'

That quizzical look appeared again in her eyes. 'It wasn't Peter,' she said slowly. 'It was Teddy who murdered Tricia.'

I sat there staring at her, thinking that she must be confused.

'Surely it was Peter who murdered Tricia? That's why he ran away.'

'It was Teddy who murdered Tricia,' she said again quite clearly.

I sat there stunned. 'But why?' I asked pitifully.

'Because of the baby,' she said, equally clearly. 'Your grandfather was the baby's father.'

I STAYED WITH my grandmother for another hour, trying to piece together the whole sorry story. Trying to pull accurate details out of her fuzzy memory was like trying to solve a Rubik's Cube while blindfolded. Not only could I not see the puzzle, I didn't know when, or if, I'd solved it.

But now that she had started to give up the secret that had burned within her for so long, she did so with a clarity of mind that I didn't realise she still possessed. The awful knowledge poured from her, almost in relief, it seemed, at being able to share her hitherto private horror at last. I learned more in that one hour about my parents and my early life than I'd managed to extract from her at any time in the previous thirty-seven years. And I didn't like it.

I discovered that the five of us had lived together in my grandparents' house in Surrey, my mother having moved in on the day of her marriage. And if I read correctly between the lines of what my grandmother had said, extreme tensions had existed between my mother and father throughout their short marriage. There had also been considerable friction between my parents and my grandparents. It had obviously not been a happy family home.

I found out that it hadn't only been my mother and father who were staying in Paignton at the time of Tricia's death. Both my grandparents had been with them, and I had been there as well. It seemed that the holiday in Devon had been my father's idea, an attempt to make things better between them all, but it had actually made them much worse.

'Peter and Tricia argued all the time,' my grandmother said, placing her head to one side and closing her eyes. 'On and on they went. They physically fought more than once. Peter slapped her and she scratched his face.'

Hence the traces of my father's skin and DNA under Tricia's fingernails, I thought. The DNA that the police had wrongly believed was her killer's.

'Then she told him that her baby wasn't his,' Nanna said. 'She told him that it was your grandfather's baby. He went completely wild.'

'Peter went wild?' I asked.

'Yes,' she replied. 'But Teddy went wild as well because she threatened to tell everyone and to get it in the newspapers.'

'Was the baby Tricia was carrying really Grandpa's child?' I asked.

'Yes,' she said, opening her eyes and looking at me again. 'I believe so.'

'But are you certain?' I pressed her.

'Yes,' she said. 'I had suspected it even before she said anything. I'd been telling Teddy over and over for months that we would be better off without her around, but he wouldn't have it. He thought he was in love with her. Then, the morning after Tricia tells us that he's the father of the baby, Teddy walks into the hotel where we were staying and tells me it's finished between them. Then he calmly tells me that he's strangled the little bitch.'

I stared at her, almost in disbelief.

'But why did my father run away if he hadn't killed her?'

'Because I told him to,' she said, quite matter-of-factly.

'But why?' I asked her.

'So that Teddy wouldn't get arrested for murder.'

'But why didn't you go to the police?'

'Because then we would have been ruined,' she said, as if it was obvious. 'What would I have lived on with your grandfather in jail?'

The faithful, practical wife, I thought. She'd let her only son be blamed for her daughter-in-law's murder, banished him to the other side of the world, not only to protect her husband from justice but to protect her income.

'How about me?' I said with passion. 'Why didn't my father take me with him?'

'He wanted to,' she said. 'But I told him he couldn't. I said I'd look after you. He wanted to come back for you but I told him to go and start somewhere else and forget that you ever existed. It was for the best.'

'Not for me,' I said with barely contained fury.

'Oh, yes. It was the best for all of us.' She said it with unshakable conviction. 'And I decided that it was also the best for me.'

It was like a knife to my heart. How could this woman have sent my father out of my life like that? He had done nothing to deserve it. And how could she have then kept silent about it for so long? Just because she thought it was the best for her.

I had sat in the chapel of Slough Crematorium only the previous afternoon with my head bursting with anger. Now I felt totally bereft. I had been cheated of my right to grieve properly for my father, and I further believed that I had been cheated out of my rightful life.

I stood up. I didn't want to hear any more. I looked down at her, this frail, demented eighty-year-old woman who, with my grandfather, had raised me. I had loved them, trusted them and believed what they had told me as being the truth, only for it now to emerge as a web of lies and deception.

I walked to the door without turning back, and I went away.

I would never visit her again.

I WENT STRAIGHT from the nursing home to Leicester Racecourse, but afterwards I couldn't recall a single moment of the journey. I was too preoccupied trying to come to terms with what I had been told.

As I had so hoped, I was, after all, not the son of a murderer. But I was the grandson of one. I had stood alongside my grandfather on racecourses for all those years as his assistant, unaware of the dreadful secret he and my grandmother had concealed. Far from being the ones who had cared for me in my time of need, they had been the very architects of my misery.

Automatically, as if on autopilot, I parked the Volvo and began to unload the equipment. I pulled out our odds board with TRUST TEDDY TALBOT emblazoned across the top. I would have laughed if I didn't feel so much like crying. Trust Teddy Talbot to ruin your life.

LUCA AND DUGGIE were waiting for me in the betting ring.

'How did you get on yesterday?' I asked. 'With the delinquents?'

'Great,' said Luca. 'We're all set.'

'Do you think they will do it right?' I asked.

'Should do,' said Duggie. 'And they're not all delinquents.'

I smiled. I suppose I was pleased he was standing up for his friends.

'And besides,' he said, 'I told them you were a mean bastard and would come looking for them in the night if they spent your money on drugs.'

I stared at him and he smiled. I couldn't tell if he was kidding or not.

'Good,' I said finally. 'Let's hope the horses are not all withdrawn at the overnight declarations stage.'

'How about you?' Luca asked as we set up. 'Did you have a good day?'

'No,' I said without clarification.

'Not Sophie?' he asked with concern.

'No,' I said. 'Sophie's doing well. I was just dealing with some other family business. Don't worry about it.'

He looked at me with questioning eyes but I ignored him.

'I've decided that we are going to change our name,' I announced. 'From today, we shall be known as Talbot and Mandini.'

Luca beamed. 'But we haven't done the partnership papers yet,' he said.

'I don't care,' I said. 'If you're still up for it, then so am I.'

'Sure,' he said with real pleasure showing on his face.

'How about Talbot, Mandini and Masters?' said Duggie, joining the fun.

'Don't push your luck,' I said. 'You're still on probation, remember.'

'Only until Monday,' he said with a pained expression.

'That will be up to me,' I said. 'And to Luca,' I added quickly.

Leicester was a long, thin, undulating track with the public enclosures squeezed together at one end. The betting ring was in front of the glass-fronted grandstand and several other bookies were also setting up.

'Where's Larry?' I asked Luca, noting his absence.

'Nottingham,' he said.

'But he's all set for Monday?'

'Sure is,' said Luca with a grin. 'Norman Joyner's coming, too.'

'Good,' I said. 'Do they know?'

'They think it's the same as last time, at Ascot,' he said.

'Good,' I said. 'It will be, as far as they are concerned.'

The Saturday crowd was beginning to build, with cars queuing for the popular car-park-and-picnic enclosure alongside the running rail. Even the weather had cooperated, with blue skies and only the occasional puffy white cloud. A glorious English summer's day at the races. What could be better?

I suppose six losing short-priced favourites would be good.

Just as I'd begun to enjoy the day, my two non-friends from Kempton and Towcester turned up. Once more, they wore their 'uniform' of short-sleeved white shirts, black trousers and work boots. I was on my platform, which gave me a height advantage for a change. It also gave me some courage.

'I thought I told you boys to bugger off,' I said down to them.

'Our boss wants to talk to you,' said the spokesman of the two.

'Well, I don't want to talk to him,' I said. 'So go away.'

'He wants to make you an offer,' said the spokesman.

'Which part of "go away" didn't you understand?' I said to him.

They didn't move an inch but stood full square in front of me.

'He wants to buy you out.' It was like a stuck record.

'Tell him to come and see me himself if he wants to talk,' I said, 'rather than sending a pair of his goons.'

Thoughts of poking hornets' nests with sticks floated into my head. And I'd been the one to warn Larry against doing it.

'You are to come with us,' the man said.

'You must be joking,' I said, almost with a laugh. 'I'm not going any-where with you two. Now move out of the way. I've got a business to run.'

They didn't move.

Luca and Duggie came and stood on the platform on either side of me and a staring match ensued. It was like a prelude to a gunfight at the O.K. Corral.

'Sod off,' said Duggie suddenly, breaking the silence. 'Why don't you two arseholes go and play with your balls somewhere else.'

They both turned their full attention to him, this young slip of a lad, who I still thought looked only about fourteen years old.

The talkative arsehole opened his mouth as if to say something.

'Save it,' said Duggie, beating him to the draw. 'Now, piss off.'

There was something about the boy's assured confidence that had even me a little scared. The two men in front of me definitely wavered.

'We'll be back,' the talkative one said.

But Duggie wasn't finished with them. 'The man here told you he wasn't coming with you to see your boss, so go away now, and stay away.' He sounded so reasonable. 'And you can tell your boss it's no deal.'

The men looked at him like two big sheep under the gaze of a tiny border collie puppy and then, slowly, they walked away.

Luca and I watched them go out of sight round the grandstand; then we turned to Duggie in astonishment.

He was smiling. 'All brawn and no brain,' he said. 'Guys like them need orders to follow. Can't think for themselves.'

If I hadn't seen it myself, I wouldn't have believed it.

'My God, Duggie,' I said. 'You were brilliant.'

'I think he just completed his probation,' Luca said.

'Damn right he did,' I said. 'Welcome to the firm.'

THE SIX FAVOURITES didn't all lose, but our afternoon was both profitable and enjoyable, with Duggie warming to his new-found permanent status.

He was a natural showman with a quick wit, and as his confidence grew he became a great success with the punters. He hardly stopped talking and bantering with them all afternoon. There was no doubt in my mind that we did far more business because of it.

The two goons didn't reappear at our pitch, but I was worried that they might be waiting for us in the car park and I didn't exactly relish another of their 'messages' being applied to my solar plexus.

'Where are you parked?' I asked Luca as we packed up the equipment.

'Across the road in the free car park,' he said.

'Good, so am I. Let's keep together when we go, just in case.'

'Too bloody right,' he said.

'Wait for me, then,' said Duggie. 'I'm just going for a pee.'

He ran off towards the Gents, leaving Luca and me with the trolley.

'Any movement on the Sister Millie front?' I asked, unable to contain my curiosity any longer.

He smiled broadly. 'Negotiations are continuing,' he said, 'but no break-through as yet. She wants to, but she thinks Betsy will murder her if she does. And she's probably right. But it certainly makes life interesting.'

'Just don't let her meet Duggie,' I said, 'or you'll have no chance.'

He pulled a face at me. As we fixed the last of the cords over the tarpau-lin, Duggie appeared from the Gents.

'OK, then,' Duggie said cheerfully, 'let's go get 'em.'

Much to Duggie's disappointment, there was no sign of the goons in the car park. But I kept a wary eye out for a black BMW 4x4 all the way home.

ON SUNDAY, Alice went back to her home in Surrey. Sadly, she wasn't going permanently, just to do some washing and to gather some different clothes.

'How about your job?' I asked her over breakfast.

I knew that she had taken a week's holiday from her position as a local radio producer in Guildford, but her week was up.

'A few days more won't worry them,' she said.

I made no fuss, even though I yearned for the time when I didn't have to make the bed every morning, or put my dirty coffee cup immediately in the dishwasher; when I could walk around the house in my underwear, and lie on the sofa to watch football on the television. In the five months Sophie had been in hospital, I had become quite used to living on my own.

It wasn't that I didn't want Sophie at home. Of course I did. I just wasn't sure about her sister being here, too. Still, her presence had at least made me feel a little better about Sophie being alone in the house when I was at work.

We closed the front door and went back into the kitchen.

'I can't believe I've been home a week already,' Sophie said. 'It seems like only yesterday I left the hospital.'

I thought it felt like a month, but I didn't say so.

I went up to my office while Sophie pottered around in the kitchen, relishing being able to do things without Alice constantly offering advice.

I logged on to the *Racing Post* website and checked the declarations for Bangor-on-Dee Races for Monday. It was good news. The short-priced favourite in the two-mile hurdle race for maidens was still running.

Sophie came into my office with a cup of coffee for me.

'Thank you, my darling,' I said.

She stood behind me, stroking my shoulders. 'What are you doing?'

'Just checking the runners for tomorrow,' I said.

'Can I come with you to the races?' she asked.

'Of course,' I said, pleased. 'We're going to Bangor tomorrow. It's quite a long way, but you can come if you like. Or we're at Southwell for the evening meeting on Tuesday.'

'Maybe I'll come to Southwell on Tuesday if the weather's nice.'

'That would be lovely,' I said, meaning it. I shut down my computer. 'Why don't we go out to lunch?'

'What, now?' she said.

'Yes. Right now.'

'Great idea.' She smiled.

WE WENT TO THE PUB in the village of Avon Dassett, where their speciality was sixty-four different ways to have a pie. Sophie and I, however, opted to go for the Sunday roast lamb, which was delicious.

After lunch I drove the few miles to the Burton Dassett Hills Country

Park, where I stopped the car on a ridge with a view all the way to Coventry.

And there we sat in the car while I told Sophie about my father.

I had lain awake for much of the night, going over and over in my mind the secrets I had gleaned from my grandmother, and weighing up whether I should tell Sophie. I was painfully aware of how easily in the past her behaviour had changed for the worse at times of stress or anxiety, and I desperately didn't want to cause her either of them unnecessarily.

However, there was a real need in me for her to know the truth. I realised that I was bottling up my pain and my anger. I feared they would overwhelm me and I needed, perhaps selfishly, to ease the burden by talking things through. Maybe I should have sought out one of the hospital psychiatrists to give *me* some therapy, but Sophie was the one I wanted to help me.

I started by telling her about my father's sudden appearance at Ascot and the shock of finding that he hadn't died in a car crash as we had thought.

'That's great,' she said. 'You always wanted a father.'

But then I told her about him being stabbed in the racecourse car park, and about him dying at the hospital.

'But why was he stabbed?' she asked, clearly upset on my behalf.

'I think it was a robbery that went wrong,' I said.

I still considered it prudent not to mention anything about microcoders, false passports or bundles of cash. Best also, I thought, not to refer to my father's black-and-red rucksack, collected from our home by his murderer.

'But *you* could have been killed,' she said.

'I would have given the thief the money,' I said. 'But my father told him to go to hell and kicked him in the balls. I think that's why he was stabbed.'

She was a little reassured, but not much.

'But why didn't you tell me about it straight away?' she implored.

'I didn't want to upset you just before the assessment,' I said. And she could see the sense in that. 'But that's not all, my love. Far from it.'

I told her about my mother and the fact that she hadn't died in a car accident, either. As gently as I could, I told her about Paignton pier and how my mother had been found murdered on the beach beneath it.

'Oh, Ned,' she said, choking back the tears.

'I was only a toddler,' I said, trying to comfort her. 'I have no memory of any of it. In fact, I don't remember a single thing about my mother.'

'How did you find out?' she asked.

'The police told me,' I said. 'They did a DNA check on him. At the time everyone thought my father had been responsible, and that's why he ran away, and also why Nanna and Grandpa made up the story of the car crash.'

'How dreadful for them,' she said.

'Yes, but it wasn't actually that simple,' I said.

I told her about my mother's pregnancy and, eventually and carefully, I revealed the whole story about the baby being my grandfather's child and how it had been he who had strangled my mother to stop anyone finding out.

She was silent for some time as I held her hand.

'But why, then, did your father go away?' she asked finally.

'He was told to,' I said.

'Who by?'

I laid bare the awful truth that my grandmother, our darling Nanna, had been responsible for me having had no father to grow up with.

Sophie just couldn't believe it. 'Are you absolutely sure?' she asked.

I nodded. 'I found out most of it yesterday,' I said. 'When I went to see her. For once she was quite lucid. She didn't remember who you were, but there wasn't much wrong with her memory of the events of thirty-six years ago.'

'Was she sorry?' Sophie asked.

'No, not really,' I said. 'I think that's what I found the hardest to bear.'

We sat together silently in the car for some while.

All around us were happy families: mums and dads with their children, running up and down the hills, chasing their dogs and flying their kites in the wind. All the things that normal people do on Sunday afternoons.

The horrors were only inside the car, and in our minds.

CHAPTER 11

On Monday morning, I picked up Luca and Duggie from the Hilton Hotel car park at junction 15 on the M40 and the three of us set off for Bangor-on-Dee with mischief in mind.

The bruises on my abdomen, inflicted by fists and steel toecaps at Kempton Park, had finally begun to fade, but the fire of revenge still burned in my belly. I had told Larry Porter that I would get even with the bastard who had ordered the beatings, and today was going to be the day.

'Did you check with Larry?' I said to Luca. 'Has he got the stuff?'

'Relax,' Luca said to me. 'Don't worry. Larry will be there in good time.'

'Did you speak to your friends?' I asked Duggie. 'To remind them.'

'All OK,' he replied. 'As Luca said, relax, everything is fine.'

I hoped he was right.

We arrived at the racecourse early and I parked in one of the free car parks. I went to pay the fee at the bookmaker's badge entrance while Luca and Duggie unloaded the equipment and pulled it through to the betting ring.

'Where's the grandstand?' said Duggie, looking round.

I laughed. 'There isn't really a grandstand at Bangor.'

'How do the punters see the racing, then?' he asked.

'It's a natural grandstand,' I said, pointing to where the ground fell away towards the track. 'The people stand on the hill to watch the racing.'

'I've seen it all now,' he said.

'No, you haven't,' I said. 'In southern Spain they race along a beach with the crowd wearing swimming trunks and sitting under sun umbrellas. It's proper racing with starting stalls, betting, the lot. It even gets TV coverage.'

'And, in St Moritz, in Switzerland,' Luca said, 'every year they race on a frozen lake covered in snow. I've seen it. It's amazing.'

'Then why do they cancel racing here when it snows?' Duggie asked.

'Good question,' I said. 'Obviously the wrong kind of snow.'

We giggled nervously as we set up our pitch. Luca commented favourably on the new name on our board. I had spent the previous evening painting over the TRUST TEDDY TALBOT slogan and had replaced it with, it had to be said, some pretty poorly painted white letters saying TALBOT AND MANDINI.

'I'll change the wording on our tickets as well,' Luca said.

He set to work on his computer while I went to the Gents. The nerves were clearly beginning to get to me.

'There's a public payphone on the wall round there,' I said when I got back. I pointed down the side of the building between the seafood bar and the lavatories. 'I don't want anyone to use it when the mobiles stop working.'

'That's easy,' said Duggie. 'I'll go and fix it.' And off he went before I had a chance to stop him.

He was back in a couple of minutes.

'All done,' he said. 'No one's going to use that phone today.'

Luca and I looked at each other. 'What did you do?' I asked Duggie.

'I broke it,' he said simply. 'Then I went into the office and complained that the phone wouldn't work. They've put an out-of-order sign on it now.'

I laughed. 'Well done.'

'Yeah,' he said. 'But they offered me the use of the secretary's phone instead, if it were urgent, like.'

'Ah,' I said. I didn't want anyone using the secretary's phone, either.

'It's simple,' said Duggie. 'I got the secretary's phone number, so I get a few of my mates to call it at the right time and then not hang up. It will tie up any lines they have on that number.'

'But won't your mates' numbers show up on caller ID?' I said.

'So I'll get my mates to withhold their numbers, or they can call from the phone boxes in Wycombe,' he said. 'It's dead easy.'

'OK,' I said. 'Fix it.'

Larry Porter arrived and began to set up his pitch alongside ours.

'Have you got the equipment?' I asked him.

'Yes. All set,' Larry said. 'Bill's coming separately, later.'

Bill, I assumed, was the man I had seen at Ascot in the white shirt and fawn chinos who had placed the 'two monkeys' bet with me when the Internet and phones went down just before the Gold Cup.

Monday-afternoon racing anywhere was always quiet and today was no exception. I counted sixteen bookmakers in the main betting ring, all chasing meagre pickings from the sparse crowd. Other than Larry and Norman I didn't recognise any of the other bookies, as we were at the northern extent of our usual patch, and I wouldn't normally be standing at Bangor.

At long last, it was nearing the maiden hurdle race time, the fifth race of the afternoon. There were nineteen runners, with Pool House the fairly short-priced favourite at six-to-four. The horse had raced three times previously and finished second on the last two occasions. And today it was being ridden by a many-times champion jockey, who had made the journey from Lambourn especially to ride this one horse, so he, for one, expected it to win. And all the newspapers agreed with him.

With the horses in the parade ring, and with precisely six minutes before the scheduled start time, I nodded to Larry, who pushed his out-of-sight switch to turn on the phone jammer. At the same time I nudged Luca, who activated his virus on the racecourse Internet server, effectively putting it out of action and isolating the racecourse from the outside world.

I thought of the thirty juvenile delinquents and hoped that they were all poised to place their bets.

A man in a white shirt and fawn chinos suddenly appeared in front of me. Bill, I assumed. 'Grand on number four,' he said, thrusting a wad of banknotes at me. Number four was the second favourite.

'Grand on number four at three-to-one,' I said loudly over my shoulder.

'Offer at eleven-to-four,' Luca said, equally loudly.

'OK,' said the man. I gave him the TALBOT AND MANDINI printed ticket and the price changed on our board.

'Give me a monkey on four at threes,' Luca bellowed at Larry Porter.

'You can have it at five-to-two,' Larry shouted back.

'OK,' said Luca, who then turned the other way towards Norman Joyner. 'Give me a monkey on number four,' he shouted even louder.

'Fine,' shouted Norman back. 'At nine-to-four.'

The price of number four was tumbling all over the betting ring and, as a result, Pool House, the favourite, drifted longer.

The panic from the boys from the big outfits wasn't as dramatic as it had been at Ascot but it was fairly impressive, nonetheless. They rushed around trying desperately to get their phones to work, but without success. One rushed off to use the payphone but was soon looking frustrated.

They had all obviously been well briefed, however, after the incident at Ascot. They clearly knew that the price of the hot favourite had, on that occasion, lengthened during the time when the Internet and phones were down. They would also know that, when the favourite then won, they all got hit badly because the bets in the high-street betting shops were paid out on the starting price, and that had been artificially made too high.

Consequently, the big-firm boys now took it upon themselves, in the absence of orders from their head offices, to back the favourite heavily, to bring its price down again to six-to-four.

There was almost panic to get their money on with the ring bookies before the start. I took a number of big bets and, reluctantly, we brought the price of Pool House down from seven-to-four, first to thirteen-to-eight, then to six-to-four, and finally to eleven-to-eight. The horse had actually started at shorter odds than it would have if we had done nothing.

The race began and Larry switched off his phone-jamming device, while Luca cured the Internet server of his virus.

'That didn't bloody work, did it?' said Larry angrily. 'Now if the favourite goes on and wins, I stand to lose a packet.'

But the favourite didn't win.

A complete rank outsider called Cricket Hero beat it by two lengths, and was returned at the surprisingly long starting price of a-hundred-to-one. We hadn't taken a single bet on the horse, so, from the paying-out point of view, it was a very satisfactory result.

'Hold the fort a minute,' I said to Luca.

I went over to watch Cricket Hero being led into the winner's unsaddling enclosure. There was a distinct lack of enthusiastic applause from the crowd, few, if any, of whom would have backed it. The horse's connections, however, were beaming from ear to ear as their horse circled the enclosure, steaming gently from under its rug. I looked in the racecard to see the name of the trainer. Miles Carpenter, it said, from Ireland.

I leaned on the rail close by to the person I assumed was Mr Carpenter. He was smiling like the cat that got the cream.

'Well done, Mr Carpenter,' I called to him.

He turned towards me. 'Thanks,' he said in a thick Irish accent.

'Nice horse,' I said, nodding at the bay, but the truth was it didn't look that good. Unlike the well-groomed coats of the other horses, the winner's seemed matted and dull. His tail was a jumble of knots and his hoofs were not nicely blackened like most racehorses' are when they run. In fact, the horse looked like an old nag. That's partly why his price had been so high. Horses that don't look good in the parade ring don't generally run well, either.

But appearances can be deceptive.

'Yes,' the Irishman replied with a big smile, coming a step closer to me. 'I think he's going to be a champion.'

I spoke directly to him, quietly but clearly. 'Oriental Suite, I assume.'

The smile instantly disappeared from his face.

'And you,' I went on, 'must be Paddy Murphy.'

'And who the feck are you?' he said explosively, coming right up to me and thrusting his face into mine.

'Just a friend,' I said, backing away and smiling.

'What do you want?' he snarled.

'Nothing,' I said. I turned away, leaving him dumbstruck behind me.

He had already given me what I wanted. Confirmation that Oriental Suite was, indeed, now called Cricket Hero. Not that I had really needed it.

I assumed that the real Cricket Hero, whose official ratings had been so low as to be almost off the bottom of the scale, was dead. Switched with Oriental Suite using fake RFID tags, then killed for a large insurance payout.

The horse now running as Cricket Hero was actually Oriental Suite and one thing was certain. It should never have started any race at odds of a-hundred-to-one, let alone a low-quality maiden hurdle at Bangor-on-Dee.

I thought about the two photocopied horse passports I had found in the secret compartment of my father's rucksack. One of them had been in the name of Oriental Suite. The other had belonged to a horse called Cricket Hero, and I had been struck by the similarities in the markings and hair whorls of the two horses as recorded on the diagrams.

And I had been waiting for the name Cricket Hero to appear in race entries ever since.

'YOU CALL THAT getting even?' Larry Porter said loudly to me as I made my way back to our pitch.

'Keep your voice down, you fool,' I said to him.

'But it didn't bloody work, did it?' he said, at only slightly lower volume.

'I can't make the favourite win every time, now can I?' I said.

'Bloody good job it didn't,' he said. 'Norman and I took so much money on it in those last minutes we would have been well out of pocket.'

Norman Joyner stood next to Larry, nodding vigorously.

'But you aren't,' I said, smiling. 'So what are you worried about? You both ended up in profit on the race, didn't you?'

'No thanks to you,' Larry said, still grumbling.

'I reckon we'd better not try it again,' said Norman.

'Fine,' I said. That would suit me very well.

'Those big firms must be laughing all the way to the bank,' he went on.

True, I thought. But I knew of one firm that wouldn't be laughing.

Tony Bateman (Turf Accountants) Ltd, the high-street betting-shop subsidiary of HRF Holdings Ltd, employers of the two bully-boys with their steel toecaps, would be far from laughing all the way to their bank.

There were more than fifty Tony Bateman betting shops in the chain, scattered throughout London and the southeast of England. If all had gone to plan, at precisely five minutes before the due time of the race, and therefore exactly one minute after we had isolated the racecourse, thirty members of Duggie and Luca's electronics club, the juvenile delinquents from High Wycombe, had each gone into a different Tony Bateman betting shop and placed a £200 bet on Cricket Hero to win, payable at the starting price.

Even now, I hoped, each of the thirty would be collecting £20,000 in winnings; that was £600,000 in total. And all the bets had been financed by the £6,000 in cash that I had taken from the blue-plastic-wrapped packages hidden beneath the lining in my father's black-and-red rucksack.

The deal with the delinquents had been easy. Luca and Duggie had handed over £200 in cash to each of them, together with an address of one of the Tony Bateman betting shops. They were given strict instructions. Go to the shop at that address and at exactly 4.25 p.m. make the bet: £200 to win on Cricket Hero. If the horse lost, they were simply to walk away, curse their luck, and otherwise keep quiet. If it won, they were to try to collect the winnings, and a quarter of it, £5,000, would be theirs to keep. Luca and Duggie would take the other three-quarters from them that night.

I expected that a few might have simply pocketed the £200 and hoped that the horse lost. But enough of them would have placed the bets, and a single £200 bet, even on a hundred-to-one long shot, should not have raised too many suspicions at each separate betting shop. If the head office did notice that £6,000 had swiftly gone on to such a rank outsider, they would have been powerless to do anything about the starting price. Larry's mobile-phone jammer and Luca's Internet-server virus had seen to that, helped by Duggie's expertise with the land lines.

'They may not pay out,' Luca said. Bookmakers, particularly the big chains, had a nasty habit of not paying out on bets if they thought someone had been up to a fiddle. Not that we had, of course. We had simply piggy-backed on someone else's fiddle.

'Maybe not immediately,' I said. 'But I think they will in the end.'

I could say that with confidence because I knew something that he didn't.

The owner of Oriental Suite, the same owner who had been quoted in the *Racing Post* as being distraught over the death of his horse, and the man who had pocketed the large insurance payout, was none other than a Mr Henry Richard Feldman, director and shareholder of Tony Bateman (Turf Accountants) Ltd and sole shareholder of HRF Holdings Ltd. The very same man who had sent his bully-boys to give me a 'message' at Kempton Park Racecourse with their fists and steel toecaps.

Getting even had, indeed, required considerable cunning.

And almost the best part of the whole scheme was that Larry Porter and Norman Joyner firmly believed that it hadn't worked.

I was certain that Mr Feldman would eventually see sense and pay out on all the bets, just as I was sure that he would decide not to pursue his plans to take over my business. Both would be the price for my silence. And he would know that a letter had been lodged with my solicitors, to be handed to the British Horseracing Authority in the event of my sudden or suspicious death.

Just to be on the safe side.

LUCA, DUGGIE AND I could hardly contain ourselves as we packed up the equipment after the last race. Larry had been so frightened that he gave the electronic phone jammer back to Luca and swore he'd never try anything like that again. I bit my lip hard so I wouldn't smile.

We loaded the stuff in my Volvo and I drove back south towards Warwickshire, Luca next to me as usual, with Duggie behind him.

'I heard one of those suits saying that he knew something was up as he couldn't get a line on the secretary's phone,' said Duggie.

'Thanks to you,' I said, looking at him in the rearview mirror. 'Well done.'

He beamed. We drove in silence for a while, wallowing in our success.

'What are you going to do with the money?' Duggie asked eventually.

'Well,' I said, 'I thought of donating it to charity. Perhaps the Injured Jockeys Fund.'

'Good idea,' said Luca very seriously. 'It's a very good cause.'

I went on driving.

'But then I thought it would be more fun if we had it,' I said.

We all burst into laughter.

'Much better idea,' said Duggie, banging the back of Luca's seat in his excitement.

We discussed the money for the next twenty minutes.

Provided Tony Bateman paid it all out, and assuming that all the thirty bets had actually been placed, and at the hundred-to-one starting price, then the total winnings would be £600,000. A quarter of that would go to the delinquents, and we decided that we would split half the total, £300,000, jointly between us. The other quarter would go anonymously to two charities, the Injured Jockeys Fund and Racing Welfare, to ease our consciences.

'Can we do this every week?' asked Duggie. 'Biggest pay cheque I've ever had, I can tell you.'

'Better than that,' I said. 'Gambling winnings are tax-free in the UK.'

We all laughed again.

I had decided that splitting the money equally among the three of us was the only way. Duggie's help had been crucial, and his little intervention with the bully-boys at Leicester had made me grateful that he was on my side. I wanted to keep it that way.

We were still all in high spirits when I finally turned into the Hilton Hotel car park at junction 15 on the M40, where Luca had left his car.

He and Duggie gave me a wave as they headed for the bar for a quick celebration drink, and I drove away. I thought it was a good job you couldn't lose your licence for having euphoria-induced adrenaline in your bloodstream. I would be well over the limit.

My telephone rang as I accelerated away. It was in its hands-free car cradle and the number of the caller was shown across the green display at the top. It was Sophie's mobile number.

I pushed the button. 'Hello, my darling,' I said cheerfully into the microphone. 'I'll be home in about ten minutes.'

But it wasn't Sophie's voice that came back at me out of the speaker.

'Hello, Mr Talbot,' said a man's voice, and a chill ran down my spine. 'You still have something of mine,' he said. 'So now I have something of yours.'

I became cold and clammy all over. 'Let me speak to my wife,' I said.

There was a slight pause, then Sophie came on the line. 'Ned, Ned,' she screamed, sounding very frightened, 'help me.'

'It's OK, Sophie,' I said, trying to calm her. 'Everything will be all right.'

But she wasn't there any more and the man came back on the line. 'Do as I say, Mr Talbot,' he said calmly, 'and she won't get hurt.'

Not only did I fear for Sophie's safety, I feared for her state of mind.

'What do you want?' I asked him.

'I want the rest of the items that were in that rucksack,' he said. 'I want the chips, the chipwriter and the rest of the money.'

My fears that I'd not seen the last of Kipper were clearly well founded

'I haven't got the items with me,' I said.

'Go and get them, then,' he said, just as if he was telling off a miscreant schoolboy who had forgotten his books.

'Where are you?' I asked.

'Never you mind,' he said. 'And don't hang up. Keep on the line. If you hang up, I will hurt your wife. Do you understand?'

'Yes,' I said.

'Good. Now, where are my things?'

What was I to say? Telling him that I had given the RFID chips and the microcoder/chipwriter to Mr John Smith was unlikely to help get Sophie released unharmed. As for the money, it was still spread among the juvenile delinquents. True, I had the take from the afternoon's racing at Bangor-on-Dee, but at best that only amounted to half of the £6,000.

'They're at my house,' I said.

'Where in your house? I couldn't find them.'

I didn't like the sound of that.

I thought quickly. 'In the cupboard under the stairs. In an old paint tin.'

'Go and get them,' he said. 'Now. But don't hang up the phone. If you hang up, I will kill your wife.'

A fresh wave of fear swept over me. 'All right, all right, I won't hang up,' I said quickly. 'But what happens if I lose mobile signal?'

'You had just better hope you don't,' he replied.

I realised why he didn't want me to hang up. As long as I was on the line to him, I couldn't call the police.

'OK,' I said. 'Where shall I bring them?'

'Just get them first,' he said. 'Then I'll tell you what to do.'

I turned off the A46 into Kenilworth, and was soon drawing up outside my house alongside Alice's car, which stood alone in the parking area.

'I've arrived at my house,' I said into the microphone.

'Good,' he said. 'Go in and fetch the stuff. Take your mobile with you. But don't hang up, or I will kill your wife.'

'But it hangs up automatically when I take it out of the hands-free system.'

'Take it out now,' he ordered.

I lifted the phone out of its cradle and, of course, it immediately hung up. Oh God, I thought, now what do I do? Do I call back or what?

Before I had a chance to decide the phone rang in my hand.

'Hello, yes,' I shouted into it. 'I'm here.'

'Good,' said Kipper. My heart rate went down by at least half. I would never have thought that I would be relieved to hear his voice.

'OK,' I said. 'I'm getting out of the car and going in.'

The front door was open about two inches, and I began to fear that he might actually be inside the house waiting for me.

'Are you in my house?' I asked him.

There was no reply.

'Stop playing games with me.' I spoke firmly into the phone. 'I am not going through my front door until you tell me where you are.'

'I'm in charge here, not you. Now, go into your house and get my things.'

'No,' I said, my heart rate climbing again. 'I will not go through my front door only for you to knife me like you did my father at Ascot.'

There was a long pause from his end.

'How come your name is Talbot and not Grady?' he asked eventually.

I suddenly realised he hadn't known that the man he knew as Alan Grady, the man he had murdered in the Ascot car park, had been my father.

'My father's name was really Talbot, not Grady,' I said.

'Ah,' he said. 'That's why I haven't been able to find out about him.'

He obviously hadn't traced me through the inquest records because he hadn't known which records to look at.

'Are you in my house?' I repeated into the phone.

'If I was, I'd have gone to the paint tin and taken what's mine by now.'

Did I believe him? But did I have any choice but to go in anyway?

I pushed the front door open wide with my foot until it was almost flat against the wall. There was not enough space for him to be hiding behind it.

I stepped into the hall. I could hear nothing. I walked down the hall, past the cupboard under the stairs and into the kitchen. Everything from the kitchen cabinets was strewn across the floor. I stepped carefully through the mess to the house telephone, but the wire had been cut through. I had no doubt that the extension in the bedroom would have suffered the same fate, but I still started up the stairs to check. For once I trod on step three. It creaked.

I thought I could hear a faint knocking.

I stopped to listen. I could definitely hear it. It was below me.

'Have you got my things yet?' Kipper asked, making me jump.

'No,' I replied.

I rushed back down the stairs and opened the cupboard beneath them.

Alice lay there on her side with her arms tied behind her back. She was banging her tied-up feet on the floor. A tea-towel gag had been wrapped round her face, so I pulled it down, and she spat out a dirty dishcloth.

'Ugh,' she said, and was promptly sick on the floor.

'You bastard,' I said into the phone.

Kipper laughed. 'Ah, you've found my little surprise.'

I went back into the kitchen, fetched a pair of scissors and cut through the plastic garden ties that had secured Alice's wrists and ankles. She sat on the hall floor, rubbing where the plastic had dug into her flesh. I put a finger up to my mouth in the universal 'be quiet' gesture and pointed at the phone.

'Phone the bloody police,' she shouted, ignoring me.

'I wouldn't do that if I were you,' said shifty-eyed Kipper through the phone. 'Not if you want to see your wife again.'

'Alice, I can't,' I said.

'Why the bloody hell not?' she demanded.

'He's got Sophie,' I said. 'And he's on the other end of this phone.'

Kipper laughed again at Alice's stunned silence.

'Now get my things,' he said, 'and go back to your car.'

What was I to do? I had to make him think that I still had them or he would kill Sophie. And I needed to set up a swap, I thought. That would be a good start but, so far, I hadn't actually worked out how to do it.

First I needed something to swap for Sophie. I took a blue canvas shopping bag off the hook on the back of the kitchen door and started putting things into it. First, the wad of banknotes, the takings from Bangor Races, came out of my trouser pocket and into the bag. Next, I took a clear polythene sandwich bag and put ten grains of rice in it. Finally, the instruction booklet for the kitchen television, together with the TV remote control, went into the bag as well.

Alice stood in the kitchen doorway, watching me with wide eyes. 'What are you doing?' she said. 'Call the police.'

I again put my finger to my mouth and this time she understood. I also held up the cut phone wire and she nodded.

'OK, I've got it all,' I said into the phone.

'Go and get into the car and drive back onto the A46 towards the M40.'

'OK,' I said. I put my hand over the microphone and spoke to Alice. 'I've got to go and give this to the man.' I held up the blue shopping bag. 'I'll come back here with Sophie. Are you OK?'

She nodded, but I noticed tears on her face. I stroked her shoulders in reassurance and then went back out to my Volvo with the shopping bag.

'OK,' I said into the phone. 'I'm back in the car. I'm going to put the phone back in the hands-free cradle, but it may hang up again.'

'Leave it, then,' he said. 'Keep it in your hand.'

I reversed out onto Station Road and retraced my path.

'OK,' I said, holding the phone to my ear. 'I'm now on the A46.'

'Leave the A46 and take the A425 towards Warwick,' he said. 'Take the third turning on the right, Budbrooke Road. Follow it round to the right. Go to the very end of the road.'

'OK,' I said to him. I still wasn't sure what I would do when I got there.

I took the A425, then turned into Budbrooke Road. It was an industrial estate sandwiched between a canal and a railway line. No doubt during the day this area was busy, but at 8.15 on a Monday evening it was deserted.

I drove slowly down to the end of the road and stopped between two big metal buildings. I turned the car round so I was looking back up the road, but my Volvo was the only car about. I wondered if I was in the right place.

'Are you here?' I asked.

'I'm here,' he said. 'Just shut up and wait.'

I wondered if he was waiting to see if I'd been followed. I sat there for what seemed like ages but it was probably only a couple of minutes.

'OK,' he said finally through the phone. 'Open the car door, put the things out on the ground and drive away.'

'What about my wife?' I asked.

'When I am satisfied that I have everything, I will let her go.'

'No way,' I said. 'If you want your things, you will have to let her go now, and we'll do an exchange.'

'An exchange?' He laughed. 'Mr Talbot, this is not a spy movie. Leave the things on the ground and go.'

'No, I will not,' I said again firmly. 'I want my wife back now.'

He didn't answer and I began to fear that he'd gone. But then a small silver hatchback moved slowly down the road and stopped, facing me, about thirty yards away. The driver's door opened and Kipper got out.

He lifted the phone to his ear. 'Where's my stuff?' he said.

I opened the door to the Volvo and stood next to it. 'Where's my wife?' I said into my phone.

He reached down into the car and pulled her up from the back seat. She stood up next to him. I could see that her hands were tied behind her back. He held her in front of him with his right arm over her shoulder. And he had his twelve-centimetre-long knife resting against her neck.

'Where's my stuff?' he asked again through the telephone.

I could feel my heart pumping in my chest. I put my hand into the Volvo, picked up the blue shopping bag and held it up.

'Show me,' he said.

I pulled the wad of banknotes out of the bag. I held it up above my head and waved it at him. Most of the notes were tenners and twenties, but he wouldn't be able to see from his distance that they weren't all fifties.

'Show me the chipwriter,' he said.

With a dry mouth, I put the money back in the bag and carefully picked up the television remote control. I held it up with the back of it towards him. I hoped that from where he was standing it would appear to be a black box of approximately the right size and shape.

'And the chips?' he asked.

I held up the sandwich bag with the grains of rice in it. I could hardly tell them apart from the real RFID chips, so he would have had no chance of doing so from thirty yards away. I put them back in the bag.

'And here are the horse passports,' I said, waving the TV instruction booklet around so that he couldn't see it clearly. 'Now release my wife.'

'Go over there and put the bag on the ground.' He pointed towards a building to my right.

I walked over to where he was pointing. I put the bag down on the ground and stood next to it. I was still twenty yards or so from where he stood holding Sophie, the knife at her neck glinting in the sunlight.

'Now go back to your car,' he said.

'Let my wife walk away from you,' I said to him. 'When she starts walking, I will walk away from the bag.'

He laughed. 'You really have been watching too many spy films.'

It may have amused him to think that we were taking part in a spy movie but I didn't feel at all like laughing. Not with my humble TV remote control acting the part of an electronic microcoder/chipwriter, and a bag of simple rice grains appearing as some programmable RFID tags. And certainly not when my wife's life depended on them not forgetting their lines.

'Let my wife go and then these are yours.' I pointed down at the bag.

The recovery of the items must have become an obsession with him. He looked longingly at the bag. He removed the knife from Sophie's throat and gently pushed her towards my car. I let her go a few strides, just enough to be out of his reach; then I started slowly moving backwards towards the Volvo, watching Kipper intently for any sudden movements.

He walked round the front of his car, and started towards the bag.

Sophie was now about halfway to my car, relief showing in her face, but she wasn't going anywhere near fast enough for my liking. Kipper was almost at the bag, and a single glance would tell him instantly that my kitchen TV remote control was not the microcoder/chipwriter he was expecting.

'Sophie, run,' I shouted at her. At the same time I sprinted for the Volvo and opened the rear door. Sophie ran towards me. I took a couple of strides forward, grabbed her and literally threw her across the back seat. I slammed the door and was in the car almost before Kipper realised he'd been fooled.

I started the engine, threw the car into gear and shot past Kipper's silver hatchback with my back wheels spinning on the loose surface. I could see him shouting something at me but I couldn't hear what it was.

He ran over to his car and, all too soon, the silver hatchback appeared in my rearview mirror as I waited at the junction with the Birmingham road for a gap in the traffic. He came right up behind me at speed and rammed the Volvo forward, right into the path of a speeding white van.

I closed my eyes and waited for the crash, but somehow the van driver managed to swerve round me with a squeal of his tyres.

Sophie was lying full-length across the back seat where I had thrown her, still with a black plastic tie binding her hands behind her back. 'Ned, what's happening?' Her voice was remarkably calm for someone who had just had a knife at their throat. Where, I thought, was the expected panic?

The answer was that the panic was up here in front, with me.

I SUPPOSE IF one had to be involved in an impromptu stock-car race along the highways and byways of Warwickshire, an old Volvo 940 2.3-litre turbocharged estate might actually be one's car of choice. They hadn't been nicknamed the 'Volvo Tank' for nothing.

At the A46 junction I debated with myself which way to go. Kipper was right up against my tailgate and the Volvo lurched every time he hit me. If I went down towards the M40, I would have to deal with the traffic lights on the motorway junction. Equally, if I went straight on the A425 towards Birmingham, there were traffic lights within a few hundred yards. I decided to turn right onto the A46 back towards Kenilworth.

I swept onto the roundabout so fast that my mobile phone slid off the passenger seat where I'd dropped it and into the gap between the seat and the door. Sod it, I thought. I'd wanted to call the police with that.

Kipper kept darting back and forth around the rear of the Volvo like an annoying insect. Twice he gave me such a big nudge that I feared I would lose control completely, and my car was still fishtailing badly as it sped down the slip road and onto the A46 dual carriageway.

In spite of being thrown around by the constant lurching of the car, Sophie had managed to get herself into a fairly upright position on the back seat. I smiled at her in the rearview mirror.

She looked back at me with wide, frightened eyes. 'Can you untie me?'
'Not just at the moment, darling. I need both hands to drive.'

Fortunately, the A46 was quite empty at that time of the evening and I was able to put my foot down. The Volvo speedometer climbed to well over ninety miles per hour, but still I couldn't get away from Kipper's car, which seemed to be stuck to me like a limpet. Twice he tried to get alongside but both times I swerved to cut him off, forcing him back. Soon, the road would open up to three lanes. Keeping him back then would not be so easy.

Our two cars raced along the road together towards the next junction. At the very last moment I jerked the steering wheel to the left and went onto the slip road, hoping that Kipper wouldn't be able to make the turning. Sadly, he did, slowing only momentarily to cross the grass verge, which sent up a shower of earth and stones.

I shot up the slip road to the roundabout at the top of the rise. I hoped that nothing was coming round it for I wasn't about to slow down. My tyres squealed in objection as I took the first exit along a single-track country road towards the village of Leek Wooton.

I thought the best plan was to drive to the nearest police station and park right outside the door. Surely even shifty-eyed Kipper wouldn't be crazy enough to try anything there. The only police station I knew well was in Kenilworth. I knew it didn't operate round the clock, but it would have to do. It might be enough to put Kipper off, even if it was closed.

I tore down the road towards Leek Wooton with the silver hatchback seemingly glued to the back of the Volvo. At one point he tried to overtake me, so I pulled right into the middle of the road, swerving back to my side only at the last second to avoid an oncoming truck.

I ignored the thirty-mile-per-hour signs at the entrance to the village, hoping desperately that a child didn't step out into my path. At more than double the speed limit, I would have had no chance of stopping in time.

I realised that I didn't even have my seat belt on, so I reached for it and clicked it into place. But Sophie had no chance of doing the same.

'Darling, please lie down on the floor behind the seats,' I said firmly. 'Get as low as you can and brace yourself with your feet. Just in case we have an accident.' I glanced over to her and tried to give her a reassuring smile.

'When will all this stop?' she cried.

'We're going to the police station right now,' I said. 'It will stop there.'

But it didn't. Because we never reached the police station.

SO FAR we had not encountered much other traffic, but our luck ran out as we left Leek Wooton. A line of four cars was following a slow-moving builder's lorry that was piled high with sand. I could see a van coming the opposite way, but it was still some distance off. I swung out and overtook all four cars and the lorry with my hand firmly on the horn to stop anyone pulling out. Kipper tried to come through behind me but he had to brake hard and dive in behind the lorry in order to miss the oncoming van.

Suddenly, I was away from him. But not for long, and not by much, and I watched in the mirror as he quickly swept past the lorry in pursuit.

I looked ahead in horror. In the distance, there were some roadworks with a set of temporary traffic lights, and a line of vehicles was waiting.

I was doing about eighty miles an hour and the roadworks were beginning to loom large. I glanced in the mirror. Even at this speed, the silver hatchback was gaining on me fast. I looked ahead. Traffic was coming the other way, headed by a huge articulated lorry.

I made a quick decision.

'Sophie,' I shouted, 'brace yourself against the seats as hard as you can.'

With about 400 yards still to go to the temporary traffic lights, I took my right foot off the accelerator and stood hard on the brake.

My old Volvo 940 estate weighed a little over one and a half tonnes, but the brakes were in excellent working order. With a little shuddering from the anti-lock system, the car pulled up in a much shorter space than that shown as the stopping distance for eighty miles per hour in the Highway Code.

Kipper hadn't a hope of stopping in time. He had been going even faster, and had still been accelerating in his attempt to catch me.

I looked up into the rearview mirror. The Volvo had almost stopped before Kipper realised what I'd done. White smoke poured from his tyres as all four wheels locked up, but by then it was far too late.

I'd hoped that he would hit a tree, or the oncoming truck, but his locked front wheels meant he couldn't steer, and he came thundering on, straight towards the Volvo. I watched him coming ever closer almost as if it was happening in slow motion and, in the last moments before the impact, I clasped my hands firmly together in my lap and put my head back against the headrest. All the while shouting at Sophie, 'Brace! Brace!'

There was a tremendous bang as the vehicles collided and the Volvo was thrown violently sideways onto the grass verge. At the same time, the air bag in front of me inflated with another bang and a cloud of white gas.

Then there was another huge thump from somewhere behind me. Something else had collided, but not with us; the Volvo hadn't moved again.

'Sophie, Sophie,' I shouted urgently, fighting to undo my seat belt and turning round in my seat, 'are you all right?'

'Yes, Ned, I'm fine,' she said, almost calmly, from the back. 'Is it over?'

'Yes, my darling, it's over.'

But I didn't know that for certain. I couldn't even see the silver hatchback from where I was, let alone know the state of its occupant.

'Can you untie me, then?' she asked, sounding remarkably unfazed.

The driver's door wouldn't open and I began to panic as I could smell petrol. I pushed and shoved but still the door wouldn't budge, so I struggled over the centre armrest into the passenger seat. Thankfully, the passenger door opened easily. I scrambled out onto the verge.

'You all right, mate?' shouted someone from behind me.

'Yes, fine,' I said, turning round. 'How about him?' I pointed at the crumpled silver mess some ten yards or so behind the Volvo.

'Doesn't look too good, I'm afraid,' he said. 'I've called the ambulance.'

I looked around. The road was blocked and traffic queues were building up in both directions. I tugged open the nearside back door of the car.

Sophie was curled up on the floor, still with her hands tied together with the plastic garden tie. I needed something to free her, before anyone came snooping around asking why I had a tied-up woman in the back of my car.

I knew there was a pair of scissors somewhere among our bookmaking equipment in the back of the estate. Our equipment boxes, which had been neatly stowed at Bangor, were now in a jumble. The collision had buckled the big top-hinged back door of the Volvo but, amazingly, the rear window was still intact. I slithered on my stomach over the back seat into the luggage space, and found the scissors in the second box I tried.

I soon had Sophie cut loose and safely out of the car. I sat her down on the grass verge and told her to wait.

'Please don't leave me, Ned,' she wailed.

I looked lovingly at my battered and frightened wife. 'There's no chance of that,' I said, kissing the top of her head. 'I'll be back in a moment.'

The road was filling with people from their cars as I went to inspect the damage to my Volvo. The rear off-side corner was staved in, the back wheel on that side was at the wrong angle, and I could see petrol dripping out onto the road. But it was not half as bad as the silver hatchback.

It seemed that Kipper's car had collided not only with my Volvo Tank but also with the oncoming traffic, the first impact having bounced the hatchback straight into the path of the huge truck. The driver was wandering among the crowd in a daze. 'I had no chance,' he kept saying to everyone. 'That car came straight across the road. I had no chance.'

Nor had shifty-eyed Kipper. The truck had ploughed into the driver's door of the hatchback, mangling the vehicle beyond recognition.

Another James-Bond-style car chase was over and, this time, I thought, 'M' might have been fairly proud of me. I was only shaken, not stirred.

But I suddenly felt quite ill. This was reality, not a spy movie.

SOPHIE AND I sat side by side on the grass verge while a team of firemen, police and ambulance staff did their best to remove Kipper from the twisted wreckage of his car. He was still alive, but only just. The emergency crews were trying to keep him that way. I rather wished they wouldn't bother.

Sophie and I had been assessed by a paramedic as being physically unharmed before being wrapped in red blankets and asked to wait.

We waited. After a while, a yellow-and-black helicopter landed in the cornfield alongside the road and soon a doctor in an orange flying suit came over and asked us if we were both OK. 'Yes,' we said in unison. He went over to join the team working on the hatchback.

Sophie took my hand. 'We are OK, aren't we, Ned?' she said.

'Yes,' I said with certainty. 'We are definitely OK.'

EPILOGUE

Six months later, Sophie and I went to Australia to look for my sisters while Luca, my new, fully documented, legal business partner, and his young full-time assistant, Douglas Masters, carried on our flourishing business at home without me.

'Don't hurry back,' Luca had said the day before I left. 'Duggie and I will do just fine. And Millie will help us when she can.' Millie, it seemed, had moved in with Luca and hadn't yet been murdered by her sister, Betsy.

Since that glorious Monday in July at Bangor-on-Dee, I had discovered renewed energy and enthusiasm for my work. Bookmaking had become fun again, not least because Sophie had often stood with me, paying out winning tickets and bantering with the crowds as she'd never done before. She had clearly been taking lessons from Duggie.

It had actually been Sophie's idea to go to Australia, but I'd jumped at it.

Understandably, she'd had one or two problems after the events involving Kipper and the car crash. At the time I'd been amazed at her calmness but, according to the psychiatrists, this had been due to her brain bottling up the stress and switching off some of her emotions. Only afterwards did the fear and panic manifest themselves in a physical reaction. Four days later in the middle of the night, I had found her lying awake in our bed, shaking uncontrollably and soaked in sweat. Fortunately, the panic attack had been short-lived, and since then she had been doing well. The new drugs really were working and both of us had begun to hope and to make plans for a future.

Slowly, over the months, I had recounted to her the complete story of those three weeks in late June and early July. I told her the full details of my father's murder, about finding his rucksack and its hidden contents. I told her about Mr John Smith and the microcoder, about finding him in our house, and breaking his wrist. I even told her about Luca and Larry's little games with the phones and Internet at Ascot, and how I had exacted revenge for the attack on me at Kempton by the big-firm bully-boys.

Once or twice she told me off for not having contacted the police straight away, and she was, justifiably, quite cross that I had placed myself, and her, in such danger from a known murderer.

I had gone to see Chief Inspector Llewellyn the day after the car crash, at the Thames Valley Police Headquarters near Oxford. He'd told me that the driver of the silver hatchback, identified as a Mr Mervyn Williams, had indeed survived the crash, but was still in a critical condition. Apparently, he hadn't been wearing his seat belt at the time of the accident.

'It wasn't an accident,' I'd said flatly. 'The man was trying to shunt me off the road at the time, and I was just lucky that the truck hit him and not me.' I had decided against telling the chief inspector about me making an emergency stop in order to precipitate the crash in the first place.

'But why?' he had asked me.

'Because I think he's the man who murdered my father. I presumed that he was trying to do the same to me, to eliminate me as a witness.'

'What makes you think he's the man who murdered your father?'

'I think I recognised him at one point, when he tried to pass me.'

'How very interesting,' the chief inspector had said, and he'd lifted the telephone on his desk.

Mervyn Williams, I discovered at a second meeting with the chief inspector just a week later, was a qualified veterinary surgeon, who for the past ten years had worked as some sort of veterinary investigator for the RSPCA. A police search of his house had uncovered a red-and-black rucksack, still with an airline baggage tag attached with GRADY printed on it. Results were eagerly awaited for a DNA test of blood spots discovered on the sleeve of a grey hoodie from Mr Williams's wardrobe and consistent with my description of the Ascot attacker's clothes. And a further search of the mangled remains of his car had uncovered a kitchen knife of the correct proportions to have inflicted the fatal wounds to my father's abdomen.

I chose not to ask the chief inspector if they had also found the remote control to my television, although I could really have done with it back.

'So what happens now?' I'd asked instead.

'That depends on if, and how well, Mr Williams recovers,' the chief inspector had said. 'He's been formally arrested on suspicion of murder, but the doctors are saying he has massive brain damage, so he'll probably never be fit to plead, even if he survives.'

'What does that mean?' I'd asked.

'If he's unfit to plead, there would be no criminal trial as such. But there would be what is called a trial of the facts, when the evidence is placed before a jury and they effectively decide if he had done it or not. He'd technically be a free man, but if he recovers enough so that he becomes fit, he could still be tried for murder. There doesn't seem to be much doubt that he was the man responsible, and the DNA should prove it.'

'So is that it?' I'd said.

'For the moment,' the chief inspector had replied cautiously. 'But I still have a niggling feeling you haven't told me the whole truth.'

He was, I supposed, quite a good detective really.

THANKS TO THE NEARLY £600,000 generosity of Mr Henry Richard Feldman, Sophie and I travelled in Club Class, from London to Sydney on a British Airways jumbo jet, sipping vintage champagne for most of the way.

It had taken a little while for Tony Bateman (Turf Accountants) Ltd to pay out on the juvenile delinquents' bets, but they had been persuaded by HRF Holdings Ltd, their parent company, to see sense in the end.

Only two of the thirty delinquents had failed to make the bet, having pocketed the £200 stake instead. They were now ruing their mistake to the tune of 4,800 smackers.

Duggie and Luca had given a portion of their own winnings to refit the electronics club with some new equipment, and I'd spent a couple of thousand of mine on some new dining chairs for the mental-hospital grand salon.

The source of all our riches, the horse Oriental Suite, now running as Cricket Hero, had raced twice more since Bangor-on-Dee, winning easily on both occasions, but at starting prices far shorter than our hundred-to-one bonanza of July. His trainer, Miles Carpenter, also known as Mr Paddy Murphy, had stated in a television interview that he hoped the horse would win at the Cheltenham Steeplechase Festival the following March.

However, according to reports in the *Racing Post* in early December, Cricket Hero had suffered a massive heart attack at home on the gallops and had dropped down, stone dead. 'Just one of those things,' the paper had said. 'Sadly, it happens all too often in racing.'

I, meanwhile, wondered if it had actually been that particular horse that had died, and whether or not he'd been insured for a small fortune.

SOPHIE AND I landed in Sydney at six in the morning on a glorious January southern-hemisphere summer's day, just as the sun began to peep over the horizon to the east. I had a wonderful view of the city as we approached from the north, with the still-dark Sydney Harbour Bridge spanning a ribbon of early light reflected from the water beneath.

We spent the first few days in Sydney, getting over jet lag and doing the things all tourists do. Courtesy of Tony Bateman, we stayed in a magnificent five-star hotel overlooking the busy harbour. After three days of dawn-to-dusk tourism, including climbing to the very top of the Harbour Bridge, Sophie and I were exhausted, and our sore feet were grateful for the short breather as we flew the hour or so to Melbourne.

Before we'd left England, I had engaged a private detective to help in the search for my sisters and he was waiting for us at the airport.

'Lachlan Harris?' I asked a young man holding up a TALBOT sign at the baggage claim.

'Sure am,' he said. 'But call me Lachie.' He was short, about thirty, with a well-bronzed face and spiky fairish hair, with highlights.

'Ned Talbot,' I said, shaking his hand. 'And this is my wife, Sophie.'

'G'day,' he said in typical Australian fashion. 'Good to meet you both.'

'Any news?' I asked eagerly. I had purposely not called him from Sydney, although at times I had been desperate to do so.

'Yes,' he said. 'As a matter of fact I have some good news for you. But let's get out of the airport first. I'm taking you to see your father's house.' And, with that, he picked up our suitcases and turned for the exit.

We followed, but I was rather frustrated by his lack of explanation.

'All in good time,' he said when we were in his car, leaving the airport.

'But what's the news?' I asked him again.

'I've found the two daughters of Mr Alan Grady,' he said.

'My sisters,' I said, all excited like a young child on Christmas morning. 'When can I meet them?'

'There's a slight problem,' he said.

'What problem?'

'They don't believe you're their brother.'

'What?' I cried. It wasn't something that I had even considered.

'They say they have documentary evidence that shows their father, Alan Charles Grady, was born in Melbourne in March 1948. I've checked with the State of Victoria records office,' Lachie said. 'Alan Charles Grady was indeed born in the Royal Melbourne Hospital on March the 15th, 1948. I have a copy of his birth certificate.' He handed me a folded sheet of paper.

Mr John Smith, or whoever he was, had told me in my car near Stratford, that my father's 'Alan Grady' birth certificate had been genuine, but I hadn't really believed him.

'My father must have stolen the identity of the real Alan Grady,' I said.

'I've checked in the register of deaths,' Lachie said. 'No one called Alan Charles Grady who had that birthday has been recorded as dying.'

'Perhaps he died somewhere else, not in Australia. Maybe on the ship where my father worked.' I looked at the birth certificate. Both of Alan Grady's parents were named, together with their addresses and occupations. 'How about these parents shown on the certificate?' I asked.

'Both dead,' said Lachie. 'I checked. It seems they both died in the swine flu epidemic that struck Melbourne in 1976. They were in their seventies.'

'Did they have any other children?' I asked him.

'None that I could find.'

'So where does that leave me?' I asked, somewhat deflated.

'I didn't say the Grady daughters wouldn't meet you,' he said. 'Simply that they don't accept that you are their brother.'

'Oh,' I said. 'That's all right, then. I'll just have to convince them.'

Lachie Harris drove Sophie and me to Macpherson Street, in Carlton North, and pulled up outside number 312.

It was the middle property of a terrace row of single-storey houses, all with verandahs and elaborate wrought-iron railings.

'These houses are known as Boom Homes, because they were built during the boom time of the nineteenth century, after the gold rush of the 1850s.'

'They're very pretty,' Sophie said.

'Can we see?' I asked. 'I've got the keys.' I showed him the ring and the three keys that had been in my father's rucksack.

'Ah,' said Lachie apologetically. 'I'm afraid we can't.'

'Why?' I asked. 'I am his son.'

'His daughters have taken out an injunction to prevent you from entering the property.'

'They've done what!' I was astounded.

'Sorry,' said Lachie. 'These types of property are worth quite a lot these days, and the Grady daughters believe that you're only here because you're after their inheritance.'

I sat there with my mouth open.

'I don't want money,' I said, exasperated. 'I want family.'

'Nevertheless,' Lachie went on, 'this whole business is going to be a legal can of worms. Alan Grady left a will and, as we all know, where there's a will there's a disgruntled relative.' He laughed at his little joke.

'But if there's a wil,l, then what's the problem?' I said. 'Surely he would have left everything to them anyway.'

'The will is in the name of Alan Charles Grady,' Lachie said, 'and, according to the registry here, he's not dead. You, meanwhile, claim that the man who owned this house was your father, a Peter James Talbot, now deceased, but it doesn't say that on the property deeds.'

I peered at the house, dark behind the lacy ironwork. The earlier excitement of my arrival in Australia had evaporated completely. I felt dejected and lost. 'So what's next?' I asked miserably.

'Well, let's look on the bright side,' he said. 'The Grady girls have agreed to meet you and I've set up the meeting for tomorrow. It's Australia Day and we're going to meet them at Hanging Rock Races tomorrow afternoon.'

'What are their names?' I asked.

'Patricia and Shannon. Patricia's the elder. She's twenty-nine. Shannon is two years younger.'

I was astounded. My much maligned, but innocent, father had named his first Australian daughter after his murdered English wife.

LACHIE PICKED UP Sophie and me from our hotel at eleven o'clock the following morning and drove us the hour and a half northwest from the city to Hanging Rock Races.

'Why exactly are we meeting my sisters up here?' I asked.

'They live up this way.' It seemed like a good reason.

'How many meetings do they have a year at Hanging Rock?' I asked.

'They race only two days. New Year's Day and Australia Day. It's country racing. Quite small. It's not like Flemington.' Flemington was where the Melbourne Cup was held each November.

Hanging Rock Racecourse was, indeed, no Flemington, nor a Royal Ascot either. But it was lively and bustling with people on their Australia Day out.

The racecourse was dominated, as its name might suggest, by the hanging and other rocks of a 500-foot-high volcanic outcrop behind the enclosures. It was a delightful setting, with great elm trees providing shade for the punters as they gathered round the bookmakers. Gambling was gambling, the same on both sides of the globe.

Lachie had obviously spun some yarn to the Hanging Rock Racing Club, because we were met at the entrance by a small delegation.

'Welcome to Hanging Rock Races,' said Anthony, the club chairman, shaking my hand. 'Always a pleasure to welcome a fellow racing enthusiast from England.'

'Thank you,' I said, shaking his hand back and feeling a bit of a fraud.

And they had laid on lunch for us in one of the hospitality marquees.

'What on earth did you tell them?' I asked Lachie in a quiet moment.

'I told them that you ran one of the biggest bookmaking firms in the UK and were looking to possibly expand over here.' He smiled broadly. 'It got us a free lunch, didn't it?'

The lunch was excellent and would have easily rivalled anything served at Royal Ascot. We were at a table laid for ten that included the club dignitaries as well as the chairman, who was seated on the far side of Sophie. I, meanwhile, had been placed next to an official from the Australian Racing Board

174 | DICK FRANCIS AND FELIX FRANCIS

who, I discovered during the meal, was the head of their security service.

'I wouldn't have thought there was enough skulduggery going on here to warrant the presence of the head honcho,' I said, smiling at him.

'I hope you're right,' he said. 'But I have a holiday home just down the road and I'm here simply to enjoy myself today.' He took a swig of his beer.

'Busman's holiday?' I said.

'Exactly.'

We ate in silence for a while.

'Do you have any undercover staff in the security service?' I asked him quietly, while the others were deep in conversation.

'A few,' he said, draining his beer glass.

'How about an Englishman?' I asked. 'Someone called John Smith?'

He smiled. 'There are lots of Englishmen called John Smith.'

'This particular one was interested in something called a microcoder.'

The smile disappeared from his face, but only for an instant. He stood up from the table, and said, 'Anyone for another beer?'

'Lovely idea,' I said, also standing up.

We walked together down to the bar at the end of the marquee.

'What do you know about a microcoder?' he asked me intently. The busman's holiday was over. This was now a workday after all.

'That it's used to write fake RFID chips.'

'Oh God,' he said, clearly disturbed. 'Do you know where it is?'

'Not any more,' I said. 'I gave it to this Mr John Smith.'

I could tell that the head of Australian racing security wasn't pleased to hear that. Not one bit. 'For God's sake, why did you give it to him?'

'Because he told me he worked for you,' I said in my defence. 'But he also told me you'd deny it.'

'I do deny it,' said the security man. 'If he's the person I think he is, then he did use to work for us. At least, we thought he did, but about a year ago we began to suspect he'd been abusing his position by investigating only those people who wouldn't pay him handsomely to overlook things. There probably wouldn't have been enough evidence to win a court case, but we fired him nevertheless. We've since discovered he was involved in a group that was switching horses using fake ID chips. Horses were being killed.'

'For the insurance money?' I asked.

'Yes,' he said, surprised that I knew. 'Some illegal off-course bookmakers were also involved in the scam.'

I decided that it would not really be a good time to tell him that my father had been one of those illegal bookmakers.

'We feared he was up to the same tricks back in the UK,' the security man said. 'And now you've just confirmed it.'

'What's his real name?' I asked.

He was clearly reluctant to tell me. 'We're still investigating the affair and are trying to recover the device before it's used again.'

'I wouldn't bother if I were you,' I said.

'Why on earth not?' he demanded somewhat crossly.

'The microcoder doesn't work any more,' I said, smiling. 'I made some significant and incurable alterations to its circuitry before I gave it away.'

'But why?' he asked.

'Because I didn't altogether trust Mr John Smith.'

The head of Australian racing security thought for a moment and then smiled back. 'You mean, you didn't altogether trust Mr Ivan Feldman.'

'Ivan Feldman,' I repeated slowly. So that was his real name. 'I wonder if he's any relation to Henry Richard Feldman of HRF Holdings Ltd.'

I decided that he probably was.

MY SISTERS were to join us in the marquee for afternoon tea, and Lachie went away after lunch to collect them. Presently, I saw him waiting in the doorway. Most of the official party had left by this time, gone off to do other things like watch the races, make presentations to the winners, or chase the kangaroos away from the finishing straight.

I waved Lachie in, and he was followed closely by two young women, both of them with brown hair and high cheekbones, just like me.

I didn't need to convince them that I was their brother. They both knew instantly that it was true. The three of us looked so much alike. Introductions weren't necessary. We simply hugged one another and cried.

Finally, I managed to introduce them to Sophie, who was also in tears.

'Ned has always wanted sisters,' she said to them, wiping her eyes.

I was simply too overcome with emotion to say anything.

Sophie turned to me. 'And they're going to be aunties as well,' she said, crying huge tears of joy. 'Because I'm pregnant.'

dick **francis** and felix **francis**

To find out more about the 'junior partner' in this hugely successful father-and-son writing partnership, we have turned the spotlight onto Dick Francis's son, Felix:

RD: Which was the first book you wrote with your father, and do you enjoy writing with him?

FF: The first book with both our names on the cover was *Dead Heat* in 2007, but I have been helping with the writing of the Dick Francis books for most of my life. I designed the bomb that was used to blow up an aircraft in *Rat Race* back in 1970 and I wrote the computer program in *Twice Shy* in 1981, as well as many other bits. I began to help more from *Under Orders* in 2006 and, yes, I do greatly enjoy it.

RD: As a boy, what were your interests and did they include horse riding?

FF: I rode most days when I was a young boy but I developed a serious hip problem when I was thirteen and I had to give up riding. However, my teenage passion wasn't horse racing, it was the space race. Yuri Gagarin became the first man in space when I was eight, and Neil Armstrong walked on the moon when I was sixteen. What magical years of pressing my ear to a crackly radio, or studying flickering black-and-white TV images.

RD: Where did you go to university and what did you study there?

FF: London University. I read Physics and Electronics.

RD: What career caught your imagination and did you pursue it?

FF: I always wanted to be a pilot and I learned to fly as soon as I was old enough. I flew solo before I drove myself alone in a car. But my hopes were dashed by my bad left hip. First the RAF turned me down, then British Airways, just before my finals. It was a devastating blow, but I picked myself up and went into teaching, mostly because I saw a notice on the university physics department notice board asking for physics teachers. I thought I would do it for a short while, but I loved it and went on teaching for seventeen years.

RD: How was your own interest in physics sparked?

FF: I was always interested in how things worked and that developed into a passion for physics. It is the study of the great invisibilities of life—electricity, magnetism, radiation, gravity, sound—forces and energy, in other words. To understand physics one needs imagination, something that also helps in writing. The subject is full of enigmas.

RD: What made you decide to become your father's full-time manager? And did you miss teaching after you took on this role?

FF: I started helping my father soon after he'd moved to the United States in 1986. My mother was very concerned that he was struggling with his US tax return and she asked me to help. For the next five years I spent my school holidays and half-terms going to Florida to help him with his finances. Eventually, I was spending so much time helping him that I was worried I might be neglecting my day job, so I gave up teaching to become his manager and to help both my parents. I did miss teaching but, in truth, after seventeen years I was looking for a change in direction. I did not give up contact completely with young people as I became deputy chairman of World Challenge Expeditions Ltd, one of the largest youth leadership training companies in the UK, a role I retained until 2005.

RD: Do you have children of your own?

FF: I have two sons of my own as well as two stepchildren, a boy and a girl. The eldest is now thirty and the youngest nearly eighteen. I love them all. *Even Money* is dedicated to my son Matthew, who will marry his Australian fiancée in Melbourne in October, and to William on his passing out of the Royal Military Academy, Sandhurst. I am so proud of them both.

RD: To achieve the harmony you have when writing with your father, you clearly get on with him very well. Do you manage to enjoy free time together?

FF: The whole family—some thirty-five of us—stay in the same hotel in south Devon for a week over the first weekend in August every year. My father absolutely loves it and he lives the whole year just for that time together. We have been going to the same place every summer since I was born and we never get bored with it. I have been so lucky in life that my father and I get on so well. We never row—just as long as he does what I say!

RD: In *Even Money* there's a lot of information about bookmakers and betting. Have either you or your father ever had any big wins on the Tote?

FF: I don't bet on horses, except perhaps a small wager if I am in a group of friends at the races. I don't think my father has ever bet much although he did win a big sweepstake on the Epsom Derby in 1964. I remember that the win paid for a new carpet in the living room.

RD: Do you have a favourite bolthole, a place to go where you can relax?

FF: No. All I need to relax is a large glass of red wine and a comfy chair.

RD: Have you got any special hopes and dreams for the future?

FF: To go on writing the 'Dick Francis' books for at least another ten years.

RD: What advice would you give to a teenage son about how to build a good relationship with his father?

FF: I think the best advice I can give is to have a dad like mine. Then it's easy!

THE SIGN

RAYMOND KHOURY

When a mysterious apparition forms in the skies over the South Pole, directly above a spot where the polar ice-shelf is crumbling as a result of global warming, millions watch on TV screens across the globe, spellbound.

What does the sign herald? Is it an earthly phenomenon, or something supernatural?

Either way, anchorwoman Gracie Logan and her film crew, stationed on a nearby ship, are ready to run with this breaking news story . . . wherever in the world it may take them.

Skeleton Coast, Namibia—two years previously
As the bottom of the ravine rushed up to meet him, the dry, rocky landscape hurtling past Danny Sherwood miraculously slowed right down to a crawl. Not that the extra time was welcome. All it did was allow the realisation to play itself out, over and over, in his mind that he would be dead in a matter of seconds.

And yet the day had started off with so much promise. After almost three years, his work—and the rest of the team's—was finally done. It had been a hard slog. The project, which he'd been told was being developed for the military, had been daunting from a scientific point of view, but the tight deadline, the security, the virtual exile from family and friends for all those lonely months were even more of a challenge. Today, though, as he had looked up at the pure blue sky and breathed in the dry, dusty air of this godforsaken corner of the planet, it had all seemed worthwhile. A significant on-success bonus had been promised to every member of the team. In his case it was enough to provide financial security for him, his parents and for any wife he might end up with. For the moment, though, a wife wasn't on his radar. He was only twenty-nine years old.

Danny wished he'd been allowed to share the excitement of it all with a few people outside the project. He could just imagine how proud his parents would be. His older brother, Matt, would get a huge kick out of it. There were also a few in the business he would have loved to gloat to, but he knew that any disclosure was strictly not allowed. The project was covert. The nation's defence was at stake. The word *treason* had been mentioned. And so he'd kept his mouth shut. When it came down to it, the choice between an eight-figure bank account and a cell in a federal penitentiary was a no-brainer.

That morning, as he was about to knock on the project director's rigid-wall tent, he heard angry voices inside it that made him pull his hand back.

'You should have told me. It's my project, goddamnit.'

Danny knew that voice well: Dominic Reece, his mentor, and the project's lead scientist. A professor of electrical engineering and computer science at MIT, Reece occupied hallowed ground in Danny's world.

'What would your reaction have been?' The second man's voice, which wasn't familiar to Danny, was inflamed.

'The same,' Reece replied emphatically. 'I can't help you do this. I can't be a party to it.'

'Dom, please . . . think about what we can—'

'Forget it,' Reece interrupted. 'There's no way.'

Danny heard the second man say, 'I wish you hadn't said that.'

'What the hell does that mean?' Reece shot back. There was no reply. 'What about the others? When were you planning on letting them in on your revised mission statement?'

'I was hoping you'd help me win them over.'

'Well that's not going to happen,' Reece retorted angrily. 'As a matter of fact, I'd like to get them all the hell away from here as soon as possible.'

'I can't let you do that, Dom.'

'What are you saying? You're not going to . . .' Reece's voice trailed off for a beat, then came back with added urgency. 'Jesus. Have you lost your mind?'

The outrage in his mentor's tone froze Danny's spine. He heard the second man call out to Reece, 'Dom, don't,' then a third voice said, 'Don't do that, Reece.' It was the voice of a man who'd creeped Danny out from the moment he'd first met him: Maddox, the project's stony-faced head of security, the one with the missing ear and the star-shaped burn around it, the man nicknamed 'The Bullet' by his equally creepy men. Then he heard Reece say, 'Go to hell,' and the door to the tent swung open, and Reece was suddenly there. Danny heard a distinctive, metallic sound he'd heard in a hundred movies, the sound of a gun slide, and the second man, whom Danny now recognised, turned to Maddox and yelled, 'No . . .'

A muffled cough echoed from behind Reece, then another, before the scientist jerked forward, his legs giving way as he tumbled onto Danny.

Danny struggled to support the stricken Reece. A thick, dark-red liquid was gushing out of him, soaking Danny's arms and clothes. He couldn't hold him. Reece thudded heavily onto the ground, exposing the inside of the tent, the second man standing there, frozen in shock, next to Maddox, who held a gun. Its muzzle was now levelled straight at Danny.

Danny dived to one side as a couple of shots cleaved through the air, then he tore off. He was a dozen yards away when he glanced back and saw Maddox emerging from the tent, radio in one hand, gun in the other, bolting after him. Danny sprinted through the campsite, almost slamming into two other scientists, who were emerging from one of the tents.

'They killed Reece,' he yelled. 'They killed him.' Maddox was closing in. Danny took off again, glancing back to see crimson spouts erupting from his friends' chests as Maddox gunned them down.

He ducked behind the mess tent, his mind churning desperately for escape options, when he noticed the project's two ageing Jeeps. He flung the first car's door open, spurred the engine to life and stormed off in a spray of sand and dust just as Maddox rounded the tent.

Danny kept an eye on the rearview mirror as his Jeep charged away across the harsh gravel plain, all the while fighting for a way round the horrifying truth that there was nowhere to run. They were in the middle of nowhere—that was the whole point of being there.

A loud buzz burst through his frazzled thoughts. He looked back and saw the camp's chopper coming straight at him. He pegged the gas pedal to the floor, sending the Jeep bounding over the undulations of the outback.

The chopper was now on his tail, its rotor wash drowning the Jeep in a swirling sandstorm. Danny strained to see through the tornado of dust as the chopper dropped down heavily towards the car's roof. Danny veered left, then right, fishtailing the car as he fought to avoid the flying predator, the car careering wildly over rocks and cactus bushes. He was running on pure adrenaline, an irrational hope of escape propelling him forward.

Just then, he sensed the chopper pulling up slightly and the cloud of sand around his Jeep lifted—and that's when he saw the canyon dead ahead, a vast limestone trench snaking across the landscape like something from the Wild West. The Jeep flew off the canyon's edge and into the dry desert air.

Amundsen Sea, Antarctica—present day
The static that hissed through the tiny earpiece was replaced by the voice of the show's anchorman, Jack Roxberry. 'Talk us through why this is happening, Grace.'

Grace Logan—Gracie, to her friends—turned away from the camera

184 | RAYMOND KHOURY

and watched as a wall of ice plummeted into the grey-blue water.

Under normal circumstances, this would have been a pleasant, sunny, late-December day, but today nature was in turmoil. It felt as if the very fabric of the earth was being ripped apart. The slab of ice that was tearing itself from the rest of the continent measured thousands of square miles.

The cold was starting to get to Gracie, who'd been out for over an hour on the observation deck of the RRS *James Clark Ross*, a beefy three-hundred-foot floating oceanographic and geophysical laboratory operated by the British Antarctic Survey project. She could see that the rest of her team—Dalton Kwan, the young Hawaiian cameraman, and Howard 'Finch' Fincher, their veteran producer—were also far from comfortable, but the footage they were airing was worth it, especially since theirs was the only news crew around.

Gracie had been on the continent for a couple of weeks, shooting footage in the Terra Firma Islands for her big global-warming documentary. They had been ready to head home for Christmas when the news desk back in Washington, DC, had informed them that the ice shelf's breakup had started. Gracie and her crew had jumped at the opportunity for an exclusive. The BAS had agreed to have them on board to cover the event.

Gracie turned back to the camera. 'Jack, this breakup was probably caused by a number of factors, but the main suspect is meltwater, pools of water that build up on the surface of the ice. This meltwater is heavier than the ice it's sitting on, so—basic law of gravity—it finds its way down into the cracks and acts like a wedge. If there's enough meltwater to keep pushing through, the ice shelf eventually just snaps off.'

There had been a handful of major ice-shelf breakups in the past decade, but none this big. Also, they were rarely captured live on camera. In twelve years in television news, Gracie had witnessed a lot of tragedies, but now she was watching the planet fall apart—literally.

'Why is it happening now?' the anchorman asked.

'Because of us, Jack. Because of the greenhouse gases we're generating. We're seeing it at both poles and it isn't just part of a natural cycle. Almost every expert I've talked to is convinced we're close to a point of no return—because of man-made global warming. Until now, ice shelves like this one have been keeping back the glaciers, like a cork holding in the contents of a bottle. Once the ice shelf breaks off, there's nothing left to stop the glaciers from sliding into the sea—and, if they do, the global sea levels rise.

This melting is happening much faster than forecasts had predicted . . .'

Her voice suddenly trailed off as something distracted her: a ripple of sudden commotion, shrieks and gasps and outstretched arms pointing out at the ice shelf. She saw the cameraman Dalton's head rise from the camera and look beyond her. Gracie spun around and that's when she saw it. A shimmering sphere of light a couple of hundred feet above the ice. It had a spherical shape, but it didn't seem . . . physical. It had an unstable, fragile quality to it, like water suspended in midair and lit up, if that were possible. Only, Gracie knew it wasn't.

She darted a look at Dalton, who was angling the camera towards the sighting. 'Are you getting this?'

'Yeah, but what the hell is it?'

'I don't know.' A surge of adrenaline spiked through her as she struggled to process what she was seeing.

She glanced at the knot of scientists crowding the railings. They were talking and gesticulating excitedly, trying to make sense of it too.

'What is that?' Anchorman Jack Roxberry's voice boomed through her earpiece.

For a second, she'd forgotten this was going out live. She faced the camera. 'I don't know, Jack. It just suddenly appeared. It seems to be some kind of corona.'

She scanned the sky. Nothing else was out there apart from their ship and the . . . what *was* it? Its texture reminded her of a gargantuan jellyfish, floating in midair, rotating. It looked . . . alive.

She focused her mind on getting a handle on its size, making a comparison with the height of the cliff face below. It seemed to be around a hundred and fifty feet in diameter, maybe more.

Dalton asked, 'You think it's some freaky aurora borealis thing?'

She'd been thinking the same thing, wondering if it was an illusion caused by a reflection off the ice. In Antarctica, the sun never set during the summer and it played tricks on you, but somehow Gracie didn't think that explained what she was seeing. The corona seemed more substantial. 'Maybe,' she replied, almost to herself, lost in her thoughts, 'but I don't think it's the time of year for them. Maybe someone else on this ship knows what it is. We've got quite a few experts on board.'

Dalton lifted his tripod and camera, and followed Gracie as she edged over to the scientists and crew members on deck, who were discussing the shape in excited, heated tones. Gracie got the impression that they weren't comfortable with what they were seeing.

She was about to speak when a wave of gasps broke out across the deck. She turned in time to see the shape suddenly pulse, brightening up to a blazing radiance before dimming back to its original pearlescent glare.

Roxberry's excited voice crackled. 'Did it just flare up?'

'Jack, I don't know how clearly it's coming through to you, but it's not like anything I've seen before.' Her heart was racing.

She turned to the producer, Finch. 'Can you get the bird up?'

Finch nodded. 'Let's do it.'

'We're sending the Skycam up for a closer look,' Gracie confirmed into her mike, then clicked it off. 'Tell me you know what this is,' she asked Jeb Simmons, a palaeoclimatologist she'd met on arrival.

Simmons shook his head. 'I'm stumped.'

A few of the others congregated around them, equally bewildered. She darted a look behind them. Finch had the Skycam's arms clicked into place while Dalton was double-checking the second camera's harness. She noticed the captain coming out on deck. Two crew members hurried to join him.

Dalton shouted, 'We've got liftoff,' over the whirr of the Skycam's rotor blades.

The Draganflyer X6 was an odd-looking but brilliant piece of engineering. It looked like a matt-black alien insect, and consisted of a central pod the size of a large mango that housed the electronics, gyroscopes and battery. Three small collapsible arms extended out from it horizontally. At the end of each arm was a motor driving two parallel sets of rotor blades. Any type of camera could be fitted to the rig under its belly. The Draganflyer weighed less than five pounds and gave great aerial shots.

Gracie was watching the contraption glide away towards the ice shelf, when a female voice yelled out, 'Oh my God,' and Gracie saw it too.

The shape was changing. It shrank until it was barely a tenth of its original size, then slowly flared back to the way it had been. And then its surface seemed to ripple, as if it was morphing into something else.

The second it started changing, something deep within Gracie knotted. The sighting had clearly come alive. It was shape-shifting, taking on different compositions and melting from one to another at a dazzling rate. Gracie felt a deeply unsettling sensation, as if she were staring at the very fabric of life itself.

The small gathering froze. A range of emotion, from awe and wonder to confusion and fear, was etched across their faces. Two people—an older man and woman—crossed themselves.

Dalton was holding the Skycam's remote-control unit at waist level, his fingers expertly controlling both joysticks.

She caught his gaze. 'Jesus, Dalton. What's going on?'

He looked up at the sighting. 'I don't know.'

She heard a few gasps, and someone said, 'It's slowing down.'

The brighter zones of the sphere were consumed by a darkness that spread until the sphere's entire surface looked blackened and coarse, as if it had been carved from a lump of coal. A ripple of terror spread among the crowd. In the blink of an eye, the apparition had gone from being strangely wonderful to sinister and lifeless.

Finch moved close to Gracie, both of them riveted by the ominous sight. 'This isn't good,' he said.

Gracie didn't reply. She glanced down at the Skycam's control box. The image on its LCD monitor was clear. With the Draganflyer now more than halfway to the shelf, Gracie was able to get more of a sense of scale. The apparition dwarfed the approaching flying camera, like an elephant looming over an ant. It held the dark, lifeless skin it had assumed for a minute or so, then the sphere flared up again, burning brightly. It now looked unquestionably three-dimensional. At its core was a bright ball of light and around it were four equal rings, evenly spaced. Rays of light were projecting outwards from the core.

The sight electrified the crowd and brought some of them to tears. The couple who had crossed themselves were holding each other close. Gracie could see their lips trembling in silent prayer. She felt a confusing surge of euphoria and fear, which seemed to be echoed in the faces around her.

She held the mike up and faced the camera again. 'I hope you're still getting this, Jack, because everyone here is just stunned.'

The Skycam was closing in on the apparition. 'How far from it do you think it is?' she asked Dalton.

'A hundred yards. Maybe less.'

Gracie couldn't take her eyes off of it. 'It's just magnificent, isn't it?'

'It's a sign,' someone said. It was the woman Gracie had noticed crossing herself. Dalton panned over to her.

'A sign? Of what?' another asked.

'I don't know, but . . . she's right. Look at it. It's a sign of . . . something.' It was the older man with her. Gracie remembered being introduced. He was an American glaciologist, Greg Musgrave, and the woman was his wife.

Musgrave turned to Gracie, waving towards the Skycam. 'Don't send that *thing* any farther. Stop it before it gets too close.'

'Why?' Dalton was incredulous. 'It can help us figure out what it is.'

'I'm telling you, pull it back,' Musgrave said, reaching out to grab the remote-control console.

'Hey,' Gracie yelled at him, just as Finch and the captain stepped in to restrain Musgrave.

'Calm down,' the captain snapped at Musgrave. 'He's going to pull it back before it reaches it,' then, to Dalton, 'aren't you?'

'Absolutely,' Dalton replied. He checked out the monitor, as did Gracie. The Skycam was very close to the apparition, which now filled the screen.

'You shouldn't be messing with it before we know what we're dealing with,' Musgrave blurted out sharply. Dalton ignored him and the Skycam glided on. It seemed tantalisingly close now, perhaps fifty feet or less, when the sign suddenly dimmed right down and disappeared.

The crowd heaved a collective gasp.

'You see that? I told you,' Musgrave rasped.

'What, you think I scared it?' Dalton fired back angrily.

'We don't know. But it was there for a reason, and now it's gone.' The scientist put an arm round his wife, dismay clouding their faces.

'Get real, man,' Dalton shrugged, turning away.

Over the shelf, the Draganflyer continued on its trajectory through the air that the apparition had occupied. Dalton slid a glance at Gracie. He looked thoroughly spooked. Gracie had never seen him react that way and they'd been through some pretty gut-wrenching times together.

She peered out into the sky. There was no trace of the sign. It was as if it had never happened. And then, all of a sudden, Gracie felt a momentous weight above her and looked up to see the massive ball of shimmering light hovering over the ship itself. She flinched as the crowd gasped and Dalton pounced on the main camera to try and get it on film. Gracie just stood there, staring up at it in complete bewilderment, fear and wonder, every hair on her body standing rigid for a brief moment that felt like an eternity.

And then, suddenly, the sign faded out, vanishing as inexplicably as it had appeared.

Bir Hooker, Egypt

Yusuf Zacharia glanced at his watch. It was time to head home. The wiry old taxi driver was pushing himself to his feet when the TV set on a rickety shelf behind the counter of the small café caught his eye. At this hour, in the small village of Bir Hooker, at the sleepy edge of the Egyptian desert, the TVs were all tuned to some news programme or other.

The screen showed a woman in heavy winter gear reporting from one of the poles. Behind her, something shone in the sky. Something bizarre and otherworldly. It was just floating there over a collapsing cliff of ice.

The scene was surreal, unimaginable, only that wasn't what disturbed Yusuf most. What really troubled him was that he'd seen the sign before.

He edged forward for a closer look. His mouth dropped by an inch, his skin tingled with trepidation. The camera cut to another angle and, this time, the illuminated symbol took over the whole screen.

It was the same sign! There was no doubt in his mind. Unconsciously, he crossed himself.

He rushed out of the café, clambered into his old Toyota and churned its engine to life. Yusuf rode the pedal hard, rushing back to the monastery as quickly as he could, muttering the same phrase to himself, over and over and over. *It can't be.*

Cambridge, Massachusetts

The crowd massed outside a window display of the latest plasmas and LCDs caught Vince Bellinger's eye as he ambled across the mall in Cambridge, Massachusetts. Some people were talking animatedly on their cellphones, others were waving friends over to join them. Bellinger veered towards the store, wondering what all the fuss was about.

He peered over the heads and shoulders. As usual, the screens were all tuned to the same channel, in this case a news network. He didn't quite understand what he was looking at—a spherical light hovering over one of the polar regions. He was watching with curiosity when his cellphone trilled. He fished it out of his pocket.

'Dude, where are you? I just tried your land line.' Csaba—whose name was pronounced *Tchaba*, but who was more often nicknamed 'Jabba'—sounded excited. Which wasn't unusual. The big guy had a hearty appetite for life. 'Put the news on, quick. You're not gonna believe this.' A brilliant chemical engineer of Hungarian extraction who worked with Bellinger at the Rowland Materials Research Laboratory, Jabba Komlosy had a passion for all things televisual.

Bellinger couldn't resist a little dig. 'Since when do you watch the news?'

'Would you stop with the inquisition and put the damn thing on,' Jabba protested.

'I'm looking at it right now. I'm at the mall, outside Best Buy.' Bellinger's voice trailed off as some heads in front of him shifted and he caught sight of a banner at the bottom of screen, which read, UNEXPLAINED PHENOMENON OVER ANTARCTICA. He recognised the reporter. He'd caught some of her specials over the years and remembered her: Grace Logan with the unforgiving green eyes, the earnest voice and the blonde curls.

Bellinger's eyes, though, weren't on her. The camera zoomed in on the phenomenon again, sending an audible shiver through the crowd.

'Dude, it's unreal,' Jabba exclaimed. 'I can't take my eyes off the screen.'

'Where is this exactly?'

'West Antarctic Ice Sheet. They're on some research ship off the coast.'

'How long has it been up?' Bellinger asked.

'About ten minutes. It came on out of the blue while la Logan was yapping about the breakup of the ice shelf. First it was like this ball of light, then it morphed into a dark sphere. Totally creeped me out.'

'Then it turned into this?'

'Yep. What do you think?'

'I don't know,' Bellinger answered, as if in a daze. The crowd oohed as an airborne camera gave a closer look at the unexplained apparition. 'How are they doing this?' he asked. As a scientist, his mind was instinctively sceptical and he was immediately trying to figure out ways it could be done.

Jabba was obviously thinking along the same lines. 'Must be some kind of laser effect.'

'No way,' Bellinger countered. 'You'd need a generator the size of an aircraft carrier sitting right under it for something this big. Plus it wouldn't explain the sustained brilliance or the way it's so clearly defined.'

'What about other kinds of projections? Spectral imagery?'

Bellinger stared at the screen. 'I don't think 3D projectors actually exist.' Which was true. Something that could achieve a free-floating, uncontained, three-dimensional, moving image still eluded the best brains in the business.

'Besides, it's daylight.' Bellinger added. 'Not exactly projector-friendly.'

'Nope,' said Jabba.

'OK, so we can forget about lasers and projectors,' Bellinger said.

'Unless there are a couple of monster mirrors on either side of it they're not showing us,' Jabba mused. 'Hey, maybe it's generated from space.'

'Nice idea, but how exactly?'

'I don't know, dude. I mean, this thing doesn't compute, does it?'

Bellinger and Jabba bounced around several other ideas, trying to pin down some plausible explanation, but nothing stuck. Bellinger's excitement soon gave way to a sense of unease. Something was bothering him.

Suddenly, the camera image jarred as an altercation took place on the ship's deck. Then the aerial camera closed in on the apparition, which faded away, only to reappear directly over the ship. The crowd around Bellinger recoiled in shock.

'It's spherical,' Bellinger marvelled. 'It's not some kind of projection. It's actually physical, isn't it?'

'I think you're right. But how . . . ? It's almost like the air itself is burning up, but . . . that's not possible, is it? I mean, you can't light up air, can you?'

Bellinger felt a sudden rush of blood to his temples. Something clicked, rushed in on him out of nowhere and made a connection.

An unhappy one. He went silent.

'Dude, you there? What? What're you thinking?'

'I've got to go. I'll call you when I get home.'

'Dude, hang on, don't just—'

Bellinger hung up. He stood there, contemplating the disturbing idea that had clawed its way out from the darkest recesses of his mind. No way, he thought. Be serious. Finally he tore himself away from the screens and drove home.

He got himself a beer and switched on his TV. The images it threw back at him were spine-tingling. Snarled traffic in Times Square, people in bars and stadiums, their eyes peeled, focused on the screens; and similar chaotic images from around the world. He fired up his laptop and spent a couple of hours scouring Internet chat rooms while flicking around various news reports, trying to get a clearer picture of what was going on, hoping to come across some ammo to dismiss his theory.

It was insane, outlandish . . . but it did fit. It did just fit.

Which brought up an even bigger problem: what to do about it.

His instinct told him to forget it. If what he was imagining was really happening, then he'd be far better off expunging the thought from his mind and never mentioning it to anyone. But a friend had died. His best friend. And that was hard to ignore.

Visions of the tragic accident on the Skeleton Coast two years ago sparked in his mind's eye, images his imagination had conjured up long ago, after he'd been told how Danny Sherwood had died.

He couldn't ignore it. He retrieved his phone and scrolled down his contacts list until he found the entry he was looking for, a number he hadn't called for almost two years. He hesitated, then hit the call button.

'Who's this?' Matt Sherwood's voice had a detached, no-nonsense ring to it. It brought Bellinger a modicum of solace. A palpable connection, however fleeting, to his long-dead friend.

'It's Vince. Vince Bellinger,' he answered. He paused, then added, 'I need to see you, man. Like, now.'

Boston, Massachusetts

No one in the crowded arena could tear their eyes away from the huge video scoreboards. And certainly no one watching the basketball game from Larry Rydell's perfectly positioned luxury suite at the Boston Globe sports arena.

His guests, the design team working on the ground-breaking electric car he hoped to launch within a couple of years, had been enjoying the treat. The car was just one of several world-beating pet projects he had running. He had teams working on more efficient wind farms, solar cells and better wiring to ferry the resulting power around. Renewable energy and clean power were going to be the next great industrial revolution, and Larry Rydell was nothing if not visionary.

The only resource his projects fought over was his time. Money certainly wasn't an issue, even with the recent turmoil in the markets. He was well aware of the fact that he had more of it than he'd ever need. Every computer and cellphone user on the planet had contributed his or her share to Rydell's fortune. But although Rydell enjoyed the good life, he'd found better things to do with his money than build himself five-hundred-foot yachts.

They'd just heard the first-period buzzer go, when the screens had flicked over to a live news feed and all noise had drained out of the arena.

As Rydell stood there, mesmerised by the surreal display before him, he felt his BlackBerry vibrate in his pocket. His nineteen-year-old daughter Rebecca was calling.

'Dad, are you watching this?'

'Yeah,' he replied, somewhat dazed. 'We're all standing here watching it like zombies.'

'Same here.' A friend in LA called to tell us about it.'

'Where are you anyway?'

'Mexico, Dad.'

At the family villa, he thought.

'Dad . . . what do you think it is?'

And, in what was probably a first for a man who was feted around the world as nothing less than a genius, Larry Rydell had no answer for his daughter. At least, not one that he could share with her.

Washington, DC

A light rain peppered the nation's capital as a black, chauffeur-driven Lexus slipped out of the underground garage into the late-evening traffic. Keenan Drucker stared out in silence, contemplating the events of the momentous day.

His mind chewed over his plan, once again dissecting it, looking for the fatal flaw that he might have missed, but he couldn't find anything. There were a lot of unknowns, but that didn't trouble him. A lifetime of making questionable deals in smoke-filled rooms had taught him that unknowns weren't worth worrying about until they materialised. His BlackBerry nudged him out of his reverie. The ring tone told him who it was.

The Bullet got straight to the point. 'I got a call from our friend at Meade. He got a hit. A phone call, between two of the peripherals on the watch list.'

Drucker mulled over the news. Brad Maddox—The Bullet—had suggested using one of his contacts inside the National Security Agency to monitor the airwaves for unexpected trouble. It looked like Maddox had made the right call. Which was why he was in charge of the project's security.

'Is it anything to worry about?' Drucker asked.

'It might be. The call was too brief to read either way, but its timing raises concerns. One of the peripherals is a techie in Boston, Vince Bellinger. He was Danny Sherwood's college room-mate. The other's Sherwood's brother, Matt. Last communication we have between them goes back almost two years.'

Drucker thought for a moment. Two years ago, these two connections to Danny Sherwood would have had a natural reason to chat. The timing of this new call, though, was troublesome. 'I take it you've got it under control?'

Maddox sounded detached. 'Just bringing you up to speed.'

'And the girl?'

'Waiting to be plucked.'

'You're going to need to handle that one with even more discretion,' Drucker cautioned. 'She's key.'

'My boys are ready. Just say the word.'

'It's imminent. Keep me posted on the room-mate.'

Drucker hung up. He looked out at the streaks of red and white light gliding past the wet car window, and played out the next moves in his mind.

It was a good start, but the hardest part was yet to come.

Amundsen Sea, Antarctica

They'd stayed on deck, scanning the skies, for about an hour after the apparition had vanished before heading inside for some warmth. Some crew members had stayed out on watch in case it reappeared, while Gracie and the others had crowded into the scientists' lounge and watched the footage from both of Dalton's cameras on a big plasma screen. Several viewings and countless cups of coffee later, they still weren't anywhere close to explaining what they'd witnessed.

The comfort of ascribing it to some spectacular but natural weather phenomenon was quickly dispelled. The obvious candidates—aurora australis, fogbows and green flashes—didn't fit the bill.

Looking around, Gracie could see that this group of qualified scientists had all been seriously shaken up by what they'd seen. If it wasn't natural, it was either man-made—or supernatural.

Dalton frowned. 'Maybe it's some goofballs messing with us.'

'You think it could be a prank?' Gracie asked.

'Remember those UFO sightings in New York a few years back? Turns out it was a bunch of guys flying some ultralights in formation.'

'On the other hand, no one's been able to explain the lights over Phoenix back in 1997,' Theo Dinnick, a geophysicist with a goatee, countered. The sighting he was referring to, witnessed by hundreds, remained unexplained.

'You're forgetting this was in broad daylight,' Gracie remarked.

Jeb Simmons, the palaeoclimatologist, nodded. 'If it's a prank, I want to meet the guys behind it and find out how the hell they pulled it off.'

Gracie glanced around the room. Her eyes settled on Greg Musgrave, the glaciologist who'd become testy, and his wife. They were not participating, clearly discomfited by the conversation.

Musgrave finally stood up. 'For God's sake, people. Let's be serious,' he announced. 'You really think something that . . . *sublime* . . . could just be a vulgar prank?'

'What do you think it is?' Simmons asked.

'Isn't it obvious? It's a sign from God.'

A leaden silence greeted his words.

'Why not aliens?' Dalton finally asked. 'That's the first thing that popped into my mind when I saw it.'

'Don't be ridiculous.' Musgrave didn't mask his contempt.

'Why is that more ridiculous than what you're suggesting?'

'Maybe it's a warning,' Musgrave's wife suggested. 'It appeared here, now, over this ice shelf, during the breakup. It can't be random. There's got to be a reason for it.'

'I'm guessing we're all pretty convinced that what we saw out there is *way* beyond any technological capability we know of,' Simmons put in. 'The fact that I can't explain it excites me and scares me in equal measure. If it didn't originate on this planet then it's either, as Greg says, God—or, as our friend here was saying, extraterrestrial. Frankly, either one would be just extraordinary, and I don't see that the difference really matters right now.'

'You don't see the difference?' Musgrave was incensed.

'I don't want to get into a big theological debate with you, Greg, but—'

'—but you obviously don't believe in God, even if you're presented with a miracle, so any debate is pointless.'

'That's not what I'm saying,' Simmons insisted. 'Look, if you're saying our maker has, for some reason, chosen to appear to us, here, today, then I've got to think He must have a damn good reason.'

'Half the West Antarctic Ice Shelf is slipping into the sea. You need more of a reason?' Musgrave's wife said, irritably.

'Why do you think we're here?' Musgrave added. 'Why are we all here?' His eyes darted feverishly around the room before settling on one of the British scientists. 'Justin, why are you here?'

'England's at the same latitude as Alaska,' the man replied. 'The only thing that makes it habitable is the Gulf Stream. Take that away—which is what happens if the ice melts—and that movie, the one with Manhattan swamped with ice and snow? That'll be London.'

'Exactly,' Musgrave insisted. 'We're all here because we're worried. All the signs are telling us that we've got one hell of a problem, and maybe this—this *miracle* is telling us we've got to do something about it.'

'OK,' Simmons conceded, 'all I'm saying is, if it's a warning . . . why couldn't it be coming from a more advanced intelligence?'

'I agree,' Theo Dinnick said. 'If we're talking about some entity making contact with us to warn us . . . if you accept the notion of a creator of intelligent design . . . why couldn't that intelligent designer be from a more advanced race?'

Musgrave's wife was clearly riled. 'It's pointless to discuss this with either of you. You're not open to the possibility.'

'On the contrary, I'm open to *all* possibilities,' Dinnick countered.

Musgrave was incensed. 'Believe what you will. I'm out of here.' He stormed off.

Musgrave's wife got up. 'I think we all know what we saw out there,' she said, before following her husband.

An uncomfortable silence smothered the room.

'I've got to say,' the British scientist finally offered, 'while I was out there, looking at it . . . there was something rather . . . *divine* about it.'

The honesty of his simple words struck Gracie, their significance chilling her. What they'd witnessed was beyond explanation. It was beyond reason. It would have been beyond belief if she hadn't seen it with her own eyes.

Her mind drifted to the possibilities. *Could* it be? Had they just witnessed a watershed moment in the history of mankind? Her innate scepticism dragged her back from conjecture with a resounding *No*. And yet . . . she couldn't ignore the feeling that she'd been in the presence of something transcendent. She glanced at Finch. 'What did the news desk say?'

Finch said, 'They're getting everyone they can think of to check it out. But they're getting calls from broadcasters all over the world wanting to know what's going on. Ogilvy wants us to send him a high-res clip pronto,' he added, referring to Hal Ogilvy, the network's global news director.

'OK,' she nodded. 'We need to make some calls. Let's grab the conference room.' They walked down the hall in silence, the sheer magnitude of the discussion sinking in.

Dalton stopped suddenly. 'What if that Bible-thumping nut is right?'

Gracie considered the question. 'If it's really God,' she said, 'then He sure picked one hell of a moment to show Himself.'

Wadi Natrun, Egypt

Laboured breaths and sluggish footfalls tarnished the stillness of the mountain as the three men trudged up the steep slope. The early dawn light and the chilling solitude weighed heavily on them.

Like many other devout Coptic Christians, Yusuf donated as much as he could afford to the monastery, delivering free fruit and vegetables from his brother's stall at the market and helping out with odd jobs. He knew the monastery like the back of his hand, and he'd been to the cave delivering supplies, every few weeks, to the recluse who was its sole inhabitant. Which was why he'd seen what was inside it.

He'd already made the trip to the monastery once, earlier in the evening, when he'd roused the monk he knew best, a young man with alert grey-green eyes by the name of Brother Ameen, with his startling news. Ameen knew Yusuf well enough to take him at his word and had led him to the monastery's abbot, Father Kyrillos. The abbot had agreed to accompany them back to the café and they'd watched the footage on the TV in shock.

Yusuf had driven them back to the monastery, where they'd counted down the hours anxiously. Then, at dawn, he drove them to the edge of the desert, where the barren, desolate crags rose out of the sand. From there, the three men had climbed the steep slope of the mountain for over an hour. It was hard enough to navigate by daylight, let alone in near-darkness. Visits to the caves were a rare event, and access to the area was discouraged out of respect for the occasional driven soul who elected to retreat into its harsh seclusion.

They reached the small wooden door that led into the cave. The abbot paused for a moment. He gave the door a hesitant knock. A moment passed, with no answer.

'Wait here,' he told them. 'Maybe he can't hear us.'

Ameen and Yusuf nodded.

The abbot gently lifted the latch and pushed the door open.

The interior of the cave was dark and cold. It was empty, save for a few furnishings. Beside the window was a writing table and a chair. The abbot aimed his flashlight towards them. The table had a lined notebook on it. A small stack of similar notebooks sat on a ledge by the window.

The abbot's mind flashed to the notebooks, to the dense writing, only fleetingly glimpsed, that filled their pages, to how it had all started, several months earlier. To how they'd found him. And to the *miraculous*—the word suddenly took on a wholly different ring—way he'd come to them.

The abbot shook the thoughts away and turned. That could all wait.

He took slow, hesitant steps deeper into the cave until he reached a small nook that housed a narrow bed. It was empty.

'Father Jerome?' he called out.

No answer. Perplexed, he retreated to the main chamber. He raised the flashlight, lighting up the wall that curved into the cavern's domelike roof.

With his heart pounding, he surveyed its surface.

One symbol, painstakingly painted onto the smooth rock face, repeated over and over, covering every available inch of the cave. A clearly recognisable symbol. The same symbol he had just seen on television, in the skies over Antarctica.

Yusuf was right.

The abbot dropped to his knees and began to pray.

PERCHED ON THE CREST of the barren mountain, high above the caves, Father Jerome contemplated the majestic landscape spread out before him. The thin, ageing man with the wire-rimmed glasses and closely shaved white hair spent most of his mornings and evenings up here.

He still didn't know what had drawn him to this place. Much as he thought about it, in those endless nights in the cave, he still couldn't explain what it was that had led him to walk away from the orphanage he had just opened, several hundred miles south, and to wander into the desert, unprepared and alone. Perhaps it was a calling. And yet, it scared him. The nights scared him most. The loneliness was, at times, crippling. Still, he had to embrace the challenges and not resist them.

The days were better. When he wasn't up on the mountain, he spent them in prayer, or writing. And that was something else he didn't understand: the writing. There seemed to be no end to the words, to the thoughts and ideas and images—*that* image, in particular—which flooded his mind. He couldn't write down the words fast enough. And yet, somehow, he wasn't sure where they were coming from. It was as if they were flowing through him, as if he were a conduit. And the words were beautiful, even if they didn't necessarily concord with his own personal experience within the Church.

He drank in the view before closing his eyes and clearing his mind, preparing himself for what he knew was coming.

Moments later it began. A torrent of words that flowed into his ears, as clearly as if someone were kneeling right beside him and whispering to him. He drank in each wondrous moment of revelation.

Boston, Massachusetts

Snowflakes dusted the sidewalk as Bellinger climbed out of the cab outside a small bar on a quiet street in South Boston. As he turned to duck into the bar, he slammed into a woman who emerged from the shadows, explaining that she was trying to grab the cab before it drove off. Bellinger had a fleeting glimpse of an attractive face and shoulder-length auburn hair. Before he could spew out any clumsy words, she'd hopped into the cab.

Matt Sherwood had chosen the low-key rendezvous. The place was busy, but not mobbed, which was good. The conversation Bellinger needed to have was one he'd prefer to keep as private as possible.

He paused by the door and realised that he was subconsciously scanning for some unseen threat. He tried to quash his unease as he made his way deeper into the bar and spotted Matt sitting in a corner booth. As he wove his way through the pockets of drinkers to join him, his cellphone rang. He pulled it out of his pocket. Jabba. He decided to ignore the call.

Even hunched over his drink, Matt Sherwood's hulking stature was hard to miss. The man was six foot four, a full head taller than Bellinger. He hadn't changed much in the two years since Bellinger had last seen him. He still had the same brooding presence, the same close-cropped dark hair, the same quietly intense eyes that surveyed and took note without giving much away. Bellinger had last seen him around the time of Danny Sherwood's funeral. Matt and his kid brother had been close, Danny's death sudden and unexpected.

As Bellinger slipped onto the bench, Matt acknowledged him with a nod. 'What's going on?'

Bellinger remembered that Matt was a man who didn't pussyfoot around. Time was something he appreciated. He'd had enough of it taken away from him already.

Bellinger found a half smile. 'How are you?'

'Terrific.' He gave Bellinger a sardonic look. 'You said we needed to talk.'

Bellinger hesitated. It was a tough subject to broach. 'I was thinking about Danny.'

'What about Danny?'

'Well, last time I saw you, after the funeral . . . we never really got a chance to talk about what happened to him.'

'He died in a helicopter crash. You know that. Why are you asking me this, Vince? Why now?'

'I know, but . . . what else do you know about it? What did they tell you?'

Matt shrugged. 'The chopper came down off the coast of Namibia. Mechanical failure. They said it was probably due to a sandstorm, but they couldn't be sure. The wreck was scattered all over the ocean floor.'

'What about the bodies?'

Matt winced. The memory was painful. 'They were never recovered.'

'Why not?'

Matt's voice rose a notch. 'The area's swarming with sharks, and if they don't get you, the rip tides will. It's the goddamn Skeleton Coast.'

'So you—'

'That's right, there was nothing to bury,' Matt flared. He was angry now. 'The casket was empty, Vince. We cremated an empty box but we had to do it that way. It helped give my dad some closure. Now are you going to tell me why we're really here?'

Bellinger looked away. His head throbbed with the strain of his confused thoughts. 'Did you watch the news today?'

'No, why?'

Just then, Bellinger's cellphone beeped, alerting him to the receipt of a text. He ignored it. He didn't have the patience to deal with Jabba now.

He fixed on Matt. 'I think Danny may have been murdered.' He paused. 'Or worse.'

Matt's expression curdled. 'What could be worse?'

'Maybe he's being held somewhere. Maybe they all are.'

'What?' Matt looked like he'd been winded. 'What the hell are you talking about?'

Bellinger leaned in closer. 'Maybe they killed Danny and the others and faked the chopper crash. Then again, maybe they've still got them locked up, working on it against their will.' His eyes were anxiously scanning the bar. 'Think about it. If you got a bunch of geniuses to design something secret for you, wouldn't you want to keep them around long enough to make sure nothing went wrong when you finally used it?'

'To design what? You're not making sense.'

Bellinger's voice dropped to a whisper. 'Something happened today,

Matt. In Antarctica. There was this thing, in the sky. It's all over the news. I think Danny had something to do with it.'

'Why would you think that?'

Bellinger was shaking visibly now, the words tumbling out of him nervously. His phone beeped again, but he ignored it. 'Danny was working on something. He showed me some of his stuff and the possibilities were just mindblowing. But then Reece showed up and whisked him away to work with him on that project of his, the biosensors and—'

'Reece?'

'Dominic Reece, his guru at MIT. He was also in that chopper with Danny.' He stared at Matt. 'It was a great project; the sensors would have saved tens of thousands of lives—'

His phone beeped for the fourth time.

Bellinger lost his train of thought and irritably fished out his phone. He saw that three messages had come in from the same number.

Not Jabba's. The messages were all from a number he didn't recognise. But the words on the small screen hit him like a sledgehammer.

They simply read, IF YOU WANT TO LIVE, SHUT UP AND LEAVE THE BAR NOW.

THE PENNY-SIZED MIKE, rapidly placed under the lapel of Bellinger's coat by the auburn-haired woman he'd bumped into on his way into the bar, rocketed his words to the earpieces of the three operatives who sat in the van parked outside the bar: 'I think Danny may have been murdered.' Two other operatives inside the bar heard them too.

In the van, the operative leading the surveillance team looked pointedly at his auburn-haired colleague. She had done well. Her hands had been lightning quick, the tag unnoticed.

The voice of one of the men in the bar shot through their earpieces. 'He's not going for it.'

The lead operative scowled and brought up his wrist mike. 'I'm giving him another prod. Get ready to move in if he still doesn't take the hint.'

He hit the send button on his cellphone again.

THE WORDS on the screen of his phone seared Bellinger's eyes. His alarmed gaze raked the bar. Everyone around him suddenly looked suspicious.

'What is it?' Matt asked.

Bellinger stumbled to his feet, his eyes bristling with fear. 'Forget I said anything, all right? I've got to go.'

Matt shot to his feet and grabbed hold of Bellinger's arm. 'Cut the crap, Vince. What's going on?'

Bellinger spun around, yanking his arm free.

His frenzied reaction surprised Matt, who fell heavily, jarring his head against the booth's wooden edge. Then Matt staggered to his feet and bolted after Bellinger to the bar's entrance.

He burst out onto the pavement and stopped in his tracks at the sight of Bellinger being dragged into the back of a van by two bulky men.

Matt shouted, 'Hey!' and charged at them, only his feet had barely left the ground when something heavy slammed into him from behind, sending him flying face first onto the snow-speckled pavement. Before he could push himself back onto his feet, two sets of strong arms grabbed him, pinned his arms behind his back, and threw him into the van.

He landed hard, face down on the metal floor. He heard the doors slam shut and felt his body slide back as the van took off. He angled his head up to glimpse Bellinger, two bulky men and the vague outline of a woman with a shoulder-length bob looking back from the driver's seat. One of the men was sitting on Bellinger's back, pinning him down, one hand covering his mouth. The other loomed over him, holding something that looked like an oversized electric shaver.

Matt tried to shift himself over but one of the men stomped down heavily on his back. A jolt of nausea rushed through him as he heard a vaguely familiar, high-pitched whine reach a fevered intensity and realised what it was.

Straining to raise his head, Matt caught sight of the second man bringing his hand down onto Bellinger and branding him with a pocket Taser. Bellinger screamed in agony as a faint blue light flickered inside the van. A two-second burst was usually enough to bring a fit man down, but Bellinger's hit lasted well over five seconds, and Matt knew what the effect on the scientist would be. He'd been at the receiving end of those prods. It wasn't a pleasant sensation, especially not when they were wielded by neolithic prison guards. His skin bristled at the memory.

Bellinger's tormentor put down the Taser and brought out a syringe, which he swiftly plunged into the stricken man's back, just below the neck. Bellinger's struggling stopped.

'He's done,' the man announced.

The bulldozer sitting on Matt asked, 'What about this one?'

The man who'd dealt with Bellinger mulled over the question for a moment. 'Same deal,' he decided.

Not the answer Matt was hoping for. He glimpsed the man moving off Bellinger and making his way over, the pocket Taser in his hand.

Just then, the van made a turn. The weight of the bulldozer sitting on top of Matt shifted slightly and he suddenly heaved back as hard as he could. The move caught his captor by surprise, sending him flying against the wall of the van. Matt followed through with a full twist, weaving his fingers together and locking them as he swung round and used his extended arms as a baseball bat.

He caught the bulldozer flat across the nose. The man's head ricocheted against the van's wall before he curled over, writhing with pain.

Matt didn't pause to watch. The bulldozer's partner was already leaping at him, so he quickly grabbed the rear door handle, yanked it open and, despite glimpsing a car not too far back, flung himself out of the moving van.

Hitting the asphalt was beyond brutal. His left shoulder and hip took the brunt of it, a lightning bolt of pain shooting through him as he landed and rolled over. Confusing glimpses of streetlights and tarmac flooded his senses, every inch of his body getting a beating. An ear-piercing shriek filled the air as a car's front bumper came to a stop only a few feet behind him.

Matt could feel the heat radiating from the car's grille, and the air was thick with the smell of burned rubber. He glanced down the road. The van was quickly receding.

He pushed himself to his feet and staggered over to the driver's window. An old man was staring at Matt in trepidation and disbelief.

'Open the window,' Matt shouted.

The man hesitated, shook his head, then just hit the gas. Matt reeled back and watched, dumbstruck, as the car disappeared into the darkness.

Wadi Natrun, Egypt

Golden light rose from the distant horizon as the three men climbed down the mountain. They'd waited for close to an hour for Father Jerome to show up, and when he still hadn't appeared, they'd finally given up.

Yusuf offered to stick around in case he was needed. The abbot told him he wasn't and thanked him, then said gravely, 'I need you to keep what you know about all this to yourself. No one else must be told. Do you understand?'

Yusuf nodded somberly. 'As you wish, Father.'

'What are we going to do?' Brother Ameen asked, as Yusuf drove away.

'First, I need to pray,' answered the abbot. 'This is all too . . . unsettling.'

They entered the monastery through a small gate in the forty-foot wall that surrounded it. Just inside the enclosure, the large *qasr*—the keep—squatted proudly in the dawn light, its timber drawbridge now permanently lowered and welcoming. The valley of Wadi Natrun held a special resonance for the faithful: it was there that Mary, Joseph and their infant son had rested while escaping from King Herod's men. For centuries, the profoundly religious had been drawn to its desolate wilderness. And on the dawn of this portentous day, the abbot thought, it seemed eminently possible that the valley hadn't yet exhausted its relevance to the faithful.

The monk followed the abbot through the courtyard and into the Church of the Holy Virgin, the monastery's main place of worship. None of the other monks was there yet, but he knew the solitude wouldn't last long. His eyes drifted up to a wall painting adorning a half-cupola overhead, a thousand-year-old depiction of the Annunciation.

The abbot, on the other hand, found his gaze drawn to the first prophet to the right of the Virgin, Ezekiel, and a chill crawled down his neck. For the next hour, as he desperately prayed for guidance, he couldn't shake the prophet's celestial vision from his mind: the heavens opening up to a whirlwind of amber fire folding in on itself, the wheels of fire in a sky 'the colour of a terrible crystal', all of it heralding the voice of God.

The two men prayed, side by side, for close to an hour.

'Shouldn't we have waited longer for him?' Brother Ameen asked eventually. With the sun setting fast, they were now in the monastery's museum. 'What if something's happened to him?'

The abbot shrugged. 'I think he knows how to handle the mountain by now.'

The younger monk cleared his throat and asked, 'What are we going to do, Father?'

'I'm not sure what we should do,' the abbot replied. 'I don't understand what's happening.'

'A miracle. That's what's happening. What other explanation is there?'

The abbot shook his head, lost for words. He thought back to that day in the desert when their guest had been found, before he took to the caves. The terrible state he was in. His recovery. The word *miraculous* glided into his thoughts again.

'It doesn't fit any of the prophecies of our holy book,' he finally said.

'Why does it need to? We're living a miracle, Father,' Ameen exclaimed, his voice flushed with excitement. 'Not reading about it hundreds of years after the fact. Living it, in this modern age. With all the power of modern communication at our disposal,' he added, pointedly.

The abbot's face was uneasy. 'You want people to know about this?'

'They already know about the sign. You saw the woman on the news service. Her images and words will have reached millions.'

'Until we understand what is happening, we can't allow this to come out.'

Ameen spread out his hands questioningly. 'Isn't it evident, Father?'

The abbot nodded thoughtfully. He understood the younger man's exuberance, but it needed to be reined in. 'We need to study the scriptures more closely. Consult with our superiors.' He paused. 'Most importantly, we need to talk to *him*. Perhaps he will know what to make of it.'

Ameen stepped closer. 'We can't keep this to ourselves. People need to know, Father. The world needs to know.'

'Not yet,' the abbot insisted, firmly. 'It's not up to us to decide.'

The younger monk's voice rose. 'Forgive me, Father, but I believe you're making a mistake. Others will try to claim the sign as their own. Our message could be drowned out by impostors and opportunists. We can't wait.'

The abbot sighed wearily. The young monk's words rang true, but he couldn't bring himself to take that step. The consequences were too frightening to contemplate. The painting in the chapel crept back into his mind's eye, and he thought again of Ezekiel's vision.

'It's not up to us,' he repeated. 'We need to consult with the councils. They will decide.'

AN HOUR LATER, Brother Ameen watched from a dark hallway as the library's curator stepped out of his office. He'd failed to convince the abbot. The old man seemed incapable of grasping the enormity of what was happening, but Ameen wasn't about to let that stop him. He needed to take matters into his own hands.

He waited patiently, his eyes tracking the curator as he walked away and entered the refectory.

Moments later, the young monk sneaked into the curator's office, picked up the telephone and started dialling.

LESS THAN A MILE from the ridge that Yusuf and the two monks had just climbed down, a boy of fourteen ambled on tired feet after his small herd. Humming a tune, he rounded an outcropping of rocks and stopped in his tracks at the unexpected sight before him. Three men—soldiers, it seemed, from their outfits—were loading equipment into a pick-up truck. Equipment he'd never seen before, including a sand-beige, drumlike object, perhaps three feet wide but only five or six inches deep, that snared his attention.

Even though the boy froze, the men spotted him instantly. He barely had time to register the familiar gear he'd seen on countless news broadcasts of the war in Iraq—the camouflage BDUs, the boots, the sunglasses—before one of the men spat out a brief word and the others dropped what they were doing and took quick strides towards him.

The boy started to run, but didn't make it far. One of the men tackled him from behind, bringing him down into the soil head first. In a frenzy of terror, the boy tried to squirm around, but the man who sat on him was too heavy.

He heard another man's footsteps crunching their way closer, then glimpsed a pair of military boots from the corner of his eye.

He didn't hear a word. And he didn't feel a thing after the big hands of the man sitting on top of him tightened their grip around his neck.

Amundsen Sea, Antarctica

Gracie gave out her satphone number, hung up and heaved a sigh of frustration. Another dead end. She'd called contacts at NASA, Caltech and the Pentagon, as well as the editor of *Science* magazine and the network's science and technology guru. They were all as baffled as she was.

She'd hardly hung up when the satphone rang. Another reporter, angling for a comment.

'How are they getting hold of this number?' she groaned to Finch.

Her producer pulled a 'who-knows?' face and grabbed the phone for yet another polite, but firm, rebuff. For the moment, it was still their exclusive.

It was not that Gracie didn't like being in the public eye. Far from it. She'd wanted such a break since she'd first started as a TV correspondent, and she'd worked damn hard at grabbing her share of air time. She loved stepping in front of that camera and telling the world what she'd found out, and, undeniably, the camera loved her back.

She'd gone from being a local reporter to becoming the anchor and special correspondent for the network's flagship Special Investigations Unit.

In the process, she'd become a face America trusted, whether she was reporting from Kuwait in the run-up to the invasion of Iraq, or following Hurricane Katrina in New Orleans.

She breathed a sigh of exasperation. 'I'm getting nothing here. You having better luck?'

Finch had been talking to the news desk back in DC and trawling through his contacts list. 'Nope. If it's natural, no one's seen anything like it. And if it's not, they're all telling me the technology doesn't exist.'

'We don't know that,' Dalton objected, looking up from his monitor. 'I'm sure there's a lot of stuff out there that we don't know about.'

'Sure. But there doesn't seem to be any technology out there that we can point to and say, 'If we took that and made it bigger or more powerful, it could explain it. This is a whole different ball game. Everyone's trying to figure it out. Every station from London to Beijing is running it. Same for the big news blogs. And the chat rooms are just going nuts.'

'What are they saying?'

'Some people think it's a harmless stunt, a *War of the Worlds* kind of thing. Others see something more sinister in it, and they're throwing out all kinds of crazy ideas about how it could have been pulled off.'

'Is there anyone who doesn't think we're behind it?'

'Yep. The ones who believe it's the real thing—real as in God, not ET. One of them called us "the heralds of the Second Coming".'

'Well that makes me feel so much better,' Gracie groaned. Part of her was thrilled by the idea of being the face of the hottest story around, but the more reasoned side of her was clamouring for restraint, uncomfortable with how it was all spiralling out of control.

Finch tapped some keys on the laptop. 'Speaking of ET, a guy at the Discovery Channel sent me these pictures. Some of them are ones you'd expect, like clouds and Concorde contrails that make people think they're seeing UFOs. He tells me there are over two hundred reported UFO sightings a month in America. And there's a whole slew of historic references to unexplained sightings going back thousands of years. Check out these historical records: Japan, 1458—an object as bright as the full moon and followed by curious signs was observed in the sky. Or this one: London, 1593—a flying dragon surrounded by flames was seen hovering over the city.'

'None of these references is even remotely verifiable,' Gracie said.

'Sure, but there are so many of them. Even the Bible's got them.'

'So what are we saying? What do you think we saw?'

'I'd have said mass hallucination if it wasn't for the footage.' Finch shook his head. 'I can't explain it.'

'Dalton?' she asked.

His face clouded with uncertainty. 'I don't know. There was something ethereal about it. Like the sky . . . like the sky itself had lit up, you know what I'm saying?'

'I do,' Gracie agreed uncomfortably. The vivid sight of the glowing sign materialised in her mind's eye. It was as if the air itself had been summoned by God, she found herself thinking. Which didn't sit well with her. She'd stopped believing in God when her mother died. Get a grip. There's got to be a logical explanation.

But a nagging question kept coming back: what if there isn't?

The satphone rang, and as Finch stretched across to answer it, her mind migrated to a UFO hoax from a year earlier. Millions were taken in by it on YouTube until it turned out to be something a French computer animator had put together on his MacBook. With advances in special effects and the proliferation of faked videos of such high quality, Gracie wondered: would people even recognise a 'true' event of this kind if it really happened? Or would it be drowned in a sea of cynicism?

'Gracie,' Finch called out, covering the phone's mouthpiece with his hand. 'It's for you.'

'Now what?' she grumbled.

'I'm not sure, but it's coming from Egypt. And I think you need to take it.'

Boston, Massachusetts

There were no cabs around, but it didn't take too long for Matt to stagger the short distance back to the bar where he was relieved to find his car, a 1968 Mustang GT 390, where he'd left it. His keys, miraculously, were still in the pocket of his coat. Less miraculous was the fact that he'd lost his cellphone. It had probably flown out of his pocket during his landing.

He leaned against the car and the images of Bellinger getting fried and injected roared back into his mind. He had to do something to try and help him, but he couldn't see a move that made sense. He couldn't report it to the cops. The van was long gone and the questions he'd be asked, given his prison record, would only cloud the issue. More to the point, he didn't think the cops would be able to find Bellinger anyway.

The traffic was light and he was on the expressway within minutes, and from there it was only a short hop to his studio apartment over his workshop. As he cruised south, he tried to make sense of events and figure out what the right move would be. Every bone in his body felt like it had been hammered by a blacksmith on steroids. And, as if to add insult to injury, it was snowing again.

Bellinger had asked for a meeting, then hit him with the news that his brother might have been murdered, or that his death might have been faked and that he might be locked up somewhere . . .

Danny, alive—but locked up somewhere? The thought flooded Matt's gut with equal doses of elation—and rage. He and Danny had always been close, which never failed to amaze their friends given how different they were. Matt, three years older, had inherited his dad's dark hair and solid build, whereas Danny—fairer and fifty pounds lighter—took after his mom. Matt had no patience for schoolwork, whereas Danny had an insatiable appetite for learning. Matt was irreverent, wild and reckless; Danny was introverted and preferred his computer to company. Despite it all, they'd had a bond that was unshakable. Their friendship had also survived Matt's repeated collisions with the law.

He remembered how it had all started. He'd built his first car at the age of thirteen, hooking up an old washing machine engine to an old wreck. It became something of a fixture around his neighbourhood. Even the most hard-headed of cops couldn't quite bring themselves to take away his pride and joy—but his relationship with law enforcers would change dramatically over the years. For, as he grew older, the disparity between his love of cars on the one hand and the bleak part-time work prospects available to him became more frustrating. Headstrong and impatient, Matt sought to redress that imbalance his own way.

His early escapades were classic Matt. He didn't go after any old ride. He would trawl the more affluent neighbourhoods of Boston for specific cars on his hit list. He also never crashed or trashed the cars he stole, nor did he ever try to sell them. He would merely abandon them in some parking lot once he'd had the chance to sample them. He managed to test drive quite a few before he got caught. The judge he came up against on his first conviction wasn't amused.

Upon his release from jail, trouble seemed to come looking for him. Matt ended up dropping out of high school before graduation and, from there, his life spiralled out of control. He spent the next few years in and out of jail for theft, criminal damage to property and battery, his future withering away while Danny's blossomed, first at MIT, then at a highly paid job in a tech company.

Matt ruefully remembered how he hadn't seen much of Danny just before his death. Matt had been released from jail only a few months before Danny was offered the job with Reece, and he had been busy setting up in business—with the help of a life-altering loan from his kid brother, he thought with a twinge of shame. In a sense, he owed him his life.

It was Danny who'd got him to go straight, suggesting he turn his passion for cars into something positive. And Matt listened. He found a small car shop that was closing down, and took over the lease. The plan was for him to find and fix up classic cars and, in the heady days before the credit crunch, Matt had built up a solid reputation in car-enthusiast circles. Things had been looking up. Meanwhile, Danny had been sucked into his new job. A black hole that had ultimately swallowed up his life.

Or had it? Was it possible that Danny was still alive? Bellinger had made a convincing argument for it. And he'd been grabbed seconds after making it. That had to mean something.

Whether Danny was still alive or not, the idea that they'd all been lied to—*the idea that someone, not fate, had taken Danny away*—felt like acid in his throat. He wasn't about to let it slide.

His fury swelled as he thought back to how Danny's death had devastated their parents. It was bad enough when they learned their eldest son was a convicted felon. To lose Danny—their pride and joy—was too much to bear. Their mom had died a couple of months later. Matt's dad hadn't fared much better. They had hardly spoken at his mom's funeral and, almost a year to the day later, the local sheriff had tracked Matt down to his garage in Quincy and given him the news of his dad's death from a stroke.

Bellinger's words now echoed in Matt's mind. Someone had taken Danny, and it was linked to something that had just happened in the skies of Antarctica. It sounded outlandish. Only it clearly wasn't. The guys he'd just gone up against were highly professional. Well equipped. Ruthless.

With no other cars around, the snow had had time to settle. He motored on until he reached the alleyway that led to his apartment and workshop tucked away about a hundred yards back from the main road. Just before turning into the alleyway, a corner of his mind registered a set of tyre tracks in the fresh snow. He couldn't see down the alley, but the tracks could only have been heading to his place. There was nothing else down there.

Problem was, he wasn't expecting anyone.

Amundsen Sea, Antarctica

'You need to come here. There's something you need to see.'

The caller wasn't a native English speaker and Gracie couldn't place his accent. But his words were laced with an urgency that came through loud and clear, despite the satellite link.

'Slow down a second,' Gracie said. 'Who are you exactly?'

'My name is Brother Ameen. From the Monastery of the Syrians, in Egypt.'

'And how'd you get this number?'

'I called your Cairo bureau. I told them I was calling on behalf of Father Jerome.'

'What, *the* Father Jerome?'

'Yes,' he assured her. 'The very same.'

It suddenly occurred to her that she hadn't read anything about the world-famous humanitarian for quite a while. Which was unusual, given his high public profile.

'Now you've got me on the line,' she said, 'what's this about?'

'You need to come here to see Father Jerome. We saw your broadcast. The symbol you witnessed, there, over the ice. It's here too.'

Her pulse rocketed. 'You've got it there too? In the sky?' Her words got Dalton and Finch's attention.

'No, not in the sky. You need to come here. To see it for yourself.'

'I'm going to need a little more than that.'

Brother Ameen seemed to weigh up his words for a moment. 'Father Jerome came to us several months ago. He was . . . troubled. After a few weeks, he went up into the mountain. There's a cave, you see. Men of God go there when they're looking for solitude.'

'What does that have to do with me?'

The man hesitated then said, 'Since he's been up in the cave, he's been writing, filling one journal after another. And there's a drawing, one he's painted all over the walls of the cave.'

Gracie's skin prickled.

'It's the sign, Miss Logan. The sign you saw over the ice.'

Gracie's mind scrambled to process what he'd just told her.

'No offence, Brother, but—'

He cut her off. 'Of course, you've every right to be sceptical. I wouldn't expect any less. But you need to hear me out. There isn't a television up in the cave, and Father Jerome hasn't seen your broadcast.'

'I'm not sure your word on that is going to get me hopping on a plane.'

'You don't understand,' Brother Ameen added. 'It's not something he just started to do. He's been drawing the sign over and over again for seven months.'

Quincy, Massachusetts

Matt turned, pulling into the lot of a 7-Eleven just before the alleyway. He flicked the Mustang's lights off but left the engine on, and sat there, taking stock of the situation. They were here. Waiting for him. Had to be. How? It had not even been an hour since he'd leaped out of their van.

They must have been watching Bellinger. Maybe even listening to his calls. If they were, they knew about his call to Matt. And if this was about Danny, then they knew all about Matt already.

And Matt had obviously become a problem for them. Wonderful.

He gave his immediate surroundings a quick scan but didn't notice anything that jarred. They had to be waiting for him near his garage. He could picture the perfect spot where they might have parked, out of sight, ready to ambush him on his return.

He switched the engine off and climbed out of the car, alert to any movement. He took a few quick steps over to the store and huddled under its awning, giving the area another quick once-over.

Nothing. Just the single set of tracks headed down the alleyway to the side of the 7-Eleven.

He stepped inside the store, triggering an electronic chime that brought him to the attention of Sanjay, the store's congenial owner, who smiled. 'Hey, Matt.'

Matt just nodded absently, while he made sure there was no one else around. 'Sanjay, I need to go out the back way.'

Sanjay stared at him for a moment. 'Whatever you need, Matt.'

They'd known each other ever since Matt had taken the lease on the apartment. Matt had been a good customer and a reliable neighbour and by now Sanjay knew him well enough to know that Matt wouldn't be asking if it wasn't important.

He led him to the back of the store and unlocked the door.

Matt paused. 'Don't lock it just yet, will you? I won't be long.'

Sanjay nodded. 'You sure you're OK?'

'Not really,' Matt shrugged, then slipped out of the door.

There were no cars around in the back lot of the store, so he headed away from the main road. Light from the store quickly petered out, and he was soon in total darkness with only a diffused moon glow to guide him. He ducked into a patch of trees and over to a low brick structure that housed a small law firm. With his left leg and hip blazing with pain with every step, he scuttled along the back wall of the building until it ran out.

He bent down and chanced a peek around the corner. He'd read it right. A dark Chrysler 300C was parked in one of the law firm's spots, about twenty yards from the entrance to his place. He could just about make out the silhouettes of two figures inside. They were waiting for him.

Matt's first instinct was to charge in and pound the truth out of them. A few years back, he might have done just that. But much as he was desperate to take them on, he forced himself to accept that it would be the wrong move. His left leg was barely holding him up. He wouldn't stand a chance.

Besides, the guys in the Chrysler seemed to have a solid set-up, which meant they had connections. All he had was a rap sheet.

Another idea elbowed its way into his mind. He decided it was his best option, then made his way back to the 7-Eleven.

He cut through the store, past Sanjay, who gave him a quizzical glance.

'I need some tape,' Matt told him. 'Something solid and sticky, packing tape, that kind of thing.'

'I'll get you what I have,' Sanjay said as Matt disappeared out of the front door. He walked to the back of the Mustang and popped the trunk, pulled back the lining, reached in and found a small black box, not much bigger than a packet of cigarettes. A tracking device. Matt stuffed it in his inside breast pocket. He then pulled out the lug wrench from the tool kit, closed the trunk, and went back into the store.

Sanjay was waiting for him with a roll of two-inch-thick duct tape. Matt grabbed it, blurted out, 'Perfect,' and kept going.

He crept back to the corner of the brick building. The Chrysler was still there. He slipped into the shrubs and trees behind the parking bay, keeping low. He manoeuvred to a spot around fifteen yards behind the Chrysler. From there, he dropped to the ground and crawled the rest of the way on elbows that were still suffering from his leap out of the van. He ignored the pain and kept going until he was right behind the Chrysler. He rolled onto his back and quietly pulled himself under the car. He quickly found a metal strut that would suit his purpose, pulled out the tracker, and taped it to the strut.

He was almost done when he felt weight shift in the car, then heard the click of an opening door. He froze as he saw first one foot, then another, drop to the ground, faintly illuminated by the car's inside light. The light dimmed as the man swung the door back quietly.

Matt felt a surge of panic. He angled his head to look behind the car and saw the trail he'd left: it led right up to the car, a black streak through the shimmer of the snow.

His body tensed as he watched the man take a few steps towards the back of the car. With his heart in his throat, Matt followed the man's feet past the rear wheel—then they stopped. Matt's fingers tightened against the handle of the lug wrench. He was about to swing his legs out in an attempt to kick the man off-balance when he heard a zipper open. The man was just out there to take a leak.

He waited for the man to get back into the car, made sure the tracker was solidly attached, then retreated along the same path he'd taken, pausing only to commit the car's licence plate to memory.

He found Sanjay standing by the cash register, clearly worried. Matt gave him a nod of gratitude as he scribbled down the Chrysler's licence plate on a flyer. He tucked it into his pocket. 'Anyone asks, you haven't seen me, not since lunch time. OK?'

Sanjay nodded. 'You gonna tell me what's going on?'

'Better you don't get involved. Safer for you that way.'

Sanjay acknowledged his words sombrely, then hesitated and said, 'You'll be careful, won't you?' in an uncertain tone.

Matt smiled. 'That's the plan.' He took a few steps to the fridge, and pulled out a can of Coke. 'My tab still good?'

Sanjay visibly relaxed. 'Of course.'

And with that, Matt was gone.

Amundsen Sea, Antarctica

'So what's the verdict? Do we believe this guy, Ameen?' Gracie leaned her head against the cold glass of the conference room's window.

'Gracie, come on,' Dalton replied. 'He's talking about Father Jerome.

The guy's a living saint. He's not going to fake something like this.'

Father Jerome had begun his life in 1949 as Alvaro Suarez, the son of a humble farming couple in northern Spain. His father died when he was five, leaving his mother with six children. Young Alvaro showed great resilience and generosity of character, especially during a harsh winter when a viral epidemic almost took away his mother and two of his sisters. He credited his faith with giving him the strength to forge ahead despite overwhelming odds. By the time he was in his teens he knew he would devote his life to the Church. He left home at seventeen, joining a seminary in Andalusia before crossing into Africa, where he soon founded the first of many missions. He took his first vows a few months short of his twenty-second birthday, choosing the name of Jerome, after the patron saint of orphans. The modern Jerome's hospices and orphanages were now scattered across the globe. His army of volunteers had turned around the lives of thousands of the world's poorest children. The man was indeed a living saint, and Dalton's point was hard to ignore.

'But that wasn't Father Jerome on the phone, was it? We don't even know if the caller was really calling from Egypt,' she argued.

The reports they'd pulled up after the call confirmed that Father Jerome himself was in Egypt. He'd fallen ill while working at one of his missions, close to the border with Sudan, a little over a year ago. After his recovery, he'd retreated entirely from public view.

'And how could he actually have drawn what we saw? I mean, how would you draw it?' Gracie argued.

'We need to get a copy of that tape,' Dalton suggested.

Before ending his call, Brother Ameen had offered them a tantalising piece of corroboration. A BBC film crew had visited the monastery several months earlier and had managed to get a peek inside the cave to shoot some footage before being turned away by Father Jerome. Brother Ameen assured Gracie it included the priest's handiwork on the ceiling and walls.

It was proof that Gracie desperately needed to see. The problem was, getting hold of it would most likely alert the film-makers to its significance and Gracie could lose the lead on the story. A story that was still virtually exclusively hers.

She heaved a sigh of frustration as she pondered Dalton's suggestion. 'No. We can't risk it.'

Finch said, 'So what do you want to do?'

216 | RAYMOND KHOURY

'I don't know what's really going on here, but, like it or not, we're caught up in something exceptional. And the story's not here any more. It's in Egypt. It's in that monastery. And that's where I need to be.'

Finch smiled. 'Let's do it.' A lesser producer would have debated the point to death before covering his back by getting his news director's approval. Finch was rock solid and, right now, Gracie was hugely grateful to have him in her corner.

Gracie turned to Dalton. He nodded. He was in too.

Gracie beamed back. 'Great.'

'I'll go talk to the captain,' Finch said. 'See how quickly he can get us choppered off this ship. You guys start packing.'

She crossed over to the window again and looked out. The shelf was still disintegrating, but the sign was long gone.

With her back to Dalton, she asked, 'Are we making the right call here?'

He joined her at the window. 'We're talking about Father Jerome. If you're not going to believe him . . . who *are* you going to believe?'

Boston, Massachusetts

Matt guided the Mustang back onto the expressway and headed towards the city. He felt shattered and he was having trouble making sense of what had happened since Bellinger had called him. He needed to rest and think things through, but there were no obvious spots where he could crash out, no friends or family to take him in. He was on his own.

He ended up at a fifties-style diner, the only place in town that he knew would be open this late. He looked a real mess and drew a couple of contemptuous glances as he stepped inside. The last thing he needed right now was to get noticed. He disappeared into the men's room and cleaned himself up as best he could, then grabbed a stool at the far end of the bar. He ordered coffee and a cheeseburger.

He sifted through his options. He was facing pros with serious resources, and his options were limited, especially given that he didn't really know much beyond the cryptic words Bellinger had left him with. He needed to find out more about what was going on. He could think of two threads to follow. One was the tracker. The other was Bellinger. Or whatever it was that he knew which had put him in their cross hairs. His heart sank at the thought of the dire situation Danny's best friend must now be in and he seethed with frustration at not being able to do anything about it. Not yet, anyway.

He needed to check the tracker's position, and he also wanted to see what he could find at Bellinger's place. And for both lines of attack, he needed to go online. He got directions from the waitress to a nearby Best Western and pulled into the hotel's parking lot fifteen minutes later. The business centre was restricted to hotel guests, so he gave the receptionist a fake name, took a single and paid in cash. He was soon ensconced at a workstation with a high-speed connection pumping information to his screen.

He logged onto the tracker's web site. Having been a car thief, he appreciated the value of such devices more than anyone, especially when it came to covetable, high-value classics like his Mustang.

The Chrysler hadn't moved. Which was both good and bad. If the goons were still there, it meant they weren't on his tail, but, then again, it also meant they weren't giving up easily. He trawled the online directory for Bellinger's home address, which was over in an upmarket enclave that Matt had visited a few times. At this hour, it would be only a quick hop to get there.

Matt jotted down the address and Googled 'Antarctica', 'sky' and 'news'. He clicked on the first link and read through a news report of a huge section of ice shelf breaking off.

It was less than enlightening. He sat back, perplexed as to how it could possibly be linked to Danny. Another link caught his eye, mentioning an 'unexplained sighting' on the frozen continent. It took him to a related article that had an accompanying video clip.

He felt a tightening at the back of his neck as he viewed the clip. He initiated a new search, and got a geyser of hits related to the unexplained sighting. This was no small event. If Danny was involved in it—against his will, Bellinger had insinuated—then the stakes were much higher than Matt had imagined.

Minutes later, he was in the Mustang, crossing the Longfellow Bridge and trying to stay focused as he made his way to Bellinger's address.

The lights of a lone Christmas tree blinked out of a bay window on the ground floor of the three-storey Victorian house, but, otherwise, the rest of the building was dark. The snow outside was undisturbed.

He pulled into a small alley and switched off the throaty V-8—not the most discreet of engines. Everything around him was eerily quiet. He rummaged through his glove box and found his trusted Leatherman multitool and a short, stiff piece of wire, then walked over to the house's front porch.

The labels on its buzzer showed three occupants, one apartment per floor. Bellinger's name was at the top. The lock on the communal entrance didn't pose too much of a challenge. Getting past the lock on the door to Bellinger's place on the third floor was equally effortless. Matt had had way too much practice over the years.

He slipped in quietly without turning the lights on, wishing he had a flashlight. The small entrance hall opened onto an open-plan living room. Moonlight bathed the bay window and he advanced carefully, all senses on high alert. He spotted a halogen lamp with a dimmer switch and decided it wouldn't be too visible from the outside on a low setting. The dimmer buzzed slightly as the lamp suffused the room with a yellowish gleam.

A sleek, glass-and-chrome desk was covered with newspapers, books and unopened mail. Matt spotted a box of Bellinger's business cards and pocketed one. He could see that something was missing—a computer. A large flat screen was still there, as was the docking station for a laptop. The laptop itself was gone.

Had they been here already? They had Bellinger, which meant they had his keys. If they had been here, they were probably already long gone. It had been around three hours since he and their van had parted company.

He crept across the hallway and checked the two bedrooms, both empty. He made his way back to the living room, where a blinking light on a coffee table caught his eye. It came from the base unit of a cordless phone that had a waiting message.

He clicked the playback button. A digital voice informed Matt that the message came in at 12.47 a.m. People didn't normally get calls at that hour.

'Dude, where the hell did you disappear to?' a hyper voice on the machine quizzed. 'Pick up the damn phone, will ya? This thing's gathering some serious mass. The blogs are going loco over it. Anyway, call me back.'

Matt hit star-69. Another voice recited the caller's number to him. It was local. As he wrote it down on the back of Bellinger's card, a faint noise intruded—a car pulling up outside the building.

He crossed to the window and saw two men walking away from an unmarked sedan into the building. Coming to check out Bellinger's place. Either they were more goons, or they were plain-clothes cops and Bellinger's body had already turned up. Matt could just imagine how that one would play out . . .

He flinched as the entry phone in Bellinger's apartment buzzed, then sprinted to the front door and cracked it open. It buzzed again.

The hit team had Bellinger's keys. They wouldn't need to ring up. He waited by the door, his mind racing through possible outcomes, none of which seemed promising.

Leaving the door slightly ajar, he scuttled back to the bay window and peeked out. He could see the two men standing by their car. One of them was on his cellphone. Matt relaxed somewhat. They came, they buzzed, no answer, they'd leave. Or so he hoped.

Then he saw the other man disappear under the porch again.

Matt slipped back to the door and quietly picked up the entry phone's handset. He eavesdropped, coming in in midconversation.

'—on the second floor,' a woman's voice was explaining. 'Bellinger's got the penthouse directly over me.'

'Does Mr Bellinger live alone, ma'am?'

Does, Matt thought. Not *Did*. Present tense. Maybe Bellinger was all right.

The woman's voice had a nervous quaver to it. 'Yes, I think so. But I'm surprised he's not picking up. I'm pretty sure he's home.'

'What makes you say that?' the man asked.

'I think he came in earlier,' she said with more urgency. 'And then he went out again. But then he came back.'

'When did you hear him come in?'

'Not long ago. Ten minutes, maybe? He should be upstairs.'

He heard the man's tone take on a much harder edge. 'I need you to let us in, ma'am, right now,' followed by the distinct sound of the entrance door snapping open. Seconds later, heavy footsteps were charging up the stairs.

Amundsen Sea, Antarctica

Gracie's stomach fluttered as she watched Dalton being winched off the deck of the ship. The *James Clark Ross* wasn't endowed with a helipad and transfers could be made only by transferring passengers to and from a hovering chopper, which wasn't for the fainthearted.

It was six hours since the sign had first appeared. After Gracie's clip was broadcast, the news had simply exploded across the world's TV screens. Armies of reporters and pundits were talking about it, offering wild theories. And it was still the middle of the night across North America. The next day, Gracie knew, was when the real frenzy would begin.

One expert after another was being wheeled in to try and explain it. Physicists, climatologists, all kinds of scientists, dragged in from every corner of the planet. None of them had a clue. The religious pundits were faring better. Faith was one explanation that didn't carry the burden of proof. Priests, rabbis and muftis were voicing their thoughts on the sign with increasing candour, and the view that faith, not science, was the true explanation was gaining ground. The thought consumed Gracie as she shielded her eyes to watch Dalton's slow ascent.

The ship's captain joined her and Finch, taking stock of progress.

'I got a call from someone at the Pentagon,' he informed them. 'They wanted me to make sure no one left the ship before their people got here. You in particular,' he specified, pointing his finger at Gracie.

'What did you tell them?'

The captain grinned. 'I said we were in the middle of nowhere and I didn't think anyone was going anywhere for the time being.'

Gracie breathed out in relief. 'Thanks,' she said and beamed at him.

The captain shrugged it off. 'It wasn't even a request. It was more like an order. And I don't remember signing up for anyone's army. I'll expect you to kick up a big stink if they ship me off to Guantanamo.'

Gracie smiled. 'You've got it.'

He leaned in closer. 'We're getting flooded with requests from reporters. I'm thinking we should bump up our room rate and rake in some cash.'

'What are you telling them?' Finch asked.

He shrugged. 'We've hung up a no-vacancy sign for the moment. It's hard to say no, but this is a research ship. I don't want to turn it into a Carnival Cruise. Trouble is, we're the only ones out here.' His eyes twinkled mischievously at Gracie. 'Looks like it's still your exclusive.'

'What can I say? I must be blessed.'

'I'm kind of surprised you're in such a rush to get off my ship while everyone else seems so desperate to get on.'

Gracie grinned, 'That's what makes us the best damn investigative reporting team in the business. Always one step ahead of the story.'

As if to rescue her, the harness reappeared and a crew member helped Gracie strap herself into it. Once she was safely locked in, he waved to the winch operator in the chopper, and the slack in the cable began to tighten.

'Thanks again, for everything,' she yelled to the captain.

He flicked her a small parting wave. 'Just let us know what you find out there. We'll be watching.'

The cable yanked Gracie into the ice-speckled air.

West Antarctic Ice Sheet

The four ghosts on the ice shelf watched as the Royal Navy chopper glided over the ship, just under half a mile west of their position.

They weren't worried about being spotted. They just hugged the snow, invisible in their full 'snow-white' camouflage parkas and trousers. Four snowmobiles squatted nearby. Hidden under white camouflage netting, they were virtually undetectable from the sky.

The team leader monitored the chopper through his binoculars as it lifted the last of the news crew off the ship. A smile of satisfaction flitted across his lips. Things were going as planned.

The operation had gone live four days earlier. They'd left their training camp in North Carolina and flown to New Zealand, where they'd been whisked down to McMurdo Station, on Ross Island. From there, an LC-130 Hercules aircraft had ferried them to the ice shelf itself, fifteen miles south of their current position.

To say the job was a priority-one assignment was an understatement. The team leader had never experienced anything quite as intense, as uncompromising, as the rigorous interview process and psychological profiling he'd undergone before getting the job. No expense had been spared in either the training facilities or the gear that was made available to him and his team. The client obviously didn't have budget issues.

It was clear to the team leader that the stakes were higher than on any of his previous assignments. Beirut, Bosnia, Afghanistan, then Iraq—they'd led him here, to the gig of a lifetime. And now it was finally underway.

Something in his pack warbled. He pulled out his satellite phone and pressed the answer key. He waited for the red LED to tell him the call was secure, then spoke.

'This is Fox One.'

A computerised male voice responded. 'What's your status?'

He knew his own voice sounded just as robotic to the caller. Only another phone fitted with the same chip could decode their transmissions.

'We're ready to roll,' Fox One replied.

'Good. Pull your men out and initiate the next phase.'

The team leader terminated the call and glanced up at the sky. It had returned to a monotone, off-white emptiness.

Not a trace, he mused.

Perfect.

Cambridge, Massachusetts

Matt eased the door shut and darted through the hallway into the main bedroom. He had to get the hell out of there. They were only seconds away.

He went straight to the back wall where he'd earlier spotted a half-glazed door that gave onto a ten-foot-square balcony. With his heartbeat throbbing in his ears, he saw that, as he'd suspected, it led to a fire escape.

The door was locked. He looked for a key, but there was nothing in sight. He pulled and yanked at it, but the door stubbornly refused to budge.

A heavy knock pounded the front door. 'Open up, police.'

He didn't want to get caught in the apartment of a possibly dead man who was last seen running away from him after they'd had a bust-up in a crowded bar, so his reflexes took over. He grabbed a side table by the bed, swung it back, and hurled it through the window of the balcony door. Glass exploded as the heavy wooden console thudded onto the decked floor outside. The posse outside the door must have heard it, as a more pointed shout of 'Open up, police' echoed from the stairwell.

Matt dashed across the room and dived behind the door to the bedroom, squeezing himself tightly against the wall just as the front door erupted inwards.

Two men thundered in and charged into the master bedroom, rocketing up to the shattered balcony door. Matt heard one of them yell, 'He's gone down the fire escape. Check out the rest of the place,' before the man disappeared into the darkness outside. His partner darted past Matt and was halfway back through the dark hallway when Matt tackled him from behind. As they tumbled onto the floor, something metallic clattered across the floor. A handgun. The man fought back, lashing out with rapid-fire blows. Matt let loose with an anvil of a punch that caught the downed man just below the left ear and pounded the air out of him. The man curled over, groaning heavily. Matt rolled him back onto his front and felt something under his jacket. He found a pair of handcuffs in a belt pouch. He quickly locked the man's arms around a radiator pipe.

Without glancing back, he flew out of the apartment, hurtling down the stairs. He stopped suddenly at the main entrance to check out the front. There was no sign of the man who'd gone down the fire escape. He took a deep breath to clear his senses, and slipped out into the cold night.

The street was disconcertingly quiet. He crept over to the parked sedan, pulling out his Leatherman and slashing one of the car's front wheels with its blade. He leaped over the small picket fence by the pathway that led up to the house and skirted the front until he reached the alley.

The Mustang was still there. He slid into it as quietly as he could and spurred the engine to life without switching on the headlights. Just as it ticked over, the other cop appeared at the mouth of the alley behind him. He hollered, 'Stop!' reaching for his handgun. He was blocking the way, leaving Matt no way out.

Matt cursed, slammed the car into gear, and floored it. The Mustang leaped forward. Matt strained to see what waited for him at the end of the alley. It wasn't good—a mound of bushy terrain that rose into a thicket of trees. The Mustang didn't have a hope in hell of making it through.

He glanced in his rearview mirror. He could see the shadowy silhouette of the cop coming at him, weapon raised.

Matt was out of options. He slammed the car into reverse. The car lurched backwards through the alley. He hugged the passenger headrest as he steered the car, riding virtually blind. All he could do was keep the car in a straight line and hope the cop didn't have a death wish. A shot reverberated in the narrow space, followed by several more, one of them drilling through the rear windshield and slamming into the passenger headrest.

Matt twitched the steering wheel to angle the car right up against the wall, away from where the cop was firing. The Mustang squealed furiously as it scraped the side of the house, and the cop flattened himself against the opposite wall.

More shots followed him as the Mustang bounced out of the alley and onto the main road, where Matt spun the car so it was aimed right, and powered away.

He glanced in his mirror and saw the cop rush to his car, but Matt knew he wouldn't be following. Still, he wasn't in the clear. An APB concerning his less-than-low-key car would be heating up the airwaves any second now. He had to ditch the Mustang quickly and lie low until dawn.

What he'd do the next day, though, was far less certain.

Washington, DC
Keenan Drucker felt electric. Over a breakfast of waffles and fruit, he'd gone through the newspapers with a quiet satisfaction he hadn't felt for years.

Sitting in his tenth-floor office on Connecticut Avenue, he pivoted in his plush leather chair and looked out across the city. He loved being in the nation's capital, playing a role in shaping the lives of the citizens of the most powerful country on the planet. He'd spent twenty years serving as senior policy advisor and legislative director to a couple of senators, then he'd left the Hill to create and run a well-funded think tank, the Center for American Freedom. A ruthless and imaginative political strategist, he was made for this life, his effectiveness enhanced by easy-going charm that masked an iron resolve.

He checked his watch. A late-morning meeting had been hastily scheduled with the available fellows of the Center to discuss the unexplained apparition over the ice shelf. After that, he'd monitor the news channels to check on the project's status. Which seemed well on track, apart from that small complication in Boston. Drucker wasn't worried. He could trust the Bullet to take care of it.

His BlackBerry pinged. The ring tone told him it was the Bullet. Drucker smiled. *Speak of the devil.*

With his habitual curt efficiency, Maddox updated Drucker on Vince Bellinger's fate, Matt Sherwood's escape, and his foray into the now-dead scientist's apartment. Drucker absorbed the information with detachment.

MADDOX DIDN'T LIKE much about Drucker but he liked the way that he didn't second-guess when it came to matters in which he was no expert. Drucker knew to leave the dirty work to those who were comfortable trudging through the muck, something Maddox had never shied away from.

Maddox was a hands-on kind of guy. He had a single-minded work ethic and unwavering discipline forged out of a twenty-year career with the Marines, where he'd earned the sobriquet 'The Bullet' because of his shaved, slightly pointed head. It was a name that took on an even more disturbing connotation after his squad was cut to bits in a savage firefight in Fallujah. Maddox lost fourteen men and an ear that horrific afternoon. It was the tragedy that had first brought him and Drucker together and united them.

He relived that day every time he caught a glimpse of himself in the mirror. It was branded on his face, in the form of a star-shaped burn that spread out from the small mangled flap of ear that the surgeons had been able to salvage. He also relived the aftermath and the way his superiors had let him down, the way he'd been mistreated and spat out by the system. He found out he'd been lied to. The whole country had. The war was a sham. He watched as the same lying bastards who'd sent him to war voted against funding increases for those who had come home with debilitating injuries. And with each new revelation about the lies behind the war he got angrier. And out of the anger came a realisation that he had to take matters into his own hands if he was going to change anything.

His wounded status made it easier for him to set up shop. Before long, he had dozens of men on his payroll in the hellholes of Afghanistan, Iraq or anywhere else people were paying him to do jobs that no one else wanted to touch. And when this job came up, he immediately realised it was one he couldn't delegate. If this thing could really achieve what Keenan Drucker thought it could, then he sure as hell was going to make sure nothing went wrong.

Still, Drucker didn't sound thrilled by his news. 'I'm not comfortable with Sherwood out there, running around,' Drucker told him. 'You need to put him away before it gets out of hand.'

'Shouldn't take long,' Maddox assured him.

He set his phone down and stewed on the night's events. Matt Sherwood had proved far more resilient than his brother. He was taking impulsive, unexpected initiatives like breaking into Bellinger's apartment. That could prove to be a major nuisance.

Maddox cleared his mind and put himself in Matt's shoes. He extrapolated ahead, looking for the straws at which Matt would be grasping.

He turned to his screen and brought up the phone logs linked to Bellinger and Matt. His eye settled on the phone call from a coworker of Bellinger's by the name of Csaba Komlosy. He clicked on the small icon by the entry and listened to the message left on Bellinger's home phone. He went back and listened to the first call between the two scientists. The one that had precipitated the previous evening's confrontations.

The Bullet checked his watch and picked up his phone.

Boston, Massachusetts

Larry Rydell had just got off the phone with Rebecca. Again. Two calls from his daughter in less than twenty-four hours, far more than usual. They were close, despite the divorce from her mother almost a decade ago, but Rebecca was nineteen and regular phone calls to Daddy had been increasingly crowded out of the whirlwind of activity in her life.

He loved chatting with her. But he hated lying to her. And he had. Twice now, in less than a day. And he'd have to go on lying to her for the rest of his life. It was out there now. There was no turning back. The thought terrified and elated him in equal measure.

It had seemed surreal when he'd first considered the possibility four years earlier. And it had come about fast. The breakup of the ice shelf had been expected, though it had come sooner than they projected. But they'd been ready to capitalise on it. Ready to change the world.

He thought back to that fateful evening with Dominic Reece, three years earlier. A great dinner. An inspired late-night chat about the possibilities of the manufacturing breakthrough that Reece had achieved. The many and diverse applications it could be used for. And then, the mere mention of a word: *miraculous*. One word. A catalyst that sent Rydell's mind tripping into uncharted territory. And here he was now, and the impossible had become a reality.

Reece. The brilliant scientist's face drifted into his consciousness. Other faces materialised alongside it—young, talented, dedicated, all of them—and with them, a cold feeling deep inside. He felt his very soul shrivel at the memory of that last day in Namibia. He could still see Maddox pulling the trigger. He could hear himself shout, hear the bullet thumping into Reece's back, see his friend's body jerk before toppling into Danny Sherwood's arms.

The images of that day had been gnawing away at him ever since. He hated himself for not having been able to stop it. And, despite what the others told him about the greater good or about sacrificing the lives of the few for the lives of the many, the platitudes did not work.

He hadn't realised to what lengths the others were prepared to go. And it was too late now to do anything about it. If everything he'd worked for was to succeed, he just had to swallow it all and keep going. Maybe, if all went well, their deaths would amount to something in the end. Although he knew their ghosts wouldn't let go of him, even then.

SHELTERING BEHIND a tall hedge in the early-morning chill, Matt waited and watched, trying to make sure no unpleasant surprises were in store for him at the hotel before making his way in. He slipped past a few bleary-eyed businessmen, took the elevator to the fifth floor, and reached the refuge of his room. He was as tired as he was pissed off.

He'd had to dump the Mustang a few blocks from Bellinger's place. The car represented a personal milestone for him, a notable step on his road back from the edge. And now he had been forced to abandon it because of the same bastards who had taken Danny away. He was seriously pissed off.

After parking the Mustang, he'd hot-wired a decade-old Ford Taurus then headed out of town before looping back on the turnpike, on the lookout for any blue-and-whites. He'd parked behind a shopping centre around the corner from the hotel.

His muscles and nerves were ravaged by tension and fatigue, so he took a long, hot shower to reinvigorate himself and, twenty minutes later, he was back at a workstation in the business centre.

He used the phone directory web site to do a reverse listings search on the phone number he had got from Bellinger's answering machine. It yielded the curious name of Csaba Komlosy, with a home address in the same geek-central catchment area that Bellinger lived in. He thought about calling Komlosy, but decided against it. The goons seemed to be avid wiretappers. A face-to-face would be better anyway. He jotted down the address, then, deciding he couldn't duck it any more, pulled up the web site of the *Boston Globe*.

It was the first item in the local, breaking news section. His face contorted with sadness and rage. A stabbing close to a bar in South Boston, shortly after midnight. They'd identified the body as Bellinger's. A murder investigation was under way. The report didn't mention Matt—yet. But he knew there'd be more to come on that front. They'd make sure of it.

He took in a deep breath and let it out slowly, willing his fury to subside. A moment later, he keyed in the home page of his tracking device, and logged in.

The Chrysler was no longer outside his place.

A detailed map displayed the car's itinerary in thirty-second increments. Matt saw that the goons had given up their stakeout—or passed the baton to the next team—almost an hour ago. He wondered if this meant that they were already aware of his little excursion to Bellinger's place. If they were, it meant they had insights into police activity, either through radio scanners or someone inside the department. He made a mental note of it and zoomed in on the Chrysler's current location.

It was parked on a street in Brighton, not far from St Elizabeth's Medical Center, and hadn't moved for twenty-three minutes. The tracker's web site featured a link-up with Google Maps. Matt clicked on the 'street view' option and a wide-angle shot popped up of a narrow, residential street. The fix fell on a tired-looking, seal-grey house with a small balcony and a gabled window in its roof. He needed to take a closer look.

It didn't take long to get there at this early hour. He hit a red light at a big intersection and as he sat there behind a tattered pick-up truck, his gaze was drawn beyond it. A Chrysler 300C was waiting at the opposite light, facing him, left indicator on.

He focused on it, trying to ascertain whether it was 'his' 300C. The opposite light changed to green and the Chrysler cut across the intersection. As it streaked past, Matt got a look at the guy in the front passenger seat. Although his hard features fit the bill, Matt wasn't sure. Sealing it for him, though, was the 300C's licence plate. *It was them.*

He spun the wheel and hit the gas, steering the car around the pick-up truck and following in the Chrysler's wake. It was more of an instinctive reaction than a rational move, but, a few car lengths behind, his decision grew on him. There were only two of them in the car, and he didn't mind those odds. Not with the way he was feeling right now.

As they headed up River, an uncomfortable feeling twitched inside him, flaring into full-blown dread when he saw the name of the street the Chrysler had turned into and spotting the number of the building where it had pulled up.

They were parked right outside Csaba Komlosy's place.

Matt coaxed the Taurus past the Chrysler, turning away to hide his face as he drove by. He took the first side street he found, and pulled over.

He sat in the car, unsure what this meant. Was this Csaba character working with them? Had he helped them set up Bellinger? Somehow that didn't ring true. The message Csaba had left for Bellinger sounded genuine enough.

If Csaba wasn't working with them, then they had to be here for the same reasons they'd gone after Bellinger. Which didn't give Csaba much of a rosy future. The fact that the goons were after him meant that he knew something, something that could shed light on what had happened to Danny.

Matt had to do something. He slipped out of the Taurus and crept over to the corner. He edged out carefully and looked down the street. The Chrysler hadn't moved; the two silhouettes were still inside, stalking Csaba.

Matt had to get to him first, but the guys in the Chrysler had a controlling view of the street and a clear line of sight to the entrance lobby of Csaba's six-storey block. There was a ramp at the side of the building, the kind that led to an underground garage. Problem was, it too was within their sight line.

He pulled back from the corner and sprinted farther up the side street, and found a narrow alley that ran between two houses. He cut into it and advanced cautiously, closing in on Csaba's block—only to hit a five-foot-tall wooden fence. He clambered over the fence and kept going. He reached a side passage that ran alongside the ramp and led back to the street.

The Chrysler was still there, and he still couldn't make it onto the ramp without them seeing him. Just then, Matt heard a low, creaking rumble—the garage door opening. He edged back. The nose of a large, black Escalade emerged from the garage. The SUV charged up the ramp and stopped where it met the street, momentarily blocking the Chrysler's view.

Matt seized the opportunity. He leaped over the low wall that gave onto the ramp. He dived through the garage door as it closed, and took cover to one side, hoping he hadn't been spotted.

The apartment numbers were listed next to the floor buttons in the elevator. He rode it to the third and made his way to Csaba's door and rang the bell. A shadow fell across the bottom of the door.

'Who is it?' It was the same slightly wired voice from the answering machine.

'I'm a friend of Vince Bellinger.'

Csaba's voice had a stammer in it. 'What do you want?'

'We need to talk. Something happened to him.'

More shuffling, then Csaba said, 'Vince is dead, man. I don't know what you want, but—'

'Listen to me,' Matt interjected bluntly, 'the same guys who killed him are parked outside your building right now. They heard your phone calls last night and that's what got him killed. So if you want me to help you not end up like him, open the goddamn door.'

The door cracked open. A wide, boyish face surrounded by a shock of shaggy hair peered through the slit. Csaba's eyes widened in panic at the sight of Matt's face and he tried to push the door shut.

Matt shoved the door back and charged in. The big man raised his arms defensively, tripping over himself as he backed away from Matt.

'Don't kill me, man. I don't know anything.'

'Calm down,' Matt shot back. 'I'm not here to kill you.'

Csaba stared at him in terror, droplets of sweat all over his face. Matt studied him for a brief moment—then his attention was torn away by an image on the TV. It was on one of the twenty-four-hour news networks and showed the same glowing sign he'd seen earlier, only this wasn't the same footage. A banner at the bottom of the screen proclaimed, SECOND UNEXPLAINED SIGHTING, NOW OVER GREENLAND.

Matt inched closer to the screen, his forehead furrowed in confusion. 'This isn't the same one as before, is it?'

'No,' Csaba stammered. 'This one's in the Arctic. Don't kill me, dude.'

Matt was missing something. 'Stop saying that, all right? What is wrong with you?'

Csaba hesitated, then said, 'I know you killed Vince. Your face is on the news.'

Alarm flooded through Matt. 'My face? Show me,' Matt ordered.

Cairo, Egypt

Gracie spotted the man in the black cassock angling for her attention among the throngs of people lining the arrivals hall at Cairo International Airport. She caught Brother Ameen's eye, and the monk moved through the crowd to meet her, Dalton and Finch.

The journey there had been fretfully long. They'd used the time to read up about the Coptic religion and the monastery's history. No one back in DC, apart from Hal Ogilvy, the network's global news director, had been told they'd left Antarctica, or where they were headed. The exclusivity of their story had to be ferociously guarded from the rest of the pack.

Gracie, Dalton and Finch were aware of the new apparition over Greenland. The electrifying news had shaken the tiredness out of their bones and injected them with renewed vigour. And as they sat in the back of Yusuf's Previa, inching their way through the early-evening traffic and into the city, they couldn't put their questions to Brother Ameen fast enough.

He confirmed that, as far as he could tell, it was identical to the apparition they'd seen over the ice shelf—and to the symbols lining the walls of Father Jerome's cave. The ones he'd started drawing seven months earlier.

Gracie was now certain she'd made the right choice in heeding the monk's call and coming to Egypt. She couldn't remember the last time she'd felt this energised by the thrill of an exclusive. There were many questions she needed answered. Starting with Father Jerome.

'Why did he come here in the first place?' she asked.

Brother Ameen hesitated. 'The truth is,' he said, 'We're not sure.'

'He was working in Sudan before, wasn't he?' Finch queried.

'Yes. Father Jerome was very concerned with what was happening in Darfur. Earlier this year, he opened another orphanage near the border with Egypt. And then . . . he doesn't quite understand it himself. He left the orphanage one night on foot. He just walked out, into the desert.'

'Weren't they worried he'd be kidnapped or killed? He was very critical of the warlords,' Gracie said. 'He would have been a big prize for them.'

'The massacres in Darfur affected him deeply. He got very sick—it was a miracle he pulled through. The night he left, he told his aides he needed to go away to "find God" and asked them to make sure their good work continued during his absence. Five months later, some bedouins found him in the desert, a few kilometres south of here. He was in a simple robe, torn and filthy. His bare feet were cut and calloused; he was delirious, barely alive. It seemed that he'd crossed the desert. On his own. On foot.'

Gracie's eyes flared in puzzlement. 'But it's, what, six hundred miles from here to the border, isn't it? How did he survive?'

The monk looked at her with an expression that mirrored her confusion, but said nothing.

'What does Father Jerome say?' Gracie asked.

'He doesn't remember. But he believes he was meant to come to our monastery. He believes it was part of God's plan.' The monk paused. 'You can ask him yourself, when you meet him.'

'What about the documentary?' Gracie asked. 'How did it came about?'

Brother Ameen shrugged. 'There's not much to tell. They contacted us. They said they'd heard about Father Jerome being in the cave, and could they film him. The abbot wasn't keen, but they were coming from a very respectable network. They kept on asking and, eventually, we accepted.'

'Lucky you did,' Finch told him. 'We wouldn't be here otherwise.'

'Oh, I don't know,' the monk replied. 'God works in mysterious ways. I imagine he would have found another way to bring you here, don't you?'

Cambridge, Massachusetts

Csaba's desk was a mess of magazines and coffee cups. A large flat screen rose out of the morass. It, too, showed the light over the ice shelf. Csaba tapped in a few keys and brought up a brief crime report.

Bellinger's body had been found in an alleyway not far from the bar. The report featured two black-and-white shots from a security camera. One was a wide shot, showing Matt and Vince in mid-tussle. The other was a close-up of Matt's face, taken from another frame. He was pretty recognisable.

Matt didn't see his name anywhere, although he knew that wouldn't last. The article mentioned several witnesses, including an 'unnamed woman' who claimed she was outside the bar when she saw Matt chase Bellinger down the street. Matt frowned, his mind flashing back to the woman in the van, the shoulder-length auburn bob framing her face. One and the same, he was certain. He pictured the police showing up at his place, search warrant in hand. He also pictured them finding the murder weapon that bob-girl and her buddies must have planted there.

'I know how this looks,' Matt told Csaba, 'but that's not what happened. These guys came after Vince Bellinger because of this thing in Antarctica.' He pointed angrily at the TV screen. 'He thought my brother might have been murdered because of it. *They* killed Vince. I didn't. You have to believe me.'

Which, reading Csaba's jittery eyes, seemed like a tall order.

'You and Vince,' Matt asked. 'You were talking about it, weren't you?'

Csaba nodded reluctantly.

It was all Matt had time for right now. 'I need you to tell me what you guys said, but that can wait. They're outside. We need to get out of here.'

'"We"?' Csaba flinched, reaching for his phone. 'Hey, I'm not going anywhere. You can do what you want. I'm calling the cops and—'

'We don't have time for that,' Matt grabbed the phone and slammed it down. 'They're here. If you want to live, you're going to have to come with me.'

Csaba hesitated, then he nodded.

'Do you have a car?'

'No.'

'Doesn't matter. Come on.' Matt sprinted towards the door.

'Wait,' Csaba blurted, grabbing a backpack off the floor. 'Gimme a sec.' He stuffed his MacBook laptop, charger and iPhone into the backpack.

'Switch off your cell,' Matt told Csaba. 'They can track us with it.'

Csaba's mouth dropped an inch. 'You're right,' he said, as he fished out the phone and turned it off.

They took the elevator down to the garage. It was home to a dozen or so cars. Matt settled on a Toyota RAV4, grabbed a fire extinguisher off the wall and smashed the driver's window with it. 'Get in,' he ordered.

The big man stood there, slack-jawed. 'That's Mrs Jooris's car. She's gonna be seriously pissed, dude.'

'Get in.'

In the time it took Csaba to cram himself into the passenger seat, Matt had got the engine running. He threw the car in gear, and screeched up to the garage door. An unseen sensor had already instructed it to open. As it rose, the ramp appeared ahead, curving to the left.

'Hang on,' Matt said.

His fingers tightened against the steering wheel as he nudged the RAV4 up the ramp slowly. The goons would see him soon enough—which happened the instant the small SUV cleared the side of the building.

Matt locked eyes with the two startled men facing him in the Chrysler, committing as much of their features to memory as he could in that nanosecond, his foot poised on the accelerator.

He was about to floor the pedal when he spotted a car coming down the street towards him and, just as the approaching car was almost level with him, Matt charged right in front of it, cutting it off. The car, a lumbering old Caprice, scraped against the Toyota and bounced off it, its driver swerving into the opposite lane and screeching to a stop right alongside the Chrysler. Matt hit the gas and tore down the street, headed in the opposite direction to the one in which the Chrysler was facing. He watched in the rearview mirror as the goons climbed out of the Chrysler to get the man to move so they could turn round to take up pursuit.

Matt pulled a screaming left before charging down one empty street after another, changing directions often as he wove his way out of the city, all the while keeping a wary eye on his mirrors for the Chrysler. It was gone.

He glanced at Csaba. 'How do you pronounce your name anyway?'

'Call me "Jabba",' he replied. 'Everyone does.'

Matt shrugged. 'OK, then. Let's ditch this car and find a safe place. Then I'm going to need you to tell me exactly what you and Vince were talking about and help me figure out what the hell is going on.'

Deir Al-Suryan Monastery, Wadi Natrun, Egypt

The Previa had left the desert behind and was cutting through the traffic leading into Cairo. It was early evening, and the low sun's fading light punctured the mist of exhaust fumes and dust.

'Does he know what's going on yet?' Gracie asked Brother Ameen. 'Have you told him about the signs?'

'Not yet.' The monk glanced at her uneasily. 'Actually, he doesn't know you're coming. The abbot doesn't know either—he didn't want the outside world to know about it.'

'But you did,' Finch prompted.

The monk nodded. 'Something miraculous is happening. We can't keep it to ourselves. It's not ours to keep.'

Gracie looked over at Finch. They'd been around such situations before: travelling into trouble spots to talk to reluctant interviewees. Sometimes, Gracie and Finch managed to get through; other times, they were locked out. In this case, they had to make it happen. They hadn't flown halfway round the globe to leave empty-handed.

The chaotic mess of Cairo quickly gave way to sleepier, scattered clusters of houses and, as they passed the last town before the desert and the monasteries, they lost the signals on their cellphones. The monk informed them that they'd be limited to the satphone from there on.

Before long, the monastery of Deir Al-Suryan appeared at the end of a dusty lane. It looked like an ark adrift in a sea of sand. Detail soon fell into focus as the Previa drew nearer: two tall bell towers; the squat, four-storey keep; the small domes with crosses on them strewn around the chapels and structures inside the walled complex; all of it surrounded by a fortified wall.

They got out of the Previa, then Brother Ameen led them across the inner courtyard. Every surface, wall and dome alike, was covered with a clay-and-limestone adobe of a pleasing, sandlike beige. The walls of the keep were dotted with tiny, irregular openings in place of windows—to keep the heat out—and narrow staircases led in all kinds of directions.

As they approached the entrance to the library, a monk stepped out and looked at them, first curiously, then with a dour expression. Gracie guessed it was the abbot.

'Please wait here,' Brother Ameen told Gracie and Finch. They stayed behind while he intercepted the clearly irate abbot. A moment later, Brother Ameen came back with the elderly man.

'I'm Father Kyrillos,' he told them dryly. He didn't offer his hand. 'I'm afraid Brother Ameen overstepped his bounds by inviting you here.'

'Father,' Finch said, 'please accept our apologies for arriving like this. We certainly don't mean to inconvenience you. If you'd like us out of here, just say the word and we'll head home. But I ask you to keep two things in mind. One, our boss is the only one who knows where we are. So you mustn't worry about this suddenly becoming a media circus. We won't let it happen.' He paused, waiting to see if his words were having any effect. He thought he detected a softening in the man's frown.

'Two,' he pressed on, 'we're only here to help you and Father Jerome understand the extraordinary events that we're witnessing. We were in Antarctica. We saw it all right in front of us. So we're here foremost as expert witnesses. We won't broadcast anything without your permission. What we see here remains between us until you allow otherwise.'

The abbot studied him and glanced over at Gracie and at Dalton. After a moment, he seemed to reach a verdict. 'You want to talk to Father Jerome?'

'Yes,' Finch replied. 'We can tell him what we saw. Show him what we filmed. And maybe he can make sense of it.'

The abbot nodded. 'Very well.'

He invited them into a simple building dating from the seventies. Finch and Gracie followed while Dalton scooted off back to the courtyard. Brother Ameen had told them the monastery didn't have a television, and they were aching to see the new footage from the Arctic and the reaction to it.

Gracie and Finch gratefully accepted a drink of water and a small platter of cheese and dates. They'd barely had time to exchange pleasantries when Dalton popped his head through the door. 'We're up.'

Dalton had linked his laptop to a collapsible satellite dish and was on the news network's web site. Gracie, Finch, the abbot and the monk huddled around him while he played the news clip of the sighting over Greenland.

A graphic showed the location of the sighting, by the Carlsbad Fjord, four hundred miles north of the Arctic Circle. The footage that followed was eerily familiar, and had been captured by a team of scientists who were studying the effects of meltwater on glaciers. The apparition had taken them by surprise. A white-bearded glaciologist was interviewed live.

'First, Antarctica, and now here,' the offscreen anchorman's voice came through. 'Why do you think this is happening?'

'Look, I don't know what it is,' the scientist answered with a gruff voice. 'What I do know is that it can't be a coincidence that this *sign* is showing up over disaster areas. That ice shelf in Antarctica and this glacier here— they're ground zero. I've been studying these glaciers for over twenty years. It used to be nothing but snow and ice, year-round. Now it's melting so fast that we've got lakes and rivers all over the place, and that water's loosening the bases of the glaciers, which is why they've started to slide out to sea. And if this one goes, we're talking a three-foot rise in global sea levels. So,

I think nature's flashing us a red alert here, and I think we need to take that warning seriously, before it's too late.'

The report cut away to a montage of reactions to the sign's second appearance. A large crowd had congregated in Times Square, watching the scenes unfold on the huge screen. Similar scenes were captured in London, Moscow and other major cities. The world was sitting up and taking notice.

The satphone dragged Gracie's attention away from the screen. It was Ogilvy.

'I just got a call from the Pentagon. Two DIA guys just landed in McMurdo and found out you'd skipped town. They're pretty pissed off.'

Gracie frowned. 'What did you have to tell them?'

'Nothing. It's still a free country. But they'll track you to Cairo Airport pretty quickly. From there . . . who knows. Switch off your phones.'

'There's no signal out here anyway,' she told him.

'Check your satphone every hour; I'll text you if anything comes up.'

'We'll do that. I'll get you the land line of the monastery too.'

Ogilvy's voice took on a serious tone. 'Talk to Father Jerome, Gracie. Quickly. We've got to keep our lead on this thing. It's ours for the taking.'

Gracie glanced uneasily at the monks and turned her back to them, lowering her voice. 'We've got to be careful here, Hal. This is a Muslim country. I'm not sure they'd react kindly to something that smells like a Second Coming, especially not in their own back yard.'

'It's where it happened the first time,' Ogilvy remarked drily.

'Hal, seriously, we need to tread carefully. I don't want to put Father Jerome in any danger.'

'I don't want to put anyone in danger, either,' Ogilvy countered, slightly testily. 'We'll be careful. Just talk to him. We'll take it from there.'

Gracie relented. 'I'll call you after I meet him.' Then she snapped the phone shut and turned to the abbot. 'The documentary footage they filmed in the cave. Can we see it?'

'Of course. It's on the DVD they sent us—I haven't watched it as we don't have a player here.'

'This laptop'll play it,' Dalton told him, tapping his computer. The abbot left them and reappeared quickly, DVD in hand. Dalton loaded it up and fast-forwarded until the screen showed the small film crew climbing up the mountain and approaching an old door cut into the rock face.

'There,' the abbot exclaimed. 'That's Father Jerome's cave.'

Dalton reverted to play mode, and the screen showed the cameraman's point of view as he entered the cave. Gracie watched, heart in mouth, as the camera tracked through the dark chamber. Then it banked around and covered the curving ceiling of the chamber.

'Right there,' Gracie burst out. 'That's it, isn't it?'

Dalton backtracked a few frames, and played the clip again in slow motion. They all leaned in for a closer look. It was just a brief shot, but it was all they needed. Dalton froze the image on one of the painted symbols, an elegant construction of concentric circles and intersecting lines that radiated outwards. Despite its simplicity, it managed to convey what they'd seen over the ice shelf. It was unmistakable.

Gracie turned to the abbot. Her nerves were buzzing with anticipation. 'When can we go there? Given what's happening, I don't think we should wait. We ought to talk to Father Jerome tonight.'

The abbot held her gaze. 'Very well. In that case, we should go now.'

LYING UNDER a sand-coloured camouflage net four hundred yards west of the monastery's gate, Fox Two watched through high-powered binoculars as Gracie, Finch and Dalton, accompanied by the abbot and another monk, climbed into a waiting people carrier.

His satphone vibrated. The text message told him Fox One and his team had just landed. As expected.

He watched as the Previa drove away in a swirl of dust and waited until they were half a mile away before pushing himself to his knees. Crouching low, he stowed the netting in its pack, then slipped away to rejoin his two men, who waited nearby. The mountain beckoned.

Woburn, Massachusetts

The motel was grubby and run-down, but it provided Matt and Jabba with the basics: shelter and anonymity. And, right now, that was what they needed most. That, and some answers.

Matt was sitting on the floor, leaning against the bed. Jabba, on the other hand, was pacing around, making repeated checks out of the window.

'Just sit the hell down,' Matt snapped.

'I'm sorry, all right?' Jabba fired back. 'I'm just not used to this. It's insane. Why can't we just go to the cops and tell them what you know?'

''Cause what I know is nothing compared to what the cops think they know. Now do me and this carpet a favour and sit down.'

Jabba stared at him, then set himself down on the bed. He palmed the remote and changed channels on the TV bolted onto the wall.

News of the Greenland apparition was on every channel. The world was, simply, entranced.

Matt exhaled wearily. 'Tell me what you and Vince talked about last night.'

'We were watching this thing,' Jabba pointed at the screen. 'The first one, anyway. Trying to work out how it could be done.'

Matt sat up. '"Done"? You think it's a fake?'

Jabba gave him a look. 'Dude. Come on. Something like this happens, your first instinct has to be it's a fake. There's so much bullshit out there, whether it's from the government or from people who are out to make a fast buck, you've got to look at things with a cynic's eye. And we're scientists, man. Our instinct is to ask questions first.'

Matt nodded. 'You and Vince come up with anything?'

'Nothing at all. We couldn't even begin to figure it out. If this thing is a fake, then whoever's doing it is using some pretty advanced technology.'

Matt frowned. 'What is it you guys do, anyway? I mean, if it *was* a fake, what made you think you and Vince could figure it out?'

'We're electrical engineers. We design computer circuits, microchips, that kind of thing.'

'That doesn't sound particularly relevant to this thing.'

'What we do is not just a job,' Jabba explained. 'It's a calling. It takes over your life. And part of it is keeping track of everything that's going on. You've got to know what everyone else is doing, whether it's at NASA, in Silicon Valley, or in some lab in Singapore. Because everything's interconnected. One of their breakthroughs could be combined with what you're doing and send your work in a completely new direction.'

'Well if you couldn't figure it out, why was your conversation a threat to anyone? Do you think you might have hit on something without knowing it?'

'I doubt it. Everything we talked about is public knowledge.'

'So why come after Vince? And why did it make him think that my brother was somehow involved?'

The word threw Jabba. 'Your brother?'

'Vince thought my brother might have been killed because of it.'

'Who was your brother?'

'Danny Sherwood.'

The name had clearly struck a chord. 'Danny was your brother?'

Matt nodded. 'You knew him?'

'I knew of him, sure. Vince said he was the most brilliant programmer he'd ever met.' He let the words settle as his mind tried to see the connections. 'What did Vince tell you, exactly?'

'He said someone called Reece hired Danny to work with him on something. You heard of him?'

'Dominic Reece. They all went down in the chopper, didn't they?' Jabba's expression tightened. 'Vince told you he thought they'd been murdered?'

'Maybe. He said they were working on some kind of biosensor project. Does that mean anything to you?'

'No. But Vince and Danny were close. He might have told him something he wasn't supposed to spread around. In our business, one slip of the tongue could lose you a billion-dollar advantage.'

Matt rubbed the exhaustion from his eyes. 'You and Vince. That night. What was the last thing he said?'

Jabba concentrated. 'He didn't say it. I did. I was just saying that it looked like the air itself was being lit up. Like the air molecules themselves were on fire. Only that's not possible.'

Matt studied the grainy image on the screen. 'What about a laser, a projector, something that needs the skill set of one hell of a programmer.'

Jabba just shook his head. 'Nothing I know of can do that.'

Matt shut his eyes and leaned back, frustrated. 'There's a reason they killed Vince. And it has to do with what happened to Danny and the others. Whether this damn sign is real or not, someone's doing something.'

Jabba's face sank. 'And you want to find out who's doing it.'

'Yep.'

'Are you nuts? I mean, what are you, an ex-cop or something? Ex-FBI? Some kind of ex-SEAL special ops hard-ass maybe?'

Matt shook his head. 'You've got me pegged on the wrong side of that fence.'

'Oh, that's just wonderful,' Jabba groaned. 'Dude, these are bad people. We're talking about guys who kill by the chopper-load. We're screwed, aren't we?'

Matt ignored the question. 'Can you find out who else was on that chopper? What their specialities were? And also . . . who was funding them?'

Jabba sighed. 'Like I have a choice?' He pulled out his laptop.

'Think you can get an Internet connection in this dump?'

'I seriously doubt they have WiFi here, but . . .' Jabba held up his iPhone and flashed Matt a knowing look. Then his face clouded. 'Forgot. Can't use this.' He thought about it. 'I can fire it up for forty seconds. Any longer than that and they'll get a fix on where we are.'

'OK. But just to play it safe, maybe the guy at reception'll let you use his computer. I need a little update on where our friends with the Chrysler are hanging out.'

Mountains of Wadi Natrun, Egypt

Father Jerome looked very different from how Gracie had imagined: thinner, more gaunt-faced, more fragile. But even here, in the light of the gas lanterns in the oppressively dark cave, his piercing green-grey eyes, blazing out of his tanned face, were captivating.

'So you don't remember anything at all of your journey?' Gracie asked him. 'You were out there for weeks, weren't you?'

'Three months,' he answered. Gracie, Finch and Dalton had been pleasantly surprised by the fact that he hadn't refused to see them. Far from it. He'd been welcoming, and Gracie had immediately warmed to him.

She had decided not to ask for this first interview to be filmed. She felt it was best to spend a bit of time getting to know him. She also wasn't sure how he'd react to seeing the footage of the signs in the sky. And she felt uneasy at the thought of springing the news on him with a camera rolling.

She glanced up at the roof of the cavern. The white swirls, unsettling representations of the sign she'd witnessed over the ice shelf, were all over it.

'Tell me about these,' she asked him.

The priest looked upwards thoughtfully. 'Shortly after I arrived here, a clarity that I'd never experienced before came over me. It was as if my mind were suddenly freed to see life for what it really was. I just need to close my eyes and these ideas start flowing through me. It's beyond my control. I've been writing them down.' He pointed at a few notebooks on his desk. 'Like a faithful scribe,' he added.

Gracie couldn't take her eyes off him as he spoke. Most unsettling was how utterly normal he sounded, as if he were describing the most mundane of experiences. She pointed upwards. 'You painted these, didn't you?'

He nodded slowly. 'It's something I can't explain. I found myself drawing the symbol, over and over. I'm not sure what it means, but . . . it's there, in my head. I just need to close my eyes and I can see it. Anytime.'

'So you've never actually seen it physically? Could it be something you saw while you were out in the desert? In the sky?'

'Anything's possible. Those weeks are nothing but a blur.'

Gracie glanced at Dalton, who was keying in commands on his laptop.

'I'd like to show you something we filmed in Antarctica before coming here. It has to do with this symbol you've been drawing. Would you like to see it?'

The priest nodded. 'Please,' he said.

Dalton hit a button. The video from Antarctica played. Gracie kept her gaze locked on Father Jerome as he absorbed the images unfurling before him. The clip seemed to confuse him. He leaned in for a closer look, his forehead furrowed.

When it was finished, he was lost for words. 'What does this mean?'

Gracie didn't have an answer. From the silence around her, it didn't seem like anyone else did either. She said, 'There was another sighting like that in Greenland just a few hours ago.'

Father Jerome picked up one of his notebooks. He rifled through its pages. 'I don't understand it,' he mumbled. 'It's what I've been seeing. And yet . . .'

Gracie hesitantly reached out. He placed the book in her hand.

She leafed through a few pages. They were all packed densely with an elegant, handwritten script and elaborate renderings of the sign.

'When I see it,' the priest continued, 'it speaks to me. It's as if it's putting the words and ideas in my head.' He studied their faces intently, his eyes jumping from one to the other. 'Don't you hear them too?'

Gracie didn't know what to answer. The abbot placed a comforting arm around Father Jerome's shoulder. 'Perhaps we should take a small break,' he suggested.

'Of course,' Gracie agreed. 'We'll wait outside.'

She, Dalton and Finch stepped out into the small clearing outside the cave's entrance. The last vestiges of day were now gone. The ink-black dome above them blazed with a dazzling array of stars.

Gracie suddenly remembered Ogilvy. 'Where's the satphone?' she asked.

Finch retrieved it from his bag, which he'd left at the entrance to the cave, and switched it on. Within seconds, it pinged with several text messages. One was from Ogilvy. It said, CALL ME AS SOON AS YOU GET THIS. Finch handed it to Gracie. 'Something's up.'

The curtness of the message unsettled her as she thumbed the redial key. Ogilvy picked up inside of one ring. 'They just aired the documentary footage from the cave.'

Gracie froze. 'What?'

'The whole thing's out. Father Jerome, the monastery, the symbol he's painted all over his cave. It's on every TV screen from here to Shanghai,' he told her, clearly struggling to process the implications himself. 'This thing's just blown wide open.'

Boston, Massachusetts

Larry Rydell strode down the wide hallway to his office. As he reached the secretarial pool stationed outside his door, he saw Mona, his senior PA, and three other assistants clustered around the bank of wall-mounted LCD screens that were tuned to the major international news channels.

Mona waved him over. 'Did you see this?' she asked. 'It's from a documentary they filmed six months ago in an old monastery in Egypt.'

The blood drained from his face as the significance of what was showing on the screen sank in. He managed to mask his unease and feigned sharing their excitement for a minute before retreating into his office, where he studied the news reports in private. He was familiar with Father Jerome, but he'd never heard of the monastery. Close-ups of the markings on the cave wall showed they were definitely renderings of the sign. Which sent Rydell's mind cartwheeling in all kinds of troubling directions.

The news networks were competing to make sense of it. 'If what we're seeing here is true,' one pundit was saying on screen, 'then, clearly, there's an association between this unexplained phenomenon and a Christian man of faith who somehow foresaw these events we've been witnessing . . .'

The implications of the footage were creating a huge stir. Evangelists and born-again Christians had begun staking their claim to the sign and making all kinds of prophetic proclamations. More would inevitably come from other religions, Rydell was certain.

Which wasn't part of the plan.

They'd expected crazies to make all sorts of nonsensical declarations. But this was no nutcase. This was Father Jerome. Something was very wrong.

He'd misjudged them again. The certainty sent a bracing shot of ice through his veins. He did all he could to keep his anger in check as he picked up the phone and dialled Drucker.

Washington, DC

In his office on Connecticut Avenue, Keenan Drucker marvelled at how quickly the media pounced on any development. He felt a deep-rooted satisfaction at how things were unfolding, then dropped his gaze to a framed picture on his desk. Jackson, his son—his dead son—beamed back at him.

Drucker felt the same stab of grief every time he glanced at the picture. He tried to keep that image of Jackson in his mind—alive, handsome, proudly turned out in his crisp officer's dress uniform—eyes blazing with a sense of pride and purpose. But he never could. The images from the visit to the mortuary, when he and his wife were presented with what was left of their son, were permanently chiselled into his soul. I'll make things right, he thought. I'll make sure it never happens again.

He tore his eyes off his son's face and looked up at the screen. He surfed away from the mainstream news networks and trawled the Christian channels. The footage from the caves was whipping up a storm of excitement and the people in the street were lapping it up. The preachers, however, were being more cautious. He watched as one televangelist after another gave a cagey response. Typical, he thought.

'If he's the real deal,' he heard one pundit remark, 'these preachers will soon be falling over themselves to claim him as their own.'

They'll get there, he mused. They just need some encouragement.

Covert encouragement, to be precise. Which was something Keenan Drucker excelled at.

His BlackBerry pinged. It was Rydell—as expected. Time for damage control. He picked up and immediately heard Rydell's voice—agitated.

'Keenan, what the hell's going on?'

'Not on the phone,' he replied curtly

'I'll fly down in the morning. Meet me at Reagan. Eight o'clock.'

Drucker nodded to himself. Anticipating Rydell's reaction was simple. But it meant he needed to initiate an effect of his own.

Maddox picked up his call within two rings.

'Where are we with Sherwood's brother?' Drucker asked him.

'It's under control,' Maddox said. 'I'm dealing with it myself.'

Drucker frowned. He didn't expect the Bullet to dive in himself unless things were getting out of hand. He decided now was not the time to delve further on that front. He had a more pressing message to convey.

'Get the girl,' he said. Then he hung up.

Mexico

Almost two thousand miles east, Rebecca Rydell was enjoying a late lie-in. It was past lunch time, but at the Rydells' sprawling villa on the sun-kissed Mexican coast, life was unfettered by such mundane limitations.

The door to her room swung open and two men hurried in: Ben and Jon, the bodyguards her father insisted should accompany her whenever she left the country. They were normally very discreet and stayed well out of sight, so for them to be barging into her bedroom like this meant that something bad had happened.

'Get dressed,' Ben told her bluntly. 'We have to get you out of here.'

He picked up a floral-patterned dress that was strewn across the foot of her bed and flung it at her. 'Let's go,' he ordered.

Something about the way he said it made her uneasy. She grabbed her phone. 'Where's my dad? Is he OK?'

Ben snatched the phone out of her hand. 'He's fine. You can talk to him later.' He slipped her phone into his pocket.

She nodded and reached for her dress. The two men turned to give her some privacy as she pulled it on. They were professionals. She knew her dad hired only the best of the best. She was in safe hands.

She slipped her sandals on. Seconds later, they were rushing her out of the house and into a waiting car.

Everything's going to be fine, she told herself, although deep inside a voice was telling her she was wrong.

Brighton, Massachusetts

Matt had been parked across the street from the target house for over an hour, thinking about his options. Not liking any of them.

He'd ditched the RAV4 and picked up a bathtub-white Camry. Probably the blandest car he'd ever stolen. He'd felt a pang of guilt as he'd hot-wired it. Still, he didn't really have a choice.

The grey house he was watching was equally unremarkable. Run-down, two floors, gabled roof. Probably leased in the name of a shell company. A small driveway ran alongside it and led to a covered garage at the back. The Chrysler was parked outside, as was the van he'd escaped from earlier.

No one had gone in or out of the house, but the cars, and the lights in the front room, suggested the goons were in. He tried to think how many had been in the van—four, he thought. Which was bad enough. He didn't know if the two in the Chrysler were part of that crew or additional, in which case there'd be six. Which would be even worse.

Matt thought of waiting till it got dark, to give him more cover, but he didn't feel like loitering around that long.

He decided to chance it.

He skulked behind the Chrysler. The back of the house was just dark and still. He looked through the car's window, but he couldn't see anything of interest. It was a new car, high-specced and not the easiest to break into.

He crept over to the van. It was slightly older and had a basic locking mechanism that would surrender more easily. He knelt by the passenger door and was about to start jemmying the lock when he heard a car turn into the driveway—a black S-Class Mercedes.

Matt crouched low. He heard the Merc's door open and watched as a man climbed out and walked up to the back door of the house. He was close to six feet tall, packed with muscle and walking with purpose. He had a shaved head and wore a dark suit.

As he turned, Matt saw the man was missing an ear. He wondered if he was ex-military. Maybe they all were. And judging by the step, the suit and the car, this guy was their boss. As if to confirm it, the rear door of the house creaked open as the man in the suit approached it. One of the goons stepped out and took a glance around as the hard case walked right past him without acknowledging him. A moment later, the goon followed, shutting the door.

Matt stayed down, his mind working double-time at interpreting this new variable. One move sprang to the forefront of his mind immediately. He embraced it, sneaked over to the 300C, and slid under

Mountains of Wadi Natrun, Egypt

Gracie quickly relayed to the three holy men what Ogilvy had told her.

'It's not safe,' she said. 'The news vans are already on their way. It'll be a zoo out there before sunrise. At least at the monastery you'll have four walls around you to keep the world at bay until we figure things out.'

Father Jerome's face sagged in dismay, but he didn't object. The abbot and the young monk didn't argue with Gracie's reading of the situation either. What she was suggesting seemed sensible.

'We should take what we can with us,' she told them. 'Everything you wrote, Father. And anything else that's of value to you. I don't know what condition the cave will be in next time you see it.'

She got Dalton to shoot a quick take of the cave and its ceiling while the others helped Father Jerome gather his belongings.

Before long, they were back under the stars, heading down the mountain.

Brighton, Massachusetts

Matt was just sliding out from the big Mercedes when he heard the back door of the house creak open. He huddled against the car's front passenger door and froze. He was stuck. There was more than one set of footsteps, so he figured there were at least two of them approaching. Headed for the Merc. The car beeped and the locks popped open with a loud snap.

A figure appeared on his side of the car, a guy with a brush cut. Matt sprang up before the guy could react and landed a crushing fist on his chin. Brush Cut tried to fight back, but Matt hooked him with a ferocious uppercut that lifted him off his feet before sending him staggering backwards.

From the corner of his eye, Matt saw the hard case in the suit reaching under his coat. Matt grabbed Brush Cut from behind, curling his left hand around the guy's neck while diving his right hand under the guy's jacket, searching for a gun. The hard case had his own gun out. He raised it at Matt, with Brush Cut between them.

Matt hit pay dirt. Brush Cut had a handgun in a belt holster on his right hip. Matt yanked it out and raised it.

'Get back,' he shouted, swinging the gun to his hostage's head.

He sidestepped to his left, putting the Merc between him and the hard case, who raised his left hand in a calming gesture. 'Easy, Matt,' he said.

'Who are you people?' Matt yelled, edging sideways, keeping tabs on the front and rear of the house.

'I'm impressed that you made it here, Matt,' the hard case said, clearly trying to work out how Matt had found them.

Matt was now at the back corner of the Merc. The hard case was actually tracking Matt, moving closer to the Merc, eyeing the surroundings with radar-like focus. There was something deeply unnerving about him.

'What's going on?' Matt rasped. 'What happened to my brother? Is he still alive?'

The hard case stayed calm, his cold eyes assessing Matt's position. 'You're messing with something you don't want to be messing with,' he told him. 'My advice to you is to let it go. Find yourself a deep hole and forget any of this ever happened. Or better still—' he squeezed the trigger, once, without a trace of emotion, and the round hit the guy Matt was holding squarely in the chest '—let me put you in it.'

Matt felt Brush Cut jerk and felt a sudden burn by his left ribs. The man started to fall just as the hard case fired again. Matt struggled to keep him up, using him as a shield while firing back at the hard case, who ducked behind the Merc. He faltered backwards, the burning sensation in his left flank getting stronger with each step.

Two more goons rushed out of the house, guns out. They crouched into firing positions, but Matt got one of them in the shoulder—the auburn-haired girl from the van. The other shooter dived behind the Merc. Matt kept moving, still using the not-yet-dead Brush Cut as a shield. A couple of shots whizzed by and he retaliated, then his gun's magazine spat out its last round.

He looked around frantically and realised he was now only a couple of yards from the sidewalk. Summoning whatever energy he could muster, he let go of Brush Cut and bolted into the street.

He didn't look back. He just kept running, putting a barrier of cars between him and the shooters' line of fire, hoping one last round wouldn't find him before he got to his Camry.

Wadi Natrun, Egypt

As Gracie had predicted, they'd barely managed to beat the news crews to the monastery. A growing number of cars and vans were gathering outside the gates. The abbot dispatched Brother Ameen to tell the crowd that Father Jerome had no comment as yet.

The siege had begun. And less than half an hour after getting back from the cave, they were sending their first live footage from the roof of the keep that abutted the monastery's entrance.

Gracie chose her words carefully as she faced the lens of Dalton's camera. 'He hasn't yet made a statement, Jack. All I can confirm to you at the moment is that Father Jerome is indeed here with us at the monastery.'

'But you've talked to him, haven't you?' Roxberry asked, through her earpiece. 'What did he tell you?'

Roxberry's frustration was clear, and Gracie's cagey replies weren't helping. She and Finch had decided that it wasn't their place to announce things that the priest had said in confidence. Hard as it was to keep a huge scoop like this to themselves, they'd agreed that it was more appropriate to give Father Jerome the chance to tell his story himself. They'd approach him for a live interview as soon as he'd had a chance to rest.

'He asked us to respect his need for peace right now.'

She could sense Roxberry's blood pressure rising, so she signed off, expecting an irate callback from the news desk, and stepped over to the edge of the flat roof. The roof had nothing but a low, three-inch lip around it, and Gracie felt a bit uneasy looking at the sharp drop-off. As she gazed beyond at the flat, barren landscape outside the monastery's walls, she watched the trickle of headlights bouncing across the desert, growing ominously as more and more cars converged on the monastery. She went to join Finch and Dalton, who were huddled around the laptop watching an Al Jazeera reporter's live broadcast from outside the gates.

'Weird, isn't it?' she observed. 'Sitting here, inside the gates, watching ourselves from the outside in.'

Brother Ameen climbed up the rickety ladder to join them.

'How's Father Jerome?' Gracie asked.

He shrugged wearily. 'Confused. Praying for guidance.'

He kept his eyes on the screen for a moment, then turned to her. 'I don't understand Father Jerome's visions but there are some things I do know. Egypt's not a rich country. Half the people around here have little or no education and live on less than two dollars a day. They take comfort in their religion because they don't have faith in their politicians. They have no one to trust but God. Religious identity matters more to them than their common citizenship. And we're on a knife edge as far as sectarian differences are concerned. There's a lot of tension between the people of this country.' He paused. 'Bringing Father Jerome down from the cave might not be enough to protect him.'

She'd been thinking the same thing. An alarming vision coalesced in her mind: of two seriously antagonistic groups outside the gates—Coptic Christians on a pilgrimage to hear what Father Jerome had to say, and Muslims out to repel whatever outrage the blasphemers were perpetrating.

'Where's the army?' she asked. 'Shouldn't they be sending people here to protect the monastery?'

'Not the army,' the monk said sombrely, 'the internal security forces. They're twice as big as the army but they don't usually send them out until after a problem catches fire. And when they do show up, things generally get worse. They don't have a problem with using a lot of force.'

Finch said, 'Might be better to get out of here before it gets out of hand. And that goes for Father Jerome too.'

Dalton indicated the crowd below. 'It's not going to be easy.'

'We have a car and a driver. And it's still calm out there. We should leave at first light.' Gracie faced Finch again. 'We can take Father Jerome to the embassy. We'll figure the rest out from there.'

'What if he doesn't want to leave?' Finch asked.

Brother Ameen gave an uncertain shrug. 'I'll talk to him.'

'I'll go with you. We've got to convince him,' Gracie insisted

Houston, Texas

The Reverend Nelson Darby's cellphone rang just as he was stepping out of his chauffeur-driven car in front of the handsome manor that housed the administrative core of his sprawling 'Christian values' empire.

'Reverend,' the caller said. 'How are things?'

'Roy,' Darby answered heartily, pleased to hear Roy Buscema's measured voice. With his perfectly coiffed jet-black mane and designer suits, Darby looked more like an investment banker than a preacher. Which wasn't inappropriate, given that both jobs involved managing multimillion-dollar enterprises in a highly competitive marketplace.

Buscema, a gregarious journalist for the *Washington Post*, had met the pastor a little over a year earlier, when he'd been commissioned to profile him for the Sunday magazine. The highly complimentary article that he'd written had laid the groundwork for the friendship that followed. The pastor saw in Buscema a savvy analyst who had the pulse of the people—an invaluable man to have at hand. Especially now.

'You been watching that thing over the ice caps?' Buscema said. 'What do you think?'

'To be honest with you, I'm a bit befuddled by the whole thing,' the pastor confided. 'What is going on out there?'

Buscema's tone took on a serious edge. 'I think we ought to talk about it. I'm gonna be in town tomorrow.'

'Come to the house,' Darby replied. 'I'm curious to hear your take on it.'

I bet you are, Buscema thought as they agreed on a time. He hung up, then made a second, almost identical, call. A third followed. As did six other carefully coordinated calls, made by two other men of a similar profile to his, to other evangelical leaders across the country.

Woburn, Massachusetts

The bullet had clipped Matt just below his bottom-left rib, punching a small hole less than an inch in from his side. Not exactly a graze, but not a major organ-buster either. Still, he needed stitches. And given that going to a doctor was out of the question, whatever sewing talents Jabba had would need to be summoned.

Jabba was holding up surprisingly well. He'd managed not to throw up when Matt staggered back into their room, his clothes soaked with blood. He'd made it to the closest drugstore and picked up the list of items Matt had hastily dictated to him: iodine, sewing needles, nylon thread, painkillers, bandages. He'd so far completed three sutures without puking.

They were huddled in the far-from-antiseptic bathroom of the motel room, and Matt was in his shorts grinding down his teeth as Jabba pushed the needle through the skin that rimmed his open wound. The sensation was far worse than getting shot. He blinked away tears of pain as the needle came out.

'This look right to you?' Jabba's fingers trembled as he cut off the end of the thread. It wasn't a particularly elegant piece of stitching, but at least the wound wasn't bleeding any more.

Matt shrugged. 'Don't sweat it. I hear the ladies love the hard-ass scars.'

Seven stitches and half an hour later, they were done.

As he cleaned up, Jabba filled Matt in on what he'd discovered. He'd given the receptionist ten bucks to let him use the motel's computer and, burrowing through the Internet, he'd tried to find out more about the team that had died in the helicopter crash. He'd come up with two other names— a chemical engineer by the name of Oliver Serres, and a biomolecular engineer named Sunil Kumar.

'It's weird, dude. What's a biomolecular engineer have to do with this? Those biomolecular guys rearrange DNA and play around with the building blocks of life, pulling apart atoms and molecules like they were Lego bricks. They're always getting flak for messing around in God's closet. Who knows what they found in there.'

Matt frowned. 'You've spent too much time watching *The X-Files*.'

Darkness was closing in fast outside their room, which suited Matt just fine. He needed to rest. Jabba went back out and picked up some blood-free clothes and food. They wolfed the food down greedily while watching the news. Footage from the cave in Egypt was hogging the airwaves.

'This is getting bigger,' Jabba noted glumly. 'More elaborate.'

Matt nodded. 'They know what they're doing.'

'That's not what I mean. These people have got serious resources. Think about what they're doing. First, they rustle up some major brain power—Danny, Reece and the rest—put them to work somewhere for, what, a couple of years? Then they kill them all off. Or, maybe, lock them up and fake their deaths—even more complicated to pull off. The one thing that's sure is that there's some serious moolah involved. That kind of research ain't cheap.'

'OK, so where'd the money come from?'

Jabba thought about it for a second. 'Two possibilities. Reece could've raised the money privately. Not easy, given the scale of it. Or, Reece was doing this for a government agency. A highly classified project. Which sounds about right to me.'

Matt's expression darkened. 'A government op?'

'It's pretty obvious, isn't it? If what we're saying is true, if they've really faked this thing, they're on their way to convincing everyone out there that God's talking to us. Maybe even through the good Father Jerome. Who else would try to pull off something like this?'

Matt could see the sense in what Jabba was saying but something was nagging at him.

'I don't know. The guys in the van. Their place in Brighton. They're a small unit. Working with good resources, but not overwhelming ones. I don't know . . . If it is a black op, it's way off the books.'

'Even worse, then,' Jabba added. 'Officially, they don't exist. Whoever sent them's got full deniability. They can do anything they want to us and no one will ever know.' He fixed Matt with a sobering stare. 'We need to disappear, dude. I know he's your brother and all, but we're outgunned.'

Matt said, 'What if Danny's still alive?'

Jabba took in a long, sobering breath. 'You really think he might be?'

'I don't know, but you want me just to forget about him and run?'

Jabba held his gaze for a moment. Then he nodded. 'OK.'

Matt acknowledged his acceptance with a small nod of his own and asked Jabba if he could check the tracker's web site.

Jabba came back a few minutes later armed with some printed screen shots. The tracker had moved within minutes of Matt's escape from the safe house. They'd obviously vacated it in a rush. Which was to be expected. Neighbours would have reported the shooting. The place would have been swarming with cops. And the goons would have panicked. Which lit a tiny fire of satisfaction deep in Matt's gut.

He checked the tracker's current position. It was at a location in the Seaport district of the city. Which meant the big Mercedes—the hard case's car, the one he'd moved the tracker onto—was there.

Matt let his head loll back against the pillows. The last image that floated into his mind before everything went quiet was the hard case's face. The man had the answers Matt needed. And, one way or another, Matt knew he'd have to wrest them out of him.

Wadi Natrun, Egypt

By dawn, the desert plain outside the monastery was teeming with life. Dozens of cars were strewn across the parched wasteland beyond the monastery's walls and all along the narrow approach road. People, men mostly, milled around by their cars or stood in small groups, tense, waiting.

Gracie and Finch sat on either side of Father Jerome in the middle row of the people carrier, with Dalton next to Yusuf and Brother Ameen in the back.

Music wafted from small groups of worshippers, their heads down in prayer as they chanted traditional Coptic hymns. Firebrand clerics spouted invective, denouncing the priest and the sign. It was clear that violence could erupt at any moment.

Gracie watched as the abbot pushed the people carrier's door shut, his face etched with concern. Father Jerome returned a forlorn look. He seemed even more lost now than in the cave. The abbot waved to two monks manning the gate. They pulled its huge doors open and a rising cacophony of noise gushed in as the crowd outside sprang to life.

The old people carrier lurched forward out of the gate. It advanced quickly along the monastery's wall and, almost immediately, people started converging on it. As the van turned down the approach road, the crowd around it swelled. Yusuf had to slow down. With his hand pressed against the horn, he managed to keep going for another thirty yards or so before coming to a complete stop, blocked by a wall of people.

Desperate faces were pressed against the Previa's tinted windows, calling out Father Jerome's name. Pleading with him to talk to them. They rattled the door handles, shaking the locks.

Father Jerome shrank into his seat as he darted nervous glances at the threatening faces behind the dark glass.

'We've got to go back to the monastery,' Finch urged Yusuf.

'We can't,' Gracie said as she saw the mass of bodies pressing against the car from all sides. 'We're boxed in.'

AT THE EDGE of the crowd, on a small rise by the crumbling remnants of an old wall, three men in a canvas-topped pick-up truck surveyed the chaos through binoculars.

As the people carrier disappeared behind the swarm of bodies, Fox Two signalled to his men. One peeled up a corner of the canvas top to expose the tripod-mounted, drumlike device underneath. Another man aimed it at the scrum of people crowding the back of the Previa. Then he hit the trigger.

The crush of people pressed against the people carrier recoiled as if struck by an unseen force, their hands rising to block their ears.

As the mob jerked back, a clear space opened up behind the Previa.

'Go back now,' Brother Ameen shouted.

Yusuf slammed the car into reverse, and—with his hand still on the horn—eased the car backwards. The mob flinched back in surprise, widening the opening behind the Previa.

Yusuf kept his foot down and they swerved around the bend at the far corner of the monastery in reverse gear, chased by the frenzied horde. Father Jerome's followers tried to block the followers of the Islamic firebrands from getting to the van. The Previa finally made it to the monastery's gates, which swung open just as it reached them.

They tumbled out of the car in a daze. Dalton was filming, capturing every moment of their escape.

Gracie turned to Father Jerome. 'Please go inside, Father. You need to be somewhere safe.'

Father Jerome didn't acknowledge her words. He was staring beyond her at the people crowding the gate and shouting out his name.

'I need to talk to them,' he said finally. Then he headed towards the keep and began marching up its stone steps.

They followed him to the top floor. Moments later, they were all standing on the roof. The scene below was unnerving. Hundreds of people were massed against the gates of the monastery, chanting, shouting and pumping their fists into the air. Behind them, pockets of fighting spread like wildfire, threatening to engulf the entire plain.

While Dalton got the live feed hooked up, Gracie grabbed her earpiece and mike, mentally running through what she would tell a world audience while watching the priest. The abbot and the young monk were pleading with him to move back, telling him someone below could easily have a weapon and might take a shot at him. Father Jerome was having none of it. He met Gracie's gaze, and started moving forward to the edge of the roof.

The crowd erupted in a mix of cheers and angry shouts, calling out his name. The euphoria of the faithful at the front only served to rile those who were opposed to Father Jerome farther back.

He stared down at the raging maelstrom below.

'Please,' he yelled out in Arabic. 'Stop and listen to me.'

His pleas had no effect. With rocks pelting the wall of the keep and flying past him, he remained steadfast, his arms held high—and, suddenly, the crowd gasped in shock. Gracie saw people pointing at the sky and she spun her head up to see a ball of light swirling no more than twenty feet over the priest. It hovered for a moment, then started to rise and, as it did, it suddenly morphed into the sign she'd seen over the ice shelf—a kaleidoscope of shifting light patterns.

The throng below froze, staring up in awe. The stones stopped flying.

Father Jerome was staring at the blazing apparition above him, dumbfounded. Then, a few seconds later, he turned to face the crowd. He spread his arms expansively and basked in the sign's radiance. The masses below stared in silence, their arms stretched upwards towards him. He maintained his outstretched stance for the better part of a minute, then he opened his eyes to face the crowd.

'Pray with me,' he bellowed. 'Let us all pray together.'

And they did. Every single person outside the monastery—Christian and Muslim, believer and protester—prostrated themselves in fearful adulation.

Washington, DC

'What the hell are you doing? I thought we had an agreement.'

Rydell had been up through the night, monitoring the news. The images from Egypt had exploded across his TV screen and, right now, pacing the cabin of his private jet near a quiet hangar at Reagan Airport, he was seething.

'We never agreed on it, Larry,' Drucker replied smoothly from his lush, padded seat. 'We both have a lot invested in this. I wasn't about to jeopardise it all because of your stubbornness!'

'So you just went out and did it anyway? Have you even thought about where this goes from here?'

'It's working, isn't it?'

'It's too early to tell.'

'It's working, Larry, because it's what people have been used to for thousands of years. You know how the world works. There are only two sure-fire ways to get people to do what you want them to do. You either put on an iron glove and make them do it. Or you tell them God wants them to do it. People like to follow. They need a guide. A prophet. Always have.'

'So you create, what, a Second Coming?'

'Not exactly, but close,' Drucker said.

'What about the other religions? How do you think they're going to react to your manufactured messiah?'

'He won't be exclusive. His message will embrace all.'

'Embrace all and encourage them to follow Jesus?' Rydell said acidly.

'Well,' Drucker mused, 'That's not the main message, but I suspect it may well be a secondary effect of his preaching.'

'Great,' Rydell retorted fiercely. 'You'll turn every born-again politician and every televangelist into a saint. And before you know it, they'll reclassify the pill as a form of abortion and we'll have a creationist museum in every town. If that's the trade-off, I think I'd rather stick with global warming.'

'You're forgetting one thing,' Drucker pointed out. 'We control the messenger. A messiah that we own. Think of what we can make people do.' He studied Rydell through calculating eyes. 'People don't question what the preachers say, so we need these windbags to sell our message. And what better way to get them on board than to give them a new prophet to sell on to their flocks?'

Drucker paused, gauging Rydell for a moment. 'Our focus hasn't changed. This is still about the singular threat facing the planet. About leading people away from the dangerous path they're on. It's a story of salvation after all, isn't it? We took this perfect Garden of Eden that God bequeathed to us and desecrated it with our orgies of consumption. Now we have to make huge sacrifices by driving smaller cars and using less electricity and cutting down on flying and other luxuries. We have to defeat pollution and seek out the salvation of sustainability and save ourselves before Judgment Day wipes us out in an Armageddon of climate change. That's how it's playing out, Larry. People like these religious myths. They thrive on them. Sooner or later, they turn everything into a crusade. And this crusade needed a prophet, not just a sign, to get the word across and make it happen.'

'And where does it end?' Rydell countered. 'Do you really think you can keep Father Jerome in line forever? Sooner or later, something'll screw up, someone'll slip up, and it'll all come out. What happens then?'

Drucker shrugged. 'We'll keep it going as long as we can. Then we'll figure out a graceful exit.'

Rydell sat, hobbled by the shock of it all. 'No,' he told Drucker, his voice thick with dismay. 'This is wrong. This is a huge mistake.'

Drucker's eyes narrowed. 'Take some time to think this through properly, Larry. You'll see that I'm right.'

'It's wrong,' Rydell flared. 'The plan was to scare them. To make them sit up and think about what they're doing. A few carefully chosen appearances, kept mysterious and unexplained and scary. We agreed that it would be a good thing if people didn't know where this was coming from, if they ended up thinking it was coming from some unidentifiable higher intelligence out there.'

Drucker was unmoved. 'This was the only way it was ever going to work, Larry. The world's not ready to give up its obsession with religion.'

'We have to stop it, Keenan,' Rydell insisted.

Drucker shrugged. 'We might just have to agree to disagree on that one.'

'I still have a say in this.'

'Within reason. And right now, you're being unreasonable.'

Rydell thought for a moment. 'You need me for the smart dust.'

'I know that. So I had to take out some insurance.'

Rydell studied him. 'What have you done, you son of a bitch?'

Drucker let him stew on it for a moment, then said, 'Rebecca.'

The word stabbed Rydell like an ice pick. He yanked out his phone and stabbed a speed-dial button. After two rings, a voice answered. Rydell instantly recognised Rebecca's bodyguard.

'Put Becca on,' he ordered.

'I can't do that, Mr Rydell.'

The words coiled around his gut.

'Put her on,' he growled.

'Only if Mr Drucker gives the word, sir.'

Rydell charged at Drucker. 'Where is she?' he yelled.

Drucker sprang out of his seat and deflected Rydell's attack, twisting his partner's arm back. As he did so, he kicked out Rydell's leg from under him. The billionaire tumbled to the floor.

Drucker took a couple of steps back. 'She's fine,' he said. 'And she'll stay fine. As long as you don't do anything foolish. Do we understand each other?'

Wadi Natrun, Egypt

Tucked away behind the crumbled wall four hundred yards west of the monastery, and veiled by their desert camouflage netting, Fox Two and his men watched and waited. Beside them, nestling under the truck's canvas top, the long-range acoustic device unit, aka the LRAD, sat patiently, ready to wield its unseen power again.

Fox Two studied the crowd below. So far, he'd been able to push the right buttons and generate the responses he needed without a problem. Father Jerome had reacted as expected to the gentle prodding he'd given him on the rooftop, after the sign had appeared above him—but then, he'd been well primed to react that way. A few whispered words, aimed at the more visibly heated pockets in the mob, were also enough to trigger a reaction. A high-frequency, ultraloud pulse using the crowd-control setting was more than enough to hobble their fervour when it was no longer needed.

Remarkable, he thought, even though he'd used the device so often it had become second nature to him. A simple concept, really—projecting noise in a tightly focused audio beam so that only the person in the device's cross hairs could hear it. It was possible either to make it appear as if someone's voice was actually inside the target's head, or—using the less subtle crowd-control mode—send an unbearably loud sound pulse into the target's ears that, at its highest setting, crippled the toughest enemy.

The power of suggestion was particularly effective when the subjects were already burning with the desire to do what was required of them, as in the case of Father Jerome, who had undergone weeks of forced indoctrination, electroshocks and sleep-deprivation sessions, followed by cocktails of drugs to take the edge off. Transcranial mental stimulation. A complete psychochemical breakdown. Disarming the brain before implanting visions, thoughts, feelings. Conditioning it to accept an alternate reality—like hearing the voice of God.

He panned his binoculars across the desert to locate Fox One and his unit. Their contribution had been flawless.

Fox Two turned his attention back to the hordes at the monastery's gates. He'd soon be able to leave this dump for good. Soon, he thought. But first he needed to make sure that the mission ended smoothly.

Woburn, Massachusetts

The smell of fresh coffee coaxed Matt out of a dreamless sleep. Jabba was sitting by the table next to the window, watching the TV. He grinned at Matt, a cup of coffee in one hand and a half-eaten doughnut in the other, with which he pointed at the box of doughnuts on the table.

'Breakfast is served,' he said, in between mouthfuls.

'How long was I out? What time is it?'

'Almost eleven. Meaning you've been out for sixteen hours or so.'

Which Matt had needed. Badly. He noticed a couple of newspapers on the table. A photograph of the apparition, in colour, was emblazoned across the front pages, next to file portraits of Father Jerome.

Jabba nodded. 'The Eagle has landed,' he said soberly.

Matt watched the footage from Egypt in disbelief. Breathless reports coming in from around the world showed the explosive reaction to what had happened at the monastery. Father Jerome's face was everywhere, beamed from every channel. The frail priest had been thrust into megastardom.

Jabba filled Matt in on what he'd been up to. He'd got an update on the tracker's position, and handed Matt the print-outs. They showed that the Merc had left the Seaport district, the last position they had for it, some time before ten the previous night. It had travelled to the downtown area where the signal had been lost. It had appeared again soon after seven that morning and returned to Seaport. Jabba had then spent most of his time beefing up the few bits of information they had managed to compile on the doomed research team. He'd made calls to contacts in the industry and had given Google's search algorithms a real workout. However, no one knew anything. The project had been born, and had died, in total secrecy.

He had, however, managed to unearth a real nugget, one he kept for last.

'I tracked down Dominic Reece's wife,' he informed Matt. 'Maybe she has some idea of what her husband and Danny were doing in Namibia.'

'Where is she?' Matt asked.

'Nahant, just up the coast,' Jabba replied. 'We can be there in half an hour.'

Matt nodded. 'Sounds good. But let's see what the tracker's got for us at Seaport first.'

Wadi Natrun, Egypt

Gracie had faced Dalton's lens every half hour, feeding the world's insatiable hunger for new information. Her throat felt numb, her legs rubbery, but she wouldn't have had it any other way. Every news broadcast was carrying the story and she was at the heart of it.

They'd brought Father Jerome off the roof for safety and he had been escorted into the bowels of the monastery by the abbot and Brother Ameen.

Dalton, Finch and Gracie had climbed back up onto the roof on a couple of occasions, and Dalton had filmed the scene outside the monastery's walls where the crowd had grown tenfold. So far, the violence hadn't flared up again, but the rival camps were eyeing each other nervously and the threat of a bigger eruption of violence was palpable.

Gracie gratefully accepted some fresh lemonade from one of the monks and sat down. Dalton and Finch joined her.

'Weren't we just freezing our nuts off in the South Pole like yesterday?' Dalton asked in a weary, incredulous tone. 'Weird how these things happen, isn't it? Imagine if you hadn't taken that call from Brother Ameen, back on the ship. If the documentary guys hadn't been here before us and shot Father Jerome's wall paintings. We wouldn't be here now, and maybe none of this would have happened.'

Gracie shrugged. 'Someone else would be. It'd just be their story.'

'But would it? What if the documentary guys hadn't shot that footage? The mob wouldn't be out there. Father Jerome wouldn't have been up here on the roof. There'd be no sign up there.' He raised his eyebrows in a 'think-about-it' manner. 'Makes you wonder if there were others before him.'

'Others?' Gracie asked.

'You know, nuts with voices in their heads, painting weird signs all over their walls or filling journals with their ramblings. Others who no one knew about. And what about the timing of it?' he added. 'Why now? Why not before Hiroshima? Or during the Cuban Missile Crisis?'

'You always get this lucid with lemonade?' she asked.

'Depends on what the good monks put in it.'

Just then, Brother Ameen popped his head through the roof hatch, his expression knotted with concern. 'Come with me, please. To the car. You need to hear this. Come now.'

They followed him to the Previa, which was still parked by the gates. The abbot arrived as they did. The car's doors were open, and Yusuf and a couple of monks were huddled around the vehicle, listening to an Arabic broadcast on the radio. They looked thoroughly spooked.

'It's an imam, in Cairo,' Brother Ameen told them. 'One of the more hotheaded clerics in the country. He's saying Father Jerome is either a fabrication of the Great Satan America—or he's an agent of the devil. And that either way, they should consider him a false prophet who's been sent to sow fear and confusion among the true believers.' He listened some more, then added, 'He's telling them to do their duty as good Muslims and to remember the preachings of the one true faith.'

'Which is?' Finch asked.

'He's asking for Father Jerome's head. Literally.'

Houston, Texas

'I've got to tell ya,' the pastor grumbled as he set down his tumbler of bourbon. 'This isn't how it's supposed to happen.'

'How what's supposed to happen?'

'The Second Coming, Roy. The End of Times.'

They were seated across from each other in the large conservatory of the pastor's massive mansion. An oval-shaped pool lay beyond the windows. The fence around Darby's tennis court winked out from behind a row of poplars.

Roy Buscema still studied the man before him with the fascination of an anthropologist discovering a new species. The Reverend Nelson Darby was modern in all things technological and where business was concerned, but immovably medieval when it came to anything relating to scripture. In his fiery sermons he took on homosexuals, abortion, evolution, stem cell research, even directing his bombastic rants at the Girl Scouts, whom he'd branded agents of feminism.

'Maybe this isn't the End of Times?' Buscema suggested.

'It sure as hell isn't,' the pastor agreed huffily. 'The Bible tells us the messiah will return only *after* we've had the final battle between God's children and the army of the antichrist out there in Israel. Hell, we're still waiting for the Israelis to bomb the crap out of Iran and kick-start the whole thing.'

'God's giving us a message, Nelson,' Buscema put in thoughtfully. 'He's given us a sign over the ice caps. And he's sent us a messenger. A Christian. More importantly, the messenger happens to be one of the holiest men on the planet. He's spent the last few months holed up in some cave near a monastery in Egypt.'

'What about all that Coptic business?'

'The monastery where he's staying is Coptic, but he's not. Anyway, the Copts are the purest, oldest, uncorrupted Christians you'll find. And those monasteries out there are the oldest in the world. It's a deeply religious place, Nelson. And Father Jerome . . . well, you know all about him. If God was going to choose someone, it seems to me like Father Jerome fits the bill nicely.'

Darby nodded grudgingly. 'But why now? And why the signs over the poles? You don't really believe these greenhouse gases are gonna end up by wiping us all out with their tidal waves or with that new ice age they've been harping on about?'

Buscema gave him a noncommittal shrug. 'It could happen.'

'Hogwash,' Darby shot back. 'Nuclear war between the forces of good and evil's gonna bring about the End of Times, Roy. Not global warming.'

'All I'm saying is,' Buscema countered, 'there's a sign popping up over the planet's climate-change tipping points. And I just saw the first national polling numbers.'

The pastor's face sharpened with keen interest. 'What do they say?'

'People are taking notice. It's in the Bible: "The Lord God took the man and put him in the Garden of Eden to work it . . . *and to take care of it.*" People are worried about the kind of world their kids are going to grow up in.'

'They're misguided. We've got to be careful, Roy. Are we saying the planet's holy? Are we supposed to worship nature? That's a slippery slope. We can't go out and tell people to love Mother Earth and look after her. Hell, that's what the Indians believed in.'

Buscema smiled. The man understood the subtleties of faith. And he was smart, a mesmerising orator who knew how to entrance his audience. There was a reason why millions tuned in to his slick TV broadcasts.

'Think of it more in terms of man's sinful desires having led him astray,' Buscema said. 'He needs to see the road to salvation. And it's your job to hold his hand and show him the way.' He leaned in for emphasis. 'You're pro-life, right? That's what saving the planet's all about, isn't it? Life?'

Darby breathed out heavily. 'What do you think I should do?'

'Grab him. While you can.'

'You want me to endorse him?'

Buscema nodded. 'Others are thinking about doing it. Schaeffer. Scofield.' He knew mentioning the names of two of Darby's biggest competitors in the soul-saving sweepstakes would generate a reaction. Judging by Darby's expression, the names hit the sweet spot he was aiming for.

'You sure of that?' the pastor asked.

Buscema nodded enigmatically. I should know, he thought to himself. I spoke to them before coming here to see you. He said, 'You've got to endorse him. Look, you're already lagging on this front. Your fellow church leaders who signed up for the global-warming initiative two years ago, they're on board. This is your chance to leapfrog over them and take control.'

Darby frowned. 'But what about that sign that keeps popping up? If it was a cross or something Christian, then fine . . . but it's not.'

'It doesn't matter what it is. What matters is that it's up there and everyone's looking at it. You're right it's not a cross, but it's not linked to any of the other major religions either. Right now, there's just a man and a sign in the sky. But people are coming to him in droves. You need to decide whether you want to be part of it, hitch your wagon to him before the rest of them. If you don't embrace this now, you might find yourself with a bunch of empty pews. You don't want to be left behind, now, do you?'

'DID HE BUY IT?' Drucker asked Buscema.

'Please,' the journalist said mockingly. 'He's so into it it's almost painful to watch.'

'You gonna see Schaeffer again?'

'He's left me two messages since I spoke to him,' he confirmed. 'Same with Scofield. I'll let them sweat it out a little bit before calling them back.'

Good man, Drucker thought. It sounded like they'd already reeled in one major marlin. With a bit of luck, they'd be bringing in a record haul.

Boston, Massachusetts

Matt and Jabba were parked outside a modern office block in the Seaport district. They'd been parked there for half an hour, and had seen only one person. There had been no sign of the hard case.

'I'm going to have a look,' Matt told Jabba. He reached for the Camry's door handle, grimacing with discomfort as he pulled on it.

Jabba reached out to stop him. 'Not a good idea, dude. You shouldn't even be here. I'll go.'

Matt looked at him.

'I'll go', he insisted. 'If I'm not out in five minutes, call the cops.' Then he grinned. 'God, I never imagined I'd ever hear myself say that.'

Jabba scanned left and right as he ambled across the parking lot. Matt watched him disappear inside the entrance lobby.

Less than a minute later, he emerged, breathing fast. 'No receptionist. Five names on the roster, one per floor,' he informed Matt. 'I think I know which one we want. Just need to go online somewhere to confirm it.'

Matt thought about it, then said, 'OK. Do it here.'

'Dude, they could track our position.'

'Fine. Stay on long enough for them to be able to do it,' Matt said. 'I want to shake them up.'

Jabba looked at him as though he'd sprouted little green antennae. 'You want them to know we're here?'

'Like I said, I want to shake them up.'

Jabba looked as if he wanted to object, but turned on his iPhone. He then fired up his MacBook and connected it to the phone. He swung the laptop round so Matt could see the home page of a company called Centurion. A picture showed a guy in military gear behind a large-calibre machine gun. The 'About Us' paragraph described Centurion as a 'security provider to the US government and a registered and active UN contractor'. Jabba clicked on the 'Management' link, and a black-and-white portrait of the hard case, Maddox, leaped out at them. He was the firm's founder and CEO.

'Ouch,' Jabba said, flinching at the unsettling mugshot. 'Can we please switch this off and get out of here?'

Matt was still absorbing Maddox's biog. After a moment he said, 'Sure.'

Jabba turned off the MacBook as Matt fired up the car and pulled away. His expression was dour. 'So now we know who we're dealing with.'

'Dude, the man's got a private army. We've got a white Camry and a handgun with no bullets in it.'

'Then we've got some catching up to do,' Matt replied. 'But let's see what Reece's wife has to say first.'

'YOU'RE SURE?' Maddox wasn't shouting, but his displeasure was coming through loud and clear to his contact at the NSA.

'Absolutely,' came the answer. 'Komlosy's phone signal popped up on the grid for just over a minute before powering down.'

264 | RAYMOND KHOURY

Two unexpected appearances from Sherwood in as many days, Maddox fumed. The second one in the immediate vicinity of his office. The man was good. A bit too good for Maddox's liking. 'How long ago?'

'It just went dead.'

'Can't you track him with his phone switched off?'

'We're working on some stuff. It'll get better every time he switches it on. The tracking software will keep adding data every time. We won't need as long to get a lock.'

'OK. Let me know the second it powers up again,' the Bullet ordered.

Wadi Natrun, Egypt

'We need to get Father Jerome out of here,' Gracie said.

'I agree,' Finch said, 'but how?'

'What about bringing a chopper in to whisk him out?' she asked.

'Where's it gonna land?' Finch queried. 'There's nowhere for it to put down inside the monastery's walls.'

Gracie pointed up at the keep. 'What about up there?'

Finch shook his head. 'The roof's not strong enough. And I don't think winching him out will work either. Someone could take a shot at him.'

'There might be another way out,' Brother Ameen offered.

All eyes turned swiftly to him.

'The tunnel,' he said, turning to the abbot with a questioning look.

'There's a tunnel? Where to?' Gracie asked.

'It goes from here to the monastery of Saint Bishoi—the one we drove past on the way in.'

'What, the one across the field?' Gracie was pointing northeast, trying to visualise the second monastery's relative position.

The abbot nodded. 'Yes. The tunnel is older than this monastery. You see, our monastery was built over what was once the monk Bishoi's hermitage, the cave he used to retreat to. Because of the constant threat from invaders, the monks decided to build an escape route from Saint Bishoi's monastery, and they chose his old cave as the exit point.'

'You think it'll still get us there?' Finch asked.

'The last time anyone went down there was years ago, but it was clear then. I don't see why it should be any different now,' the abbot replied.

'If we can make it across, can we get a car to drive us away from there? Discreetly?' Gracie asked.

The abbot stepped over to Yusuf and spoke to him in Arabic. Then the abbot turned back to Gracie. 'Yusuf's brother-in-law drives a car like his. If he can use your phone to call him, we can get him to meet you at Bishoi.'

'OK, but then what? Where do we go?' Dalton asked. 'The embassy?'

'It'll be the same thing there,' Ameen put in. 'Maybe even worse. It's safer to fly him out of the country.'

Finch frowned. 'Easier said than done. Does he have a passport?'

'He can use my passport,' the abbot offered. 'With his hood down, they won't look too closely. Ameen will be with you to deflect any questions.'

'OK, I'll call DC,' Finch told Gracie, 'see how quickly they can get us a plane.' He turned to the monks. 'How long do you think this tunnel is? Half a kilometre?'

'I'm not sure,' the abbot said. 'Maybe a bit more.'

Finch frowned. 'We're not going to be able to lug all our gear through.' He turned to Dalton. 'Let's bring it all down. We'll grab as much as we can.'

'We'd better get moving,' Gracie said.

Houston, Texas

'They're trying to get Father Jerome out,' Buscema informed the Reverend Darby. 'I just got a call from my guy at the network. They've still got that news crew there with him. They're handling him themselves.'

'Of course they are,' Darby chortled. 'How are they going to do it?'

'They're scrambling to get a plane out to them as soon as possible.'

'Where are they planning on taking him?' Darby asked.

'I don't think they know. They just want him out of there before the whackos rip him to pieces.'

The reverend said, 'Let's bring him here.'

'It's not gonna be easy. Everyone else will want him. Did you see footage of the rallies in Rome?'

'We've got to get him over here. Like you said, he's polling through the roof. People want to hear what he has to say.'

'The government hasn't even made an official statement about him yet.'

'Just as well,' Darby said, gloating. 'Gives me a chance to do it myself and save him from ending up with those heathens back east.'

'You want to handle this yourself?'

'God's sending us a message,' Darby asserted. 'I'm going to make sure everyone hears it, loud and clear.'

'If you want to make it happen, you're gonna have to move fast.'

The reverend's tone was as smooth and sharp as a blade. 'Watch me,' he replied.

Egypt

Gracie, Dalton and Finch had brought the rest of their gear down from the roof of the keep and were now sorting through it.

Finch had spoken to Hal Ogilvy, who had gone to work on rustling up a jet that could fly them out without their being asked too many questions. They'd still have to get past whatever security checks were in place at the airport, but they'd got out of trickier places before.

As Finch clicked his backpack shut, Dalton's earlier observations were still bouncing around in his mind. Something was nagging at him. As Dalton had noted, everything had hinged on the pre-existence of the BBC's documentary footage of the cave. Without it, he thought, none of this would have happened.

He considered putting in a call to the documentary's producer to find out how it had all happened. After making a quick mental calculation of the time difference between Egypt and England, where the producer was based, he picked up the satphone, then patted his pockets. 'You seen my BlackBerry?'

Dalton glanced around. 'No, why?'

'I thought I'd put a call in to the documentary guys.'

'So use the satphone. Your phone doesn't work here, remember?'

Finch gave him a grin. 'It's got my contacts list on it, numbnuts.'

Dalton said, pointing at the keep, 'Last I remember, you had it out when we were up there.'

Finch frowned. 'Be right back.' He cut across the courtyard and disappeared.

The BlackBerry was there on the roof in the dust. Finch picked it up, found the phone number of the producer and called him on the satphone.

Gareth Willoughby was a respected film-maker with an impressive CV. Finch got through to his voicemail, and left him a brief message asking him to return the call, then headed back down.

As his foot settled on the bottom rung of the ladder from the roof, he heard a voice from one of the rooms behind the chapel. Something about it made him listen closely. He followed the voice—to a room that faced out from the monastery.

A man was inside, alone. It was a monk, wearing the traditional black cassock and hood. He had his back turned to Finch, and was talking on a cellphone. In English.

'We should be leaving in ten, fifteen minutes. Shouldn't take more than twenty minutes to get through.' He paused, then said, 'OK,' and hung up.

Finch stiffened as he recognised the voice.

The monk sensed his presence and turned. It was Brother Ameen.

Finch relaxed his face into a sheepish smile. 'I, um, forgot my phone.'

Brother Ameen didn't answer. He didn't return the smile either. He just stood there, in silence.

Finch's eyes drifted down to the phone. It wasn't just a regular cellphone. They didn't work there. It was a satphone, with its flip-up antenna. Not only that, but it had a small box plugged into its base, which Finch knew to be an encryption module.

Nahant, Massachusetts

'More than anything, Dom lived for his work,' Jenna Reece was telling Matt and Jabba. They were in her house in Nahant, a small town on a tiny crescent-shaped peninsula fifteen miles north of Boston. It had once been their summer home, she'd told them, but, following her husband's death, she'd moved there full-time, turning the living room into a workshop, where she lost herself in her sculpture.

'I imagine your brother was the same, wasn't he?' she asked. 'They all seemed consumed by their work. And look what it got them in the end.'

Matt held her gaze and nodded solemnly. 'What do you know about the project they were working on when they died?'

'Not much. Dom didn't go into much detail about his work with me. It was his world. And, well, you must know how obsessive he and the rest were when it came to secrecy.'

Matt shifted in his seat, clearly discomfited by what he needed to ask. 'Mrs Reece . . .'

'It's Jenna, Matt,' she softly corrected him.

'Jenna, I need to ask you something, but you might find it a bit weird . . . Did you actually see your husband's body?'

Jenna Reece blinked a couple of times. 'No,' she said. 'I mean, not his whole body. But you know how they died, and . . . the conditions out there . . .'

'I know,' he offered.

'All they had for me was his hand,' she said. The words caught in her throat and she shut her eyes for a moment. 'His left hand. His wedding band was still on it. I didn't have any doubts.'

'You're sure of it,' Matt probed, despite his misgivings.

Jenna Reece nodded.

'He had fine hands. Like a pianist's. I noticed them the first time we met. Of course, it had been . . .' She brushed a painful thought away. 'I still knew it was his. Why do you ask?'

'Well, there wasn't anything left of my brother, so I wondered if . . .'

'You think your brother might still be alive?'

The way she cut to the heart of his thinking surprised him, and he couldn't help but nod.

She gave him a supportive smile. 'I wish I could tell you something that would help, but all I can tell you is what I know about my Dom.'

'Do you know who Dom was working for?' Matt asked.

'He didn't share that with me. Not that he wasn't very excited about it. He . . . he felt it could really change things on a fundamental level. And the day he got the green light on the funding—it was like the next phase of his life had begun. Like he was on a mission. He was more secretive than ever after that. I hardly ever saw him.'

'Did you know who was backing him?' Matt pressed.

Jenna eyed him hesitantly. 'I'm not sure I should be telling you this.'

'Please, Jenna,' Matt said. 'My brother was part of it.'

Jenna heaved a sigh.

'Well . . . He let it slip only once, and that was by accident. The money was coming from Rydell.'

Matt looked at her, confused.

Jabba took up the slack. 'Larry Rydell?'

'Yes,' she confirmed. 'No one was supposed to know. I don't know why, but that's how they wanted it. Still, I was surprised—and more than a bit pissed off when he didn't even show up at Dom's funeral. I mean, I can't complain, they took good care of me, but still . . .'

Jabba looked at Matt pointedly. Matt knew the name—most people did—but didn't quite grasp the significance it seemed to have for Jabba.

'You're sure of this,' Jabba pressed.

'Yes,' Jenna Reece replied.

Jabba's expression told Matt they had all they needed to know.

Wadi Natrun, Egypt

'So you've got a satphone?' Finch asked.

Brother Ameen didn't respond.

'I thought the whole point of being here was to isolate yourself from the rest of the world, to allow you to concentrate on God and . . . and yet you've got a satphone.'

'I do,' the monk finally said, almost regretfully. 'And it's got an encryption box. I know you recognised it when you saw it,' he added. 'I expect you've seen them before, given your line of work.'

'Yeah, but . . .' Finch waved it away. 'I see more of them these days. It's safer, isn't it?' His voice trailed off and it suddenly hit him that he was in serious danger. He took a step backwards.

The monk mirrored him with a soft step forward.

Finch frowned. 'What are you doing?'

'I'm sorry,' Brother Ameen said as he took another step closer.

Finch bolted backwards and turned to head back to the stairs, but he'd barely made it past the door before the monk was right with him, slamming him back against the wall while driving a hard knee straight into his groin. Finch pitched forward, exhaling heavily from the kick. His glasses flew off, and he raised his hands, hoping to stave off another blow. For a split second, he caught sight of the monk's fist bunched tight, with its middle knuckle extended. Its steely tap struck him on the side of his neck, just below his ear, pounding his carotid sinus with the force of a hammer blow. He felt his entire body lose control of its muscles and he plummeted to the ground.

'WHERE IS HE?' Gracie asked, scanning the monastery's courtyard. She was standing with Dalton, ready to go. They'd been joined by the abbot and Father Jerome, and the monks who'd be helping them carry their gear.

Dalton tilted his head up at the top of the keep and yelled, 'Finch. We're all set here. Time to move out, pal.'

No answer.

Gracie looked around, then asked Dalton, 'You sure he went up there?'

Dalton nodded. 'He's just looking for his BlackBerry.'

'I'm going to see what's keeping him,' Gracie said.

She'd almost reached the doorway when something made her look up— just in time to see Finch's body hurtling to the ground and slamming into the hard sand a few feet away from her.

Outskirts of Boston, Massachusetts

'It makes sense,' Jabba concluded. 'Rydell's got the money. He's got the technical know-how to pull off something like this. And he's a major environmentalist.'

They were heading towards the city. Jabba had told Matt what he knew about Rydell—the way he championed alternative energy projects across the globe, the passion with which he lobbied Washington to take climate change seriously, the support he gave to politicians who'd been fighting the previous administration's callous disregard for environmental concerns. Every word of it added to the goal that was forming in Matt's mind: him getting in Rydell's face and hearing what they'd done to Danny.

Matt shrugged. 'So Rydell's set this whole thing up to save the planet?'

'Not the planet. Us. The planet was here long before us and it'll still be around long after we're gone. It's *us* that need saving.'

Matt shook his head in disbelief. 'Do you think they knew what they were really working on? Do you think Rydell told them?'

'I don't know . . . They had to be aware of the power of what they were putting together.' Jabba glanced sideways at Matt. 'The question is whether they knew what it was going to be used for. What do you think? Could your brother have been part of something like this?'

Matt thought about it. 'A hoax? Scamming millions of people?' He shook his head. 'I don't think so.'

'Even if he thought it was for a good cause?'

That one was harder to answer. Danny wasn't religious any more than Matt was, so there wouldn't have been any faith issues for him. Matt didn't remember him being particularly concerned with the planet's environmental problems either, no more than most well-read, levelheaded people.

Jabba was scrutinising him. Matt noticed it. 'What?' he asked.

'I hate to say it, but it doesn't look good. It's been two years. I don't see how they could have kept him locked up and muzzled all this time. He would've found a way to sneak a word out, don't you think?'

'Not if they know what they're doing.'

'Two years, man,' Jabba added with a slight wince.

Matt felt his chest tightening. He didn't know what was better—to find out Danny was actually long dead, or that he was part of all this willingly.

'No way,' Matt finally said. 'He'd never want to be part of something like this. Not if he knew what they were really doing.'

They motored on for a mile or so, then Matt said, 'Get us another lock on Maddox's car, will you? Just don't stay on any longer than you think is safe.'

Jabba pulled out his iPhone and got up the tracker's web site.

'He's stationary. Somewhere by the name of Hanscom Field. It's a small airport. And I'm logging off before they track us.'

Matt chewed it over. A small airport. He wondered what Maddox was doing there. He glanced at the clock on the dashboard. It wasn't far, even with the Christmas holiday traffic. Forty minutes maybe. 'Check it again in fifteen minutes or so, will you? Keep making sure he's still there.'

Jabba nodded grimly, anticipating the worst.

Bedford, Massachusetts

Maddox hung up the call with his contact at the NSA and scowled. He'd received three consecutive calls. The first one was innocuous enough: the targets were just north of the city, heading into town. The second told him the targets had changed direction and were now heading west. The third call, though, was seriously troubling. The targets had turned north and were now less than five miles away from the airfield.

It was the second time Matt had managed to track him down that day. Which meant he was either psychic or he had an advantage Maddox wasn't aware of. The Bullet's mind ran a full-spectrum sweep of everything that had happened since he'd first come across Matt Sherwood. He focused on establishing causal links between that first encounter and the present moment, running them against the background skills he knew Matt possessed.

All of which drew his attention to his car. He scrutinised it, knowing now what the likely culprit could be. He wouldn't have time to have the car checked out. Which meant he'd have to leave it there for now. Which pissed him off even more. He really liked that car.

He checked his watch. The jet's arrival was imminent. He decided it was time to put an end to Matt Sherwood's unexpected intrusions—permanently—and waved over two of his men.

'I think we're about to have some company,' he told them.

Wadi Natrun, Egypt

'Finch!' Gracie's cry shook the walls of the monastery as she dropped to the ground at his side. The blood drained from her face, and her hands shot up to her open mouth. Finch's body lay in front of her, flat against the desert sand.

The others all rushed to her side. 'Is he . . . ?' Dalton couldn't say it.

There were no visible wounds, but it didn't make the sight any less horrific. His head, which must have hit the ground first, was twisted sideways at an impossible angle. He had one arm bent backwards, and his eyes were staring lifelessly at the parched soil.

'Oh my God,' Gracie sobbed. Her fingers pressed his neck, searching for a pulse or any sign of life.

She looked at Dalton through teary eyes and shook her head. He put his arms around Gracie, his eyes locked on his fallen friend's body. The monks started murmuring some prayers. Gracie sensed movement behind her, and saw Father Jerome advance hesitantly. The holy man knelt down beside her, his concentration focused on Finch's dead body.

She watched with rapt attention as he held out his hands over Finch, and shut his eyes in silent prayer. For a fleeting moment, an absurd notion rose within her—that Father Jerome was going to bring her friend back from the dead. She tried to hold onto that possibility as long as she could, flashing to all the other impossible things she'd witnessed over the past few days, clutching at it with desperation.

Father Jerome made a cross over Finch's head and turned to face her with a look of profound sadness. 'I'm so sorry,' he said simply.

His expression, Gracie saw, was riven with guilt. She nodded, but said nothing. He rose and shuffled back to join his brethren.

Gracie turned to Dalton, then glanced up at the top of the keep.

'How . . . ,' she muttered. 'How could he fall like that?'

Dalton shook his head slowly, still in shock. 'I don't know.' His eyes went wide. 'Do you think someone out there took a shot at him?'

Gracie looked at him with horror, then bent back down to Finch's side. With trembling fingers, she straightened Finch's arms and legs, then turned him over. She scanned his front, but couldn't see any bullet wound.

'It doesn't look like it,' she said. 'I didn't hear a shot, did you?'

'No.' Dalton turned his gaze back up at the top of the keep. 'The lip of that wall is so low. Maybe he was leaning over?' His voice trailed off.

Gracie scanned the ground around them. The satphone glinted at her, half-buried in the sand. She scanned wider. Spotted Finch's BlackBerry lying by the base of the keep's wall. She retrieved the satphone, then picked up the BlackBerry, imagining Finch's last moments in her mind's eye as he found it on the roof and crossed over to the edge for—what, one last look?

'What are we going to do?' she asked.

'We've got to go,' Dalton told her, his voice hollow.

'What about Finch? We can't leave him here like this.'

'We can't take him with us,' he replied softly. 'We just can't.'

After a brief moment, she nodded. 'You're right,' she said. She looked over at the abbot. 'Can you . . . ?'

The abbot nodded solemnly. 'Of course,' he told her. 'We'll take care of him until we can send him home . . . properly.' He glanced over at the Previa and the men huddled around it. 'You should go now,' he added, 'as planned.'

Gracie and Dalton watched as a few monks lifted Finch's body onto a makeshift stretcher and carried him inside to the main chapel.

Four other monks picked up the rest of the news crew's gear, and the small troupe followed the abbot out of the sun-soaked courtyard and into the cool darkness of the monastery.

They reached an ancient stairwell. 'You'll need the lamps from here on,' the abbot instructed. The monks lit up a succession of small, camping-gas lanterns. Slowly, they descended a narrow staircase and landed in another passage that led them past a couple of olive-oil cellars.

The abbot pushed the crumbling timber door open and led them into a cave no bigger than a small bedroom.

'It's this way,' he said. In a corner of the cave, to the left of the doorway, was another rotting timber door. Two monks helped the abbot pull it open. Gracie edged closer and spotted the entrance to the tunnel. It was no more than five feet high and three across.

'God be with you,' the abbot told Father Jerome as, one by one, they clambered into the tight passage. Gracie was the last one in. She hesitated for a moment, still choking inside at the thought of abandoning Finch, before disappearing into the tunnel's oppressive darkness.

Bedford, Massachusetts

Matt slowed the Camry right down as the woods on either side of the two-lane road gave way to a handful of low office buildings. He scanned the area. There were no other cars on the road. They cruised past the entrance to a small air-force base tucked away to their right, where a lone guard manned its flimsy red-and-white barrier. The base shared its runway with the adjacent civilian airfield, but little else. The approach road led to the civilian air terminal, then looped back on itself, ringing an asphalted central space that served as the visitors' parking lot. Matt counted fewer than a dozen cars.

The hangars and planes were to his right, across from the parking lot. The high-pitched whine of a taxiing jet could be heard behind one of the two main hangars. The low-level security was surprising: a basic chain-link fence, seven feet high at best, with an extra foot on top sloping outwards, was all that separated the road from the apron. As he drove around the return leg of the road, Matt saw two entry points to the airfield: chain-link rolling fences, two cars wide, that slid sideways on small metal wheels. No guardhouses.

'Check it again,' Matt told Jabba. 'We need a tighter fix on the bastard.'

'I don't know, dude,' Jabba replied warily. 'We're too close.'

'Just don't break your forty-second rule and we'll be fine, right?'

Jabba groaned as he fired up his laptop and phone. He zoomed right in on the linked Google map, then killed the connection. The tracker was about four hundred yards ahead, beyond the second hangar.

'What's he doing in there?' Jabba asked.

'Dropping someone off or, more likely, meeting someone who's flying in.'

Matt glimpsed a small private jet rolling towards the tracker's position. His pulse quickened. His instincts told him he needed to be in there—fast. He gave his options a quick run-through, then saw the gate farther down, closer to the tracker, open up. He tensed—but it wasn't the Merc, or the Chrysler 300C, coming out. Just a silver minivan, idling as the gate rolled back.

He nudged the throttle, propelling the Camry forward. The car accelerated down the ring road, with the airfield's perimeter fence to the right. He was sixty yards away when the minivan had cleared the gate, and was driving off. Forty yards away when the gate had started to roll back.

Matt didn't lift his foot. Fifteen yards from the gate, he twisted the steering wheel left to send the car swerving wide, before flicking it right again, giving the gas pedal a violent kick. The Camry fishtailed into a position perpendicular to the gate and rushed towards it. Matt kept his foot down and threaded the Camry in, scraping the car's right side against the closing gate. They were in.

THE BULLET WATCHED attentively as the private jet veered left on the wide apron and pulled up between an outbuilding and the edge of the tree line, by the parked Merc and the 300C. He had used the spot before: it was tucked away at the far end of the airfield, away from prying eyes, well suited to whisking certain camera-shy clients in and out of the city unnoticed. In this case, things were different.

As the plane's engines wound down, a voice crackled in his earpiece. 'A white Camry just snuck in through the south gate. I think it's our boys.'

Maddox spoke clearly into his cuff mike. 'Got it. Stay with them. And take them down once the package is in the car.'

His eyes casually swept the environment. He didn't see anything suspicious, and turned his attention back to the plane, where Rebecca Rydell and her two bodyguards were now coming down the stairs.

MATT HUGGED the back of the first hangar. He reached its corner then edged forward slowly. He could hear the plane powering down but he couldn't see it, so he feathered the throttle again and crossed over to the second hangar.

About a hundred yards ahead was a low, concrete structure with no windows. He could see the tail of the jet sticking out from behind it, as well as the tailgate of a black Dodge Durango.

He decided to cut across and get behind the outbuilding. From there, he and Jabba would be able to see what was going on—and, if feasible, Matt could make his move. He pulled out his handgun.

'You do realise it's empty, right?' Jabba said.

'They don't know that. Besides, I don't plan on needing it.'

Which, judging from Jabba's expression, didn't seem to reassure him.

'You can get out here and wait for me, if you want,' Matt told him.

Jabba looked at the deserted area behind the hangar. 'I think I'll stick around. It's not exactly Grand Central Terminal out here.'

Matt nodded, sat the gun in his lap, and eased the car behind the outbuilding, just forward enough to give them a view of the plane.

Two men were escorting a young, tanned blonde off the plane.

Jabba leaned forward, his jaw dropping with surprise. 'Whoa.'

Matt slid a reproachful glance at him. 'Not now, tiger—'

'No, dude,' Jabba interrupted urgently. 'She's Rydell's daughter.'

Matt studied her with more interest. She stepped off the stairs and glanced around uncertainly as the two men led her over to Maddox, who spoke to her briefly before leading the trio to the waiting Durango. As he opened the rear door, he glanced in Matt's direction and their eyes met.

Matt flinched slightly but Maddox didn't. In fact he didn't seem rattled at all. Which could mean only one thing.

The hard steel muzzle that suddenly nudged Matt just above his ear confirmed it.

Wadi Natrun, Egypt

Half an hour after climbing into the tunnel, Gracie, Dalton, Father Jerome, Brother Ameen and their four black-robed sherpas emerged into a musty old cellar at the neighbouring monastery. There, anxious monks, led by the local abbot, greeted them.

The abbot fussed over Father Jerome. He seemed completely awed by the monk's presence as well as rattled by the turn of events. He fired off a nervous prattle of words and led them up a stairwell into the monastery.

They were offered cold water and took a moment to catch their breath before heading out into the balmy daylight. Yusuf's brother-in-law's taxi, a tired, white VW Sharan people carrier, was waiting for them in the shade by a small, multidomed structure.

'Are you sure it's safe out there?' Gracie asked the abbot.

'They're not interested in us,' he informed her. 'So far. I'll show you.'

They left the driver and the monks to pile the gear into the car and followed the abbot across the courtyard and up a maze of narrow stairs to the top of a wall.

'Have a look,' the abbot told them, 'but stay low—just in case.'

The familiar carpet of cars and trucks covered the plain between the two monasteries, but with one crucial difference now. All attention seemed focused away from them, towards the monastery they'd just left. Which meant they had a reasonable chance of sneaking out unnoticed.

They climbed back down and got into the car. Gracie felt a bubble of apprehension as she watched the gate creak open. She steeled herself and straightened in her seat as the Sharan rumbled out into the desert.

A few cars and trucks were parked on either side of the dusty trail that led away from the monastery. Men loitered by each cluster of vehicles. As their car got closer to the first group, Gracie turned to Father Jerome and raised his hood over his head, shielding him from view. Yusuf's brother-in-law kept calm, trying not to draw attention, and the Sharan cruised past slowly without eliciting more than a casual glance.

Gracie let out a small breath of relief. A few more minutes, she guessed, and they'd be free and clear. They were less than a hundred yards from the monastery when the road doglegged to the left. More cars were parked there, with another bunch of men clustered against the wall. A lone man was walking towards them, alongside the trail. Gracie tried not to look at him as the driver slowed down to a crawl. As the man drew alongside them he glanced in and Father Jerome turned in his direction. It was enough.

The man reacted as if he'd been slapped. His relaxed features took on a scowl as he put both hands against the car's side window and leaned right in against the glass, trying to see in, sidestepping alongside them.

'He's spotted us,' Gracie exclaimed. 'Get us out of here—now.'

The driver nudged the gas pedal. The Sharan's engine whined as the rear tyres bounced across the ditch. The man quickly fell back into the car's dusty trail. Gracie knew they weren't out of danger yet, though. Sure enough, she saw him start running towards the cluster of men by the wall, waving his hands. One moment he was there and then he was gone. She thought she saw him clasp his hands to his head and fall to the ground but she wasn't sure. They weren't about to stop and find out. The driver kept his foot pressed against the pedal and, fifteen minutes later, they were on the highway with a clear run to the airport.

And then Gracie's satphone rang.

She'd been steeling herself to make a call to Ogilvy, to tell him about Finch, and thought he'd beaten her to it. But as she reached for the phone, she didn't recognise the number. 'Hello?' she queried curiously.

'Miss Logan?' the voice boomed back. 'We haven't met yet, but my name is Darby. Reverend Nelson Darby. And I think I can help you.'

Fox Two watched the white people carrier streak away down the desert trail, then turned his binoculars back to the stricken man. He was still on the ground, writhing with pain, his hands pressed against his ears.

He knew the agitator would be down for a while—they'd hit him with a potent blast. Main thing was, he wasn't going anywhere or saying anything. Not for a while, anyway.

Which was all the time they needed.

He gave his men the signal to move out. Swiftly and silently, they powered down the LRAD, the long-range acoustic device, heading out as innocuously as they'd arrived, shadowing the van from a safe distance and looking forward finally to going home.

Bedford, Massachusetts

The man kept the gun pressed against Matt's temple. 'Easy.' His voice was flat. With his left hand, he reached down to Matt's lap and pulled out his gun, which he stuffed under his belt.

Matt cursed. He'd been so focused on watching the plane and Maddox that he hadn't noticed the man sneaking up on them. Another guy appeared a few yards ahead, moving towards Jabba's side of the car. He also had a gun levelled at Matt's head.

Maddox's drones couldn't kill them here, Matt thought rapidly; there had to be CCTV cameras that would have recorded their presence. It was altogether too messy. Which was good news. But they had plenty of other options. The key was getting him and Jabba off the airport grounds, quietly. The drones would likely get into the Camry and lead him and Jabba, at gunpoint, to somewhere nice and quiet where they could pump a few bullets into them. Which was definitely bad news.

It was simple. He couldn't let them get into the car. Which meant he had no more than a couple of seconds left to do something about it.

Matt moved like lightning. His left hand grabbed the man's right wrist, his gun hand, and slammed it forward, crushing it against the inside of the car's A-pillar. A shot erupted eighteen inches from Matt's face. The sound wave hit him like a lead fist in the split second that the round obliterated the rearview mirror and punched through the windshield.

Matt thought he heard Jabba yell out, but the other guy was more his concern. His foot stamped on the gas pedal and he twisted the wheel to the right. The car lunged straight at the second shooter, crushing him against the low metal fence that jutted out from the side of the outbuilding. He let out a piercing yelp of agony before a gush of blood spewed out of his mouth onto the Camry's virgin-white hood.

Matt still had the first guy's gun hand pinned against the pillar and he struggled to angle his gun inwards. Another round exploded and whizzed past Jabba's face.

Matt saw the guy reaching down with his free hand to pull the gun he'd taken off Matt from under his belt, and Matt spun the wheel to the right—once, twice, full lock, using one arm—then dropped his hand down to the gearstick, slammed it into reverse, and mashed the gas pedal again.

The car leaped back and slammed into the first shooter. He was thrown back and, with his hand still pinned to the pillar, tripped over and stumbled to the ground. The Camry's rear end crunched against the outbuilding's wall just as its left front wheel rode over the fallen shooter's ankles. The man howled with pain and let go of the gun, which tumbled into Matt's foot well. Matt threw the car back into drive and howled away in a squeal of rubber.

He threw a glance at the plane—the two bodyguards who were with Rydell's daughter were rushing towards him, guns drawn.

He floored the accelerator again and tore back up the apron, ploughed right through the gate and tore down the approach road into the shelter of its tree line.

'They knew we were coming,' Matt yelled at Jabba. 'They were waiting for us.'

'But . . .' Jabba was still in shock from the bullets slicing through the air right in front of him.

'Your phone—they're reading it,' Matt stated flatly.

'There's no way, man.' Jabba held his iPhone up, examining it curiously. 'They can't lock onto it that fast, and I haven't had it on long enough for them to download any spyware—'

Matt snatched it out of his fingers, and was about to flick it out the window when Jabba grabbed it with both hands.

'My whole life's in there. You can't just throw it away. Give me a second.'

He looked around, checked the car's side pockets, then opened the glove box and rifled through it. He found some paperwork in a plastic sleeve held together by the very thing he was looking for, a paper clip. He straightened it, and stuck one of its ends into the tiny hole on the top face of the phone. The SIM card tray popped out. He showed the card to Matt.

'No SIM card. No signal. The phone's dead for now. OK?'

Matt frowned at him for a moment, then shrugged and nodded. 'OK.' He felt his pulse slow. He'd just taken down two men. Which should have felt bad, but—strangely—didn't. It was, he told himself, a simple matter of self-defence. But he knew he'd have to be more careful if he didn't want to fall on the wrong side of that equation next time.

Jabba sat quietly for a moment, just staring ahead, then asked, 'What are we going to do now?'

'What do you think?' Matt grumbled.

Jabba studied him then nodded stoically. 'Rydell?'

'Rydell,' Matt simply confirmed.

Wadi Natrun, Egypt

'I understand you're looking to get out of there in a hurry,' Darby said.

Gracie stared ahead quizzically. 'I'm sorry?'

'You need a ride, Miss Logan, and I'm calling to offer you one.'

Her mind scrambled to make sense of the call. She couldn't count herself among the pastor's fans. Far from it. But that didn't really matter now. 'Who gave you this number?'

'I have a lot of friends, Miss Logan. But that's beside the point, which is that you need to get yourself and my most esteemed brother in Christ out of danger. And I can help you do that. Are you interested?'

She tried to figure out where they stood. Ogilvy was supposed to be arranging a plane, but she didn't even know what Ogilvy had told Finch exactly—whether or not he'd be able to get them a plane and, if so, how soon. They didn't have a specific destination either. The overriding concern had been to put as many miles as possible between them and the mobs outside the monastery. The rest hadn't been mapped out. That was Finch's domain, and he wasn't there to sort it out.

'What do you have in mind?'

'First things first. Father Jerome is with you, right?'

'Of course,' she answered, knowing that was all he was interested in.

'Can you make it out of the monastery safely?'

'Yes,' Gracie answered. 'We have a way out.'

'Good. I need you to get to the airport in Alexandria. It's as close to you as Cairo is, but it's quieter,' Darby told her. 'I'll have a plane on the ground in under two hours. How soon can you get there?'

Gracie thought about it. 'We can be there before that,' she replied.

'Perfect,' Darby shot back. 'Call me when you're on your way.'

'Where are you flying us to?' she asked, feeling a stab of discomfort at the idea of putting herself and Father Jerome in the reverend's hands.

'The one place we know we can keep the good Father safe. You're coming home, Miss Logan, to God's own country. And you can take it from me, the people out here are going to be overjoyed to see you.'

Brookline, Massachusetts

Darkness was moving in as Matt slowed down and pulled over by the side of the road. The area was heavily wooded, the traffic sparse. Just ahead, two waist-high stone posts marked the entrance to the municipal service centre.

From where he was parked, Matt could make out the low office-and-garage structure set back from the road, the drive leading up to it lined with parked cars. There wasn't much going on, which suited Matt just fine.

He hadn't driven there directly. The first priority had been dumping the Camry. They'd ducked into a mall, pulled up to a far corner of its parking lot, and exchanged the car for a decade-old green Pontiac Bonneville.

Matt had wanted to get a few things—importantly, more bullets for the handgun he'd taken off the shooter at the airfield. His options were limited. He couldn't exactly walk into a gun store in his current wanted and bruised state. So they'd rushed down to Quincy, where they'd hooked up with a deeply concerned Sanjay, who'd met them away from the 7-Eleven, at his place. He came through for Matt with two boxes of Pow'RBall rounds, some fresh gauze dressing for his wound and some cash.

They'd also used Sanjay's computer to look up Rydell's address—he lived in a big house in Brookline. Matt had also got a refresher course in what Rydell actually looked like. Then Matt and Jabba had driven across to Brookline and scouted the municipal service centre and the area around Rydell's house before staking out the house itself.

They hadn't had to wait long. Rydell's chauffeur-driven Lexus had pulled into the narrow lane that led to his house shortly after five o'clock. Matt had thought about making his move there and then, but decided against it. The bodyguard and the heavyweight riding shotgun looked to be too much to take on.

They'd watched the house for a while, making sure Rydell wasn't going anywhere, then Jabba had stepped out of the car to keep an eye on the building.

'Remember,' Matt told him, 'if this goes wrong, don't go to the cops. Don't trust anyone.'

Jabba shrugged. 'Just make sure it doesn't go wrong then.'

Matt smiled. 'I guess I'll see you in a little while.' He'd left him there and looped back to the service centre, where he was presently parked.

He double-checked the handgun, tucked it in under his coat then got out and walked up the drive to the service centre. He'd taken some painkillers, which had numbed the wound in his side, and found that he was able to walk in a way that didn't scream, 'walking wounded'. He followed the curving drive, past the entrance to the reception area and past the building's 'employees-only' door, until he reached the garage area at the back.

There were several Mack garbage trucks parked in there, side by side. Matt looked around. A couple of mechanics were working on a truck parked thirty yards away. One of them glanced over. Matt gave him a relaxed nod, then walked towards the back wall of the garage with a purposeful step, so as not to appear out of place in any way. From the corner of his eye, he saw that the mechanic had gone back to work.

Matt checked the back wall. He noticed a whiteboard with some shift lists marked up on it, then spotted the metal, wall-mounted box where the keys were kept. It wasn't locked, which wasn't a surprise—garbage trucks usually ranked pretty low on the 'most stolen vehicles' lists.

He matched the number on a key tag with the licence plate on one of the trucks, and picked the keys off their hook. He climbed into the big truck's cabin, then fired the engine. The big cab rumbled under him. He pressed down on the heavy clutch and teased the accelerator. The truck nudged forward. The mechanic looked over again, an uncertain expression on his face.

Matt leaned out of the window and said, 'Clutch might need some work. I'll be back in ten,' and pulled away. A moment later, he was turning the lumbering orange behemoth onto the main road.

FEELING NUMB as he sat in the book-lined study of his mansion, Larry Rydell stared into his tumbler of Scotch and fumed in silence, flinching at the thought of any harm coming to his daughter. *Those bastards. If she so much as gets a scratch* . . . He sagged in his chair. It was pointless. He knew he couldn't do anything. He'd never felt so helpless in his life.

With his fortune and power, he'd reached a point in his life where he felt he was untouchable. But he was powerless to deal with these . . . thugs. That's what they were. Thugs, out to pervert his vision, to take his idea and use it for . . . what, exactly? Much as he turned over what Drucker had said, it didn't make sense. They were alike when it came to what they believed in. They saw the risks facing the world—and those facing America—in the same light. And yet they were doing this, creating a fake messiah in the figure of Father Jerome.

It doesn't make sense, he thought again. And yet Drucker had confirmed it. They were actually doing it. The backstabbing bastards.

His mind latched onto Rebecca's face, on the last time he'd seen her, shortly before her ill-fated trip to Mexico. He'd wanted to join her there for the holidays, but he hadn't been able to. Not with the biggest undertaking of his life in full swing. And, bless her, she hadn't voiced her disappointment. She never did. She'd got used to having a mythical dad, in the good and bad sense of the word. Which was something he'd fix—if he ever got the chance.

He had to find her, tuck her away somewhere safe. Even saving the planet now paled into insignificance. He had to get her out of their hands. Then he had to try and stop this, to shut it down before it got too big.

But how? For years, he'd entrusted all his security requirements—personal and professional—to that rattlesnake Maddox. The security guards 'watching over him' right now, at his house; his driver-slash-bodyguard; the vetting of his pilot, of the staff on his yacht; the corporate security at his companies, email, phones. Everything was covered by one firm. Maddox's. On Drucker's recommendation.

He felt like a fool. He'd been played. From the beginning.

He stared angrily at the heavy tumbler, then flung it at the huge stone fireplace. It exploded and rained shards of glass on the carpet. Just then, he heard the sound of a large engine. He edged over to the window and looked down the drive that curved to the mansion's entrance gate.

MATT SPOTTED JABBA as he approached the turnoff. Jabba gave him a thumbs up before darting back into the trees. Matt turned into the lane, and floored the gas pedal.

The Mack's three-hundred-horsepower engine growled as it raced ahead. Before long, the mansion's entrance gate appeared up ahead. Matt wasn't exactly flying, but that didn't matter. Speed wasn't what he was after here. It was bulk. He reached the gate and didn't lift his foot off the pedal. Fifteen tons of solid steel ploughed into it and obliterated it into toothpicks.

The truck charged up the driveway, scattering gravel and leaving twin ruts in its wake. Matt could see the house through a scattering of trees: looming at the top of a manicured, landscaped rise, a Georgian revival mansion with a circular gravel drive. There was no sign of the Lexus or the muscle. Yet.

He aimed the truck at the entrance. Just as he reached it, one of the heavies rushed out. His eyes went wide as he spotted the charging garbage truck, and he was already pulling his gun out from a shoulder holster

The truck bounced over a floral bed and slammed into the bodyguard before he had a chance to fire off a single round. The man was squashed against the front door as it bulldozed its way into the house.

Brick, timber and glass exploded inwards as the Mack came to rest inside the house's cavernous foyer. Matt kept the engine running and climbed from the cabin as another heavy appeared from a side room, gun drawn. Matt had the advantage of surprise and blew him away with two rounds.

Then he stepped away from the truck and yelled, 'Rydell.'

He advanced through the house, looking for his quarry. He checked the main living room, then a media room next to that, and was on his way into the kitchen area when a double-door opened up and Rydell's head popped out.

Matt recognised him immediately. He grabbed him by his shoulder. 'Let's go.'

Rydell's mouth dropped when he saw the truck squatting in the entrance hall, a twelve-foot-square gash eaten out of the house's front façade. As Matt nudged Rydell forward, he heard footsteps and saw another guard rushing at them. Matt aimed and squeezed, dropping the man to the floor.

'Is that all you've got, huh?' he barked furiously at Rydell.

Before the shell-shocked Rydell could answer, Matt pushed him to the back of the truck and pointed at its rear-loading bay. 'Get in,' he ordered.

Rydell stared at him, terror-stricken. 'In there?'

'Get in,' Matt roared, raising the gun inches from Rydell's nose.

Rydell climbed in. Matt glared at him and hit the compacting switch. The hydraulic paddle churned to life and inched its way down, swinging over Rydell and herding him into the belly of the truck.

Matt hit the switch again to block the paddle in position, then made his way back to the truck's cabin and climbed in. Another drone in a dark suit aimed a big gun at Matt and the bullets hammered the back of the cabin behind Matt's head. Matt ducked, crunched the gear lever into reverse and floored the accelerator. The truck extricated itself from the battered house and emerged onto the gravel drive. The man followed, still shooting. Matt swung the orange beast round and slammed it into first. The truck's smoke-stack let out an angry bellow of black smoke before hurtling down the drive and out onto the narrow lane again.

Matt was halfway to the main road when the first of the armed-response cars appeared, a yellow SUV with a blaring siren and a rack of spinning lights on its roof. The driver knew he didn't stand a chance. He swerved just as the big Mack reached him, but the truck flicked the SUV into the trees like a hockey puck. The second response car didn't fare much better. Matt sent it pirouetting on its smoking tyres before coming to a violent stop in a sewer ditch.

He slowed down at the mouth of the lane, picked up Jabba, and motored on. He had Rydell, which was good, and he was still alive, which was even better.

Washington, DC

Too bad, Keenan Drucker thought. He liked Rydell. The man was a great asset, a visionary. And none of this would've happened without him.

Drucker's mind travelled back to how it had all started. Davos, Switzerland. The two-hundred-thousand-dollars-a-table black-tie dinner. A gathering of the planet's powerful elite who aspired to solve the world's big crises. Rydell and Drucker had sat together late into the night, going over the growing mountain of data on global warming. Fourteen thousand new cars a day hitting the road in China. The booming industries there and in India building new coal-fired plants every week. Congress giving the oil and gas companies back home one tax break after another.

They were both in agreement: the planet was hurtling towards the point of no return. The question was, what to do about it.

Throughout, Drucker couldn't escape the feeling that Rydell was testing him, seeing how far he'd go. Drucker smiled as he remembered how he had gestured at the lavish setting around them, 'All this won't change much. People don't really want change, not if it costs something. The "don't worry, it's all a load of crap" message the fuel lobby keeps pumping out— deep down, that's what everyone wants to hear. It's heaven-sent.'

'Maybe heaven should send them a different message,' Rydell had replied, a visionary blaze in his eye. The rest had followed on from that.

At first, it had seemed Rydell was talking theory. But the theoretical soon became the possible. And when that happened, everything changed.

As far as Drucker was concerned, what Rydell and his people had come up with could be used as a weapon that could tackle any number of threats in different ways. Problem was, Rydell wouldn't be open to that. As far as he was concerned, there was only one major threat facing humanity.

Drucker disagreed. There were other threats that required more immediate attention. For although Drucker was a concerned citizen of the world, he was, more than anything, a patriot. The Muslim world was growing bolder and wilder. It needed reining in. China was also a growing concern. Not militarily, but economically, which was even worse.

In any case, using the global-warming message as the first hook was the way to go. It was a cause that everyone could embrace, one that transcended race and religion. The secondary message would sneak in through the back door.

The strategy had to be carefully conceived, though. The deception had to be strange enough to capture people's attention and root itself firmly in their memory, but not so strange that they would dismiss it. Also, the manifestation needed to have an emotional resonance in order for belief to set in. Religions used elaborate rituals to stir up people's emotions. The environmental movement taking on a quasi-religious aspect was the perfect platform.

The timing was helpful, too. The planet was living through scary times. Economic meltdown. Terrorism and rogue nukes. Avian flu. Nanotechnology. Hadron Colliders. Everything seemed to be out of control. Which could only feed into the prophecies of some kind of a messiah showing up to sort everything out and bring about a millennial kingdom. And it wasn't just a Christian phenomenon. Every major religion had its own version of how a great teacher would appear and rescue the world from catastrophe.

Drucker would have preferred Rydell to be part of it all. He'd tried to convince him about the need to introduce a messenger—a prophet—into the mix. They'd talked about it at length. But Rydell wouldn't listen. Drucker didn't like doing what they'd had to do to Rebecca, but it'd had to be done. Rydell was too passionate. His commitment came with an inflexibility that couldn't be overcome. He'd never be able to accept the trade-off. And, besides, he couldn't be fully included, anyway. He was part of the end game. The sacrificial pawn that was crucial to its successful closure.

Drucker's phone trilled. The Bullet's name flashed up on the screen. The man whose foot soldiers were making it all happen. The deformed marine, who had been the commanding officer of Jackson, his only son. The man who'd left half his face in the same Iraqi slaughterhouse that had ripped Drucker's son to shreds.

Drucker picked up the phone. The news wasn't good.

Brookline, Massachusetts

The hydraulic compactor whined as it swivelled upwards. Matt let the compactor rise two-thirds of the way up, then killed its motor. The heavy lid just held there, cantilevered over the stinking cavity of the truck's hold.

Matt leaned in. 'Get out here,' he ordered and Rydell stumbled out.

The truck was parked in a deserted alley that ran behind a low-rise commercial street. It was six blocks from the municipal service centre where Matt had stolen the truck. The green Bonneville was parked nearby. They stood out of view, shielded by the bulk of the truck.

Rydell stank. His clothes had rips in them, and he was battered and bruised from bouncing around the empty metal box. He had to lean against the truck, breathing heavily and gathering his senses.

Matt raised the big silver handgun the shooter at the airport had lost and held it inches from Rydell's face. 'What did you do to my brother?'

Rydell raised his eyes at him. He glanced across to Jabba, his expression revealing that he didn't have a clue who Matt and Jabba were.

'Your brother . . . ?' he muttered.

'Danny Sherwood. What happened to him?'

Rydell's eyes flickered back to life. 'As far as I know, he's OK. But it's been a few weeks since I saw him.'

Matt flinched at his words. 'You're saying he's alive?'

Rydell looked up at him and nodded. 'Yes.'

Matt glanced over at Jabba, who gave him a supportive nod.

'I'm sorry,' Rydell continued. 'We didn't have a choice.'

'Of course you did,' Matt shot back. He was still processing the news. 'So this sign . . . this whole thing. You're doing it?'

Rydell nodded. 'I *was*. The others . . . my partners . . . they're doing it their way now.' He sighed. 'I've been . . . sidelined.'

'What really happened? In Namibia? Was Danny ever really there?'

Rydell nodded again, slowly. 'That's where we did the final test. But there was no helicopter crash. It was all staged.'

'So Reece, the others . . . they're also still alive?'

'No.' Rydell hesitated. 'Look, I didn't want any of that. It's not how I do things. But there were others there . . . they overreacted.'

'Who?' Matt asked.

'The security guys.'

'Maddox?' Matt guessed. 'He got rid of them, when you didn't need them any more.'

'It wasn't like that,' Rydell objected. 'None of them knew what we were really planning. And then when I finally told Reece, he didn't want to hear of it. I thought I could have convinced him . . . He would've come on board.

And the others would have joined in, too. But I never got the chance. Maddox just snapped and . . . he just started firing. I couldn't stop him.'

'And Danny?'

'He ran,' Rydell said.

'But he didn't get away.'

Rydell shook his head.

'And you kept him locked up, all this time.'

Rydell nodded. 'He designed the processing interface. It works perfectly, but it's very sensitive. It was safer having him around.'

'Why would he keep doing what you asked? He had to know you'd kill him once it was all over.' He studied Rydell. 'He's not doing this of his own free will, is he?'

'No,' Rydell replied. 'We—they—threatened him.'

'With what?'

'Your parents,' Rydell said, 'and you. They told him they'd hurt you. Badly. Then they'd get you thrown back into prison, where they'd make sure your life was a living hell.'

Matt felt a surge of anger. 'My parents are dead.'

Rydell nodded with remorse. 'Danny doesn't know that.'

Matt looked away into the distance. His kid brother. Going through hell for two years, made to wield his brilliance for something he didn't believe in . . . going through it all to protect him. After everything Danny had already done for him.

Matt thought of his parents, how they'd been devastated by the news of Danny's helicopter crash, and a crushing sense of grief overcame him. He glared back at Rydell and felt like ripping his heart out.

Jabba watched Matt struggle with the revelation but didn't interfere. Instead, he took a step closer to Rydell. He couldn't help himself. 'How are you doing it?' he asked him.

Rydell shook his head and turned away.

'Answer him,' Matt barked.

After a brief moment, Rydell just said, 'Smart dust.'

'Smart dust? But that's not . . .' Jabba shook his head with disbelief. 'How small?'

'A third of a cubic millimetre.'

Jabba's mouth dropped an inch. According to everything he'd read or heard about, that just wasn't possible.

'Smart dust'—minuscule electronic devices designed to record and transmit information about their surroundings while literally floating on air—was still a scientific dream. The idea was simple: tiny motes of silicon, packed with sophisticated on-board sensors, computer processors and wireless communicators, small enough to be virtually invisible and light enough to remain suspended in midair for hours at a time, could be used to gather and transmit data in real time—and undetected.

The concept was sound. Breakthroughs in nanotechnology were inching the dream closer to reality. Making the sensors small enough wasn't the problem. The problem lay in the processors that analysed the data, the transmitters that communicated it back to base, and the power supply that ran the whole thing. By the time they were added on, they turned dust-sized particles into clusters the size of a golf ball.

Clearly, Rydell's team had managed to overcome those hurdles.

Jabba was struggling to order the questions in his mind.

'But where are they coming from? Are you dropping them from drones?'

'Canisters,' Rydell told him. 'We shoot them up, like fireworks.'

'But there's no noise, no explosion,' Jabba remarked. 'Is there?'

'We're using compressed-air launchers.'

'So what are they running on?'

'They feed off each other. We light them up with an electromagnetic signal from the ground. They convert the transmission into power and spread it across the cloud where it's needed.'

Jabba was struggling to absorb the information. 'But even the slightest breeze pushes them around, right? And yet the sign wasn't moving.'

Rydell glanced over at Matt, his expression darkening with remorse.

'That's where Danny came in, with his distributed processing program. He came up with this brilliant optical system based on corner-cube reflectors. It lets them communicate with each other very elaborately while using up virtually no energy. It literally brought the motes to life.'

He exhaled then continued, 'We needed the shape—the sign—to stay in one place. But you're right, the motes, they're so small, so light, they're floating around, moving in the air like dandelion seeds. So we needed them to be able to talk to each other. The sign appears stationary even though the dust particles are always changing position. Factor in that we wanted the sign to morph constantly in shape to appear as though it's alive, and . . . it's a hell of a lot of processing power in a machine the size of a speck of dust. We couldn't have done it without Danny.'

'Oh, well in that case, I guess you did the right thing by locking him up all this time,' Matt retorted.

'You think this has been easy?' Rydell shot back. 'I've put everything on the line for this. The way things are going, I'll probably end up dead because of it.'

'It's a distinct possibility,' Matt confirmed drily.

'I had no choice. Something had to be done. This thing's getting out of hand, and no one's paying attention.'

'Global warming?' Jabba asked. 'That's what this is all about, right?'

'What else?' Rydell flared up. 'People out there—they've got no idea. They don't realise that every time they get into their cars, they're slowly killing the planet.' He was gesticulating wildly, all fired up. 'We're getting close to the point of no return. And when that happens, the weather will just shift dramatically and that'll be the end of us. We owe it to our kids and to their kids to do something about it. Some time in the next hundred years, people will look back and wonder why the hell no one ever did anything about it. Despite all the warnings we had. Well, I'm doing something.'

'So you decided to go out and kill off a bunch of decent guys to get everyone's attention,' Matt said.

'I told you, that wasn't part of the plan,' Rydell snapped.

'Still, you're going along with it.'

'What did you want me to do? Give up on the whole thing and turn Maddox and his people in? Throw away a plan that could change everything?'

Matt didn't waver. 'But did you ever even consider it?'

Rydell thought about it, and shook his head.

'What about Father Jerome?' Jabba asked. 'He's not part of this too, is he?'

'I don't know. He wasn't part of the original plan,' Rydell said.

'He can't be in on it,' Jabba protested.

'It doesn't matter,' Matt interjected firmly. 'I just want to get Danny back.' He turned to Rydell. 'Where is he?'

'I don't know,' Rydell said. 'I told you. I'm out of the loop.'

Matt raised the big handgun and held it aimed squarely at Rydell's forehead. 'Try again.'

'I'm telling you I don't know. But the next time the sign shows up, you'll probably find him there.'

'What?' Matt rasped.

'We needed him alive to make the micro-adjustments in real time. Onsite.'

'"Onsite"?' Jabba asked. 'He can't do it remotely?'

'He could, but data transmission isn't foolproof over such long distances, and even the smallest time-lag could mess things up. He has to be within half a mile or so of the sign. That's the transmitter's range.'

A siren wailed nearby. Matt tensed. Through a narrow passage that led to the main drag he spotted the flash of a police car blowing past.

He turned to Jabba. 'We need to move.' He flicked the gun at Rydell, herding him on. 'Let's go.'

'Where?' Rydell asked.

'I don't know yet, but you're coming with us. They've got Danny. I have you. Sounds like a good trade.'

'They won't trade him for me. They need him more than they need me. They'd probably be happy to see me dead.'

'Maybe, but if they haven't killed you yet, it means they also need you for something,' Matt observed.

Judging by Rydell's expression, that struck a nerve. But he told Matt, 'I can't go with you. They have my daughter.'

Matt scoffed. 'Sure.' Rydell was clearly a cunning liar.

'Listen to me. They grabbed her in Mexico. They're hanging onto her as security to make sure I don't rock the boat. They can't even know I talked to you. They'll kill her.'

Jabba stepped closer. 'Maybe it's true, dude. She's here.'

Rydell's head jerked forward. 'Here?'

'We saw her a couple of hours ago,' Jabba informed him. 'Maddox and his goon squad flew her into a small airport near Bedford. We thought they were her bodyguards.'

Rydell's expression clouded.

'They have your daughter, and you think you've only been sidelined?' Matt's expression was heavy with contempt. 'Me, I'd take it as a definite sign that you guys are now enemies. Let's go.' He motioned to Rydell with his gun.

Rydell shook his head. 'I can't.' He took a step back. 'They'll kill her.'

Matt's anger flared. 'You should have thought of that before you started looking the other way while your people got bumped off.'

Rydell shook his head stoically. 'Even if I wanted to help you, I can't as long as they have her. Do what you want, but I'm not going anywhere with you.'

Matt raised his gun, but Rydell didn't stop. He kept inching backwards.

'Stop. I mean it,' Matt ordered.

Rydell shook his head and kept backing up. He was now at the mouth of the small passageway that led to the main drag.

Matt hesitated. Rydell saw it. He bolted into the passageway.

Matt took off after him, Jabba in tow. They burst onto the main road and Matt stumbled to a halt. A few pedestrians stood on the sidewalk, eyes locked on Matt, taken aback by his sudden appearance and his gun. Behind them, Rydell was backing off.

Matt felt too many eyes on him. Rydell was slipping away, and he couldn't do anything about it.

'Let's get the hell out of here,' he told Jabba.

He'd lost Rydell, but Danny was alive and, right now, that was all that mattered.

Alexandria, Egypt

The plane was waiting for Gracie and the others when they got to Alexandria Airport. Darby had come through, as promised. They kept Father Jerome well out of view, only too aware that the merest glimpse of him could trigger a stampede. He was perhaps the most recognisable face on the planet right now.

The clerk manning the civil aviation office turned out to be a Copt. One look at Brother Ameen's cassock did the trick. Within minutes, their passports had been stamped, the gates had been opened and they were climbing up the stairs of the chartered jet. The plan was for the driver to wait until the plane took off before letting the abbot know it was safe to announce that the priest was no longer at the monastery.

Gracie started to relax as the fourteen-seater Gulfstream G450 streaked upwards to its cruising altitude, but her relief was short-lived. It allowed only darker thoughts to surface. Thoughts about Finch lying dead in the sand. A veil of grief descended over her.

'I wish we hadn't left him there,' she told Dalton in the seat opposite her.

'We didn't have a choice,' Dalton comforted her. 'We've got to tell the folks back home.'

Gracie nodded quietly.

'We need to give Ogilvy an update on our ETA,' he added. 'I'll go talk to the pilot. See if he can patch us in to the desk.'

He pushed himself to his feet, but Gracie's hand reached out and arrested his move. 'Not just yet. Let's just take a few minutes for ourselves.'

'Sure.' He glanced at the galley. 'You want some coffee?'

'Thanks.' She nodded, then added, 'If they're out of coffee, a couple of fingers of Scotch will do.'

THE FALSE PRIEST who had chosen to be called Brother Ameen watched Dalton rise from his seat. He acknowledged the cameraman with a friendly nod as he walked past.

Finch had been Dario Arapovic's first kill on this mission, though he'd killed many times before. The war in his homeland had been brutal. It had turned a lot of young Croatian men like him into heartless killers. And some of those, also like him, discovered that their talents were in demand by people like Maddox and were richly rewarded.

He would much have preferred not to have had to kill the producer. The risk of detection was high. Equally dangerous was the risk of disrupting a plan that had been working smoothly up until then. The news team couldn't have done a better job had they been a covert unit. They were professionals who could be counted on to follow a well-thought-out methodology. Finch had been an integral part of that. Someone would have to replace him. A new producer. A hardhead who might not be as easy to steer as Finch had been.

Still, Dario had had no choice. He knew Finch wouldn't have bought into anything he could have come up with to explain his having a satphone, much less one that was encryption module-equipped.

He glanced at Gracie. He knew she wouldn't bow out because of Finch's death. Like all pros, she had the cold, rational ability to compartmentalise tragedies like her producer's death and carry on.

Which was good. She still had an important role to play.

HALF AN HOUR after the Gulfstream had taken off, another aircraft followed it into the sky and was now shadowing it, a couple of hundred miles back.

The chartered Boeing 737 was a much larger aircraft. Its hold carried a selection of state-of-the-art technology, including a long-range acoustic device, canisters of nanoengineered smart dust and ultrasilent compressed-air launchers. The jet's cabin held a load that was no less exceptional: seven men whose actions had entranced the world. Six were highly trained professionals: one three-man team that had spent over a year in the desert, another team that had endured extreme weather all over the globe. The seventh man wasn't highly trained, nor did he share their sense of purpose.

Danny Sherwood was there only out of fear. He'd been their prisoner for close to two years. Two years of coming up with plans of escape, of fantasising about them, of ditching them. And then, finally, it had begun. It was why they'd kept him alive.

He thought he knew what they were up to, but he wasn't sure. He'd thought of sabotaging their plans, of rejigging the software so that a giant Coca-Cola sign appeared instead of the mystical sign they had designed. But he knew they'd probably figure out what he was up to. He also realised it would mean a death sentence for him and, probably, for Matt and for their parents. And so he never went through with it. He wasn't a tough guy. If they'd taken Matt, things would have been different.

He sometimes wished his survival instincts hadn't kicked in just as the Jeep was launching itself off the canyon's edge. Wished he hadn't leaped out of it just as its front wheels ran out of ground. Wished he hadn't ended up clinging to life at the edge of the abyss. But he had. And here he was now, shackled to his seat, wondering when his nightmare would end.

Framingham, Massachusetts

Matt and Jabba sat facing each other in a booth in a small diner in Framingham, about fifteen miles west of Brookline. They'd polished off a burger each and hadn't spoken more than ten words throughout.

A small, wall-mounted TV was rerunning an old *Simpsons* episode. The end credits eventually segued into the evening news, starting with the latest update from Egypt. The volume was low, but a banner on the bottom of the screen informed them that Father Jerome hadn't been seen since the sign had appeared over him earlier that day. Unconfirmed reports said that he had left the monastery. Reporters around the world were scrambling to figure out where he was. They wondered whether he might be headed to Jerusalem, or the Vatican, or back home to Spain.

Crowds massed in St Peter's Square, and in Sao Paulo and in many more cities, holding vigils. The world was waiting for Father Jerome's next appearance. Pockets of violence had cropped up in Pakistan, Israel and Egypt, where men and women of all religions had taken to the streets. Riot police had been deployed, cars and shops had been set alight, and there had been deaths.

Matt stared at the screen for a moment, then finally said, 'Wherever that priest's going, that's where we'll find Danny.'

Jabba's shoulders sagged. Their fates were now intertwined, there was no escaping that. And though he hardly knew Matt, he'd seen enough of him to recognise a distant, frowning look that indicated something was bothering him. 'What is it, dude?'

Matt said, 'We need Rydell. They screwed him over. They've got his daughter. Right now he's real angry. Which makes me think he could help us get Danny back.'

'Not as long as they've got his daughter,' Jabba reminded him.

'Maybe we can change that.'

'Dude, come on,' Jabba protested.

'She's got herself caught up in this thing just like we have,' Matt argued. 'You think this is going to end well for her? They're hanging onto her to get her dad to play nice. Once they're done, they're not going to let her live.'

Jabba gave him a look.

'You like the idea of Maddox and his storm troopers keeping her locked up? Besides, maybe that's where they've been keeping Danny too.'

Jabba tilted his head at him, dubiously. 'You don't really believe that, do you?'

'Not really,' Matt conceded. Then he gave Jabba a slight grin. 'What, you got something better to do?'

Jabba shook his head in defeat. 'Even if I did, this is bound to be *so* much more fun.'

Just over three hours later, Maddox took the second call that night from his contact at the NSA.

'I just got another hit. Very brief. Under twenty seconds.'

'Location?'

'Same place,' the caller told him. The GPS lock had placed Jabba's iPhone on a busy little commercial strip leading out of Framingham.

'OK. Keep me posted.' Maddox hung up and hit a speed-dial key. The man on the other end picked up. 'How far away are you?' Maddox asked.

'Should be there in less than ten,' the operative replied.

'OK,' Maddox said. 'We just got another lock. Same location. They're probably in a hotel or a motel on that block. Let me know what you find.'

Boston, Massachusetts

The presidential suite on the sixth floor of the Four Seasons was as comfortable as it got in the city or pretty much anywhere else in the world, but, as far as Rydell was concerned, he could have been sitting in a motel room. His mind was elsewhere.

He'd returned to his house after getting away from Matt. It had been swarming with cops and armed-response guys—and Maddox, who'd had Rydell give the cops a bullshit story about an attempted kidnapping. Rydell had told them the men had worn balaclavas and that he'd managed to escape when they'd tried to transfer him from the garbage truck and hadn't operated the compactor properly. He'd left it at that and had checked into the Four Seasons. His lawyers could deal with the rest.

Maddox had arranged to have two of his men stationed outside the suite. That angered Rydell, but there was nothing he could do about it. Not as long as they had his daughter.

If they haven't killed you yet, it means they also need you for something, Matt had told him. Which rang worryingly true. But what did they need him for? When he had told Drucker they couldn't do it without him, Drucker had agreed. But it wasn't true. They had the technology. They had Danny. They didn't need him to make it happen any more.

He and Drucker had gone into this together, brothers-in-arms united for a worthy cause. Was that still the case? It suddenly dawned on him that maybe they weren't after the same thing any more. Maybe the others were after something else. After all, they had created a messenger who transcended the message. The story was no longer about God's warning. It was about His messenger.

Drucker wouldn't make such a mistake unless he had a different message in mind. *Think of what we can make people do*, he had said.

A final thought confirmed Rydell's worst fears. Again it was born out of something Matt had said: *Me, I'd take it as a definite sign that you guys are now enemies*.

It suddenly dawned on Rydell that Matt was right. There was no way this was ending well for him. Those bastards had Rebecca. There was no going back from that. They were the enemy.

His cellphone rang. It was Drucker.

'What did you tell him?'

'All he wanted to know was what happened to his brother,' Rydell said.

'I told him I thought he was still alive, but I didn't know where. Then I ran.'

'Nothing else?'

'Don't worry. He doesn't care what you're up to. He doesn't know about you, for that matter, though maybe I should have mentioned it.'

'Wouldn't have been ideal for Rebecca,' Drucker reminded him coldly. 'Stay at the hotel and avoid the press. We might have to find you somewhere more discreet until you can move back into the house.'

Rydell hung up and thought about Rebecca again. Matt was right. He and Drucker were enemies now. And maybe Matt was the only one he could turn to in order to do something about it.

Above the Eastern Mediterranean

The cobalt-blue sea stretched out as far as Gracie could see. She leaned forward and drank in the tranquil view. Looking out from an aircraft at high altitude never failed to instil a sense of wonder in her.

The dulcet tones of Father Jerome intruded. 'How are you feeling?'

She managed a partial smile and a shrug. 'Frankly . . . a bit lost.' She gestured at Dalton's empty seat. 'Please. Won't you join me?'

He sat down. 'Since I left Sudan, I've often felt adrift myself.'

She studied him. 'Up on that roof . . . What did it feel like?' She remembered his mystified look when the sign was suspended over him in midair. 'Did you have any control over what was happening?'

He shook his head. 'It feels as strange to me as it does to you and to everyone else,' he said. 'There's only one thing that's clear. If I've been fortunate enough to be chosen, then I mustn't shy away from it. It's happening for a reason. It has to be.' He eyed her reaction. 'What do you think is going on?'

'I don't know. But it's weird actually to have proof of this miracle. Not just some questionable writings from a couple of thousand years ago.'

Father Jerome's brow furrowed. 'Questionable?'

'I have to be honest with you, Father. I don't believe in God. On the few occasions I did go to church, I never met a preacher I felt I could trust. Or who could ever give me a convincing answer to the simplest questions.'

'Like what?'

'How much time have you got?' she joked.

He smiled back. 'Not to believe in one religion or another, that's entirely understandable for a well-educated woman like you. But why not believe in God? The idea of something wondrous and unknowable.'

She paused, thinking about something close to her heart. 'My mom died when I was thirteen. Breast cancer. I couldn't see why anyone would create something that nasty or take away someone so wonderful.' Her eyes glistened with the memory.

'I'm sorry.'

'It was a long time ago.' She hesitated, then, 'I talked to a couple of pastors who just gave me the standard remarks about her "being with God" and all kinds of other platitudes. Their words meant nothing to me.'

Father Jerome nodded thoughtfully. 'The reason they couldn't help you is they're lost. They're using the same words preachers used to comfort people five hundred years ago. That's the problem with religion now. It hasn't evolved. Instead of looking for ways to be relevant in today's world, it's regressed into lowest-common-denominator sound bites—and fundamentalism.'

'But you can't reconcile religion with science,' Gracie said. 'I mean, do you believe in evolution?'

Father Jerome smiled. 'I've seen the fossils, I've studied the science. Of course I believe in evolution. Does that surprise you?'

'You could say that,' she laughed.

'It shouldn't. But religion in America is so focused on fighting science that your preachers have lost track of what religion is really about. In our Church—the Eastern Church—religion isn't there to offer theories or explanations. We accept that the divine is unknowable. But for you, it's become a choice. Fact or faith. Science or religion.' He paused, then added, 'You shouldn't have to choose.'

'But they're not compatible,' Gracie insisted.

'Of course they are. We need science to understand how everything on this planet works. But we need religion to fill the need for meaning. Your preachers don't understand that their job is to help you discover an inner sense of meaning and not behave like a bunch of zealots intent on converting the rest of the planet. "God is on our side"—that's all I hear coming out of your churches. Everyone claims Him at one point or another.'

'The way they're now claiming you,' she pointed out.

'Are they?' he asked, curiously.

'We're in this plane, aren't we?'

Her comment seemed to strike a nerve, and he pondered it for a bit.

'Although,' she mused, 'they might be in for a bit of a surprise. You're much more open-minded than I imagined.'

The priest smiled. 'I've seen a lot. I've seen good people do the most charitable things. And I've seen others do the most horrific things you could imagine. And that's what makes us human. We make our own choices and live by them. How we behave towards others shape our own lives. And we feel God's presence every time we make a choice. Everything else is just . . . artifice.'

'But you're a priest of the Church. You wear that,' she said, pointing at a cross around his neck. 'How can you say that?'

He looked at her thoughtfully. 'When the sign appeared . . . did you see a cross up there?'

Gracie wasn't sure what he meant. 'No.'

He smiled somewhat uncomfortably. 'Exactly.'

Framingham, Massachusetts

At around midnight, the Chrysler 300C swung into the front lot of the Comfort Inn. Two men got out. A third stayed behind the wheel. He kept the engine running. They weren't planning on staying long.

The two men entered the austere lobby and strode up to the reception desk. Behind it, a lone man of advancing years was watching a soccer match on a fuzzy screen. The lead man beckoned him over and pulled out three items, which he spread on the desk: head shots of Matt and Jabba— and a fifty-dollar bill.

The receptionist scanned the items and nodded. He pocketed the fifty. Then the lead man got his answer, but it wasn't the answer he wanted. They had checked in earlier that evening for a couple of hours; then they'd paid and left.

They'd just missed them.

The man frowned. He studied the receptionist for a beat, decided there was nothing more to be gained, and walked out. Something about it didn't sit well with him. Why take a room for just a couple of hours?

He led the other man back out and gave the parking lot a once-over. Nothing suspicious caught his eye. He pulled out his phone and informed his boss what he'd been told. Heard the anger in his boss's voice. And was ordered to head back to the safe house and wait for further instructions.

The two men climbed back into the 300C and drove off, oblivious to the green Pontiac Bonneville that was now tailing them.

MATT AND JABBA kept their eyes peeled on the taillights of the 300C and didn't say much. The traffic was sparse, the cars few and far between. It made the risk of them being spotted that much greater.

They'd baited their pursuers by lighting up Jabba's iPhone. The Chrysler's appearance had confirmed Matt's suspicion that Maddox had been able to track them, despite Jabba's precautions. Which gave Matt an opening to draw them in.

They weren't in the least bit sure what they'd find when the 300C got to wherever it was headed. Matt didn't think he'd find Danny, but there was a chance they'd find Rebecca Rydell. Beyond the possibility of finding Rebecca, this was also a chance to throw a wrench into Maddox's plans, which sounded pretty satisfying to Matt right now.

The 300C threaded through some residential streets before finally turning into an unlit driveway. Matt killed the motor and watched. Two men headed into the house. The driver hung back and gave the street a cursory sweep before following the two other goons in.

The house was a small, two-storey structure. Matt knew those houses well—it wasn't far from where he'd grown up in Worcester and the internal layouts were pretty standard. Front entrance to a living room, kitchen at the back, stairs in the middle going up to two or three bedrooms upstairs. There was also a basement, and Matt was pretty sure that was where they'd be keeping any prisoners.

Matt glanced at Jabba and nodded. There was another car in the driveway. The black Durango they'd seen at the airfield. The one Maddox's goons had stuffed Rebecca Rydell into.

The easy part was over. It was time to crash that party.

THE GUYS from the Chrysler were in the kitchen at the back of the house, going over the events of the day. Talking, sipping cold cans of Coke. Winding down. Not really expecting to be called out again that night.

The loud crash changed things. It came from the living room. The sound of something thumping heavily against the wall and landing in a dull thud while a shower of glass cascaded down onto the floor.

The lead guy from the hotel barked orders as he rushed to the front of the house, his gun drawn. One guy stayed behind in the kitchen, another stopped at the central staircase. The third was hot on his heels as he burst into the living room.

Glass shards crunched noisily under the man's heels as he advanced into the empty room, sweeping his gun around. He looked up at the bay window and saw that its central portion had a large hole punched out of it. He spotted a big rock at the foot of the back wall. Then something bulkier came crashing in. It splashed him with a sour-smelling liquid before it tumbled to the ground. It was a polyethylene gas can. It didn't have a lid and it had spewed fuel as it spun through the air on its inward flight, hosing him along the way and now spilling its load all over the floor. Then a third projectile came flying into the room. This one was coming right at him and it was lit.

MATT FLICKED the lighter on. In his other hand, he held a water bottle that he'd emptied then refilled, half with gasoline, half with motor oil. A wick, in the form of a strip of dust cloth that was soaked with gasoline, was stuffed tightly into its neck, waiting for the flame. Two other identical projectiles were ready by his feet.

He knew he had to hit the men before they understood what was going on. He lit the rag and lobbed the bottle in. The petrol bomb arced through the cool night air and flew into the room through the broken window. A flash of light lit up behind the shutters, followed almost instantly by a fireball as the flames caught the fuel from the gas can. He heard a scream, lit a second bottle, hurled it, grabbed the third bottle, and sprinted round to the back of the house.

THE LEAD GUY shrieked as his arms and legs caught fire. He twisted around furiously, trying to bat the flames down with his bare hands. He dropped to the ground and rolled around, trying to suffocate the flames. The second guy took off his jacket, looking to wrap it around him. The third guy, who'd been stationed by the stairs, was also in the room, watching his burning partner in horror. He looked around frantically to find something to smother the flames, but the room was bare. No carpets, no curtains, no throws over sofas.

'What's going on?' a fourth guy shouted from the back of the house.

'Cover the back,' the second guy ordered. But it was too late.

The guy in the kitchen had edged right up to the door by the hall, trying to see what was happening. The screams and smoke billowing through the house panicked him enough to draw his attention away from the back door.

Matt was peering in through the kitchen window. He recognised the man as one of the guys who'd escorted Rebecca Rydell off the plane, and it gave him confidence that she might be there. He lit the last bottle and hurled it with all his strength. The bottle punched its way into the kitchen and exploded against the wall inches away from the guy. Matt kicked the door in and caught the guy flat-footed. The guy was still swinging his gun hand around when Matt put him down with two rounds to the chest.

He pushed through the house, scanning for a locked door. His guess was they'd be keeping Rebecca in the basement and, sure enough, the door that led down, by the stairs, was shut. Someone was desperately hammering against it from the inside and yelling. A girl's voice.

He didn't veer off to help her. There were at least two goons to deal with. Matt was easing past the stairs when another guy slipped out of the living room. Matt had a flash of recognition from the airfield. He didn't stop to ponder it. He let the handgun rip. A round caught the guy in the thigh and he buckled and collapsed.

Matt watched the smoke and the flames wafting out from the living room. He knew the fourth guy had to come back out. Then he heard the sirens, distant but closing in. He'd told Jabba to call 911 the instant the first petrol bomb exploded, figuring he'd have enough time to storm through the house before the fire engines got there, and thinking they could come in handy if things hadn't gone according to plan.

The sirens grew louder, and he crouched low, expecting that the guy inside had heard them and would be needing to make a desperate break-out.

Then he heard a loud crash and he understood. The guy had decided to bail out through what was left of the bay window.

He scrambled back to the closed door. Rebecca—it had to be her—was still banging and shouting.

'Hey! What's going on? Get me out of here!'

'Step back from the door,' Matt yelled. 'I need to shoot the lock off.'

He fired—once, twice. It did the trick. The locks were old, the doorframe soft with age.

He kicked the door in. Wooden treads led down to the basement, where an attractive, tanned girl was cowering against the wall.

'Come on, we've got to go,' he hollered over the crackle of the flames.

They stormed out of the house, past a fire truck that was swinging into the driveway. Matt peered through the darkness, scanning for the Bonneville, and a stab of dread cut into him as he saw that it was no longer there. He ran faster, imagining the worst. As he drew nearer, he spotted Jabba flat on his back outside a nearby house.

A couple of onlookers were huddled beside him, the man checking him out hesitantly, the woman staring down, riveted with fear.

'Jabba,' Matt yelled as he slid to the ground beside him.

In the darkness, it was hard to see where the wound was, but a pool of blood was spreading out from under him. He caught sight of Matt and sputtered, 'Did we get her?'

Matt said, 'She's right here,' turning to give Jabba a glimpse of Rebecca. 'Don't talk,' he told him. 'Just hang on. You're going to be fine.' He turned to the couple looming over him. 'Call 911,' he shouted.

Matt just stayed there, hanging onto Jabba—cursing himself for having dragged him along—until an ambulance showed up and the paramedics bundled him onto a stretcher with breathtaking efficiency.

Matt asked, 'Is he going to be OK?' but he couldn't get a straight answer out of them. He watched as they wheeled Jabba into the back of the ambulance, shut the doors and stormed off.

He heard another siren—a police cruiser this time—and glanced at Rebecca. She was huddled on the lawn, shivering.

'Come on,' he said as, mouthing a silent prayer for the life of his new friend, he took her hand and led her away from the horror-struck crowd that had gathered around the blazing house.

Houston, Texas

'Where are they now?' Buscema asked.

It was late, but Reverend Darby didn't mind Buscema's call. He owed him for giving him the heads-up on Father Jerome's predicament.

'They should be landing in Shannon, Ireland, about an hour and a half from now,' he told the journalist.

'So what time will they get here?'

'I make it around six a.m., Houston time.'

Buscema went silent, then said, 'Well, I suppose you could sneak him in under the radar. Might be safer to play it that way.'

'Or we could turn his arrival into a major event,' Darby said, completing Buscema's train of thought. He pondered it for a moment. 'You're right. We shouldn't be sneaking him in like some petty criminal. The man's God's emissary, for crying out loud. We're going to welcome him with open arms.'

304 | RAYMOND KHOURY

'I can help leak it,' Buscema told him. 'Just delay their arrival as much as you can.'

'I'll give you enough time,' Darby said.

'What about beyond that? Any progress on your Christmas offering?'

'The stadium's booked,' the preacher confided. 'I'm going to give the people of this country a Christmas they'll never forget.'

Buscema went quiet. He knew Darby would pick up on it.

Sure enough, Darby said, 'What is it?'

'I'm hearing grumblings. From other pastors and church leaders.'

'I know. Every preacher from here to California's been on the line. Even the governor wants in.'

'Wouldn't be a bad idea to share that platform, Reverend. Turn this into a much bigger event. The country could use it right now.'

'I'm the guy flying him in, Roy,' Darby noted calmly.

'And you'll be the one greeting him when he steps off that plane,' Buscema reassured him. 'You. No one else.'

'The governor's also pushing to be there.'

'Doesn't matter, Reverend. There won't be any other pastors at the airport. It'll be your moment. That's the image people will remember. But after that, it's in your interest to show generosity and invite other church leaders to join you on the big day. America doesn't have a spiritual leader, but the country needs one.' He paused to let the words settle. 'You don't want it to look like just another service at your church. This one's for the whole country. For the whole world. By extending a welcoming hand, you'll be elevating your own position as a gracious host . . . and leader.'

TOUGH PART'S OVER, Buscema thought after hanging up with Darby. Now he'd have to wait and see if the self-obsessed blowhard would play nice. He needed him to share his new toy with the other kids.

He picked up his phone and hit another speed-dial key. The man on the other end had been waiting for the call.

Buscema just said, 'We're on. Leak it,' then hung up.

Shannon, Ireland

The Gulfstream was parked by a service hangar at Shannon Airport. Gracie was pacing near the plane as she spoke on her cellphone to the abbot, who was on his way back from Cairo after delivering Finch's body to the

American embassy. He told her that fierce clashes had erupted outside the monastery once the news of Father Jerome's departure had been made public. Internal security men had contained the outburst and were now clearing away the last troublemakers, but the situation had repeated itself in Cairo, Alexandria and other cities.

Gracie saw Dalton coming towards her, indicating there was a call for her. She was thanking the abbot when he remembered something and said, 'I'm also very sorry about your friend's glasses.'

Dalton mouthed, 'Ogilvy' to her.

Gracie asked him to wait one second while she tried to make sense of what the abbot was talking about. 'I'm sorry, Finch's glasses?'

'One of my brothers stepped on them by accident. They were in the keep and it's dark in there. I know it's the kind of personal belonging that matters to loved ones at times like these. Would you please apologise to his wife on my behalf?'

'Of course,' Gracie said. 'Thanks for everything, Father.' She clicked the off button and took the other phone from Dalton.

It was Ogilvy. His news pushed any thought of Finch to the sidelines. 'The word's out that Father Jerome's on his way here.'

Gracie frowned. This wasn't good. 'We've got to fly in somewhere quiet. People are going to go nuts. We'll get mobbed.'

'I called Darby. He told me he's got the cops lined up to help. They're going to cordon off the tarmac, provide a rolling escort. It'll be fine.'

'You're not serious?'

'This is still our story, *Your* story, Gracie. Think about it. Every single TV set in the country is going to be watching you as you walk off that plane right alongside Father Jerome. And Darby wants you and Dalton to stick around. He's going to put you up with them. I'm flying out too. So just get some rest and get ready. We've got a show to do, and you're about to get the biggest scoop of your life.'

Boston, Massachusetts
'Dad?'

Rydell couldn't believe his ears. 'Where are you? Are you OK?'

'I'm fine,' Rebecca said. 'They got me out. I'm fine.'

Rydell's heart cartwheeled. Her voice had a quaver in it, but she didn't sound afraid.

'Hang on,' she said.

He heard some shuffling as the handset changed hands, then came the last voice he was expecting. 'Are you alone?'

He recognised Matt's voice and panic seized him. 'What have you done?'

Matt ignored his question. 'She's safe. Can you get out without any escorts?'

'I don't know.' Rydell faltered. 'I . . . I can try.'

'Do it right now,' Matt ordered. 'And meet us outside the place you took Rebecca for her eighteenth birthday.'

The line went dead.

Rydell didn't know what to think. Was she Matt's hostage now? He wasn't sure what he preferred—knowing she was in his hands, or in Maddox's. What he was sure of was that now that Rebecca was out, Drucker didn't have any hold over him. He had to get out.

He picked up the hotel phone and hit the button for reception. 'This is Rydell. I need security up here right now. As many guys as you can send. My bodyguards are up to something; I need protection from them.' His tone left no room for doubt.

He darted to the bedroom, found his wallet and coat, and pulled his shoes on; darted back to the door and peeked through the peephole. He could see the two bodyguards, looking bored. About ten seconds later, he heard the elevator and four men rushed out. Rydell saw the bodyguards step towards the security guys, arms raised in a 'what's-going-on' gesture.

Rydell swung the door open and sprinted past the surprised bodyguards and through the wall of security guys shouting, 'Stop them. They're trying to kidnap me. Help me get out of here.'

The bodyguards were caught off-guard by Rydell's exit. One of them reached for his holster, but the security guys stood their ground, creating a barrier across the corridor. One of them had his handgun out too, and a 'you-really-don't-want-to-do-this' grimace across his face.

Rydell didn't wait for the outcome. He slipped into the elevator and rode down to the lobby, his nerves on fire. He flew out of the lobby, and hurtled into a waiting cab. He made the driver take a few rudderless lefts and rights, then, when he was satisfied that they were on their own, he told him where to go.

IT WAS A SHORT HOP to get to the Garden sports arena. As he pulled into the arena's parking lot, Rydell spotted Matt across the street, leaning against a dark sedan. Rydell got the cabbie to drop him off at the gate. He was halfway across when his daughter clambered out of the car and ran to him.

He hugged her tight. He still couldn't quite believe it. Rydell kept a firm grip on Rebecca's hand as he went up to Matt.

'You did this?' Rydell said. More like a statement than a question.

'My friend's in the hospital,' Matt told him crisply. 'He's been shot. Bad. I need you to make a call and make sure they give him everything he needs. He's also going to need protection.'

Rydell nodded. 'I've got the number of the detective who came out to the house. I'll call him.'

Rydell kept hold of Rebecca as he made the calls. It didn't take long. His name usually helped speed things up. They told him Jabba was in surgery, and that the prognosis was uncertain. He hung up and informed Matt.

'He's in good hands,' Rydell told him. 'He'll get the best of care.' Rydell studied Matt. 'I can't thank you enough for doing this.'

'My friend's been shot and your buddies still have my brother.' Matt stared at him. 'I thought you might want to help me make things right.'

Rydell didn't know what to do. He looked at Rebecca. She was eyeing him with a mixture of confusion and accusation. 'They're bringing Father Jerome back,' he said finally. 'He's left Egypt. He's on his way here.'

'Where here?'

'They're saying Houston. Wherever it is, they're bound to put a sign up over him, and the odds are, that's where you'll find Danny.' He paused. 'You were right. They're planning something they need me around for. I don't know what it is, but it's all about the priest now.'

'Who would know?' Matt asked him, fixing him squarely.

'Keenan Drucker. It's pretty much his show.'

'Where do I find him?'

'DC, the Center for American Freedom. It's a think tank.'

Just then, Rydell's BlackBerry trilled. He checked its screen and frowned. It was Drucker. He hit the answer key.

'Where the hell are you? What are you doing, Larry?'

'Getting my daughter back.' Rydell let that one sink in for a beat. Then added, 'I thought I might head down to the *New York Times* and have a little chat with them.'

'Why would you want to do that?'

''Cause I don't know what you're up to, but I'm pretty sure it has nothing to do with what we set out to achieve.'

Drucker let out a rueful hiss. 'Look, taking Rebecca was way out of line. I'm sorry. But we're in this together. We want the same thing.'

'And what is that?'

Drucker went silent for a moment, then said, 'Let's meet somewhere. I'll tell you what I'm thinking. After that, you decide if you want to bring this whole thing down on top of us.'

Rydell let Drucker sweat it out. He knew he needed to hear him out. Too much was at stake. 'I'll think about it,' he replied then hung up.

'What did he want?' Matt asked.

'To talk. To convince me to play ball.'

'What are you gonna do?'

Rydell pondered his question. 'I don't know.' He gazed at his daughter. Her safety was paramount. 'We can't stay in Boston. There's nowhere to lay low. Anywhere we go will get flagged to the press—and to Maddox.'

Matt mulled it over for a moment, 'Don't you want to see your handiwork? In all its glory.'

Rydell thought about it, then said, 'Why the hell not?'

Houston, Texas

The jet banked around the small airport of Ellington Field, Houston. From a height of around a thousand feet, Gracie saw that the traffic was backed up a couple of miles in each direction. People were abandoning their cars and swarming in from all corners.

The jet touched down and came to a stop by a large hangar. A twin-jet helicopter was parked nearby. The captain killed the Gulfstream's engines and, as they whined down, the noise from outside seeped in, an eerie wave of clapping and cheering.

Father Jerome's face was tight with anxiety

Gracie put her hand on his. 'It's going to be fine,' she said.

He nodded stoically, as if resigned to his new role.

His look brought back the same unease she'd felt on the roof of the keep. She glanced over at Dalton, who was getting his camera ready.

'You ready for this?' he asked her.

'No,' she said.

REVEREND DARBY drank in the clamour rising up from the mass of onlookers. He was used to big crowds. His megachurch welcomed over ten thousand people every Sunday. But this was different; he wasn't used to being a passive observer. The crowd behind the barriers at the edge of the airfield were clapping and whooping. A large group to the left were singing '*I've Been Redeemed.*' And Father Jerome hadn't even stepped off the plane yet.

The governor was standing stiffly by the pastor's side. He gave the silver-haired politician as genuine a smile as he could muster and swivelled his gaze over to his right. Roy Buscema nodded solemnly as the plane's cabin door cracked open. The door swung outwards, retractable stairs slid down and Darby's people rolled a red carpet out for Father Jerome's descent.

Without inviting any of his guests to join him, Reverend Darby strode up to the plane, turning briefly to acknowledge the crowd with a regal wave. The hordes roared back their appreciation as the preacher positioned himself at the base of the steps.

FATHER JEROME straightened his cassock and padded to the front of the cabin. He seemed confused, an anxious look darkening his face.

Brother Ameen took his hand, cupping it with both of his. 'It's going to be fine,' he told the older priest.

Father Jerome straightened up, nodding with renewed resolve.

'Is it OK if we start rolling?' Gracie asked. Brother Ameen studied Father Jerome, then gave her a nod. Gracie lifted her BlackBerry to her mouth, and gave Jack Roxberry back at the studio a low-voiced 'go' signal. They were going out live—an exclusive for the network.

Father Jerome stepped onto the landing at the top of the stairs. The crowd's reaction was thunderous. Gracie craned her neck to get a better look. There were people stretching back as far as she could see. Some carried banners, others had their arms raised. There were cries and wails and tears of joy. Television cameras and mobile broadcasting vans were everywhere.

Father Jerome raised one hand, then another, an open embrace that spoke of humility, not of showmanship. The crowd screamed, their eyes scanning the sky. Father Jerome himself slid a glance upwards, wondering if anything was going to appear, but he didn't wait for it. He climbed down the stairs, straight into Reverend Darby's welcoming embrace.

'Are you getting this?' Gracie asked Roxberry.

'You bet.' His voice crackled in her earpiece. 'Keep it coming.'

She watched as the reverend kept the priest's hand firmly cocooned inside his own and whispered into his ear. The priest nodded hesitantly, as if out of courtesy.

Darby turned to the audience and raised his arms for quiet. An assistant handed him a microphone. 'Brothers and sisters in Christ,' he announced, 'greetings in the name of our Lord to you all, and thanks for coming out here with me to greet our very special visitor, Father Jerome.' He got a raucous reply from the crowd.

'Tomorrow is Christmas Day, a special time of celebration for us all and yet, until a few days ago, I was troubled. I've been praying for God to spare our great nation. To spare it from the judgment we deserve for our trespasses, like the killing of millions of preborn children. For allowing our scientists to experiment with stem cells. For allowing our children to be exploited by the deviant anarchists who now control public education and Hollywood. And when a great nation like ours is going through troubled times such as these, the natural and spiritual thing to do is to call upon God for guidance.' He paused to let his sombre words sink in, then he beamed a kindly smile at the mob.

'Well, guess what? I think God heard our prayers,' he bellowed. 'And I believe he's sending us a lifeline in the form of a deeply spiritual man who has devoted his entire life to helping his fellow man. So I ask you all to join me please in welcoming Father Jerome to our great state of Texas.'

Father Jerome cast his eye across the crowd, taking it all in silently. He glanced over at Gracie. He seemed clearly uneasy.

Darby put his arm around the priest. 'Now I have a special request for Father Jerome, an invitation from the heart of Texas and from the heart of the entire nation.' He turned to Father Jerome, 'I'm here to ask you, on behalf of all these people—will you honour us with a special service tomorrow?'

The crowd whooped its approval. Father Jerome looked into Darby's eyes, then gave him a nod. 'Of course.'

The crowd went nuts and Darby said, 'You're all invited. Spend the day with your loved ones. And at five in the evening, come on down to the stadium at Reliant Park. We've got room for all of you.'

Darby put a guiding arm behind the priest for the best photo op he could have asked for, then herded him away towards the hangar to their right.

'We're moving away from the crowd now,' Gracie told Roxberry as she and Dalton followed, continuing their live transmission. 'We're headed for a chopper, which is probably the only way out right now.' They all piled into the helicopter and less than a minute later the chopper lifted off the ground.

MATT'S EYES were fixed on the wall-mounted plasma screen in the executive lounge at Houston's Hobby Airport. Rydell was watching it with him. He had arranged the night flight from Boston, borrowing a jet from one of his dotcom buddies. It had dropped them off in Houston before continuing onwards to Los Angeles, whisking Rebecca off to the relative safety of an old friend and a big city.

The live coverage cut away from Grace Logan to the sight of the chopper taking off. Matt had been hoping to see the sign show up. It hadn't happened, but that didn't stop him from scrutinising every corner of the screen, looking for anything suspicious.

'Reliant Stadium,' Matt said. 'That's where the Texans play, isn't it?'

'Yes,' Rydell said. He was on his BlackBerry. 'Let's see what the weather's like tomorrow.'

'Why?' Matt asked.

'The stadium's got a retractable roof. If it's not going to rain, they'll have it open—which they'll need to do if they're planning to put a sign up over him.'

Matt felt a burgeoning optimism. He was getting closer to Danny.

'It's not going to be easy finding Danny,' Rydell added. 'The stadium's huge.'

Matt frowned. 'Maybe we won't have to. Call Drucker. Tell him you're here if he still wants to talk.'

Rydell weighed it up. 'He'll suspect something's up.'

'He'll still want to meet you, and that's something we can control. We can be ready for him.'

'You sure?' Rydell asked.

'Get him down here,' Matt confirmed. 'I think we'd both like to hear what the bastard has to say.'

River Oaks, Houston, Texas

The area around Darby's house was entirely sealed off. The back of the house looked out over the golf course, and access to the club was now under strict police control.

The governor also had the National Guard on standby, should the need for more manpower arise.

The chopper set down in the parking lot of the country club, and its occupants were shuttled across the golf course to their host's mansion under escort. Gracie and Dalton were shown to a room on the ground floor of a guesthouse that abutted the main building. Brother Ameen was in an adjacent room. Father Jerome was given a guest suite on the second floor. The plan was for them all to remain at the mansion until the big sermon at the stadium the following evening.

Hal Ogilvy, who was in town, had asked for continual updates live from inside the Darby estate. Gracie and Dalton gave the network's viewers a tour of the compound and, after Gracie signed off, Dalton headed for the airport to get the rest of their stuff.

Gracie collapsed on the bed. It had been a brutal few days, and there was no end in sight. She managed to tune out for three minutes before the phone rang. She fished out her BlackBerry, but it wasn't ringing. She burrowed deeper into her bag and saw Finch's phone. The caller's ID was flashing up. Gareth Willoughby wasn't a name she recognised—then it clicked. The producer of the BBC documentary.

She took the call. Willoughby didn't know Finch had died. The news took him by complete surprise. He told Gracie he didn't know Finch and said he was just returning his call.

There was an uncomfortable silence for a moment, then Gracie said, 'I guess you must be glad that they finally agreed to let you go up there and talk to Father Jerome.'

Willoughby sounded confused. 'What are you talking about? They came to us.'

His statement pricked Gracie like a dart. 'What?'

'They came to us. I mean, we were there making the documentary, but we didn't go looking for him. We had no idea Father Jerome was even there.'

'So how'd you end up meeting him?'

'It was just one of those serendipitous breaks, I suppose,' Willoughby said. 'We were filming at Bishoi, the other monastery, and we bumped into this monk from the monastery of the Syrians. We got chatting and he told us Father Jerome was in one of their caves acting rather bizarrely, as if he were possessed, only in a good way. Which was really timely for us.'

'Hang on a minute, I thought everyone knew Father Jerome was there.'

'No one knew he was in Egypt until after we filmed our programme,' Willoughby corrected her. 'He was on his sabbatical, remember. They wouldn't say where he was. We thought he'd died at one point. It was all rather fortuitous, in more ways than one.'

'What do you mean?'

'We wouldn't have met that monk in the first place if it hadn't been for the BBC. They handed us the assignment in the first place.'

Gracie felt a build-up of pressure in her temples. 'You're saying this wasn't your idea?'

'No. The commissioning editor proposed a three-parter that they had American partners lined up for and we ended up doing that. Comparing Eastern and Western approaches to spirituality. They were laying out a decent budget for it.' He paused. 'If I may ask, Miss Logan, why all the questions?'

Gracie instinctively put up a defensive wall, a small voice inside her telling her to protect what she was uncovering. 'I guess I'm just trying to understand what got us all out there. Why Finch died.' She felt horrible at using his death in that way, and hoped Finch would have forgiven her for it.

'Tell me something, the monk who told you about Father Jerome. Do you remember his name?'

'Yes, of course. He was from Croatia. His name was Brother Ameen.'

GRACIE FELT as if she'd fallen into a whirlpool of doubt. There was no way to gloss over it—they'd been lied to.

She focused back on the conversation in the car after they'd been picked up at Cairo Airport. She visualised the monk, Brother Ameen, telling them how the film-makers had badgered them for access to Father Jerome and how the abbot had finally relented.

A clear lie. The question was, why?

From a cobweb of conflicting thoughts and suspicions, another worry latched onto her consciousness.

She found her phone and rang the number the abbot had called her from. Yusuf, the driver, answered on the third ring. It was his cellphone.

'Yusuf,' she said, her tone ringing with urgency. 'When the abbot called, he said something about where the glasses of my friend were found. He said it was dark inside. That's why whoever it was stepped on them. They were inside the keep?'

Yusuf paused for a moment. 'They were in a passageway on the top floor. They must have fallen from your friend's pocket on his way up to the roof.'

Gracie felt a cold stab in the pit of her stomach.

Finch couldn't see without them. And hard as she tried, she couldn't see how he could have climbed up there, much less how he could have found his BlackBerry on that roof, if he hadn't been wearing them.

She hung up, eyeing the door to her room as if it were a gateway to hell. Something was very wrong. Her first instinct was to speed-dial Ogilvy.

'I need to see you,' she said, her eyes locked on the door.

Houston, Texas

Matt walked through the hotel lobby slowly. Glancing round, he checked for security guards, cameras, escape routes and vantage points. He doubled back on himself and made his way over to the café that fronted the hotel, noting its layout and making a mental list of the ways in and out. Then he went back out to check the service entrance at the back of the hotel.

He was early. The meeting between Rydell and Drucker wasn't for another two hours. Still, Matt felt he needed to check the place out long before any of Drucker's men had a chance to get there. He knew Drucker wouldn't be alone. With a bit of luck, Maddox might even be with him. And even though he knew he'd be outnumbered, Matt had something going for him that they didn't. He didn't have anything to lose. The one thing he needed to achieve was to get the muzzle of his gun pressed right against Drucker and walk out of there with him. It didn't matter who saw him. Only the end result mattered. He would wait until Rydell got the information he needed out of Drucker, and then he'd move in.

Oddly, Matt was actually looking forward to it.

SIX BLOCKS WEST of there, Gracie stood with Ogilvy in Sam Houston Park. She was rippling with nervous energy as she took the network's head of news through what Willoughby and Yusuf had told her.

Ogilvy didn't seem to share her concern. A slick-looking man with an aquiline nose and swept-back hair, he was studying Gracie patiently through rimless spectacles.

'These guys are humble, Gracie,' he remarked with a shrug. 'So this Brother Ameen character didn't admit he pimped Father Jerome out. He was probably hoping to get some screen time himself.'

'He wasn't the least bit nervous when he was lying about it. And what about Finch's glasses?'

'It might explain why he fell. If he couldn't see properly.'

'They should have been down on the ground, next to him. Or on the roof. But inside the keep? How'd he even make it up on the roof without them?'

'What if he dropped them and broke them himself. Before he got there?'

'You step on glasses, you maybe break one lens. You can still wear them for some kind of vision. You don't just leave them there.'

Ogilvy glanced away and heaved out a ragged sigh. He looked like he was losing patience. 'So what are you saying?'

'I'm saying we need to talk to the abbot and get some background on this Brother Ameen. He's from Croatia, right? How long has he been at that monastery? The guy's been pivotal to this story and we don't know anything about him.'

Ogilvy paused and looked at her like she was saying she'd been abducted by aliens. 'What are you doing? You've got the inside track on the scoop of the century. We have unparallelled access. You start poking your nose around and getting Jerome and Ameen all riled up and they could shut us out. You can't afford to mess this up right now, Gracie. So how about you put the conspiracy paranoia on hold for a while.'

'Hal, something's not right. The whole thing has been one "lucky" break after another. Think about it. We happen to be there when the shelf breaks off. Hell, we wouldn't even have been down there if you hadn't suggested it.'

And then her mind lined up the disparate thoughts so they would all fit. She saw a connection that suddenly seemed obvious to her.

Almost without thinking, she said, 'Oh my God. You're in on it too.'

And in that briefest of moments between her saying it and his responding, she saw it. The tiniest, hardly noticeable hesitation.

'Gracie, you're being ridiculous,' he said dismissively.

She wasn't listening to his words. She was reading through them. And now she was even more sure. 'It's fake, isn't it?' she blurted. 'The whole damn thing. It's a set-up.'

Ogilvy took a step forward and raised a calming hand.

She shoved his hand away. Her mind was racing. 'You played me all along. This whole assignment. The trip to Antarctica. All that enthusiasm. It was all bullshit.' She glared at him. 'What are you doing? You're setting up a new messiah? You want to convert the world?'

Ogilvy's eyes were flicking left and right now. The truth was confirmed beyond a doubt. 'You think I'd want that?' he hissed, trying to remain calm. 'You know me better than that. It's the last thing I'd want.'

'Don't tell me this is about saving the planet?'

Ogilvy gave up the pretence and framed her with a fervent glare. 'Maybe. But, first and foremost, it's about saving our country.'

And right then, another realisation burst out of the mire. 'Was Finch's death an accident?'

'Of course it was,' he assured her.

But her gut was telling her otherwise. 'I don't believe you.' She took a step back, suddenly hyperaware of her immediate surroundings. All she could register were two stony-faced guys in short haircuts and dark suits. Their body language wasn't casual.

Ogilvy acknowledged the men with a barely perceptible nod. They started towards her. Blocking any escape route.

She looked at Ogilvy in disbelief. 'Jesus, Hal. What are you doing?'

'Only what's necessary,' he replied, somewhat apologetically.

Gracie spun on her heels and sprinted off, heading straight for one of the heavies coming at her. She veered left before swinging right, hoping to slip past him, but his arm whipped out and caught her and pulled her in. The other suit was on them a couple of seconds later. The first guy spun her round and pinned her arms behind her back. She lashed out with her foot, kicking the suit facing her in the shin, but he came back with a backslap across the face that rattled her teeth. The suit facing her pressed a gauze patch against her nose. The smell from it was strong and sour. Almost instantly, she felt the strength in her body seep away before everything drifted off into a silent and hollow darkness.

THEY MET in the hotel, as per Rydell's instructions. Located just off the lobby, the café was an open, public area. Rydell felt safe there.

Drucker was already at a table by a wall of glass that looked out onto the street. It was late afternoon and a few pedestrians were promenading by.

As Rydell sat, Drucker pulled out a small black box and placed it on the table. It was the size of a paperback novel, and had a couple of small LED lights on its side.

'Just in case you were planning on taping any of this,' Drucker said and discreetly nudged a button. The LEDs lit up. Rydell shrugged and glanced around to see its effect. A couple of people who'd been talking on their cell-phones were now pressing random buttons to get a signal back. Rydell knew they wouldn't be able to until Drucker had switched off his jammer.

'I'm surprised you're down here,' Drucker said. 'Couldn't resist seeing its effect with your own eyes?'

Rydell ignored the question. 'What are you up to, Keenan?'

Drucker studied Rydell like a principal wondering what to do about a wayward student. 'Do you love this country?'

'Of course, I love my country. What does that have to do with anything?'

Drucker nodded, as if that was the right answer. 'I love it too, Larry. I've devoted my whole life to serving it. And this used to be a great country. We put a man on the moon forty years ago. We were the ones showing the rest of the world how it's done, how science and technology and new ideas can help us live better lives. And where are we now? What have we become?'

'A lot poorer,' Rydell lamented.

'Poorer, meaner, fatter . . . and dumber. We're moving backwards. We've lost our standing in the world. And you know why? It's all about leadership. We used to elect presidents who blew us away with their intelligence. Guys who used to inspire us, guys the rest of the world respected, guys who made us proud. Guys who had vision.'

'We have one of those now,' Rydell interjected.

'But we just had eight years of criminal incompetence and unbridled arrogance that brought our country to its knees, and did we learn anything? Clearly not. This was no landslide, Larry. Damn near half the country voted for more of the same—or worse. That's how blind we've become when it comes to choosing our leaders. And do you know why it almost happened?'

Rydell started to see what Drucker was getting at. 'Because God is on their side.'

'Because God is on their side,' Drucker repeated solemnly. 'That's all it takes. We'll elect any champion of mediocrity to the highest office in the land as long as they have God as their running mate. We'll give them the power to nuke other countries and destroy the planet as long as they say the magic words. We've got presidents making policy decisions based on the Book of Revelations, Larry.'

He caught his breath before pressing on. 'We were a great country once. Then they got us a guy who found Jesus but can't read a balance sheet, and now they're out there waging wars in the name of God and getting our boys blown to bits, and half the country's still marching into church every Sunday and coming out with a big smile—'

'I know you're angry about your son,' Rydell interrupted, suddenly aware of what was really fuelling this, 'but—'

'Angry?' Drucker growled. 'A soldier's job is to put his life on the line for his country. Jackson knew that when he signed up. But our country was not at risk. This is a war that should never have happened. And the only reason it did was that we had an incompetent fool with a messiah complex running the show. And that can't be allowed to happen again.'

Rydell knew how much Drucker had loved his son. He had to tread carefully. 'I'm with you on this, Keenan. But what you're doing is—'

Drucker headed him off. 'We can't allow this to go on. They've got it so politicians can't get elected these days if they say they believe in Darwin. And we need to turn that mindset on its head. We need to bring back respect for science, education, intelligence and reason. And we have to do it now. There are seventy million Evangelicals out there, attending a couple of hundred thousand Evangelical churches, most of which are run by pastors who belong to conservative political organisations, and these guys are not voting for the guy with the brains or the vision. They're voting for whoever will help them improve their standing when they get to the pearly gates.'

Drucker fixed Rydell with blazing intent and continued. 'You think global warming is around the corner? This threat's already here. At some point, these prayer warriors are going to put a televangelist in the Oval Office. And then we'll have a bunch of whack jobs running Capitol Hill and another bunch of nutcases facing off against them in the Middle East. They'll be lobbing nukes at each other before it's over. I'm not going to let that happen.'

Rydell wasn't following. 'And you're going to do that by giving them a prophet to fire them up even more?'

Drucker just stared at him enigmatically. 'Yes.'

'You're giving them a miracle man to worship and getting all the church leaders to hitch their wagons to his train?'

'Yes.' This time, a hint of satisfaction cracked across Drucker's face.

'And then you'll get him to change his message?'

Drucker shook his head. 'I'll just pull the rug out from under him.'

'You're going to expose him as a fake?'

'Exactly. We'll let it run for weeks. Months. Just let it build. Let every pastor in the country endorse him as God's messenger and when they're all on the hook—we'll show them what the sign really is.'

'And you'll show them how gullible they are.' Rydell had a faraway look on his face as he imagined the outcome.

'The preachers will have so much egg on their faces they'll have a hard time facing their people. The churchgoers will feel like they've been had—and maybe they'll start questioning what they hear. It'll open up a whole new discussion. It'll put everything about religion on the table. And it'll make people think twice about who they're willing to follow blindly.'

Rydell had been ready to convert the world to his cause, but this went much further. 'You'll make a lot of them even more fanatical than they already are,' he warned. 'You could also start a civil war, if not a world war.'

Drucker scoffed. 'Oh, I very much doubt that.'

'You're going to have a bunch of angry people out there looking to take it out on someone. You can't exactly stand up and tell them, "Hey, we did it for your own good." There'll be blood in the streets. And that's before you get the blowback from the rest of the world. It's not just Christians who are buying into your scam. Muslims, Jews, Hindus . . . they're fighting among each other over whether or not he's the real deal. And they're going to be seriously pissed off when they discover this scam's got Uncle Sam's fingerprints all over it. You're gonna end up triggering a war you're trying to stop.'

'We had a war over slavery. Maybe we need a war over this.' Drucker gave a haughty shrug. 'If it's going to happen, might as well just get it over with. Maybe then we can build something more sane from its ashes.'

'You're insane,' Rydell told Drucker. 'You've lost all sense of perspective. You can't do this.'

'No. Not without a fall guy,' Drucker conceded.

Rydell instantly got it. 'That's what you need me for.'

Drucker nodded. 'I need a visionary genius with no political motive other than trying to save the planet. Who knows? It may well end up giving people more awareness of the global-warming problem.'

'But you couldn't care less either way,' Rydell said sardonically.

'Not true, but I'm not even sure what we can realistically do about it. And bringing reason back into politics—that's going to help the polar bears, don't you think?'

'This isn't about saving the polar bears, Keenan,' Rydell said angrily. 'It's about social justice. For everyone on the planet.'

'Social justice is about freeing people from the clutches of witch doctors and superstition,' Drucker fired back.

Rydell rubbed his brow, letting Drucker's words sink in. The room was suddenly much hotter.

'How was it all meant to end for me? "Suicide"?'

Drucker nodded. 'Once the hoax is exposed. A tragic end to a heroic attempt.' He sighed. 'I'm sorry. But I hope you can see the sense in what I'm trying to do. And that, at some level, you agree that it had to be done.'

Rydell shrugged. 'I hope you won't be disappointed if I don't play along.'

Drucker gave him a dismissive wave of his hand. 'Please, Larry. Give me some credit.'

Rydell froze at Drucker's composure.

'You're going to have a stroke,' Drucker told him casually. 'A bad one. You'll end up in a coma. And, during that time, we'll massage your personality. You know, like we did with the priest. Put the right answers in your mind. Make you more amenable to our plans. And when the time comes, we'll help you take your own life, after leaving behind a contrite and moving explanation of why you did what you did.'

Drucker studied his face, as if intrigued by Rydell's reaction. 'It's the stuff of legends, Larry. No one will ever forget your name, if that's any consolation.'

Just then, Rydell noticed a man in a dark suit behind Drucker. Two more men appeared towards the entrance of the café. He was about to make a run for it when he spotted a white van on the street, its side door sliding open. Two silhouettes stood inside on either side of something mounted on a stand that looked like a projector lamp. He tried to push himself to his feet, but he never made it.

The blast of noise assaulted his senses like a hammer blow from inside his skull, overwhelming every nerve ending in his head. His hands shot up to protect his ears, but it was too late. He fell to the ground, coughing and sputtering with convulsions.

Drucker's men helped him up and bundled him out of the café. Within seconds, they'd hustled him into a waiting elevator. Its doors slid shut with a silent hiss, and it glided down to the hotel's underground parking lot.

MATT'S PULSE thundered as he saw Rydell get blasted out of his seat by an unseen force. It was as if he'd been punched backwards by a huge invisible fist. Then he was on the ground, writhing in agony.

Matt had been waiting in a corner booth, biding his time, ready to make his move. But they'd moved first. Whatever they'd done to Rydell had sent Matt's plans to the shredder.

He charged towards the entrance and caught sight of Drucker leaving the hotel with his escorts. There was no way he could get to him. He'd missed his chance.

The lights over the elevator Rydell was in scrolled down to indicate he was being taken to the parking lot. Matt chose to go after Rydell instead. If Drucker had him again, Matt would be left with no leverage. Leverage he needed if he was going to see his brother again.

He flew down the stairs three at a time and burst onto the parking level in time to see a white van turning onto the exit ramp. He heard a door click open to his left. A valet was getting out of a big Chrysler Navigator SUV. Matt sprinted up to him, yanked the car keys from his grasp, and climbed in. He slammed the selector into drive and cannoned out of the parking space and onto the same exit ramp.

The van was heading west. Matt threaded the big SUV through a rolling chicane of slower vehicles and caught up with it in no time. He held back, keeping a car between them. The road was straight and wide, the traffic sparse. Two blocks on, a sign announced the on-ramp to the interstate. Matt knew he had to do something before they hit the highway. Once they were on it, all kinds of unknowns would come into play. He had to make his move now.

The road was as wide as a runway and didn't have any cars parked on either side. The next block they were coming to looked promising. The sidewalk on the right led to a rise of a dozen or so wide, low steps outside an imposing stone-clad office building.

Matt mashed the pedal and the Navigator surged out from behind the buffering car. He went out wide to the left then veered right and aimed the Navigator's nose at the van's left front corner. A split second before he slammed into it, Matt jerked the wheel to the left and righted the SUV. It hit at a tangent, its momentum flinging the van off its trajectory. Matt brought the Navigator right up against the van's left side, nursing it along its diagonal trajectory, then he swerved right even more to close the deal. The van had nowhere to go, and bounced heavily up the stairs before slamming against one of the building's massive square pillars.

Matt ramped the Navigator over the kerb and flew out of it just as the van hit the column. He stormed up the steps, the handgun out.

The van was hit hard. Its radiator was smoking and its front end curled around the column. Matt didn't know what state he'd find Rydell in. One thing he knew was that the guys in the front wouldn't be at their healthiest.

Passersby were edging forward to check out the crash, only to reel away at the sight of Matt and his handgun. He rounded the side of the van, eyeing the doors and windows cautiously. The front was badly mashed up. He side-stepped away to the back of the van and pulled the door open.

Rydell was in there on the floor, shaken up but alive. He saw one of the guys from the hotel, his head bloodied, trying to straighten himself up. The guy saw Matt and fumbled for a gun. Matt squeezed off a round and saw a red splatter burst out from the guy's chest.

'Come on,' he yelled at Rydell, who nodded vaguely. As Matt reached in to him, he saw another body, lying face down behind Rydell. A woman. Matt climbed in and turned her over. He peeled off the duct tape covering her mouth and recognised her instantly: Grace Logan, the news anchor. He put his fingers to her neck, looking for a pulse.

She stirred at his touch, then flinched, her eyes wide with shock.

'Who . . . ?' she mouthed incoherently.

'Give me your hand.' Matt helped her up and slung her arm over his shoulders. 'Come on,' he told Rydell. He half-carried Gracie to the Navigator. He set her down in the back seat, got behind the wheel with Rydell beside him, and powered away. In the rearview mirror, Matt saw Gracie straighten up.

'You OK?' he asked her.

She stared at him blankly. Then things must have come flooding back, as her face tightened up with a worried frown. Her hands rummaged around, looking for something. 'My phone. Where's my phone? I have to call Dalton. It isn't safe.' She turned to Matt. 'I have to warn him.'

Matt looked down the street, saw a bank of phone booths, and pulled over.

'Where shall I tell him to go?' Gracie asked. 'Dalton. My cameraman. They'll be after him too.'

Matt tried to fill in the blanks. 'Where is he?'

'At Darby's mansion.'

'The preacher?'

'Yes.' She concentrated hard. 'No. Wait. He went to the airport. Either way, he's on his cell.' She picked up the handset. 'What'll I tell him?'

Matt gave it a quick thought. 'Just tell him to get somewhere safe away from the preacher's place. We'll call him back.'

She started to dial, then studied him curiously, 'Who the hell are you?'

'Just make the call,' he told her. 'We'll get to that later.'

DALTON JOINED THEM at the motel, arriving not long after they got there. They spent the next couple of hours filling each other in on how they'd ended up in that room. The conversation had been urgent as the different pieces had fallen into place, the string of troubling news brightening up only when Rydell had got through to the doctor treating Jabba in Boston. The surgery had been successful. Jabba had lost a lot of blood, but he was stable, and his prognosis was optimistic.

'I keep thinking of Father Jerome,' Gracie remarked. 'He knew something was wrong. I could see it in his face.' She turned to Rydell. 'You don't know what they've done to him?'

'I don't know the details,' Rydell admitted. 'I didn't want to hear about it when they brought it up. They mentioned stuff using drugs. Electroshock therapy. Implanting memories and adjusting character.'

'He said he heard voices up on the mountain. He thought God was talking to him,' Gracie mentioned.

Rydell nodded. 'They would have used a long-range acoustic device, an LRAD. It sends sound accurately over distance. They talked to him through it.'

Gracie glanced over to Rydell. 'You really thought you could get away with this?' she asked him.

'I had to do something,' he said with a tired shrug. 'People don't listen to reason until it's too late. I couldn't just sit back. This is about the planet losing its ability to sustain life.'

'Do you agree with what Drucker's trying to do?' Gracie asked.

Rydell gave a pained shake of his head. 'I agree with what he thinks is wrong with our country. But I don't agree with his solution, and I certainly don't agree with his methods.' He looked around the room. 'No one was supposed to get hurt. Drucker's out of control. Who knows what message he'll choose to put into Father Jerome's mouth before he's through.

He could make him say or do anything. And the whole world's listening.'

'We've got to stop him,' Gracie put in. 'We've got to go live with what we know.'

'No,' Matt said flatly from the corner of the room.

Gracie turned to him. 'What are you talking about?'

Matt shook his head. 'We can't break the story yet. If we do that now, they'll kill Danny. I need to get him out first.'

'You heard what they're planning, Matt,' Gracie argued. 'The show's tomorrow and it'll be watched across the planet. If we wait until after the show to blow the lid off, it might be too late to undo the damage it'll cause.'

'We'll be kind of doing their work for them if we expose it, won't we?' Dalton asked. 'That's their plan, right?'

'They can't expose it yet,' Matt countered, aiming his words at Rydell. 'not as long as they don't have you. They've got to blame it on someone without a political axe to grind. Plus, as long as they don't have you locked up, they'd be running the risk of you coming out with your side of the story. They've got some figuring out to do before they tell the world it's a set-up.'

'Which they will, sooner or later,' Gracie interjected. 'No way they'd let this run indefinitely. They'd be handing the Christian Right the keys to the kingdom. And we can't let that happen either.'

Although all Matt could think about was getting his brother back safely, he realised there were bigger considerations he couldn't shy away from. He said, 'We've got a small window before they figure out their fall-back position, right? Which gives me a bit of time to try and get Danny back. Even if it means letting them put Father Jerome up on that stage tomorrow night. You can't ask me to give up on him. Not when I'm so close.'

He looked around the room. The others glanced at each other, weighing up his words. He looked at Gracie.

She held his gaze, then nodded. 'Sure we can hold off till then. Besides, it seems to me that none of us would still be around if it wasn't for Matt. We owe him that much.'

She glanced round, judging the others' reactions. Rydell and Dalton each nodded their agreement. Her eyes ended up settling on Matt.

'OK, so how do we do it?'

'Do what?'

'Find your brother.' She caught his confused look and flashed him a grin. 'What, did you think we were going to bail out on you now?'

Matt glanced round the room and saw beaming support from everyone around him. He nodded to himself, accepting it. 'We've got to assume they're going to put a sign up over Father Jerome tomorrow, right?'

Gracie nodded. 'No doubt about that.'

'Then that's how we'll do it.'

THEY STAYED UP most of the night, studying plans and photographs of the stadium pulled from the Internet, trying to anticipate where Danny and the launch team were likely to be positioned.

By dawn, they'd reached a consensus on how Drucker's guys might try to stage it. They'd pretty much followed Rydell's lead. Having the guy who'd been in charge of the sign's technology gave them a head start, but there were still a lot of unknowns. Then, as the first glints of sunlight broke through the darkness, the TV started showing cars and people setting out on their pilgrimage. They had to get going too.

They loaded the gear they had into the back of the car. After they were done, Matt saw Gracie standing alone, staring out at the brightening sky. He joined her.

'What are you thinking about?'

'Father Jerome. You couldn't ask for a more decent human being. To think of the hell they must have put him through . . .'

Matt nodded thoughtfully. 'It's not going to be easy for him when this thing breaks. You're going to need to get him into some kind of protective custody. They'll rip him to shreds.'

'We're damned if we do and damned if we don't, aren't we?'

Matt shrugged. 'We don't really have a choice. We have to do this.'

'You're right.' It was clear from her haunted look that it wouldn't be that simple.

Matt let a moment pass, then said, 'I want to thank you. For backing me up in there. And not bailing out on me.'

'After everything you've been through? I owe you my life.'

'I know it wasn't easy,' he insisted. 'Putting the scoop of a lifetime on hold. You'd be the biggest face on television right now if you walked into any newsroom and just told them what you know.'

'Just how shallow do you think I am?'

'Not shallow, just . . . realistically ambitious.'

Gracie smiled. 'My Woodward and Bernstein moment. It's like, all your life, you wait for a big moment like this, then when it actually happens . . .'

'When it comes out, it'll change everything for you, you know,' he told her. 'And not necessarily for the better.'

She glanced over at him. 'I know.' For something every reporter dreamed about, it was starting to feel more like a nightmare.

He smiled. 'Let's just see how the rest of the day turns out and take it from there.'

THEY CAME BY CAR, by foot, by any means possible. METRORail was running extra trains to try and cope with the crush. The gates of the stadium itself were closed shortly after twelve. Seventy-three thousand people had already filed in by then. Most of those who had made the journey were calm and well behaved. The police were doing a commendable job in marshalling the pilgrims and keeping things civil.

Darby's people had also brought in a small army of volunteers who were distributing free bottles of water and pamphlets promoting Darby's evangelical empire. The crowds in the parking lots, the ones who didn't make it into the stadium, had come prepared and were settling into a festive mood. Turkey, eggnog and carols were on offer everywhere. Whole families, young and old, were joined in one seamless celebration.

Matt and the others left early, pulling in briefly at a gas station to pick up some baseball caps and cheap sunglasses to shield their faces. The first glimpse of the stadium gave Matt's spirits a boost. It was clear the roof was open, which meant there was a strong chance the sign would be making an appearance. Matt felt he was getting closer to Danny. He was daring to hope that he might actually see his brother alive again.

The cars weren't moving. Matt and Gracie left Rydell and Dalton in the SUV and walked the rest of the way. As they approached the centre, Matt cast his eyes across the huge complex and tried to fit Rydell's reading of the situation onto it: having the launchers outside the stadium and the transmitter inside. The reasons Rydell had drawn that conclusion were simple. It was hardly likely that the compressed-air launchers would be placed anywhere near the crowds inside the stadium. In such close proximity, someone was bound to notice the large canisters shooting up into the sky, no matter how silent they were. On the other hand, the laser transmitter that controlled the sign's appearance had to be inside the stadium.

The question was, would Danny and his master board be with the transmitter or the launchers? They planned to split up. Matt and Gracie would comb the stadium for the transmitter, while Rydell and Dalton would scour the area outside for the launchers.

The noise and the energy inside the stadium overwhelmed Matt and Gracie the minute they stepped in. With its roof wide open and the clear sky overhead, the building was simply breathtaking. Every single seat was occupied. Tens of thousands of people, talking and laughing and singing and waiting.

A large stage had been erected in the centre of the stadium floor, with the area around it off-limits to the public. A knot of TV news crews, reporters and photographers were busy setting up around the stage. It was one o'clock and the festivities were due to start at five. That gave him and Gracie four hours to do their sweep. It sounded like a lot of time, but it wasn't. The place was enormous and the sheer size of the crowd wasn't making their task any easier. Getting across the main concourse had taken for ever due to the human obstacle course they had to get through.

'Where do we start?' Gracie asked.

Matt shrugged. It was a daunting task. He needed to narrow down the search area if they were going to stand a chance. He looked around, trying to picture the invisible cone of the laser signal that would be animating the smart dust. He tried to visualise the sign appearing overhead, and worked back from there to suss out where the best vantage point would be for the transmitter. The banks of suites caught his eye. They provided both the right coverage and privacy. Matt discounted the ones on the highest level. It didn't seem to him that they'd allow enough of an angle to control the sign. That left six banks of suites in total to check out.

'Up there,' he said, pointing at the upper suites. They'd work their way down. Gracie nodded, and followed him back onto the main concourse and the stairwells.

IN A FAR CORNER of the parking lot, Dalton clicked the Draganflyer's black carbon-fibre rotor blades into place and tightened the harness around the airborne camera. He had it laid out on the back deck of the Navigator, away from curious eyes.

As he got it ready, he kept glancing round suspiciously, wary of any danger. He couldn't help it. The idea that Finch had been murdered was gnawing at him. Militias and angry mobs in Middle Eastern or African countries he could deal with. Silent, anonymous killers in black robes who threw you off roofs—the thought made him shudder.

He checked the remote-control unit again. Even though it would have been really useful to scan the surrounding areas, they'd decided not to use the Skycam before the sign came up. It was too risky. Instead, he and Rydell were going to recon the area around the stadium on foot.

Dalton tried to get the image of Finch being shoved off the roof out of his mind, and set out to begin his search.

KEENAN DRUCKER glanced at his watch. He frowned. Two hours to go. Things weren't going well. Losing Rydell was a huge blow. Right now, he couldn't read the man's state of mind. Would he act impulsively and bring the whole thing down on them all, even if he destroyed himself in the process? Or would he retreat and try to come up with a way out that kept him in the clear?

Drucker hoped it would be the latter. That would give him time to come up with an alternative. Because right now he needed one.

He frowned, his eyes burning into the framed portrait of his son on his desk. He felt as if he was failing his memory.

I won't fail you this time, he insisted inwardly.

'We might need to bring our plans forward,' Maddox's voice prompted him from his speakerphone.

'We can't do that,' Drucker grumbled. 'Not with Rydell running around out there. Any sign of his daughter?'

'No,' Maddox said. 'The plane dropped her off in LA. She's not using her cell or her credit cards. She's out of play for the time being.'

Drucker sighed. 'They'll go for the brother. That's all Sherwood cares about. Are you all set for that?'

Maddox just said, 'We're ready.'

'Then finish it,' Drucker ordered him, and hung up.

AFTERNOON TURNED to evening and the clocks skipped past five o'clock. Matt and Gracie still hadn't found anything. Checking out the suites wasn't easy. They had been allocated to Darby's personal guests and the media, and access was tightly controlled. Gracie managed to get into both banks of suites on the fourth and club levels by charming some bona fide invitees, and dragging Matt with her. They swept through them on the lookout for any high-tech gear or for men who didn't look like they were there for a spiritual experience. They didn't find either.

They had just cleared the first bank of suites on the club level when the lights dimmed and the reverend's hundred-member choir filed onto the stage. The crowd erupted, clapping and cheering.

Matt frowned. Father Jerome's appearance was drawing near, and they still hadn't found any trace of Danny. Matt had to go for the likeliest spots and forget about the rest. He settled on the two banks of suites on level two; each bank had thirty-nine suites in it.

Darby strolled out onto the stage, basking in the wild applause. 'Greetings in Christ,' he boomed.

Matt and Gracie weren't going to stick around for his speech. They pressed on with their sweep. They were on their way to level two when Gracie suddenly gasped.

'Ogilvy,' she said. 'He's right there.'

Matt's fists clenched. 'Which one?'

'By the concession stand. Greying hair, rimless glasses, in a light-coloured suit.'

The concourse was filled with people. A couple of heads parted and Matt caught a glimpse of someone fitting Gracie's description. 'Come on,' he said as he took Gracie's hand and cut through the crowd, only to slam into a couple of rancher types. One of them shoved Matt back angrily.

'Watch your step, doofus,' the man snapped. 'What's your rush?'

Matt's eyes narrowed but Gracie held him back. She turned to the angry rancher and cranked her flirt look up to eleven. 'No damage done, boys. What do you say we just forgive and forget. It *is* Christmas, right?'

The rancher scowled then grudgingly gave Matt a tiny bob of the head. Matt nodded back and pulled Gracie's into the throng of people, but there was no sign of Ogilvy.

OUT AT THE EDGE of the parking lot, Rydell looked up at the sky. The last glints of daylight had dipped down behind the horizon.

'Let's send it up,' he said.

Dalton switched the Draganflyer's engines on and guided it up. It rose quickly and disappeared in the night sky.

Rydell studied the area around them, trying to divine where he would put the launchers. 'Send it up there,' he said, pointing behind them, north of the stadium. He checked the image the Skycam was sending back onto Dalton's laptop. The detail was surprisingly clear. 'And keep your eyes on that screen.'

'DAMNIT,' MATT HISSED. 'We've lost him.' His eyes scoured the concourse around him. Ogilvy had vanished into the crowd.

'The network,' Gracie blurted out. 'Maybe they wangled a suite here. Maybe that's how they brought the transmitter in.'

'Makes sense. But how do we find out where it is?'

They also had another problem. There were two banks of suites on level two, but they were at opposite ends of the stadium.

'We won't have time to check both banks,' Gracie said.

Just then, the music changed into a heraldic burst of brass and Darby reappeared on stage. He milked the thunderous uproar for almost a minute before raising a calming hand.

'My fellow children of Christ, please open your hearts to our special guest, Father Jerome.'

Every single person in the stadium stood as the slight figure of Father Jerome appeared, looking unimaginably small on the huge stage. A blinding fusillade of flashbulbs accompanied him as he padded across to a microphone stand.

Matt and Gracie stood transfixed by the crowd's reaction. Gracie watched the close-up of Father Jerome's face on the screens. He was clearly overwhelmed. He didn't seem to know what to say. The crowd was silent, hanging on what God's messenger would proclaim. Then his expression changed. He swallowed and said, 'Thank you all for welcoming me here tonight.'

As Father Jerome embarked on his sermon, an idea burst through the chaos in Matt's mind.

'I need to call Rydell,' he told Gracie.

RYDELL PICKED UP on the first ring.

'Do you have the Skycam up?' Matt asked, his tone urgent.

'It's over the medical centre,' he informed him. 'Nothing so far.'

'What happens to its video downlink if it crosses into the transmitter's signal?' Matt asked.

'It would interrupt it, for sure,' Rydell speculated.

'It wouldn't mess it up so it couldn't fly, would it?'

Rydell thought about it for a beat, then said, 'It might. The laser signal could override the signal from the Skycam's remote controller. We could lose control of it while it's in the beam's path. Might fry it altogether.'

Matt's voice shot back. 'We've got to risk it. Send it inside the stadium. It's the only way we're going to find out where their signal's coming from.'

'OK,' Rydell turned to Dalton. 'We're going in.'

As Dalton banked the Draganflyer around, Rydell exclaimed, 'Did you see that?' He jabbed a finger at the screen, but whatever he was pointing at was gone. 'There was something, back there. On the roof.'

Dalton's face was tight with concentration as his fingers made micro-adjustments to the joysticks. 'It's gonna reach the stadium any second now.'

Rydell nodded. 'OK, keep going. We'll come back to it.'

'If it's still flying by then,' Dalton worried.

MATT AND GRACIE SCANNED the rectangular opening of black sky and waited as Father Jerome finished his sermon. 'Matt, he's doing it,' Gracie said, pointing at the stage.

Matt looked down, the cellphone still on his ear. 'Come on, guys.'

'It's almost there,' Rydell said, clearly tense.

Down on the stage, Father Jerome tilted his head back and raised his arms. All eyes turned to the empty air under the stadium's open roof.

'Pray with me,' Father Jerome beseeched his followers. 'Pray that God gives us a sign and guides our thoughts.'

A gasp reverberated throughout the giant hall as a ball of light appeared over Father Jerome. The apparition floated there for a few seconds, then started to rise. It reached the halfway point between Father Jerome's head and the stadium's full height, then it expanded into the familiar, massive sphere of brilliance. Like a breaking wave, euphoria rolled across the arena and the crowd erupted into a mighty roar. People were crossing themselves. Some fainted, others wailed hysterically. Most just stared in disbelief while tears of joy ran down their faces.

Matt's skin tingled. Its power blew him away. He had to remind himself that it was Danny's work. More than ever, he had to find his brother. He hissed into the cellphone, 'Where is it?'

'It just dropped in from the north face of the opening,' Rydell announced.

The tiny black machine was barely visible in the night sky, but Matt kept his eyes glued to it, sizing up its position.

'Bring it down so it's by the lower end of the sign and take it around the stadium anticlockwise,' he told Rydell. 'And let me know the second you get any interference.'

'Got it,' Rydell acknowledged.

Matt struggled to keep the tiny contraption in view as it began its sweep around the stadium. The cellphone was glued to his ear. Gracie was on alert too, scanning the entrance behind them, still wary of Ogilvy.

The Skycam had almost reached the southern tip of the east bank of suites when Rydell's voice shot into his ear.

'We've got something. Shit, we're losing it,' he shouted.

Matt saw the Skycam go into a wobble, then it dropped like a rock. His heart skipped a beat, but his eyes lasered in on the suites that faced its last stable position.

'Come on,' he yelled to Gracie, grabbing her hand and bolting back onto the concourse, racing for the escalators.

DALTON YELLED as he lost control of the Draganflyer, his fingers desperately playing the joysticks in search of a reaction. The image on the laptop's screen fizzled out and was replaced by grey static.

'It's gonna kill someone,' he blurted—then the image on the screen suddenly flickered back to life as it dived at a rapidly growing crowd.

'Pull it up,' Rydell yelled.

'I'm trying,' Dalton fired back. The people in the camera's sights grew bigger—then the device came back to life and swooped away, pulling up until it hovered in place by the stadium's roof.

Dalton let out a huge breath of relief. Rydell patted him on the shoulder. 'Great job, man. Now get it out of there and let's check out that building.'

A crescendo of excitement erupted around them. Rydell and Dalton stared up at the top of the stadium to see the sign now rising slowly into the night sky.

MATT RACED across the landing area that led to the entrance of the suites, Gracie close behind. There was no one around; everyone was watching the miracle taking place in the arena.

The target suite was all the way down the concourse. As Matt charged along, he saw a man walking his way, heading out of the suites area. Gracie yelled out, 'Matt,' from behind him.

The guy had on rimless glasses and a light-coloured suit—Ogilvy. He flinched with surprise as Matt slammed into him, grabbing him by the arms and shoving him up hard against the concourse wall. He let out a pained gasp as Matt's weight crashed into his back. Matt was in overdrive. He grabbed Ogilvy's right arm, yanked it way up behind him then shoved him down the concourse at a half jog.

'Which one are they in?' Matt rasped. He knew the suite he wanted was one of the last in the row and didn't really need Ogilvy to answer. He figured the target suite wouldn't be like all the others, with the doors wide open and clusters of people inside. Maddox's suite would have its door shut. Sure enough, the last suite had its door closed. Matt pushed Ogilvy up against the door and rapped on it firmly.

'Get them to open up, nice and friendly,' Matt hissed into his ear.

Ogilvy blurted, 'It's me.'

The door cracked open. Matt lifted Ogilvy off his feet and shoved him against the door like a battering ram. The door slammed backwards, hitting the guy standing behind it in the face. The impact knocked the guy off his feet and sent his gun flying. Matt stormed in, keeping Ogilvy in front of him like a shield. His eyes registered two other guys in addition to the one on the ground. They had silenced handguns trained on the door.

Matt didn't slow down. He kept charging forward. Ogilvy jerked as several rounds cut into him, but the shooters didn't have that much time to fire before Matt was on top of them. He launched Ogilvy at the one ahead of him and leaped at the other shooter, pushing his gun away while landing a heavy elbow across his jaw. He heard it snap as he spun round, still gripping the guy's gun wrist with both hands and tracking it through ninety degrees until it was facing the other shooter.

The two handguns pirouetted round to face each other, only the one under Matt's control got there a split second earlier and he squeezed hard against the guy's trigger finger. The handgun belched a round that caught the opposing shooter in the neck.

Matt felt the shooter behind him squirm. He slammed his elbow back into him, mashing his throat. He felt the shooter's body go rigid—then Gracie yelled, 'Matt.'

He spun his gaze back to the guy who'd taken the door in the face. He was on his knees, his face purple. He'd just recovered his gun when Gracie hurled herself at him. The shooter reacted fast—he just whipped up his arm and deflected her against the wall, but it bought Matt the seconds he needed to fire off a couple of rounds into purple-face.

He wrenched the handgun out of the shooter's hand, and pushed himself to his feet. Gracie, her face locked in shock, stepped over to join him.

He cast his eyes around and a grim realisation hit him. There was no transmitter in the room. And no Danny either.

He thought back to the shooters' position when he'd come through the door. It had been a trap. They were waiting for him, using Ogilvy to draw him in.

Matt's heart sank. Gracie looked out through the suite's floor-to-ceiling glass pane into the arena. The sign had risen through the open roof. Father Jerome was still on the stage, his arms outstretched. And every single person in the stadium was still standing.

A warble snapped his attention. Rydell was calling.

'We think we've got them,' Rydell blurted out breathlessly. 'Get your ass out here. They're here.'

'Where?' Matt asked, his voice racing.

'There's a tall building that backs up against the entrance on the north side,' Rydell said. 'Might be a hotel, I'm not sure. There are four guys on the roof. They've got the launchers.'

Matt glanced out of the glass wall. The sign was hovering over the stadium and his mind rocketed back to Rydell telling him it could stay up for around fifteen minutes before it burned out. And once that happened, the crew with the launchers would be gone. Taking Danny with them.

'Where are you?' Matt asked.

'At the east end of the lot, by the Center.'

Matt was recalling the park's layout. 'So if I come out the north gate—'

'Just head straight up across the lot and you'll hit it.'

'I'm on my way.' Matt turned to Gracie. 'They've got a fix on the launchers. I'm going after them.' He stepped over to the downed shooters, retrieved their handguns and stuffed them under his belt. 'Come on. We've got to go.'

THE BLAZING SIGN had now cleared the stadium's roof and was hovering in the night sky. It was a mesmerising sight.

Rydell checked his watch. He knew what was coming. And, sure enough, it happened almost on cue: the sign pulsed slightly, like a beating heart, then just faded out. The crowd reacted with an audible collective intake of breath and scattered cries of 'Praise the Lord.'

He glanced at the screen. The guys on the roof were moving fast now, packing their gear. He knew how efficient they'd be. Within a minute, they'd disappeared into the building.

He craned his neck, angling to get a better view of the stadium's north entrance, as if he could spot Matt, but the entrance was too far. He made a quick decision.

'The guns are in the glove box, right?' he asked Dalton. Before Dalton could answer, he'd already scurried over and pulled out the Para-Ordnance.

'What are you doing?' Dalton felt a stab of fear at the sight of Rydell holding the silver handgun.

'I've got to help Matt,' Rydell said, and, before Dalton could object, he was gone.

MATT EXPLODED out of the stadium's north entrance with Gracie close behind. He reached the lot and pointed her in the direction Rydell had said the big SUV was parked. 'They should be there somewhere, at the back.'

She nodded, and he was off, sprinting through the rows of cars and cutting around the clusters of revellers. One and a half minutes later, he reached the fence, then stopped in his tracks at the sight of Rydell waiting for him.

'Figured you could use some help,' Rydell said, lifting his jacket to expose the handgun he had tucked under his belt.

Matt gave him a grin. He held the phone to his mouth. 'Anything?' he asked.

Dalton's voice came back. 'No movement, but the lot on the south side of the building is crawling with people. Hang on, we've got four guys, heading for a van, by the trees in the northeast corner of the lot.'

Matt snapped the phone shut and stuffed it in his back pocket. 'You know how to use it?' he asked, pointing at Rydell's silver handgun.

Rydell nodded. 'I'll manage.'

Matt flicked him an OK nod and took off for the trees.

They hurdled the low fence bordering the parking lot and cut across the scrub that led to a Holiday Inn. They kept going, rounding the hotel and reaching its front parking lot.

The lot was wide and had poor lighting. Matt could just make out the roof of the van all the way down, on the far right. He saw movement around it, figures silhouetted in the night. Saw one of them lifting a big tube. He looked to Rydell. Rydell nodded. They were Maddox's men.

Matt felt a tightening in his gut. Danny could be less than fifty yards away. He pulled out his guns and handed one to Rydell. 'This one will be quieter than that cannon you've got there. Go wide that way.' He gestured for Rydell to move in from the left. 'I'll cut across from the right. And stay low.'

Rydell confirmed with a slight nod and slipped away.

Matt hugged the cars, slithering through the narrow gaps between them, his eyes locked on the target. He heard one of its doors clang shut and saw one of the men stepping towards the back of the van. Matt gripped his handgun in a two-handed stance, ready to pump a couple of bullets into Maddox's men—but there was no one there. They were gone. Then he heard a rustle off to the right and saw a shooter emerge, pulling Rydell along with him, a handgun pressed against the billionaire's temple.

Matt flinched—just as something hard nudged him in the back.

'Drop it,' the voice said. 'Nice and slow.'

For a split second, the notion of making a move sparked in his mind, but the guy behind him cut it short with a sudden punch to Matt's ear that sent him down to his knees. He dropped his gun. Through a bleary veil, he glimpsed the outline of someone climbing out of the back of the van. It was Maddox, and he was dragging someone with him, yanking him by the neck, a handgun pressed against it.

The recognition was instant. It was Danny.

Matt pushed himself to his feet, and the adrenaline boost coursing through him brought Danny's face into focus. Matt couldn't suppress a broad smile, even though things weren't looking too promising.

Maddox acknowledged Matt's presence with a shrug, but his eyes registered genuine surprise when he saw Rydell.

'What do you know,' he quipped, clearly pleased with the unexpected presence of the tycoon. 'And people say there is no Santa.'

GRACIE FLARED. 'What are they doing?'

The image on the laptop's screen showed the two figures they knew to be Rydell and Matt putting their guns down and stepping back from the van in defeat. Two other figures appeared from the van.

'Is that a gun?' she asked, fear catching in her throat.

Dalton brought the Draganflyer down for a closer look.

The top view of Maddox's extended arm grew bigger on the screen. And there was no mistaking the gun that was staring Matt and Rydell in the face.

'I'M SORRY, BRO,' Danny told Matt. 'I couldn't warn you.'

'Don't worry about it.' He saw that Danny's hands were tied together with plastic flex cuffs.

Danny glared at Rydell. 'What's he doing here?' he asked Matt.

'His penance,' Matt replied flatly.

Danny shook his head sardonically. His stare burned into Rydell. 'Too little, too late, don't you think? Or do you have the power to raise the dead?'

Rydell kept quiet.

Maddox swung his right arm straight out, flicking his handgun in a horizontal arc from Matt to Rydell and back.

'Sorry to have to cut this happy reunion short, boys,' Maddox said tersely, 'but we've got to get going. How about you say goodbye to your pain-in-the-ass brother one last time, Danny-boy.' He settled his gun sight on Matt. 'It's been good knowing you, kid. You did really well.'

'Not well enough,' Matt retorted gruffly.

Maddox raised the gun a couple of inches for a head shot, no emotion whatsoever registering on his face. Matt's heart stopped—then Maddox whipped back as something rocketed out of the night sky with a whoosh and batted his arm savagely to one side. His gun went flying off as the Skycam's carbon-fibre blades sliced through skin and muscle, and Maddox fell to the ground in a burst of blood.

Matt rammed his elbow back into the shooter behind him, then he spun round and pushed the man's gun hand away while battering him with a cross that sent him tumbling to the ground. Matt went down with him, fighting for the gun and they wrestled for it until the gun spat out a shot that caught the shooter in the gut.

Rydell was grappling with his shooter, his hands clasped round the man's wrist. The shooter suckered him into a head butt and Rydell's legs caved in and he rag-dolled. Then the shooter jerked back to the tune of a couple of silenced coughs. Matt blinked, then he saw Danny gripping Maddox's gun. Danny stared at Matt, his face locked in disbelief at what he'd done.

Matt's eyes went wide. 'Watch out,' he blurted, but it was too late—Maddox had already sprung to his feet behind Danny.

Maddox's eyes met Matt's for a nanosecond before he shoved Danny towards Matt and scurried back away from them, and disappeared behind the van.

Matt bolted after Maddox into the thicket of trees that edged the parking lot, but the darkness had swallowed his quarry up.

Maddox was gone.

Matt scanned the lot, then stepped round Rydell and joined Danny. He embraced him with a big bear hug, then pulled him back and ruffled his hair.

'Merry Christmas,' he told him.

'Best one ever,' Danny replied, his face lit up with nervous relief. Rydell got up and joined them. Danny faced him, a hard, angry glare shimmering in his eyes. Then he balled up his fists and whipped his still-tied arms in a big, curving swing that knocked Rydell to the ground.

'I couldn't have made it here without his help,' Matt told Danny.

Danny turned away and shrugged. 'It's a start,' he grunted.

Rydell looked towards Danny. 'I'm sorry,' he said.

'Like I said,' Danny replied, as he walked away, 'it's a start.'

THEY'D CHANGED MOTELS for safety, although with Maddox hurt and a lot of his men dead, they were starting to feel that the cross hairs had lifted.

Danny and Matt had a lot of catching up to do.

'I've got to call Mom and Dad,' Danny said enthusiastically.

Matt couldn't duck it any longer.

He held Danny's gaze as he tried to find the words to tell him what had happened, but Danny read his expression.

'Who? . . . Mom?' he asked.

Matt nodded, but his pained look held more portent than just one parent.

Danny's face crumpled with grief. Matt had already told him about Bellinger's murder. The triple whammy hit him hard.

A sombre mood enshrouded them as Danny told Matt of his despair during those two years. How he'd tried to sneak an email out to him and been caught. How he'd contemplated suicide. How they'd drugged him after that.

'You're here now,' Matt told him, 'and you're safe.' Matt smiled, 'That's way more than either of us had a couple of days ago.'

IN AN ADJACENT ROOM, Rydell stewed alone, as uncomfortable to be around Danny as Danny was around him. He also had a lot on his mind.

It was over, that much was clear. Once Gracie returned, the story would blow wide open. And then, whichever way you looked at it, his life was over too. He wasn't prepared to run. It wasn't his style. He'd be there to face up to what he'd been a part of.

The hardest part of it was thinking about what it would do to Rebecca. It would follow her for the rest of her life. His mind kept churning, desperate to find a way to keep her out of it, but there was nothing he could think of.

BY THE TIME Gracie and Dalton joined them a couple of hours later, the reunion was a bittersweet, subdued celebration. Yes, they were all safe and Danny was alive and free. And Gracie and Dalton were about to become superstars. But there was a downside to the forthcoming media feeding frenzy. A downside well beyond Rydell's very public downfall.

In the background, a TV was replaying the evening's events.

'What's this going to do to all those people who were out there tonight?' Gracie asked. 'And everyone around the country who was tuning in. Everyone around the planet, for that matter. How are they going to take it?'

'What's the alternative?' Dalton countered. 'We can't let the lie run. Finch was murdered because of it. The sooner we end this the better.'

'Vince too,' Danny added. 'And Reece. And many others.'

Gracie heaved a sigh. 'They were killed to keep it quiet until Drucker was ready to pull the cover off. And now we're going to do it for him.'

'We have to do this. The longer it runs, the more painful it will be when the truth comes out,' Danny said.

Gracie nodded grudgingly, then said to Rydell, 'I'll need you to go on record. We'll need the evidence.'

Rydell nodded sombrely. He turned to Danny. 'How were they going to expose Father Jerome?'

'They made me design a debunking software. They were going to run it over him once they were ready to out him. It simulates a breakdown in the technology. Like if you're watching TV and the signal breaks up. What you'd expect to see if the sign was a fake. It'll conjure up a broadcast that's going haywire.'

'What if it never comes out?' Gracie threw in.

'The Evangelicals get to keep their new messiah, and Darby and his friends on the far right choose our next few presidents,' Rydell observed.

'Either way, Darby and all, his pals are going to come out of this stronger.' Gracie countered. 'Once you and Drucker are exposed, all liberals are going to be demonised. We'll be giving the hard-core right their biggest rallying cry since the fall of the evil empire.'

'Hang on, we're talking about a handful of guys who put this stunt in play, not an entire political party,' Danny protested.

'It doesn't matter,' Gracie argued. 'What matters is how they'll spin it.'

On the TV, the image cut away to footage of violent riots in Islamabad and in Jerusalem.

'Turn it up,' Gracie told Dalton, who was closest to the TV.

An anchorman came back on. 'Following the unprecedented events in Houston earlier this evening,' he announced, 'a White House spokeswoman indicated that the president would be making a statement tomorrow.'

'We can't let that happen,' Gracie insisted.

Dalton asked, 'So what do we do? We're screwed whether we expose it or not.'

Rydell sat up. 'We have to expose it. But only if I take the fall for it. Alone.'

That got everyone's attention.

He pressed on. 'It's the only way. My plan was never intended to empower or undermine any religion. It was just meant to get people to listen. But now after what they've done . . . we need a fall guy with no political motive if we're going to avoid tearing this country apart. And that fall guy's got to be me.'

'Great,' Gracie grumbled. 'So Drucker wins.'

'I'll make sure he pays,' Rydell assured her quietly.

Gracie nodded. Rydell was right, and they knew it.

Matt hadn't said a word till now. 'We're forgetting someone in all this. Father Jerome. Can you imagine what's going to happen to him if this thing breaks?'

'They'll rip him to shreds,' Rydell said.

'But he wasn't in on it,' Dalton noted.

'It doesn't matter.' Matt frowned.

Gracie glanced at Matt. 'We can't do this. Not without letting him know what's about to happen to him. He needs to be part of this decision. I have to talk to him.'

'They flew him back to Darby's place,' Rydell reminded her. 'You walk in there, Drucker'll make sure you don't come out.'

'What if you say you want to interview him, one-on-one?' Danny offered.

'Too dangerous,' Rydell grumbled. 'Besides, he's got to be the most heavily protected guy on the planet right now.'

Matt turned to Danny. 'How much of their gear is in that van?'

'The full kit,' Danny said.

'What about the laser transmitter? It was inside the stadium, wasn't it?'

'One was. We had another with us for when the sign was over the roof.'

Matt nodded. 'And how much smart dust do you have left?'

'I'm not sure. Why?'

'Because we're going to need it. We can't feed Father Jerome to the wolves.' Matt glanced around the room. 'He was dragged into this and he's a good man. We can't let Drucker ruin his life until he's had his say on the matter.' He turned to Gracie. 'What does Darby's place look like?'

River Oaks, Houston, Texas

The chaotic scene outside the entrance to Darby's gated community was hardly normal, but at least it was quiet. It was five o'clock in the morning and the gathered masses were down for the night. They slept in their cars, in sleeping-bags by the side of the road, anywhere they could. A small, tireless contingent was still crowding the entrance gatehouse, waiting for their messiah to make an appearance. The news crews sheltered quietly by their vans, taking turns on watch.

The sign's appearance took them all by surprise, lighting up the night sky, pulsating with mysterious, unexplained life as it hovered just above the treetops. Right over Darby's house.

The crowd snapped to attention. The believers, the reporters, the cops, the security guards. Even the dogs went manic. Within seconds, everyone was up, shouting excitedly. The worshippers were pressing against the barricades. The cops were scrambling to contain the sudden swell of people. The news cameras were rolling.

Then it started to move. Floating away from Darby's house. Gliding over the trees towards the country club. Opening a floodgate of pandemonium.

The crowd went after it. The barricades toppled over, breached by a wave of hysterical believers who streamed through the trees, chasing the shimmering apparition.

The cops patrolling the edge of the estate's western perimeter saw it too. Their radios squawked to life seconds later. They could hear an eerie noise that subverted the stillness of the night. But the rear of the estate, where they were, was calm.

Then one of them saw something. A hint of movement, slipping across the trees at the edge of the fairway. It was hard to see anything in the darkness, but it looked like two figures, creeping along the far edge of the tennis court, heading towards the house.

'Over there,' he hissed, pulling out his handgun—then it hit them all. An anvil-punch to their eardrums that shocked them into unconsciousness.

MATT GLANCED into the darkness behind him. He couldn't see Danny, Dalton and Rydell hiding in the trees by the seventh green, manning the LRAD. So far, the diversion was working. But it wouldn't last long. They had to be in and out in fifteen minutes.

He made sure the guards were staying down, and gave Gracie a 'let's-go' gesture, knowing that she wouldn't hear him through the wax plugs shielding her eardrums.

They struck out over the lawn and crept up to the rear façade of the house. Matt pulled his ear-plugs out. Gracie followed suit.

'This it?' he asked her in a whisper.

She nodded. 'Stairway's off to the right. His bedroom's upstairs, first door on the left.'

He pulled out his handgun. He'd brought one of the silenced automatics with him, even though he wasn't planning on using it. Defending himself against Maddox's goons was one thing. This was different. The guys babysitting Father Jerome were cops and private security guards from the estate, just doing their job.

He tried the handle of the French doors; they were open. They slipped inside. There was no sound coming from the house. Matt glanced around. They were in the guesthouse's living room. It was dark except for a pale glint of light from the hallway.

They crossed the room and slithered up the stairs. Found the first door on the left. Matt cracked it open and slipped through, with Gracie on his heels.

Father Jerome was fast asleep. Gracie bent down and nudged his shoulder softly. He turned over, his eyes blinking open. He saw her and pushed himself up.

'What? Miss Logan . . . ?' He saw Matt standing by the window, peering out from behind the curtains. 'What's going on?'

She flicked on the small lamp by the bed. 'We have to be quick. You need to come with us. Your life's in danger.'

'Danger? From what?'

'Please, Father. There's no time. Trust me on this. We have to go now.'

He stared at her, his face wrinkled with uncertainty. Held her gaze for a brief moment, then got out of bed. He was wearing dark pyjamas.

'Just put your shoes on,' she said.

Matt put a friendly hand on the holy man's shoulder. 'My name's Matt Sherwood. Just stay close to Gracie and try not to make any noise, OK?'

The priest nodded his readiness, then Matt opened the door and stepped out.

HE DIDN'T SEE IT coming. The strike came flying out from the right, nailing him just behind his right ear. Matt thudded heavily to the floor as Gracie screamed at the sight of Brother Ameen moving swiftly out of the shadows and landing a heavy kick on Matt's midsection.

Matt slammed back against the wall, unsure of where the next blow was coming from, his vision blurred. He pushed himself onto his hands and knees in time for another kick to explode across his ribs. Then the monk was right up against him, his arms round his neck, choking the life out of him. Matt struggled to suck in air. He tried a rear head butt, snapping his neck back as hard as he could. The monk jerked his head sideways to avoid it, then tightened his hold on Matt even more.

Then he heard a dull thud and felt the monk's grip slacken. Gracie was holding the lamp from the priest's bedside table like a baseball bat, ready for another swing. The monk didn't give her another chance. He whipped the lamp out of her hands, then caught Gracie on the left temple. The blow sent her flying back into the room.

Matt leaped at the monk. He was bigger and bulkier, but Ameen was a tight coil of hard muscle and knew how to hit. They wrestled and punched their way across the hallway, then the monk's fist found Matt's bullet wound. A gush of pain erupted across him, causing a momentary blackout that opened him to a frenzy of sharp jabs.

He was at the edge of the stairs when he heard Gracie scream his name and he saw the monk's fist racing at his head for a final, crippling blow.

He jerked sideways without thinking and grabbed the monk's arm, twisting it savagely. The move caught the monk by surprise, lifting him off his feet as his shoulder tore out of its socket. The monk's feet left the ground as he flew into the air over the railing before landing with a sickening crack at the bottom of the stairs.

Matt looked down. The monk's body lay slack and silent. Gracie stepped over to him, followed by a shell-shocked Father Jerome.

'Come on,' Matt whispered. 'We don't have much time.'

They slipped down the stairs, past the Croatian's corpse. They threaded their way back out of the living room, and skirted the edge of the fairways just as the sign faded out.

They all crammed into the SUV and slipped away, wondering how the city—and the world—would react to their Christmas surprise.

Houston, Texas

Maddox blocked out the pain as he watched the ER team deal with his own Christmas surprise. He'd insisted on having only local anaesthetic. The surgeons had been working on him for over three hours, cutting and drilling and sewing away at his mangled arm.

They'd just about succeeded in saving the arm, but the doctors had told him that he'd have very limited use of it. The blades had hacked their way through muscle and tendons. It would be little more than a decorative limb. So he'd settle for one working arm. He'd just need to train it to compensate.

Even in his weakened state, Maddox registered the commotion in the hospital as news of the sign's appearance over Reverend Darby's house had spread. He knew that wasn't part of the plan. He wondered if Drucker was behind it and, if so, what he was doing. He realised things were unravelling. He knew when the time was right to cut his losses. And with Rydell, the Sherwood boys and that reporter running free, that ship wasn't just sinking, it was about to be torpedoed into smithereens.

He thought back to Jackson Drucker and the rest of his men, thought of their chewed-up bodies littering that Iraqi ghost town, thought about how he'd failed them all. But he'd lived and he was fighting on. And that didn't involve him spending any more time in ER than he had to.

Less than an hour after they'd finished patching him up, Maddox was making his way to downtown Houston.

THEY WERE STILL debriefing Father Jerome by the time dawn finally made its appearance, all five of them—Matt, Gracie, Rydell, Danny and Dalton. They told him about Rydell's original plan. About the smart dust and the launchers and the planet reaching its tipping point. About Drucker's taking hold of it and perverting it to his agenda.

Then they got into what Drucker's people had done to him. The treatments. The drugs. The LRAD talking to him up on the top of the mountain.

By the end of it, he was holding up better than Gracie had expected. For all his physical frailty, the man had a remarkable inner strength.

'The voice on the mountain,' he finally said, looking into the distance. 'It was amazing. Like it was inside my head. Like it knew what I was thinking.'

'That's because they put those thoughts in your head in the first place,' Gracie told him, her tone careful and soft.

Father Jerome nodded. He sighed heavily, and lifted his gaze towards Rydell. 'And you're going to say it was all your idea?'

Rydell nodded. Father Jerome's brow furrowed. 'I'm tired,' he finally said in a hollow voice. 'I need to rest.'

IN THEIR ROOM, Danny and Matt stretched out on their beds. They'd caught the early-morning news on TV. The top story was the sign's appearance over Darby's mansion, but there was no mention of Father Jerome going missing.

After a while, Danny said, 'It really gets my goat, you know? That Drucker might weasel out of this without damage.'

'You want to go put a bullet through his skull?'

Danny tilted his head to one side. 'Not really my style. But if Rydell doesn't take care of him in a big way, I might want to reconsider.'

'We could grab him and lock him up in my cellar for a couple of years as payback,' Matt remarked flatly. 'Just feed him dog food and toilet water.'

'Nice to know we've got options.'

Matt tilted his head over to him. 'It's good to have you back, man.'

Danny nodded warmly. 'It's good to be back.'

IN HIS ROOM, Rydell was racking his brain, trying to think of another way out. What an end, he thought. Everything he'd achieved was about to be flushed down the toilet.

He had to talk to Rebecca. He pulled up her number. Poised his finger on the call button. But he couldn't do it. He didn't know what to tell her.

He set the phone back down.

WHEN MATT STEPPED OUT of his room to hit the vending machine again. Gracie was there too, a cold can of Coke in her hand. He put in some coins and pulled out a can of his own.

'Can't sleep?' he asked.

'Nope.' She smiled. 'My body clock's out of whack.'

Matt said, 'You should get some rest. You're about to have the most intense few months of your life. Of anyone's life.'

'Even worse than the last few days?'

'Oh yeah.' He shrugged. 'That was a cakewalk.'

'Some cakewalk.' After a moment, she said, 'It seems like such a waste, don't you think? All those people, at the stadium. Hanging on Father Jerome's every word. They were loving it. For a moment, they'd forgotten about their problems. They were happy and hopeful. He gave them all hope.'

'False hope,' Matt corrected.

'What's wrong with that? Hope isn't real by definition, is it? It's just a state of mind. If it wasn't for all those self-serving leeches using something as inspirational as that to fill their own pockets and grab more power . . .'

He shrugged. 'It's the way of the world.'

She nodded ruefully. Stood there quietly for a moment, then asked, 'So what are you going to do? You're part of this story too, you know. People are going to want to hear your side of it.'

He cocked his head towards her. 'Good,' he said.

'Why?'

'I thought I might knock out a book about it. Maybe flog the movie rights to some studio.' He flashed her a grin.

'Yeah, well, get in line, bud,' she countered.

He let out a slight chuckle. Turned to look at her. It suddenly occurred to Matt that she was a great-looking girl and, with all the rest of it, everything any man could ask for. Much as he wanted to put the whole nightmare of the last week behind him, the thought of it keeping them involved in each other's lives for a while longer had taken over as the preferred option. But they had to get through the tough part first.

'When are you going to hit the button?' he asked her.

Her face tightened at the thought. 'How about we let everyone out there enjoy a few more hours of peace. Tomorrow.'

He nodded. They dunked their empty cans in the trash and trudged back to their rooms. They were outside Father Jerome's door when it cracked open. The old priest stood there. He didn't look as if he'd slept at all. He said, 'Can you get everyone together? We need to talk.'

THE FIRST PEOPLE to see the ball of light were the families and couples and joggers enjoying a day out in Houston's Hermann Park. It was hovering innocuously over the south end of the pool by the Pioneer Memorial obelisk. Curious onlookers gravitated towards it. They soon spotted the man in the black cassock underneath it as he walked away from the obelisk and made his way up the steps to the platform that looked down over the pond.

The park was hugely popular and, before long, hundreds of people had their eyes locked on the tiny figure with the sphere of shimmering light floating above him. The park police set up a protective cordon around the platform, and the news vans rushed over too.

Once everything was in place—the crowd, the coverage, the protection—Father Jerome took a step forward and raised his hands. The entire park was shrouded in silence. He tilted his head up to look at the sphere of light floating over him, nodded thoughtfully and addressed the crowd.

'Friends, something wonderful has been happening these past few days. Something amazing and strange . . . something I don't understand.' A murmur of surprise coursed through the crowd. 'Because the honest truth is I don't know what this is,' he said, pointing upwards at the hovering ball of light. 'I don't know why it's here. What I do know, though, is that its meaning hasn't been properly understood. Not by others. Certainly not by me. Not until last night. And now I think I do understand what it's trying to tell us, I'm here to share that with you.'

KEENAN DRUCKER STARED at the TV screen in his hotel room, wondering what the hell was going on.

He'd been on edge since he'd got news of Father Jerome's disappearance. He'd wondered why Rydell and his new friends hadn't gone public. The sight of Father Jerome on the screen wasn't making things any clearer.

He heard his doorbell ring, and crossed to see who was there.

'Jesus,' he said when he saw Maddox's heavily bandaged arm and his sweaty face. 'You didn't tell me it was that bad.'

Maddox pushed into the suite, ignoring the comment. 'There's a lot of commotion in the lobby. Have you seen what's happening?' He saw the live coverage on the TV and turned to Drucker with a suspicious frown. 'What are you doing?'

'It's not me,' Drucker protested. 'I don't know what's going on.'

Maddox studied him dubiously. 'It's not you?'

'This has nothing to do with me. It's got to be Rydell. He's running things now. They got the priest out last night.'

'I tried Dario's phone and got some cop, and that didn't add up.'

'Dario's dead,' Drucker confirmed.

Maddox nodded. Things were unravelling even worse than he'd thought. He turned to the screen. 'So what are they doing?'

'I don't know. Maybe Rydell's got the others convinced the global-warming message is too important to kill.'

'But he knows you can blow it all up for him,' Maddox remarked.

'He can also take me down with him,' Drucker reminded Maddox, then added, 'and you, too, in case you forgot. He was the fall guy, remember?' Then his face relaxed. 'They're not going to expose him yet. Not before they figure out who they're going to pin it on. Which gives us time to come up with a way out.'

Maddox came to a quick conclusion. If he was going to live to fight another day, he had to make sure he didn't leave anyone behind who could ruin things for him. Like a career politician who wouldn't think twice about selling someone out to save his own skin. But what he was seeing brought back to life a far more attractive option. One he thought had been wiped off his list.

He pulled out an automatic and shoved it against Drucker's forehead. 'Sit down.'

He herded Drucker into an armchair facing the TV, then, in one swift movement, grabbed Drucker's shaking hand with his gun hand, and arced it up so the silencer's muzzle was jammed against Drucker's mouth.

Drucker stared at him, terrified.

'I never thought exposing Jerome was a good idea,' Maddox told him. 'He's much more useful this way. The truth is, we're not out of options here, Keenan. You are.' And he pulled the trigger.

The bullet ripped out the back of Drucker's head. Maddox placed the gun in Drucker's limp hand, pressed his fingers tightly against the grip and the trigger, then let it drop as it would have done had Drucker been alone.

He pulled out his cellphone and hit the well-worn speed-dial number. 'I think we're back in business. How's our boy?' he asked.

'He's at home,' his NSA contact told him. 'Watching the live coverage from the park.'

'Good. Let me know if he moves. I need him to be at home.' He slipped out of the room, calculating the quickest route to Hermann Park.

FATHER JEROME STARED at the crowd and hesitated. Other thoughts started rising out of the caverns of his mind, fighting for attention. Then a familiar voice echoed in his ears.

'You're doing great,' Gracie told him. 'Just keep going. Remember everything we talked about. Think about what you really want to tell these people. Block everything else out. We're right behind you, Father.'

A ghost of a smile broke across his face and a renewed resolve blossomed within him. He pressed on.

IN THE BACK of the van, Gracie put her binoculars down and turned to address Matt across the big drum of the LRAD.

'This thing's just incredible.' She grinned, patting it. 'I want one.'

'Why not. It is Christmas,' Matt said with an easy grin. Then his expression tightened. 'Let them know I'm going in. And keep your eyes on Father Jerome in case he wobbles again.'

'Good luck.' She smiled.

He smiled back and said, 'I'll see you in a little while. He pushed his phone's earpiece into place and glanced across at Dalton behind the wheel. They exchanged a nod, then Matt slipped out of the van and headed for the plaza.

ACROSS THE FIELD from the plaza, Danny watched the proceedings while Rydell liaised with Gracie on the phone. The Navigator was parked nearby, its rear door open. The launch tubes were huddled beside them, now freshly stacked with the last of the smart-dust canisters.

'Matt's on his way,' Rydell told Danny.

Danny nodded. 'Launchers ready?'

'They're all set,' Rydell told him. 'You sure you had enough time to write the new programs?'

'They'll be fine,' Danny said flatly.

Their eyes met. An unspoken anger still festered behind Danny's gaze. Then he turned his attention back to Father Jerome. 'Let 'em rip.'

'OTHERS HAVE COME before me,' Father Jerome announced. 'Blessed with wise and noble thoughts that they tried to share with those around them to help humanity. But all it's done is turn man against man. Their wise words and selfless deeds have been misinterpreted, twisted, hijacked by others for their own glorification. Institutions have been built in their names—temples of intolerance, each one of them claiming to be the true faith and pitting man against man.'

He paused, sensing the unease spreading among the crowd, and redoubled his concentration, pushing the conflicting thoughts back. 'We have to try and fix that.'

Just then, the sphere of light spread out until it dwarfed the piazza below it. The audience gasped, staring in wonderment as the sign pulsed and rippled with life before morphing into a blazing cross.

Shouts of 'Praise the Lord' and 'Amen' burst through the throng of onlookers, but their joy was cut short when the sign started morphing into the Star of David. The crowd flinched with surprise, confused and caught off-balance—but the sign changed again. It kept shape-shifting into a rotating sequence of symbols associated with other religions—Islam, Hinduism, Buddhism, Bahaism—reaching back into history.

The changes sped up until the symbols became almost indistinguishable—and then it just vanished.

The stunned onlookers stared at each other, mystified—then the sign burst out in its former glory, assuming the shape first seen over the ice shelf, and shimmered above the priest's head.

'INTERESTING SHOW you're putting on,' the voice rasped.

Danny and Rydell turned and froze at the sight of Maddox approaching them from behind. He had a long, black case slung over his shoulder and held a gun in his left hand. He stopped about ten feet away. It hadn't been that hard for him to find them. Not for someone who knew what to look for.

'I'm feeling all warm and cuddly inside,' he chortled, gesturing for them to raise their hands. 'Love and peace—is that what you're selling them?'

'It's working,' Rydell told him, as he set down his phone without killing the line. He raised his hands slightly. 'They're listening.'

'You think that's going to make a difference?' Maddox's voice rose with anger. 'You think our enemies are going to buy into that too? Wake up, Larry. They may be listening, but it's not going to change anything.'

'It could. I don't want them to stop believing in God,' Rydell said, volleying the anger back. 'I'd just like them to use their own minds a bit more. Just listen to Father Jerome.'

'It's an admirable thought,' Maddox said mockingly. 'We are the world, we are the children, right? Everything he's saying out there, it's just great— but you know what it's going to do?' He set his pack down on the ground, reached into it, and pulled out a sniper rifle.

'It's going to get him killed.'

GRACIE STIFFENED the second the words echoed through the headset of her cellphone. Maddox was alive. And, by the sound of it, he'd taken them by surprise.

An icy panic stabbed the back of her neck. She turned to Dalton in alarm and said, 'I need to call Matt. We've got trouble.'

'MATT.' Gracie's voice burst through his earpiece. 'It's Maddox. He's got Danny and Rydell.'

Matt's feet froze for a beat, then he was suddenly hurtling through the crowd, a tangle of horrific images tumbling through his mind.

MADDOX SWUNG the rifle at Rydell and Danny. 'As soon as he's done talking, he's going to get his head blown off. 'Cause that's how all good prophets end up, isn't it? If you really want his words to be seared into the minds of millions, he needs to die. 'Cause martyrs are so much harder to ignore, aren't they?'

Danny studied him, then said, 'And after he's dead . . .'

Maddox nodded. 'Yep. With both of you out of the picture, it'll clean things up, nice and tidy. They won't find you. They find the Iranian whacko who shot Jerome, though. A card-carrying fanatic we've been watching for a while. He'll have his head blown off, of course. Self-inflicted.'

'You weren't planning to expose Father Jerome?' Rydell asked.

Maddox shook his head. 'Nope.'

'But Keenan . . .' Rydell got it. 'He didn't know.'

Maddox flashed him an icy smile. 'Of course not.'

'So the Iranians, the Muslim world,' Danny said, 'will get the blame?'

'Of course,' Maddox smiled. 'Beautiful, isn't it? The prophet who wanted to set us free, shot by an agent of intolerance.'

'You'll start a war,' Danny blurted.

'I'm counting on it,' Maddox replied coolly.

Rydell took a step forward. 'Think about what you're doing—'

'I've thought about it,' Maddox hissed. 'I've done nothing but think about it. We're too weak. We're playing by the rules against an enemy who knows wars don't have rules. We're getting our asses handed to us and you know why? Because they know how to get things done. They know that if someone slaps you, you don't turn the other cheek. You rip their arm off. The only way we're going to win this thing is to get people so angry that they'll be baying for blood.'

'You'll be dragging millions of innocent people into a war just to punish a few extremists—'

'It's not just a few extremists, Larry. It's the whole region. You weren't out there. They're our enemies, plain and simple. It's a holy war. And to win a holy war, you need a crusade. We have to go after them no holds barred. And the death of your fake prophet will make it happen. It'll be one hell of a call to arms.' He levelled the gun at them. 'So you just keep that sign up there and settle back until he's done. Then we'll finish this.'

FATHER JEROME FIXED his eyes fervently on the massed onlookers.

'We all pray to the same God. That's all that matters. Everything else— all the institutions, all the rituals and public expressions of faith—we created those. But God doesn't care about what you eat or what you drink or how often you pray or what words you use. He cares only about how you behave towards one another. That's all that matters. Every day, each and every one of you is faced with a choice, and it's how you choose to behave that matters. It's that simple.'

RYDELL WATCHED MADDOX prop the rifle on the SUV's side mirror. He turned to Danny. 'Run the debunking software.'

'What?' Danny asked.

'Run the damn software,' Rydell yelled. 'Better to expose him than get him killed and start a war.'

'Don't,' Maddox growled, spinning the rifle at them—

'Wait,' Danny blurted out, raising his hands. 'Calm down. I'm not doing anything.'

'Danny, listen to me,' Rydell urged him. 'He can't kill us both. He needs the sign to stay up. Run the goddamn software.'

'Don't even try it, Danny-boy,' Maddox warned. 'It doesn't matter to me if the sign dies out right now. It's done all I needed it to do.'

Rydell turned to Maddox in exasperation. 'Listen to me,' he pleaded. 'This is good. It'll achieve what you're trying to do without—'

'Enough,' Maddox yelled. 'You know what, Larry? You're no longer needed here.' He raised the gun and squeezed the trigger—just as Matt tackled him from the side. The bullet flew wide, missing Rydell. Matt fell against the ground. Maddox spun around and lashed out with a fierce kick.

Matt recoiled in pain as Danny and Rydell rushed Maddox. The soldier scrambled to push himself off the ground, but he instinctively used his mangled right arm, causing a torrent of agony to flood through him. He fell back again and glared at Matt as his left hand dived under his jacket. Matt saw the grip of an automatic sticking out from behind Maddox's belt, saw the rifle he'd dropped lying a few feet away, and dived for it.

Maddox's hand had less distance to travel and came up first—but he didn't count on Danny, who shoved him to one side, hard. Maddox landed on his right arm and his scream sliced through the empty lot before Matt shut him up permanently with three rounds to the chest.

'YOU DON'T NEED ANYONE to tell you what to believe or who to worship,' Father Jerome told the crowd. 'You don't need to follow any set of rituals. You don't need to worry about an angry God not allowing you into heaven. All I know is that if there is a God, and I believe there is one, then you are all God's children. Each and every one of you. You need to look after each other. You need to look after the land that feeds you and gives you the air you breathe. You need to assume your duty towards all of God's creation. And you need to accept the credit for the good and take the blame for the bad.'

He looked across the stunned crowd. 'Enjoy your lives. Look after your loved ones. Help those less fortunate. Make the world a better place for all.'

He shut his eyes and raised his hands. The sign held there for a moment longer—then it dropped down, until it engulfed the entire platform around Father Jerome in its dazzling light, obscuring him from view. The massed audience flinched backwards—then the sign divided itself into smaller balls of light that shot outwards, over the crowd. A horizontal field of hundreds of smaller signs, each no more than three feet across, hovered over the sea of onlookers, almost within reach.

It took a couple of seconds for the first gasp and the first shout to draw the crowd's attention back to the platform at the top of the steps.

Father Jerome was gone.

ACROSS TOWN in his mansion, Reverend Nelson Darby glared at his massive TV. His land line was ringing again. As was his cellphone.

The preachers he'd invited onto the stage with him were clearly watching the live telecast too. And they weren't thrilled either.

He sucked in a deep, angry breath. Grabbed the phone, ripped its power cord out of the wall and hurled it straight through his TV screen.

THEY ALL WATCHED the endless replays of the coverage in the executive lounge at Hobby Airport with relief. So far, there was no sign of any vicious reaction from anywhere around the world. They knew they'd opened a debate that would rage on for months and years ahead.

The plane bringing Rebecca from LA was due any minute. It would then take them all to their destinations: DC for Gracie and Dalton; Boston for Rydell, Matt and Danny. Father Jerome would be Rydell's guest until they figured out how to reintroduce him into public life—if at all.

Gracie studied Father Jerome as he watched himself on TV.

'No regrets?' she asked him.

He looked at her with warm, smiling eyes. 'None whatsoever. Who knows? Maybe it'll work.'

'You have more faith in human nature than I do, Father,' Rydell commented.

'Do I? You created this.' He pointed a bony finger at Rydell. 'You created something wonderful with the best intentions. Which tells me you also had some faith in mankind doing the right thing, no?'

Rydell smiled. 'Maybe, Father.' He paused, then told him, 'I owe you my life, Father. Anything you want, just name it.'

'I can think of a few places that could use hospitals and orphanages.'

'Just write me up a list,' Rydell told him. 'It'll be my pleasure.'

Gracie gave Father Jerome a soft pat on the shoulder. She looked over at Dalton, who was listening as Danny told him about the technology behind the sign. Then she spotted Matt by the coffee machine and joined him.

'So your Woodward and Bernstein moment's gone up in smoke,' he said.

'Thanks for reminding me,' she groaned.

Something in her eyes told him it wasn't that much of a light-hearted retort. 'You OK?' he asked her.

'I don't know. Pulling off a big scam like this feels a bit condescending. Like we know better. I feel like Jack Nicholson on that stand barking out, "You can't handle the truth."'

'You're way hotter,' he ventured.

It was just the disarming comment she needed. 'I sure as hell hope so.' She beamed a melting smile at him. 'Thanks for noticing. Now, would you do me a favour and find something else for us to talk about?'

He basked in her smile for a moment, then said, 'You like classic cars?'

raymond **khoury**

RD: Where were you born, and what do you remember about the place?

RK: I was born in Beirut, which feels like a long, long time ago in a galaxy far, far away. This was prewar Beirut, with all the wonderful Mediterranean old-world city charms that remain fond memories, and the underlying social problems that, as a child, one is unaware of.

RD: How old were you when you went to America in 1975, after civil war broke out in Lebanon, and did you take easily to life in the US?

RK: I was fourteen when, after a two-week summer holiday in Greece, I started at a New York high school. It wasn't too hard an adjustment, as I'd grown up with an American best friend in Beirut and been immersed in American popular culture—comics, TV, movies—but it was a bit brutal to be yanked out of a tight-knit social circle with tons of family around and to be suddenly alone in a school of strangers.

RD: Was there a catalyst that led you to want to study architecture?

RK: I may not have excelled at physics or chemistry in school, but art was something I could count on to bump up my average. I have been a graphic artist and an illustrator ever since I was barely in my teens, painting the covers for my high-school yearbooks and illustrating children's book for Oxford University Press's Middle East division. Architecture seemed a natural to me, combining art with a more 'serious' career.

RD: Eventually, though, after you'd moved to London in the mid-1980s, you decided to do an MBA and go into banking. Why the move?

RK: It was a bump in the road. There was no work for architects in London; the few I knew were barely scraping by, and I needed to earn a living. Bankers were (and still are, more than ever, it seems) being paid staggering amounts of money for work that didn't seem like rocket science, so I cynically decided that's what I would do. I lasted three years.

RD: Do you consider that it was fate that then led you to screenwriting?

RK: It happened through a chance meeting—someone I barely knew saying I could, and should, write. It was one of those fortuitous moments that totally change your life.

RD: Now that your first novel, *The Last Templar*, has been made into a TV drama, are you pleased with the result?

RK: Not really. I watched the first ten minutes and decided I couldn't watch the rest. It was too different, in feel and content, to what I had written. But that's what happens when you sell film rights—you never know how it's going to turn out.

RD: Do you have plans for many more novels, or will the screenwriting take up most of the time?

RK: Happily, I'm no longer writing screenplays.

RD: Are you now dividing your time between LA and London or do you have a more permanent base in one or other city?

RK: I spend most of my time in London, but I travel a lot, and tend to spend a lot of time in the Greek islands.

RD: What was the initial inspiration behind _The Sign_?

RK: A general frustration with the way religion is still being used to manipulate people for political ends. I'd grown up with, and witnessed, hatred fuelled by religious intolerance and fundamentalism in the Middle East, and now, in 2009, there's no real change. The vast majority of people are desperate for a peaceful, prosperous life, but a handful of psychopaths on all sides keep the conflicts brewing. I started wondering what would happen if some unexplained, miraculous event occurred that could take away the thunder from all the fundamentalist and inflexible zealots and unite the planet under a new, simpler faith. And it grew from there.

RD: What would you change about the world if you could?

RK: I believe that the people of the world are criminally underserved by their leaders. The vast majority are ruled either by psychotic dictators, deluded (often owing to religious beliefs) fantasists, incompetents, egomaniacs, or simply dishonest crooks. In almost every country, the level of scandal and corruption in the governing parties is mind-boggling. So the first thing I would do is to find a way to make politicians actually serve the interests of the electorate and make them accountable. This is why Obama's winning the election was so important, in that he genuinely represents hope and gives the impression of being honest, intelligent, hard-working and well-meaning. We'll see if that turns out to be true.

RD: What traits do you most admire in others?

RK: Honesty, wit, and the ability to be self-deprecating.

RD: And three things that really annoy you?

RK: Selfishness, closed-mindedness—and bad personal hygiene.

RD: Do you have any major ambitions that you'd like to fulfil?

RK: I'd still love to make a movie or two one day; I'd like to go back to architecture, and I'd like to paint. I'd also like to compete in Le Mans, which a friend did this year, but I guess that's not likely to happen. Like Austin Powers said, 'Some things just ain't in the cards, baby.'

Endal

Allen & Sandra Parton

'I looked down at the handsome, clever Labrador who had given me so much, and my chest ached as I watched him lying there, sleepy but trying to keep his eyes open to see if I needed anything.

'Then I realised that the aching feeling was actually *love*. It was immense, overpowering . . . as though Endal had opened a little window in my brain that let me care about people around me again.'

Allen Parton

ALLEN

I opened my eyes. The room was fuzzy and the bright overhead lights were surrounded by blurred haloes. Something hard and uncomfortable was round my neck, digging into me.

'Are you all right, Allen? Glad to see you're with us again.' The voice was cheerful. A woman. I could make out her dark shape by the bed.

'Where am I?' I tried to say, but my throat felt tight and the words came out like a harsh coughing sound.

'You're in Haslar Royal Naval Hospital in Gosport. You had an accident, remember? In the Gulf?'

The Gulf of what? Gulf of Mexico? Gulf of Bothnia? Persian Gulf? Didn't this woman know how many gulfs there were in the world? And then I remembered. I'm in the Navy. I'm a chief petty officer. I've been serving in the Gulf War.

'You flew back from Dubai overnight and got here this morning. You must be tired after the journey.'

I struggled to sit up and the nurse took my arm to help. I grabbed at the plastic collar round my neck.

'Better leave that for now until you've been checked over,' she said.

I wanted to ask when I would be seeing a doctor, but my mind went blank on the word 'doctor'.

'Medical . . .?' I stuttered, then a twitch made my shoulders shudder.

She answered for me: 'A doctor will be round to see you shortly. Do you want to have a wash first?'

I nodded yes, and swung my legs round to put my feet on the floor.

Everything about the way I was moving was odd and unconnected. My body felt as though it belonged to someone else and I was struggling to control it. I leaned on the bedside cabinet to push myself up and noticed there was no sensation in my hand or arm, only a kind of pins and needles.

'The toilet is this way,' the nurse pointed. 'I'd better come with you.'

'No!' I waved her away rudely and forced my left foot to take a step forwards, then followed with the right. I had to think consciously about each step, willing my feet to move. This was very strange.

In the bathroom, I pushed the door shut and leaned against it, breathing heavily with the effort of crossing the room. There was a mirror opposite so I lurched across to peer into it.

I looked more or less the same: a bit tired maybe, but otherwise OK. There was a large bruise on my temple that felt tender when I pressed it. I splashed water on my face, trying to remember what had happened and why I was there. I'd been in an accident in the Gulf, the nurse had said. What kind of accident? Nothing at all came back to me. I must have had a bump on the head. That would explain the bruise.

When I emerged, a doctor came over to watch me walking across the ward. 'That looks like a bit of a struggle,' he said. 'How are you feeling?'

'Strange,' I slurred.

'Can you remember your name?'

Of course I could. Whom did he think he was talking to? 'Chief Petty Officer Parton,' I barked out, the words sounding all mangled and muddled.

'And the name of your ship?'

I opened my mouth to reply and realised I had no idea. It had gone. I shook my head blankly.

'Do you know what age you are?'

I racked my brains. My mind raced back over countries I'd seen, ships I'd sailed on, weapons systems I'd helped to design, but I couldn't think what age I was.

'Missiles,' I said, trying to communicate to him that that was my job.

He nodded, and then guided me to the bed where he began to examine me, taking my blood pressure, shining a torch in my eyes, pricking my arm for blood. It hurt. Why couldn't he have done it on the right side where I seemed to have no feeling?

'What's happened?' I asked eventually.

'We think your brain has had a traumatic injury. There's no damage to the skull. It's all internal.' He made some notes on his chart, then folded his arms. 'I don't think there would be any point operating. We have to wait till the inflammation dies down and we'll see what happens next.'

I was irritated. Just do your job, I thought. And get me back to work. I haven't got time to sit round here for weeks on end. My men need me.

'The staff nurse will give you something for the pain. Take it easy now.' He turned and walked off.

I blinked. Yes, there was pain. My head and neck were aching. I let the nurse help me back onto the bed and swing my feet up for me.

'Lunch is ready,' she said. 'Then your wife's coming to see you later.'

I stared at her blankly. I had a wife? That was news to me.

She frowned. 'You don't remember, do you? Her name's Sandra. You'll know her when you see her. She's been very worried about you.'

I lay back on the pillows trying to trigger my memory. Wife. Wedding. Married. I was married. I could remember that it was a good thing to be married. You were in love, and you looked out for each other. But I had no memories of my wife at all.

And then visiting hour came, and a very attractive woman with dark hair and a curvy figure was hurrying across the room. I peered hard as she came into focus. She was definitely heading towards me. It must be her.

'Allen,' she said. 'Oh my God.' She kissed me and looked into my eyes. 'How are you feeling?'

And I thought she seemed like a nice person, but she was a complete stranger to me. I didn't remember ever seeing her before, never mind marrying her. I had no feelings for her whatsoever. Inside my head there was a vast hazy blankness.

SANDRA

Allen sailed off to the Gulf in April 1991, leaving me at home to look after our two children: Liam, aged six, and Zoe, aged five. It was always hard when he went away but after seven years of marriage I was beginning to get used to it. It goes with the territory when you're a naval wife. Although the fighting was over and Saddam Hussein's troops had been chased out of Kuwait, I was still nervous. Every time I read news stories about random shootings or friendly fire incidents, a knot tightened in my stomach.

I'd been suffering from anxiety and panic attacks since I had a severe case of postnatal depression following Zoe's birth. Some days I found it hard to look after myself, never mind two children, and I struggled to cope with the chores and responsibilities that come with running a house. Allen was my rock, the person who could always calm me down and make everything all right. He'd walk in the front door and cook a nice meal, and whatever I was stressed about, he'd say, 'Don't worry. I'll take care of it. I'll go and get the shopping, I'll pay the bills, I'll pick the children up from school.' He was a calm, capable, very caring kind of man.

Now that Liam was at school and Zoe's difficult baby years were past, I was managing a lot better but I still missed Allen very badly. Silly things, such as the central heating breaking down or one of the kids falling and scraping their knees, could reduce me to a panicky wreck again. He called from the ship when he could, but it was a complicated process.

Then tragedy struck when my sister Valerie died of liver failure on August 12, 1991. For most of her adult life she'd been battling complex health issues, but the end came suddenly and shockingly and I was distraught. She left behind a little boy who was just five.

I contacted the Navy's Family Services and asked if I could speak to Allen urgently. They called the ship and a few hours later he was able to ring me briefly.

'I'm so sorry,' he said, his voice breaking up across the crackle of international airwaves. 'I just wish I could be standing there right now with my arms round you.'

I started crying so much I could hardly speak. 'Please come home, Allen,' I begged. 'Please.'

'I'll put in a request with Family Services. When's the funeral?'

'I don't know yet. Early next week.'

'I'll do my best to get there. I love you,' he said. Then the line was abruptly cut off.

'Love you too,' I sobbed into the vast distance between us.

I'd never needed him more in my life, but the next day I got a call from Family Services to say that he couldn't get leave because it wasn't a member of his family who had died.

I argued, but they had made up their minds, so I just got on with trying to deal with it myself, along with my mum and my two remaining sisters, Marion and Jennifer. There were the funeral arrangements to make, Valerie's little boy to look after, her possessions to deal with; I staggered through each day, barely coping.

The following week, on August 21, I got another phone call from Family Services. I assumed they were ringing to see how I was managing.

'We're calling to tell you that Allen's back in hospital again,' a woman's voice said.

'What do you mean he's *back* in hospital?' I was stunned.

'After his accident,' she said.

My heart started pounding hard. 'What accident?'

I heard an intake of breath. 'Didn't anyone call you? Last week. He was involved in an accident. He's OK, but he's had a bang on the head.'

'*When* last week? Why wasn't I told?'

There was a rustle of paper. 'Last Friday, the sixteenth. I thought you knew. I'm sorry. He was admitted to hospital with concussion but then the ship was sailing and they didn't want to leave him behind so they took him back on board to treat him there. But I suppose his condition has deteriorated a bit so he's been transferred to a hospital again.'

'Where is he? I need to speak to him. Do you have a number I can call?'

'I'll have to get back to you on that. But honestly, don't worry, it doesn't sound serious.' She obviously couldn't wait to get off the phone.

Honestly, don't worry? I got on the line to HMS *Nelson*, the naval base he was attached to, but no one there seemed to know anything. They all just promised they'd get back to me. I paced the house waiting for the phone to ring. Zoe was playing with a jigsaw on the floor and when Liam got in from school they started fighting with each other. Kids always seem to sense when you are anxious, which makes them seek even more attention, which adds to your stress. I was making their tea when I finally got a phone call.

'You'll have to call the British Embassy tomorrow morning and they'll arrange for a call to be put through to your husband's hospital ward.'

When I finally reached the hospital in Dubai, a nurse said she would get Allen. I waited and waited, trying not to think about how much a phone call to the Middle East must cost per minute. I was about to hang up when I suddenly heard breathing down the line.

'Allen, is that you?'

There was a pause. 'Yes, it's me. Who are you?'

'It's me! Sandra.' I guessed it must be a bad line at his end. 'How are you? What's happened?'

'Well, I haven't got any clothes,' he said.

'What do you mean?' Was this a joke?

'I haven't got anything to wear.' His voice sounded panicky.

I frowned. 'You must be wearing something just now. Won't that do?' In the Navy they often lived in the same set of clothing for weeks on end and just learned to live with the smell of themselves and each other. Besides, Allen wasn't the kind of person to bother about having a clean set of clothes. If he only had one pair of underpants for a week, he'd joked to me, he'd wear them right way round, wrong way round, back to front, upside-down, and make do.

'I've got no clothes,' he repeated.

I was starting to get alarmed. 'Allen, what's happened? Why are you in hospital?'

'I don't know why I'm here. I can't remember.'

I asked more questions but couldn't get anything out of him. He just kept returning to his anxiety about his clothes.

'I have to go, darling,' I said at last. 'I'll ring you back tomorrow, OK?'

'Right, bye!' he said and the line went dead.

This was very strange behaviour, and not like him at all. He hadn't asked about Valerie's funeral or how I was coping or mentioned the kids. I started phoning around everyone I could think of to find out what had happened, but I just kept hitting blank walls.

The next day I called the hospital again, hoping to get more sense out of Allen, but someone told me that he'd been moved. Eventually I discovered from the British Embassy that he was in a hotel room in Dubai. It was hours before I could get through to him, and we had another brief, bizarre phone call in which he sounded vague yet on edge.

'Someone's stolen my stuff,' he said.

'I'm sure they haven't. It'll be on the ship waiting for you.'

'It's gone,' he said, slurring a bit, which I presumed must be a side effect of the painkillers he was taking. He still didn't seem to have a clue how he had been injured. It was most peculiar.

'Should I fly out to see him?' I asked the woman at Family Services. 'I could find someone to look after the children for a few days.'

'There's no point in you going out because I think they are planning to medevac him home.'

'When will that be?'

'We don't know yet.'

I had a conversation with an officer at the base, who said something I found very strange. 'We've got no idea what he was doing off the ship that night. He and a friend seem to have gone ashore without permission and been involved in a car accident.'

'But how is that possible?' I asked. 'How did they get off the ship? Where would they have got a car from?'

'We don't know. We're running an investigation and we'll find out more in due course.'

I didn't believe for one second that Allen had gone AWOL. I knew it would have been totally out of character for my ambitious, responsible husband. There had to be more to it than that.

During the next two weeks, I only had a few more worrying phone calls with Allen, but dozens of frustrating calls with the naval authorities, without getting to the bottom of what was going on. I tried to keep myself busy, doing endless housework, cooking, sewing, covering school notebooks with coloured paper—anything to keep my mind occupied. I couldn't bear silence and stillness because then the anxiety fluttered in like a big black moth. If they were going to medevac him home that meant it must be serious.

On September 7 the call came to say that his plane had taken off and on arrival in the UK he would be admitted to Haslar, the military hospital in Gosport, where I could go in to see him the following day.

I tossed and turned, wide awake all night long, and my heart was in my mouth as I drove to the hospital. I couldn't wait. I was as nervous as a teenage girl on a first date. I found the ward and picked him out straight away, sitting up on top of his bed and wearing a neck brace. He saw me at the same time and watched as I walked across the room, but he didn't smile at me or wave hello.

'How are you?' I asked, and kissed him on the lips. There was a big bump on his temple that looked more recent than three weeks old. 'How did you get that bump?'

'Fell,' he said, and the word was oddly slurred.

'When did you fall?'

He thought about this and shrugged.

'How are you feeling?'

'Funny,' he said, and I could hear it was an effort to get the word out. He was almost barking, forcing his throat to emit sound. Then he twitched compulsively, his right shoulder jerking and his face contorting.

I looked into his eyes but could see no spark of my husband, my rock, the man who always looked after me. He looked blank. There was something seriously wrong.

I chatted for a bit then went to find a doctor. 'What's wrong with my husband?' I demanded. 'I'm a nurse and I'd appreciate it if you'd tell me straight.'

'We don't know exactly,' he said. 'There's obviously been some trauma to the brain and we're keeping him under observation, and running tests.'

'How did he get that bruise on his temple?'

'I'm told he fell the day before yesterday. Have you seen him walking yet?' I shook my head.

'He's having significant problems controlling his legs. We'll just have to keep an eye on it all. Meanwhile, I see no reason why you can't take him home today, for the weekend. With your nursing background, you should be able to care for him.'

'Are you sure?' I asked, feeling hopeful. Surely he couldn't be too bad if they were letting him out?

'Why not? Just bring him back on Monday morning and he can see a consultant then. Have a nice family weekend together.'

The doctor smiled and I felt reassured. Everything was going to be all right. They wouldn't let him home otherwise, would they? I rang home, and we set off.

On the way back to the house, I drove slowly and cautiously. I did all the talking, telling Allen about Valerie's funeral and the children and everything that had been happening, but I got no response at all.

As we pulled into our street, I said, 'The kids are really excited about seeing you. They're at Julie's but I said I'd go and get them as soon as we arrived.' Julie was my wonderful next-door neighbour who had four kids of her own but was always happy to look after my two as well.

We pulled into the driveway and I walked into the house behind Allen, noticing that he had an odd, rolling gait. He picked his right foot up high and flopped it down then pulled the other one through.

Allen plonked himself down on the sofa and sat looking around him.

'Do you want something to drink?' I asked.

'Yeah.'

'Do you want tea or coffee?'

He screwed up his face, unable to think. 'The stuff that comes in bags,' he slurred.

Tea, then.

At that moment there was a burst of squealing and running feet and the children erupted into the house.

'Daddy!' they shrieked, over the moon to see him. Zoe leaped onto his knee and Liam snuggled onto the sofa beside him.

'Get off me!' he snapped loudly as he pushed Zoe away. The look of bewilderment on her little face was heartbreaking.

'Kids, Daddy's not feeling very well. Don't climb all over him.'

'I've got a new train, Daddy,' Liam said excitedly. They used to play together with his Playmobil train set.

'And I've started ballet,' Zoe joined in, not wanting to be left out. 'And I've got a new dolly as well.'

'Go away!' Allen snarled, putting his hands over his ears.

They were devastated. Whenever Allen had come back from postings in the past, he'd burst in the door bringing them presents, swinging them in the air and tickling them. They just didn't have a clue what had happened.

'Daddy's got a bad headache,' I said gently. 'You know what it's like when your head hurts. Just leave him in peace for a little while and maybe he'll play later.'

I took them back to Julie's, just telling her briefly that Allen wasn't very well. When I returned, he was examining two tubes of cream he'd been given on prescription. He had a nasty rash on his feet and another one on his groin and they'd given him a different cream for each rash, but he couldn't remember which was which. There was nothing written on the boxes and he was very anxious about it.

'Which cream is which?' he mumbled. 'I don't know.'

The old Allen would have made a joke out of it. He'd have said, 'I'll start by putting them on my feet because if my feet fall off that will be fine, but I don't want the other bits to fall off.'

But he was incapable of joking now.

'I'll go to the pharmacy and ask,' I offered. 'I'll just get your tea first.'

Two minutes later, as if I hadn't spoken, Allen asked, 'What about this cream for my feet? What am I going to do?' That weekend Allen asked me about his creams at least twenty times a day and he never seemed to hear the answers I gave. It was like being with an old person who had Alzheimer's.

I showed him the photos from a holiday we'd had in Singapore and Penang just a couple of months earlier, but there was no spark of recognition. He just looked at each one and handed it back to me without comment.

He didn't seem to remember where anything was in the house either. I had to show him where his clothes were kept, where his shaving stuff was and how to turn on the shower. My sense of alarm grew by the minute.

I couldn't wait to get him back to Haslar on the Monday morning so that they could start treating him. Despite all my nursing training, I felt utterly helpless. I had no idea what I could do to help him. Whatever it took, I would do it—but I didn't have a clue where to start.

ALLEN

Over the days and weeks after the accident, I realised that I had lost a huge chunk of my memory. In particular, my entire childhood was a blank, so I asked Sandra to tell me what she knew about it.

She said that when I was a kid I lived in a council house in Haslemere, Surrey, with my mum and my sister Suzanne. Mum and Dad split up when I was two years old and we lost contact with Dad, which must have been really tough for Mum. In my teens, I got a boarding-school place paid for by the council and that helped to ease the burden.

My gran lived in London where she used to work for Sir Samuel Hood, the sixth Viscount Hood, who came from a family long associated with the Navy. At Christmas time, Lord Hood used to let us come up to London and stay with my gran in his house in Eaton Square while he and his family were out at their estate in the country. There were huge oil paintings on the walls, of battleships at Trafalgar and great storms at sea. I used to love just standing in front of them staring and pretending I was on deck, clinging to the rails as huge waves lashed the sides. I'm sure it was there that I formed my ambition to join the Navy.

Sir Samuel heard about my plans and offered to send me to Officers' College, but I decided I would rather work my way up from the bottom. So I signed up when I was just sixteen years old, did my basic training, and then I went to HMS *Collingwood* naval school at Fareham, where I was given technical training in electronics, radar systems and mechanics.

I joined my first ship, HMS *Hermione*, at Portland in Dorset and we soon set off on a year's cruise round the world, following the kind of itinerary you'd pay tens of thousands of pounds for as a tourist. The most vivid early memories I have now are from this tour of duty; there are clear pictures in my mind of many of the places we visited. We went down past Gibraltar, through the Panama Canal, up to San Diego and Vancouver, then across to the Far East, Singapore, and right round the globe. Whenever we docked somewhere, I'd catch a train and go exploring instead of sitting in the nearest pub getting hammered, like some of my shipmates.

I was a bit of a swot, always putting myself up for exams, and before I left HMS *Hermione* I'd achieved my first promotion. Gradually, I was put in charge of other men, and I think I was pretty fair as a boss.

That was all before I met Sandra. I have no recollection of how we met, what we did on our first date, or when I asked her to marry me—none of that stuff remains. I know what she's told me but I have no first-hand memories at all, which is very distressing for her and just plain weird for me.

I know that soon after we were married, in 1983, I was posted up to Rosyth in Scotland. We had married quarters that looked out over the Forth Road Bridge and the view was amazing. My job was to maintain the minesweepers and repair any other ships that came in with problems. We were there for a year, I think, and then we were transferred down to Portsmouth where I worked on a guided-missile destroyer.

The kids were born in these years, first Liam in 1985 and then Zoe in '86. After Portsmouth, I was moved to Bath, where I was working for the Director of Engineering Support, basically designing new weaponry systems. I was the only non-commissioned officer there. I'd passed the exams and so forth but I hadn't actually gone to Dartmouth to get my commission, and I was aware that I was being watched by all the other officers to see whether I fitted in. I had to wear a jacket and tie instead of running around with the lads. But I was ready for it. Being an officer would mean that I could better provide for my family.

After Saddam Hussein invaded Kuwait, I volunteered for the Gulf straight away. It was never going to be a naval battle, so it was more about making sure supplies were getting through to our troops, intercepting any shipments of arms to the Iraqis, that kind of thing.

On arrival, we found we weren't really needed, so we sailed on to Singapore and Malaysia. Sandra told me she came out and joined me there. That was the last time she saw the 'old me'. I've no memory of ever being in Malaysia or the Gulf. It's all gone.

When I woke up in Haslar in September 1991, I was determined to get straight back to work. I just needed the doctors to fix me up. I hadn't had an operation, there weren't any scars or blood and gore, I hadn't broken my back or my neck, so why was I having such trouble walking?

'Your brain is not sending signals to your legs,' I was told. 'That's why they don't respond effectively. There's nothing actually wrong with them.'

It was the same with my eyes. There was nothing the matter with them, but because my brain wasn't working properly it wasn't picking up signals from the optic nerve as efficiently as it should have been. The squint I'd had as a young child appeared to have come back. And I had no feeling in my right arm and the right side of my body, although I seemed to be able to move them; there were intermittent pins and needles but I couldn't feel my hand if I dug a nail into it.

'You experienced a huge traumatic internal brain injury when your spine was forced up into the brain cavity,' the doctors told me. 'There's no treatment we can give you. We just have to wait and see.'

I was so determined to astonish them all with my miraculous powers of regeneration that I didn't listen to anyone who warned me it might not be possible to get back the life I'd had before. They didn't know me. They didn't have a clue what I was capable of. They were just plain wrong.

IT WAS A HUGE SHOCK the first time Sandra took me home for the weekend after the accident. I'd overheard the medical staff saying that she was a nurse but I was still anxious she wouldn't know how to look after me properly. What if I needed help with things like undressing myself? Would this woman do it? Was she really my wife?

Then, in the car, she mentioned that we had children, and that was most peculiar. I didn't feel like a person who had children. I had no memory of them, no idea of their names or what ages they were.

When we got back to the house, I didn't remember any of it, but there were photos of Sandra, the children and me all over the walls so I knew I was in the right place. When would my memory come back?

Then the door opened and two children burst in shouting and squealing. I couldn't bear the noise they made. I didn't feel as though I was their father. There was no bond there; they were strangers.

I found that I couldn't remember words. I could bark out an order—such as 'Coffee!'—but I certainly couldn't speak in sentences, or remember any of the niceties such as 'please' or 'thank you'.

That first weekend, Sandra was incredibly patient. She tried to jog my memory by showing me photos from a holiday we'd had. I recognised myself in the pictures and I could tell that we looked happy in them, but they brought back no emotions.

A doctor had explained to me that after it's been damaged, the brain favours some types of memories over others. The 'favoured areas' are different for everyone. Some might keep their love of music, or sporting prowess, or the ability to do complex mathematical calculations. As for me, I think I retained a lot of my technical knowledge, because I could remember precise details about the weapons systems I'd worked on in my various postings for the Navy, but I'd lost all my memories of the people in my life.

The problem was that memories are the basis for emotions, and love is based on shared history. Because I couldn't remember any of our history I no longer felt any 'love' for Sandra and the kids. I knew nothing about the woman and the two children who were trying to get through to me. It was as though I was visiting strangers, and I didn't feel well enough to be polite or friendly to them.

After being taken back to Haslar, I was transferred to Headley Court rehabilitation centre near Epsom in Surrey for assessment. And that's where I stayed on and off for the next year, just coming back to visit Sandra and the children at weekends.

Originally an Elizabethan farmhouse, Headley Court was expanded into a huge mansion in the early twentieth century. During the Second World War, Canadian forces were based there; after the war, money was raised to convert it into a forces rehab centre. They have doctors, nurses, physiotherapists, occupational therapists, speech and language therapists, a cognitive therapist, and several hydrotherapy pools and gymnasiums, as well as workshops where they make artificial limbs.

Right! I thought when they showed me round. Let's get started.

AN ORDERLY HANDED ME a newspaper. 'Here you go, Allen,' he said brightly. 'Just have a read through and pick out a story that interests you. Any little nugget will do. When I ask you later, you have to try to remember what it was you picked out. OK?'

I grunted and opened the newspaper: the *Sun*. Every morning in Headley Court they brought you a newspaper and asked you to memorise a single item. The *Sun* had little square boxes of two-line stories: simple things, like amazing animal feats, or vicars who streak through their churchyards. I picked one of these and repeated and repeated it in my head, over and over again.

The other patients were sitting round the day room scanning their own papers but I tried not to look at them, focusing hard on remembering my news item. I ignored the other voices and the general chatter about the day's news, and I tried not to look at anyone else.

Then the orderly turned to me and asked, 'What was your story today, Allen?'

I opened my mouth—and it was gone. Just a blank space where the words had been minutes before.

I often thought that if you had to have a brain injury, it would be better to have a more catastrophic one so that you no longer retained any awareness of your state. The worst thing was that I knew I wasn't stupid. I had flashes of complete memories, but they were like tiny islands in a vast dark sea. I couldn't put them in order or get them to join up. I knew that I used to have a lot of people working under me, and that thousands of colleagues relied on my expertise every time they went to sea. But now I couldn't remember one paltry item in a newspaper for half an hour. It drove me nuts.

Then the orderlies handed out boxes of Lego along with pictures of things we were to try to build. I peered at the picture of a Lego ship I'd been given, trying to work out how to make a mast, and the irony made me feel very bitter. From someone who was in charge of high-tech weaponry, I was now back in my second childhood, dependent on carers and struggling with the most basic tasks.

'Bollocks!' I muttered as part of the prow broke off and fell to the floor beyond my reach. I swore a lot, and that was the word that seemed to come out most often.

I saw a speech therapist most days because my words were coming out like a bark or a harsh cough, and I had the most terrible stutter that was painful to listen to. We had to go back to basics and retrain my voice box, tongue and lips with a laborious series of exercises so that I could get words out clearly—if I could remember them, that was. I still forgot lots of words, and I still resorted to snapping 'Bollocks!' in my frustration, but the speech therapy started to help, and that was a positive step.

The physiotherapists worked out a programme for me to try to deal with the spasms that caused me to twitch and flinch so frequently. I'd lost a lot of weight during the weeks of bed rest and my muscle tone was poor but I threw myself into a compulsive exercise routine. I found that I could swim using my upper body strength, and I could lift weights and raise myself up on the climbing wall.

Sometimes we were taken to the theatre, but I had no patience with anything that didn't contribute directly to me being cured. Sod Shakespeare, I thought. Just make me well and get me back to work, and hurry up about it!

SANDRA

Allen and I met in November 1982 in a nightclub in Haslemere, Surrey. I was twenty-three years old and living near there in a village called Clanfield, where I was working as a live-in nanny for the children of a surgeon at the hospital where I'd trained as a nurse.

I liked nursing, and knew I wanted to end up working in some kind of caring profession, but I'd recently been posted on a couple of difficult wards, including a unit for people with severe burns, which had been very traumatic and upsetting. I had decided to take a bit of time out from nursing to decide what to do with my future, and the nanny job was ideal. I got on well with the surgeon's wife, and when I mentioned to her that I was finding it hard to meet new people in the area, she arranged for me to go to the nightclub and be introduced to some of the locals by the club owner, who was a friend of hers.

'I need to get you up to that naval base and meeting some of those young officers,' she said, prophetically.

That night, I tried on lots of different outfits and spent ages doing my hair and make-up. It seemed like a long time since I'd made the effort, and the surgeon's wife sat and chatted to me as I got ready. I was very apprehensive about turning up at a club on my own, even though she said the doorman would look after me when I arrived. I'd led quite a sheltered upbringing and wasn't really a clubbing type. The whole thought of it made me feel very awkward.

My shyness wasn't helped by the fact that when I arrived the doorman who was supposed to be looking after me wasn't there, but I hadn't been in the club long before a scruffy-looking guy in ripped jeans and a tatty old duffel coat came up to me, somewhat the worse for wear.

'You've got beautiful eyes,' he said. 'Will you marry me? I'm pregnant, and I need you to marry me or I'll get into trouble with my mum.'

I thought it was a great opening line, and liked his handsome boyish looks and the twinkle in his eye. But when he kept drinking and became incoherent, scarcely able to stand up, I made my excuses and walked away. In the next week I found myself thinking about him and wondering if I'd see him again. Despite the alcohol, he definitely had charm.

When I went back to the club the following week, hoping to see him, I was delighted when he came bounding over as soon as I walked in.

'I'm sorry if I said anything rude last week. I hope I wasn't too offensive.'

'I'm surprised you even remember meeting me,' I commented.

'How could I forget that I was talking to the most beautiful girl in the room?' he said, and I blushed.

WE GOT MARRIED in November 1983 but it was December before we moved into our first marital home together in Rosyth. I found a job working at a local hospital. Around June 1984, they wanted to give me a routine chest X-ray at work and asked if there was any chance I could be pregnant. I had come off the pill and my periods were a bit erratic so I didn't think there was, but they decided to run a pregnancy test to be on the safe side and, to my complete astonishment, it was positive.

I couldn't get through to Allen on the phone to tell him, so I went to Mothercare and bought a tiny babygro and when he walked in the door that evening I just handed it to him and said, 'Guess what?'

Baby Liam was born on Valentine's Day 1985. Allen was fantastic in those early weeks. I fed the baby and he did everything else: nappy changing, winding, housework, meals for us, laundry, shopping. He was always good around the house, and he obviously doted on Liam as well.

Liam was only a few months old when I discovered I was pregnant again. It was totally unplanned and a huge shock, if I'm honest. I was still learning how to cope with one baby and couldn't imagine doing so with two.

While Liam had been a lovely lazy baby, who slept through the night at five days old, took his feeds well and was happy to have a nap whenever you put him in his cot, Zoe was more difficult. She flatly refused to feed from me after about two weeks. She wailed endlessly and nothing seemed to calm her.

Meanwhile I had Liam crawling round my ankles, having to be watched constantly in case he tried to stick his fingers in an electric socket or bashed his head. Allen was away on a long trip right through this period and I had no idea when he would be back. Suddenly it all got too much.

My doctor diagnosed me as having severe postnatal depression, and Zoe was placed in foster care to give me a chance to get back on my feet. The foster family lived nearby so I could go round and visit Zoe whenever I wanted. She stayed there for five or six weeks, and after she came back to live with me again they continued to look after her one day a week to give me a break. I genuinely don't know how I could have got through that period without their help.

Allen came back to work on shore when Zoe was a year old, but he was based in Bath from Monday to Friday and we only saw him at weekends. With that job he was promoted to chief petty officer, and in 1987 we moved to a nicer house in a place called Emsworth, between Chichester and Portsmouth. Once the kids were at nursery school I went to work part-time in a nursing home on Hayling Island, and I really enjoyed it there.

When Allen announced in 1990 that he'd volunteered for the Gulf War, we didn't discuss the possibility of him being killed or injured but I suppose it was in the back of our minds. I resigned from my job and during the last weeks before he left we spent a lot of time with the kids. They'd just got bikes so we taught them how to ride them. We had day trips to London and a holiday in Center Parcs and we had loads of fun. I liked creating a close-knit unit, with our own family jokes and traditions and games. I've got so many pictures in my head of us all smiling and messing about in those last weeks before Allen set off, and they're very precious.

Allen sailed for the Gulf in April, but in early July I was invited to go and join him for a holiday in Singapore and Penang. I was reluctant at first because I'd never left the children for any length of time before, but my sister Marion offered to have them. I'm so glad I did have that last, very special time in the sun with Allen, just the two of us.

We talked about the future while we were in Malaysia. Basically, we decided that I would continue to move around following Allen's postings until the children were at secondary school, at which point I would stay in one place with them so their education didn't suffer. Allen would serve his contractual twenty-two years with the Navy; then we would decide where we wanted to live and buy our dream home there. We'd only be in our forties and we could start a whole new life doing whatever we wanted.

And then the news of his accident filtered through and everything changed overnight.

THE EXTENT OF ALLEN'S brain damage sank in gradually over weeks and months, rather than straight away. When he came home from Headley Court for weekends, I watched him like a hawk, straining to find any glimpses of the old Allen and the relationship we used to have, hoping and praying that any day now he would snap out of it and get back to normal.

'Do you want to watch TV?' I'd ask. 'That programme you like is on.'

'OK.' He'd shrug, and we'd sit down to watch it together, but when I glanced at his face it would be blank and I could tell he wasn't following it at all. He didn't laugh at funny moments, or react in any way to what was happening on the screen.

One day I pointed to our wedding photograph on the wall.

'You remember our wedding day, don't you? It was Guy Fawkes Night. Your friend Kevin was best man.'

Allen shook his head. 'Don't remember.'

It was then that I finally realised that he didn't remember me at all from before the accident. I burst out crying, covered my face and ran upstairs.

It made me feel grief-stricken and terribly lonely. I'd lost Allen's love and I didn't know when—or if—I would ever get it back again. I was burdened with someone with whom I couldn't have a conversation, who needed me to be a nurse and carer, and had nothing to offer in return.

ALLEN ARRIVED ON FRIDAY EVENINGS, sat down on a chair in the corner and hardly moved until it was time to go back on the Sunday. I tried to chat to him about what had happened during the week, about the news on TV, about the children, but I got monosyllabic responses. He only spoke when he wanted something from me: food or drink, or for the children to stop being so noisy.

After a while the children tended to give him a wide berth in case he shouted at them, or tried to grab them for a hug and squeezed too hard, misjudging his own strength.

About two months after the accident, I found out that Allen's salary had been stopped. I rang *Collingwood* naval base to request his pay slips and found that he had only been paid for the first two weeks of August. His income had been stopped on August 16, the day he was injured, because when he went into hospital he wasn't attached to a ship or a base so he wasn't clocked as being at work. I ranted and raved to the authorities at *Collingwood* until eventually, a couple of months after the accident, they sorted out the problems and got him back on the payroll.

I didn't feel I was coping at all. I was frightened and vulnerable but I was angry as well and I suppose that drove me. First of all I was determined to find out exactly what had happened to Allen and see if there would be any kind of compensation for the injuries he'd suffered, to help us pay for his care in the future. I consulted a lawyer, who wrote to the captain of Allen's ship.

A reply came on November 1, and it was only then that I found out how the accident had happened. Ex-pats who lived in the countries bordering the Gulf liked to entertain service personnel when they pulled into port. I remember Allen mentioning this before. He'd said that none of them was especially keen on those evenings, when conversation could be an effort, but it was considered good PR to go along. On August 16, his ship was moored in Muscat in the Gulf of Oman. Some ex-pats issued an invitation for two men to come to dinner and Allen ended up being press-ganged into it, along with another chief petty officer.

The ex-pats picked them up from the ship in a four-wheel drive. The captain didn't know precisely what happened, but it seems that there was an accident, the car overturned and Allen's head slammed at high speed into the roof. He said that after the accident the driver had made every effort to make sure Allen was all right and had taken him back to the ship. However, he said, no one could recall the names or address of the ex-pats he had been visiting, so we couldn't contact them to try to claim compensation through their insurance company.

Allen was taken to hospital in Muscat but X-rays didn't show any damage to his skull or spine so they released him back to the ship. They sailed from Muscat but his condition deteriorated. When the ship pulled into Dubai he was admitted to hospital there, then he was placed in a hotel room under the care of the British Embassy for a week. He was brought back on board ship on August 31, and on September 7, three weeks after the accident, they arranged to medevac him back to the UK.

My lawyer concluded that there would be a lot of obstacles to surmount if we wanted to take legal action for compensation. In February 1992, I got another letter from the captain suggesting that it could be damaging to the Navy's relations with the ex-pat communities in the Gulf if I continued to pursue a claim. I knew I couldn't take on the might of the Royal Navy. If they weren't going to help me to track down the driver, we had to accept the fact that Allen wasn't going to get any compensation for his injuries.

I cried a lot in those early days. I felt like a widow with two young children to bring up, yet every weekend I had the additional responsibility of caring for a hostile, sullen, incapacitated man who inhabited my husband's body. I tried my best to stay positive when he was around and not to engage in arguments, but I could sense his frustration mounting. He was angry a lot of the time because of his lapses of memory, and he got angry with me because there was no one else he could take it out on.

His sense of humour had disappeared, and his illness made him very selfish. The man I'd married was generous and considerate. Now Allen seemed to have lost any ability to think about how his actions might affect me or the kids. This man was like an irritable stranger to us.

It was a very sad and difficult time: I missed the old Allen so badly that it hurt physically. But he'd looked after me when I was struggling to cope with my second pregnancy, and now it was my turn to be there for him.

ALLEN

I had started to become paranoid and accused Sandra of snooping on me and telling tales. I wondered if they were bugging me. I decided that I couldn't trust anyone; they were all against me, all trying to stop me getting back to work for their own ulterior motives.

I must have conveyed this paranoia to the doctor, because he said to me one day, 'I know you think people are spying on you and discussing you behind your back, but you should be aware that it is a common symptom of brain injury to experience paranoid thoughts. I'm going to give you an extra pill to put a stop to this because it can't be very pleasant for you. You have to believe that we are all here to support you, Allen. We all want the same thing, and that's for you to get as well as you can possibly be.'

I didn't trust him. I thought he was trying to brainwash me and he would report the details of any conversations we had to my superiors in the Navy, so I kept quiet. I also started hiding my pills and not taking them, if I could get away with it. I didn't want them to drug me up. I needed to think clearly.

I didn't realise it at the time, but I was slipping further and further into deep depression. Then, in March 1992, I suffered a major collapse and woke up in the Atkinson Morley Hospital in London with a drip in my arm and a load of monitors ticking away all round me and I thought: What the hell?

When a doctor came, he explained to me that they didn't know exactly what had happened but they were running tests. I couldn't follow what he was saying, but when I tried to get out of bed I realised my legs weren't working any more. I used to be able to make them do roughly what I wanted with a huge effort of will, but now that had gone.

I kept rolling myself out of bed and trying to force my legs to take my weight, but I'd end up a crumpled heap on the floor. More than once I broke down in tears of sheer frustration. It was so bloody unfair. Why me? Why should this have happened when I'd been going to a stupid ex-pat's dinner I hadn't even wanted to go to? I wanted to shout at the top of my lungs in my rage at the universe.

A physiotherapist came to visit me, bringing a wheelchair. She was just a young girl, full of false cheerfulness.

'Hi there! I've come to show you how to use a chair.'

'I don't want a chair! Teach me to walk again, not to be a cripple!' I snapped. 'You've got the wrong man. I refuse to be disabled. I will not use a wheelchair! Got it?'

SOMEONE SUGGESTED that I be given a job at HMS *Collingwood* for a while on a trial basis to see how I coped. At last! I thought. A chance to prove I can still do the job.

I would live at home with Sandra and the kids, and I would be picked up in a minibus every morning. It would be my responsibility to check the car passes of everyone coming on and off the base, as well as doing some other bits and pieces of copying and admin. I could use the gym and facilities at *Collingwood* and have lunch there, then go back home in the evening.

Fantastic! I started my new job, and never was there a more fastidious car-pass checker. I did everything by the rule book. Normally if someone had lost their car pass, they would just come and ask for another one to be issued, but I filled out all the proper paperwork. I suppose that didn't make me very popular with some, but the bosses were delighted. Another of my jobs was copying out instructions on special forms, and I was very slow but I was painstaking. I worked hard at my writing because obviously I had to get back to normal before I could go back to my old job.

There was an Olympic-sized swimming pool there, where I used to go just about every day. I liked swimming because it was good for building upper body strength. I'd given in and was using a wheelchair whenever I had to travel any distance at all, because it was impossible to drag myself round by the arms all the time. In the water I floated easily and could pretend for a few moments that I still had the use of my legs. The difference between me and an able-bodied man wasn't quite so obvious.

I had regular appointments with a psychologist at *Collingwood*, who tried to help me to improve my social graces and think about how others might be feeling. I still used to bark out my words and offend people without having any awareness that I had insulted them, and then I'd be puzzled when they stopped chatting to me.

And I couldn't seem to understand other people's emotions. When Sandra burst into tears, it went right over my head. The psychologist taught me just to put my arm around her, even if I didn't know why she was crying.

I'd only been working at *Collingwood* for four months when they decided I had to go back to Headley Court for a month's reassessment. I argued against it—I'd had enough doctors and hospitals to last me a life-time—but their minds were made up.

I think the staff at Headley Court were a bit shocked at the physical and mental decline I'd experienced since they'd last seen me, and that was very depressing. Also, they seemed to be taking a psychiatric rather than a neurological view and, in my opinion, they were barking up the wrong tree.

'There's nothing wrong with my mind,' I kept repeating every time they harped on about depression and anger. 'It's my body that needs fixing.'

I just wanted to get back to my job at *Collingwood*, but instead they decided to send me somewhere else—to a psychiatric unit at RAF Hospital Wroughton near Swindon. By that stage I had reached rock bottom.

I felt as though I was in a huge pit of despair and it was getting deeper and darker. It made me think of films where you see someone stepping into quicksand and the more they struggle, the deeper they sink. I was ready to give up the struggle because I could sense it wasn't getting me anywhere.

I was still stashing away any pills I didn't want to take in a drawer in my bedside cabinet. I can't remember anything except that one night, when everyone else on the ward was asleep, I quietly slid my drawer open and began swallowing the paracetamol they'd been giving me, one by one, washing them down with water. I took all the pills I had, and then I lay back on my pillows and closed my eyes, waiting to die.

SANDRA

Some Navy people were fantastically helpful, and one of these was my family support worker, Isabel. She'd been an absolute rock ever since Allen was first flown home from the Gulf. When I saw her car pull up outside the house one morning while Allen was in hospital in Swindon, I thought maybe she had some news for me about my claims for more money. But it wasn't that.

'I'm afraid I've got some bad news for you, Sandra. I don't know how to tell you this, but Allen took an overdose last night.'

I opened my mouth to say something but tears started to come instead. I was so shocked. Although I knew Allen had been very depressed, I'd never thought he was the type to commit suicide. It was totally out of character for him—or at least it would have been for the old Allen, the one I had married.

They kept him at Wroughton for just over a month then discharged him and he went back to the job at *Collingwood*, but there was a continuing pro- gramme of assessment and investigations he had to go through. And then, just when it seemed things couldn't get any worse, I picked up the post in the morning to find some eviction papers. The Navy wanted us out of our house.

Family Services told me that after Allen was discharged from Headley Court he was no longer attached to a naval base and so was not entitled to married quarters any more. If I had fought hard, I might have got the eviction order overturned, but there was a part of me that was beginning to realise Allen didn't have a future in the Navy.

I found out about a charity called Housing 21, an offshoot of the British Legion that specialises in housing ex-service personnel. They told us that it could take a long time before they found something in either of the areas I'd specified we would like to live—near my mum, who lived in Salisbury, or near Allen's mum in Haslemere—but as it happened we were offered a house within two weeks.

It was perfect, on a new estate in Clanfield, Hampshire, the village where I had been living when I first met Allen. Housing 21 would buy it and rent it back to us at an affordable rate. It was a small but pretty three-bedroom end-of-terrace house that was still being built, and after I saw it I said, 'Yes, please,' straight away. In April 1993, we moved to Clanfield as a family.

And then, when we'd only been there a month, I had two family tragedies, one after the other. My father died suddenly of a massive heart attack, and then my sister gave birth to a premature baby at thirty-two weeks. Little Alice, as she was called, lived for less than twenty-four hours.

I asked Allen if he would come to Alice's funeral with me and he said no, he didn't want to. I didn't push him, but I felt very hurt and unsupported.

Shortly after that, we were at a case conference to talk about Allen and in the middle of it he complained that it was 'all doom and gloom at home'.

I didn't say anything at the time but as soon as we got back to the house I really let him have it for the first time since he'd been injured. 'How can you be so bloody selfish?' I ranted. 'My dad's just died, my sister's baby's died, and you're complaining about doom and gloom?'

And I yelled at him for being so selfish as to think he could just take an overdose and walk away from us all like that. 'What did you think you were doing? How dare you try to leave us? I know things are hard for you, but did you think for one minute about how you committing suicide would affect me and the kids? Did you? Don't you think you have some kind of responsibility towards us? Or is it just all about you, you, you?'

I was utterly at the end of my tether and I let rip with everything that was on my mind, then I threw my wedding ring at him and stormed out of the house, slamming the door behind me.

I drove to my friend Judy's house and sat with a cup of tea at her kitchen table, telling her all about it.

She listened, and when I'd finished she asked, 'Where is he now?'

'He's back at the house . . .' I replied. Then I started to panic. I shouldn't have left him alone when he was already psychologically fragile. What if he did something silly? I asked Judy to phone and see if he was still there, but there was no answer.

Seriously alarmed now, Judy and I drove back at full speed. We let ourselves into the house and searched it from top to bottom, including the garage. Every time I opened a door, my heart was pounding; I was terrified that Allen would be lying inside, collapsed on the floor. But he wasn't there. I noticed he had picked up my wedding ring and put it on the side. But where was he?

Not long after, the phone rang. It was *Collingwood* saying that Allen had admitted himself to the sick bay. I asked if I could speak to him and when he came on the line, I said, 'Why did you leave?'

'Because I'm stuck with a woman I don't want to be with,' he replied. 'An angry woman whom I don't know and don't love.'

It was a complete slap on the face. I went to bed that night wondering if I should take the children and leave Allen. Where would I go? What would we live on? What would happen to him? But when I woke up the next morning I knew I couldn't do it. Maybe it was because of the love I'd had for the man he had once been. Maybe it was for the sake of the children.

IN NOVEMBER 1993 Allen was discharged from the Navy as no longer fit for active duty, and I was given the forms to apply for a war pension. I had to compile medical reports and service reports and all sorts of pieces of paperwork. I sent it all off and waited a few weeks. The request was refused on the grounds that what Allen was doing at the time he was injured—going for dinner with ex-pats—wasn't considered 'active duty'. I burst into tears. They tried to make out that it was his time off and that he was at leisure when it happened. How were we expected to live?

I suppose I was becoming quite good at battling authority, one way or another. It's not in my basic nature but when you have to do something to protect your family you just find the strength somehow. Once again I sought legal advice. I discovered that war pensions are notoriously difficult to procure. It took months before they finally accepted that when service personnel are away from home on a tour of duty, they are officially considered to be on active duty twenty-four hours a day. It was a huge relief to get it sorted out. We also received a lump sum payment from the Navy, known as gratuities, based on the number of years of Allen's service. I decided to spend some of this on a family holiday, and we went to Disney World in Florida. Everything on the trip went reasonably well.

Once we were home, however, the holiday mood quickly evaporated and Allen was back to his usual grumpy, taciturn self. I needed to find something for him to do during the day, because he would have driven me to distraction if he'd been under my feet the whole time. Thankfully, I found out about a day-care centre in Portsmouth called the Horizon Centre, where he could be looked after, which gave me a break.

He didn't go every single day—we also had what I called our Darby and Joan days when I dragged him round to help with whatever I was doing. We went to the supermarket, the garden centre, clothes shopping, or visiting my mum, his mum or his granddad—just normal everyday stuff. He was very antisocial, though, and not very communicative if well-meaning folk tried to engage him in conversation. They'd be more likely to get snapped at than greeted.

Allen wasn't good at putting names to faces. If we bumped into our next-door neighbours in the high street, chances are he wouldn't recognise them and would blurt out: 'Who are you?' I was always telling him that sounded rude but he couldn't see it. Our neighbours got used to it after a while and would even make a joke out of it, introducing themselves mock-formally every time we met.

At home he was still struggling to manage without a wheelchair; just dragging himself round by the arms, hanging on to furniture and walls and the like to support his weight, while his legs trailed uselessly behind. This was all very well and I could understand it, but it was painfully slow if he tried to manage without a chair when we went to the shops. He could get himself out of the car and haul himself round it by holding on to the roof rack but he would then be stuck if there was nothing else to hang on to.

'You'll tire yourself out that way,' I cajoled. 'Why not use a wheelchair when we go out somewhere and you can get yourself around when you're back at home?'

'I am *not* disabled!' he yelled at me.

'I know you're not,' I said. 'It's just for now, just for today.'

Eventually he agreed—he knew he couldn't go out without one any more—but he sulked about it whenever he was in a chair.

We had absolutely no social life in those days. We didn't go out to the cinema or to restaurants, although I suppose we could have done if we'd wanted to. It just seemed too complicated to get a baby sitter and go to a restaurant where they would seat you at the back beside the toilet so the wheelchair didn't get in anyone's way.

Allen's social difficulties meant I was reluctant to have people round to the house because he might upset them by being abrupt, or brutally honest. He wouldn't hesitate to say something like, 'That colour makes you look really fat,' for example, and few people could cope with him. His speech still wasn't very clear so quite often, fortunately, when he was being blunt people couldn't make his words out, but it could be extremely awkward.

He couldn't follow a normal conversation very well, so we might be chatting about politics, say, and Allen would burst in with a comment on the weather. We never even had conversations with each other beyond simple domestic things like, 'What do you fancy for dinner tonight?' I became a hermit, seeing my own friends for coffee while Allen was at the day centre, and staying in at weekends and in the evenings.

It was a basic, sterile existence, two strangers rubbing along side by side and occasionally erupting into furious argument. He looked at me sometimes with an expression of pure irritation that bordered on hatred, and I felt like bursting into tears. What had I ever done to deserve this? What more could I do for him?

Allen's sister Suzanne took him out a couple of times to take the pressure off me, but they fell out and so that stopped. His mum wasn't strong enough to cope with him on her own so it was hard for me to get a break. All the responsibility for looking after my husband and children lay at my feet and I just had to get on with it.

WHEN ZOE WAS SEVEN, I had a wake-up call that I needed to focus on the children more. My arrangement that a neighbour would pick Zoe up from school fell through and she was left standing in the playground for two hours before I realised what had happened. The teachers had tried to phone but hadn't been able to track me down—those were the days before we all had mobiles. When I got there she was in floods of tears, her little face bright red, and I felt dreadful that she had been so badly let down. I hugged her tight but she couldn't stop shaking with fear and sobs.

I think she lost faith in grown-ups after that. Her daddy had gone away, and when he came back he was different from who he had been before; her granddad (my father) went away and didn't come back; and so she started to worry about being left anywhere in case no one came back to get her. She refused to go to Brownies any more unless I stayed in the hall throughout and she became very reluctant to go to school. It took a lot of coaxing and one-to-one chats to try to help her to feel secure again.

Allen didn't help because he started to clash with Zoe. She's noisier than Liam and more likely to stick up for herself, and she used to pester Allen sometimes, just looking for attention. One evening I heard them arguing in the kitchen.

'Will you stop that bloody racket?' he shouted.

I couldn't hear her reply, but seconds later there was an ominous thudding sound. I hurried into the kitchen and saw that Allen had pinned her to the wall.

'Stop it! Leave her alone!' I screamed, grabbing his arm.

His grip loosened and Zoe wriggled away and ran out of the room crying. He swivelled the chair round so his back was to me.

'Allen, she's only little. You can't do that to her.'

He didn't reply, just started bashing pots around in the sink to drown out my voice.

I don't like to think what might have happened if I hadn't intervened. He frequently lost his temper when Zoe was winding him up, and didn't seem to make allowance for the fact that she was only a kid. Anyone else would just have said, 'Oh, for goodness' sake, clear off!' but Allen exploded and scared us all.

Zoe just wanted her dad back the way he used to be and she'd push and push for him to do the things he used to do, unable to comprehend that he wasn't capable any more. She'd climb onto his lap on the wheelchair but he would pinch her legs to make her get off again. Sometimes he pinched too hard and gave her nasty bruises, just because he didn't know his own strength any more.

Around this period, I must admit I consulted a solicitor to find out what the position would be if I left Allen. Would I be entitled to maintenance payments for the children from his war pension? Where could we live? I got the information and tucked it away in the back of my mind in case things got any worse. I didn't want to split my family up; I would much rather bring them closer together if I could, but I was running out of ideas.

ALLEN

As the day-centre minibus drove over the hill on the outskirts of Portsmouth, I could see all the way down to the dockyard and the sea, and that was like rubbing salt in the wounds. It was painful to accept that my naval career really was over, and that I was now an outsider. One of my main emotions was guilt: guilt that I wasn't still out there with the other lads serving my country but had skulked home injured, no use to anyone any more. It felt as though I was on the scrapheap at the age of thirty-four.

Although there were a few naval people at the Horizon Centre, it was mainly men who were coming up to pensionable age. The activities were very unchallenging: we'd sit and listen to classical music, which was known as 'music therapy'. Sometimes we did baking and I became a dab hand at making rock cakes, which the kids scoffed when I took them home.

It was depressing. I hated being lumped in with the elderly as though I had no further purpose in life. From fine-tuning missile systems I was reduced to stirring cake mix.

One useful thing was that I got to practise using a computer. We'd had some big complicated computers in the Navy back in 1991, before I was injured, but I'd never run Windows or surfed the Internet. I was immediately interested and started spending as much time as I could teaching myself all the functions. I couldn't remember how to spell and my words came out all scrambled, but someone introduced me to a fantastic programme designed for dyslexics that made sense of the words I did type, and a whole new method of communication was opened to me at a time when I couldn't speak very fluently.

I still felt alienated from Sandra and the children once I was back at home full-time. We were strangers forced to live under the same roof. I really hated being dependent on them if I dropped something and couldn't reach it; for example, if it rolled under the table. I could get myself to the loo or make myself a snack, and I could get from my chair into bed, or into the car, but everything was slow and laborious and draining.

The big old red hospital wheelchair was so difficult to manoeuvre Sandra suggested I should use some of the gratuities money to buy a custom-made chair. I didn't need much persuading. Using a hospital wheelchair is like wearing someone else's pants; it didn't fit my bottom. I did some research and bought a stunning white chair with a jazzy splash of colour on the wheels, all measured and fitted exactly, and it was incredibly comfortable. I suppose that was an important moment: I was beginning to accept I was wheelchair-bound and likely to remain that way for the foreseeable future.

My short-term memory was appalling. I could get to the end of a sentence now without forgetting the beginning but I couldn't remember what I'd done the day before, so if I woke up in the morning and Sandra seemed to be in a huff with me I'd have no idea why.

We slept together in a big double bed, but there was no cuddling. We just put the lights out and fell asleep. To me she was my nurse and my carer, and sometimes she could be a bit of a nag. I know I irritated the hell out of her with my short-temperedness and stroppiness but I was burning up with frustration and she was the only person I had to take it out on.

My old Navy friend and best man, Kevin, knew that Sandra needed a break but it was hard to think of what I was capable. In 1997, he offered to take me to a sporting event in the States organised by the Paralyzed Veterans of America. The British Legion were sending out a team to the National Veterans' Wheelchair Games in San Diego and they invited me to go as a guest, so Kevin kindly agreed to come along to look after me.

I remember several of the events from the Games. There was an archery contest for people in wheelchairs, and their dogs were trained to go and fetch their arrows for them, which was useful. And I saw one guy sending his dog over to get him a drink, which impressed me. In retrospect, I probably spent more time watching the dogs than the athletes.

Kevin and I talked a bit about my disabilities and he was good at teasing out my worries and getting me to talk. I tried to explain to him that I still saw life as black or white, good or bad, and basically the life I was capable of since my accident wasn't good. It wasn't good at all.

He tried to point out all the things I could do from a chair and mentioned the fulfilling lives that the athletes we'd been watching had, but I wasn't ready to listen. I was definitely in a glass-half-empty—or a glass-totally-empty—frame of mind.

My disabilities were like a cancer at the heart of the family, eating away at us all. I found out from the British Legion that out of ninety-eight married servicemen who were seriously injured in the First Gulf War, only five of their marriages survived. They had a range of injuries, but it was the emotional aspect of the return to civilian life as a disabled person that destroyed their families.

Our children were brought up by their mother. I never looked after them, got them drinks of juice, helped with homework, played with them or took any responsibility whatsoever for their care. My excuse was that it took me all my time to look after myself, but it meant that the family unit as a whole wasn't working. We only kept going because Sandra looked after all the practicalities and bent over backwards to keep us together.

No one would have blamed Sandra if she had left me.

SANDRA

Part of the problem I faced in trying to improve our home life was that the house we were living in was too small for two lanky kids who were growing up fast, and a man in a wheelchair. I approached the charity Housing 21 again and asked if there was any chance we could be moved to a bigger house. Some new houses were being built locally that had adjoining garages, and I had the idea that I could convert the garage into a room for Allen where he could get away from the kids and do his own thing.

I found a house I liked that hadn't been sold and sent the details to Housing 21 to see if they would buy it then rent it back to us. They considered it for a while but then pulled out. I was upset and frustrated because I'd set my heart on it by this time.

I tried to get a mortgage, but the first question building societies asked was: 'Are you or your husband employed?' and they slammed the door in my face when the answer was 'No'. Allen's war pension was for life and would continue to be paid to me after his death so it was a guaranteed income, but no one wanted to give us a mortgage based on it. Allen couldn't get life insurance either and I didn't like to think about the implications.

Then Allen's friend Kevin offered to lend us the deposit, and the builders of the house, who hadn't found any other buyers, said they would reduce the price and help us to get a mortgage deal. It all fell into place and we

packed up and moved to our lovely new house, just round the corner from
the old one, in April 1995. It was the first home we had actually owned
ourselves and I was over the moon.

A YEAR AFTER WE ARRIVED in the new house, it was time to start thinking
about choosing a secondary school for Liam, who was eleven years old.
I went to visit the local comprehensive, which had 2,500 pupils, and I didn't
think it would be good for him. Since his father's accident, Liam had
become quite introverted. He never talked about what had happened but he
had lost his male role model and his best Lego mate and that's hard for a
young boy. He didn't cry and have tantrums but he never talked about what
he was feeling either. I think he became very private because he felt he
couldn't express himself freely in the house with Allen around, so he just
decided to keep his thoughts to himself.

Unlike other kids their age, mine couldn't invite their friends over to play
and I think Liam became a bit of a loner. When I met any of his peers,
I realised his social skills weren't as well developed as theirs. He certainly
wasn't one of the 'in' crowd.

Anyway, I did my research and decided that I wanted him to go to an
independent school in Petersfield, which would be small enough for him to
get individual attention from his teachers, and where the crowds in the playground wouldn't be so overwhelming. They had government-assisted
places on offer, but when I phoned up I was told they had all been allocated.

'Can we come and see you anyway?' I asked, just to get a foot in the door.

Allen, Liam and I went for a family interview with the headmaster, but
Liam hardly said a word, and when he was asked for a private one-to-one
chat with the headmaster he flatly refused to go in on his own. First he tried
to run out of the door, and then he crumpled in a heap and burst into tears.
I think he found the atmosphere very intimidating.

The headmaster said, 'I don't want to be cruel, but I'm afraid this is not
the kind of school for someone who can't cope with pressure.'

I said, 'Yes, I quite understand. But I wonder if I could have five minutes
of your time to explain our situation?' Allen and Liam were shown out and
once the door closed behind them, I gave the speech of my life. My son's
future was at stake.

I told him about Allen's accident and what it was like for the children
growing up for the last few years without a proper, hands-on father,

although they had someone who looked the same as their old dad sitting in a wheelchair in the corner. I explained that if Liam was a bit immature it was because he had had a very disrupted childhood to date. I said that he was bright but he needed personal encouragement and I was scared that he would disappear into the system as just another number if he went to the local comprehensive. I talked and I talked and finally, when I had finished, the headmaster said that Liam could come and do a trial day at the school to see how he got on.

Fortunately the trial day must have gone well because in the end the headmaster not only agreed that Liam could come to his school, but he also said that he would find an extra government-assisted place for him.

I'D ASSUMED THAT I WOULD work part-time once the kids were at school, and my earnings would pay for extras like holidays, but that Allen would always be the main wage-earner. We'd hoped that Allen would have a couple more promotions before he retired and we'd have had a lot more money to play with. Once we found out the extent of his war pension, however, we realised that money was going to be tight. We'd be hard-pressed to support two teenagers and see them through college to whatever careers they decided they wanted to pursue, but how could I take a job when I had Allen to look after? We'd just have to scrape by somehow.

A year after Liam started secondary school, it was Zoe's turn. She is quite a different personality from Liam—a complete chatterbox, very trusting and outgoing. In fact, she's just like Allen used to be before his accident. Her confidence was dented by Allen's problems, though, and they continued to argue a lot at home.

When it was time for Zoe to go to secondary school, a charity called the Royal Naval and Royal Marines Children's Trust came up trumps and paid for her to go to an excellent girls' school, the Royal School in Haslemere. About a third of the girls there are boarders and Zoe liked it so much that after a couple of years, when she was fourteen, she asked us if she could become a weekly boarder. I didn't want her to. I'd always felt that boarding school forces children to grow up too quickly when they should still be allowed to be children and I knew I would miss her terribly. But our house was so cramped that her being away from Monday to Friday helped to relieve some of the pressure at home, and at least it stopped her clashing with Allen.

WE SOMEHOW MANAGED to co-exist over the years. When he got back from San Diego, I remember Allen talking about the assistance dogs some disabled athletes used. He was impressed by their intelligence and dedication to their owners and the way he went on about it may have planted a little seed in my brain. I remembered having seen an item in our local paper about an organisation called Canine Partners for Independence, which trained assistance dogs for people with disabilities. The article said that they were desperate for volunteer puppy walkers.

I found the number, and nervously rang it. 'I want to find out about becoming a puppy walker.'

The woman said there was a puppy class going on, and would I like to come right away? She gave me the address and I drove straight there. In a big old shed were six puppies—Labradors, golden retrievers, poodles, and labradoodles—along with their puppy walkers and a couple of instructors. One woman was calling: 'Endal! Endal! Endal!' in an excitable tone and I remember thinking to myself what a stupid name that was for a dog.

I noticed that all the older dogs had names beginning with 'E'—Echo, Errol, Endal—while the younger ones had names beginning with 'F'— Ferdy, Flame, Flynn. Someone explained to me that every six months they start a new team, and the puppies are given names beginning with the next letter of the alphabet. They were all wearing a red Canine Partners 'puppy in training' jacket. I learned that once they graduated and got an assistance dog jacket this gave them legal rights of access to shops and so forth under the Disability Act. When a dog is wearing the jacket, they can't be refused entry anywhere their owner goes.

After the class was over, I had a chat with the puppy trainer, Tessa. I explained about our home situation and she said that it was ideal that we were there during the day and that we had children, because it was good for the puppies to get accustomed to kids. She said the fact that Allen was in a wheelchair could also be good because the puppy would get used to being around disability, although that wasn't something they would look for in every family.

She explained that you kept puppies for fourteen months and during that time you had to attend weekly training classes. It was very important that you stuck to all the techniques you learned and were strict about the puppy's training at home, because that could make all the difference to whether it would be able to work as an assistance dog one day. She said they'd have to come and check the house to make sure our facilities were adequate.

Ten days later I got a phone call. 'Is there any chance we can come to your house to vet you today? It's just that there's a puppy we need to rehome as soon as possible and I think it might be a suitable one for you.'

They came and had a look round the house and met Allen and agreed that everything was fine, and the next day an eight-week-old yellow Labrador called Ferdy was delivered to us. He was a lively fellow, and the children adored him. This was the first dog they'd ever had and they would sit on the floor playing with him for hours on end, teasing him with a bit of rope and wrestling toys from his mouth.

Ferdy was a character, who used to carry his own pillow around with him and, when he was tired, would lie down and have a sleep on it. Zoe made him a cushion of his own and embroidered his name on it. I'd been worried about how the rabbits we kept in the garden would cope with the new arrival but they seemed to accept each other's presence without question.

What a puppy learns in the first sixteen weeks is crucial. First of all, Ferdy had to learn to use a special toilet area I created in the back garden. Then he had to become accustomed to spending time lying quietly in his crate, without chewing or barking or running wild. Assistance dogs need to learn good basic manners, such as not barging ahead of you through doors, not barking inappropriately, sitting when asked, coming when called, and walking nicely on a loose lead. They can't be allowed to tear up your kitchen lino or run amok in public. It's crucial that they don't get over-excited and rush off suddenly in a way that could pull a disabled person from their wheelchair. You have to be very strict with them, as with a toddler, and my role was to do the obedience training.

As a first-time puppy walker, I made some mistakes with Ferdy and maybe wasn't as strict as I should have been. Unless you are 100 per cent consistent with the rules, the dogs get confused and don't know what they are supposed to be doing, but Ferdy turned out just fine. He was a very nice dog, eager to do the right thing.

Allen seemed pleased to have a dog in the house. He liked to sit with Ferdy on his lap where he could pet him, but he made it clear he didn't want to get involved in any of the training.

He still didn't accept that he was going to be disabled for the rest of his life, but he had slipped into the role of the invalid, letting other people do things for him and not taking any responsibility. We often argued because I felt that he could be doing more—peeling potatoes, doing the washing-up, hanging out laundry, and so forth—whereas he was happy to be waited on hand and foot. I was getting tired of being his carer instead of his partner.

However, I found a new focus for myself once I started training Ferdy. I looked forward to my weekly puppy class and spent a lot of time working with him, trying to make sure he knew all the techniques well in advance so that he would shine in front of the trainers. I was so keen that it wasn't long before Tessa asked if I would like to become a puppy-class helper. Then Canine Partners asked if I would be prepared to give talks at various local events to help them to recruit more puppy walkers.

'It's easy,' Tessa said. 'All you need to do is chat about what it's like being a puppy walker, and answer any questions as best you can.'

I agreed to give it a try and found that it wasn't too hard after all, because I was talking about something I felt passionately about. It was a relief to get out of the house and to be involved in the charity.

ALLEN

W hen Ferdy came to live with us, I didn't pay much attention at first. I'd always liked dogs in the past: my mum kept Yorkshire terriers and my granddad had Labradors, but there was no way I could have been a puppy walker myself because I couldn't even look after myself, never mind take responsibility for a dog.

One day in October 1997, about a month after Sandra started going to Canine Partners, the morning bus didn't come to take me to day care. I waited and waited but there was no sign and Sandra was getting impatient.

'It's my puppy class day today,' she said, 'and I'm blowed if you're going to make me miss it.'

She loaded me into the car and drove me down to the converted chicken shed that Canine Partners used as a headquarters. I wheeled myself off into a corner feeling irritated by the bustle and noise level in the room.

A few people shouted 'Hello!' and a woman called Tessa came over to try and make me join in.

'Just clap your hands, and see if you can make a puppy come to you,' she suggested.

I shook my head and snarled something bad-tempered and she soon backed off and left me on my own.

The class began. Some bowls were being placed on the ground and one by one the dogs had to go and pick up their own bowl and take it to their puppy walker. Treats were placed in the bowls but the dogs had to wait until they were given permission before eating them. I soon lost interest and just sat frowning, annoyed with the bus driver who had forgotten to come for me. I didn't particularly like the day centre but I liked my routine.

Out of the corner of my eye, I noticed that a yellow Lab kept turning round to look at me, and after a while it broke away from the crowd and came over towards me. I could see it was limping slightly but I didn't feel any sympathy. At least it could limp. I couldn't even do that any more.

When it drew close to me, it ducked down, picked something up from the floor and deposited it on my lap. It looked me in the eye, its tail wagging, obviously waiting for a response.

I didn't even glance down to see what it had brought me. Didn't this dog realise I wanted to be left on my own?

The puppies were used to getting a reward when they completed a task properly, so this Lab looked puzzled when it got nothing from me. It gazed round the room and noticed some units that were set out to look like supermarket shelves with different goods: tins of soup, bread, biscuits, cereal.

The Lab went over, picked something off the shelf, brought it back and dropped it in my lap. It stared up at me again, waiting for praise, but still I didn't respond. Just leave me alone, I was thinking. Give me a break!

That puppy wasn't giving up, though. He went back to the shelves and picked up another item, and I began to watch him. Mild irritation turned to amusement as he dropped a soup tin on my lap then immediately turned to go and get something else.

He had my attention now as he trotted back and forth bringing more and more items; all of them were deposited on my lap until there was a huge, teetering pile. Finally, I looked down and the sight of all these foods, wobbling and about to capsize onto the floor, was hilarious. I found my lips stretching into a smile for the first time in ages. My face muscles hurt with the unaccustomed movement.

'Good boy!' I whispered, and a pair of big brown eyes looked eagerly up into mine. What a handsome dog, I thought. He had a large, teddy-bear head and a very gentle expression. 'Aren't you lovely?'

'I see you've met Endal,' a woman said. 'I think he's taken a shine to you.' She stretched out her hand. 'Judith Turner—I'm Endal's puppy parent.'

I hesitated then shook her hand. A packet toppled from my lap to the floor. 'Allen Parton,' I stuttered self-consciously. I really hated my stutter.

She carried all the goods from my lap back to the shelves and I took the opportunity to lean down and give Endal's tummy a rub underneath his red assistance jacket. He looked up at me with such a happy, trusting gaze that something in my stomach turned over. He really was the most handsome dog I'd ever come across and it was touching that he'd singled me out like that without any encouragement.

I STARTED ASKING SANDRA if I could come along to Canine Partners with her more often. Every time I arrived Endal would come bounding over to see me, his big eyes gazing up at me from beside my chair, and I suppose I would be looking out for him as well. At home I started paying more attention to Ferdy, testing him on the skills he was supposed to be learning, such as picking things up from the floor and bringing them to me.

It got to the stage when Sandra said, 'Allen, you're going to have to back off with Ferdy. I'm supposed to be his trainer and the one he takes orders from, but he's starting to listen more to you.'

If I'm honest, I was secretly quite pleased about this, but what I didn't realise was that it jeopardised Ferdy's training. There has to be one person in charge and that has to be their trainer, in other words Sandra, but by this stage, Ferdy seemed to think he was working for me. Tessa eventually decided that Ferdy would have to go to someone else.

Tessa and Sandra asked me if I would like an assistance dog of my own, but I was adamant I didn't. I didn't want to be labelled as 'disabled'. I didn't think I needed a dog to help me with anything.

Sandra tried to talk me into it. 'Allen, think of the extra freedom it would give you. You'd be able to go out to the shops on your own without worrying about whether or not you'll get knocked over when you step out into the road. It would mean you could stay at home on your own if you didn't feel like going to the day centre,' she continued.

At that time I couldn't be left alone because I could be a danger to myself. I'd put the gas on and forget about it, so a strong gust of wind could cause a fire that burned the house down. If I fell out of my chair and banged my head, I could be stuck there for hours till Sandra got home again.

'And if you dropped something and couldn't reach it, the dog could get it for you so you wouldn't have to be dependent on the kids or me the whole time,' she finished.

These arguments were all tempting, but I still resisted, clinging to the hope that one day I would be completely fine again. My brain would heal, I would walk and talk fluently and get my memory back as good as new.

'Don't want a dog,' I snapped.

'What if you could have Endal as a pet?' she suggested one day. 'He might not pass the tests to be an assistance dog because of the lameness in his right front leg, but he's a bright dog and he'll need a home.'

I hesitated. 'What about Ferdy?'

'Ferdy's being rehomed, and I'm getting a new puppy to train—Gracie, a sixteen-week-old golden retriever. The problem is that maybe the same thing will happen again and Gracie will think she's working for you rather than me if you don't have a dog of your own. So you'd be doing everyone a favour if you took Endal. They'd both come into the house at the same time so there'll be no established hierarchy. What do you think?'

ON THE MORNING OF FEBRUARY 28, 1998, we met Judith Turner in the car park outside the training centre to pick up Endal. She was in floods of tears and I remember looking at her and wondering what her problem was. I was still having trouble understanding other people's emotions.

She told me a bit about Endal's background and babyhood. 'He's a pure breed,' she said. 'His granddad was one of the highest-achieving Labradors ever at Crufts, but he was the result of an accidental mating between father and daughter in the kennels, the only surviving offspring in a litter.'

Sniffing back her tears, she listed some of the things he liked: 'He's partial to a bit of cheese with his dinner. He likes sleeping with his teddy bear'—she handed over a ragged, smelly creature—'and he's very loving. He's a great licker. I'm always losing earrings that way.'

She told me he was an intelligent puppy who learned easily and liked thinking things through and solving problems for himself. He understood a lot of human language: 'He can be dead to the world, but if you say, "I'm thinking of going for a walk soon," he'll be right there by your side within nanoseconds.'

400 | ALLEN AND SANDRA PARTON

'He's a big softie,' she sobbed, tears trickling down her cheeks. 'Please take good care of him.'

Judith gave Endal one last cuddle and Sandra lifted him into our car, then handed Ferdy's lead to Judith, because it had been arranged that he was going to complete his training with her.

I saw Endal watching me with an intelligent look in his eyes as if he already knew what was happening and was ready for it. He wanted to look after me. He'd been brought up to look after people in wheelchairs and now he was ready to start.

What I didn't realise was that Endal's ambitions were far greater than that.

I WASN'T SURE THAT I would be capable of looking after a puppy—but Endal made it easy. Judith had given me the little tin bowl he ate his dinner from and at mealtimes he would pick it up from the kitchen floor and bring it to me. If we went out for a walk, I hooked him onto my wheelchair and he trotted along obediently beside it. Even if I let him off the leash, he never went far, always keeping an eye on me in case it was time to go home again. In the early days, he was showing me what to do, rather than the other way round.

Maybe it was because Endal had health problems, just as I did, that he managed to get through to me on an emotional level. Before he'd arrived, I just felt a kind of numbness, but he opened the door by doing little things that made me happy. The first time I threw a ball for him and he brought it back again, I knew we had a connection that didn't require communication. I liked it when he put his front paws up on my lap so that I could give him a hug. He was reaching out to me and all I had to do was respond.

After that, Endal's training was something I did instinctively. I'd put an object on the floor and say, 'Look! Look!' then ask him to bring it to me. Next time maybe I would hide it. He seemed to know intuitively what I wanted so I didn't follow any formal training methods. But I would only give a treat when a command was carried out correctly. If Endal was giving me something but just left it on the side of the wheelchair, that wouldn't do. I'd put it back down again, and he'd have to keep trying until he placed it squarely in my lap, and then he got his treat.

On the days when Endal was limping badly he was 'off duty', but still he hovered by my chair waiting to see what he could do to help me. During his waking hours he never took his eyes off me, always alert to whatever

I might need, and that devotion was touching. It can't have been very rewarding for him in those early months because I rarely spoke, so he wasn't getting any praise or interaction.

ONE DAY I HAD CROSSED my legs by using my hands to pull my right leg across the left. As soon as Endal noticed, he bustled over and nudged my legs uncrossed again because, as far as he was concerned, that was the way they were meant to be. It's important for assistance dogs to be able to move your limbs back onto the wheelchair if they fall off, and Endal had decided that my legs being crossed didn't look right to him, so he fixed it.

I tested him by crossing my legs again and once more he nudged them back straight. As often as I crossed them, he would uncross them again. His persistence and dedication to duty made me laugh.

Another time, I was sitting downstairs when I rubbed my chin and realised I had forgotten to shave that morning. I decided to ask Sandra or one of the kids to go upstairs and get my electric razor so I could do a quick tidy-up, but I had one of my all-too-frequent lapses of memory and couldn't think of the word 'razor'. Cursing to myself, I kept fingering my chin in case that triggered my memory.

Endal had been watching, and suddenly he leaped up, ran out of the door and up the stairs, then returned and dropped the razor onto my lap.

Good grief! I thought, too stunned at first to remember to reward him with a doggy treat. That was extraordinary!

I told Sandra about it and she was surprised too, because reading my homemade sign language obviously wasn't something that had been covered in Endal's training. She was concerned that he shouldn't try to do too much, which could exacerbate his lameness, but she was reckoning without Endal's enthusiasm.

He quickly learned more signs I invented and could soon fetch my hat for me if I patted the top of my head, my coat if I patted the left side of my chest, his 'puppy in training' coat if I patted the right side of my chest, or my wheelchair gloves if I touched my hands.

I kept a rucksack on the back of my wheelchair in which I put anything I might need. However, the lack of sensation in the right side of my body meant that when I stretched round to reach into it I could never tell what I was feeling with my fingers. I might as well have been plunging them into a bowl of jelly. I spent some time training Endal to retrieve items from the rucksack for me and that was a huge help: he could get my wallet, keys, gloves, hat or mobile phone, in response to either spoken commands or sign language.

While I was sleeping, Endal kept watch over me, opening one eye from time to time to check I was still in the bed. Occasionally I suffered from spasms that made my legs start kicking out and when this happened I'd go and sleep on the sofa downstairs so as not to disturb Sandra. Endal would follow and find a spot in the sitting room so I was never out of his sight, even though he loved sleeping upstairs. His duty was 24/7 and he wouldn't dream of letting me down.

As soon as he saw any signs that I was awake in the morning, he would jump up to lick my face. I might keep my eyes closed if I fancied a lie-in but Endal always seemed to be able to tell if I was awake; there was no fooling him. Next he would pull over my wheelchair using a little cord attached to it that we called a 'tuggie'. When I got to the toilet, he would push the loo seat up for me—although Sandra complained that like a typical male he never put it down again.

He could help to fetch clothes for me to get dressed, and when we got downstairs to the kitchen he would bring the cereal packet out of the cupboard for me, by using the tuggie attached to the handle to pull the door open. Soon virtually everything in our house had a tuggie tied onto it. Then the minute the post came through the letterbox, Endal skidded out into the hall to pick it up and bring it to me.

He was very good at walking by the side of the chair when we were out. He had great road sense and would sit down on the kerb to stop me making the wrong decision and moving out into oncoming traffic. Only once did I doubt his abilities, when he stopped halfway across a road and paused to pick something up off the tarmac.

'Come on,' I hissed, tugging at his lead, worried that a car might come. When we got to the other side, Endal dropped a pound coin in my lap. He'd seen it lying there and thought it was the kind of thing he should pick up for me. It was actually one of the first early indications that I had a dog who wasn't just unquestioningly obedient but could actually think for himself.

I taught him some fun things as well. He would bark if I said 'Bark!' or roll over on the ground when I circled my finger, or kiss me on the mouth if I asked him to. Other dogs might manage to offer a paw when there's a treat on offer but Endal would do anything I asked for the fun of it (not that he ever turns down a treat, of course).

My relationship with Endal became the focus of my day. I wanted to be with him the whole time, either petting him or playing with him or testing him on his skills. It was the centre of my life.

'You're in a good mood,' Sandra said when she got home from Canine Partners one day, a couple of months after Endal arrived. 'What have you been up to?'

'Look!' I said, and showed her how Endal would roll over on demand.

She laughed and called Liam and Zoe to watch. Endal was happy to perform again and soon had them all laughing. He had a natural clown's instinct and seemed to like an audience.

'Why don't you do the Canine Partners training course and learn all the advanced skills?' Sandra asked. 'I'm pretty sure Endal could pass the exam.'

I thought it sounded like a good idea, so I applied to go on their residential course in May 1998. It was usually two weeks long but I only had to do a week because I already knew all the basics about grooming and feeding.

IT WAS FAIRLY EASY STUFF that Endal had to do on the course: walking with the wheelchair, retrieving objects, coming when called. One of the tests involved teaching your dog a new skill. For us, it was entering and leaving a room. Endal had to open the door for me to get through and then pull it shut behind me. There was a tuggie attached to the door handle to make it easier for him. He'd never done this before and for some reason he pushed the door shut leaving himself inside the room. He was still a very young dog and it was quite a difficult trick to master.

We tried several times and Endal kept shutting the door with himself inside the room until I came up with a plan. As I wheeled myself out, I dropped my hankie on the floor, so Endal followed me out in order to pick up the hankie, and then he could pull the door shut from the outside. The testers saw what I was doing but we got away with it.

In another part of the test, Endal and I were secretly watched as we travelled around Chichester facing different challenges. One of them was getting into and out of a lift in the local Marks & Spencer. Now, Endal and I had been there before and somehow he had worked out that when we wanted to get in he could stop the lift door closing by sticking his nose into the little laser beam at floor level. As soon as he did it, the doors opened again.

He also figured out that with this particular lift there was a bit of reflective glass at floor level and if he nudged it with his nose it would summon the lift from another floor without me having to press the button. I think this particularly impressed the trainers who were watching us at the time.

I had to make Endal lie down on the pavement outside M&S and wait for me while I went round a corner and out of sight. People hidden in the crowd kept an eye on him to make sure he stayed down, despite all the shoppers milling around, and he managed it just fine.

We passed the test with flying colours and I was really proud of him. It was the first time I had achieved anything at all since I got back from the Gulf War. I loved the independence it gave me; I felt as though I was less of a burden to Sandra and, with Endal's help, I even managed to do bits and pieces of housework and contribute to the running of the household.

AFTER HE PASSED the advanced training course, Endal and I began to accompany Sandra to events where she was giving talks to publicise Canine Partners, and we would do little demonstrations of his skills—picking things up for me, uncrossing my legs or fetching his bowl. Then, one day, we were at a fête and Endal had been jumping up and showing off what he could do, when he suddenly went very lame.

Sandra lifted him into the car and we drove him straight to the vet, who said he needed complete rest for several weeks. No jumping up, no climbing stairs, no going out for walks, just enforced bed rest. Easier said than done. Back at the house, Endal wouldn't stop following me about. At night we shut him in the kitchen, and he registered his protest by becoming very naughty. He jumped up on the work surface and took a carton of rabbit food out of a cupboard and started eating it, so it spilled everywhere. We reckon he got through about 2.5 kilos of it, because everything he passed for the next two weeks looked like a health food bar!

Another time when he was left alone in the kitchen he capsized the swing bin and got his head stuck through the lid, which could have been very dangerous. Basically, he was objecting to being rested and having a fit of temper. The problem was he needed complete rest for his legs to improve, so reluctantly we had to agree to put him in the charity's kennels.

He was kept still in a small area with a rubber mat on the floor. Without space to run around, he was like a bear with a sore head. He couldn't understand why I was doing this to him, and lay there whining and chewing his rubber mat to pieces. You can't explain to an eighteen-month-old dog that it's for their own good.

I remember that while he was in kennels I went with Sandra to a graduation ceremony in which a number of other dogs were made official assistance dogs, and I missed Endal badly. There was an aching in my chest, I missed him so much. I withdrew into myself again and didn't want to talk to anyone there or join in with the events. It was as though a part of me had been torn away. I hadn't realised how important his companionship had become to me.

After two weeks, Heather, one of the training centre managers, took Endal to the vet for another check-up, then came round to tell me the verdict. 'I'm afraid it's bad news, Allen. Endal isn't any better and we don't know what to do. It may be that he'll always have this joint problem, which would mean he can't be a full working dog.'

That struck fear into me. I was lame myself and I couldn't have a dog that was lame. It could inhibit my recovery if I had to go back to being a prisoner in my own home because I was looking after him. I needed a dog I could take to the shops, who would increase rather than decrease my mobility and independence.

'Take him back then,' I blurted out, and turned away from her. 'I don't want him.' My throat tightened and I felt like crying but I was too stubborn to back down. I wheeled my chair out of the room and shut the door.

SANDRA

All the staff at Canine Partners had been hoping that Allen would apply for Endal. When he was a puppy, there was some doubt whether Endal would ever pass the test to be a full working assistance dog because he had a condition called osteochondritis, or OCD, in his front elbow joints. This means that as the dog develops, the cartilage does not turn into bone as it is meant to, causing swelling in the joint and intermittent lameness.

Endal wouldn't have been able to work for someone who didn't have much upper body strength because they would need a dog that could jump up on its hind legs to fetch things for them. Allen has always had very good upper body strength, so we thought they were a good match. Apart from anything else, there seemed to be a strong attraction between them. As soon as Allen arrived at a puppy class, Endal would leave Judith's side and go over to see him. There was a definite spark there.

When Allen took Endal to do the residential training course, I worried that he might be grouchy and demanding with the staff, the way he was with me at home, but they said he was fine. He was, however, a bit arrogant at first, thinking that he knew it all, so one day they taught him a lesson by 'stealing' Endal away from him.

'Didn't he explode when you did that?' I asked. 'He'd go berserk if I did that at home.'

'No,' they said, 'he took it all in good spirit.'

I was astonished to hear this. I couldn't imagine him being the butt of a joke without growling at someone, but it seemed that he was regaining his ability to laugh at himself. That was one of the moments when I really sensed things were changing for the better. When I thought about it, I realised he'd been getting more fun-loving at home as well. There had been a few times when we'd had a laugh together, usually because of something to do with the dogs.

It was a huge setback when Endal went badly lame. When he came back from the kennels, I knew there was still a question mark over his fitness, but I was very upset when I heard from Heather that Allen was refusing to take him back again. I couldn't believe it. I thought Allen really cared about the dog.

'Maybe they haven't bonded as well as we thought?' Heather suggested.

'But they have!' I insisted. Then I thought about it. 'The only reservation Allen has expressed to me is about the fact that Endal isn't *his* dog. He's worried that if things go wrong, for example if Endal gets so lame that he can't work, you might come and take him away again.' All Canine Partners dogs were owned by the charity, not the individuals they worked for.

'We could reassure him about that. I'm sure we could come to an agreement that Endal is his for as long as he wants him.'

'That might make a difference,' I said. 'Leave it with me.'

I waited until Allen and I were in bed that night. 'What's this nonsense I hear that you're refusing to take Endal back?'

'He's lame. He can't help me any more.' Allen was sullen and I knew he could get very obstinate when he was in this kind of mood.

'Will you stop being so selfish!' I shouted. 'Try thinking of someone else apart from yourself for a change. That dog needs you, and he's done a lot for you, and you're prepared to just throw it all away.'

'I can't have a limpy dog,' he muttered.

'*Why* can't you?' I demanded. 'Why not give Endal a chance to get better? What are you so scared of?'

He didn't say anything.

'If you're worried that Canine Partners might take him away, that's not a problem. They've said that Endal can be your dog for life, whether he can work or not.'

Still he said nothing.

'You think about it, Allen. That dog didn't ask to have joint problems any more than you asked to be brain damaged in a car accident.'

He didn't say any more, but I could hear that he lay awake for quite a while and I hoped he was thinking about what I'd said.

The next morning, I didn't help him to get up. I left him to pull his own chair over to the bed, get his own clothes and then stretch to get his own breakfast cereal out of the cupboard. I wanted him to remember how much tougher life was for him without a dog.

As we were eating, Allen said quietly, 'I think I'll come with you to the training centre.'

As soon as we arrived, I saw Allen looking round for Endal.

'Where is he?' he asked Heather.

'Endal? He's back at the kennels.'

'I've changed my mind. Do you think I could have him back, please?'

He even said 'please'. I felt like punching the air in triumph.

Heather smiled and said, 'Of course you can.' She went on to explain that they were happy for Endal to remain with him as a pet in the worst-case scenario that he couldn't work, and they went off to have a chat together. Later that day we picked up Endal and brought him home again.

For the first few days, I was watching them closely and I noticed that Allen was very affectionate with Endal, cuddling and patting him and giving him constant attention. It was very sweet to watch, actually. When you live with someone it can be a while before you are aware they are changing—although someone who sees them less frequently might notice straight away—but I definitely felt that Allen was happier than I had seen him since before the accident. Happier, and easier to live with.

Endal was utterly devoted to Allen and very focused on getting him whatever he needed. When Allen couldn't remember a word and used sign language instead, some dogs would have given up but Endal kept trying until he worked out what was wanted. He never gave up. Some dogs will pick up a pencil from the floor once, twice, maybe three times and then they think: I'm not picking that up again. Endal would have kept doing it as long as Allen kept dropping the pencil, even if that was a hundred times. He was totally consistent and totally reliable.

When I went out and left Allen at home with Endal, I knew he was safe. If anything had happened, for example if Allen had fallen out of the chair, Endal would have alerted the neighbours straight away. If they went down to the shops together, Endal had good road sense and stopped him rolling out into traffic. It was a huge weight off my mind to be able to leave him without worrying. Even though Allen stopped going to the Horizon Centre once he had a puppy to look after, I still had more freedom.

Allen and Endal were great buddies, totally focused on each other. It was a real boys' club and they could be quite exclusive: Endal really didn't want to take orders from me, and Allen certainly didn't. It was funny for me seeing my husband getting so close to someone else in a way that he wasn't close to me, but I wasn't jealous for a second. My overwhelming emotion was relief that Allen's mental outlook was getting so much healthier. I felt a stirring of optimism for the first time in seven long years.

ALLEN

After Endal's problem with lameness, we had to take it very easy when he came back to stay with me. He couldn't run for a ball and he wasn't supposed to jump up on his hind legs. He was only allowed a minute's walk the first day, then two minutes, then three, and it was several months before he was able to come out of the house and down to the shops with me. It was particularly important that we kept his weight under control, so I put him on a strict diet and he was weighed once a week. I had explicit instructions that if he went over thirty-one kilos he was to be given smaller portions until his weight went back down again.

Even stuck indoors, Endal was a very responsive companion, and we started playing lots of games together. He loved his Kong, a hardened rubber toy on a string that I would put a biscuit inside. He would swing it around as if it was a wild creature he was trying to subdue and he'd chew away at it until he had wrestled the treat out of the middle. If I got hold of it or tried to yank it out of his mouth, he would run off round the room with it before bringing it back again.

Another game he enjoyed was hide and seek. If he was in the garden, I'd sneak into the house and find a hiding place—not easy with a wheelchair in a small house—then wait as he came scurrying in to find me. It never took him long and he'd be overjoyed and bark happily when he saw me again. I started hiding behind bushes when we went out for a walk but he'd always find me within thirty seconds.

Endal wasn't really supposed to climb the stairs at first because of his lame front legs, but he was so unhappy if I left him downstairs that I gave in and let him come up at night-time only. His bed was just by my side of the bed in our bedroom, and it was made up of a king-size duvet folded several times and stuffed inside a single duvet cover, with a big, smelly doggy cushion on top. His favourite position for sleeping was on his back with his legs splayed wide. I liked to watch him while he wriggled in his sleep in the midst of a doggy dream, probably chasing something.

When he was off the lead in an open space, Endal would set off at a run to try to catch any birds, squirrels or cats he caught sight of, but his training was such that if I called him to 'stop' then he'd do so immediately. When he was on the lead, I could feel the tension when he noticed a small animal, but he would never pull too hard and risk me falling out of the chair.

He was keen on eating any cat pooh he came across on our walks but a doggy expert told me that it is full of protein and good for them to eat so I didn't stop him, even though his breath was horrible afterwards. And, like most Labs I've come across, he loved rolling in fox pooh and impregnating his entire coat with the scent. It must be the Chanel No. 5 of the doggy world.

Endal can smell a biscuit at fifty paces. At the Canine Partners training centre, he always used to nose around an old corner cabinet and we couldn't work out why until it was moved one day and we found a manky bit of left-over biscuit underneath. He had been able to smell it, and it really used to bug him until he could finally claim it.

He would never steal food: he was too well trained for that. The only time Endal was really naughty was when once I took him for a walk round a nearby lake. He dived straight into the water and despite all my calling, offering of treats and then angry shouting, he didn't come out for hours. He just loved swimming. It's the only time he's abandoned me when we've been out, but I reckoned it might be good for his joints so after that I usually let him have a swim whenever we were near somewhere suitable.

Gradually, over the course of a year or so, I noticed that Endal was limping less, and then barely at all. Once the vet had given him the all-clear, he was able to start accompanying me to events promoting the charity. He always liked going out and about and meeting new people, especially children, and I enjoyed a break in my normal routine.

WE STARTED to become known in the Clanfield area. When we went into the grocer's shop, I would point to the goods I wanted and Endal would pick them up for me, much to the other customers' amazement. The chemist didn't have disabled access at that time so I would wait outside while Endal went in to pick up my prescription. At the post office, he could post letters in the letterbox or push forms into the service tray under the glass security panel. And if we stopped for a pint in the pub on the way home, Endal would jump up at the bar and hand my wallet to the barman so he could take out the money for my drink.

I hadn't ever learned to drive before the accident and it was out of the question afterwards because of the brain damage I'd suffered, but once the local buses got a disabled ramp I could travel on them. Endal would take my wallet to the driver so he could extract the right money. Endal would then tear off the ticket and bring it and the wallet back to me while I parked myself in the wheelchair space.

Having Endal made my confidence grow in all sorts of ways. Apart from playing with him, I spent most of my time learning new functions on the computer. Out of curiosity I decided to take it apart and figure out how everything worked. Computers are basically just a mechanical box with a power supply and lots of microchips and they hold the same kind of fascination for me as Lego had done when I was a kid.

One day I saw an advert in a computer magazine for a casing that you could buy to build your own computer in. I bought it by mail order, and when it was delivered I hid it in the garage. Gradually I started buying more bits and pieces and hiding them all from Sandra. I used to disappear out there and started putting them all together, working it out through trial and error. I didn't have a monitor at first so I couldn't see if it was working properly but the lights went on and it seemed to be making the right noises. Endal barked, as if congratulating me.

I remember one of my old Navy bosses saying, 'Divide a problem into bits.' That's what you do with engineering. If a signal is coming in but the device isn't working, you look at the next bit of wire, use logic to find any faults and go through it slowly. It took a while, but finally I got my computer working all by myself. It was such a proud moment when I plugged everything in, booted up and the screen came to life.

IN MARCH 1999 I took Endal to Crufts, where Sandra and I were helping to do talks and demonstrations at the Canine Partners stall. I was starting to say a bit more at these events, but I was very nervous about it in the early days. I knew I could talk fairly fluently but I couldn't memorise a speech and, as I didn't remember what I'd said two minutes before, there was a real risk of me repeating myself. What they really wanted to see was Endal doing his stuff: nudging my leg back onto the chair when it fell off, picking up things I had dropped and so forth.

After the Crufts competition finished and everyone was packing up, Endal and I went to have a play in the main ring. Some spectators were sitting round the sides as we began messing around with his Kong. We tugged, Endal ran off round the ring with it, then brought it back to me to tug again. We had extended our sign language so that if I circled my finger in the air, he would roll over three or four times, and he would respond to hand signs for 'Sit', 'Wait', 'Come' and so forth, even when I was some distance away.

I signalled to Endal to run round the ring again and he set off, and I was stunned to hear the onlookers clapping. I didn't realise anyone had been watching our game, but they were laughing at his antics and seemed to be amazed at this dog who understood sign language. From across the ring I signed to Endal to roll over again, and he did. There was no hint of the lame dog of a year ago. He was playful, intelligent and a born performer.

As we were leaving, I slipped Endal's Kong into the rucksack on the back of my wheelchair, knowing that he would immediately go in there to retrieve it. Sure enough, as I wheeled myself away Endal pulled out the Kong again and the audience erupted into laughter.

While I was making my way back to the Canine Partners stand to find Sandra, a Crufts official came hurrying over to introduce himself.

'That was a fantastic display you did there,' he said.

'It wasn't a display. We were just playing.'

'Well, I wondered whether you would come and do it again next year as a demo? People would love to watch you two together.'

What could I say? I was delighted to be asked.

More and more, this dog was bringing fun and joy back into my life. Dogs are utterly non-judgmental so if I woke feeling irritable one morning, while Sandra might snap back at me and storm out of the room, Endal was endlessly patient and accepting. If I was depressed, he came up on my lap for a snuggle. If my chair got stuck, he would try to clear obstacles out of the way. He was always ready to pick up whatever objects I dropped. From the moment he arrived in my life he gave me unqualified, unconditional love that shone out of his gentle face.

SANDRA

Right from the start, we made a good team at the Canine Partners public demonstrations. I was the 'straight' one who got the facts across, and Allen and Endal were the comedy showmen. I enjoyed it and I could tell that Allen did as well. He was interacting with members of the public, forgetting to be embarrassed about his stammer—although when I listened closely, I realised that was happening less and less. I also noticed that his compulsive twitching was becoming much less frequent.

Gradually Allen was doing more and more of the talking at charity fundraising events. One day I stood back and listened as he spoke to a member of the audience at one of our demonstrations. He was describing the time when Endal had piled objects on his lap at the training centre, and I realised he wasn't stuttering at all and he didn't forget any of his words. What's more, he was smiling at the woman who had asked the question, and acting like a normal, sociable human being. As I watched, I got goose bumps. In the way he was chatting, I could see the friendly, gregarious man I had fallen for—the man I thought I'd lost for ever.

Where speech therapists had failed to get him speaking clearly in sentences during the seven years since his accident, it seemed that the relationship he had formed with Endal had increased his desire to communicate and had somehow helped his brain to re-form a link that had been missing. That's the only explanation I can come up with and the doctors couldn't come up with anything better.

Once he could speak more clearly, Allen began to engage with the world again. He'd chat to people we met, and although he could still be tactless and harsh, his natural cheerfulness, which had been absent for the previous seven years, came back. Of course, the huge gaps in his memory still hadn't been filled in, and he still forgot the names of people he'd known for years, but I felt a real sea change in his mental outlook.

There were just a few little signs that he was beginning to think about the children and me, and to care about all the memories of us that he had lost. He asked me questions about what happened at our wedding, about the birth of the children, and about what they had been like as toddlers, and the fact that he was starting to care again made me start to fall back in love with him. I'd never fallen out of love with the man he used to be, and it all came flooding back as I recognised that person in him again.

When Endal first came to live with us Allen was still very serious and humourless, but gradually at the puppy classes he learned to laugh at himself again—and to try to make others laugh as well. The corny jokes crept back and along with them, the practical jokes.

One day I was in the kitchen preparing dinner when Allen wheeled himself in with a bar of soap in his hand.

'Does this smell funny to you?' he asked, holding it out.

I bent down to smell it, and he tipped it up so I got soap on my nose. I remembered the first time he played that trick on me, back in 1982 when we'd first started dating. I laughed and quickly turned away so that he wouldn't see my tears.

One of the best things for me was that he began to bond with the children, through playing with the puppies together. Although Endal really only took orders from Allen, Liam and Zoe would fall about laughing as they watched him perform all the skills he had mastered and would whoop with delight every time he barked on demand or rolled over in response to Allen.

Endal naturally had a range of different barks and Allen had been teaching him to produce them on demand. An expert once told me that the normal dog has only eight voice patterns but Endal has at least twenty, all with different meanings.

There was a little bark he used with children, a soft, gentle mouth bark that makes people laugh because it sounds funny coming from such a big dog. There's his 'Hello' bark, which always surprises people: if you say 'Hello' to Endal, he will answer you with a kind of 'wuff' sound. There's his, 'I love you' bark and his, 'Turn over the TV channel bark' and his, 'Can I have another treat?' bark. There's a louder and more assertive 'ruff', a hound-like 'yaowww', a full-on big bark, and many more besides.

If Allen said 'Gentle!' he got the children's one that was almost like a coughing sound; if he said, 'Big bark!' he got the loudest one; and he had different commands for most of the others in between. He also taught him to bark whenever there was a toast to the Queen, just as a party piece!

Around this period, Allen's granddad Roger was admitted to hospital. He was ninety-odd and very sprightly but he fell in his bathroom one night, broke his femur and then his kidneys started to fail. Allen had been very close to this granddad, his mother's father, who had been an important figure in his childhood after his dad walked out on them—but he had no memories of him from before the accident. He just knew him as a lively old man whom we visited sometimes.

We went to see Roger in hospital but by the time we got there he was in a coma, and several family members were gathered round the bed because the end was near. If Allen had recalled all the closeness they'd had in his childhood, he'd probably have been very upset. As it was, he lightened the mood of the gathering by suggesting we send out for beer and pizza. Everyone was hungry so they agreed and we sat by the old man's bedside with an almost festive atmosphere, munching our pizzas. It may sound odd but it's exactly what Roger would have wanted. He had an amazing sense of humour—it's probably where Allen got his from—and I think he would have been tickled by that scene round his hospital bed.

I was delighted with the way Allen dealt with the situation that night. He couldn't relate to the grief people were feeling, but he sensed it and was respectful of it. There were no inappropriate comments at all. I remembered when he had refused to come to baby Alice's funeral back in the bad old days. We seemed to have come a long way since then. His memory hadn't returned but he was looking outside himself and learning to be more considerate towards other people.

I FELT MORE RELAXED and happy at home, and my spirits were also lifted by the work I was doing at Canine Partners. As well as helping at the groups for puppy walkers and their dogs, I started getting involved in the advanced training that was done when the dogs were between fourteen and eighteen months old.

The dogs learned lifesaving skills tailored to the person they were going to take care of. They might be trained to get help if someone has an epileptic fit, in particular pulling out the plug in the bath if they lost consciousness. If we lay down on the floor with our eyes shut during training, they had to find another trainer, stand in front of them and bark or even grab their clothes to try to pull them over to help. We used to get them to sit in front of someone, bark and paw at their leg, but this was stopped after one dog hurt a trainer's knee during a demo when they got just a little bit too enthusiastic!

I came home every day and told Allen what we had been doing, and he was curious and asked lots of questions, then really listened to the answers. It was wonderful to realise that we had this new interest in common. If anything had happened that upset me during the day, Allen listened and seemed to care. It made me feel less lonely than I had been. Our relationship was beginning to feel like a friendship, although it still wasn't a marriage.

Gracie had passed her advanced training and moved on to live with a wheelchair-bound QC, where she leads a very starry, high-powered life, moving in royal circles on occasion.

After her, I had a puppy called Indie for six months and then I took on a golden retriever called Ikea, who suffered damage to his immune system after a gut infection. He wasn't strong enough to become an assistance dog, but rather than have him put down we adopted him as a pet.

Gradually I was doing more and more volunteer work for Canine Partners, and I was over the moon when they asked if I would like a full-time, paid position with them. It was a Monday to Friday, nine-to-five job, with decent holidays and a whole week off between Christmas and New Year. It suited me down to the ground.

As a member of staff I learned how to choose from a litter of puppies the one that will make a good assistance dog. We were looking for a puppy that was not so bold that it would dash off and do its own thing, but confident enough that it wouldn't panic at any slight noise.

To test their responses, we would start by taking the puppies, one by one, to a place they hadn't been before. We'd give them a quick cuddle then put them down in a corner and run and hide somewhere. Some puppies would stay where they had been put down, get very anxious and even start crying. Others would get straight up and hurtle off in all directions, unconcerned about the fact they had been left alone. The ones we were interested in were the ones who would sit for a while then get up and start looking around in the immediate area trying to find the person who had brought them there.

After about a minute, we would go up to the puppy and clap loudly to see what the reaction was. Some would ignore us, some would approach us warily, others would be delighted to see a person again and would come up close to try to jump on our knees and say hello.

As I immersed myself in my wonderful new job, Allen became engrossed in dealing with the charity requests, and by supper time we always had a lot of news to discuss. We were starting to like each other again, I mused one day. I no longer saw that look of irritation and sheer hatred on his face. We were arguing less and talking much more.

ALLEN

Endal had an incredible appetite for learning new skills to help me. One day I went to get some money out of a cash machine. It was slightly tricky because the sun was shining on the screen, so I put the card in and then had to manoeuvre my chair to the other side to shade the keyboard so I could key in my PIN number. The machine spat my card back out before I had shifted myself back into the correct position to reach it and, without being asked, Endal jumped up and grabbed it in his mouth then turned and handed it to me.

'Wow! Good boy,' I said, and gave him a treat from my pocket.

Of course, once he saw that it earned him a treat, he was keen to repeat his new skill. When the money slid out, Endal leaped up to retrieve it before I could stop him. I took it from him rather nervously, hoping that his teeth hadn't torn any of the notes, but I needn't have worried. He was usually very gentle when picking anything up for me, and the worst that would happen was that items could be a bit slimy from his saliva.

Endal was delighted to have found a new way to assist me, so the cash point became part of our routine whenever we were in town. I thought I would see if he could go a step further, so one day when we arrived at the machine I put the card in Endal's mouth the right way round and he jumped up and tried to insert it in the slot. It took a bit of effort and a slight helping hand from me before he pushed it in and the machine sucked it away for processing. After that, Endal became an expert at positioning my card into all kinds of cash machines, whether they had slots on the sides or front.

One day in the summer of 1999, we were getting cash from a machine in Havant. I was quite blasé about it by now because Endal always did it perfectly. He put the card in the slot, waited while I keyed in my PIN number and then retrieved the card and the cash for me, in return for which I gave him a doggy treat. I was just tucking the money in my wallet when I felt a hand on my shoulder.

'Excuse me,' a man's voice said. 'Did I really just see your dog using the cash machine?'

'Yes. He always does it for me.' I turned the chair round.

'I'm a reporter for the *News of the World*. I'd be interested in running a story about this, but I wonder if you would mind getting your dog to do it again so I can take a photo?'

'Sure.' I shrugged. 'Why not?'

Endal performed impeccably, even holding still with the card in his mouth, poised at the entrance to the slot so the journalist could get the picture he wanted.

The journalist asked some questions about our relationship then said, 'Thanks very much,' and told us the article would be in the paper the following Sunday.

We bought the paper and there we were on page five. It felt nice, and I was glad that Endal was getting recognition for being so special.

Then, a month or so later, I got a letter through the post saying that *Dogs Today* magazine wanted to photograph Endal for a calendar they were producing for the new millennium. I can only assume they heard about us through the *News of the World* article. The letter said that they would then choose one of the twelve dogs they photographed to be their 'Dog of the Millennium'.

Sandra, the kids and I stayed in a hotel in Slough with Endal the night before the magazine photo shoot. At the photographer's studio the next day,

I was slightly disappointed when they decided Endal didn't need any grooming—he was handsome enough as he was. Endal was very cooperative and did whatever they asked him to.

After the photography, there was to be an announcement about which dog was to be the Millennium Dog. I hadn't really paid much attention to that part of the letter; I was just happy that Endal was going to be in a calendar at all. Then a woman came over and told us that Endal was the Dog of the Millennium and I couldn't believe my ears.

I was even more amazed when we were told that there was an award of £500, but straight away I said that the money would go to Canine Partners. Endal was their dog, and I certainly didn't intend to profit from him.

Several TV cameras and journalists appeared clutching notepads, tape recorders and microphones, and everyone was shouting: 'Where's Endal?' 'How does it feel to be the Millennium Dog?' 'Can we have a shot of the two of you?' and 'Look this way, please!'. I felt that Endal deserved it.

NEXT WE GOT an invitation to be interviewed on GMTV with Eamonn Holmes and Fiona Phillips. Everyone at the Canine Partners training centre was jumping up and down asking us to get their autographs, which I did. I don't remember much about that first TV appearance. Sandra did most of the talking and I just answered a few quick queries, in the same way we did at Canine Partners presentations. Endal sat sagely on the sofa, looking with interest at all the camera equipment and sound men with mics scurrying across the floor. He barked when asked to and behaved impeccably.

The Canine Partners management were delighted about the Dog of the Millennium award and the publicity it generated. Not long afterwards they invited me to become a trustee of the charity, which was an incredible boost to my confidence, still dented by the way the job at *Collingwood* had turned out. Maybe there was useful work I could do despite my faulty memory, damaged cognitive powers and unresponsive legs. Maybe I wasn't ready for the scrapheap just yet. I decided to devote myself to raising money for them as best I could, using Endal's media profile if that helped.

A Japanese film crew came to visit us at home. They had heard that Canine Partners dogs were taught to open washing machines and take the washing out so they asked if I could get Endal to demonstrate that. Now, this wasn't a skill that I had ever taught him so I was a bit concerned but I said we could have a go.

We put on Endal's jacket and I demonstrated opening the washing machine door and pulling out some clothes, then asked Endal to do it.

To my astonishment, he went straight up to the machine, opened the door, pulled out the washing into a basket positioned just below and pushed the door shut, before turning to me for a treat.

'I thought you said he couldn't do that!' the cameraman exclaimed.

'I didn't think he could . . .' I was as amazed as they.

'It was all a bit too fast, though,' they said. 'Do you think you could ask him to do it again so we can get it all on film?'

Endal was happy to oblige and pulled out the washing several times, opening and shutting the door with ease.

My life seemed to have turned round from misery and gloom to pride and achievement in just a couple of years. Where psychologists and therapists and doctors had all failed, a very talented Labrador had changed my world and made my life worth living again.

I LEARNED TO USE the trains to get up to London to keep up with all the media appointments. Every new journey I managed added to my confidence. I could never have gone without Endal, and I knew he would protect me.

One dark evening after a day's filming at a studio in London, we were making our way back through the streets towards Waterloo Station when a man came out of the shadows and walked towards me. As he passed I saw him checking out my rucksack. He got to the end of the street, then turned and came back in our direction. I unhooked the bag from the back of the chair, clutched it to my chest and wheeled myself faster. The street we were in was deserted so, my heart pounding, I made towards a road several blocks further along where I could see traffic flowing.

Suddenly Endal turned towards the man and started barking more loudly than I'd ever heard him bark before. The man stopped and Endal advanced towards him without any let up in the barking. I began to worry that the man might produce a knife, but after a moment's hesitation he turned and legged it. Without Endal, I've got no doubt I would have been mugged.

WE ALWAYS ENJOYED our annual trips to Crufts, held at Birmingham's NEC, but in 2001 the competition was delayed due to the outbreak of foot and mouth disease that swept the countryside in the early months of that year. It was May before it was finally held and Sandra was too busy with work to come along. Undeterred, Endal and I went along with the Canine Partners team to help on their stand.

By this, our fourth Crufts, we had our little routines and places where we liked to chill out. There was a mattress where we could lie down for a rest near the press centre, and little patches of grass where I took Endal. 'Better go now!' I'd say, and he'd obligingly empty his bladder. We booked in to a dog-friendly motel not far from the NEC and met some colleagues for dinner on the first night, May 24.

Afterwards we left the restaurant to cross the car park back to our chalet-style room. The light was fading and there were sounds of revelry from a nearby pub. All of a sudden I heard a car engine starting and before I knew it a car had reversed out of its parking spot and straight into us. In the split second when I realised what was happening, I tried to push Endal clear but then the car hit my chair and toppled me out onto the tarmac.

I think I lost consciousness briefly, winded by the fall. I only know what happened next because there is CCTV footage of it all.

Despite having taken quite a blow when the car hit him, Endal sprang into action. First of all, he grabbed my jacket in his teeth and pulled me on to my side, into the recovery position. Then he retrieved a blanket that had been on the wheelchair and pulled it over me. My phone had got knocked under the car as I fell, but Endal found it and placed it by my head. When I didn't start talking into it straight away, he realised more help was needed and he ran across to the pub, barking furiously to get attention.

I had come round by this stage but was dazed. I'm not sure what the driver of the car was doing, but I think he was very shocked. At any rate, it was Endal who got someone to summon an ambulance, and then he came back and waited by my side till help arrived. I tried to talk to him to show him I was all right but I think my voice was very shaky. I looked round and saw that my chair was badly buckled where the car's wheel had gone over it. I was lucky it hadn't gone over me as well.

An ambulance drew up and the men checked me out where I lay on the ground, then they lifted me onto a stretcher and into the back. Endal immediately climbed the ramp to follow. Once we got to A & E, a nurse tried to stop Endal coming through to the cubicle where I lay awaiting assessment, but he wasn't having it. He planted himself by my side, less than a foot away from my head, where he could see everything that went on, and he wouldn't budge.

It was one in the morning by this time and a child was sobbing loudly in the next-door cubicle. Poor kid! I thought. I wonder what he's doing in here at this time of night?

Suddenly Endal poked his nose under the curtain that divided us and stuck his head into the other side. The crying stopped immediately.

'Oh, there's a doggy here,' the child's voice said in amazement. The sight of a big yellow Labrador seemed to calm him down as the crying didn't start up again.

When the doctor came, he checked me for concussion and broken bones, but the only injury I'd incurred was bad bruising down my right side. The wheelchair was a write-off, though. Fortunately I had a power chair with me that was charging back at the motel, so I wouldn't be stranded.

I was taken back to my room in the early hours of the morning. I rang to tell Sandra that I was all right, and she was relieved to hear from me because someone had already phoned to tell her about the accident. The next day a vet checked Endal and said he was OK. It had been a shock but it was all over as far as I was concerned.

I WAS SO PROUD of Endal that I wanted to tell the whole world about him. I remember one time a film crew met us at Waterloo to film him opening and closing train doors, getting in and out of taxis and so forth. At lunchtime they offered to take me to a restaurant but I said, 'Actually that wouldn't be much fun for Endal. He needs to be a dog again just now.'

Instead of our posh lunch we went to Hyde Park to let him have a run-around and chase a few squirrels while we sat on a bench and ate some sandwiches. The director watched for a bit and then he said, 'This is really nice. We should try to get some footage of Endal running around like this.'

They stood up to discuss where the shots should be and Endal came over thinking he was on duty again.

'It's a bit windy,' the sound man was saying. He turned to his assistant. 'Can you get the boom mic out of my bag?'

Before the assistant could move, Endal had gone to the bag, pushed his nose in and pulled out the large furry microphone. They were all speechless and I was surprised as well. Earlier I'd noticed that Endal was interested in the mic, probably because it was grey and furry like a small animal, so I suppose he just tuned in to the name. That's the kind of dog he is. His brain is always switched on.

When I was away from home overnight, I could stay in hotels quite confidently knowing that Endal would look after me and keep me out of harm's way. If I fell asleep without switching the lights off and closing the curtains, he would do it for me. He could manage pull switches and push ones, and he didn't wait to be asked; he thought of what was needed to be done and just went ahead and did it. I wouldn't have had the courage to stay away from home on my own without him.

WHEN CANINE PARTNERS wanted to expand to cover the Yorkshire area, Yorkshire Electricity agreed to sponsor them, provided that they got plenty of local support. Endal and I went up to help raise the charity's profile and we made an appearance on Yorkshire TV's afternoon show and in a local pantomime. I've got photos of him meeting Snow White and the Seven Dwarfs—he barked at the dwarfs, which was somewhat embarrassing.

Back at the hotel, I let Endal out for a walk on the grass outside and he must have trodden on a piece of broken glass because when he came back in, the pad of his paw was bleeding heavily. I scooped him up and wheeled him across to the bed, then looked around for a *Yellow Pages* to find a local vet. There was one on a shelf in the bedside cabinet. I stretched but couldn't reach it from my chair and, before I could stop him, Endal had jumped down and picked it up for me. There was blood everywhere and for a horrible moment the thought occurred to me that he might die. It was as though a vice were tightening round my heart.

I bandaged him up as well as I could, then found the local duty vet who said to bring him straight in. A kind taxi driver came all the way up to the room and helped me to carry him downstairs. It was a deep cut but the vet managed to stop the bleeding, using some kind of spray.

'Would he like a biscuit?' the vet said when he'd finished and, on hearing the magic word, Endal jumped down off the table to look for the promised biscuit, thus opening up his wound yet again. You have to be careful when you use the 'b' word around him.

Finally, we were able to go back to the hotel, Endal limping heavily, and I felt as though I had been through the wringer emotionally. I hadn't had any dinner and I was exhausted, but all of that faded into the background compared with the anxiety I'd felt for Endal. He was the most unselfish creature in the universe. Even with a sore paw, he would jump off the bed to try to help me by getting the phone book.

I looked down at the handsome, clever Labrador who had given me so much and my stomach just turned over. It was an unfamiliar feeling that I couldn't place at first. My chest ached as I watched him lying there with his sore paw, sleepy but trying to keep his eyes open to see if I needed anything. Then I realised what the feeling was.

Sandra had told me about a night when she sat and kept watch over Liam, aged three, when he was in hospital with suspected meningitis. She'd described the intensity of her love for him that night and I realised that I was feeling the same kind of thing. That aching sensation in my chest was actually *love*. I don't know if it is the same way I'd experienced love before the accident but it was an immense, overpowering feeling.

It was gradual, of course, but once I started rediscovering these lost emotions, I began to look at my children and realise how smart and funny they can be. I'd missed so much of their lives when our relationship wasn't good because they just got on my nerves, and I can never get that time back. But I began to want to get to know them better and understand what made them tick. For example, it used to bug Zoe that I could never remember her teachers' names, so I made a concerted effort to write them down and ask her about her day at school and take an interest. I listened to her practising her clarinet and Liam playing his drums and asked questions about their tastes. I'll never remember their first words and first steps but I hope I'll always remember the sound of them laughing at a TV show or messing around together in the back garden.

And I started to look at Sandra as a person again rather than a carer. One day I remember I noticed how pretty her eyes were, and another day I sat admiring her kindness to beginners at the puppy classes. Then I started noticing what a nice laugh she has. I began to watch her when she didn't know I was looking, and thinking about how lucky I was to be married to her, and how extraordinary it was that she had stuck by me all those years since the accident. I'd thought this before, but in an intellectual way, and now I really began to feel it emotionally.

It was as though Endal had opened a little window in my brain that let me care about the people around me again. For eleven years I had been shut in my own selfish world where I only cared about other people in so far as they affected me. Now I realised I was interested in them for themselves and it mattered to me what happened to them. It might not sound much, but it was actually a huge leap forwards.

SANDRA

W ord of Endal's heroism in the car park incident spread like wild-fire because it happened at Crufts, which is full of dog-lovers. Journalists pricked up their ears and it quickly made national news. Soon Allen was getting more interview requests than ever before. They all wanted to ask how Endal had known about the recovery position. Was he trained to do that?

The answer was that he wasn't. Canine Partners dogs were trained to go and get help if their owner fell unconscious. Maybe Endal was trying to tug on Allen's clothes to wake him up in the car park that night, but I think he just instinctively realised that lying on his side was the safest position.

They've done demonstrations since then, and any time Allen lies on his back Endal will grab his jacket and pull him over onto his side.

Endal was always diligent, even when it wasn't necessary. Since he had learned so much about computers, Allen had started helping Canine Partners to set up new networks to connect their machines. There were times when that involved lying on the floor and stretching underneath desks to push plugs into sockets. Endal used to get really distressed when he saw Allen in that position and would try to tug him out. The staff and I stood in fits of laughter one day watching as Allen was trying to reach a socket while Endal was trying to pull him away. When he couldn't shift him, Endal began licking his face, making the job virtually impossible!

As the story of Endal's lifesaving skills appeared in doggy magazines, he began to be nominated for all kinds of awards. *Dogs Today* readers voted him 'Assistance Dog of the Year'; he won an internet vote to be 'Coolest Canine'; and then in 2002 Bonio dog biscuits ran an entry form on the side of the boxes where people could nominate a dog to win a new award they had created called the 'Golden Bonio'. Endal was given a special Lifetime Achievement award. We sent Endal up to collect the trophy himself—a big golden bone—then Allen wheeled himself up the ramp to the stage and said thank you.

And then came the one that meant the most to us: the PDSA Gold Medal, which is the animal equivalent of the George Cross. It's the UK's highest honour for animal bravery and the medal bears the inscription: 'For gallantry and devotion to duty.'

Three dogs were given the Gold Medal in 2002, the year it was introduced. Two of them—Monty and Bulla—were police dogs who had been injured in the line of duty trying to protect their handlers while they apprehended dangerous criminals. Endal's award was for outstanding devotion to duty and all his remarkable skills, in particular for getting help for Allen when he was knocked from his wheelchair despite the fact that he had been hit by the car himself.

Princess Alexandra presented the medal at the awards ceremony. We were immensely proud and the award sparked off a whole new onslaught of media requests. Other Canine Partners dogs won awards of course, but in 2002 none had achieve as much recognition as Endal. He was become a figurehead for the charity, a recognisable symbol of the good work they did.

Endal took all the celebrity in his stride with his usual good nature. He loved meeting people and showing off and would happily have turned up to the opening of a paper bag so long as there was a doggy treat for him.

Sometimes I'd hold Endal's head and look into his big brown eyes to try to see what made him tick. The truth is he has no side. He is a bit of a show-off who enjoys demonstrating what he can do, but above all he is a sensitive, compassionate dog who genuinely likes helping people in need. That's his character. And he utterly dotes on Allen with every fibre of his being. I think he knows how much he has done for Allen, but I shouldn't think he has any idea how much he has done to help me as well.

AFTER A NICE MEAL one evening we were sitting on the sofa watching TV and I slipped my fingers towards where Allen's hand lay on the seat. Immediately he took my hand and squeezed it, and tears came to my eyes. We carried on watching the show without saying a word, but we kept our fingers intertwined.

We started to become more physically affectionate with each other: just a cuddle in bed, or a quick kiss in the kitchen, but it was wonderful. There wasn't the high passion of the early years but no couple keeps that for ever anyway. We were companions who enjoyed each other's company for the most part, and that was pretty good going after all we'd been through.

One day we were at a Canine Partners event. One of the girls had just got engaged so there was lots of chatter about weddings. Someone asked Allen about our wedding and he said, 'I don't remember getting married.' It was just an offhand comment, something he was no longer concerned about, but it bugged me.

'You may not remember the first wedding but you'll remember the second,' I told him quietly, without thinking it through. He looked puzzled, not understanding my meaning.

It was a throwaway comment on the spur of the moment, but over the next few days I gave it more thought. You read about lots of people who renew their vows or have their union blessed and I realised I wanted to do something like that. I thought it all through before I broached the subject with Allen again.

'How would you feel about us getting remarried?' I asked. 'So that we have a wedding day you can remember.'

He looked startled at first, and then he said, 'Was that what you were hinting about the other day? Are you serious?'

I nodded. 'Perhaps we could look into it and see what we can do.'

'Yes,' he said thoughtfully. 'I'd like that.'

On our nineteenth wedding anniversary we had a second ceremony, one that Allen could remember. There had been three Allens in my life: the high-flying, infinitely capable yet romantic man I had first married; the angry, taciturn, selfish one I had nursed for years; and now the contented partner with whom I had a shared interest in our dogs. When I looked into Allen's eyes I knew he loved me, although he was no longer demonstrative or spontaneously affectionate. It wasn't the marriage I had thought I was signing up for nineteen years earlier but it was good in a different way.

ALLEN

Sandra made all the arrangements for our second wedding and I was happy to let her. It was her big day and, as far as I was concerned, she could have it just the way she wanted it. I kept pinching myself because I felt so lucky that she was still prepared to stick by me after everything we'd been through. I knew I'd been awful to her in the eleven years since my accident. I'd been moody and unresponsive for most of that time, and I hadn't any right to expect her to stay with me; I'm just incredibly fortunate that she did because I'd fallen in love with her all over again. I woke up the next morning and turned to look at her sleeping in bed beside me and was filled with a warm glow. This is what I wanted for the rest of my life.

My early charity work was all for doggy charities but, as the story got out about how I had been injured, I began to get requests from military charities to give talks to men who had lost limbs or suffered spinal injuries that left them paraplegic or quadriplegic. I was happy to go along if they thought I could be of use, but I didn't realise at first just how powerfully it was going to affect me. Meeting guys who were going through the same experiences that I had gone through after my injury took me right back to those times.

Like me, at first they were all convinced they would one day walk again, and resisted being labelled as 'disabled'. Like me, they became furiously angry when progress was slow and they often took their anger out on those closest to them. And, also like me, the majority of them became suicidal at some stage. It shone a harsh light back on some very dark years and made me realise just how impossible I must have been to live with—and I had had no idea at the time.

I sat and listened to their stories, letting them pat Endal as they talked, and when I looked into their eyes I saw a ghost of myself. Sometimes I felt a bit sick and panicky when I wheeled myself into a unit but I owed it to the men there to listen and keep calm and tell them a bit about my own story, if they were interested.

In 2004, Canine Partners was asked to take a team up to meet the Queen at Windsor Castle and tell her a bit about our work. I was overjoyed when they asked if Endal and I would come along, although sadly Sandra wasn't part of the delegation.

We drove up there in a minibus and were led out to the castle's stable yard, where they had laid ramps to make it wheelchair-accessible for me. The Queen appeared and some of our young puppies did a display of their skills, then I was asked to come up in front of Her Majesty and tell her a bit about my experiences.

She seemed genuinely moved when I told her my story. The Queen was very understanding, and I found her to be a genuinely sympathetic human being. She took a real liking to Endal and kept petting him as we were talking. What's more, I got a lovely letter afterwards saying that she had been very touched by our visit.

AN ARMED FORCES CHARITY asked me to come along to an event they had organised for the families of men who had recently lost their lives in Iraq and Afghanistan. When we arrived I could see the hurt, anger and bewilderment on the children's little faces and wondered what on earth I could do. There was one girl in particular who, the helpers told me, hadn't spoken a single word since she'd been told about her father's death.

Endal soon noticed the silent little girl and obviously decided he wanted to get a reaction from her. She was ignoring everyone, turning away from us with abrupt, dramatic gestures, and Endal started copying her. She looked up; he looked up. She looked down; he looked down. She noticed what he was doing out of the corner of her eye but didn't want to react, so he kept going: putting his head to one side, shifting, even lifting his paw when she raised a hand to rub her face. Before long, she started moving deliberately to test him. He kept copying her and I saw a smile creep onto her face as she realised the power she had. Finally, the whole situation was so comical that she burst out laughing and the barriers came down.

Endal walked up to her and she got down on the floor and flung her arms round him. The helpers whispered to me that it was the first time they had seen her smile since her dad died. I decided to go over and have a word.

'He's copying everything you're doing,' I said, 'so I hope you're not going to do something rude like burping.'

She giggled, and we started to chat. I told her that Endal had a friend called Ikea back at home and she wanted to know more about how they got on. I described what they were like together, and then I said, 'Endal is missing his friend. Are you missing your daddy?' And she looked down and nodded. 'Give Endal a big cuddle,' I said, and she did. It was very moving. Yet another example of 'the Endal effect'.

Endal has always loved children of all ages, particularly ill or vulnerable ones. When we were invited to visit a home for autistic children, I knew they would enjoy meeting him. It can be difficult for people with autism to relate to human beings because they aren't able to read the social signals that most of us take for granted, but with Endal none of that matters. He doesn't put any stock in social rules.

When we first walked into the room, I got him to perform some of his wide range of barks, all at different commands from me, and that got the children's attention. It made them look outside the little protective shells they exist inside.

'Does he bite?' a little girl asked.

'Not once in his whole life,' I said truthfully.

Nervously they came forward to stroke him and he lowered his head to let them. We showed him playing games with his Kong, and picking up things I dropped, and the kids were totally engrossed. Some of them wanted to hug him and I was worried they would squeeze too tightly but Endal put up with it all uncomplainingly.

Endal encourages people to feel warmth and affection again in the same way he did for me: by being totally non-threatening and non-judgmental and just offering a level of communication that it is impossible for them not to respond to. I'm always very proud and humbled when I see him reaching out like that. Other people might get the benefit of the Endal effect for a few hours or an afternoon, but I was lucky enough to get it for his whole life, more or less.

The core of Endal's life has been his devotion to me, which is absolute. He will put up with just about anything so long as I am nearby. If I have to go to the toilet without him and ask someone else to hold his lead, he will sit gazing in the direction I went until I get back, and no earthquake or hurricane could shift him from his post. When I have to be lifted up to an aeroplane on the hydraulic lift, a stewardess will usually walk Endal up the steps for me and he sits on the top step peering out until I'm beside him.

I'd like to think I have earned this devotion, but I haven't. No one could. Endal would lay down his life for me in a heartbeat, as he's shown on the occasions he has protected me in the past without any thought for his own safety. In the early years, I was surly and ungrateful and took him for granted. Once I had learned to love him, I tried my best to be a playmate and to make sure he has everything he wants.

After Endal's tenth birthday in December 2006, Sandra tentatively asked me if I had thought about what I would do when it was time to retire him. He still occasionally went a bit lame, he was going slightly deaf and he got more tired than he used to. I realised that I was going to need a new dog, but I just couldn't face thinking about life without Endal.

We talked and talked about it and meanwhile Sandra mentioned to the people at work that we were looking and asked the breeders they worked with to let us know if there was a suitable litter. I was clear that I wanted another yellow Labrador and that I wanted a boy.

'We'll call the new one EJ,' I said. 'Short for Endal Junior.' We also agreed that there should be a good overlap period so that EJ could learn from Endal what I needed and how to go about things. I wasn't optimistic that we would find a dog with a tenth of Endal's qualities, but I accepted that it was only fair to let him retire.

SANDRA

It was summer 2008 when we got a call to say there was a litter of yellow Labradors we might like to come and inspect. Allen and I drove over to the breeder to have a look. As soon as we arrived one puppy came straight out of the litter pen with mud all over his head, so we nicknamed him 'Dirty Head'. Instinctively I thought to myself that he was the one.

Allen was very quiet, just sitting and observing, so I did the usual Canine Partners tests on all three boys in the litter. We took them out into a field and two of them made a dash for freedom, but Dirty Head came over and tried to climb onto us, wanting to play. He was obviously the one that wanted to be with people, and I said to Allen I thought we should take him.

'I don't know,' he said. 'I'm not sure if this is what I want.'

I asked the breeder to keep him while I talked Alan round, but I couldn't persuade him to make a decision. It was he who would have to be stuck at home looking after a new puppy so I could understand that was something he had to think about. The weeks went by, but Allen was having real difficulty with the concept of replacing Endal. We reached the eight-week limit when the puppies were ready to go to their new homes, and it was not until I told him that the puppy would probably go to someone else that he finally made the phone call and said, 'Can we come and pick him up?' A brand-new bundle of uncontained energy exploded into our peaceful household.

What was strange was that Endal seemed to know what was going on. People say you shouldn't attribute human emotions to dogs but I swear that Endal looked at this puppy coming into the house and thought: Hey, I can relax now. The next morning when Allen got up, Endal had a lie-in for the first time in his life. He had such a long sleep that we had to go and check up on him to see he was all right. It was the first day of his retirement and he'd decided to take it easy—and he had every right.

Of course, EJ couldn't work for Allen straight away. He had to learn the basics, such as toileting, sitting in his crate, not jumping up and barking, and that takes weeks to achieve. Allen has always used different voices to get each dog's attention, and he developed a high-pitched squeaky one for EJ that had me in stitches. He also started using a hand-held clicker. When there are three dogs in the house you need to be quite clear which one you are talking to and be able to make them stop in their tracks at any time, and Allen's got that down to a T.

EJ is a lively but bright toddler who seems keen to learn and will copy whatever he sees Endal and Ikea doing. If they pick up the post from the mat, the next day EJ will rush to get it first. He'll probably slobber all over it and destroy it before it reaches us but the instinct to help is there. He watched Endal opening cupboard doors for Allen in the kitchen when he was putting the washing-up away and, one morning, EJ just came in when I was there, pulled on the tuggie and opened the door for me. I looked round and Endal was watching from his bed, as if pleased with his star pupil.

I'd bought EJ outright from the breeders, and Ikea had been mine since we'd adopted him, but on paper Endal still belonged to Canine Partners. As he approached retirement we asked if he could be officially signed over to us, and they were happy to agree.

I know it meant a lot to Allen that Endal was finally 'his' dog and no one could take him away again. He was very moved. After that we talked about setting a retirement date for Endal when he would stop making public appearances and stay at home to rest more. We decided on a date just a few weeks later because he'd seemed very old and slow recently. But as it turned out, events were about to force us to take action sooner than we'd thought.

ALLEN

In early September 2008, Endal and I had a busy week. Endal was presented with his wings by British Airways after having made fifty flights with them, so we squashed into a car and drove to Southampton airfield to get the award. Then we went up to London for a business-award ceremony in the Albert Hall, at which Prince Charles was present.

Afterwards there was a school to visit, and at all these events Endal had to put on a bit of a show. The next morning when he woke up he could hardly drag himself out of his bed. He'd always had osteochondritis, of course, but he hadn't gone lame this badly for years, even after long photo shoots. It wasn't just the front paws; he seemed to be having trouble with all four.

Endal had two vets—one for everyday things, and another who specialised in joint problems. We took him to see the specialist first. There was a veterinary student with him that day.

'Let's see him walking,' the vet asked, so we took Endal outside to the road and he managed to walk.

'Now let's see him trotting,' he said, but Endal froze completely when he tried.

The vet and his student had to lift him back inside and put him up on a table. The vet started feeling Endal's legs, which made him yelp with pain. The vet pointed out to us that both Endal's left and his right front legs were very swollen. 'What's happened is that although the right leg is the main problem, he has tried to compensate by over-using the left and now it's in trouble as well. Because of this he's been trying to use the back legs and they're giving up too, making him quadrilaterally lame.'

As well as the leg problems, Endal had ongoing problems with ankylosing spondylitis, a disorder in which the vertebrae of his back were fusing together. A bone specialist from another part of the practice came in to join the discussion.

Sandra and I were expecting that they would perhaps increase his medication and ask me to let him rest for a week or two, so the next words came as a complete bolt from the blue.

'Basically,' the first vet said, 'if you were to ask me to put this dog down now, I would support that request.'

I couldn't believe my ears. I looked at Sandra. Her eyes were welling up and she was gripping the edge of her chair. I looked at Endal, worried that he might understand what we were saying, but he lay there oblivious.

'Quality of life is an issue here,' the vet continued, 'and while the threshold has not quite been reached, it could be very close.'

I started to shake. Neither of us said a word, but I suppose the vet saw from our reaction that this wasn't an option we were ready to consider. To me, it sounded barbaric. How could I think of killing my best friend and faithful companion when he still loved his life?

The vet continued, 'It's either that or a question of managing the pain as long as he has a decent quality of life. I can give you some morphine-based painkillers that will take the pain away but they'll make him quite dopey. I'd suggest you give them to him in the evening, before bedtime.'

Endal had been taking a non-steroidal anti-inflammatory drug for easing his arthritis for years, and they said we should increase the dosage. The vet suggested he should sleep downstairs rather than trying to climb the stairs, that he should only have very short walks and, in particular, he should stop jumping up and putting his feet on my lap as I sat in the wheelchair—the classic Endal and Allen pose—because it jarred his joints every time he jumped down again.

'If we can manage the pain and make the lifestyle changes, he could have a bit longer—how long, nobody knows. You need to find the level at which the painkillers work but don't knock him out too much. There's a plateau the dog can find for himself.'

I concentrated hard, determined to remember every instruction. Sandra seemed numb with shock still. I reached over and squeezed her hand.

Afterwards, we lifted Endal into the car and drove away in complete silence, Sandra especially careful to avoid bumps in the road that might jar his joints. Neither of us could bear even to repeat the words the vet had said. We carried Endal into the house and laid him on his bed and gave him an extra-special dinner that night and lots of doggy treats.

We started him on the painkillers but not on massive doses. We wanted to take the edge off the pain but not medicate him to the extent that he would stop feeling any twinges and might do something stupid like trying to chase a squirrel or swim across a lake. You can't cure arthritis but you can manage it if you're careful, and I think Endal realises he has to be circumspect now.

When I take Endal and EJ out for a walk together, Endal lets EJ take his traditional place at my right side and he stands further out, protecting both of us. EJ absolutely adores him. When I open his crate in the morning, he'll go straight over to Endal and lick his face to say hello. I'd always hoped they'd have longer to work together, so we could go out and about as a threesome and EJ could learn from Endal how things are done—but it wasn't to be. Endal's just not up to coming out on trips with me any more. Ikea does more for me now than Endal does and EJ is learning fast.

It became a lot harder for me when Endal stepped down. It was a complete pain when I dropped something and couldn't reach it, or needed to dig something out of my rucksack or reach up to pay for a pint in our local without his help. It was much slower to get on a bus, wheel myself to the front to pay the driver, then turn round and go back to park myself in the wheelchair space, and it meant the bus had to stop for longer while I did all this. I'm not confident enough to catch a plane somewhere and stay overnight in a hotel on my own without Endal, so I miss the busy social aspects of the life we were leading before.

I'm getting more tired now though, and often fall asleep on the sofa in the evenings, with Endal beside me. He's earned his rest. All the signs are that EJ will be able to take over his role bit by bit and in a year's time I'll be able to get out and about again as much as I ever did.

EPILOGUE—SANDRA

Every evening when I leave work, I ring Allen from the car. It's our catch-up time when we share the details of our day—where we've been, who we saw. Allen tells me what he's got planned for dinner and maybe I'll make a suggestion about what vegetables could go with it. We talk about everything so that when I arrive at the house I can switch off. It's become part of our routine, and it's one of the ways I unwind from the stress of my job.

When I get in Allen will have the dinner on and EJ will be running around playing. He's learning fast but, like any toddler, he can still be incredibly foolish. I once saw him trying to steal a food treat out of Ikea's mouth but he got his comeuppance fairly quickly with a sharp bark and a nip. Endal is more like an over-indulgent parent, smiling as he watches his favourite child learning the ways of the world.

Liam has a managerial career with a supermarket but he still lives with us, although you'd hardly know it from the amount of time he spends at home. Zoe qualified as a nursery-school teacher and has her own flat, but she will call on me if she needs a room repainted or a loan to get her to the end of the month. They don't need us much any more and that means Allen and I have more time to be a couple.

In November 2008 it was the twenty-fifth anniversary of our first wedding, and that made me stop and reflect on the huge life changes we've been through. The man I married in 1983 was an ambitious, competitive, high-flying naval officer, with a wicked sense of humour and a deeply compassionate side. Today he is still competitive and he still has a great sense of humour but his life is focused on helping others. I'm so proud of everything he's achieved.

Even though Endal is retired, we still get invited to media events, but most evenings you'll find us at home, just relaxing together. We've got two sofas but we indulge Endal by letting him lie on one of them if there aren't any guests. He dozes on his back, legs akimbo, looking very comfy and occasionally making gentle little snoring noises. His condition is stable now and he's enjoying a comfortable retirement.

We didn't celebrate our silver wedding anniversary on the day but we are planning a cruise that will take us from San Diego down through the Panama Canal. Allen has described to me the way the jungle encroaches on either side of the ship, and it sounds beautiful.

I prefer to look to the future now instead of the past. We've been through a lot, but we've survived and now we have so many good things to look forward to. I'm lucky enough to have found the man I want to grow old with, and that is a great blessing. The fact that he's good at doing silly voices and training dogs to use cashpoint machines is just the icing on the cake.

ENDNOTE: *In March 2009, Endal died peacefully in Allen's arms. He is literally irreplaceable, but on April 6, ten-month-old Endal Junior attended his first official engagement taking Allen up to a lunch at the Stationers' Hall in London, happily coping with train, tube, ticket barriers and a taxi ride. EJ dutifully barked once at the loyal toast, and twice at the thanks. Allen said: 'A few eyes in the room filled up, including mine, and I guess Endal would have been looking down with pride.'*

allen and sandra **parton**

1: Sandra and Allen Parton celebrate their wedding in 1983; after his accident in 1991, Allen would have no memory of this happy day.

2: Liam and Zoe Parton, aged three and two.

3: The Parton family on holiday.

4: Endal posting a letter for Allen—one of many valuable tasks he performed for his master.

5: His ability to use a cash machine brought Endal to the attention of the media.

6 and **7**: Helping with daily chores.

8: As he neared retirement, Endal took the training of his replacement, EJ, very seriously.

9: 'The team'.

10: In 2002, after nineteen years of marriage, Sandra and Allen celebrated their 'second wedding'.

5

8

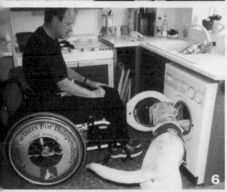

6

9

7

10

HELL BENT

WILLIAM G. TAPPLY

Boston-based lawyer Brady Coyne finds his past returning to haunt him when an old flame, Alex Shaw, shows up at his office asking if he will represent her brother Gus in his divorce proceedings.

Brady sees no reason to turn down the case—or the chance to be with Alex again. But when his new client, a photojournalist recently back from Iraq, is found dead, the questions mount. And Brady finds himself dealing with something far more sinister than matrimonial wranglings . . .

UNIVERSITY OF MASSACHUSETTS BLAST KILLS SEVEN, LEVELS PHYSICS BUILDING
ANTIWAR GROUP THOUGHT RESPONSIBLE

AMHERST, MASSACHUSETTS, AUGUST 24, 1971: At 3.04 a.m. on Tuesday morning, an explosion believed to be set off by antiwar extremists destroyed UMass's Cabot Hall, which housed the university's physics department. Seven people died in the blast.

The school's fall semester was scheduled to begin in ten days, and summer sessions ended a week ago, so the campus was largely deserted. 'We hate to even imagine the possible loss of life if school had been in session,' said university spokesperson Eva Shallot.

Of the seven who died in the explosion, six were graduate students whose names have yet to be released. The seventh victim has been tentatively linked to the Soldiers Brigade, a radical antiwar organisation.

FBI investigator Martin Greeley, in a prepared statement, said: 'The timing of this unspeakable action is no coincidence. The Sterling Hall explosion at the University of Wisconsin occurred one year ago almost to the minute. There is no doubt that last night's event is also the work of radical left-wing antiwar terrorists.' Greeley indicated that arrests are imminent.

Last summer's Wisconsin explosion, which occurred at 3.42 a.m. on August 24, was linked to a student antiwar group called the New Year's Gang. Four people, all students, have been arrested in connection with that event. A fifth remains at large.

UMASS BLAST TERRORISTS ARRESTED,
VICTIMS' NAMES RELEASED
FBI: 'CASE CLOSED'

AMHERST, MASSACHUSETTS, AUGUST 29, 1971: The final two members
of the Soldiers Brigade, a radical antiwar group of Vietnam veterans
believed to be responsible for the deadly explosion at the University of
Massachusetts last Tuesday morning, were arrested without
incident last night at a motel in White River Junction, Vermont.

'All of our suspects are now in custody,' said FBI spokesman
Martin Greeley.

The alleged leader of the terrorist group, a decorated Vietnam
veteran from Keene, New Hampshire, named John Kinkaid, was
identified as one of the seven victims of the UMass blast. The other six
victims were graduate students working on a laboratory project.

'Kinkaid was the brains,' said Greeley at a press conference. 'He
was a fugitive, wanted for the explosion a year ago in Wisconsin. In
both cases, Kinkaid procured and set up the explosives, which he was
familiar with from his military experience. It appears that he was
rigging them inside the University of Massachusetts building when an
electronic malfunction of some kind detonated them prematurely. We
believe Kinkaid's intention was for the explosion to occur at 3.42 a.m.,
the same time as the Wisconsin event that he masterminded.'

When asked to compare the UMass explosion with the one at the
University of Wisconsin a year ago, Greeley said: 'The Wisconsin
explosion was caused by a crude homemade bomb. The perpetrators
of that crime, aside from Kinkaid, were student radicals. This
Massachusetts event was the work of a misguided group of Vietnam
veterans, including Kinkaid, all of whom appear to be suffering from
depression, shell shock and disorientation from their military
service. In addition to the timing and their apparent aim of bringing
attention to the war, the one commonality between the two explosions
was the target.'

Both university buildings housed military research projects funded
by government contracts.

No information has been made available about preparations for
trials of the alleged terrorists.

ONE

It was a few minutes before five in the afternoon on the second Thursday in October. I had just hung up the phone from my last client of the day, a paediatrician who was getting divorced and wanted to hang on to as much of his money and dignity as the law would allow. He had plenty of money, but he was running short of dignity. Divorce does that to people.

It does it to their lawyers, too.

I had swivelled my desk chair round so I could look out of my office window. The low-angled late-afternoon October sun was washing the tops of the Trinity Church and the Copley Plaza Hotel with warm orange light, and dusk was beginning to seep into the floor of the city. It was the last gasp of Indian summer in Boston. Already the scarlet leaves were losing their grip on the maples that grew along the walkways that intersected the plaza. A bittersweet time of year in New England. Evie had been gone for nearly four months, and I had no plans to go trout fishing again until next spring.

There came a soft one-knuckle tap on my office door. Without turning round, I said, 'Come on in, Julie. I'm off the phone.'

I heard the door open and close behind me.

'You notice how early it's getting dark these days?' I swivelled round. 'You can—' I stopped. Blinked. Shook my head. Smiled.

It wasn't Julie, my faithful secretary, standing on the other side of my desk with an armload of manila folders.

It was Alexandria Shaw.

I got up, went round my desk and opened my arms.

She smiled, stepped forward and gave me a hug.

'Julie could've warned me,' I said. 'What's it been?'

'Seven years,' she said. 'It's been a little over seven years.'

'Seven years since you dumped me.' I stepped back from her. 'You look great.' I frowned. 'Something's different.'

She smiled. I remembered that lopsided, cynical smile. 'Everything's different after seven years, Brady.'

'Yeah, but there's something. What is it?'

'My hair's a little longer. Some of them have turned grey. A few new wrinkles. I got contacts. Gained a couple of pounds.' She waved her hand, dismissing the subject of her appearance. 'I'm actually here on business. I need a good lawyer.'

'It's the glasses,' I said. 'You used to wear glasses. They kept slipping down to the tip of your nose.'

'That's why I got contact lenses.'

'I used to think it was sexy,' I said. 'The way you'd keep poking at them with your forefinger, pushing them back.'

She shrugged. 'That was a long time ago.'

'You need a lawyer, huh?'

'Maybe I could buy you a drink?'

I glanced at my watch, then shook my head. 'I've got to get home, feed my dog. He's expecting me.'

'Your dog.'

'His name is Henry. Henry David Thoreau. He's a Brittany. He knows when it's suppertime, and he sulks if I'm late.'

'I should've made an appointment,' Alex said. 'Julie didn't say anything about a dog needing to be fed.'

'I bet she said a lot about other things.'

She shrugged. 'We caught up.'

'She always liked you.'

'It took her a while, if you remember,' Alex said. 'Julie is very protective of you. Still is. Wanted to be sure my intentions were honourable today before she let me see you. I had to convince her I didn't come here to seduce you.'

'She told you about Evie?'

Alex nodded. 'I'm sorry to hear . . .'

'Yeah,' I said. 'Oh, well.'

'How're you doing?'

'I'm getting used to it.' I smiled at her. 'You don't need an appointment. I'm a little off-balance here. I meant it about Henry, but the drink is a good idea. Why don't you come home with me. I've got a nearly full jug of Rebel Yell. You always liked Rebel Yell.'

'You sure? I mean . . .'

'What exactly did Julie tell you?'

'She said you bought a town house on Beacon Hill and were living with a hospital administrator named Evie Banyon. Julie said Evie is smart and quite beautiful, and she implied that you love her. But Evie's gone now, and you don't know when—or if—she'll be back.' Alex smiled. 'Julie said you've been lonely and sad lately.'

'I should fire that woman,' I said. 'She talks too much.'

'She certainly does,' said Alex. 'But she cares about you.'

'So what else did Julie say?' I said.

'She said she likes Evie,' Alex said, 'but she's quite angry at her for deserting you.'

'Evie's out in California taking care of her father,' I said. 'On his house-boat in Sausalito. He's dying of pancreatic cancer. I support what she's doing. She didn't desert me.'

'But she's gone.'

'Yes,' I said. 'She's gone.'

Alex looked at me for a minute. 'This was a mistake. I'll go make an appointment with Julie.' She turned for the door.

'I meant it about the drink,' I said. 'I want to hear about your problem. You'll like Henry.'

She turned back to face me. 'I didn't come here to seduce you. Honest. And for the record, I didn't dump you.'

'Well,' I said, 'in the final analysis, you did. But I suppose it was more complicated than that.' I shrugged. 'It's easier for me to think of it that way, that's all. Anyway, it was seven years ago. I've forgiven you.'

She glared at me. '*You've* forgiven *me*?'

I held up both hands, palms out. 'I'm kidding.'

'It was you who kissed that woman, Brady Coyne.'

'Do you want to pick at old scabs,' I said, 'or do you want to come meet my dog and have a smooth glass of sippin' whisky and tell me why you need a lawyer?'

She looked at me for a moment, then nodded. 'The drink and the dog. We can save the scab picking for another time.' She smiled. 'You always did know how to piss me off.'

'And vice versa,' I said. 'It was one of the strengths of our relationship.'

ALEX HAD LEFT her car at the Alewife T station and taken the train into the city, and I had walked to work. It was warm and pleasant, so we decided to walk from my office in Copley Square to my town house on Mt Vernon Street on Beacon Hill. There was between us the awkwardness of intimate old friends who hadn't even spoken for seven years. We had once loved each other. Now we were strangers, getting to know each other all over again.

So we exchanged some facts about our lives as we poked along Newbury Street. Alex still lived in her little house on the dirt road in Garrison, Maine. I used to drive up from Boston to spend weekends with her. A couple of years after she and I parted ways, she married a Portland land developer, and a couple of years after that, they divorced amicably.

She'd finished the book she'd been working on when we were together. It was a collection of case studies about domestic abuse that got her a few talk-show appearances and made it onto the bottom end of some best-seller lists, and then she published a novel inspired by one of the cases. The novel got good reviews, and her publisher was encouraging her to write another one. Now she was trying to get a handle on her story.

I told her about buying the town house from the family of a client who'd been murdered, how a dog had come with the house, how Evie and Henry and I had been cohabiting there for the past few years, and how Evie had bought herself a one-way ticket to California the previous June.

Alex didn't offer to tell me why she'd come down to Boston from Garrison, Maine, or why she needed a lawyer, or why she thought I should be that lawyer, and I didn't ask.

WE SAT BESIDE each other in my wooden Adirondack chairs in the little walled-in patio garden behind my house. I'd put my jug of Rebel Yell and a platter holding a wedge of extra-sharp Vermont cheddar and a handful of Wheat Thins on the picnic table, and we drank the whisky on the rocks from thick glass tumblers. Alex had slipped Henry a hunk of cheese, making her his friend for life.

'This is nice,' she said. She was looking up at the darkening autumn sky. 'Quite a change from that dump you used to have on Lewis Wharf.'

'That wasn't a dump,' I said. 'I was just a dumpy housekeeper.'

She didn't say anything for a few minutes, and neither did I. We sipped our drinks. Then she said, 'It's my brother, not me. Why I need a lawyer. It's for him. Do you remember Gus?'

'I never met him,' I said. 'You used to talk about him. Your big brother, Augustine. Alexandria and Augustine. Your parents had fun with names. He's a photographer, isn't he?'

'A photojournalist, to be precise,' she said. 'He didn't create art, and he didn't do weddings or proms. He told stories.'

I nodded. 'Telling stories runs in your family. Gus travelled a lot, I seem to remember. So what's he need me for?'

'He's getting divorced.'

'Wait a minute,' I said. 'You used the past tense. You said Gus *told* stories. Meaning . . .?'

'It's kind of a long story.'

'And I bet it's connected to why he wants me to represent him.'

'Sure it's connected,' Alex said. 'Everything's connected. But this is me. I'm the one who wants you to represent him.'

'He doesn't?'

'He doesn't know what he wants.'

'Well, consider it done,' I said. 'Just have him give me a call.' I hesitated. 'This is nice, seeing you again. But really, I do divorces all the time, and it's not as if I'm likely to refuse to represent him. It wasn't necessary—'

'Like I said,' she said. 'It's a long story, Brady.' She put her hand on my wrist. 'You'll represent him?'

'Assuming he's getting divorced in Massachusetts, where I'm allowed to practise law, sure.'

'He's renting a place in Concord now. He works in a camera store there. His wife and kids live in Bedford.'

'How long have they been separated?'

'A little over six months. It's . . . Why don't I just tell you.'

I slouched back in my chair. 'Proceed,' I said.

'Gus came back from Iraq a little over a year ago,' she said. 'He doesn't say much about it. He lost his right hand. He's—he *was*—right-handed. So now he's given up photography. Says he can't manipulate a camera one-handed.' Alex took a sip from her glass. 'He's got two little girls. My nieces. Clea and Juno. His wife, a really nice woman named Claudia—Gus travelled all over the world, and he ended up marrying the girl he took to his senior prom—Claudia asked him to leave back in the spring, and now she's hired a lawyer and she wants a divorce, and Gus, he's not doing anything.'

'He needs to be represented,' I said.

'I know,' said Alex. 'That's why I'm here. Can you represent somebody who doesn't want to be represented, says he doesn't care what happens?'

'Not unless he asks me to,' I said. 'He sounds depressed.'

'Oh, he's depressed, all right. He has been ever since he got back, if depressed is what you want to call it.'

'Post-traumatic stress disorder, huh?' I said. 'He lost his hand. Probably saw a lot of horror.'

She nodded. 'I guess so. That's why he went over there. To take pictures of the horror.'

'Was he embedded?'

Alex shook her head. 'Not Gus. He was independent and proud of it. He believed that being embedded meant being controlled. Being censored. He went on his own, at his own expense. It's what he always did. He was always off somewhere looking for a story to take pictures of. That was his career. Finding the stories that weren't being told, the shadows and angles that he believed needed to be exposed. He thought it was important.'

'So what stories did he find in Iraq?'

Alex shrugged. 'I don't know. He was over there for about a year, and then he came home without his right hand, and he hasn't said much of anything to anybody.'

'Is he being treated for it?' I said. 'The PTSD?'

'He's in some kind of support group. Or he was. I don't know if he's still going. He's on medication, I do know that.' She shook her head. 'There's a lot I don't know. It was Claudia who called me, told me she was divorcing my brother and he refused to retain a lawyer and, as much as she couldn't live with him and didn't want him around her kids, she was worried about him and thought he should have a lawyer. So I called Gus, told him I was coming down. I figured I'd stay with him for a few days, try to get him pointed in the right direction.'

'Get him a lawyer,' I said.

'Yes,' she said. 'Ideally, you. And see how he was doing and if there was anything I could do for him.' She blew out a breath. 'When we were growing up, Gus was my hero. I called him Gussie. Everybody loved him, or that's how it seemed to me. He was a really good athlete; he was strong and handsome; he laughed all the time. He made me laugh. He was nice to me. I was just this bratty little four-eyed sister. But he didn't tease me or get mad at me or ignore me, even though he was eight years older than me. He read to me at bedtime, taught me how to play checkers . . .'

I could see the glitter of tears in her eyes.

'So I drove down from Maine a few days ago, and basically he said

I couldn't stay with him, that he had to be alone. Said he was working on some things. It was pretty obvious that me being there made him edgy. So I got a room at the Best Western there by the roundabout in Concord. I've had supper with him a couple of times, and he pretends that everything's all right. I know he's just trying to protect me, the way he's always done.'

'But you're worried about him,' I said.

'His life has gone all to hell, Brady. I guess he's going to have to work most things out for himself, but the least I can do is make sure he gets a fair shake in this divorce. Now he's saying he doesn't care. I figure someday he will care.'

'That's exactly right,' I said. 'I see that a lot. One of the parties—usually the husband—he's racked with guilt or just overwhelmed by the whole thing, he thinks he doesn't care what happens. He thinks if he gets screwed, it's what he deserves.'

'That's Gussie exactly,' said Alex.

'He said he was working on some things?' I said.

'I think it was just his way of getting me off his back.'

'Why did Claudia kick him out of the house?'

She shrugged. 'I'm sure he was pretty hard to live with. I figure that's none of my business.'

'If I'm going to be Gus's lawyer, it will have to be my business. Anyway, if he doesn't agree to have me represent him, it's all moot.'

'He'll agree,' said Alex. 'I'll take care of that. And just to be clear about it, I intend to pay you.'

'Right. Of course.'

'I *do.* And don't you patronise me, Brady Coyne.'

'I'd never patronise you, Alexandria Shaw.' I laughed.

'Damn you,' she said. 'What's so funny?'

'It's just like old times, isn't it?'

Then she laughed, too. 'You still get under my skin.'

'So what about a sandwich or something?' I said. 'Or I can throw something on the grill, call out for a pizza.'

'Do *I* still get under *your* skin?' she said.

'Pizza it shall be. You still like it with artichoke and eggplant?'

'See?' she said. 'Nothing ever gets under your skin. That always drove me crazy. No wonder I dumped you.' She blew out a big, phoney sigh of exasperation. 'Don't forget the goat cheese on my half of the pizza.'

TWO

Back in May, Douglas Epping and his wife, Mary, moved from the split level in Chelmsford to their retirement condo on the waterfront in Charlestown. Now, five months later, on the day after my reunion with Alexandria Shaw, Doug Epping was pacing round my office, his face getting redder and redder. He was about seventy, tall, bald and stooped. He looked like a stroke waiting to happen.

'Calm down,' I said. 'Sit. Take a deep breath.'

He smacked his palm with his fist. 'Mary told me it wasn't worth getting all upset,' he said. 'But damn it, Brady, I *am* upset. I want to murder those sonsabitches.' He plopped himself on my sofa.

'Let's talk about suing them,' I said. 'You shouldn't ever mention murder to your lawyer. Start over, OK? Slowly.'

'OK.' He took a deep breath, blew it out. 'So these movers—this outfit from Lowell, AA Movers, which my wife Mary hired because, she said, they seemed nice—first thing they do on the day of our move is, they show up in a truck that isn't big enough. And the crew boss, he says not to worry about it, sir, which turns out to mean that they're committed to cramming all of Mary's precious stuff in there whether there's room or not.' Doug resumed pacing. 'So the next thing we know—'

'Doug,' I said. 'If you're planning on having a heart attack, take it somewhere else, will you?'

'Sorry. You're right.' He sat down again. 'So, anyway, the second thing was, they took all Mary's paintings and laid them out on the lawn. I mean, these oils and watercolours she's been collecting for the past forty years are lying there, and these guys are stepping over them while they're lugging other stuff out of the house. The third thing was, I'm talking to one of them, young Hispanic guy, and I'm asking him about the training he had to be a mover, and he laughs and says, "No training, man. Me, I'm a roofer. Sonny at Double A needs to load a truck, he got a bunch of guys like me he calls."'

'All the movers are part-timers?' I said.

'I don't know about all of them,' said Doug, 'but it wouldn't surprise me. Day labourers, you pay 'em under the table.'

'I'm getting quite interested in your story.' I made some notes. 'This outfit's based in Lowell, you said?'

'Right. AA Movers, Inc. So, they managed to squeeze everything into the truck. The rest of it seemed to go OK. We got to Charlestown, and they unloaded us, and it wasn't until after they were gone and we started unpacking that we found all the damage. For example, Mary's got this dresser, been in her family for five generations. Big gouges on the top. Antique rocking chair, cost more than my Volvo. Rocker busted clean off. Puncture in the oil painting that used to hang over our fireplace. You want me to go on?'

I stood up. 'I'm going to get us some water. You relax for a minute.'

I went out to the reception area. Julie had her headset on. She was talking on the phone and tapping at her computer. I took two bottles of spring water from the refrigerator in the alcove and went back to my office. I handed Doug a bottle and resumed my seat behind the desk. 'Drink,' I said to him.

He unscrewed the top of the bottle and took a swig of water. 'Where was I?'

'When you unpacked, you found a lot of damage.'

He nodded. 'Right. So I called them, talked with some guy named Delaney. President of the company. I told him we had a lot of damage from the move, said I assumed he'd want to make good on it. He said something like, "Yes, sir. Absolutely, sir. We stand by our work," blah blah. Tells me to get an estimate of the damage, send it to him. So I found a guy in Charlestown who does antique restoration and he wrote it all up for me. I photocopied the estimate, overnight-mailed it to Delaney. Waited a week. Didn't hear anything.'

'What was the estimate?' I said.

'Little over thirteen grand.'

'You never make antiques as good as they were by filling in gouges, replacing a rocker, painting over scratches.'

Doug nodded. 'I figured there'd be some give-and-take. Anyway, when Delaney doesn't call me back, I try calling him. Keep getting voicemail, leaving messages. Finally, I figure out he's reading my name off his phone, just refusing to talk to me. So I use my cellphone and Delaney answers. Yeah, sure, he says, he got the estimate. It's outrageous, he says. Can I prove his movers caused the damage? Best he can do for me, he says, is what's covered by his insurance as per our contract, which is sixty cents a pound, take it or leave it.'

'So how did your conversation with this Delaney guy end?'

Doug smiled. 'I told him he'd be hearing from my lawyer. I hung up on him and called you.'

'And you haven't heard from AA Movers since then?'

'No. Nothing.'

'I'm sure you won't.' I paused. 'You didn't sign any waiver about the antiques, didn't even agree orally that they were absolved of risk?'

'No. The subject never came up.'

'You signed a contract agreeing to the sixty-cents insurance, though.'

'Yes. Mary did. Sixty cents per pound per article liability. There were other options on the contract, but Delaney told her just to initial that one.'

'Too bad.'

'You mean, that's all we can collect?'

'Didn't say that, because if it's true that they hire roofers off the street, pay them as part-timers and under the table, use the wrong-size vans, lay the paintings out on the lawn, all that, we've got a lot going for us. You've got to do some due diligence, though, OK?'

'Sure. What?'

'I want good photos of the damaged items,' I said. 'And if you've got any photos showing what the damaged stuff looked like before the move, that would be great.'

He nodded. 'We photographed everything for our homeowner's insurance.'

'You should talk with them, too,' I said. 'Your homeowner's policy might give you some coverage.'

'I'll check it out.'

'I want two estimates for the cost of repairing all your stuff,' I said. 'They've got to be reputable outfits. I also want two estimates from antique and art experts on the market value of all those items—both as is, with the damage, and as they would be if they hadn't been damaged. Tell them what you're doing, what it's for, and make sure they'd be willing to testify in court, if it ever came to that, which is unlikely.'

'Unlikely why?'

'Because the last thing your movers'll want is a court case. They'll want to settle,' I said. 'You get me everything I asked for and I'll take it from there. You got any questions?'

Doug Epping shrugged. 'Just one. You think we can win?'

'I never promise anything like that. But I wouldn't take the case if I didn't think we had a good shot.'

I stood up, and he did, too. I steered him into the reception area. 'Soon as you get everything I asked for, let me know.'

'Sure. Meanwhile . . .'

'Meanwhile,' I said, 'I'll write AA Movers an official lawyer letter, try to find out who their lawyer is, see if he might want to have a talk with Mr Delaney, make things easier for all of us.'

We shook hands and Doug left.

'Hey, Brady,' said Julie, waving a piece of paper at me. 'Alex rang and left a message.'

I took the paper from Julie, went back into my office, sat at my desk and looked at it. Julie had written: 'Ms Shaw called. It's about her brother. Call her cell.' She'd added a phone number.

I leaned back in my chair and closed my eyes. I remembered how the previous night Alex and I had sat in my back yard and polished off a large pizza and a bottle of Chianti. Alex had got me talking about Evie, and I'd finally told her that when she left for California, Evie had urged me to live my life, by which she meant I should feel free to 'see other people'. I told Alex how thus far I'd had no particular desire to see other people and how, in spite of what Evie said, I did not feel very free. I still felt committed, probably because I still loved her, although it might've just been out of habit. I was pretty sure that Evie didn't feel committed to me.

All the time I talked to her, Alex watched me solemnly, and I couldn't help remembering how she used to look at me out of her big round glasses, and how sexy I used to think she was . . . and how sexy she still was, even with contact lenses.

Between the Rebel Yell and the wine, Alex and I both ended up a little drunk, so I brewed coffee and we moved into the living room. We sipped coffee, and our conversation shifted to the old days, how we met when she was a reporter chasing me for a story she was working on, the years we'd been together. I remembered having the impression that if I'd asked, Alex would have agreed to spend the night. I found the idea powerfully tempting.

After a while we decided she was sober enough to drive, so I walked with her across the common to the Park Street T station so she could take the train to Alewife, where she'd left her car.

At the top of the stairs she hugged me, thanked me for agreeing to help her brother, said it was really nice to see me, touched my cheek, kissed the side of my throat, then turned and walked quickly down into the subway.

When I got back home, I wanted desperately to call Evie.

But I didn't. That was our deal. She might call me, but she didn't want me to call her. She had to focus on her father. She didn't want to feel torn.

I guess I understood. But there were times when it didn't seem fair.

THREE

I pulled into the Rib 'n' Fin in Acton a few minutes after seven on Saturday night. It had rained all day, but in the afternoon a sharp northerly wind had blown the clouds away, and now a skyful of stars peppered the October heavens.

The restaurant was a giant A-frame with lots of glass and a wide deck all round. It looked like an orphaned ski lodge. Inside, just about all the tables were occupied. The Rib 'n' Fin was a local chain. Blond pine panelling, tables and chairs to match, booths upholstered in rust-coloured vinyl.

I spotted a hand waving at me from a booth against the wall and weaved my way among the tables. Alex was sitting across from a bulky man about my age. He had an unkempt reddish beard and thinning hair. He was peering at a menu and did not look up at me.

I slid in beside Alex. 'Gussie,' she said to the guy, 'this is Brady.'

'How're you doing?' I said. I held my hand out to him.

Gus put down his menu, nodded at me without smiling, then took my right hand with his left one, and we shook awkwardly. I only remembered then that he didn't have a right hand.

'So you're the old boyfriend,' he said.

I nodded.

'She dumped you.'

'She did,' I said. 'I deserved it. My loss.'

'Screwing around on her, were you?'

I glanced at Alex beside me. She was frowning at her menu.

'It was more complicated than that,' I said.

'She can be a bitch,' he said.

I studied his face and saw no hint of humour or irony in it. 'It was me,' I said. 'Alex was never a bitch.'

'Shall we have a drink?' said Alex. 'Gussie? Want something?'

'Nobody calls me Gussie any more,' he said. 'I can't drink. You know that.'

'I meant a Coke or something.'

'If the damn waitress ever comes back,' he said.

'To me you're Gussie,' said Alex. 'Deal with it.'

He frowned at her, then shrugged and looked at me. 'She always was a bully. I'm not sure what this is all about, are you?'

'What?' I said.

'This, I don't know—reunion? Me getting to meet you finally, now that your relationship's over with.'

'I just thought you guys would likc each other,' Alex said.

I looked questioningly at her. She gave me a little roll of her eyes that asked me to just go with her flow.

Gus pointed his finger at me. 'You're not back together again, are you?'

I smiled. 'No. Alex and I are old friends. We've been out of touch for a few years.'

'So what's the point? Why are we here, us three?'

I assumed that Alex would remind him that I was the lawyer who'd agreed to help him with his divorce. That was why she'd called on Friday and asked me to meet her and Gus at the Rib 'n' Fin on 2A in Acton tonight.

Instead, she said, 'Come on, Gussie. Lighten up.'

'Sure,' he said. 'That's my problem. Too heavy all the time. Sorry.'

At that moment a waitress appeared at our table. Alex ordered a Coke, and so did Gus. I asked for a mug of coffee.

The waitress returned with our drinks, took our orders—the rib eye with a baked potato for me, the shrimp scampi with French fries for Gus, and the halibut with rice pilaf for Alex—and left.

Beside me, Alex was watching her brother.

I leaned my shoulder against hers. 'Henry sends his love.'

'Dear old Henry,' she said. She looked at Gus. 'Brady has a dog named Henry David Thoreau. He's a darling.'

Gus nodded. 'A dog. Nice.'

'He's a Brittany,' she said. 'Isn't that right, Brady?' Her eyes seemed to be pleading with me.

'Right,' I said. I turned to Gus. 'Henry's a Brittany. They used to be called Brittany spaniels, but now they're officially called Brittanys. They're not, technically, spaniels, I guess. Brittanys are pointing dogs. Great bird dogs. I don't hunt birds, although sometimes I think I should, just so that Henry could fulfil his destiny. All dogs have something in their genes that gives meaning to their life. Retrievers have got to fetch ducks. Terriers need to dig rats out of holes. Like that.'

I was watching Gus as I talked. He sat there unmoving, holding himself together with his two big arms crossed over his chest. I had the powerful impression that he was struggling against the urge to scream.

We fell into silence, until Gus lowered his eyes and said, 'That's interesting. About the dogs. People are like that, don't you think? Destined to do something? Like me. I was made to take pictures. And you, you're—' I sensed that he had relaxed a little. 'What are you? What do you do?'

'I'm a lawyer,' I said.

'A lawyer.' He nodded. 'So do you feel like you've got the law in your DNA? You think this is what you were born for?'

'My old man was a lawyer,' I said, 'and I guess that's why I became one. I think what I was born for, my destiny, is trout fishing. Not the law. The lawyer in me was made, not born. It was a choice. I don't think I had any choice about fishing.'

Gus nodded. 'You are what you are,' he said, 'and there's no getting away from it.' He put his right elbow on the table and folded back the cuff. Where his hand and wrist should have been was a stump with a flesh-coloured plastic cap over it. 'My new destiny,' he said. 'This is how I'm made now.'

'You could still take pictures,' Alex said softly.

'No,' he said, 'I really couldn't. My group keeps reminding me I've got to accept who I am now, which is to say a guy with one hand, and it's nothing but frustrating when people like you keep pretending that I'm still what I used to be.'

Alex blew out a breath and leaned back in the booth. 'People like me,' Alex muttered. 'I'm sorry. I'm your sister.'

'Everybody's sorry,' Gus said. 'It's no help.' He looked at me. 'My hand hurts all the time. Which is quite a trick, since I don't even have a hand.'

'Phantom pain?' I said.

'Phantom like hell,' he said. 'It's real, believe me.'

We lapsed into silence again.

A few minutes later our waitress arrived with our meals. We began to eat and, after a minute, Gus said, 'So, Brady, I get the picture. You want to handle my divorce. You're soliciting business, huh?'

I turned to Alex. 'What did you tell him?'

She shook her head. 'I'm sorry. If I told him, he wouldn't have agreed to meet you.' She looked at Gus. 'Would you?'

'No,' he said.

'Brady's not soliciting your business,' she said. 'It's my idea. You've got to have a lawyer. Brady's the best.'

'You lied to me,' he said. 'You know I wouldn't have come here if you told me you were hooking me up with some lawyer.'

'It wasn't really a lie. But, OK, I guess I manipulated you. You need a lawyer, and I can't sit back and watch you wreck your life. I'm sorry, Gussie,' Alex said. 'I love you. You're my big brother.'

'I don't need a lawyer. This is between me and Claudia.'

'Talk to him, Brady,' said Alex. 'Please.'

I looked at Gus. 'Does Claudia have a lawyer?'

'Oh, sure. Good one, she says. Gonna take care of her.'

'You have kids?'

He nodded.

'A house? Credit cards? Bank account? Insurance? Retirement plans and savings?'

Gus waved his left hand. 'I know what you're saying. But, see, I don't want any of that stuff. She can have it. She deserves it.'

'What about Claudia?' I said. 'Does she work?'

'She's an accountant. Works for a company in Lexington. It's a good job. Pays pretty well. Health insurance, benefits.'

'Unlike you, huh?' I said.

'Freelance photojournalists don't work on salaries.'

'Any chance of you two reconciling?' I said.

'Not hardly.' He shook his head. 'Trust me, Claudia's done with me and I don't blame her. She can have everything as far as I'm concerned.'

'And the kids?' I said.

He shrugged. 'Whatever.'

Alex leaned towards him. 'You say this now,' she said, 'but think about a year, five years, from now.'

'I can hardly think about tomorrow,' he said.

'See?' said Alex. 'That's why you need a lawyer.'

He looked at me. 'No offence. I appreciate what you're doing. Both of you. But really, I'd rather everybody just left me alone.'

'I feel the same way a lot of the time,' I said. 'But it doesn't work that way. Especially when you're in the middle of a divorce. Listen. I'm here because I like your sister, and she loves you, and she's right about your needing representation with your divorce. Look at it like this: the best way for you to be left alone is to have a lawyer handle it for you.'

He narrowed his eyes. 'I thought a lawyer was so you could fight it. I don't want to fight it.'

'A lawyer is to steer you through it,' I said. 'Handle the paperwork. Do the negotiating. Watch out for your interests.'

'I don't have any interests except being left alone. What were you getting at about my kids?'

'Your wife could go for full custody,' I said. 'She could try to deny you visitation rights. She could move to California—or Australia, for that matter—and take the kids. You have two girls, right?'

He nodded.

'Juno and Clea,' said Alex. 'They're eight and five.'

'Look,' I said to Gus. 'Let me take care of this for you. I won't do anything you don't agree to. You can't just do nothing, though. The system won't allow that. It'll be a big fat hassle for you. What do you say?'

He said, 'What's in it for you?'

'Me?' I gave him a hard look. 'Nothing's in it for me, as far as I can see, except another pain-in-the-ass, neurotic, self-destructive client'—I pointed my finger at him—'of which I already have more than my share. I know what I'll be getting into with you. You'll piss and moan all the time and be late for meetings and refuse to answer the phone and lie to me and generally refuse to cooperate with me, and I'll just end up with one more big stack of paperwork on my desk. You think I drove out here on a Saturday night because I'm hard up for clients? Believe it or not, I turn away clients if I don't like them or if I don't think their cases will be fun for me. You think another screwed-up client in a crappy divorce is going to bring joy into my life?'

Gus Shaw was staring at me. Then he smiled. 'OK.'

'What do you mean, OK?' I said.

'I want you to be my lawyer.' He looked at Alex. 'I like this guy.'

She smiled at him. 'I do, too.'

'Nobody talks to me like that any more,' said Gus.

'You had it coming to you,' she said.

He turned to me. 'Your job is to do what I want, right?'

'I'm your lawyer, not your slave,' I said. 'My job is to help you figure out what you want, what's in your best interest, and then to try to get it.'

'And you are obliged to keep my secrets?'

'What passes between us is privileged, yes,' I said. 'If you're my client, you can trust me to keep your secrets.'

He reached his left hand across the table. 'It's a deal, then.'

I shook his left hand with my right one. 'OK. A deal.'

'We need to talk,' he said. 'Right?'

'We do,' I said. 'First order of business, you've got to tell your wife that I'm representing you.'

'Why?'

'She's got to tell her lawyer. We two lawyers will need to talk. You don't know who her lawyer is, do you?'

Gus shook his head.

'It's important,' I said. 'Give her my name and phone numbers. Do it right away. Her lawyer will want to call me.' I handed him one of my business cards. 'Don't forget.'

He took my card. 'So when should we talk?'

I shrugged. 'We can start now. Otherwise you're going to have to trek into the city or I'm going to have to drive out here.'

'I can't drive,' he said. 'I don't have enough hands.'

'So let's get started,' I said. I looked at Alex. 'You can't be here.' I stood up so she could slide out of the booth.

Alex eased past me and whispered, 'Thank you.'

'Let's get the hell out of here,' said Gus, 'I don't like being around all these people. We can go to my place, talk there. It's not far.'

GUS AND I piled into my BMW and headed towards Concord. He said he was renting an apartment over a garage behind a big old colonial house not far from the Old North Bridge, where the American War of Independence began on April 19, 1775.

He directed me to a long driveway off Monument Street, about a mile outside the centre of town. The garage appeared to be a refurbished carriage house. It was separated from the main house by a lawn and a screen of hemlocks. A set of wooden stairs had been built onto the outside wall. We climbed them, and Gus fished a key from his pocket and let us in.

It was one large room with slanting walls and a dormer, with triangular windows on the ends and a couple of skylights. There was a galley kitchen with stainless-steel appliances; an alcove with a leather sofa, two leather chairs and a flat-screen television set; a table under one of the windows, with a laptop computer and a telephone; a dining table; a bathroom; and a bed behind a half-wall partition. Everything looked new.

'Not bad,' I said to Gus. 'Comfortable.'

'I'm the first tenant. It came furnished, too. TV, microwave, everything. All I had to move was myself.'

In addition to the door from the outside stairway, there were two other doors. One was ajar, and I could see it led to a small closet with some clothes hanging inside. I pointed at the other one. 'Another closet?'

Gus shook his head. 'Goes downstairs to where Herb keeps his carriages.'

'Carriages?'

'Joke, man. This used to be a carriage house.'

'Sorry,' I said.

No pictures hung on the photojournalist's walls. Aside from two dirty mugs and an empty plate on the coffee table and some dishes in the sink, it looked as if nobody lived here.

'How long have you been here?' I said.

'Since Claudia kicked me out. Last April. Mr and Mrs Croyden—my landlords, Herb and Beth—they'd just finished having it fixed up around the time I needed a place. A mutual friend told me about it. Herb and Beth were happy to have me, I think. Someone who'd been over there. They lost a son.'

'In Iraq?'

He nodded. 'Roadside bomb. Random, senseless, stupid, like everything over there.' He went over to the coffee table, piled the two empty mugs on the plate, balanced them against his chest and took them to the sink. 'You want a Coke? Or I could make some coffee. I don't have any booze.'

'A Coke is fine,' I said. I went over and sat on the sofa.

Gus came over a minute later holding two cans of cola against his chest with his left hand. He put them on the coffee table and sat across from me. 'So, what do you need to know?'

'What do you want out of this divorce?' I said.

'Me?' He shook his head. 'Nothing. It's for Claudia, not me. I want it over and done with, is all.'

'You don't want to lose your kids, right?'

'Of course. I would've thought that goes without saying.'

'Nothing goes without saying. That's why you need a lawyer.'

'I just can't take any more hassle, you know?'

'You want me to leave,' I said, 'I'll leave.'

'No,' he said. 'We need to talk.' He looked at me. 'You want me to tell you my life story?'

'I'm your lawyer,' I said, 'not your confessor. This is about your divorce. The main thing is, you can't lie to me.'

He nodded. 'Fair enough, I guess. So what can I tell you?'

'I don't know you,' I said. 'I don't want to be blindsided by your wife's lawyer. There can't be any surprises. So you tell me. What do I need to know?'

'I've got PTSD. That pretty much defines me these days.'

I nodded. 'You're getting help for it?'

'I've got meds, and I've got a support group, although I'm not sure how supportive they actually are. They try. They're keeping me going, I guess.' He held up the stump on the end of his right arm. 'I had it before this happened. The traumatic stress. Had it the moment my plane touched down in that godforsaken place.'

'And what happened between you and your wife?'

Gus shook his head. 'Sometimes I don't recognise myself. It's like I'm floating around in the sky watching myself, and I wonder who the hell that whacked-out, one-handed, evil-tempered guy is down there, doing things I'd never do.'

'What did that guy do?' I said.

He gave me a wry smile. 'He lost it. He accused his wife of cheating on him. He made his kids cry. He made his wife cry. And he made himself cry, and he got the hell out of there. See? That's not me. Except, now I guess it is me. The one-handed part, anyway.'

'Your wife,' I said. 'Was she cheating on you?'

'I don't know,' said Gus. 'Wouldn't blame her, huh?' He paused. 'I can't prove it, but I think she was. Is.'

'Did you hurt anybody?' I said.

'Of course not. I never . . .' He stood up and went over to the window. He looked out into the darkness. 'Do we have to do this?'

'I need to know everything,' I said.

'There's nothing else to know.'

'OK,' I said. 'Another time.'

Gus came back and sat down again. 'It's about all I think about,' he said. 'This man who lost it in front of his family. This stranger I've turned into. But, yeah. Let's not talk about it.'

'You're not taking pictures any more?'

'Can't,' he said. 'Can't do it one-handed. My sister keeps saying I could, but she's wrong. Drives me crazy. I'm trying to get used to the new me, and she keeps insisting that nothing's changed.' He shook his head. 'So I've got this job at the camera shop in Concord. Minuteman Camera. They're doing me a favour, I know, giving me this job. I sell cameras, picture frames, shit like that. I think they hired me because I'm—I used to be—a fairly well-known photojournalist, published in *Time*, *Newsweek*, the *Geographic*, won some prizes. The lady who owns the shop, Jemma, nice lady—she hired me, I'm positive, because she feels sorry for me—she's trying to get me to teach some classes. I tell her, the only thing I know about taking pictures is, be in the right place at the right time, always have your camera with you and hope the light's good.' He smiled. 'It'd be a very short course.' He leaned forward. 'You remember the photos that came out of Vietnam?'

'Sure,' I said. 'There were some absolutely indelible images.'

'Buddhist monk immolating himself,' Gus said. 'Viet Cong soldier, looked about twelve years old, mowing down people with a gun bigger than him. VC officer getting shot in the head. Caskets being offloaded from airplanes. Iconic photos. Better than a thousand words. That's what I was after over there. Images that would tell a story. How much of that do you see coming out of Iraq?'

I shrugged. 'Not much, I guess.'

Gus sighed.

'See, Brady,' he said after a minute, 'the thing is, it was those images that made all the difference in Vietnam. People wouldn't put up with it. Embedded journalists are controlled. They're good, dedicated reporters, most of 'em, don't get me wrong. They work hard, and they encounter plenty of danger. But they only see and hear what the military and the politicians approve. Everybody knows that. They get the stories the brass want them to have, and the brass take their orders from Washington. They use the media to promote their own agendas. You ever see a photo of body bags coming out of Iraq?'

'I don't think so, no.'

'That's because they're off-limits to the media. So all the American kids who've been killed over there? Numbers, that's all.' He blew out a breath. 'There are a lot of good journalists over there. But if they're not allowed to be in the right place at the right time, it doesn't matter how good the light is, you know what I'm saying?'

I nodded. 'So what about you, Gus? Were you in the right place at the right time?'

'I've always been independent,' he said. 'Not embedded. There were a bunch of us freelancers. They hated us.'

'Who did?'

'The brass. They couldn't control us. Couldn't censor us. They knew we were after the stories they didn't want told. The senselessness of it. The failure of it. The friendly fire fatalities. The crappy equipment. The wrong-headed decisions. The dead children. They were all about covering up. Getting their own version of the story out there. Not the truth.' He looked at me. 'You probably think I'm paranoid. The PTSD, huh?'

I shrugged. 'I don't know.'

'Yeah, well, maybe I am. They tell me I am. Paranoid and depressed and unpredictable. That's why I went nuts on Claudia. It's why I don't trust you or Alex. But what it was like over there? That's not paranoia.'

I touched my right hand, indicating his missing one. 'Are you saying . . .?'

'Huh?' He frowned. 'Oh.' He patted his stump. 'This was an accident. One of the things that happens over there all the time. Nothing special. Ordinary, actually. Just another random little thing that changes somebody's life. You might say it happened because I was in the right place at the right time. When I woke up, my camera was gone, and so was my hand.' He shook his head. 'Look. I went over there to take pictures. To do what I'm meant to do, like your dog with birds. I thought I could make a difference. Get the truth. Then this happened, and I can't do it any more.'

'So you didn't get any photos?'

'When I woke up in hospital after the explosion,' he said, 'my camera was gone. I assume it suffered the same fate as my hand.'

'All your photos were in your camera?'

He narrowed his eyes at me for a minute, then said, 'Let's change the subject. OK?'

'If you've got some photos, some iconic images—'

'I don't want to talk about photography right now.'

I shrugged. 'Up to you.'

'Another time, maybe.' He paused, and looked at me. 'I can really tell you anything,' he said, 'and you've got to respect my privacy. Right?'

'Yes, that's right.'

'Because sometimes . . .' He shook his head. 'Not now.'

'You shouldn't do anything without talking to me,' I said.

He smiled. 'Don't worry about me.'

'That's easier said than done,' I said.

I LEFT a few minutes later. Gus walked out to my car with me. Through the screen of hemlocks, orange light glowed from the old colonial house where Herb and Beth Croyden lived. I pointed over there. 'Do you see much of your landlords?'

'They leave me alone,' he said. 'Nice folks. I see them now and then when they take their dog out for a walk. They've got a golden retriever, I think it is.' He gestured off towards the back of the property. 'The Concord River's right over the hill there. They throw sticks for the dog.' Then he turned back to me. 'I'm thinking of getting a dog.'

'You can't beat dogs for companionship,' I said.

'I'm not quite ready for it. It's a goal of mine. To feel confident enough, to feel like I could take care of a dog.'

'Sounds like a worthwhile goal,' I said.

We talked idly for a few minutes, and then I reached into the back seat of my car and came up with an envelope with some forms that I'd brought with me for Gus to fill out. He said he'd do the forms and fax them back to me.

He asked me how it worked. Divorce, he meant.

I told him that Claudia's lawyer and I would hammer out a separation agreement, make sure the two parties agreed to it, and bring it to the court. Division of property, insurance, custody, child support, alimony. If the judge signed off on it, there would be a 120-day waiting period, during which he and Claudia would be legally separated. During that period, they could change their minds about the terms of the agreement or even about whether they wanted to go through with it. If they didn't, the divorce would automatically become final.

I told him he could call me anytime—if he had questions about the forms or anything else.

We agreed to meet again after I'd had a chance to talk to Claudia's lawyer.

He recited two phone numbers—one at the camera shop where he worked, the other for his apartment over the garage—and I scribbled them on the back of one of my business cards.

I held out my hand to him.

He looked at it, then smiled and gripped it with his left hand. 'Most people won't shake hands with me,' he said.

'Don't forget,' I said. 'Anything you need to talk about . . .'

He nodded. 'I won't forget.'

I LEFT MY CAR in the Residents Only space in front of my town house on Mt Vernon Street. Henry was waiting inside the front door. His whole hind end was wagging. I squatted down so he could lick my face, then let him out of the back door. I stood there on the deck and waited for him to finish snuffling in the bushes and locating the places where he needed to mark.

I still hadn't got used to the vacuum left by Evie. As long as I'd lived in this place, Evie and Henry had been there, too.

Sometimes I couldn't conjure up the image of her face or the sound of her voice. At other times, though, the feel of her skin and the scent of her hair were so vivid that I'd have to blink to remind myself that the smells and textures existed only in my memory.

After a while, Henry came padding up onto the deck and we went inside. I gave him a dog treat, then checked my phone for messages. There was one.

I hesitated before listening to it. It might've been Evie. She'd called maybe half a dozen times since she'd been in California. Not once had I been there to answer the phone. I was pretty sure that she made a point of calling when she figured I wouldn't be there. Leaving messages was easier than talking to me.

Typically, Evie's messages were brief and impersonal. Reports on her father's health, mostly. She always asked me to give Henry a big hug for her, and one for me, too. That was all. No 'I love you' or 'I miss you'.

This message wasn't from Evie. It was Alex. 'Brady? Will you call me when you get back? I'm dying to hear how it went with Gussie.' Then, in a softer tone, she said, 'I can't tell you how grateful I am that you're doing this. I want to buy you dinner. Call me, OK? Even if it's late. I'm wide-awake.'

Alex's voice, and the unavoidable image of her lying in a king-size bed in the Best Western hotel, brought old memories and images bubbling into my brain. We'd been together for over three years. We'd loved each other. When we split, I believed that I'd never find another woman to love.

So now Evie was a continent away and Alex was in Concord, barely half an hour's drive, and she was calling me on a Saturday night with that husky voice of hers, telling me how grateful she was and asking me to return her call.

I stood there in my kitchen holding the phone in my hand. After a minute, I set the phone back on its cradle and gave Henry a whistle, and we went upstairs to bed.

FOUR

On Monday afternoon I was working on my letter to AA Movers, on behalf of Doug and Mary Epping, when Julie tapped on my door. 'Enter,' I called.

'I brought you coffee.' She put a mug on my desk, then sat in the chair across from me. 'How goes the composing?'

'More like decomposing,' I said. 'I'm semicolon-ing and whereas-ing myself to death here. I'll have a draft for you to edit before the sun sets.'

'Goody,' said Julie. 'I love deleting your semicolons. Meanwhile, Attorney Capezza called.'

'Lily Capezza? What's she want?'

'She represents Claudia Shaw. She seemed to think you'd know what she wants. I told her you'd get back to her.'

'You could've put her through,' I said.

Julie cocked her head and smiled.

'Oh,' I said. 'Right. Promoting the illusion that I am too busy to take a phone call.'

'We've got a new client, then?'

'I guess we do,' I said. 'Sorry. I should've given you a heads-up. Gus Shaw. Augustine. Alex's brother. He's getting divorced.'

'You're going up against Attorney Capezza, huh?'

'I guess so,' I said. 'The formidable Lily Capezza. Why don't you see if you can get her on the line for me. Might as well start the ball rolling.'

Julie stood up, headed for the door and left.

A few minutes later the console on my desk buzzed.

'I have Attorney Capezza on line one for you,' said Julie.

There was a click on the line. 'Lily,' I said. 'How are you?'

'Hello, Brady Coyne,' she said. Lily Capezza had a soft, girlish voice that belied a heart of granite and a will of titanium. 'I'm well, thank you. I do have a rather unhappy client, however.'

'Me, too,' I said. 'What are the chances, from your client's point of view, of a reconciliation?'

Lily laughed. 'You're joking, right?'

'No,' I said, 'I'm not joking. We always go for reconciliation. You and I have always been of one mind on this.'

'The 209A makes reconciliation moot, don't you think?'

I said nothing. Gus hadn't mentioned a restraining order.

I heard Lily chuckle into the phone. 'He didn't tell you about the abuse prevention order, did he?'

'Come on, Lily. That's between me and my client.'

'He didn't contest it,' she said. 'We got it extended till May 15th, by which time I'm hoping the divorce will be final.'

I said, 'Why don't you give me your perspective on it?'

'It's public record,' she said. 'An unbalanced man suffering from post-traumatic stress disorder, back from Iraq having lost his right hand to some kind of explosive device, terrorising his wife and children? You've got to feel bad for the poor man. But first and foremost, you've got to worry about the wife and kids.'

'Terrorising,' I said. 'Strong language, Lily.'

'The man brandished his side arm, Brady. Come on.'

'Oh shit,' I said before I could stop myself.

Lily was silent for a moment. Then she said, 'Look, Brady. I don't mean to tell you how to do your job, but between you and me, and entirely off the record, you've got to talk to your client.'

'I intend to. So why wasn't Gus arrested?'

'My client refused to report it and wouldn't let me use it with the judge. She knows he's a sick puppy. She stuck by him for as long as she could. She's scared, Brady. She needs to be divorced, and she had to go for the 209A. Fortunately, as your client didn't contest the order, the brandishing part's not in the public record. But if it should be necessary . . .'

'I hear you.' I cleared my throat. 'Off the record, I confess that I'm kind of embarrassed, Lily. My client is an unstable man, seriously depressed, and obviously not entirely forthcoming with his attorney. I hope we can find a way that works in the interests of both of our clients. For the sake of justice.'

'Look,' she said. 'Let's have lunch, talk it through, OK? Let's figure out what they both want, and see if we can reconcile that with what makes sense, what's right and just, and what the judge will accept.'

'Sounds good to me,' I said.

'You know,' said Lily, 'contrary to popular belief, I am not a monster. I do believe in justice.'

'For your clients,' I said.

She laughed. 'Sure. But I sleep best when things work out for everybody. Why don't you put your secretary back on to talk to mine, and we'll let them make a date for us.'

'Yes,' I said, 'I will.'

'Just don't lose track of the fact that Mr Shaw brandished a weapon at his family in the living room of his home,' said Lily.

'It kind of puts Mrs Shaw's extramarital adventures into perspective,' I said, 'doesn't it?'

Lily was quiet for a moment. Then she chuckled. 'Why, Attorney Coyne, I came this close to underestimating you. This might turn out to be more fun than I thought. I'm going to put my secretary on now. Let's make it sometime this week, OK?'

'I look forward to it,' I said. I hit the intercom button and told Julie that Attorney Capezza's secretary was coming on the line and they should set up a lunch meeting for us attorneys.

I hung up the phone. My first impulse was to call Gus and blast him for not telling me the truth and putting me on the defensive with his wife's lawyer. But one of the things I've learned is to resist my first impulse. In fact, it's best to resist all impulses.

I'd talk to Gus later.

A FEW MINUTES before closing time, Julie came into my office. 'You got a lunch date with Attorney Capezza,' she said. 'In the spirit of give-and-take, her secretary picked the time—one o'clock on Friday—and I picked the place. Marie's. OK?'

'OK,' I said. 'Good. Marie's gives me the home field advantage.'

Julie put two sheets of paper on my desk. 'See how this reads.'

It was my letter to AA Movers, now edited and neatly typed and formatted and printed out on our official stationery.

'You let a few semicolons slip through, I hope.'

She smiled. 'Read it over. Feel free to mark it up.'

When Julie left, I looked at the letter, then took it out to her in the reception area.

'It's great,' I said. 'There's a lovely sequence of semicolons there, and you preserved several of my "pursuants" and "hereins". I couldn't have done better myself.'

'I changed hardly anything, actually,' said Julie. 'You can take full credit for this masterpiece of empty threat and muddy obfuscation. They'll ignore it, of course.'

'Probably,' I said. 'I would. They don't know what we've got up our sleeve.'

'So what exactly *do* we have up our sleeve?'

'According to Doug Epping,' I said, 'this Double A outfit hires day workers off the streets of Lowell. They're untrained and poorly supervised. Probably get paid under the table. I'm guessing no withholding or Social Security taxes are paid by Double A, Inc., to the Commonwealth or to Uncle Sam. I'm curious about their insurance. Doug can testify to their lack of professionalism.' I tapped the letter. 'Fax a copy of this to Doug and Mary with a note just saying that we've got the ball rolling and we'll be in touch. Certified mail to Double A, as usual.'

Julie nodded, then smiled. 'If I didn't know better, I'd guess that you're itching for a battle with this outfit.'

THAT EVENING, as Henry and I were watching *Monday Night Football*—the Detroit Lions were playing the Chicago Bears at Soldier Field—the phone on the table beside my chair rang. I hit MUTE on the remote, picked up the phone and said, 'Hello.'

'Hey.' It was Alex.

'Oh,' I said. 'Hi.'

'Did you get my message the other night?'

'I did,' I said. 'Yes.'

'Were you planning on returning my call?'

'No,' I said. 'I guess not.'

She laughed quickly. 'You never did pull your punches.'

After an awkward moment, Alex said, 'Well, maybe I should be flattered.'

'Maybe,' I said. 'Yes.'

'Then you miss my point,' she said. 'This is all about Gus, OK? I mean, I am flattered. But I'm not here to complicate your life.'

'Don't worry about it.'

'I just wanted to buy you dinner,' said Alex. 'See how it went with Gussie. Thank you for taking his case. That's all.'

'You call me in that sleepy whispery voice of yours,' I said, 'make sure I know you're in bed, conjure up a million old memories? What am I supposed to think?'

She said nothing.

'I would like to have dinner with you,' I said after a moment. 'We do need to talk about your brother's case.'

'That's the only reason you'd like to have dinner with me?'

'You didn't tell me that Gus's wife took out a 209A on him. You didn't tell me that he threatened his family with a gun.'

'Would you have taken his case if you'd known that?'

'You did know, then.'

'I did,' she said. 'Gussie told me. He was very shaken up by it. Said it was like he was somebody else. It's why he's not interested in defending himself.'

'I would've taken the case,' I said. 'I don't limit my clientele to angels. Or cases I'm sure I can win, either.'

'I should have known that,' she said. 'I'm sorry.'

'More to the point,' I said, '*he* should have told me. He's the client. He's the one who has to tell me the truth, not you.'

'I have to, too,' said Alex. 'I'm the friend.'

'So instead,' I said, 'I got blindsided by his wife's attorney.'

'I'm sorry. What are you going to do?'

'Have dinner with you,' I said. 'How's Friday work for you?'

'I meant about Gus.'

'He's my client,' I said. 'I'll give him hell and we'll move on.'

I heard her blow out a soft breath. 'Thank you,' she said.

'I feel bad,' I said, 'not returning your call. You're my friend. That's not the way I treat my friends. You still staying at the Best Western?'

'I got this room for two weeks, which I may extend.'

I said, 'So, Friday, dinner is here. I'll mix a pitcher of gin and tonic, grill some chicken. We can eat out in the garden. Dress casual.'

She chuckled. 'I remember how you used to love to grill burgers on that greasy old charcoal grill on your balcony when you lived on Lewis Wharf.'

'I've got a spiffy gas grill now. Around seven, OK?'

'Perfect,' said Alex in that husky bedroom voice of hers.

After we disconnected, I sat there and thought, What the hell do you think you're doing, Coyne?

Henry and I stayed up till almost midnight watching the rest of the Bears–Lions game. It wasn't adrenaline from watching a football game that kept me awake. It was thoughts of Alex, my old love, coming to my house—Evie's and my house—for drinks and a cookout, ping-ponging with thoughts about how Gus had pointed a gun at his wife and daughters, resulting in an abuse prevention order.

I was angry at Gus, but the poor guy's life was spinning away from him and his best chance of regaining some control over it rested on my shoulders. I decided I'd clear the air with him first thing the next morning.

I didn't know what to do about Alex.

I CAUGHT GUS at home at eight o'clock on Tuesday morning and arranged to meet him at the Sleepy Hollow Café in Concord an hour later. The café was within walking distance of the camera shop where he worked. He had to be there at ten. That would give us an hour.

I didn't tell Gus what I wanted to talk to him about.

I steered my car onto Storrow Drive. It was another postcard New England autumn day. The maples and oaks along the Esplanade glowed in shades of gold and orange and the sun glittered off the Charles River. I was heading out of the city while most of the traffic was heading in, so I made good time, and I pulled into the parking lot beside the Sleepy Hollow Café ten minutes early.

Besides its indoor dining room, the café featured a dozen umbrella-shaded tables on an outdoor patio. Gus Shaw was seated at one of them, and he wasn't alone. A Hispanic-looking man, mid-thirties, I guessed, sat across from him. A compact, fit-looking individual, he had black hair and a black moustache and wore sunglasses. Both men had their forearms on the table and were leaning forward, talking intently. Their body language told me that this wasn't a good time to interrupt, so I stopped outside the patio.

Gus was doing most of the talking. The other guy kept shaking his head, and then he suddenly pushed back his chair and stood up, put his hands on the table, and bent forward. From where I was standing, I heard the passion in his voice, though I couldn't tell what he was saying.

Gus leaned back, crossed his arms and shook his head.

The Hispanic guy stared at him for a moment, then smiled and nodded.

That's when I approached them.

Gus looked up and saw me.

'Sorry, I'm late,' I said to Gus, although I wasn't.

'Just leaving,' said the Hispanic man. Up close, I saw that he was older than I'd thought.

'Brady,' said Gus, 'this is Pete. Pete, Brady.'

I shook hands with Pete.

He looked me in the eye and nodded once. Then he lifted his chin at Gus. 'Later, man.'

Gus nodded. 'Later.'

'Everything all right?' I said.

'All right?' He shook his head. 'Nothing's all right.'

I sat at the table. 'Anything you want to talk about?'

'Nope. No problems, man. Life is good.'

'Sarcasm doesn't really suit you,' I said.

He smiled. 'A man can try, huh?' Then he said, 'You want something to eat? I'm having a muffin. The date-and-nut's my favourite. The bran's good, too. They're all good. Homemade. I ordered us a carafe of coffee. I remember you like coffee.' Gus's knee was jiggling like he was keeping time to a very fast piece of music.

I smiled. 'Relax, Gus. You're all wound up.'

'You make me nervous.'

'Me?' I said. 'You seemed pretty keyed up before I arrived.'

'OK,' he said. 'I make myself nervous. I feel strung out all the time. But you didn't tell me what you wanted. So what's up, huh?'

'I had a phone conversation with Lily Capezza yesterday.'

'Who?'

'Your wife's lawyer. She told me something that disturbed me.'

'I don't—' His eyes shifted to someplace behind me.

A waitress appeared. She put a muffin on a plate in front of Gus, and a stainless-steel carafe and two mugs and a little pitcher of cream on the table between us. 'Would you like a menu, sir?' she asked me.

I pointed at Gus's muffin. 'One of those date-and-nut muffins, please,' I said. 'Can you heat it for me?'

'They're already warm,' she said. 'Fresh from the oven.'

She left, and I poured two mugs full of coffee.

Gus watched her walk away, then looked at me and said, 'So what did Claudia's lawyer say?'

'I bet you know.' He looked down at his muffin and said nothing. I reached over and touched his arm. 'Dammit, Gus. You've got to be straight with me. I came this close to firing you.'

'Can you do that? Fire me? I didn't think . . .'

'Sure, I can. It's tempting.'

'That restraining order, huh?'

'Threatening your wife and kids with a gun? Do you ever want to see your children again? How am I supposed to help you if you keep things like that from me?'

'I was afraid you wouldn't take my case.'

'The only reason not to take your case is if you lie to me.'

He looked up at me. 'I didn't threaten them.'

'You didn't wave a gun around in your living room?'

'Well, I did, sort of, yeah, but—'

'And Claudia kicked you out and took out a 209A against you, right?'

'Yes, she did. But it wasn't like that.' He looked down and muttered, 'I threatened myself.'

'You saying you threatened to shoot yourself?'

'I didn't mean it,' Gus said. 'I wouldn't do that. The damn gun wasn't even loaded. It was just . . . I was frustrated, you know?'

'Frustrated,' I said.

'Nothing was going right. I couldn't sleep. My non-existent hand ached all the time. I couldn't take pictures. The kids didn't want to hug me. And Claudia . . . I was sure she was involved with somebody.' He shook his head. 'I don't know why I did that. Just trying to get Claudia's attention, I guess.'

'What about your group?' I said. 'Is it helping you?'

'That's what I was talking about with Pete. Our group.'

'He's in your group?'

Gus nodded.

'Problems?'

'There's stuff I don't want to talk about, OK?'

'No problem for me,' I said. 'I'm just your divorce lawyer.'

The waitress brought my muffin. When I broke it in half, steam wafted from it. I spread some butter on it and took a bite.

'I'm meeting with Attorney Capezza on Friday,' I said. 'At that time I'll get a sense, at least, of what Claudia wants from this divorce. And I'll tell her what we want from it. I'm going to go for joint custody of the girls, all right?'

He nodded.

'Joint custody is more than we'll probably be able to get,' I said, 'given what you did. I also intend to do what I can to protect your rights to your intellectual property.'

'You mean, like my old photos?'

'Your old ones,' I said, 'and your future ones. Whatever income they generate needs to be accounted for. Your rights need to be protected.'

'What makes you think there'll be future photos?' he said.

'You're a photojournalist,' I said. 'You said it. It's in your DNA. You can't use losing a hand as an excuse for ever.'

Gus smiled. 'You can be pretty harsh, you know that?'

'You can be pretty negative.'

He shrugged. 'OK, so my intellectual property. That's good. I never really thought about that.'

I took another bite of my muffin. 'Tell me about your gun.'

'It's gone,' he said. 'I threw it in the river. Behind where I'm living now.'

'Was it registered?'

He shook his head. 'I brought it home.'

'From Iraq?'

He nodded. 'It was in my duffle.'

Another triumph for airport security, I thought. 'What were you doing with a gun?'

'Standard side arm over there. M9 Beretta. Everybody carries a gun. Reporters, cooks, chaplains, doctors.'

'There's no record of your owning this gun, huh?'

He shook his head. 'I bought it from a soldier over there. Never registered it when I came home.'

'And no record that you divested yourself of it, either.'

'No. I just threw it away.'

'So tell me, Gus,' I said. 'What other secrets and lies do you need to straighten out with me?'

Gus looked straight into my eyes. 'None. Nothing. Honest to God, Brady. That's it.'

I returned his gaze, looking for deceit. The fact that I saw none, I knew, didn't mean it wasn't there.

'How are you making out with those forms I gave you?'

'Truthfully,' he said, 'I haven't looked at them. I dread them. I don't want to think about them. They depress me.'

I smiled. I was quite certain that this, at least, was the truth. 'Everybody feels that way,' I said. 'You've got to do them.'

'I got a lot of other stuff on my mind, Brady.'

'Like what?'

Gus looked at me for a moment, then shook his head. 'Stuff, that's all. I'll do the damn paperwork, I promise.'

'You have no choice,' I said.

He nodded. 'You know,' he said, 'at first, I was really depressed about Claudia wanting to divorce me. But I'm not any more. I've caused her and the kids nothing but problems ever since I got back, and all the pressure I was feeling . . . well, since I moved out? It's better. I feel like I'm finally getting better.' He looked at me. 'Can I ask you something?'

'Sure. Of course.'

'I'm thinking of bagging the whole thing.'

I frowned. 'Meaning what?'

'Getting the hell away from here. Starting over someplace far away from here. I mean, like Tahiti or Bali or Dubai or something.'

'Are you asking for my opinion?'

Gus laughed quickly. 'Of course not. Nobody would say it's a good idea. I don't need to hear that.'

'Why are you telling me this, then?' I said.

He shrugged. 'You're my lawyer. You could help me. I mean, if I asked you to, you'd have to help me. Right?'

'*Are* you asking?' I said.

He grinned. 'Nah. Forget it.' He looked at his watch. 'I gotta get to work.'

WHEN I GOT HOME from the office that afternoon, I found a business-sized envelope with actual handwriting on it amid the bills and credit card promotions on the floor under the mail slot in my front door. I couldn't remember the last time somebody sent me a letter.

This envelope had been addressed with green ink in Evie Banyon's distinctive curvy penmanship. I thought, Uh-oh. A letter. This can't be good.

I found a bottle of Long Trail ale in the refrigerator and took it and Evie's letter out to the patio. I slouched in my chair, took a long pull from the bottle, stuck my finger under the envelope flap and tore it open.

The letter was written on two sheets of lined white notebook paper.

Dear Brady,

It's a little before midnight here in foggy Sausalito. I figure if I called on the phone, you'd be home and you'd answer. I don't want a conversation. I just want you to listen to me.

Daddy's asleep. He's not doing very well. He has morning naps and afternoon naps and he goes to bed right after supper and sleeps fitfully at night. Me, I don't sleep much at all these days. I mostly sit around and think, though I can't say I've solved any of the world's great problems. Or even any of my own little ones. We smoke a lot of dope, Daddy and I. Him for his pain, me to keep him company. And for my pain, too, I guess. And to prevent me from thinking too deeply. We try to take it day by day.

Yesterday I extended my leave at the hospital. Truthfully, I don't know that I ever want to go back to that job. I'm thinking I'll just stay here after Daddy's gone. It feels disconnected from the world. I like that. I'm sorry.

I hardly remember you, Brady. I'm sorry to say that, too. But it's true. I do remember that I loved you. Maybe I still do. I don't know.

I hope you are doing what I ordered you to do. Are you? Are you having any fun? I worry about you. I know you don't believe in this stuff. Maybe I don't, either. But when I woke up this morning, still lying in bed, I had this vision. It wasn't a dream. I was wide-awake, and this image came popping into my brain. It was you and some other woman. I didn't recognise her, but she was pretty, and the way she was looking at you I could see that she loved you. I could see that the two of you were happy together. And seeing the two of you smiling at each other made me happy. Made me feel free.

So that's why I'm writing to you. Because this vision has haunted me all day. I know there's truth in it. It's important to me that you listen to what I'm trying to tell you.

Here it is: I want you to forget about me, if you haven't already. Our lives are separate now. That's it.

Goodbye, then, Brady Coyne. Be free and be happy, please. Don't forget to give Henry a hug for me.

Evie xxoo

I folded Evie's letter and stuck it back into its envelope. She said she'd seen a vision. The Evie Banyon I knew was a rock-solid hardheaded rationalist. I supposed the California houseboat culture—and smoking a lot of dope—could change that.

I looked at the postmark on the envelope. She'd mailed it the previous Friday, meaning she'd written it late Thursday night. She'd had that dream just before Alex had appeared in my office.

For some reason, I accepted the idea that the woman Evie had seen in her vision was Alex. Which meant that on some level I accepted the validity of the vision itself.

Evie wasn't coming back. She was ending it.

Reading her letter, I heard her voice. She wrote the way she talked. But now when I tried to visualise her, to conjure up her image in my mind's eye, her face was blurry. Evie Banyon was an absence, not a presence. There was a place in me where she used to live. Now nobody lived there.

Henry was lying beside my chair. I reached down and stroked his back. 'Evie sends a hug,' I said to him.

He looked at me with those intelligent dog eyes of his.

'So now it looks like it's going to be just the two of us,' I said. 'How about some supper?'

FIVE

On Thursday, near closing time, Julie came into my office. 'We got a problem,' she said. She put an envelope on my desk.

It was addressed to AA Movers, Inc., at their address in Lowell. It had a green CERTIFIED MAIL sticker on it. The post office had stamped it with a pointing finger in red ink.

'It came back?'

'It did. AA Movers have moved and left no forwarding address.'

'I hope they broke all their own stuff,' I said. 'So where'd they move to?'

'It took some research. This is what I found out. As of August 31st, AA Movers, Inc., ceased to exist. They closed their Lowell office and terminated their Massachusetts corporation.'

'So the legal body is dead and buried,' I said.

'Well, yes and no. They registered as a New Hampshire corporation, effective September 1st, at which time they opened new accounts and moved their entire operation to their office on Outlook Drive in Nashua. Still using the same name. AA Movers. When the Eppings used them, they were a Massachusetts corporation. That corporation no longer exists.'

'We can't sue a corporation that no longer exists,' I said.

'And this new legal body has no incentive to continue a business relationship with anybody connected with the old body,' she said. 'The Eppings have no leverage with them.'

'In other words, we're screwed. I've got to talk to Doug.'

'Want me to get him on the phone for you?'

I shook my head. 'No, first off, let's resend this letter to the Nashua address, see if we can get a rise out of them. Make the necessary changes, reprint it and I'll sign it. Then find out who their lawyer is.'

MARIE'S WAS A QUIET ITALIAN restaurant just outside Kenmore Square. It was always dark and cool and subdued inside, with the mingled aroma of roasted garlic and fresh oregano and grated Parmesan wafting in from the kitchen. Marie's was my favourite place within walking distance of my office for a private conversation with a friend or a client or another lawyer.

I got there fifteen minutes early on Friday afternoon. I wanted to be there before Lily Capezza arrived so I could play the role of genial host at our first sit-down on the Shaw divorce.

Lily arrived on the dot of one o'clock. 'Am I late?' she said.

I smiled. 'You know you're exactly on time.'

Lily Capezza was a fiftyish woman with glossy black hair, high cheekbones, big dark eyes, wide mouth and imposing bosom. She could charm any judge or jury—or opposing counsel—if you weren't on your guard.

She picked up a menu, scanned it and put it down. 'You want to eat before we talk?'

'I'd like to hear what you want to say,' I said. 'I trust it won't spoil my appetite. We can eat and talk, I bet.'

Our waitress came over. Lily ordered a Caesar salad and iced tea. I asked for a grilled chicken panino and coffee.

When the waitress left, Lily said, 'We should be aiming to settle this case. To make an agreement that the judge will accept. We both know how that works. Child support, division of property, alimony, insurance, all by formula. As I see it, we are left with two issues of potential contention.' She held up two fingers. 'Custody of the children and Mr Shaw's intellectual property. Do you agree?'

'At least those two,' I said. 'You're not suggesting we give one in exchange for the other?'

'Claudia Shaw is thinking about moving to North Carolina to be near her parents.'

'Taking Gus's kids with her.'

'Of course.'

'In exchange for which,' I said, 'she'll let him hold on to his intellectual property. Is that it?'

'That's one way we might make it work,' she said.

I shook my head. 'I don't think so, Lily.'

At that moment our waitress arrived with our lunches.

When she left, Lily said, 'Maybe we should just let the judge decide it. Is that what you want?'

'No,' I said, 'of course not. You and I should work this out.'

'I agree,' she said. 'But I don't want you to think for one minute that I'm not prepared to go that route.'

I started to speak, but Lily held up her hand. 'My client is not having an affair. She was a good and faithful wife and she's a terrific mother. You won't get anywhere accusing her of infidelity, because it's not true.'

'Whether it's true or not,' I said, 'I wouldn't want to use it.'

Lily shook her head. 'I won't hesitate to use his behaviour with his gun,' she said. 'I want you to know that.'

'It was an empty suicide gesture,' I said. 'Pathetic and scary, granted, but he'd never harm his wife or kids. The gun wasn't even loaded.'

Lily shrugged. 'Enormously traumatic for the little girls. I can provide expert testimony to that fact.'

'Gus is a very sympathetic figure,' I said. 'He's suffering from post-traumatic stress disorder. He had his right hand blown off, for God's sake. He's in a support group. He's taking prescription medication. It's a serious illness, and he's doing everything he's supposed to do to get better. I've got plenty of expert testimony for that, too.'

Lily was poking at her salad with her fork.

'My point is,' I said, 'he's sick and he's working hard at getting better.'

Lily impaled an anchovy, ate it, wiped her mouth with her napkin and took a sip of her iced tea. 'I won't quarrel with that,' she said, 'but it doesn't make him any less dangerous or scary.'

'He's getting it under control,' I said. 'He's recovering. That's important. He's not drinking. He's holding down a job. He's doing what he needs to do to heal.'

Lily nodded. 'I see where you're going with this.' She smiled. 'I was hoping we could work out something for these nice people and their two sweet kids. Save them from themselves.'

'I'm hoping the same thing,' I said. 'Maybe we need to go back and talk to our clients some more.'

'Yes,' she said. 'We should probably do that.'

'Claudia relocating to North Carolina with the girls isn't acceptable.'

'I hear you,' Lily said.

ON FRIDAY EVENING, a little before seven, Henry and I went outside and sat on my front steps. The streetlights had come on.

Alex came strolling up the sidewalk a few minutes later. She was wearing sneakers, snug-fitting khaki-coloured trousers that stopped halfway down her calves, and a light windbreaker.

I got up and went to meet her. Henry followed behind me.

She gave me a hug and a peck on the cheek, which I returned, then stepped back and frowned at me. 'Are you all right?'

'Sure,' I said. 'Why wouldn't I be?'

'Gussie says you're really pissed at him. Anyway, that wasn't much of a hug.'

'I don't bring my business home with me,' I said. 'Come on in. I made a pitcher of gin and tonic.'

We went into the house, paused in the kitchen to fill two glasses from the pitcher and grab a dog treat for Henry, and went out onto the patio.

We sat in the wooden Adirondack chairs. I handed the dog biscuit to Alex. 'Give it to Henry. Tell him to sit or lie down, then reward him for it, and it will predispose him to obey you for ever.'

Alex showed the treat to Henry. 'Can you sit?' she said.

He sure could. He sat and gazed lovingly into her eyes.

She laughed and gave him the biscuit.

I held up my glass to her. 'Cheers.'

She clicked her glass against mine and we both took sips.

'Let's not talk about Gus tonight,' said Alex. 'OK?'

'He's my client now,' I said. 'I couldn't talk about him even if I were inclined to.'

'Technically,' she said.

'No,' I said. 'Really.'

She put her hand on my wrist. 'What's wrong, Brady?'

'What makes you think something's wrong?'

'I used to know you pretty well,' she said. 'I've seen you, been with you when you're upset, or sad, or frustrated, or angry. I know how you hold it inside. I'm getting all those vibes from you now.'

'You shouldn't place too much stock in your vibes.'

Alex patted my arm. 'None of my business,' she said.

'I'm glad you're here,' I said. 'It's just . . . awkward. It feels like a date.'

She nodded. 'I know. It does to me, too. Like a first date. I got those old butterflies. I don't know what to expect.'

'Food,' I said. 'You can expect to eat.'

'Evie, huh?'

'Evie and I are over,' I said, 'and I don't want to talk about it.'

Alex's eyes were solemn. She looked at me for a long moment. Then she nodded and her eyes slid away from mine. She took a sip of her drink, then put her head back and looked up at the sky. It was full of clouds and it smelled like rain.

'So, OK,' she said, 'we won't talk about Gus, and we won't talk about Evie. What do you want to talk about?'

'Tell me about your novel,' I said.

'I'll try,' she said, 'but there's not much to tell yet.' As she talked about her characters and what she knew so far about her story, I could hear the enthusiasm bubbling in her voice, and it reminded me of Alex back in the days when I knew and loved her. She'd been full of energy and passion and conviction in those days.

I was beginning to see that she hadn't changed very much.

When our glasses were empty, we went inside. I put out a box of crackers and a plate of pâté. Henry looked on longingly, so I dumped some dog food in a bowl for his supper.

I refilled our glasses and Alex perched on a stool, sipped her drink and spread pâté on crackers for both of us. I took out the chicken breasts that had been marinating. I peeled and sliced an aubergine, two yellow onions and a couple of big Idaho potatoes, brushed olive oil on all the slices, salted and peppered them, and wrapped them in aluminium foil.

'You can throw a salad together while I'm grilling this stuff, if you want,' I said to Alex.

Then I took the chicken and veggies out to the deck. Being with Alex in the house I'd been sharing with Evie had me feeling edgy. Yet it felt comfortable and familiar to be out on the deck cooking while Alex was bustling round in the kitchen making our salad.

By the time the chicken and vegetables were grilled, the wind had shifted. Now it came out of the east, off the water, and it brought a chilly nip to the autumn air, so we decided to eat inside at the kitchen table.

A COUPLE OF HOURS LATER we were munching some Pepperidge Farm cookies and sipping coffee at the kitchen table when a tune began playing in Alex's shoulder bag on the floor beside her chair.

She fished her cellphone out of her bag, frowned at the little screen, then flipped it open and said, 'Claudia? . . . Hi . . . Sure, no problem. What's up? . . . No, he's not. I'm at a friend's house, and . . . Not since yesterday . . . He seemed, you know, normal for him. Why? . . . *What?* Say that again?'

Alex glanced at me as she listened. Then she closed her eyes and I saw something like horror spread across her face. After a minute, she said, 'I'm sure there's nothing to worry about. I'll let you know . . . Right. Bye.'

She snapped her phone shut and placed it on the table. 'That was Claudia,' she said. 'Gus sent her an email. She didn't get it until she got home from work today. It said, "I'm sorry for everything. I don't think I can do this any more." She's been trying to reach him. He's not answering his house phone or his cellphone.' Tears welled up in her eyes. 'Claudia's pretty upset. I guess I am, too.'

'"I don't think I can do this any more"? That's what he said?'

Alex nodded. 'Claudia's afraid of what Gus might do. I am, too. It sounds like, you know . . .'

I nodded. 'When did he send the email?'

'She didn't say. It was waiting for her when she checked her emails after supper tonight. Around six thirty.'

I looked at my watch. It was a little before ten. 'She's been trying to reach him since then?'

Alex nodded. 'No answer.'

'Maybe he's screening Claudia.'

Alex nodded. She picked up her phone, pressed some numbers, then put it to her ear. She waited, then shook her head. 'He's screening me, too, then.'

I took out my cellphone. 'His phone won't recognise my number.'

Alex gave me his number, and I dialled it. It rang five or six times before the recording invited me to leave a message.

I looked at Alex. 'What do you want to do?'

She stood up. 'I don't know about you,' she said, 'but I'm going to go find my brother.'

'Me, too,' I said.

A SOFT AUTUMN RAIN was falling when Alex and I left the house. Mt Vernon Street was slick and shiny. Alex reached for my hand and gripped it hard as we walked down Charles Street to the parking garage where I stow my car.

By the time we crossed Route 128 in Lexington, the rain had stopped, and a little less than an hour after we'd left my house on Beacon Hill, I steered onto the long curving driveway off Monument Street that led to the apartment over the carriage house that Gus Shaw was renting.

I stopped in front and turned off the ignition.

No lights shone inside or outside Gus's apartment.

'He's not here,' said Alex.

'Let's go check,' I said.

We got out of the car and climbed the outside stairway to the little porch at the first-floor entry above the garage. I knocked on the door, waited and listened, knocked again. Nothing.

Alex stepped up and banged hard on the door. 'Gussie,' she called. 'Come on. Open up. It's just me and Brady.'

There was no sound. Nobody came to the door.

'I know where he hides a spare key,' Alex said. She reached over the railing, moved her hand across the shingles that sided the carriage house, then showed me a house key. 'Four over from the light, then four down,' she said. 'He keeps it wedged up under a shingle.'

She handed me the key. I unlocked the door, then gave the key to Alex. She stuck it back under its shingle.

When I pushed open the door and started to step inside, I whiffed an unmistakable smell. It was burnt gunpowder.

I turned to Alex. 'You stay here,' I said.

'But—'

I held her by the shoulders. 'I'm going to go look,' I said.

She looked at me wide-eyed, then nodded. 'Yes, OK.'

I went in and closed the door behind me, leaving Alex out on the porch. Inside the apartment, the smell of cordite was stronger.

I felt along the inside wall, found the light switch and turned it on. When my eyes adjusted, I looked around.

Gus was sitting in the shadows in a leather-backed armchair at his desk by the window at the end of the room. His arms were dangling at his sides and his head was slumped onto his right shoulder. Even from where I stood, I could see that there was a lot of blood.

Now mingled with the smell of a gunshot was another odour. I'd smelled it before. It was the dank odour of recent death. I put my hands in my pockets to remind myself not to touch anything. It was already too late to do anything about the doorknobs and the light switch.

I went over to Gus, took a quick look and turned away. I swallowed hard and forced myself to look again. The bullet had entered his head at the soft place behind his jawbone under his left ear and exited from the upper right side of his skull.

The entry wound was small and black and round. The skin round the hole was red and blistery, and it looked like the hair behind his ear was singed. The exit wound was big and jagged and bloody.

A square automatic handgun lay on the floor under Gus's dangling left hand. I was willing to bet that it was the M9 Beretta that he'd waved at his wife and daughters. The gun he told me he'd thrown into the Concord River.

On the desk in front of Gus was a closed laptop computer, an empty tumbler and a small paper bag. Inside the bag was a bottle. I pulled open the end of the bag with my fingertips and saw that it was a pint of Early Times bourbon. A little skim of amber liquid coated the bottom of the tumbler. The booze smell was strong.

I went out onto the porch and closed the door behind me. Alex looked at me with big eyes.

I shook my head and held out my arms.

Her arms went round my chest and she pressed herself against me. I held her tight.

After a minute, Alex looked up at me. 'I want to see him.'

'We've got to call the police.'

'They'll tell us to stay outside, won't they?'

I nodded. 'But you don't want to see him, honey.'

She made a fist and punched my chest. 'Don't tell me what I want, Brady. I need to see my brother.'

I looked at her. Fire sparked in her eyes. I remembered that fire. 'He shot himself,' I said. 'It's pretty bad. There's a lot of blood. It looks like he drank a glass of bourbon and then shot himself behind the ear.'

Alex narrowed her eyes at me. 'If you're trying to convince me not to go in there, it's not working. Come with me, will you?'

'OK,' I said. 'I'll go with you.' I took her hand.

Alex stopped inside the doorway. 'I can smell it,' she said. 'Gunpowder. Something else, too.' She let go of my hand and went over to where Gus was sitting. I followed.

She put her hand on Gus's shoulder. She looked down at him and shook her head. 'Oh, Gussie' was all she said. She sighed heavily, then looked at me. 'I've got to tell Claudia.'

'Later,' I said. 'First, if you can handle it, look around, see if you notice anything.'

'Like what am I supposed to notice?'

I shrugged. 'Is anything out of place? Anything missing? Anything here now that wasn't here last time you were here?'

She pointed at the bottle in the bag and the empty glass. 'Bourbon was what he used to like. He stopped drinking a long time ago. He said it made him crazy. I didn't think he had booze in the house.'

'This is still in its store bag.'

She nodded. 'As if he bought it for this occasion, you mean.'

I bent closer to Gus. A light scattering of white flakes had fallen onto his shoulders and on the back of the leather chair he was sitting in. I looked up. In the angled plasterboard ceiling directly over Gus's head was a round bullet-sized hole.

'Look,' I said to Alex. I pointed at the ceiling.

She looked. 'What is it?'

'I'd say it's a bullet hole.'

'So what does it mean?'

I shrugged. 'I don't know.'

She muttered, 'To remind himself that his gun worked? Or maybe, just at the last minute, he's trying to shoot himself, but his hand refuses to cooperate, moves the gun away just as he pulls the trigger. So maybe that does it . . . gives him courage or something . . . so then he puts the gun back against his head and . . . and this time he does it.' She squeezed my arm. 'Brady, I've got to go outside now.'

We went outside and sat on the steps. I took out my cellphone.

'Calling the police?' said Alex.

'I'm calling Roger Horowitz,' I said. 'He's a state homicide detective. He'll handle it.'

'Horowitz,' she said. 'I remember him. Always crabby. You used to like him.'

'I used to respect him,' I said. 'Still do. He's pretty hard to like, though over the years he's kind of grown on me.'

I accessed Roger Horowitz's secret cellphone number in my phone's memory and hit SEND. He gave me this number several years ago and warned me never to use it unless it was urgent, by which he meant that it related to a homicide.

He answered on the third ring. 'Coyne,' he growled. 'It's Friday night. I've been home from work less than an hour.'

'Sorry,' I said. 'I'm here with the body of a man named Gus Shaw. It appears that he shot himself.'

'You couldn't call 911 like any other citizen?'

'Not when I could call you.'

'So where's here?'

'Concord. It's an apartment over a garage off Monument Street. I don't know the street number. The people who own it live in the house in front. Folks named Croyden.'

'Your body's inside?'

'Sitting at his desk.'

'So you've been in there.'

'I'm here with Alex Shaw, Gus's sister. We went in. We didn't touch anything except the doorknobs and the light switch.'

'Alex?' he said. 'Your old girlfriend? That Alex Shaw?'

'That's right.'

'I remember her.'

'Yes,' I said. 'She's hard to forget. She remembers you, too.'

He snorted a laugh. 'OK. The Concord cops'll be there in a few minutes, and the rest of the troops'll be right behind them.' And then, typically, he disconnected without a goodbye.

After a minute, Alex stood up and fished her cellphone from her pocket. 'I'm going to call Claudia now,' she said.

She moved over to where I'd left my car, leaned against the side, pecked out some numbers on her phone, then pressed it against her ear. After a moment, I heard her speaking softly.

A few minutes later Alex folded her phone and shoved it back into her pocket. She came back and sat on the step beside me.

'You OK?' I said.

She looked at me. Her face was wet. 'I'm hardly OK.'

'How'd Claudia take it?'

'She seemed . . . I don't know. Not surprised. She said some part of her had been expecting it for a long time.'

A minute later we heard the distant, muffled wail of a siren. It grew louder, and then the beams of headlights cut through the darkness and a cruiser pulled up next to my car.

A pair of uniformed officers got out and came over to where Alex and I were sitting. 'You're Coyne?' said one of them.

I nodded. 'This is Alexandria Shaw. It's her brother up there.'

He looked at Alex. 'I'm going to ask you to come over to the cruiser with me, ma'am. You, sir, stay with Officer Guerra here.'

Alex turned to me. 'Don't you go anywhere without me.'

'I won't,' I said.

She stood up and the cop touched her arm, then she followed him over to the Concord PD cruiser. He opened the passenger door and held it for her, and she ducked her head and slid in.

I remained sitting on the bottom step. Officer Guerra stood there with his back to me.

Pretty soon the place was swarming with people. There were local cops and state cops, and there were other officials—technicians from the medical examiner's office and forensics experts.

After a while, a bulky guy in a dark suit, no necktie, came over to me. 'You Brady Coyne?' he said.

I nodded.

'I'm Detective Boyle,' he said. He had flipped open a notebook and was holding a pen in his other hand. 'You're the one who found the body?'

I nodded.

'You were in the apartment up there?'

'Yes.'

'Did you remove anything?'

'No.'

'Touch anything? Move anything?'

'Touched the doorknobs, inside and out. And the light switch. I didn't move anything.'

'And the victim? His name is Shaw?'

'That's right. Gus Shaw. Augustine. I'm a lawyer. I was handling his divorce. I came here with his sister.'

He looked at his notebook. 'That would be Alexandria Shaw?'

'Alex, yes. She's in that cruiser.'

'OK. We'll get your story later.' He flipped his notebook shut. 'For now, I want you to stay out of the way.'

Officer Guerra motioned for me to stand up, and I followed him away from the garage to the edge of the clearing. Guerra was not inclined to talk to me. We stood there watching the people go up and down the steps to Gus's apartment. After a while, I found a big boulder to sit on.

A little while later a man with a flashlight in one hand and a dog on a leash in the other came down the driveway. He stopped beside me, flicking off his flashlight. 'What's going on?' he said. 'All these vehicles . . .'

I pointed up at the apartment. 'A man up there is dead.'

The dog was a golden retriever. It sniffed my trouser legs.

The man shook his head. 'Dead,' he said. 'Oh, dear. Gus, is it?'

'Yes,' I said. 'It's Gus.'

'I'm Herb Croyden,' the man said. 'I own this property.'

Herb Croyden was a stocky, fit-looking guy with silvery hair and rimless glasses. 'So, what happened?' he said.

'Gus apparently shot himself.'

'*Apparently?*'

'How well did you know him?' I said.

'Me?' He shrugged. 'Not very well, evidently. I know he had his problems, but you never think a man's going to . . .'

I nodded.

'He liked Gracie here,' he said. 'He'd sometimes take her down to the river and throw sticks for her.' He gave Gracie's ears a scratch. 'She'll fetch sticks all day, and she loves to swim. The river runs right behind our property. Gracie seemed to give Gus a lot of pleasure.' He shook his head. 'I can't believe this. Beth—that's my wife—she'll be devastated. I've got to go back to the house and tell her what's going on.' He cocked his head. 'I didn't get your name.'

I held out my hand to him. 'Brady Coyne. I'm Gus's lawyer.'

'You found him? His body?'

I nodded. 'Alex and I. Alex is his sister.'

Herb Croyden shook my hand, then started to walk away.

Officer Guerra shone a flashlight on him. 'Who are you, sir?'

'I live in that house at the end of the driveway,' Herb said.

'You better stay here,' said Guerra. 'They'll want to talk to you.'

'Well,' Herb said, 'they can find me at my house. My wife is there waiting for me, and I'm going to go back to her now.'

'I'm sorry, sir,' said Guerra, 'but you'll have to wait here.'

'Shoot me, then,' said Herb, and he flicked on his flashlight and headed towards his house with Gracie heeling nicely.

Officer Guerra stood there watching the beam of Herb Croyden's flashlight move away. Then he turned to me and smiled. 'Oh, well,' he said.

'I'm glad you didn't shoot him. He seems like a nice guy,' I said.

AFTER A WHILE, two men lugged a collapsable gurney up the steps to the apartment. A few minutes later they carried it back down, this time with a plastic body bag strapped onto it. They loaded it into an emergency wagon, slammed the doors and got in. Then the wagon rolled down the Croydens' driveway.

A minute or two later Detective Boyle came over. He said something to Officer Guerra, who moved away from us, then sat on the boulder beside mine. 'I sent him for coffee,' said Boyle.

I nodded. 'Great. Thanks.'

'I need to know everything, Mr Coyne.'

'Alex got a call from Gus's wife,' I said. 'Claudia got an email from Gus that worried her, so she—'

'Worried her why?'

'It said something like, "I can't take it any more."'

'A suicide note, huh?'

I shrugged. 'It could be interpreted that way, I guess.'

'You don't think it should be?'

'I don't know. No, I don't think so. I wouldn't've thought Gus Shaw would kill himself.'

Boyle nodded. 'So his wife got that email. Then what?'

'Claudia was worried, of course,' I said. 'She tried to call Gus, got no answer, so she called Alex, who was at my house. Alex tried to call him, got no answer, so we came here.'

'You live where?'

'Boston, Mount Vernon Street.'

Boyle scribbled in his notebook. Without looking up, he said, 'What's your relationship with Ms Shaw?'

'Alex and I are old friends,' I said. 'She's the one who asked me to handle Gus's divorce.'

'So, tell me about Gus Shaw,' said Boyle.

I said, 'I only met him a week or so ago. Met with him just twice. He lost his hand in Iraq. He was a photojournalist and, next thing he knew, he couldn't handle a camera. He was suffering from post-traumatic stress disorder. His wife was divorcing him. She'd taken out a restraining order on him.'

Boyle made some more notes, then looked up at me. 'The man sounds like an ideal candidate for a bullet in the brain,' he said, 'but I'm hearing a "but" in your voice.'

'I guess you are,' I said.

Right then Officer Guerra came over with a lidded foam cup in each hand. He handed one of them to me. 'Black, OK?'

'Thanks, yes,' I said.

He gave the other one to Boyle, then wandered away.

Boyle peeled off the cap, took a sip, set the cup on the ground and said, 'Do you want to tell me about that "but"?'

I took the top off my coffee and sipped it. It tasted good. 'Nothing you could call evidence,' I said. 'He told me he felt like he was getting better. He talked about the future. He seemed to accept what was happening with his family. The divorce, I mean. Given everything he'd been through, he seemed OK to me. As if he had things he was looking forward to.'

'You having no expertise whatsoever in the field of mental health,' said Boyle.

'You're certainly right about that,' I said. 'Just my gut.'

'Well,' he said, 'it looks like your gut was off base this time.'

'Not the first time. I sure didn't see it coming, though. So case closed or what?'

'It's in the hands of the medical examiner,' Boyle said. 'Don't quote me, but, yeah, based on what I saw up there, that would certainly be my prediction. We gotta wait for all the forensics, of course.'

Boyle snapped his notebook shut, then stuck it into the inside pocket of his jacket.

'OK, I guess I'm done with you for now,' he said. 'As soon as my partner's finished talking to Ms Shaw, you're both free to go. Might need to ask you some more questions in a day or two.'

'Will you keep us posted?' I said.

He shrugged. 'As soon as the ME comes up with his verdict, I'll make sure someone lets you know. You being the deceased's lawyer. Wait here.' He stood up and stalked over to the cruiser, where his partner was questioning Alex.

I sipped my coffee, and a few minutes later Alex climbed out of the cruiser and came over to where I was sitting.

I stood up and hugged her. 'You OK?'

'Hardly,' she said. 'Can we get out of here now?'

We went over to my car.

Alex said, 'You mind dropping me off at my hotel?'

'Listen,' I said. 'Why don't you stay at my house tonight?'

'You think that's a good idea?' she said.

'It's no night to be alone.'

'You sure?'

'I'm sure,' I said.

I felt her fingers touch the back of my neck. 'Thank you,' she said softly. 'I accept.'

I LEFT MY CAR in the Residents Only slot in front of my house on Mt Vernon Street. Henry was waiting in the hall. Alex scootched down so he could lick her face.

I got two bottles of Samuel Adams lager from the refrigerator, and the three of us went out to the patio at the back. Alex and I sat side by side in the Adirondack chairs. Henry marked his territory, then lay down on the deck beside me.

An easterly breeze had blown away the rain clouds from earlier in the evening and the sky glittered with a billion stars. We said nothing for a long time. It was a comfortable silence. The two of us had always been comfortable with silences.

Then Alex said, 'There's Elvis. See him?' She was pointing up at the stars. 'You can see his guitar. And over there's Snoopy, with his two ears hanging down.'

I found myself smiling. 'Elvis and Snoopy constellations?'

'Yes. And look. That's the Green Ripper, with his scythe.'

'You mean the Grim Reaper?'

'No. The Green Ripper. That was Gus's name for the Grim Reaper. See?'

I looked where she was pointing, but I couldn't make out the starry outline of the Green Ripper any more than I was able to see Snoopy or Elvis. So all I said was, 'Oh, yeah. Sure enough.'

'When I was little,' she said, 'our family used to rent a cottage on the Cape in the summer and, on a clear night, Gussie and I would go out on the back lawn and he'd sit me on his lap and show me his own constellations. He used to say, "Why shouldn't we have our own constellations? We shouldn't have to go along with the Greeks and Romans." Gussie rejected all conventional wisdom. He questioned everything. He had to see it and make sense of it for himself. It's why he was a good photographer, I think.'

'I'm really sorry,' I said.

'I never felt safer than when I was sitting on my big brother's lap with his arms round me, looking up at the sky when he told me about the stars.'

Alex took a sip from her beer bottle. Then she pushed herself up from her chair. She stood there looking down at me.

I held up my arms.

She smiled and snuggled sideways on my lap.

I wrapped my arms round her and held her while she cried.

SOMETIME LATER we went inside. We made up the day bed in my ground-floor office and I put out some clean towels in the downstairs bathroom for her. I found a new toothbrush she could use and gave her one of my T-shirts to wear to bed.

'Will you be OK?' I said.

She shrugged. 'Probably not.'

'I'll be right upstairs.'

She arched her eyebrows at me.

'If you can't sleep. If you want to talk. That's all I meant.'

She smiled. 'I'll be all right.' She put her hands on my shoulders, tiptoed up and kissed my cheek. 'Thank you, Brady. I know I'm lucky to have you here for me.'

'I'll be here for you tomorrow, too.'

'I know,' she said. 'That's what I used to love about you.'

Henry followed me upstairs to my bedroom. Mine and Evie's. Well, now it was just mine. I lay awake for a long time.

SIX

It was nearly eight thirty when I woke up the next morning. I pulled on a pair of jeans and went downstairs. I found Alex sitting at the kitchen table. Henry was sprawled on the floor beside her.

'I made the coffee,' said Alex. She was wearing the T-shirt I'd given her and a pair of old sweatpants that she must have found in my downstairs closet.

'Did Henry wake you up?' I said.

She smiled. 'I was awake when he came into the room. It was obvious that he wanted me to let him out. So I did.'

I poured myself a mug of coffee and sat across from her. 'Did you sleep at all?' I said.

She shrugged. 'Not much. How about you?'

'I didn't sleep so well, either.' I took a sip of coffee. 'So what's your programme today?'

'Fetch my car,' she said, 'stop at my hotel for a shower and a change of clothes, then go see Claudia.'

'I'll go with you, if you like.'

'You don't need to, Brady. You must have better things to do.'

'Nothing more important. I'm offering. But I understand if it's something you want to do by yourself.'

She smiled quickly. 'It would be nice. And I'd like you to meet Claudia and the girls. Thank you.' She gazed out of the back window into the garden and said, 'He didn't do it, you know.'

'Gus?' I said.

She turned and looked at me. 'I lay awake thinking about it, trying to be objective. I guess I knew Gus better than anybody.'

'In my experience,' I said, 'what seems objective in the middle of the night has a way of seeming far-fetched in the light of day.'

'Well,' she said, 'here it is, and the sun's shining, and I still don't think he killed himself. Gussie just wouldn't do that.'

'Honey,' I said softly, 'he wasn't the same man who told you about the constellations while you snuggled in his lap.'

'You don't think I know that?' She shook her head. 'Look, in a lot of ways, I barely recognised my brother. But Gussie wasn't a suicidal person.'

'I'm not sure what a suicidal person is,' I said, 'unless you mean somebody who actually commits suicide.'

'I think some people just have it in them to kill themselves,' she said, 'and some don't. How else do you explain why somebody whose life isn't any worse than somebody else's does it and the other person doesn't? I think it's like a gene. You're either born with it or you're not.'

'You're saying Gus didn't have it,' I said.

'That's right. He didn't.'

'So,' I said, 'if Gus didn't kill himself, it means . . .'

'I know. It means somebody else did.'

'Like who?' I said. 'Why?'

She shook her head. 'I have no idea.'

'We can talk to Detective Boyle, but . . .'

She shook her head. 'He probably won't put much stock in my theory about the suicide gene. He'll just look at the evidence.'

'You've got to admit, the evidence is quite compelling.'

She narrowed her eyes at me. 'What do you think?'

I shrugged. 'He had a lot of good reasons to kill himself.'

'That doesn't answer my question.'

'Well,' I said, 'just from being with him, if I didn't know any of the facts of his life, I guess I'd say that he was a fighter and a survivor. Some of the things he told me, it seemed as if he was planning on living. He was thinking about the future.'

'He *was* a fighter,' Alex said. 'Exactly. So let's start with the assumption that he didn't kill himself.'

'We can't ignore the evidence,' I said.

'That's what I'm saying. Let's take the evidence and see how it can be explained if we assume somebody murdered my brother.'

'Start with his email to Claudia yesterday, then,' I said.

Alex shrugged. 'Easy. Somebody else sent it. Whoever killed him. A note, to make it look like suicide. What else?'

'All of it,' I said. 'The who, what, where, when, why and how of it. I mean, who'd want to kill him? And why? What would anyone gain by killing Gus Shaw? Where's the motive?'

'That's exactly the question, isn't it? Are you going to help me, or what?'

'Help you?'

'Figure out who killed my brother.'

'Look,' I said. 'Let's see what the medical examiner comes up with first. If his verdict is suicide, then we can decide what to do.'

WE STOPPED at the parking garage at the Alewife T station so Alex could retrieve her car. Then I followed her to the Best Western hotel in Concord. She pulled into the parking area in front, and I slid my car in beside hers.

She got out and came over to my window. I rolled it down. 'You want to come up?' she said. 'I'll be a while. I've got to wash my hair. There's a coffeemaker in the room and a TV.'

'Don't worry about me,' I said.

She turned and went into the hotel.

There was a little gas station/convenience store next door to the Best Western. I walked over, bought a cup of coffee and a skinny Saturday *Globe*, and took them back to my car.

An hour later, Alex came out and climbed into my car. 'I just talked to Claudia,' she said. 'She didn't sound that pleased about us going over.'

'I imagine she's totally blown away,' I replied. 'Maybe the idea of entertaining company . . . Why don't you go ahead without me.' I patted her arm. 'Give me a call afterwards, tell me how it went.'

'I wanted you to meet Claudia and the girls,' she said.

I nodded. 'I would like to meet them. There will be a better time.'

Alex sighed. 'It's going to be hard. For Claudia, I mean. I know they were getting divorced, and I know Gus behaved badly, but I'm sure she still loved him. She has to be feeling . . .'

'Guilty?' I said. 'I'd be surprised if she weren't. I'm feeling guilty. I bet you are, too.'

Alex nodded, then leaned over and kissed my cheek. 'I think you're right. It's better if I do this by myself. I'm sorry you had to drive all the way out here. I'll call you later, OK?'

'Please do.'

She smiled. 'Well, thanks for everything. I don't know how I could've got through last night without you.'

'That's what friends are for.'

SINCE EVIE LEFT, my weekends had been empty. I'd managed to get away for a few Sundays of trout fishing. Mostly, though, I spent my weekends ploughing through the paperwork that Julie always insisted I bring home, and watching a lot of ball games on TV, and reading some books. Before Evie came along, I lived alone and never felt lonely. Now I felt lonely much of the time.

That afternoon, Henry and I piled into my car and drove out to Bolton Flats, which was a several-hundred-acre expanse of field, forest and marshland near Clinton. He ran and I walked, and after about three hours of fresh air and exercise, both of us were panting.

When I got home I checked my voicemail for messages. There were none.

I spent a couple of hours at the desk in my home office slogging through some paperwork, and then, as a reward for my diligence, I heated a can of Progresso minestrone soup for my supper. I was watching a Saturday night college football game and sipping a glass of bourbon when Alex called.

'I just wanted to say good night,' she said.

'How'd it go with Claudia?'

'I ended up spending the whole day and staying for supper,' she said. 'They aren't quite sure what it all means. The girls, I mean.'

'Did you get a sense of Claudia's, um, take on it?'

'She's the one who got that email yesterday, don't forget. I think by the time she called to tell me about it, she'd already decided Gussie had done something to himself.'

'So what are your plans? You going to hang around for a while?'

'Until we figure out what happened with Gus,' she said.

'We'll have dinner,' I said.

'That would be nice.' Alex was quiet. Then she said, 'Well, good night, Brady. Thanks for everything. Sleep well.'

'I think I will,' I said. 'You, too.'

I SLEPT WELL and woke up late on Sunday. I took a carafe of coffee and the Sunday *Globe* out to the patio and read all of it.

In the afternoon I watched the Patriots clobber the Dolphins. Then I spent an hour fooling around with my paperwork. I made an omelette for supper and found *From Here to Eternity* on a cable channel.

The movie ended at eleven. Eight o'clock on this Sunday evening in California. I picked up my cellphone. I had stopped trying to call Evie a long time ago. I didn't like imagining her screening her calls and not answering when she saw it was me. I didn't like hearing her voicemail inviting me to leave a message and deciding not to leave one because I knew she wouldn't call me back.

Well, I wanted to do this. I poked out her cellphone number. I hit SEND. It rang five times. Then came her familiar, businesslike message. 'It's Evie. I can't come to the phone. Leave a message and I'll get right back to you.'

I took a deep breath, and after the beep, I said, 'Hey, babe. It's me. I got your letter. I guess it didn't surprise me. It's OK. I want you to do what you need to do. And I'm good. You don't need to worry about me.' I hesitated. I wasn't saying any of the things I wanted to say. 'Look,' I said. 'We really could talk. I wouldn't beg you to come home or tell you how lonely I am. Nothing like that, honest. It would just be nice to talk. Well, I just wanted to tell you that. I hope Ed's doing OK. I hope you're doing OK. We're good here. Me and Henry. I'm trying to live my life, just like you want me to.' I stopped, then hit the END button on my phone.

Before bed, I let Henry out. While he sniffed around and squirted on the bushes, I stood on the deck, looked up at the sky, and tried to locate Snoopy and Elvis and the Green Ripper. But it still just looked like a random chaos of stars up there.

I SPENT all of Monday morning in court and didn't get back to the office until around two in the afternoon. Julie was on the phone when I walked in. I gave her a wave, poured myself a mug of coffee and went into my office.

She came in a minute later. 'How'd it go?' she said.

'Judge Kolb was his usual pissy self,' I said, 'but we got it done. Gus Shaw has been weighing heavily on my mind.'

Julie nodded. 'I'm sorry. And Alex? How's she taking it?'

I shrugged. 'He was her big brother. So, did anything happen in my absence this morning?'

She pushed a list of messages and reminders across my desk to me, then said, 'I tracked down the lawyer for AA Movers. Charles Kenilworth. Office on Route101A in Amherst, New Hampshire.'

'That's good work,' I said.

'I know. So I bet you want to talk to Attorney Kenilworth, huh?'

'You bet I do,' I said.

Julie went out to her desk, and a few minutes later my telephone console buzzed.

'I've got Attorney Kenilworth on line two,' Julie said.

'His secretary can't be much good,' I said, 'if she didn't give you the runaround.'

'He answered the phone,' she said. 'I told him who you were, who you were representing, and he said to put you on.'

'OK,' I said. 'Thanks. Got it.' I hit the blinking button and said, 'Attorney Kenilworth? You there?'

'I'm here,' he said, 'and you can call me Chuck.'

'OK,' I said. 'I'm Brady. I wanted to talk to you about—'

'The Epping complaint with some non-existent Massachusetts corporation,' he said. 'I've got your letter here on my desk.'

'I assume you were intending to talk to me about it,' I said.

'No,' he said. 'Actually, I wasn't. My client, assuming you're referring to AA Movers, a New Hampshire corporation with headquarters in Nashua, has no reason to respond to your letter.'

'Assuming your client has broken no laws,' I said, 'I guess you're right. Nothing to discuss.'

Kenilworth hesitated one beat too long before he said, 'You're not threatening me, are you, Brady?'

'Me? Certainly not,' I said. 'Just keeping you informed. Your client wrecked a lot of valuable stuff of my clients and refused to accept responsibility. So my clients are very upset, and on their behalf, so am I. I just thought you might want to get back to Mr Nicholas Delaney at Double A Movers, formerly a Massachusetts corporation, now incorporated in New Hampshire, and tell him that there is an angry Boston attorney who knows people in the state attorney general's office and has friends at the IRS who's thinking about looking into their business practices. I promise you that before we're done, I will know everything there is to know about Nicholas Delaney.'

Kenilworth chuckled. 'Sounds like a threat to me.'

'I'll wait to hear from you, then?'

'I'll get back to you,' he said. 'Good talking to you, Brady.'

'You, too, Chuck,' I said. 'I enjoyed it.'

I then called the number for Doug and Mary Epping. When Mary answered, I asked to talk to Doug.

'You can talk to me,' she said. 'It's really my furniture.'

'Of course,' I said. 'Sorry. OK. Here's the thing, Mary. Back in the spring when this Double A outfit moved you and wrecked your stuff, they were a Massachusetts corporation. Now they're not. Legally, they no longer exist. We can't touch them.'

'I understand about corporations,' she said. 'And limited liability. But you're saying they have no responsibility for what they did?'

'I'm afraid that's right, yes. No legal responsibility.'

'Doug will be beside himself,' she said.

'I don't blame him.'

'You've got to think of something, Brady. It's not even the furniture, or the money. It's . . .'

'The principle of it,' I said. 'I agree.'

'It's just that it's not *right*,' said Mary Epping. 'We're not done with this. I guarantee that.'

ALEX AND I talked by phone on Monday evening and then again on Tuesday and Wednesday, a little before eleven, when both of us were thinking of heading for bed. It was eerily reminiscent of the time years earlier when we were a couple but living apart, Alex at her house in Garrison, Maine, and I in my rented condo on the Boston waterfront. Back then, during the week, we talked on the phone every night before bed but saw each other only on weekends.

Somewhere along the way we decided to get together on Friday, just as we used to do in the old days. We'd have dinner at my house. Alex insisted on doing the cooking. She said she wanted to show me that she'd become a better cook, and I said I believed it, because she'd never cooked anything before.

We didn't talk about where she'd sleep that night, or how we'd spend the weekend, or how much things between us had changed in the past seven years, or how much things hadn't changed.

I'D HUNG UP my office pinstripe, pulled on a pair of jeans, and was giving Henry his supper on Thursday when my phone rang. It was Roger Horowitz. 'In five minutes I'm going to knock on your front door,' he said. 'Wanted to be sure you were there.'

'I'm here,' I said. 'You want something to eat?'

'Just coffee,' he said, and hung up.

So I made a fresh pot of coffee, and five minutes later, almost to the second, my doorbell rang. Henry scurried to the door and stood there pressing his nose against it. I told him to stay, then opened the door for Horowitz.

He stepped in. A big manila envelope was tucked under his arm. 'I got the ME's report on the Shaw thing,' he said. 'Figured you'd want to hear it.'

'I do. I appreciate it.'

We went into the kitchen. I poured some coffee and we sat at the table.

Horowitz slid a folder out of the envelope. He opened it. 'Suicide. That's the verdict. I bet you're not surprised.'

'No, not really,' I said.

'The evidence was unequivocal,' he said.

'I'm not arguing with you,' I said.

He nodded. 'The weapon they found on the floor under the victim's left hand—a military-issue M9 Beretta, nine millimetre—fired the bullet that killed him. Shaw's were the only fingerprints on the weapon, which matches the description of the handgun that he, um, allegedly brandished before his wife and children several months ago, the same weapon he brought back illegally from Iraq.'

'How'd you hear about that?'

'Boyle got it from Mrs Shaw.'

I shrugged. 'OK. What else?'

'Two empty shell casings on the floor. One evidently a practice shot into the ceiling.'

'Explain the practice shot,' I said.

'We see it sometimes with handgun suicides,' he said. 'For courage, maybe. Or just to be sure he knows how the weapon works. Unfortunately, we've never had the opportunity to ask the victim to explain it to us. But, anyway, there were those two cartridge casings. Ceiling, then head.'

'So,' I said, 'the bullet entered here'—I put my finger against the soft place just below my left ear and behind my jawbone—'and exited . . .'

Horowitz touched the top of the right side of his head. 'Here. The gun was held at an angle, pointing slightly upwards. The bullet angled through his head. It expanded as it went. Made a helluva big exit wound.'

'Did he press the barrel against his head?'

'No,' said Horowitz. 'There was some burning and blistering of the skin around the entrance wound consistent with the gun being held an inch or so away.'

'Is that what a man shooting himself in the head would do?'

He frowned. 'You got some kind of a problem, Coyne?'

I shook my head. 'No. No problem. You're answering my questions. I'm just trying to envision it. Thanks. Carry on.'

He took a sip of coffee, then glanced at the papers on the table in front of him. 'Gunpowder residue on Shaw's left hand which, as it happens, was his only hand.' He moved his finger down the page. 'I'm skimming here. A lot of technical stuff. Traces of legal prescription drugs in his system. Antidepressants, matching what they found in his bathroom, quantities consistent with a prescription dosage. Um, OK, he had about two ounces of bourbon in his stomach, which was otherwise empty. There were about four ounces gone from that bottle of Early Times he had there, which just about computes with his blood alcohol level, which was .04.'

'You lost me there,' I said. 'Explain.'

'Two two-ounce shots of whiskey, one maybe half an hour after the other,' he said, 'what you might call a couple of stiff drinks, would give a big guy like Shaw a BAL of around .04, which would result in partial impairment. Not legally drunk, but enough to affect your judgment, retard your reflexes. Enough, probably, to give a man who wants to kill himself the courage. The two ounces still in the stomach, not yet metabolised, had to've been taken within a minute or two before he pulled the trigger. See? He took a drink, waited for it to hit him, got relaxed, maybe fired a bullet into the ceiling, then took another drink and did it.'

I was shaking my head.

Horowitz frowned at me. 'What?'

'Just that Gus had quit drinking,' I said.

'I guess when you're about to put a bullet in your brain, you don't worry about things like that. Or maybe he was lying.'

'Did they find any other booze in his apartment?'

'No. Just that Early Times. He probably bought it for the occasion.' He shuffled through the papers. 'OK,' he said. 'Moving on. Shaw's fingerprints were the only ones on the tumbler. They couldn't pull any prints off the paper bag the bottle was in. Several smudges and partials on that bottle, but nothing they could use. As I said, the only fingerprints on the gun were Shaw's. They put time of death at between five thirty-five and eleven ten on Friday.'

'Those are fairly strange estimated times,' I said.

'The time on the email he sent his wife was a little after five thirty. He was alive then. You called me at eleven fifteen reporting he was dead. QED.'

'You don't need a medical degree to arrive at that estimate,' I said. 'I mean, I assume the body temperature, lividity, rigor mortis, digestion, things like that were in line?'

'They were in line, yes. The ME's science actually put it at between six and nine p.m.'

'That email was sent from Gus's computer, then?'

He nodded.

'What else did they find on his computer?' I said.

'Shaw's fingerprints,' he said. 'Nobody else's. It doesn't say anything about his computer files in this report, which I take to mean they didn't find anything relevant except for that email at the top of his SENT list.' He lined up the sheets of paper he'd been looking at, put them back in the folder and closed it.

'That's it?' I said.

'Those are the forensics of it,' he said. 'It's quite a lot, I'd say. Everything points to Shaw killing himself.'

'What about his frame of mind?'

'Everybody they talked to said about the same thing. The man suffered from post-traumatic stress disorder. He got his hand blown off in Iraq. He probably saw more horror over there than he could comprehend.'

'Can I ask who they talked to?'

'Now you're pushing it, Coyne. I'm telling you all this out of friendship, not so you can second-guess the medical examiner and the cops. I figured that Alex has a right to know before it's in the newspapers or something.'

'You want me to share this with Alex?' I said.

'I'll do it,' he said, 'if you'd rather.'

'No,' I said. 'I will. She's not going to like this verdict.'

He shook his head. 'The poor guy couldn't take it any more. Simple as that. It's always tough for the loved ones. They never want to hear it.' He stuffed the folder into the manila envelope, tucked it under his arm again, pushed his chair back from the table and stood up. 'Well, thanks for the coffee.'

'What about his apartment?' I said. 'Can we get back in there?'

'The police tape is gone,' he said. 'It was a quick and straightforward investigation, Coyne. Gus Shaw killed himself and everybody's going to have to get used to the idea.'

I nodded. 'I guess I misjudged the man.'

Horowitz smirked. 'Wouldn't be the first time, huh?'

'No, you're right. I'm not very good at judging people.'

'I mean,' he said, 'just look at your personal life.'

'Sure,' I said. 'It's a mess.'

SEVEN

Alex showed up around six thirty on Friday lugging two big paper bags. She banished me to my den while she worked in the kitchen. She said she got nervous when anybody watched her cooking.

She served a baked casserole of Martha's Vineyard scallops and portabello mushrooms in a creamy port wine sauce, with risotto, acorn squash, a salad of field greens and a baguette of French bread, washed down with a bottle of pinot. It was a chilly late-October evening, so we ate at the kitchen table.

I hadn't told Alex that I'd talked to Roger Horowitz and that the verdict was in on Gus. I didn't mention Gus at all, in fact, and neither did Alex. A week had passed since we had found him dead in his apartment in Concord, but it still felt like a raw, oozing wound.

When the food was gone and the wine bottle was empty, we loaded the dishwasher and took mugs of coffee into the living room. I put an Oscar Peterson CD on the player. Alex prised off her sneakers with her toes and nestled herself into the corner of the sofa. She was wearing black jeans with a long-sleeved pale blue jersey top and dangly turquoise earrings. I sat beside her.

'So where'd you learn to do that?' I said.

'Do what?'

'The food. It was great. Excellent. If I'd known you were a gourmet cook, I'd never have let you go.'

'Oh, ha ha,' she said. '*You* let *me* go. That's *so* not funny.'

'You're right,' I said. 'Sorry.'

'So were you planning on not mentioning Gussie at all tonight?' she said.

'I thought we'd wait till after we ate,' I said.

'Now's the time, then.'

I nodded. 'I talked to Roger Horowitz yesterday. The ME has issued his verdict.'

'They're saying he killed himself, huh?'

'Yes. Everything points to it.'

'Well,' she said, 'they're wrong.'

'Look, honey—'

'Don't give me that "honey" stuff, Brady Coyne. Just tell me. Are you going to support me on this or not?'

'I'm going to support you,' I said. 'Yes.'

'And help me prove that they're wrong about Gus, right?'

'About all I can do is talk to people,' I said. 'I'll do that.'

'*We* can do that, you mean,' she said.

I shook my head. 'No. If I'm going to do it, it's going to be just me, my way, by myself.'

'What about me?' said Alex. 'What am I supposed to do?'

'You're supposed to trust me,' I said. 'Because I'm better at this sort of thing than you are, and I've done way more of it than you have, and I'm more objective than you, and if you were involved you'd surely get in my way and be a pain in the ass and screw it up.'

She glowered at me for a moment. Then she shook her head and smiled. 'Does that mean that you agree with me? That Gus didn't kill himself?'

'I don't know,' I said. 'My mind is open. I'm sceptical. Logically, it makes sense. Gus had many reasons to—to do this. The evidence all points to it. On the other hand, knowing him, having talked with him, I do find it hard to believe.'

'The evidence is wrong,' said Alex. 'You've got to prove that.'

'I don't intend to prove anything,' I said. 'I just want to find the truth of it, if I can.'

'I honestly didn't expect you to agree to do this,' she said.

'I'm fairly big on truth,' I said.

'I thought I'd have to argue and wheedle.'

I patted my stomach. 'You seduced me with good food.'

She rolled her eyes.

'Plus,' I said, 'I hate the idea that there might be a murderer out there who's clever enough to fool the medical examiner and the police and get away with it.' I smiled at her. 'Plus, you're very cute and I don't want to let you down.'

'Cute,' she said.

'Wrong word? Is cute some sexist insult?'

'No,' she said. 'I love cute. I haven't been cute since I was a chubby eight-year-old.' She reached over, gripped my arm and pulled me towards her. Then she reached up and cradled my face in both of her hands and kissed me on the mouth. 'You're kinda cute yourself, you know,' she said.

She kissed me again and I kissed her back, and then Alex put her arms round my neck and kissed me hard and deep and pressed herself against me. After a minute, she put her hand on my chest and pushed herself away from me. 'I'm sorry,' she said.

'Don't be sorry,' I said. I hadn't kissed a woman since Evie. My pulse was pounding in my head. 'I'm not.'

'No,' she said. 'I'm all emotional about Gus, and you're being awfully nice to me. It's like we're still what we used to be. I wasn't thinking about Evie or . . . or the past seven years.'

'Evie and I are over with,' I said.

She tapped her chest. 'In here?'

'I'm still getting used to it.'

'So the last thing you need is me barging into your life.'

I touched her face. 'The *first* thing I need is you,' I said. 'I just don't know where it's going to end up.'

'Nobody ever knows that,' she said.

I ENDED UP LYING on the sofa with my feet in Alex's lap. She massaged my toes and told me about the past seven years of her life. It had been a writer's life, full of solitude and stress and self-discipline, interrupted by an ill-conceived marriage to a wealthy older man whom Alex had never really loved and, as far as she could tell, had never truly loved her. She said they might've just stayed married anyway if he'd let her continue to live in her little house on the dirt road in Garrison and work on her books, but, of course, that would have been no kind of marriage.

I talked about Evie and how when you don't get married, it's easy to split up, but you don't have the finality of divorce. Our relationship had just seemed to peter out, with her on the West Coast preoccupied with taking care of her father and me still in Boston.

Alex didn't ask any questions about the future, and since I had no wisdom about the future, I didn't talk about it. I didn't know whether Evie and I were over with for ever or just temporarily.

Around midnight we let Henry out for his bedtime rituals. It was a clear, brittle autumn night. Alex and I stood on the deck. The sky was pin-pricked with stars. She put her arm round my waist and laid her cheek against my shoulder.

'Show me Snoopy again,' I said.

She pointed, and I leaned over and sighted along her arm.

'See?' she said. 'His left ear—that's those three stars in a kind of pyramid shape—and there, see? His right one?'

I squinted, and I did see that left ear, but I was quite certain that without Alex's help, I'd never be able to locate Snoopy or Elvis or the Green Ripper in the night sky.

We went back in, and I gave Henry his bedtime dog treat.

Alex leaned against the sink and looked at me.

'You'll stay here tonight?' I said. 'With me.'

'Yes.'

'We'll sleep in the bed in my office, OK?'

'I understand,' she said.

'It's fairly comfortable,' I said, 'but it's kind of narrow.'

She smiled. 'I don't see why that should be a problem.'

I WALKED into Minuteman Camera in Concord centre a little after ten the next morning. A sixtyish man with a ponytail and a grey beard was sitting behind the counter peering at a computer monitor. It was just one large rectangular room. Along one wall was a glass case with shelves lined with cameras and lenses. There were picture frames and telescopes and tripods. The walls were hung with photographs.

The man looked up and said, 'Something I can help you with, sir?' He wore a plastic name tag that said *Phil*.

'I'm looking for Jemma.' I gave him one of my business cards. 'Tell her I'm Gus Shaw's lawyer.'

Phil looked at the card, then at me. 'Terrible thing.'

I nodded. 'Awful.'

He went to the door, knocked, opened it halfway, leaned in and said something. Then he pulled the door shut and came back to his place behind the counter. 'She'll be right with you, Mr Coyne.'

A minute later the door opened and a woman came out. She looked about thirty. She had black hair cut short, dark Asian eyes and skin the colour of maple syrup. She wore khaki trousers and a man's blue Oxford shirt.

She held out her hand. 'Mr Coyne? I'm Jemma Jones.'

I shook her hand. 'I want to talk to you about Gus Shaw.'

She nodded. 'Let's go have coffee.' She turned to Phil. 'I'll be at the Sleepy. If you need me, I've got my cell with me.'

It was a five-minute walk to the Sleepy Hollow Café on Walden Street. Neither of us spoke until we got there. Then Jemma said, 'The patio or a booth inside?'

'The patio,' I said. 'I met Gus here the other day.'

We chose a table near where Gus and I had sat a week and a half earlier. A waitress appeared instantly. I asked for one of their date-and-nut muffins and black coffee. Jemma Jones ordered a cinnamon-apple muffin and a pot of tea.

When the waitress left, I saw that Jemma's dark eyes brimmed with tears. 'It's my fault, you know.'

'What's your fault?'

'That Gus . . . killed himself.'

'He killed himself because of you?'

She nodded. 'That day—Friday, a week ago he dropped a camera. Ruined it. Before I could stop myself, I yelled at him. See, the thing was, I had stopped thinking about him as a man with only one hand. Anyway, I yelled something like, "If you can't be more careful, you can't work with cameras."' She shook her head. 'I'm saying this to one of the best photo-journalists in the business. So he looks at me, and he says, "You're absolutely right." Then he just walked out of the store. And that was the last time I ever saw him.'

'You think that's why he killed himself?' I said.

She shrugged. 'Gus had a lot of baggage, all right. But I guess that's probably what pushed him over the edge.'

'About what time was that?'

'When I yelled at him? Around noontime, I guess.'

'So you weren't surprised to hear that he'd committed suicide?'

'I was shocked. But not surprised. If that makes any sense.'

'You think he was suicidal, then?'

She shook her head again. 'He didn't seem suicidal. Oh, I knew about what was going on. The PTSD. His wife filing for divorce. He was depressed and paranoid and . . . he was a disaster, Mr Coyne. But he always seemed to me to be a pretty tough guy, too. A fighter, you know? I guess I was wrong about that.'

'How well did you know him?' I said.

At that moment, our waitress came with our order, and Jemma Jones and I paused to butter our muffins.

She poured her tea, took a bite of her muffin, sipped her tea. 'How well did I know Gus Shaw?' She smiled sadly. 'I knew him pretty damn well.'

'You worked with him every day.'

'That, too.'

'More than that, then? You were . . . what? Lovers?'

'I think we loved each other, but we didn't . . . you know. He had a lot of guilt about his wife and kids, and I didn't feel too good about loving a married man. So we were holding back. Trying to do the right thing. It wasn't easy. We had a lot of chemistry, Gus and I. We'd both been through a lot.' She sighed. 'I don't know why I'm telling you this. It's not anybody's business.'

'You said you'd both been through a lot,' I said.

'Gus lost his hand over there,' she said. 'I lost my husband.'

'I'm sorry.'

'I hate that war.' She narrowed her eyes at me, and I saw the passion in them. 'There are victims everywhere. Not just American soldiers getting killed, but all the poor innocent Iraqis. And people like me and Gus, and Gus's wife and kids and sister, and my dead husband's parents, and his unborn children, and it goes on and on.'

I found myself nodding.

Jemma cocked her head and looked at me. 'So Gus Shaw and I had all that in common. But don't get me wrong. He was a helluva man and I guess I would've loved him no matter what.'

'But it was a secret.'

'He wanted to do the right thing.' She looked at me again. 'I think it would be best if it remained a secret, don't you?'

I nodded. 'I'm very good at discretion. You went to his apartment, right?'

'How did you know?'

'The first time I went there with Gus, there were two empty mugs on his coffee table,' I said. 'I figured someone had been there.'

She smiled. 'One of the mugs was probably mine. I went over there a lot. Anyway, he didn't have a lot of friends.'

'He told me he was in a support group.'

'He was. I doubt if any of the people in his group were his friends, though. It would be like a conflict of interest, you know?'

'You sound like you know this from personal experience.'

'After Burt was killed, I was in a group for a while. But there was too much anger in it for me.'

'What about Gus's group?' I said. 'Did he talk about it?'

Jemma shook her head. 'Not really. He wouldn't. It's a rule. What happens in the group stays in the group. I had the feeling that towards the end he'd got turned off by it.'

'Turned off how?'

She shrugged. 'I don't know. Gus wasn't very specific. Like I said, it was just a feeling I got.'

'Did he ever mention a guy named Pete?'

'Not that I remember. Who's Pete?'

'The time I met Gus here, this Pete was with him. I think he might be in the group. He's somebody I'd like to talk to, that's all.'

'You want to talk to everybody, huh?' she said.

'I'm trying to figure out if Gus really did kill himself,' I said.

She looked at me. 'You don't think he did?'

I said, 'I don't know. I have no opinion. I just want to know. The police have concluded that he did. All of the forensic evidence points to it.'

Jemma was frowning. 'If he didn't . . .'

'Right,' I said. 'It means he was murdered. So, I'm wondering if you have any ideas about who could have done such a thing.'

'No,' she said, 'I don't. No ideas.'

I watched her face, looking for the lie, or the evasion, or just the hint of doubt. Her eyes held mine steadily.

I finished the last bite of my muffin. 'If anything occurs to you,' I said, 'Phil has my card back at the shop. Will you call me?'

'Sure,' she said. 'Of course. I loved Gus Shaw. If somebody murdered him, I want to know it. I don't like thinking he did it because I yelled at him.' She looked at her wristwatch. 'I really should be getting back.'

'Tell me how you and Gus found each other,' I said.

'You mean, why I gave him a job?'

I nodded.

'One of the people in his group called me,' she said. 'Said there was a new guy, used to be a photographer, needed a job. This person who called me, he'd been in my group. It was kind of a code that we helped each other if we could. So I said sure, I could always use somebody who understood cameras and photography. When he told me it was Gus Shaw, I was really interested. I was familiar with his work. Gus was a pro. I figured he could do some workshops, bring some business into the store.'

'Who was this person?' I said. 'The one who called you?'

Jemma shook her head. 'I can't tell you that.'

'That's part of the code? Keeping your identities secret?'

She shrugged. 'It's a very private, personal thing, being in a support group. That's the only way it can work.'

'Sure,' I said. 'I guess I understand.' I fished a twenty-dollar bill from my wallet and left it on the table. Then I stood up. 'I'll walk you back to your shop,' I said.

Jemma stood up and smiled. 'Thank you.'

When we got there, she turned. 'I had this thought,' she said.

'What's that?'

'Well,' she said, 'if somebody did murder Gus, and if you're going around questioning people, second-guessing what the police said, aren't you worried that the murderer will go after you?'

'Are you suggesting that I shouldn't rock the boat?'

'Just . . . be careful, that's all.'

I nodded and smiled. 'I already thought of that.'

I'D NOTICED a liquor store on the corner diagonally across the street from the camera shop. After I said goodbye to Jemma Jones, I crossed Main Street and went in.

The assistant seemed to be the only employee there. He wore a red shirt with PATRIOT SPIRITS and MIKE embossed over the pocket.

I showed Mike my business card. 'I hope you can answer a couple of questions for me.'

He frowned at my card. 'You're a lawyer?'

I nodded. 'Do you know Gus Shaw?'

'Gus Shaw.' He shook his head. 'No, I don't think so.'

'Used to work in the camera shop across the street? He lost a hand in Iraq,' I said. 'Big guy, red beard.'

'I don't think so,' he said. 'Not a regular customer. I know all my regulars.' He hesitated. 'Wait a minute. That the guy who committed suicide last week?'

'That's him,' I said. 'Were you working here that day? A week ago yesterday. Friday.'

'I work here every day except Sunday. I own the place.'

'I'm wondering if Gus Shaw came in, made a purchase.'

'Not that I remember.'

'You have records, right?'

'Sure. Every bottle that goes out of here has to be recorded. If they pay with a credit card, we got their name, too. But—'

'Check for me, would you?'

Mike shook his head again. 'I don't know . . .'

'I just want to know if he bought a pint of Early Times bourbon. It would've been sometime around noon last Friday.'

'Say I did sell him a pint of Early Times,' he said. 'Would I be liable or something? For what he did to himself, I mean?'

'Certainly not. I'm just trying to learn the truth.'

He looked at me, then said, 'Ah, what the hell. It'll just take a minute. It's all on the computer.'

Mike's computer was next to the cash register. He pecked at some keys and made some notes on a yellow legal pad. 'I sold two pints of Early Times that day,' he said. 'One at two thirty-five in the afternoon, the other at five past six. Both cash. I'm sorry. I don't remember who bought them.'

Two thirty and six o'clock didn't fit with what I knew of Gus's activities that day. Jemma said that he walked out of the camera store around noon. I guessed that if he bought a bottle that day, it would've been right after that, not two and a half hours later. And he was at his apartment writing his email to Claudia before six, when the second bottle was sold.

I stepped out onto the sidewalk. The sun was bright and it was warming the late-October air. I headed for my car, which I'd left in the big municipal lot off Main.

I WAS DRIVING DOWN Monument Street to the old colonial where Herb and Beth Croyden, Gus Shaw's erstwhile landlords, lived. It was a little after noon and maybe I'd catch them having lunch. If they invited me to join them, I wouldn't refuse, no matter how insincere their invitation might be.

It wasn't that I suspected the Croydens of anything. At this point, I didn't suspect anybody of anything, which was just another way of suspecting everybody of everything.

A gravel driveway led up to a barn beside the house. I guessed the house had been standing right there on the morning of April 19, 1775, when the local militia force of Minutemen had repelled the British redcoats at the Old North Bridge, which was less than a mile down the street.

The barn looked like it might have been standing there for over two hundred years, too. The carriage house where Gus had lived was not visible behind the thick screen of hemlocks.

I pulled up beside a green Range Rover in front of the barn. When I opened the car door, a lawn mower came chugging round the corner. Herb Croyden was driving, and his golden retriever—Gracie was her name, I remembered—was bounding along beside him.

Herb waved, disengaged the blades of the machine, drove over to where I was standing and turned off his tractor.

Gracie came to me and dropped a slimy tennis ball at my feet. I picked it up and threw it. She went galloping after it.

'She won't let you alone now,' said Herb. He got off his mower and held out his hand. 'Mr Coyne, right?'

I shook his hand. 'Yes. We met the night Gus . . .'

He nodded. 'I remember. You haven't met Beth, have you? My wife?'

'No. I'd like to.'

'She's around back planting bulbs,' he said.

Gracie came back with her ball. She pushed her nose against my leg.

'I'm telling you,' said Herb. 'Ignore her now or you're sunk. Come on. This way.' He led me round to the back of the house.

Beth Croyden was kneeling alongside a kidney-shaped flowerbed in the middle of the lawn. She turned and looked at us, and I saw that she was quite a bit younger than her husband. Early forties, I guessed. Herb was pushing sixty.

'This is Mr Coyne,' said Herb. 'He was Gus's lawyer. I mentioned meeting him the other night, remember?'

Beth Croyden smiled and pushed herself to her feet. She tugged off her gardening gloves and held out her hand to me. 'It's nice to meet you, Mr Coyne.'

We shook. 'I'm sorry to intrude,' I said.

'You're not intruding,' she said. 'How about something to drink? Beer? Coffee?'

'Coffee would be great,' I said.

'I'll bring it out.' She turned and went into the house. Herb gestured to a circular glass-topped table on a fieldstone patio. We went over and sat down. Gracie followed us.

'So, what brings you round?' said Herb. 'It's about Gus, of course. Terrible thing. We're both devastated.'

I nodded. 'I wanted to get your take on what happened, and I was hoping I could take a look at his apartment.'

'Sure, no problem.' He frowned. 'I thought it was a suicide, though. Didn't the police make that official?'

'There are still some legal loose ends.'

At that moment, Beth Croyden came out carrying a tray that held a big stainless-steel carafe, three coffee mugs, some spoons and napkins, and containers of sweetener and cream. Herb leaped up, took the tray from her and put it on the table. Beth poured coffee into the three mugs. Then she sat down.

'Mr Coyne was just saying that he's tying up some loose ends about what happened to Gus,' Herb said.

She looked at me. She had green eyes with smile lines at the corners. 'The police were here, you know. Asked us questions.'

'I assumed they did,' I said. 'I hope you don't mind if I should happen to ask you some of the same ones.'

'No, that's OK,' said Herb. 'We want to help.'

'I'm wondering if either of you was home on that Friday between five in the afternoon and eleven at night.'

They looked at each other, then Herb said, 'I had a golf match and then stayed for dinner at the club, as I always do on Fridays. It was dark when I got home—'

'It was after nine,' Beth interrupted. 'You told me you had a couple of drinks and played a few hands of gin rummy after dinner.' Beth turned to me. 'Since he retired, Herb's become quite the country clubber.'

'You were here when Herb got home, then,' I said to Beth.

'I volunteer over at the DeCordova Museum in Lincoln on Tuesdays and Fridays. I knew my husband would be late, so I had supper with a friend. I probably got home around seven thirty.'

'Did either of you notice if Gus had company that day?'

'We tried to make it a point not to notice things like that,' said Herb. 'Gus took his privacy very seriously.'

I nodded. 'But if a car drove in or out . . .'

'Sure,' he said. 'It would go right past our house. Unless we were in the bedroom or watching TV in the family room, which are at the back of the house, we'd most likely notice.'

'And you noticed nobody that evening?'

Beth and Herb both shook their heads.

'I'm wondering about other times, too,' I said. 'Cars coming or going, people who might've visited Gus at his apartment.'

'He had visitors,' Beth said. 'Not often, but occasionally.'

'Do you know who they were?'

Beth and Herb exchanged glances.

'Gus's privacy is a moot point now,' I said.

Beth said, 'There was that woman he worked with. She came by now and then.'

'Jemma Jones,' said Herb. 'Asian lady. She owns the camera store.'

'What do you mean, now and then?' I looked at Beth.

'I shouldn't have mentioned her.' She shook her head.

'It might be important,' I said.

Beth said, 'Ms Jones spent the night with Gus on more than one occasion. She'd always leave very early in the morning.'

Herb nodded. 'We saw her drive out of our driveway a few times shortly after sunrise. She's got a yellow Volkswagen Beetle. Hard to mistake it. Gus was separated, in the process of getting a divorce, and if it made him happy, good for him.'

'What about other visitors?' I said.

Herb glanced at Beth, then said, 'There was somebody in a dark SUV. He came by a few times that I know of.'

'It was a man?'

He shrugged. 'I don't know. I guess I assumed it was.'

'Can you describe the vehicle?'

'Black or dark blue,' Herb said. 'One of those big ones. Like a Lincoln Navigator. It looked pretty new.'

Beth said, 'There was a pick-up truck that went in there a few times. I'm afraid I can't give you much of a description. The truck looked old and battered. I don't even recall what colour it was.'

I nodded. 'Did either of you ever meet a friend of Gus's named Pete?'

Herb said, 'We didn't meet any of his friends.'

'Did you folks socialise with Gus?' I said.

'No,' said Herb. 'He kept to himself. The path down to the river goes past the carriage house, and once or twice he walked down there with me and Gracie. He liked Gracie. Otherwise, we didn't see much of him.'

I looked at Beth. She shook her head.

'So Ms Jones in her yellow VW and somebody driving a dark SUV and somebody else in an old pick-up,' I said. 'Any other visitors that you can remember?'

Beth nodded. 'Yes, of course. There was a woman in a small SUV-type car, come to think of it. A Subaru, I think. She came by a couple of times recently.'

'That was probably Gus's sister,' I said. I took a sip of coffee. 'I'm just wondering if there's anything you folks can think of that might cause you to question what the police have concluded.'

Herb looked at his wife. They both shook their heads.

'You never think anybody you know is going to do something like that,' Herb said. 'There's no doubt that Gus was depressed, though.' He frowned. 'Anyway, the alternative is what? That somebody murdered him? That's even more unthinkable than suicide.'

I shrugged. 'I don't know. I would like to talk to the man in that dark SUV you mentioned. And the person in the pick-up, too. If either of them should come by again, would you see if you can get their names for me, or at least copy down their licence plates?'

The Croydens both nodded.

I drained my coffee mug and stood up. 'Will you show me Gus's apartment now?'

Herb stood up. 'I'll do it,' he said to Beth.

'Good,' she said. 'I'm never going to set foot in there again.'

Herb and I started walking down the driveway to the carriage house. Gracie led the way.

'How did Gus hear that you had an apartment to rent?' I asked.

'A friend of mine called me up,' Herb said. 'He knew I was renovating the place, said he knew a guy whose marriage was falling apart and needed an apartment. It was Gus. He came over and met us, we showed him round and he took it. We liked him very much. We were happy to do what we could.'

'What did he tell you?'

'Gus?' Herb shook his head. 'Nothing, really. Just that he needed an apartment within walking distance of Concord centre. The friend who contacted me was from a support group I used to be in. I lost my son in Iraq two years ago. Anyhow, this friend is still in the group, and Gus had been in it for a while, too.'

'I'm sorry about your son,' I said. I was remembering that Jemma Jones had lost her husband over there. And there was Gus, who had survived, but minus his hand and his sanity, though one could now say that the war had killed him, too.

'I wonder if you could tell me your friend's name,' I said. 'I'd like to talk to him and maybe others in the group.'

Herb shook his head. 'Sorry. I can't do that. It's our code.'

I said, 'Maybe you could give your friend my name and number, see if he'd be willing to talk to me.'

He nodded. 'I could do that. Sure. No harm in that, I guess.'

I gave Herb my business card.

When we arrived at the carriage house, Herb came up the stairs behind me. 'We had the apartment cleaned as soon as the police gave us the OK.' He produced a key and unlocked the door.

I stepped inside. Herb remained in the doorway. The apartment smelled of Lysol and emptiness. The bottle of Early Times was gone. So was Gus's laptop computer. Probably locked up in a police evidence vault.

I opened and closed every kitchen drawer and went through all the kitchen cabinets. I found pots and pans, dishes and glasses, silverware and cooking utensils.

The medicine cabinet in the bathroom was empty. I figured the police took all of Gus's pills for when they did his blood work.

There was only one small closet in the place. Some clothes hung in it. Shirts and trousers and a couple of jackets. I fished through the pockets. They were all empty.

The small bureau beside the bed held socks and underwear and some sweaters. There was a handful of change in one of the top drawers. No business cards, no address books. Anything like that the crime-scene investigators would have taken.

There was one drawer in the table where Gus kept his laptop computer. The table where he'd been sitting when he shot himself. The drawer held some blank envelopes, a few pencils, a box of paperclips. That was all.

I went outside, shut the door and descended the stairway.

I found Herb sitting on the bottom step. Gracie was beside him.

'Find what you were looking for?' said Herb.

'Didn't find anything,' I said.

EIGHT

Alex was hunched over her laptop at the kitchen table when I got home on Saturday afternoon and, when I said hello, she lifted a forefinger without looking up and kept on typing.

Henry was glad to see me, anyway. I snagged a bottle of Samuel Adams lager from the refrigerator, and he and I went out back. I sprawled in one of my Adirondack chairs and shut my eyes. I hadn't slept much the previous night. The day bed in my office was narrow and Alex's body was warm and curvy. We'd ended up like spoons, which, after several years of sleeping only with Evie, and then several months of sleeping with nobody, was distracting and interesting enough to keep me awake much of the night.

I must have dozed off, because the next thing I knew, Alex was kissing my ear. I reached up, hooked my arm round her neck and steered her mouth to mine.

'Um,' she said after a minute. 'Nice.' She sat in the chair beside me. 'Sorry I didn't stop when you came home. I had a whole plot thread I needed to get down before it went away.' She picked up my beer bottle and took a sip. 'So what did you learn today?'

'In a word, nothing. I haven't come up with one shred of evidence to suggest that Gus did not kill himself. I'm sorry.'

'You just haven't found it yet, that's all. You will. So who did you talk to?'

I shook my head. 'Our deal was that I'd do it my way. I don't want to be debriefed every day. Right?'

Alex was looking at me out of narrowed eyes. 'Don't do me any favours, Brady Coyne. I can hire some private eye.'

'I just don't feel like recapitulating every conversation I have. I talked to a lot of people today. Based on what I know now, I'd be inclined to conclude that Gus killed himself the way the police said, but I'm resisting conclusions. I'm not done yet. For example, I want to talk to Claudia, and I need you to set that up for tomorrow.'

'Everybody thinks he committed suicide, don't they?' Alex said.

'It doesn't matter what people think,' I replied.

'No,' she said, 'they're right. This is stupid, and I'm just deluding myself. Who'd want to murder Gussie?'

'That's what I'm trying to figure out,' I said.

She said, 'I wish you'd known him . . . before.'

I reached over and gripped Alex's hand. 'I wish I had, too.'

'I'm sorry. I'll try not to nag you any more.' She drained the beer bottle. 'How would you feel if I rented an apartment in the South End?'

'Sure,' I said. 'Why not?'

'Part of my novel takes place in Boston, in that neighbourhood,' she said. 'I could be near my nieces, too. It's going to be hard for them. I saw a couple of nice places for rent today.'

'Makes sense,' I said. 'What about your house in Garrison?'

'I can rent it. What I'm saying is—'

'I know what you're saying,' I said.

For dinner, I grilled a pair of T-bones, along with some vegetables and potatoes. Alex tossed a salad and we ate out back on the picnic table.

The sky was full of stars and we wore sweaters against the cool breeze. It was a perfect late-October evening.

Our dirty dishes were in the sink and we were outside sipping coffee when I said, 'About that apartment . . .'

Alex shook her head. 'Don't worry about it.'

'All I was going to say,' I said, 'was that you shouldn't make any decision one way or the other based on me. I mean, I don't want to be a variable.'

'Of course you don't. You never did.' She chuckled. 'You don't think I learned that a long time ago?' She got to her feet. 'I'm going to call Claudia.'

She went inside and came back out about ten minutes later.

'Tomorrow afternoon around two,' she said. 'I'll take the kids for an hour. You and she can have a confidential conference.'

'Claudia's OK with this?'

Alex nodded. 'She has some things she'd like to run by you.'

'Really?' I said. 'Like what?'

'She didn't confide in me,' said Alex.

We lapsed into silence and, after a while, Alex said, 'I'm ready for bed.'

'Me, too,' I said.

Without discussing our sleeping arrangements, we both ended up in my den, I in my boxers and Alex in one of my T-shirts.

We stood there awkwardly for a moment. Then Alex crawled into the day bed, eased over to the far side and patted the empty half.

I slid in beside her, then turned off the light.

Alex rolled onto her side so that she was facing away from me. I put a hand on her bare hip. Her T-shirt had ridden up to her waist. She picked up my hand and pulled it round so that I was hugging her against me. My face was in her hair.

'I just want to go to sleep this way,' she murmured.

'OK,' I said. I kissed her neck. 'Sleep tight, then.'

CLAUDIA SHAW was a tall, angular blonde in her mid-thirties. Except for the bags under her eyes, you wouldn't be surprised to see her on the cover of *Cosmopolitan.*

After giving me solemn little curtsies, Juno and Clea, Claudia and Gus's daughters, left with Alex to look for migratory birds at the Great Meadows wildlife preserve, which was a little way down the street.

Claudia had some cookies in the oven she needed to keep an eye on, so we ended up at her kitchen table, sipping from cans of Coke. 'Alex is driving me crazy,' she said after a minute. 'She refuses to believe that Gus killed himself.'

'You believe he did?' I said.

She gave me a humourless smile. 'I believe he's dead, and there's nothing we're going to do about it, and we've all got to move on. I was kind of hoping I might convince you to talk to Alex about it.'

'We do talk about it,' I said. 'I think the only way to get closure is to find out the truth.'

'The police are quite definite about the truth,' she said. 'What about you, Mr Coyne?'

'Brady,' I said. 'Please.'

'OK, Brady. So, how do you see it?'

'Alex is my old, dear friend,' I said. 'She asked for my help, so I'm trying to help her. That's all.'

'You didn't know Gus, though, did you?'

'I met with him a couple of times right before he died. I was representing him . . .'

'Yes,' she said. 'Our divorce. So you didn't know him at all. That man you met wasn't Gus Shaw. Gus Shaw would never kill himself. Alex is right about that. But that . . . that one-handed impostor who came back from Iraq—that man was capable of anything. That man could kill his wife and daughters, and he could surely kill himself. Look, from the moment I met Augustine Shaw, I worried about him. It was just a fact of our life, our marriage. He was always taking off for places where dangerous things were happening. He was in Bosnia and Afghanistan, New York and New Orleans. Africa, Asia, Central America. You name it. Terrorism, famine, tsunami, hurricane, civil war? Gus had to be there with his camera. He fed off risk and adrenaline. That's what drove Gus Shaw.' She shook her head. 'He did get some amazing photos, but I was a perpetual basket case.'

A timer dinged and Claudia got up, went over to the oven and took out a tray of cookies.

'They smell great,' I said.

'Toll House,' she said. 'My girls' favourite.' She slid another cookie tray into the oven, then came back and sat across from me. 'When they've cooled, you can have one. Anyway, I want you to know that I got used to the idea of Gus being dead years ago. It was how I got by. It wasn't a matter of if. Only when and where. When he went to Iraq, I assumed that was it for sure. When he came home, he was a stranger. It was like he had already been killed. He didn't talk to me; he ignored the girls; he stopped working. There was no love left in him, Brady.' Tears glistened in her eyes. 'I always loved him,' she said. 'But I was petrified that we'd wake up some morning and find that Daddy had killed himself. I didn't want Juno or Clea to experience that. That's why I asked him to leave.'

'The incident with the gun,' I said.

'Oh, yes, indeed. The incident with the gun. That was the last straw.

A gun in my house? Waving it round in front of his own little girls?'
Claudia shook her head.

'Gus was in a support group,' I said. 'It didn't help, huh?'

'How much good did it do if he ended up killing himself?' Claudia
brushed the back of her hand across her eyes. 'I don't know. Maybe he'd
have been worse without his group.'

'Did he talk about it?'

'Gus didn't talk about anything. One of the men from his group called
me a few days after Gus died and asked if there was anything he could do.
That was nice. I told him no.'

'Have you ever met this man?'

Claudia shook her head. 'His name's Philip Trapelo. I had the impression
he's the leader.'

I wondered if Trapelo was the one who'd set up Gus's job and contacted
Herb Croyden about the apartment.

'I'd like to talk to him,' I said to Claudia.

'I'm not sure he'll do that,' she said, 'but he gave me his number. Let me
get it for you.'

She went over to the refrigerator, which was peppered with photos and
notes under magnets and came back with a scrap of paper. It had Trapelo's
name and a phone number.

I copied it onto the back of one of my business cards.

'Something's been bothering me,' Claudia said.

'Can I help?'

'Maybe. I don't know who to talk to about it. A lawyer, I think.' She
smiled quickly. 'Well, I have a lawyer. But I guess I don't need a divorce
lawyer any more. As far as I know, all Lily does is divorce.' She looked at
me questioningly. 'Alex said you . . .'

'I do whatever my clients need to have done,' I said. 'If I can't do it
myself, I find them a good lawyer who can.'

'So could I be your client?'

'If Gus were still alive, you couldn't,' I said. 'But now, sure.'

She nodded. 'Here's the thing. When Gus was in Iraq, every month he'd
email me a file of photos. He was adamant that he didn't want me to look at
them. He asked me to burn them onto CDs and to lock the CDs in his filing
cabinet in his office, then delete them from my computer and to never tell
anybody about them.'

'When Gus was on his other assignments,' I said, 'is that what he did?'

Claudia shook her head again. 'He'd email photos home to me routinely and I made CDs for him, but that was just for back-up. I'm pretty sure that these were the only copies of the images he was sending me, this material he was getting in Iraq. For some reason, he was super secretive about it. I had the feeling that he'd got some explosive images.'

'So what happened to the CDs?' I said.

'He never mentioned them after he came home,' she said. 'When he lost his hand, it seemed like he'd lost all interest in photography. He'd lost his interest in everything, really. But a few days after he killed himself, I get a call from a woman named Anna Langley. She was Gus's agent. She made deals for him.'

'So what did she want?'

'In a word, she wanted his photos. I told her I didn't have them. She got very upset. Said she had things in the works that would bring us money and would be a great legacy to Gus and his work. She reminded me that she and Gus had a legal agreement, and she practically accused me of . . . I don't know. Holding out on her.'

'Are you?' I said.

'I wouldn't do that.'

'So what about the photos? Do you have them?'

'No. After Ms Langley called, I went and looked. They're not where I put them. I looked everywhere in the house and they're not here. I don't know where they are.'

'Gus probably took them,' I said. 'To keep them safe.'

'To keep *us* safe, I think,' she said. 'He was very paranoid.'

'I'll be happy to talk to Anna Langley if you want,' I said.

The timer dinged, announcing that the second batch of cookies was done. Claudia took them out of the oven. She came back to the table a minute later with a plate piled with the first batch.

I took one and bit into it. It was still warm and soft, and the chocolate chips were half melted. 'Oh, my,' I whispered.

She smiled. 'Pretty good, huh?'

'You'd better not leave that plate in front of me.'

'If you can talk to Ms Langley,' said Claudia, 'please tell her that I'm sorry I was rude to her. Gus always seemed to like and trust her. Tell her I'd be happy for her to continue to manage Gus's business affairs.' She hesitated. 'And that you'll be watching out for my legal rights in the process. Is that OK?'

'A deal,' I said.

Claudia smiled again. 'It's a relief, having somebody to worry about this for me. Now I understand what Alex sees in you.'

'That,' I said, 'makes one of us.'

I HAD CLIENT MEETINGS all Monday morning, and then a work lunch with another lawyer, so it was close to two in the afternoon before I had a chance to call Philip Trapelo.

When his voicemail told me to leave a message, I said I was Gus and Claudia Shaw's lawyer and needed to speak with him on a matter of some urgency. I left my phone numbers and asked him to call me back at his earliest convenience.

The number Claudia gave me for Anna Langley, Gus's agent, was a 617 Boston area code, and it also yielded only the opportunity to leave a voice-mail message. I said I was Augustine Shaw's wife's lawyer and needed to discuss some photographs.

An hour or so later I was finishing some paperwork when Julie rapped on my door, then pushed it open. She stepped into my office and shut the door behind her. 'Mr and Mrs Epping are here. I told them you were busy. They said they were willing to wait however long it would take for you to come up with a free moment. They seem quite fired up.'

I said, 'As much as it goes against your grain to let walk-ins just walk in, let's not keep them waiting. Bring them in.'

'Right.' Julie was back a minute later with the Eppings in tow.

I went round from behind my desk and shook Doug's and Mary's hands. 'Let's sit.' I waved at the sofa in my conference area.

'I don't want to sit,' said Doug.

Mary sat on the sofa. She tugged on Doug's sleeve, and he sat beside her. I took the armchair. 'You folks seem agitated,' I said.

'He's agitated,' said Mary. 'He's been agitated for a week, Brady, ever since I told him about our conversation. What you told me about the corporation dissolving. I'm not agitated. I'm calm.'

'I want to be sure I got this straight,' said Doug. 'You're saying that we can't sue that son of a bitch? Delaney is going to get away with what he did to our stuff?'

I said, 'It's not right, but it is the law. The law can't do everything, Doug.'

He suddenly smiled. 'Exactly. I wanted to hear you say that.'

'Huh? What did I say?'

'You said the law can't do it all,' he said. 'You said that sometimes you've got to take care of things yourself.'

'That's not exactly what I said. What are you two up to?'

'We're going to picket the sleazy bastard,' said Doug. 'We're going to march up and down the street in front of his place of business until Mr Delaney acknowledges us and admits he wrecked our stuff and writes us a cheque.'

'Mary?' I said. 'You, too?'

'You bet,' she said. 'It was actually my idea.'

'We just want to be sure we don't break any laws,' said Doug. 'That's why we're here. We want to do it the right way.'

I leaned back in my chair and smiled. 'It's your sacred right. It's free speech. Just stay off private property. Don't block traffic or pedestrians. Don't cause any damage. You can hand out leaflets; you can talk to anybody who agrees to listen. Just don't harass anybody. You're going to carry signs?'

'Right,' said Doug.

'Don't use Delaney's name,' I said. 'That could be libellous. Don't use swearwords or vulgarity. Be sure anything you write is the truth. That's about it. Be sure to keep me posted.'

Doug and Mary both smiled and nodded.

I stood up, and they did, too. We went out to the reception area, where Doug and I shook hands. Mary insisted on giving me a hug.

'You kids behave yourselves,' I said. 'Dress warm and be sure to wear sensible shoes.'

After the Eppings left, Julie arched her eyebrows. 'Well?'

'They're going to picket that moving company.'

She smiled. 'How high-school-civics of them.' She rummaged around on her desktop and came up with a Post-it note. 'You had a call while you were conferring with them. A Mr Trapelo, said he was returning your call.'

I went into my office and dialled Philip Trapelo's number. After two rings, a man's deep voice said, 'Trapelo.'

'It's Brady Coyne,' I said.

'How'd you say you got my number?'

'Claudia Shaw gave it to me,' I said. 'I was hoping I could talk to you about Gus. Claudia said you were in his support group.'

'He was in my group.'

'Sorry,' I said. 'Your group.'

'We don't talk to outsiders about the group,' he said.

'I understand. But you knew Gus. I'm just trying to help the family achieve some kind of closure.'

'Gus Shaw killed himself. He betrayed us,' said Trapelo.

'I understand that,' I said. 'I was just hoping I could buy you a drink and we could talk. Off the record, whatever you feel you can tell me. Gus's wife and his sister are having a lot of trouble dealing with this, as you might expect. I am, too.'

'You don't think he committed suicide?'

'The police say he did,' I said. 'I'm still a little sceptical. It's the curse of my profession.'

He hesitated for a long moment, then said, 'As long as you don't expect me to tell you things that were said during our sessions. Gus was a good guy. You gotta feel bad for his family. You're in Boston?'

'I am,' I said, 'but I can meet you anywhere you want.'

'You know where the VFW hall is in Burlington?'

'No.'

'It's on the Middlesex Turnpike a little way past the mall heading west. You can't miss it. How's around eight?'

I looked at my watch. It was a little after four. 'I'll be there,' I said. 'How will I recognise you?'

'Just ask for the Sarge,' Philip Trapelo said.

HENRY WAS GOBBLING his dinner from his bowl, and I slid a fried egg between two slices of oatmeal bread. I put my fried-egg sandwich on a plate, sat at the kitchen table.

When I finished my sandwich, it was almost a quarter past seven. I took my jacket out of the closet. Henry was sitting there giving me that look that said, You're going to leave and never come back.

'You want to go for a ride in the car?' I said to him.

'Ride in the car' was one of the English phrases that comprised my dog's extensive vocabulary.

Henry loved to ride in cars. His ears perked up and he cocked his head at me, and when I nodded, he trotted to the door, pressed his nose against the crack and whined.

I PULLED INTO the Veterans of Foreign Wars lodge parking lot a few minutes after eight. It was a low-slung, single-storey building. I opened my car windows an inch for Henry and told him I'd be gone no more than an hour.

Inside, the VFW hall was a big pine-panelled room with a bar and some tables and chairs on the left and two pool tables on the right. A dozen or so older men sat at the tables with beer bottles and ashtrays in front of them looking at a flat-screen TV. Four younger-looking guys were playing pool.

'I'm looking for the Sarge,' I said to a bald guy.

'He's out back,' said the bald guy. 'Should be only a minute. You want a beer?'

'Sure,' I said. 'Thanks.'

He got up, went behind the bar and came back with a bottle of Budweiser. He put it on the table. 'I'm Tony.'

'Brady,' I said. 'Brady Coyne.'

Tony sat at one of the empty tables and pushed out a chair with his foot. 'Take a load off, Brady.'

I sat in the chair.

'Hey,' yelled Tony to the men at the pool table. 'One of you guys give the Sarge a holler, willya? Tell him he got company.' He jerked his thumb at the television. '*Monday Night Football.* I got fifty bucks on the Dolphins, giving three points. Vegas odds. Whaddaya think?'

I shook my head. 'I always lose when I bet on sports.'

'Me, I like the underdogs,' said Tony, 'but them Dolphins—' He stopped and looked behind me. 'Hey, Sarge.'

I turned.

The Sarge—Phil Trapelo, I assumed—had brush-cut steel-grey hair and bushy pepper-and-salt eyebrows and liquid brown eyes. His face was dark and leathery.

'You're Coyne?' He was barely five eight or nine, but his voice came from a big bass drum.

I stood up and held out my hand. 'Brady Coyne,' I said.

'Phil Trapelo.' He gripped my hand with a paw that was surprisingly big and strong. 'I see you got yourself a beer.'

'Tony got it for me,' I said.

He nodded at Tony, then said, 'Come on. We'll talk in private.'

He turned and headed for the back of the room. I noticed that he favoured his right leg with a slight limp. I followed him through a door into a living-room-sized area with fifteen or sixteen folding metal chairs arranged in a circle. There was a wooden table in one corner, with a coffee urn and two stacks of Styrofoam cups.

Trapelo sat on one of the folding chairs. So did I.

'This is where we meet,' he said. 'Tuesdays, seven thirty.'

'Gus's group?'

He nodded. 'My group. I'm the one who got it organised. It was around the time of Desert Storm. Lots of guys came home pretty messed up psychologically. Originally the group was for vets with PTSD. In my day, we called it shell shock. You don't get professional help here. Nothing like that. No headshrinking. It's just for anybody who needs support. Whoever has something going on, something they need to air out, they go ahead and talk, and everybody else chips in, and you find you're not alone, maybe get some advice. Mostly, it's a bunch of guys—well, we sometimes have a woman or two. Mostly vets. But survivors, too. Husbands, wives, parents. And people like Gus Shaw, who've been there for other reasons. We share. Make sure each other knows they've got someone they can trust, someone they can say anything to and know it ain't leaving the room.'

'What about you?' I said.

'Me? I was in Vietnam. Two tours. Made tech sergeant.'

'That where you got this?' I patted my leg.

He slapped his knee. 'Booby trap. Bum knee is all. I was lucky. Physical wounds heal. I still have bad dreams, night sweats. I came home with an addiction to amphetamines. They gave 'em to us like candy, keep you awake and alert for three or four days and nights in a row. Took me a long time to get myself together.' He smiled quickly. 'I'm still not all that together. The group helps.'

'There must be a lot of heavy emotional stuff going on.'

Trapelo nodded. 'Oh, sure. Depression, paranoia, addiction, divorce. Plenty of anger. Suicide's always an issue. Guys can't hold jobs. Frustration with the Veterans Administration, the army, politicians. Civilians in general. What we try to do is just encourage the guys to talk about it. Our rule is, nobody gets put down. If you say it, it's important.'

'When I mentioned Gus on the phone to you,' I said, 'you said that he betrayed you. What did you mean?'

'Look,' he said. 'These guys, most of 'em, they're hanging on by their fingernails. How do you think it makes them feel when they hear Gus Shaw blew his brains out? These people need success stories, you understand?'

'Did it surprise you?'

Trapelo looked past my shoulder for a minute. Then his dark eyes returned to mine. 'In one way,' he said, 'I'm never surprised. Gus Shaw wasn't a soldier—he wasn't trained for what he experienced over there. Poor bastard lost his hand. So he came home and his wife kicked him out. He couldn't use a camera any more. But I really thought Gus had a chance. He seemed to be doing better.'

'Did he talk about suicide?'

'Not specifically. Not that I remember.'

'Any chance that Gus didn't do it?'

He frowned. 'You mean, that somebody murdered him?'

I shrugged. 'If he didn't kill himself . . .'

'If you're thinking of guys in the group, you're way off base.'

'You've got a bunch of unstable men,' I said, 'ex-military, most of them, trained to violence . . .'

'Whatever happens here,' he said, 'stays here.'

'I keep hearing that,' I said. 'Seems to me, that would be expecting a lot even from the most stable, well-adjusted people.'

Trapelo narrowed his eyes at me. 'If you came here to accuse somebody of something, you better spit it out.'

'I'm just trying to understand what happened.'

'What'd the police say?' he said.

'They called it a suicide,' I said.

Phil Trapelo shook his head. 'You gotta face up to it. We all do, those of us who knew him. Gus Shaw was another casualty of that damn war.'

'I was wondering if he mentioned an enemy, somebody he was having a problem with.'

'Everybody's got enemies,' he said. 'That doesn't mean they get murdered.'

'But everybody who gets murdered has an enemy,' I said.

He smiled. 'Sure. Good point. I don't know. I mean, there was his wife. Gus thought she had a boyfriend. And there was something about some photographs that had him pretty agitated. But I don't know about an enemy who'd kill him. Except himself.'

'What did Gus say about photographs?'

'Gus didn't say much. Just he was paranoid about some photographs he took over there. He was antiwar. Antigovernment. Most of the guys are. He never said what was in those photos, but it was clear that he thought it was stuff the government and the military wouldn't want the world to see.' Trapelo stopped. 'Wait a minute. You think those photos . . .'

'What do you think?'

'Worth killing for?' he said. 'That what you're getting at?'

'If you can remember any names he might have mentioned or anything at all Gus might have said about his photographs . . .'

He frowned for a minute, then shook his head. 'Sorry. If he said anything like that, I don't remember it.'

'Phil,' I said, 'did you know Gus outside the group at all?'

'No,' he said. 'All I know about Gus was from our Tuesday nights here. I called his wife last week, just to offer my sympathies. That's all.'

'So you wouldn't say you were friends.'

He shrugged. 'I guess not. I knew a lot about him in one way. But in another way, I guess you could say I didn't know him at all.'

'What about the other people in your group?' I said.

'You mean, was Gus friends with any of them? I don't know.'

'There's a meeting tomorrow night, right?'

'Right. It's Tuesday.'

'I wonder,' I said, 'if you'd mind telling them that I'd like to talk to any-body who knew Gus outside the group. Tell them I'm just trying to help his family deal with what happened. Make sure they know that talking with a lawyer gives them absolute confidentiality, but at the same time, I only want them to tell me what they're comfortable with.'

He nodded. 'I don't see why not.'

I gave him all the business cards I had in my wallet. 'Anybody who seems like they might be willing to talk to me, give him one of my cards, tell him to call me anytime.'

Trapelo squinted at the cards, then looked up at me. 'These guys are pretty messed up, you know?'

I nodded.

'They might tell you things that aren't true.'

'I understand that.'

He shrugged. 'Well, I'll mention it to them tomorrow.' He looked at the clock on the wall, then stood up. 'I gotta get going.'

I followed Trapelo out to the big main room, shook hands with him and went out to my car.

NINE

On Thursday morning I was at my kitchen table eating an English muffin thickly spread with peanut butter, when my house phone rang. 'It's Anna Langley,' said a raspy female voice when I answered. 'Returning your call.'

It took me a minute to remember. Anna Langley was Gus Shaw's agent. 'Thanks for getting back to me,' I said.

She said, 'I just got back from out of town and found your message. You have Gus Shaw's images?'

'Me?' I said. 'No. I don't know where those photos are. I wanted to talk to you about them.'

'Oh well, then,' she said. 'What's to talk about?'

'They're pretty valuable?'

'If Gus thought they were,' she said, 'which I happen to know he did, then yes, they're unquestionably quite valuable. I have several interested parties ready to talk.'

'You heard what happened to Gus?'

'I know he killed himself, of course.'

'Maybe he did, maybe he didn't.'

'But the police . . .' She hesitated. 'Oh, I get it. You think somebody . . . those images?' She stopped. 'Are you serious?'

'They seem to be missing,' I said. 'Gus seems to be dead.'

'That's wild,' she said.

'Some of us don't think Gus would take his own life,' I said. 'You must've known him pretty well.'

'I did,' she said.

'So what did you think?'

'I was . . . surprised,' she said. 'Not really shocked. Gus always had a lot of demons. Then, what happened to him over there . . .'

'What can you tell me about those images?'

'Look,' she said, 'you want to meet for lunch or something?'

'Just to be clear,' I said, 'I'm Gus's wife's lawyer. Representing her interest in this.'

'Sure,' she said. 'I don't see any problem. I'll bring a copy of the agreement Gus and I had. So where do you want to meet?'

'Place called Marie's just off Kenmore Square?'

'I know it,' she said. 'How's one today?'

'I'll make a reservation,' I said.

I WAS AT A CORNER TABLE in Marie's at around twenty past one when across the busy dining room I saw the hostess point towards me. A slender woman with dark hair nodded and headed in my direction.

I stood up as she approached my table. 'Anna?' I said.

She said, 'I'm so sorry. The phone rang just as I was leaving.' She held out her hand. 'Anna Langley. I could use a drink.'

'Brady Coyne,' I said. 'Let's see what we can do.'

I managed to catch the eye of our waitress.

'Grey Goose, rocks, twist,' said Anna. She looked barely thirty. Older than that round her eyes, though.

When the waitress left, Anna said, 'I'm here because I'd like to get hold of Gus Shaw's Iraq images.'

'Me, too,' I said. 'Maybe we can figure out where they are.'

'I was thinking the same thing.' She reached into her shoulder bag and took out a large envelope. 'A copy of my agreement with Gus. You'll see that I have the exclusive authority to represent his work for publication. Assuming Claudia is his rightful heir, everything I might be able to do will go to her, minus my commission.'

I took the envelope. 'We're all on the same team. So what can you tell me about these missing images?'

'Just that Gus was pretty excited about them,' she said. 'He sent me several emails from over there. What I got out of it was that he was onto a story that would make Abu Ghraib look like a sweet-sixteen party. Next thing, he lost his hand and came home and commenced avoiding me.'

Our waitress came with Anna's drink. We told her we'd wait to order our meals.

After she left, Anna said, 'So I decided just to leave him alone for a while. Then when I heard he died, I remembered how enthusiastic he was about the work he was doing over there, and I got to thinking that if the photos were half as good as Gus's stuff usually was, we'd have treasure on our hands. So I put out some feelers and got a lot of good response. That's when I called his wife. I inferred that she didn't know anything about the photos, so I didn't push it. Just tried to make sure she understood how valuable they probably were.'

Anna sipped her drink. 'I've got a reputable foreign correspondent from the *Monitor* interested in writing text for a picture book, sight unseen. *Vanity Fair* will guarantee at least a four-page spread. PBS has interest in a special about Gus and his work.'

'All that?' I said.

She nodded. 'Gus was a genius. People are beginning to realise that now that he's gone.' She shrugged. 'Anyway, without the images, it's all academic.'

'Actually,' I said, 'I might have an idea. It's a long shot.'

'Better than no shot.' She drained her drink and looked round. 'I could use another one of these.'

THAT EVENING, Henry and I had just finished supper and I was debating whether to spend an hour ploughing through the paperwork in my briefcase or see what was on TV, when the phone rang.

When I answered, a man's voice said, 'This the lawyer?'

I heard male voices and other noises in the background. It sounded like a busy bar. 'Yes,' I said. 'Who's this?'

'Pedro. Pedro Accardo. Remember? Gus call me Pete.'

Then I remembered the Hispanic-looking guy who had been with Gus the time I met him at the Sleepy Hollow Café in Concord. 'OK,' I said. 'Sure. I remember you. What's up?'

'Need to talk to you. Quick.'

'About what?'

'Gus. What happen to him.'

'Gus killed himself,' I said.

'No, man.' He dropped his voice to a whisper. 'He . . .' His voice became a mumble I couldn't understand.

'What?' I said. 'What do you—'

'Hang on.' I heard Pedro speak to somebody. Then he said, 'You there, Mr Coyne? Remember John Kinkaid and eleven, eleven, eleven, OK?'

'Yes, OK,' I said. 'But tell me about—'

'Gotta go now.'

I said, 'Just wait a minute. Do you know anything about Gus's photos? And who the hell is John Kinkaid?'

'No, no, man,' he said. His voice went low and conspiratorial. 'Can't talk here. Call you later, OK?'

'OK, sure,' I said. 'Or I could meet you.'

'I gotta find another phone, man. You—'

A male voice interrupted, and then came some cackling laughter.

A moment later Pedro said, 'Call you tonight, midnight.'

'OK,' I said. 'I'll be—'

But he was gone.

I looked at the screen on my telephone. It read UNKNOWN CALLER with no return number, which meant it was either a cellphone or a payphone or a blocked caller ID. I guessed a public payphone, judging by the voices and clatter in the background.

I figured Pedro Accardo was in Gus Shaw's support group, and Phil Trapelo had given out my business cards at their Tuesday meeting, and now Pedro was calling me.

He implied that he didn't think Gus had killed himself.

Or maybe he *knew* he hadn't.

John Kinkaid was the name he mentioned. Maybe Pedro meant that John Kinkaid was Gus's murderer.

It was a name that meant nothing to me.

I went into my office, sat at my desk and Googled 'John Kinkaid' on my computer. I was instantly overwhelmed.

I found dozens of John Kinkaids, living and dead. In addition to the college athletes, real estate brokers, minor poets, local politicians and poker champions, there were, more interestingly, the bosun's mate who died trying to save his captain when their troop transport ship was torpedoed in the North Atlantic in 1918, the all-star third baseman from the Negro Leagues who was murdered in 1947, the antiwar Vietnam vet who was obliterated in his own terrorist explosion at the University of Massachusetts in 1971, and the sixties rock'n'roller who died alone on his sailboat from a heroin overdose in 1984.

Google did not identify a single contemporary John Kinkaid who had come home from Iraq, or who had reason to want to steal photographs, or who suffered from PTSD, or who seemed to have any connection whatsoever to Gus Shaw.

Pedro also said 'eleven, eleven, eleven'. Maybe it was a code or the combination of a safe, but the only thing that occurred to me was the date.

The cease-fire that ended the fighting between Germany and the Allies in the First World War was signed at 11 a.m. on November 11, 1918—the eleventh hour of the eleventh day of the eleventh month. Thereafter, November 11 was known as Armistice Day. After World War II, Congress, with the concurrence of President Eisenhower, expanded the holiday to honour all veterans and renamed it Veterans Day. Veterans Day was a little more than a week away. So why would Pedro Accardo mention it in connection with John Kinkaid and with Gus Shaw's death?

My brain swirled with information overload. The internet was a bottomless ocean of information, and I felt myself sinking and disappearing in it.

I glanced at my watch. It was a few minutes after ten. Pedro said he'd call me at midnight. Then maybe I'd get some answers. 'Come on,' I said to Henry. 'Let's see if there's something on TV.'

LATER I LET HENRY OUT, put the morning coffee together, let Henry in and we went upstairs.

I set my cellphone ringer on loud and put it on the table next to my ear. I picked up the bedside house phone extension and made sure it had a dial tone.

It was ten minutes before midnight. I was ready for Pedro Accardo's call. Henry was curled up beside me where Evie used to sleep. I scratched his ribs.

I closed my eyes and tried to think about Alex. Tomorrow, maybe, we'd sleep here, in my bedroom, in Evie's and my king-size bed—now my bed—not in the day bed in my office. Symbolically, that would be a big step.

I checked the clock. The little hand and the big hand were aligned and pointing straight up. Midnight.

Time to call, Pedro. The phone didn't ring.

Fifteen minutes later it still hadn't rung.

I turned off the light. After a while, I went to sleep.

I WOKE UP suddenly and all at once. Dim grey light was creeping in round the curtains that covered my bedroom windows.

I looked at the clock. It was ten past six in the morning.

I checked both my house phone and my cellphone for messages. No messages. No missed calls.

Pedro had not called.

BEFORE I LEFT for the office that morning, I scoured all of my Boston and Greater Boston phone books for a listing in his name.

I used a break between client meetings that morning to call Phil Trapelo. When his voicemail invited me to leave a message, I said, 'Sarge, it's Brady Coyne. I met you at the VFW hall the other night and we talked about Gus Shaw. I was wondering how I can get in touch with a member of your group named Pedro Accardo. Also wondering if the name John Kinkaid might mean something to you.' I recited my phone numbers, then said, 'Please give me a call. This is quite important.'

The only other person I could think of who might know something about Pedro was Claudia Shaw. I tried her home number, but there was no answer.

I remembered that Claudia was an accountant for a firm in Lexington. I tried Alex's cellphone, and when she answered, I said, 'Hey. It's me.'

'Hey, you,' she said. 'This is nice.' She hesitated. 'Oh, you're not gonna . . .'

'I'm not calling off our evening,' I said. 'Looking forward to it. I just wondered if you had Claudia's work number. I need to ask her something.'

'Anything I can help you with?'

'Just Claudia's number.'

'OK,' she said, and gave me the number. 'It goes directly to her desk.'

'Excellent,' I said. 'Thanks. See you at seven, OK?'

Claudia did, indeed, answer her own phone, and when I mentioned Pedro Accardo's name, she said, 'Pete, you mean?'

'That's him,' I said. 'You know him?'

'Before we, um—before Gus moved out, Pete came over to the house a few times. He seemed like a nice man. Very polite to me, sweet to the girls. He and Gus would huddle in Gus's den or out in the garage. He was in Gus's group, I think.'

'Any idea what they talked about?'

'No,' said Claudia. 'I figured they just sort of counselled each other. Why are you asking about Pete?'

'He called me last night,' I said. 'Our conversation was interrupted, and he said he'd call back, but he never did. I'd like to reach him. I was hoping you might have his number.'

'No,' she said. 'I'm sorry. I guess you could look it up.'

'Tried that,' I said. 'Oh, well. Let me run another name by you. John Kinkaid ring a bell?'

Claudia thought for a moment, then said, 'No, I'm sorry. I can't place it.'

IT WAS A DRIZZLY, grey early-November Friday afternoon. Close to quitting time. I was just tucking some papers into a folder when the intercom on my desk buzzed.

I hit the button and said, 'Yes?'

'Mr and Mrs Epping are here to see you,' said Julie.

'Good. Bring 'em in,' I said.

A minute later Julie was holding my door open for the Eppings. I took one look at them and smiled. They wore identical yellow slickers over navy-blue sweatsuits, and wet sneakers. They looked bedraggled.

'It's not funny,' said Doug.

'Sorry,' I said. 'Have a seat.' I gestured at the sofa.

I took the chair across from them. 'Picketing in the rain? You've got to be nuts, both of you.'

Doug was shaking his head. 'Four solid days. Cold, raw, nasty days. We walked back and forth in front of the AA Movers office on Outlook Drive from nine thirty or ten every morning 'til four or four thirty every afternoon. And you know what? Outlook Drive turns out to be this dinky dead-end street that goes down to some warehouses on the Merrimack River. There are no pedestrians going by, no traffic.'

'So,' said Mary, 'what we've been doing is stupid.'

'I'm ready for Plan B,' said Doug.

'He says he's going to murder Mr Delaney,' Mary said.

'Listen to your lawyer,' I said. 'Don't do it.'

'You expect us to continue picketing?'

'I never thought Doug Epping was a quitter,' I said.

'I'm not,' he said. 'OK. I won't murder anybody. Not yet, anyway. Far as I'm concerned, I'll die of old age right there on his steps, and when they write it up for the newspapers, they'll have to mention why I was there.'

'You with him?' I said to Mary.

'I don't care about my stupid furniture any more,' Mary said. 'Getting some kind of justice seems way more important. So, yes. Absolutely.'

Doug stood up. 'Well, we just wanted to fill you in,' he said. 'And I needed you to talk me out of committing murder.'

After they left, I said to Julie, 'See if you can reach Molly Burke at Channel Nine in Manchester for me.'

I sat at my desk, and a minute later my console buzzed. 'I've got Molly Burke on line two,' said Julie.

'Good work,' I said. I hit the button and said, 'Molly?'

'Hi there,' she said. 'I hope you're calling for a favour.'

Three years earlier I had handled Molly's sexual harassment case against her supervisor during her internship at a local-access cable network on the Massachusetts North Shore. We managed to get the pig fired, plus a modest settlement and heartfelt public apology from the cable company. Now she was a popular newshound on New Hampshire's biggest TV channel. I was proud of her.

'Not really a favour,' I said to her, 'although if it works out, it will make me very happy. I think I've got a story for you.'

ALEX SHOWED UP at exactly seven that evening lugging big shopping bags. She had brought a sushi assortment from a Japanese restaurant in Arlington, along with some hot-and-sour soup, salad with ginger dressing and a bottle of sake.

We warmed the sake and drank it from tiny porcelain cups without handles. We dipped the sushi in soy sauce mixed with wasabi and topped them with slices of fresh ginger.

Our one concession to our occidental culture was after-dinner coffee, which we were sipping in the living room when my house phone rang. It was Roger Horowitz.

'Detective Benetti is on her way to pick you up,' he said. 'She should be there in about ten minutes. Be ready.'

I put the phone down. 'That was Roger Horowitz,' I said to Alex. 'His partner is on her way over here to take me someplace. I don't know what's going on, but I've got to do it.'

She nodded. 'This isn't the first time he's done that.'

'You remember?'

'You and Roger go way back. He's always dragging you off someplace without explanation. Do you think you'll be gone long?'

'Hard to say,' I said. 'You'll wait here?'

'Sure. Henry and I will find a movie to watch.' She looked at me. 'Roger's a homicide detective. That means it's got something to do with . . .'

'With a homicide. Most likely, yes.'

I bent down and kissed her on the mouth. Then I found a jacket in the hall closet and went out onto the front porch to wait for Marcia Benetti.

A few minutes later an unmarked sedan stopped in front of my house.

I slid into the passenger seat beside Marcia Benetti. She'd been Horowitz's partner for several years. She was dark-haired and small-boned, with big black eyes. She looked about as much like a police officer as I looked like a sumo wrestler.

'So, what's up?' I said.

'Dead body,' she said.

'Who?'

'Don't know.'

'Where?'

'Acton.'

'I don't know about you,' I said, 'but all this clever banter is exhausting me.'

She glanced at me. 'Sorry. I've been on the go since six this morning. I was looking forward to a quiet evening in my PJs eating popcorn and watching TV with my family.'

'Murderers are inconsiderate that way.'

Benetti didn't smile. 'They sure are,' she said.

She headed west on Route 2. A few minutes later she drove past the Best Western hotel where Alex was staying, then halfway round the roundabout and into Acton on 2A/119. A few miles later she turned right, and a mile or so after that she pulled off the road into a parking area in some woods.

There were at least half a dozen vehicles parked there. Down a slope in the woods I saw some lights moving through the trees.

Marcia opened her door. 'Come on,' she said. 'Follow me.'

Her big cop flashlight lit a narrow dirt pathway that wound towards the gurgle of moving water. The sounds of voices became louder, and the flicker of lights became brighter. Then we stepped into a clearing on the edge of a small stream. Eight or ten people were standing in a cluster.

Horowitz separated himself from the crowd and came over to us. 'Thanks for coming,' he said.

'You didn't give me much choice,' I said.

'No,' he said, 'I didn't. Come on. This way.'

We approached the group of law-enforcement officials. 'Back off,' said Horowitz to them.

When they did, I saw the body lying there on the gravel and sand at the edge of the stream. The victim was sprawled on his belly.

He was wearing faded blue jeans and muddy white running shoes, with a dark blue windbreaker. He had dark hair, cut short, and a small, compact body. I couldn't tell how old he was.

Horowitz knelt beside him. 'C'mere, Coyne,' he said. 'See if you recognise him.'

I squatted beside Horowitz. He tugged on the dead man's shoulder, rolling him onto his side, and shone his flashlight on the dead man.

The first thing I saw was that the man's throat had been sliced open nearly to his spine. The second thing I saw was that the dead man was Pedro Accardo.

'I know who this is,' I said to Horowitz. 'I half expected it. His name is Pedro Accardo.'

He stood up. I stood up, too. 'I got a question,' I said. 'Whatever gave you the idea that I might know him?'

'We'll talk in the car,' he said.

When we got back to the parking area, Horowitz pointed his flashlight at Marcia Benetti's sedan and said, 'Get in.'

I got in the passenger side. Horowitz slid in beside me and pulled out a notebook. He flipped it open. 'Spell that dead man's name for me.'

I spelt Pedro Accardo. 'He had no ID on him?'

'If he did,' he said, 'I wouldn't've needed you, right? So you know him how?'

'He was a friend of Gus Shaw's.' I told Horowitz about meeting Pedro— Pete—at the Sleepy Hollow Café with Gus. I told him that Pedro and Gus were both members of a support group for people who came home from Iraq with post-traumatic stress disorder and that the group was led by an older guy, named Philip Trapelo, whom people called the Sarge. I told him that I'd talked with Trapelo about Gus because I was trying to figure out if Gus really had taken his own life. I also mentioned talking with Jemma Jones, who owned the camera shop where Gus had worked, and Herb and Beth Croyden, Gus's landlords. The Croydens, I told him, had lost a son in Iraq. Ms Jones's husband had been killed over there.

I told Horowitz how Pedro had called me the previous night implying that he knew, or believed, that Gus had been murdered. I told him that Pedro mentioned the name John Kinkaid and the number eleven, eleven, eleven, and that judging by the background noises, he was calling from a public phone and was unable to say very much.

'He said he'd call me back at midnight,' I said.

'But he didn't.'

'No. He never did call me back.'

'We figure he's been dead between sixteen and twenty-four hours,' said Horowitz. 'He might've already been dead at midnight last night.'

'Soon after he called me, then,' I said. I shuddered at the possibility that talking to me had got Pedro murdered.

'He died right there by that stream,' said Horowitz. 'Killer was standing behind him. Right-handed. Big sharp knife.'

'And didn't bother trying to hide his body,' I said.

'No. This is a popular area. They expected him to be found.' He looked at me. 'You were asking how I knew to call you.'

I nodded. 'Yes. Why me?'

'He had your business card crumpled up in his hand.'

'I left a stack of cards for Phil Trapelo to give out to his group,' I said. 'Or he might've got it from Gus.' I frowned. 'The killer left the card in his hand but stripped him of his wallet and other ID? Isn't that a little strange?'

'Not if he's trying to send you a message, it isn't.'

'Me?' I stopped. 'Oh. A warning, you mean.'

Horowitz said, 'So you think this Accardo got murdered because he knew something about what happened to Gus Shaw?'

'Makes sense,' I said.

'And he was going to tell you what he knew.'

'Maybe. He called me, couldn't talk, said he'd call again. He had my card with my phone numbers in his hand, right?'

'Why you?'

'I guess I'm the only one still asking questions about Gus.'

Horowitz grunted. 'For all we know,' he said, 'the killer put that business card in our dead man's hand. A message for you. So do you get the message?'

I nodded. 'I get it. If it is a message.'

'So you'll leave the homicide detecting to the homicide detectives.'

'The homicide detectives concluded that Gus Shaw killed himself,' I said.

'Actually, that was the ME's office.' Horowitz paused. 'If you had just let it rest there,' he said, 'maybe Pedro would be alive right now.'

'I hate to think that might be true,' I said.

He shrugged. 'In light of this new development,' he said, 'perhaps we'll have to give the Gus Shaw case a second look. Do you have any other reason to think he didn't kill himself?'

I thought for a minute. 'Honestly, no, not really. It's just about whether he was the kind of man who'd do it, that's all. I know what the evidence looks like. Alex doesn't believe it, but she's still remembering him from when they were kids. I think Claudia, Gus's wife, does believe it. People I've talked to, none of them has seemed overly surprised. Until Pedro Accardo called me last night, I'd started to accept it.'

'It's a son of a bitch, all right,' Horowitz said. 'I'm done with you for now. Lemme find somebody to take you home.'

TEN

It was a little after 1 a.m. when Marcia Benetti dropped me off in front of my house on Mt Vernon Street.

Neither Henry nor Alex greeted me at the door when I went in. I found them both snoozing on the sofa. Alex was curled up at one end. Her cheek rested on her palm-to-palm hands, and her knees were tucked up to her chest.

Henry lay at the other end in virtually the identical position.

I stood there smiling and, after a minute, Henry opened an eye. He looked at me and then yawned, slithered off the sofa and headed stiff-legged towards the back door.

I let him out and waited on the deck. When he was finished, we went back to the living room. I sat on the sofa and touched Alex's cheek.

'Oh, hi,' she murmured. 'You're back. Are you OK?'

'I'm back and I'm fine,' I said, 'and it's past our bedtime.'

'I'm pretty tired,' Alex said, her eyes drooping.

'Come on.' I stood up and held my hand down to her. She let out a sigh, took my hand and pulled herself to her feet. I put my arm round her and led her to the stairs.

She stopped. 'Up there? You sure?'

I kissed the top of her head. 'I'm sure.'

By the time I had brushed my teeth, Alex was under the down comforter in the bed that Evie and I used to share. I crawled in beside her, and she sighed. She was thoroughly asleep.

I rolled onto my back and closed my eyes. I was suddenly very tired and my mind went into free fall.

Images ricocheted around behind my eyeballs. The startling sight of Pedro Accardo's body sprawled beside the eddying water, the flash of lights blinking through the trees, the cop radios spitting static, the awful pink bled-out smile on Pedro's throat.

My business card was clenched in his fist. A message, Horowitz had suggested. A message from Pedro's killer to me.

Even half asleep, I didn't have any trouble deciphering the message, if that's what it was. *Stop asking questions about Gus Shaw's suicide* the message went. *If you don't stop, what happened to Pedro will happen to you.*

The realisation that jerked me awake and opened my eyes to the darkness was this: Gus had not killed himself. Like Pedro, he had been murdered. Most likely by the same man. Alex was right all along. Now I believed her. And now, if Roger Horowitz was right, whoever killed Gus and Pedro was threatening me.

The question that kept me awake for a long time, and for which I had no good answer, was: Who'd kill Gus in the first place, and Pedro in the second? And why?

I WENT TO SLEEP with that conundrum bouncing round in my head, and it was still there when I woke up on Saturday morning, and it lingered there all day while Alex and I drove up to Plum Island, and while we strolled the pathways and took turns spying on the late-season birds through my big Zeiss binoculars, and while we had sandwiches and beers in Newburyport, and while we bought flounder fillets at the fish market, and while we sipped Rebel Yell back at my house, and while Alex made dinner.

The only answer to the *why* part of the question that I could come up with was Gus's elusive set of photographs from Iraq. I wondered who knew about the photos besides Claudia and Anna Langley. Pedro Accardo, maybe. I wondered what they showed and who they threatened. The answer to that question might answer the *who* part of my conundrum.

I wondered where Gus had hidden them, and if he'd divulged their whereabouts to his killer before he died.

Alex poached the flounder fillets and served them with a creamy dill sauce and brown rice and steamed fresh Brussels sprouts, with a nice pinot verde for accompaniment.

Then we took coffee into the living room. Alex sat on the sofa. I remained standing.

'I've got to go out for a couple of hours,' I said to her.

Her head snapped up. '*What?*'

'There's something I've got to do.'

'You were gone all last night, too.'

I nodded. 'I'm sorry.'

'It can't wait?'

'No.'

She gave me one of her cynical smiles. 'I'm sounding like I own you. I'm sounding like some whiny wife.'

'It's OK,' I said. 'Don't worry about it.'

'I'm disappointed,' she said. 'That's all. I was hoping we'd have a nice Saturday night together. Can I go with you?'

I shook my head. 'Not a good idea.'

'Why?' she said. 'Because it's dangerous, right?'

'Don't do this, honey,' I said.

'It's about Gus, isn't it?' she said.

I didn't say anything.

'Damn it,' said Alex. 'He's my brother. I've got a right to know.'

'Wait till I get back,' I said. 'I'll explain it then. OK? I have to do this now.'

She turned her head away. 'So, go, then. Get it done.'

As I headed for the door, I heard Alex mutter, 'Same old Brady Coyne. Some things never change.'

It didn't sound like a loving compliment.

STORROW DRIVE WESTBOUND was virtually empty of traffic at nine thirty on that November Saturday night, and so was Route 2 all the way out past Route 128. Less than an hour after saying my uncomfortable goodbyes to Alex, I pulled into the centre of Concord.

I found an empty parking slot round the corner from the Colonial Inn. I fished my Mini Maglite flashlight and my Leatherman tool from my car's glove compartment and slid them both into my trouser pockets. My cellphone was in my shirt pocket, set on vibrate.

I locked the car and began walking down the sidewalk along Monument Street. Fifteen minutes later I turned down Herb and Beth Croyden's driveway. I stayed next to the shadowy edges.

Lights glowed from inside their house, although none of the windows facing the driveway was brightly lit. Two vehicles were parked in front of their barn.

I had thought about phoning them, telling them I wanted to take another prowl through Gus's apartment. But after the double hit of finding Gus and then seeing Pedro Accardo's bled-out body—with my business card clutched in his dead hand—I'd lost my faith in my ability to know whom I could trust.

I slunk through the shadows past the Croydens' house and, when I came to the carriage house, I stopped for a couple of minutes behind a hemlock tree to be sure nobody had followed behind me.

Then I switched on my little flashlight and climbed the steps on the side of the building. I counted four shingles over and four down from the light and found the key wedged there where Alex had replaced it the night we found Gus's body. I unlocked the door and pushed it open, then put the key back under its shingle.

I'd given the place just a superficial search when I was there with Herb. And at that time I didn't know what, if anything, I was looking for. Now I had my sights set on some CDs that held Gus Shaw's Iraq photos.

It was a small apartment without many nooks and crannies but, even so, searching it was time-consuming and painstaking. When I finished, I'd examined every inch of Gus's place and found no CDs.

Now what? I scanned the room and my eyes came to rest on the door that headed down into the carriage house.

I tried the door. It was unlocked. On the wall inside the doorway was a light switch. I flipped it and a dim bulb lit the narrow wooden stairway.

I went down the stairs onto the ground floor of the carriage house, where another single bare bulb in the ceiling gave minimal light. Herb Croyden did not keep colonial-era carriages in his carriage house. Instead, there were automobiles. I was instantly envious of old Herb. There was a classic white Thunderbird. Next to it sat an Elvis special, a big pink Cadillac with swooping tailfins, and beside the Caddy crouched a Woodstock-era forest-green Karmann Ghia. All three cars appeared to be in mint condition.

I shone my light around. It was a typical garage, with a row of plastic trash barrels lined up against one wall, garden tools bundled in the corners, hand tools hanging on pegs, and a workbench along the back that held tool-boxes and paint cans. A big steel cabinet stood in the back corner.

If Gus had chosen to hide his CDs in this cavernous room, it might take an expert snooper days to uncover them. I was no expert. If I were Gus, and if I believed the images that my wife had burnt onto CDs were valuable and important, and if I suspected that I had enemies who would come after them, where would I hide them?

I walked slowly round the room. I stopped in front of the high, steel cabinet in the corner near where the Karmann Ghia was parked. What interested me was the small, shiny, new-looking padlock on the paint-stained, scratched and dented old cabinet door, which closed with a loop and hasp.

I opened a couple of toolboxes on the counter and found what I was looking for—a small steel J-shaped crowbar.

I wedged a corner of the bent end of the crowbar up under the hasp and gave a hard downward yank, and the hasp broke away from the cabinet door with a loud pop.

The door swung open, and I shone my little flashlight inside.

The cabinet had three shelves. On the top shelf, which was about shoulder high on me, were some items of clothing still in their plastic wrapping. I pulled one off the top of the stack.

It was a fishing vest such as fly fishermen use for carrying fly boxes and spools of leader material and various tools and tubes and plastic containers. This one was buff-coloured with a zipper up the front, and it had dozens of pockets of varying sizes.

I looked through the other items on that shelf. All were fishing vests, the identical colour, make, model and size—XL. Six of them altogether. An odd thing to lock up in a steel cabinet.

I bent over to shine my light into the shelf under the one that held the vests . . . and at that moment, a blinding light suddenly flashed on in the carriage house.

I straightened, blinked, turned round and made a visor with my hand. 'Who's that?'

'The question is,' said Herb Croyden's voice, 'what the hell are you doing in my garage, Mr Coyne?'

'I'm not here to steal your vehicles,' I said, 'though they are gorgeous. Get your light out of my eyes, will you, please?'

I turned off my flashlight and put it in my pocket. Then he lowered the beam of his light and I saw Herb standing there beside his Ghia. Behind him, a side door to the garage was hanging ajar. He'd opened it silently.

He held his flashlight in his left hand and an ugly square automatic pistol in his other hand. The weapon looked just like the one I'd seen beside Gus Shaw's dead body. Herb was aiming it at my midsection.

'You don't need that gun,' I said.

'I'll decide that,' Herb said. 'I see some lights flickering around on my property, I'm not going to check it out unarmed. You better tell me what you're doing before I call the police.'

'I think Gus may have hidden something here,' I said. 'I think what he hid might have got him killed. And the other night a friend of his was also killed, maybe for the same reason.'

'Gus committed suicide,' said Herb.

'Maybe not,' I said.

'So did you find what you were looking for?'

I shook my head. 'This cabinet,' I said, pointing my chin at the steel cabinet I'd just broken into. 'Is that your stuff inside? Are you the one who put the padlock on it?'

He shook his head. 'It was empty except for a few old paint cans. I told Gus if he needed to store anything, he could clean it out and use it. If it had a padlock on it, it wasn't mine.'

'Come over here,' I said, 'and see if you can explain this. And maybe you'll put that gun away?'

'I don't think so,' he said.

'Well,' I said, 'just don't shoot me, please.'

Herb came over so that he was standing behind me.

I showed him one of the fishing vests.

'Maybe he was going to take up fishing,' he said.

'There are six vests,' I said. 'A fisherman needs only one. Let's look on the other shelves.'

'You look,' said Herb. 'I'm going to stand back here with my gun.'

The next shelf held three one-foot-square cardboard boxes. I put them on the floor.

Herb shone his light on them. The first box contained six brand-new shrink-wrapped television remote-control wands. The second held some coils of red, blue and white electrical wire and a handful of rolls of black electrical tape. The third box held about a dozen packs of square twelve-volt batteries and the same number of packages of double-A batteries.

I looked at Herb. 'Make any sense to you?'

'None whatsoever,' he said. 'What's on that bottom shelf?'

There were three more cardboard boxes. I slid one out and prised open the top. It held half a dozen smaller boxes, each containing shotgun shells. I showed Herb one of the small boxes.

'Shotgun shells?' he said.

I nodded. 'Six boxes. Twenty-five shells per box.' I opened one of the other boxes. It contained six rolls of nail-gun nails.

I held one of the rolls up for Herb to see.

'Nails,' he said. 'I'm getting a bad feeling.'

'Me, too.' I read the stencilled letters on the top of the third box. I did not open it. 'It says C-4,' I said to Herb.

'Plastic explosive,' he whispered. 'What in the name of hell—'

'Stand up and turn round.' The sudden loud voice echoed in the big garage. 'Move away from there.' It was a deep, booming, familiar voice, and it came from a man silhouetted in the open doorway on the other side of the Karmann Ghia.

'Sarge?' I said. 'That you?'

Phil Trapelo flicked on a flashlight. 'Put down your gun and your flashlight, Herb,' he said.

Trapelo was holding a handgun of his own. He held it out at arm's length, bracing it with the hand that held the flashlight and aiming it at the middle of Herb's face.

Herb squatted down and laid his gun and his flashlight on the garage floor. 'What the hell are you doing, Sarge?' he said.

'I've had to keep an eye on the lawyer, here,' said Trapelo. 'He doesn't seem to know when to back off.'

I turned to Herb. 'You two know each other, huh?'

'I was in a support group with the Sarge for a while,' he said. 'After my son was killed.'

'But you stopped going,' I said.

'Sarge hates war. He can be a little . . . intense,' said Herb. 'He can get kind of extreme sometimes. Right, Sarge?'

Trapelo nodded. 'I don't call it extreme, I call it clear thinking. So'—he nodded at the steel cabinet—'yeah, we thought we'd see if we couldn't introduce some reality testing into the situation.'

I remembered what Pedro Accardo said to me on the phone the night before his throat was slit beside the stream in Acton. 'On Veterans Day, huh?' I asked. 'Eleven, eleven, eleven, right? You planning to blow yourself up, Sarge? Or is the idea for your followers to blow up themselves while you pull the strings? Gus Shaw and Pedro Accardo got wise to you, right?'

Trapelo looked at me, then at Herb. 'You should tell your friend to shut the hell up.'

'Is he right?' Herb said to Trapelo. 'Is that why you killed Gus?'

'Somebody's got to fire the first shot,' said Trapelo. 'I say, let it begin here.' I heard the fervour of the true believer in Phil Trapelo's voice, saw it in his face.

'What do you know about Gus's photographs from Iraq?' I said.

Trapelo shook his head. 'He thought photographs could make a difference. We disagreed about that.'

'Do you know where they are?' I said. 'Did you take them?'

'I don't—'

That's when Herb Croyden, who was standing right beside me, suddenly yelled, 'Watch out!' He ducked and darted sideways and scrambled on the floor for his automatic pistol. At the same time, a shot exploded inside the garage and Herb staggered backwards. His gun skittered across the cement floor towards me. Just as I got my hand on it, there was another shot. I managed to get my finger on the trigger and get off a shot at Trapelo. Herb crashed into me. Then my shoulders and the back of my head smashed against the steel cabinet. The cabinet toppled and crashed onto the concrete garage floor, and my back slammed onto the ground with all of Herb Croyden's weight on my chest.

I lay there for a moment, blinking against the darts of pain in my head. Then I took a couple of deep breaths and managed to roll Herb off me and onto his back. I was still holding his gun. Phil Trapelo was gone.

I got up on my hands and knees and looked at Herb. A red blotch was spreading across his left shoulder. His eyes were clenched shut, but he seemed to be breathing all right.

'Hang in there for a minute,' I said. 'I'll be right back.'

I crept towards the open door on the side of the carriage house and darted my head outside and back in again. Nobody out there.

I fished my Mini Maglite out of my pocket and went outside.

I heard the distant, muffled sound of a car starting up. The sound came from the direction of Monument Street. Phil Trapelo, making his escape, I guessed.

I went back into the carriage house and went over to where Herb Croyden was lying and knelt beside him. He was taking shallow, gasping breaths.

'Herb,' I said. 'Hey, Herb.'

His eyes opened. 'Did he get away?'

I nodded. 'He did. How do you feel?'

'Exactly like I got shot in the shoulder,' he said.

I used my Leatherman tool to cut away his jacket and shirt. The bullet had entered where the top of his left deltoid muscle joined his arm to his shoulder, and it left a deep gouge through his flesh. It was seeping blood but not pumping it.

'No arteries were hit,' I said. I carefully wadded Herb's shirt into a tight, thick compress, and pushed it firmly against the wound. 'Can you hold that there?'

Herb reached across and held my improvised bandage on his wound with his right hand. His face was pale, but his eyes were clear. 'I'm getting a little chilly here,' he said. 'This floor is cold. You're going to call 911 and cover me with something, aren't you? You'll find a blanket on the back seat of the Caddy.'

'I'm glad you've got your wits about you,' I said. 'One of us should.' I opened the back door of the Cadillac, found a khaki-coloured army blanket and spread it over Herb. Then I folded up my jacket and tucked it under his head. 'How's that?' I said.

He nodded. 'Much better.' He closed his eyes.

I fished my cellphone from my pocket, dialled 911, and told the operator that a man had been shot and she should send an ambulance quickly and report it to state police detective Roger Horowitz. I gave her Herb's address and emphasised that they should come to the carriage house. Then I called Horowitz's cellphone number.

'Coyne,' he said. 'It's Saturday night. Almost Sunday morning. You got something against me and my wife sleeping?'

'I just called 911 and told them to contact you,' I said. 'I figured you'd want to know why.'

'What'd you get yourself into this time?' he said.

I sketched out for him what had happened.

'You talking about suicide bombers?' he said.

'Individuals wearing battery-powered fishing vests packed with plastic

explosives and nails and BB shot blowing themselves up in public places,'
I said. 'That's right.'

'And this Trapelo? He's the ringleader, huh?'

'Yes. He shot Herb and got away.'

'OK, then. You stay put. There'll be local cops along with the ambulance.
Don't say anything to them. I gotta make a couple of phone calls. Then I'll
be right along.'

'Say hi to Alyse for me,' I said.

'Your pal Coyne says hello,' I heard him say. There was a pause, and then
he said, 'She says she wishes you'd stop haunting us.'

'Boo,' I said.

I FOLDED MY PHONE and turned back to look at Herb. As I did, I noticed the
corner of a manila envelope sticking out from under the toppled-over steel
cabinet.

I picked up the envelope. It was sealed with cellophane tape. Nothing
was written on it. I moved my fingers over it. It felt like the outlines of several thin square plastic boxes. The kind of boxes that held CDs and DVDs.

If I wasn't mistaken, I'd found Gus's photos.

I glanced at Herb. His eyes were closed. His breathing came in shallow
little pants and his skin looked pale and clammy.

I unzipped my jacket and stuffed the envelope down inside the front of
my shirt.

I was zipping my jacket back up when I heard an intake of breath and the
scrape of a foot on the concrete floor behind me. I turned. Beth Croyden
was standing there hugging herself.

'What happened?' she said. 'Is Herb—'

'He was shot,' I said. 'It's a superficial wound. He'll be OK. An ambulance
is on the way.'

'*Shot?*' she said.

I nodded.

'Those *were* gunshots I heard, then,' she said. As she came towards us,
she waved her hand round the garage, taking in the overturned steel cabinet
and the cardboard boxes and her wounded husband. 'Who did this?'

'A guy named Phil Trapelo. Do you know him?'

Beth gave her head a small shake that could have meant yes or no. She
knelt down beside Herb, then bent over and kissed him. She looked up at

me. 'We were getting ready for bed. Herb thought he saw some lights down here at the carriage house. I told him, "Why don't we call the police?" But not my old James Bond here. So what happened?'

I shrugged. 'It's a long story. We'd better wait for the police.'

Beth cocked her head at me, then nodded. 'I understand. This is all connected to Gus Shaw, though, isn't it?'

'Probably.'

She returned her attention to Herb. She stroked his cheek and spoke softly to him. I heard him murmur some kind of reply.

I glanced round the carriage house. The various boxes holding what I guessed were the component parts for suicide bombs that I'd found in the steel cabinet were scattered on the floor. I wondered what would have happened if one of Phil Trapelo's bullets had hit the box containing the C-4 plastic explosive.

I heard the distant wail of sirens and went outside to wait. The sirens grew louder and then I saw the headlights cutting through the trees along the winding driveway. A minute later an emergency wagon came skidding to a stop in front of the carriage house and two medical guys hopped out.

'He's in there,' I said, pointing at the door.

They went inside. A short while later Beth Croyden came out and stood beside me. 'They kicked me out,' she said.

'They'll probably let you ride in the ambulance with him,' I said.

While we were speaking a Concord town police cruiser arrived, and right behind it came Roger Horowitz's sedan. The two local cops and Horowitz climbed out of their vehicles. They all came over to me and Beth.

Horowitz flashed his badge at the uniforms and walked into the garage. In moments, he was back. 'We got this guy,' he said to the cops. 'You boys stay with the lady.' He steered me over to his car. 'Here we go again, Coyne,' he said.

We climbed into the back seat of his car. Marcia Benetti was sitting behind the wheel. I said hello to her and she grunted at me.

Horowitz said, 'I already put the word out on Philip Trapelo, so let's start with him. Tell me everything you know about him.'

Everything I knew turned out not to be much. Trapelo was involved with the support group for post-traumatic stress disorder victims that met Tuesdays at the VFW hall in Burlington. People called him the Sarge. He appeared to be in his late fifties or early sixties. He held strong pro-veteran

552 | WILLIAM G. TAPPLY

and antiwar sentiments. He was short and compact. Grey hair, cut military style. Deep voice. He carried an automatic side arm.

No, I didn't know where Trapelo lived or worked or what kind of car he drove. Not counting tonight's encounter, I'd only met him once. All I knew was his cellphone number, which I looked up on my own phone and recited for them.

'So, Coyne,' said Horowitz, 'what the hell were you doing here on a Saturday night in the first place?'

'As you know,' I said, 'all along Alex has refused to believe that her brother committed suicide. More and more, I've come round to her way of thinking. What happened to Pedro Accardo—and finding my business card in his hand—pretty much clinched it for me.' I shrugged. 'I came here just to see if I could find something that would give me a clue about Gus.' I jerked my thumb in the direction of the garage. 'I guess I did.'

Horowitz nodded. 'I guess the hell you did. Looks like all the ingredients for a half-dozen men to dress up in fishing-vest bombs and blow themselves—plus anybody who happened to be nearby—into smithereens. You figure that was Shaw?'

'I think it was Trapelo. I think Gus just let Trapelo store his stuff here. I doubt if Gus even knew what was in those boxes.'

'Trapelo,' he said. 'So he killed Shaw?'

I nodded. 'And Pedro Accardo.'

'Why?'

'I think Gus and Pedro figured out what Trapelo was up to,' I said. 'He thought they were going to turn him in, so he killed them. He might've thought Pedro told me about it. So he followed me here and tried to kill me and Herb Croyden, too.'

'What else can you tell us?'

I told the two homicide detectives that Pedro emphasised the number eleven, eleven, eleven, and I thought that Trapelo might've had something planned for Veterans Day, just a few days away.

'Symbolic, huh?' said Horowitz.

'Profoundly disturbed, if you ask me,' I said.

He asked me a lot more questions and I answered them as well as I could. He did not ask about Gus Shaw's photographs and I didn't mention the CDs inside my shirt. Maybe I was withholding evidence, but I doubted it. That box of C-4 was evidence enough to keep the police occupied for a while.

Horowitz told me to keep my cellphone with me at all times, as he was positive he'd want to talk with me again. It was after two in the morning when they dropped me off at my car. I got in and headed for home.

I wondered if Alex was still upset with me. Knowing her, I guessed she probably was. But I figured that when I told her all about my evening's adventures with suicide bombs and gunshots and police and ambulances, and when I showed her the envelope that held Gus's Iraq photographs, she'd feel different.

I PARKED ON Mt Vernon Street and went in my front door. Henry was waiting there with his tail wagging, then turned and trotted towards the back door.

I let him out, then went to the living room.

Alex was not curled up on the sofa. I went upstairs to the bedroom. She wasn't there, either. Nor did I find her on the day bed in my den. I looked out of the front window to where she'd left her car the previous evening. It was gone. She was gone.

I stood there for a minute feeling sad and alone. And then I smiled. Of course she was gone. She was Alexandria Shaw. She didn't put up with a lot—from me, or from anybody. That was one of the things I loved about her.

Like Groucho, who said he'd refuse to join any organisation that would accept him as a member, I tended to lose interest in women who were overly tolerant of me.

I looked on the kitchen table and counters for a note. I didn't think Alex would leave one, and she didn't disappoint me. She knew I could figure it out without having it explained. It was simple. I'd treated her badly and she wouldn't put up with it.

I let Henry in. I realised that as late as it was, the evening's adrenaline was still zipping through my veins. I was wide-awake. So Henry and I went into my den. I fished the manila envelope out from inside my shirt and tore it open. Six flat plastic boxes slid out. Each held a CD on which someone—Claudia, I guessed—had used a black marker to write 'GS' and what I figured was a date, day and month—16/7, 12/9, 18/9, 19/9, 22/10, 8/12. I guessed those were the dates that Claudia had received each batch of emailed images from Gus and had transcribed them onto these CDs.

I went into my home office and put one of the CDs into my computer. When it loaded, I saw that there were 174 images. I clicked on one of them at random. It showed several men wearing military camouflage squatting and talking with a dark-skinned boy. The child was propped up by an improvised crutch. He had only one leg.

Another image showed a skinny dark-haired girl—she looked maybe fourteen—leaning back against the exploded remains of a building. She wore a skimpy tank top and a denim skirt so short that it barely covered her hips. She had the bony legs and flat chest of a preadolescent, but the look on her face was old and corrupt. If an ordinary picture is worth a thousand words, this photo of Gus Shaw's was a whole novel.

Each of the six CDs held between 142 and 179 images. Those I chose randomly to enlarge on my computer screen portrayed something Gus had seen in Iraq. Every one of them was painful to look at. Each managed to capture a psychological as well as a physical element of the human destruction that Gus found over there. Each had its story to tell.

I put the CDs back into their boxes and slid the boxes into a big padded mailing envelope and stuck the envelope into the bottom drawer of my filing cabinet. I shut the drawer and locked the cabinet. Then I leaned back in my desk chair.

Phil Trapelo said he doubted the impact of Gus's photographs. Trapelo was convinced that public attention could only be grabbed and held by something as stunningly dramatic and shocking as American veterans turned suicide bombers.

I wished I felt more confident that he was wrong.

Henry, who'd been snoozing on his dog bed in the corner, stirred, got to his feet and walked over to where I was sitting. He plopped his chin on my thigh and looked up at me with his big loyal eyes, as if he sensed that I was having deep thoughts and wanted to reassure me that all was well because he loved me.

'I wish it was that simple,' I told him.

THE SHRILL OF THE PHONE on the bedside table woke me. I opened my eyes and looked at the clock. It was ten past nine.

I groped for the phone and mumbled, 'Yes? Hello?'

'I'm on my way over.' It was Horowitz. 'I got doughnuts. Be sure there's coffee.' Then he hung up.

I rolled out of bed, pulled on jeans and a sweatshirt, splashed water on my face and let Henry out. I'd made the coffee before going to bed, so the pot was full.

I was halfway through my first mug when the doorbell rang. I went to the front door and opened it. Horowitz stood there wearing an old ski parka and holding the kind of cardboard box that would contain a dozen doughnuts. Beside him was a balding man of about sixty. He was carrying a slender oxblood attaché case.

I held the door open and the two of them came inside.

Horowitz handed me the doughnut box. 'This is Agent Greeley,' he said. He took off his parka and hung it in the hall closet.

The bald guy held out his hand. 'Martin Greeley,' he said. 'FBI.'

I shook his hand. 'Brady Coyne. Lawyer. Let me take your coat.'

Greeley let me slip his topcoat off. He was wearing a charcoal suit under it and he kept his grip on his attaché case.

I hung up his coat beside Horowitz's, then the three of us—four, actually, including Henry—trooped into the kitchen. Horowitz and Greeley sat at the kitchen table. Henry curled up under it. I poured coffee, put out plates and napkins, and sat down.

We all plucked doughnuts from the box, took bites and sipped our coffee. Then Greeley reached into his attaché case and took out a large envelope. From it, he slipped an eight-by-ten black-and-white photograph. He laid it on the table and pushed it towards me. 'Do you recognise this man?' he said.

The photo was a waist-up shot of a young guy—late teens, early twenties, I guessed. He had suspicious eyes and a small mouth, with a scruffy pale beard and long blondish hair held back in a ponytail. He was wearing a T-shirt that showed a building in flames along with the words: VIOLENCE IS AS AMERICAN AS CHERRY PIE. H. RAP BROWN.

I looked up at Greeley. 'I don't think I've ever seen this person.'

He didn't answer me. Instead, he took another photo from his envelope. It was a head-and-shoulders shot. 'How about him?'

This photo showed an older man with an angular, creased face and thinning grey hair combed straight back. I stared at the face for a minute, then looked up at Horowitz. 'You know, this could be Philip Trapelo's brother. There's something about his eyes.' I turned to Agent Greeley. 'Who are these guys?'

Greeley put the photo of the young ponytailed guy beside the second photo. 'This,' he said, poking the first one, 'is a man named John Kinkaid. And this'—he tapped the photo of the older man—'is how our computer aged him thirty-five years.'

I took another look at the two photographs. 'Your computer has the right idea,' I said. 'The shape of the face, the eyes, the set of the mouth.' I tapped the computer's rendition of the older John Kinkaid. 'Phil Trapelo's face isn't quite this wrinkled, and he wears his hair in a kind of military brush cut.'

'You see it, then,' said Greeley.

'I do, yes,' I said. 'You're telling me that the man I know as Phil Trapelo is somebody named John Kinkaid. And this'—I tapped the photo of the young guy with the ponytail—'this is Kinkaid when he was a young man.' I stopped. 'Wait a minute.' I looked at Horowitz. 'When Pedro Accardo called me that night? He mentioned the name John Kinkaid. I even Googled it. So Accardo figured out who Phil Trapelo really is, huh?'

Horowitz nodded. 'Trapelo is Kinkaid,' he said. 'Agent Greeley here has been on his tail for over thirty-five years.'

'A lifetime's work,' I said.

Greeley nodded. 'It's been an obsession.' He cleared his throat. 'John Kinkaid was a brilliant student. Graduated high school in Keene, New Hampshire, a year early. Scholarship to Princeton. Like a lot of young, um, idealists at the time, he dropped out at the end of his sophomore year and enlisted. So let me ask you something. You know this man calling himself Phil Trapelo, right?'

I nodded.

'How tall would you say he is?'

'Not very tall. Five eight, I'd say.'

Greeley nodded. 'Does he walk with a limp?'

I nodded. 'Yes. He said he had a bad knee.'

'Which leg?'

I tried to picture Trapelo the night I'd met him at the VFW hall. 'The right leg,' I said.

'Eye colour?'

'Brown, I'm pretty sure.'

Greeley looked at Horowitz. 'It's him.' He turned to me and smiled. 'John Kinkaid was responsible for the explosions of two campus buildings in the early seventies,' he said. 'The first, in 1970, was at the University of Wisconsin, the second a year later at the University of Massachusetts. Several people died. These were supposed to be antiwar protests. Kinkaid was the leader. He was a young Vietnam vet. He lost three toes to a booby trap over there. He was radicalised by the war, and then by poor care in the

Veterans Administration hospital, and then by some people he fell in with when he was discharged. Nowadays we'd diagnose him with PTSD. Back then, they tended to stigmatise those who suffered from it. Needless to say, that tended to radicalise them, too. The army had trained Kinkaid in demolitions. The Wisconsin blast was crude, though quite powerful—fertiliser and fuel oil loaded in a vehicle—but the second one, at UMass, was quite a bit more sophisticated. Plastic explosive and remote electronic detonation.'

Greeley looked at me and shook his head. 'I never for one minute believed that Kinkaid died in that explosion. We found a young man's body in the rubble of that building. He was wearing Kinkaid's dog tags, and he had Kinkaid's driver's licence in his wallet. There wasn't much left of him, but he was about the right size, shape, colour and age, so officially John Kinkaid was dead. I never bought it. Kinkaid was smart and meticulous. He'd never screw up a detonation like that. But he was perfectly capable of murdering somebody and setting up his explosion to look like an accident.' Greeley smiled. 'I've travelled to England and Canada and Argentina and Mexico, not to mention all over the United States, tracking down reported John Kinkaid sightings. I've never come close to him until now.'

'You still haven't found him, then?' I said.

Greeley shook his head. 'In our computers, Philip Trapelo doesn't exist.'

I said, 'I met him that one time at the VFW hall in Burlington. Everybody there seemed to know him. And then last night he apparently followed me to the Croydens' place, shot Herb in the shoulder and disappeared. I gave you his cellphone number. That's all I know.'

'Did he say anything about killing Shaw or Accardo?' said Greeley.

'Not really. But I'm sure he did it. I think Gus and Pedro figured out what he was up to with the suicide bombs. Pedro evidently even figured out that Trapelo was really John Kinkaid.'

'So last night in the garage,' said Horowitz, 'what did he say?'

I shook my head. 'The man was holding a gun on us. There was a carton of plastic explosive on the floor. You expect me to remember what he said?'

'Damn right,' said Horowitz. 'Think, Coyne. Come on.'

'Did you talk with Herb?' I said.

'They've got him on some big-time painkillers,' he said. 'He'll be useless for another forty-eight hours.'

'It's Veterans Day,' I said. 'That's when Trapelo plans to do whatever it is he's got in mind.'

'Help us out, Mr Coyne,' said Greeley.

'You're thinking he's still going to do this?' I said. 'Some kind of suicide-bombing demonstration?'

Greeley nodded. 'We have to think that way.'

'But he left all his supplies in Herb's carriage house.'

'John Kinkaid would never store all his supplies in just one place,' said Greeley. 'Decentralisation is one of the first principles of terrorist warfare. My guess is he's got small stashes of ingredients scattered all over eastern Massachusetts.' Greeley looked at me. 'We've got to track this man down, Mr Coyne.'

'I'm trying to help,' I said. 'Trapelo was ranting about how somebody needed to take the initiative—fire the first shot, was how he put it—and then he said . . .' I shut my eyes, trying to remember. 'Actually,' I said, 'what he said was "Let it begin here."'

'Fire the first shot,' said Greeley. 'He said that?'

'He used the term "the first shot",' I said. 'Yes.'

'And he said, "Let it begin here"?'

I nodded.

'The Lexington village green,' said Greeley. 'April 19th, 1775. Remember Paul Revere's midnight ride to warn Lexington that the British army was on its way? Remember the "Shot Heard 'Round the World"—the first musket shot of the American Revolution? It was fired on the Lexington green. And the leader of the Minutemen, Captain Parker, said to his troops, "Don't fire unless fired upon, but if they mean to have a war, let it begin here." They do a re-enactment there around sunrise every April 19th.'

Greeley said, 'Mr Coyne, I wonder if we can impose on your good nature a bit more this morning.'

I shrugged. 'It's Sunday. I have no plans.'

'I'd appreciate it,' he said, 'if you'd come to our field office and consult with our computer-imaging expert. I'd like to have a dead-on picture of John Kinkaid circulating asap.'

'Sure,' I said. 'Whatever I can do.'

'Thanks,' said Greeley. He turned to Horowitz. 'The other celebration they do on the Lexington village green every year happens at eleven a.m. on the November Monday closest to the 11th, when they officially celebrate Veterans Day. That's a week from tomorrow. Which means we haven't got that much time.'

ELEVEN

When we went out of the front door of my house, a big black van was parked at the kerb. Greeley got in the front beside the driver, whom he introduced as Agent Neal, and started talking on his cellphone. Horowitz and I climbed in the back.

The Boston field office of the FBI was housed at One Center Plaza, just on the other side of Beacon Hill from my house.

Greeley ushered Horowitz and me through a metal detector in the lobby, into an elevator, up half a dozen floors and into a small room that held two metal tables, some leather-padded wooden chairs, and several computers and other equipment. A young guy sat at one of the computers.

Greeley told me his name was Eric. Eric nodded at me.

'We want you to work with Eric,' said Greeley.

I took the empty chair next to Eric and looked on his monitor. It displayed the computer-altered version of Phil Trapelo's face derived from John Kinkaid's face at the age of twenty. It was the same image Greeley had shown me at my kitchen table.

'You know what he really looks like, right?' Eric said.

'Yes,' I said.

'You're the only person we've got who's actually seen him in the present time. We want to create a dead-on image of him to work with. Take a look at this and tell me what you think. OK?'

I nodded. 'OK.' I studied the computer-generated image for a minute, then said, 'It's not bad, but the hair's all wrong, for one thing. And Trapelo's eyebrows are way bushier than that. His ears stick out a little more and his nose is bigger. Also, his chin—'

'Slow down,' said Eric. 'Let's start with the hair and work our way down.'

While Greeley and Horowitz watched over our shoulders, I suggested tweaks and refinements, and Eric did his magic with his mouse, and the lines and shapes on the computer monitor began to resemble the man I knew as Philip Trapelo.

I sat back in my chair. 'That's it,' I said finally. 'That's exactly him. That's Phil Trapelo. It could be his photo.'

Then, as abruptly as I'd been invited, I was thanked and dismissed. Horowitz stayed there, but Greeley rode the elevator down with me and walked with me out to the kerb, where the black van was waiting.

When we shook hands, Greeley said, 'This has been a huge help. Again, many thanks. We may be calling on you again in the next week or so. Please be available. And I can't emphasise enough how important it is that you say nothing of any of this to anybody.'

'I understand.'

He opened the back door of the van for me.

'I'd just as soon walk home,' I said. 'It's not far.'

He looked at me for a moment. 'Just be careful, OK?'

THAT AFTERNOON, Henry and I shared a bowl of popcorn and watched the Patriots clobber the Jets. When the game ended, I called Alex's room at the Best Western hotel in Concord. When she didn't answer, I tried her cellphone.

She answered on the third ring. 'I'm in the middle of writing a tricky bit, and trying to get through the day uninterrupted,' she said. 'Was that you who just rang my room phone?'

'That was I,' I said.

'I'm actually quite busy.'

'Sorry. Tell me when you can you talk. I'll call you back.'

She blew out a sigh. 'What's up, Brady?'

'I've got Gus's photos.'

There was a pause. Then she said, 'That's what you were doing last night?'

'I went looking for them and I found them. Yes. Now I need to turn them over to you.'

'I'm fairly angry with you, you know.'

'I gathered that you were, yes. You left some clues. Like the fact that you weren't there when I got home.'

'Regardless of what you were up to,' she said, 'there was just too much of that old déjà vu to it. Do you understand?'

'I yam what I yam, I guess.'

'And what you are,' she said, 'as history has demonstrated, doesn't always mesh that well with what I yam.' She was quiet for a moment. 'You found Gus's photos, though, huh?'

'I got lucky, yes.'

'Claudia will be thrilled.' She paused. '*I'm* thrilled.'

'I want to give them to you,' I said. 'They belong to you. You're the one who should give them to Claudia.'

'That would mean we'd have to see each other again.'

'I could mail them, I suppose. I'm a bit reluctant to let them out of my sight, though.'

'You feel like buying me dinner?'

'That's more like it,' I said. 'Boston or Concord?'

'Definitely Concord,' she said. 'I do not intend to spend another night in your girlfriend's bed.'

'Papa Razzi, seven o'clock,' I said. 'Don't be late.'

'I might stand you up,' she said. 'You never know.'

'For the record,' I said, 'it's *my* bed.'

I WALKED INTO Papa Razzi a few minutes after seven. Alex was at the bar sipping what looked like an old-fashioned, made of whiskey and bitters. She was wearing tight-fitting jeans and cowboy boots and a rugby jersey with pale blue stripes. Her hair glowed as if it had been recently washed.

I took the stool beside her. She leaned to me and turned her cheek, which I kissed, chastely. I put the envelope holding the CDs on the bar top.

She put her hand on the envelope. 'Gus's photos?'

I nodded.

'Shouldn't you give them to Claudia yourself?' she said. 'You're her lawyer now, right?'

'You're Gus's sister,' I said. 'It's about family.'

Alex nodded. 'How did you ever find them?'

'I just kept poking around and, after a while, there they were.'

She picked up the envelope. 'Did you look at them?'

'A few, randomly,' I said, 'just to be sure they were what I thought they were. There are hundreds of images on those CDs. Those that I looked at are extraordinary. I had lunch with Gus's agent the other day. She says there's a lot of interest in them.'

Alex tucked the envelope into her big shoulder bag. Then she leaned towards me. I met her halfway and she kissed my mouth. 'Thanks,' she said softly. 'I'm kinda sorry I skipped out on you last night. Maybe if you'd told me what you were doing . . .'

'My fault,' I said. 'I don't blame you.'

The hostess came over and said that our table was ready.

Our table turned out to be a booth. Alex asked for another old-fashioned, and I said that an old-fashioned sounded good to me, too.

'You were right about Gus,' I said after the waitress left. 'He was murdered.'

Alex blinked at me. 'Who? Why?'

'I can't tell you any details. I'm sorry.'

Alex looked at me. 'Why the hell not? He was my brother.'

'The FBI is involved. They, um, they made me promise to say nothing. There's still an ongoing investigation. I probably shouldn't have told you that.'

She shook her head slowly, and I couldn't tell whether she didn't believe me or was just expressing her dismay.

'I'm sorry,' I said.

'Maybe someday you'll share what you know with me.'

'I will as soon as I can,' I said. 'I promise.'

An hour or so later we were sipping after-dinner coffee when Alex touched my arm. 'I wanted you to know that I've changed my mind about getting an apartment in the South End.'

'So where are you looking?'

She shook her head. 'Nowhere. A few more days at the hotel and then I'll be heading home. I've got just a little more research to do on this book. Then I'll be ready to start writing. I write best right there in my own house in Maine.'

'Well, sweetheart,' I said, 'it's been fun having you around.'

'*Fun?*' she said.

'I was going for world-weary and ironic,' I said. 'Say, Bogey at the end of *Casablanca.*'

Alex rolled her eyes. 'The scary thing is, I got it. I expected it, even. What does that tell you?' She looked up. Our waitress was slipping the leather folder containing our bill next to my elbow.

I paid the bill and helped Alex shrug on her jacket, and we walked out of the restaurant into a star-filled November night.

The Best Western was right next door to the Papa Razzi. Alex put her arm through mine and we walked over to her hotel. We stopped under the overhang by the front doors. She put both arms round my chest and looked up at me. 'This is the time when the girl asks the guy if he'd like to come up to her room for a nightcap.'

'Do you have the ingredients in your room with which to construct an actual nightcap?' I said.

She smiled and shook her head.

'Then I guess the guy would have to decline.'

She kissed my jaw. 'And I guess I'll have to find a different way to thank you for everything you've done for me.'

'You don't need to thank me.'

She nodded. 'You'll come visit me in Maine sometime?'

'Sure. I'd like that.'

'I've got a lot of firewood that needs to be split. You enjoy doing that. You could bring Henry. He'd love the woods.'

'He definitely would,' I said. I kissed the top of her head, then stepped away from her. 'We'll be in touch, right?'

'Of course. I don't know about you, though, but I've got some things to sort out first.'

'Yes,' I said. 'Me, too.'

Alex touched my arm, then turned and went into the hotel. I watched her pass through the two sets of glass doors and enter the lobby. She didn't turn and look back at me.

AFTER SUPPER the next evening, I was just settling in for some *Monday Night Football* when the phone rang.

'It's Mary Epping,' she said when I answered. 'I'm sorry to bother you at home.'

'No bother,' I said. 'What's up?'

'It's just so exciting,' she said. 'Doug said, "Oh, leave poor Brady alone." But I thought you'd want to know.'

'You're right,' I said. 'Tell me.'

'Just watch the ten o'clock news on Channel Nine. That's the Manchester station.'

At ten o'clock, I began toggling back and forth between the football game and the Channel Nine news, and about twenty minutes later Molly Burke's face appeared. She was saying, 'And after the break, we have a modern-day David and Goliath story that's unfolding right here in downtown Nashua. Whatever happened to, "The customer is always right"? Mary and Douglas Epping have their own answer. Stay tuned.'

After four or five commercials, Molly's voice-over came back. 'This is

Molly Burke. I'm here in Nashua to talk with a pair of retired folks from over the border in Massachusetts named Mary and Douglas Epping.' As she spoke, the camera panned across what looked like a row of grimy old brick warehouses.

. The camera then zoomed in on Molly. Doug and Mary were standing on either side of her. They were wearing ski parkas over their sweatsuits, and on their shoulders they were holding cardboard signs tacked onto wooden stakes.

Molly held the microphone to Mary. 'Mrs Epping, what are you two folks doing here on such a dreary November day?'

'We're picketing *them*,' said Mary.

The camera followed her arm as she pointed at one of the brick buildings behind them, then zoomed in on the sign in the window that read AA MOVERS, INC.

'How long have you been doing this?'

'This is our fifth day,' said Mary. 'We started last Tuesday. We took the weekend off.'

Molly smiled. 'I can't blame you.' She turned to Doug. 'Mr Epping,' she said, 'what do you hope to accomplish?'

'We want to be acknowledged,' he said.

'Acknowledged?' said Molly. 'That's all?'

'We have a dispute with those people,' said Doug, 'and they're just ignoring us. But if they think we're going to give up and go away, they're wrong. We're retired folks. We've got the time and we've got the commitment, and we're here for the long haul.'

The camera went in close on Molly's face. She looked directly at us viewers. 'I don't know about you folks,' she said, 'but I've been ignored and mistreated by businesses and bureaucracies a few times myself, and I'm ashamed to say that I haven't been very aggressive in standing up for my rights. If you ask me, we need more people like Doug and Mary Epping to remind us of the kind of country we're supposed to be living in. We've got to speak up for ourselves. Why not try some good old American picketing? I bet the Eppings wouldn't mind some company.'

Then: 'This is Molly Burke reporting from Outlook Drive in Nashua. Now back to you, Ted and Ellen.'

I hit the remote and returned to my football game. I realised that I was grinning like a fool.

AROUND THREE O'CLOCK on Friday afternoon, Julie ushered Roger Horowitz into my office. He plopped into the client chair across my desk from me and, as usual, didn't offer to shake hands or initiate small talk. 'They're gonna pick you up at your front door at seven on Monday morning,' he said.

'Monday being Veterans Day,' I said. 'A state holiday. Who's they, and why, and why should I?'

'They is all of us, us staties, and Greeley and his Feebs, plus various local agencies, and why is to maybe avert a terrorist event, and you should because you're a good citizen, and anyway, I'm giving you no choice.'

'They haven't nailed Phil Trapelo, or John Kinkaid, or whatever his name is, then, huh?'

'I ain't at liberty to say,' said Horowitz. 'Draw your own conclusions. You just be ready to go at seven on Monday. They'll have plenty of doughnuts and coffee.'

AT FIVE MINUTES TO SEVEN on Monday morning, I was sitting on my front steps sipping coffee from my travel mug when a familiar black van came to a stop at the end of my walkway.

When I stood up, the door of the van opened, and Agent Neal came round and opened the back door for me. I thought he might put his hand on top of my head as I ducked inside, but he didn't.

Agent Martin Greeley was sitting in the passenger seat in front. He was holding a cellphone against his ear. He wiggled his fingers at me without turning round.

The streets of Boston were virtually empty on this early morning of a holiday Monday, and it took barely half an hour to reach the Waltham Street exit to Lexington. Minutes later we faced the tall statue of Captain Parker of the Minutemen at the prow of the Lexington Battle Green.

Agent Neal pulled into a parking area overlooking the green. During the entire drive from my house, neither he nor Agent Greeley had spoken a word, either to each other or to me.

Now Greeley snapped his phone shut, stuffed it into his jacket pocket and turned in his seat. 'Glad you could make it.'

'Glad to help,' I said. 'Horowitz didn't give me much choice. He also didn't tell me what you wanted me to do.'

'Watch television,' he said. He pointed out of the front windshield at a big Channel Seven trailer that was parked at the edge of the lot. 'That's ours. We'll be in there.'

'Channel Seven?' I said.

'They don't mind if we use them for cover now and then.' He opened his door. 'Come on. I'll show you the set-up.'

We walked over to the trailer, climbed two portable aluminium steps and went inside, where it looked like an air-traffic control centre. No windows. Men and women hunched over big keyboards. The air seemed alive with subaudible electronic buzz and the soft murmur of voices. Along one wall there were ten stations with big computer monitors and what looked like sound-studio consoles, each attended by a tech wearing a headset. The wall above the stations was lined with television screens.

'We're monitoring the crowd,' Agent Greeley said. 'We expect that if Kinkaid makes a move, it'll be here. But there are Veterans Day events in four other Massachusetts communities this morning, too. We've got those covered.'

'And you want me to try to pick out John Kinkaid?'

Greeley nodded. 'All the agents have memorised that computer image you helped us work up the other day. But you're the only one who's actually seen him, seen how he moves, seen his gestures. You can give us a heads-up, save us half a minute, maybe save a lot of lives. OK?'

'Of course,' I said. 'Just tell me what to do.'

'Our agents out there with cameras,' he said, 'and our techs in here will be scanning the crowds looking for John Kinkaid in whatever form of disguise he may choose to wear. They'll be searching for men of a certain height who might be wearing some bulk under their jackets. They'll be looking for men with a limp. Anything at all close, we'll ask you to check him out. If you think it's even possible, you've got to say so. This isn't a police line-up. We're not waiting for a positive ID at this time. OK?'

I nodded. 'OK.'

He waved his hand at a table in the corner. 'Coffee, juice, doughnuts, muffins, crullers, Danish. Help yourself. There's a Portaloo right outside. Be sure to let someone know if you have to go.' He shook my hand. 'Good luck.'

'I'll do my best,' I said.

I ate a doughnut and sipped coffee and scanned the television screens on the wall, which I realised showed the same things that the computer monitors under them showed. The six screens on the left all displayed various areas of the Lexington village green right outside our trailer.

The other four screens showed other New England village greens where preparations for Veterans Day celebrations were under way.

Once in a while, one of the screens would zoom in on a man's face. None of the faces they put up on the screen looked anything like the man I was forcing myself to think of as John Kinkaid.

The Lexington green—and the other village greens, too—gradually became more crowded, and more faces flashed on the screens.

And then from outside the trailer I heard the muted first notes of the national anthem. On one of the TV screens, an army band was playing. I glanced at my watch: 11 a.m., on the dot.

That's exactly when the cellphone in my shirt pocket vibrated.

I LOOKED at the little window on my phone. UNKNOWN CALLER, it said. Greeley was down at the other end. I waved my hand at him. He looked up. I pointed at my phone. He nodded, then returned his attention to a monitor.

I opened my phone and said, 'Yes?'

The deep voice was unmistakable. 'Happy Veterans Day, Mr Coyne. Are you celebrating?'

It was John Kinkaid. It occurred to me that, calling my cell, he had no idea where I was. 'Where are you?' I said.

'I wanted you to know some things, Mr Coyne,' he said. As he spoke, I could hear the band playing 'The Star-Spangled Banner' through the phone. It came to my ear a fraction of a second behind the music from outside the trailer.

Kinkaid was here, in Lexington, somewhere outside.

I turned and waved my hand frantically at Martin Greeley.

'First off,' Kinkaid said, 'I hope you know that I could have killed you and Herb Croyden the other night. I chose not to.'

'I figured that,' I said. 'I'm grateful.'

Greeley came over to where I was standing. He was frowning.

I pointed at the phone, then drew a big K in the air.

Greeley mouthed the word 'Kinkaid?'

I nodded, made a circle in the air with my finger, then pointed at the floor, indicating that Kinkaid was in this area.

Greeley nodded, held up his hand and flapped his fingers against his thumb. He wanted me to keep Kinkaid talking. Then he moved to one of the techs at his monitor and spoke into his ear.

'So why did you have to kill Gus Shaw and Pedro Accardo?' I said to Kinkaid. 'I wouldn't have thought you were a cold-blooded killer.'

'I'm not,' he said. 'We had a plan. They intended to betray it. They left me no choice.' He paused, and it sounded like the band music coming from his phone was getting louder. 'Soldiers die for lesser causes all the time. Shaw and Accardo made their sacrifices.'

Greeley came over, tugged on my sleeve and pulled me to one of the TV monitors. The agent with the camera was somewhere on the battle green panning back across the street towards our trailer. The monitor showed several scraggly groups of people, including lots of people in various military uniforms, heading in the direction of the green, latecomers to the festivities.

'Aren't you tired of running and hiding?' I said to Kinkaid.

Greeley pointed at a cluster of old veterans moving up the sidewalk towards our trailer. The tech zoomed in on their faces.

'I'm not done yet,' said Kinkaid. 'I have a message for Martin Greeley. He must have been in touch with you by now. Will you deliver it for me?'

'Of course,' I said.

The camera closed in on one soldier's face.

I shook my head.

Three or four more close-ups. None was Kinkaid.

Then I noticed a man lagging behind the others a bit farther down the sidewalk. He wore army khaki and was operating an electric wheelchair. You couldn't tell how tall he was, or if he walked with a limp. He had flowing white hair under his creased cap, and thick glasses, and he didn't look much like the Phil Trapelo I'd met—but he had a cellphone pressed against his ear.

I jabbed Greeley's shoulder and pointed at the wheelchair on the monitor. The camera zoomed in on it.

'Tell Agent Greeley,' Kinkaid was saying, 'that I have never thought of this as a game. It's never been about him, or about me. Nothing personal. I have been absolutely sincere about my convictions all of these years. Will you tell him that?'

'Sure,' I said.

The man was steering his wheelchair towards our trailer while he was talking on his cellphone. I could read his lips on the TV monitor as his words came to me through my phone. The white hair and the glasses and the wheelchair weren't a bad disguise, but as I studied him, watched the way his mouth moved and his eyebrows arched as he talked, I saw past it. It was John Kinkaid.

I pointed at the image of the vet in the wheelchair and gave a thumbs-up sign to Greeley. He snatched the headset from one of the techs and began speaking into it.

'What are you up to today?' I said to Kinkaid as I watched him on the monitor. 'How are you celebrating this Veterans Day?'

'It's a day for mourning, not celebrating,' he said. 'People forget. Heroes, yes. But for every surviving hero, there are thousands—millions, probably—of forgotten martyrs. Men who've died for stupid, senseless causes at the whim of ignorant, self-serving politicians. It's been the work of my life—'

Kinkaid's voice abruptly stopped and, simultaneously on the TV screen, I saw his chin slump to his chest, his arms fall onto his lap and his wheelchair begin to veer slowly off the sidewalk.

The band was playing the final strains of the national anthem: '. . . *and the home of the brave.*' Then the sound of applause, both from outside the trailer and through my cellphone.

Almost instantly a dark-haired woman was at the handles of Kinkaid's wheelchair. She steered it behind our trailer and off the edge of the TV screen that I'd been watching.

I looked at Greeley. 'What just happened?'

He headed for the door. 'Come on.'

I followed him out of the trailer. The woman—I assumed she was an FBI agent—was wheeling Kinkaid towards us.

As they got closer, I saw the red blotch under Kinkaid's chin.

'You shot him?' I said to Greeley.

'Let's hope you didn't misidentify him,' he said.

'My God,' I said, 'Just like that? Murder him?'

'We've got sixteen snipers with silenced scoped rifles here today,' Greeley said. 'What did you think was going to happen?'

The woman who'd been pushing the wheelchair was joined by another agent, a man. They bent over Kinkaid and blocked him from my sight.

After a few minutes, the two agents beckoned Greeley over. He joined them and, a minute or so later, Greeley turned to me. 'Come here, Mr Coyne. Have a look.'

I went over and looked. John Kinkaid—the man I'd known as Phil Trapelo—was wearing a fishing vest under his khaki army jacket. The round stain at the base of his throat was crimson. The vest's many pockets were stuffed and lumpy. Plastic explosive and gunpowder and buckshot, I guessed. Strapped round the bottom of the vest at his waist was a belt of batteries linked with a patriotic snarl of red, white and blue plastic-coated wires. Two strips of one-inch nails crisscrossed his chest like bandoliers. More nails were in bags taped to his stomach.

'They disabled this rig, I hope,' I said.

Greeley nodded.

'So he was going to do it,' I said.

'He aimed to blow us up with him. He was coming right for the trailer.' Greeley showed me what he was holding. It was a television remote similar to the ones I'd seen in the steel cabinet in Herb Croyden's carriage house. 'This was in his pocket. The way it works, you press the power button and hold it down to activate it. When you release the button . . .'

'Boom,' I said. 'If he was holding the button down, even if you killed him, it would detonate. A dead man's switch.'

He nodded. 'If we'd waited till he had this in his hand, it would've been too late.' He patted my shoulder. 'Identifying him when you did and keeping him talking made all the difference.'

'I had no idea you'd just shoot him.'

Greeley smiled quickly. 'Did you have a better idea?'

'No,' I said. 'I think that was quite a good idea.'

WE WENT BACK into the trailer. I realised that 'neutralising' John Kinkaid—that was Martin Greeley's word for shooting him in the throat—had not relaxed anybody. They all continued to proceed on the assumption that there were others out there wearing suicide bombs.

I'd done what they hoped I'd do and now my job was just to stay out of the way. So I leaned against the back wall and sipped coffee and watched the TV monitors as the techs and the agents worked the crowds with their hidden cameras.

The spectators saluted the flag, and the military band played a couple of patriotic marches and 'America the Beautiful', and then, not much more than an hour after it had started, the Lexington Veterans Day celebration was over. Clusters of spectators headed for their cars, and groups of vets in uniform shook hands with each other, and band members wandered away carrying their instruments.

Agent Greeley and his cameramen and techs kept scanning the people until the only ones left on the green were the town workers disassembling the scaffolding, and the electricians rolling up their wires and stowing their gear, and the vendors packing up their wares, and a few uniformed Lexington town cops.

Then Greeley touched my arm and we went outside. Agent Neal was waiting behind the trailer at his black van. He held the back door for me, and I climbed in. Greeley slid in beside me, Neal got behind the wheel, and we headed back to Boston.

We were on Route 2 approaching the Fresh Pond roundabout before Greeley spoke. 'Your country thanks you,' he said.

'You're welcome,' I replied.

He smiled. 'There won't be any commendations or speeches or newspaper stories, I'm afraid.'

'Suits me fine.'

He was looking out of the tinted side window, facing away from me. 'Thirty-five years,' he said softly. 'I don't know who was more obsessed, him or me. He thought he'd been put on earth to end all war, and I was hell-bent on nailing him.'

'Kinkaid wanted me to give you a message.'

Greeley turned to look at me.

'He said he wanted you to know it was never a game with him,' I said. 'He wanted you to know that it wasn't about you. It wasn't personal. He said his convictions were sincere.'

Greeley smiled. 'He was a true believer, all right.'

'So he really was going to blow us up?'

'Along with himself,' Greeley said. 'Absolutely. We've managed to track down several members of his support group in the past week or so, and as well as we can figure it, Kinkaid's original scheme was to have several suicide bombers detonate themselves simultaneously, PTSD victims like Shaw and Accardo, at Lexington and other Veterans Day celebrations. Shocking, deadly, symbolic, to replicate what innocent citizens in other countries experience on a regular basis. In the seventies he blew up buildings. Now he wanted to blow up people.'

'So Gus Shaw and Pedro Accardo squelched that plan?'

Greeley shrugged. 'That's how we figure it. That's why Kinkaid killed them. We'll probably never know exactly what happened. For all we know, there are other John Kinkaids, his disciples, out there.'

'That,' I said, 'is not comforting.'

'You should never feel comforted,' he said.

AFTER LUNCH on the Friday after Veterans Day, as I was daydreaming about a quiet weekend without suicide bombers or FBI agents or old girlfriends, just Henry and me and maybe a couple of football games, Julie buzzed me. When I picked up the phone, she said, 'I've got Attorney Kenilworth on line three.'

I hesitated. 'Who?'

'Charles Kenilworth. Chuck. New Hampshire. The Epping case?'

'Aha,' I said. I hit button number three on my telephone console and said, 'Chuck. How's it going?'

'That was damn good,' he said. 'The picketing and the television and everything.'

'My clients are merely exercising their rights as American citizens,' I said.

'I've got your letter here. Mr Delaney will meet your terms. I can have a certified cheque in the mail to you this afternoon.'

'Did you see the Eppings on television?'

Kenilworth laughed softly. 'I sure did.'

'Doug said he wanted to be acknowledged,' I said.

'A fat cheque is a pretty good acknowledgment.'

'How about,' I said, 'Mr Delaney personally invites the Eppings to get together. How about he gives them the cheque himself and apologises for being tardy with it and maybe explains himself? I'm assuming he's not the complete ass that he seems to be.'

'Actually,' said Chuck Kenilworth, 'Nick Delaney's a pretty good guy. In this housing market, the moving business is shaky, and he's had to hustle to stay afloat.' He hesitated. 'I think he'll go for it. No TV cameras or reporters, though.'

'No lawyers, either,' I said.

'Wouldn't you like to be there?'

'Nope,' I said. 'Delaney walks out of his office there in Nashua and goes up to Doug and Mary, who are carrying their signs, and he says, "Why don't you folks come inside, have a cup of coffee and get warm, and we can talk about this thing?" You don't need lawyers for that, Chuck.'

Kenilworth paused, then said, 'OK. Lemme give him a call right now. Pleasure doing business with you, Brady.'

'You, too, Chuck,' I said.

WE CLOSED THE OFFICE at noon on the Wednesday before Thanksgiving, and by four o'clock, Henry and I were crossing the Piscataqua River Bridge on Route 95 entering Maine.

Alex had called the previous Sunday evening. When I answered, she said, 'So, what're you doing for Thanksgiving? No, wait. That's not really any of my business. I mean, do you have any plans for Thanksgiving? No, that's not right, either. Um, OK. You better not turn me down, Brady Coyne, because I've been thinking about this for a week and I know you'd never know it, but I've been rehearsing this stupid telephone call. So here it is. I would love for you and Henry to join me for Thanksgiving. OK? That's it. Old Mr Terry down the street gave me this huge goose he shot, and I've got big plans for it that include cranberry-and-walnut stuffing, sweet potatoes, my mother's four-bean casserole, butternut squash, mince and pumpkin pies, and . . . and I think it would be nice. Maybe you could come on Wednesday and stay through the weekend and the three of us could just relax, walk in the woods, eat, listen to music, whatever? You want to watch a football game, that's fine by me, and I've got a pile of wood that needs to be split and stacked.' I heard her blow out a long breath. 'Right. I feel like an idiot.'

'We'd love to,' I said.

'You would?'

'It sounds great,' I said.

william g. **tapply**

As professor of English and writer-in-residence at Clark University in Worcester, Massachusetts, William G. Tapply likes to describe himself as 'a writer who teaches and a teacher who writes'. He attributes much of his success in both these arenas to his father, with whom he had a very special relationship.

As a child, Tapply found writing easy. His teachers praised his stories; his grades were impressive. But one critic was a little harder to please—his dad. Tapply senior was a professional magazine writer who had published hundreds of articles and was well known for his monthly column, Tap's Tips, which appeared for many years in *Field and Stream* magazine in America. During Tapply's junior year at high school, he landed in an English class taught by the toughest teacher at the school. Getting an 'A' was nearly impossible, but Tapply was determined to earn one. When the first writing assignment was set, he worked especially hard, being sure to include lavish descriptions and elaborate vocabulary. He was thrilled with the result. But, just to ensure he'd get an A grade, he showed his work to his father.

Tapply senior asked, 'Do you want my opinion? Or do you just want me to tell you it's fine?' Confident, Tapply asked his dad for an honest opinion. The elder Tapply took out a red pencil and proceeded to cover the paper with markings. Stunned, Tapply asked what was wrong with his creation.

'Verbs,' said his dad. He proceeded to explain how active verbs were essential to good writing. And that was just the beginning of Tapply's education from his father. As the year continued, Tapply senior imparted to his son the vital rule of 'less is more', or what Tapply himself now calls the art of 'invisible writing'. Invisible writing, he explains, is the kind that leaves your readers unaware of the writing itself. The only things you want them to be aware of are the plot and the characters. Using overly fancy words and too many adverbs or adjectives can be distracting.

Now, each time Tapply sits down to write, he reminds himself of his father's words: 'Short is good' and 'Who are you trying to impress?' Clearly, this no-nonsense advice has worked, for Tapply's Brady Coyne series, to which *Hell Bent* belongs, has run to twenty-four books, all of them strong sellers in his native America. And, in addition to fiction, Tapply has written eleven nonfiction books—a number of them about fly-fishing—as well as a guide for aspiring mystery writers called *The Elements of Mystery Fiction*. He constantly passes on the fundamentals of his craft to his students at Clark University, and still recommends his father's book, *Tap's Tips,* which was reissued in 2004, as a prime resource.

When he's not teaching or writing, William G. Tapply can usually be found out of doors enjoying his hobbies of gardening and fly-fishing. He lives with his wife, novelist and photographer, Vicki Stiefel, in Hancock New Hampshire and is passionate about the great outdoors. So much so that on his website, www.williamgtapply.com, in an article entitled 'Why I Hunt', he lists no less than twenty-five reasons why he loves the sport. The first of them is yet another tribute to his paternal legacy. He says: 'I hunt because my father hunted, and he took me with him, and so we built a bond that has endured past his death, and because his father hunted, and his father's father, and all of the fathers in my line and yours, as far back as those fathers who invented spears and axes and recorded their adventures with pictures on the walls of caves.'

Further on in his list, Tapply waxes lyrical about the beauty of nature, revealing his

own powers of description: 'I hunt because the goldenrod and the milk weed glisten when the early-morning sun melts the frost from the fields, and because native brook trout spawn in hidden October brooks, and because New England uplands glow crimson and orange and gold in the season of bird hunting . . .'

Whether he is teaching or writing, it is clear that Tapply is gifted, and it's our hope that UK readers will be inspired to seek out more books in the Brady Coyne series for their enjoyment.

COPYRIGHT AND ACKNOWLEDGMENTS

EVEN MONEY: Copyright © Dick Francis 2009.
Published at £18.99 by Michael Joseph, an imprint of Penguin Books.
Condensed version © The Reader's Digest Association Limited, 2009.

THE SIGN: Copyright © Raymond Khoury 2009.
Published at £12.99 by Orion Books, an imprint of The Orion Publishing Group Ltd.
Condensed version © The Reader's Digest Association Limited, 2009.

ENDAL: Copyright © Allen and Sandra Parton, 2009.
Published at £6.99 by HarperTrue, an imprint of HarperCollins*Publishers*.
Condensed version © The Reader's Digest Association Limited, 2009.

HELL BENT: Copyright © 2008 by William G. Tapply.
Published at $24.95 by St Martin's Minotaur, an imprint of St Martin's Press, New York.
Condensed version © The Reader's Digest Association Limited, 2009.

The right to be identified as authors has been asserted by the following in accordance with
sections 77 and 78 of the Copyright, Designs and Patents Act, 1988: Dick Francis, Raymond
Khoury, Allen and Sandra Parton, William G. Tapply.

Spine: iStockPhoto; spine lozenge: Imagebank. Page 5 (top) © Allen and Sandra Parton;
6–8 images: Corbis, Imagebank; illustrator: Narrinder Singh@velvet tamarind; 176 © Apex.
178–80 images: iStock Photo; illustrator: Rick Lecoat@Shark Attack; 356 © Jerry Bauer.
358–9 courtesy of Allen and Sandra Parton (photo: Tim Rose at Martin Dawes Photography);
360 © Allen and Sandra Parton. 436–7 all photographs © Allen and Sandra Parton, except
4 and 8 © Derek Wright. 438–40 illustrator: Richard Merritt@The Organisation; 574–5
© Vicki Stiefel.

Printed and bound by GGP Media GmbH, Pössneck, Germany

020-262 DJ0000-1